BLASPHEMIES & REVELATIONS
ROBERT M. PRICE

BLASPHEMIES & REVELATIONS

ROBERT M. PRICE

2019
Exham Priory
Selma, North Carolina
United States of America

Published by Exham Priory 2019

Introduction & Stories copyright © 2008 by Robert M. Price.
First Edition: Mythos Books LLC, Poplar Bluff, Missouri 2008

Cover photo courtesy of Pixaby
Cover design by Qarol Price

Robert E. Howard material appears by kind permission of
Jack & Barbara Baum for Robert E. Howard Properties, L.L.C.

ISBN: 978-0-9991537-4-1
Copyright © 2019 by Robert M. Price

Dedicated to Brian Lumley,
whose work and whose friendship
have delighted me for many years.

CONTENTS

FUMBLERS AT THE LATCH

AN INTRODUCTION

If you know my name at all, the first thing you probably think of when you read it is "Lovecraft geek." And that might be on account of my various anthologies from Chaosium, Inc., Fedogan and Bremer, etc., or from my years-long editorial tenure at *Crypt of Cthulhu*. There is no question about it: for good or for ill, I deserve the reputation. I asked for it. I've loved HPL's writings since I first read them in 1967. They captivated me then, and I am glad to be able to say that they have not lost anything in the intervening years. In other words, Lovecraft's work, while catching adolescents just in the nick of time, before they lose the last of their sense of wonder, just before "a glory has departed from the world," is not dependent for its effect on any childish lack of taste in the reader. The same is true of Edgar Rice Burroughs, Robert E. Howard, and so many more. They are excellent writers, and their work stands the test of time. I dare say readers can enjoy them today every bit as much as those who first read the stories in the old pulps. And as adults we find we have not passed Lovecraft (and the rest) by on the way to anything ostensibly better. I will never believe otherwise. I think I know the difference between loving something out of nostalgia and making a critical value judgment.

I am typical of Lovecraft enthusiasts in that, once I had read the tales many times, I found new ways of enjoying them. One was to research and analyze them. I have done plenty of that. Another, obviously, is to write Lovecraft pastiches. Rewriting Lovecraft is a different way of rereading Lovecraft, and that is what I have done. Whether these stories possess any merit at all, you may decide more readily than I. I enjoyed writing them. I hope you enjoy reading them. But I make no critical boast on their behalf, nor do I fear any critical reviews. It's not that I imagine there won't *be* any. It's just that the prospect doesn't bother me. I don't have that sort of investment in them. Of course, I'm not ashamed of them, either! If you like them, as some say they have, I'm with you.

If I were writing here about someone else's Mythos tales, I would probably note some trends. One of them would be Price's seemingly studied avoidance of creating new Mythos tomes. "He" seems to prefer to piggyback on the latter-day gimmick of Brian Lumley and others, working with variant editions of notorious books like the *Necronomicon*, or *Feery's*

Original Notes thereupon. Or even sectarian exegesis of the Bible which, to many, is a fearsome enough book of superstition in its own right. Our author does not want to multiply the list of Mythos entities, either. It used to be, in earlier days, that a new entrant into one or another "new circle" of Mythos authors had to produce his own grimoire or demon, almost like a rite of initiation, and I'm glad they did. But somewhere along the line I, for one, reached the saturation point and figured I could best avoid cliché by leaving well enough alone. Oddly, it seemed to me that the innovation would be *not* to invent new items of Mythos lore!

I've always loved the fiction of Lin Carter, especially his tendency to find a graft point on marginal Mythos stories, enabling him to more fully develop neglected hints and to avoid going too often where others had already gone. And, like him, I prefer to emulate the scholarly element of Lovecraft's stories, but I'd rather stick with the scholarly style Lovecraft used; his stories sounded like the only kind of prose an academic like his protagonists is capable of writing. Lin, by contrast, was perfectly suited to fast-paced action; for him, the scholarly element was a big chunk of systematized Mythos lore dropped into the narrative, where it tended to dispel any mood of mystery. Secrets and mysteries became too profane and mundane in his hands. So my tales tend to stick with the lower-ichor diet.

I've also been influenced by the fine work (of which there was way too little) of James Wade, who imaginatively connected the Mythos with cults and occult fads of the 1960s and 70s as Lovecraft had done with the occultism of the 20s and 30s.

One boundary I have tried for the most part not to cross is that between traditional and what I might call New Wave Mythos stories, the authors of the latter considering it a virtue to depart from Lovecraftian precedent as far as possible by using various "hipper" and "cutting-edge" genre conventions. Well, as far as this old man (can it be I first read HPL *forty years* ago?) is concerned, you can stuff that up your non-Euclidean angle! You know, the one that looks acute but behaves as if obtuse, which sure describes a lot of people I know. To me, such writing betokens the writer's apology for liking Lovecraft in the first place: "Here, Mr. Sophisticate, if I update Lovecraft, will you stop calling me a pathetic nerd?" No, I say, gimme that old-time Lovecraftian style and mood! Who needs character? Who needs dialogue? Why not flood the reader with minutely detailed description and "adjectivitis"? It's got a charm all its own, and I for one mean to keep it that way! In conclusion, let me thank my many Lovecraftian friends and colleagues, whose company I have enjoyed over the years every bit as much as I have enjoyed reading Lovecraft himself.

They include, in no particular order, S. T. Joshi, Scott Briggs, Don and Mollie Burleson, Jason C. Eckhardt, Peter H. Cannon, Marc Michaud, Ken Neilly, Robert H. Knox, Sam Moskowitz, Colin Wilson, Gary and Jen Myers, Dick and Pat Lupoff, Steve Fabian, Joe Wrzos, Lin Carter, Ramsey Campbell, Randall A. Larson, Mary Eileen MacNamara, Will Murray, Joe Pulver, Stan Sargent, Michael Cisco, Miroslav Lipinski, Stefan Dziemianowicz, Mark Cerasini, Chuck Hoffman, Chuck Garofalo, Chris Henderson, Brian McNaughton, Peter Jeffreys, Des Lewis, Richard Dalby, Roger Johnson, David Wynn, Eric Kramer, Mark Rainey, Darrell Schweitzer, Bob and Phyllis Weinberg, Dan Gobbett, Richard L. Tierney, Karl Edward Wagner, Robert Bloch, L. Sprague de Camp, "Ankh" Schwader, Frank Belknap Long, Carl Jacobi, Hugh B. Cave, Mary Elizabeth Counselman, Fred Chappell, Steven J. Mariconda, Wilum H. Pugmire, Sam Gafford, Dixon Smith, Chris Vail, Andrew Migliore,T.E.D. Klein, Steffan B. Aletti, Donna Death, Carolyn Boyd, Robert Carey, Harry O. Morris, Jim Ambuehl, Pete von Scholly, Henry Vester, Kenneth W. Faig, Scott Connors, Steve Behrends, David Schultz, Ed O'Brien, Peter Gilmore, and Brian Lumley, to whom I dedicate this book. What a great-hearted man and a gifted yarn-spinner he is! (Sorry to those my failing memory missed!)

Robert M. Price
Hierophant of the Horde
April 6, 2008

'TWAS THE NIGHT

I had moved into the elegant old neighborhood only recently. I lived alone but found ample companionship in the magical quality of the place itself. Winter had come gracefully, like a welcome yearly guest, and I looked forward to my first Christmas in these enchanting surroundings. It arrived soon, but hardly as I had expected.

Christmas Eve I had made myself comfortable in front of the fireplace with my copy of Dickens' *A Christmas Carol*, reading through my favorite parts. I found myself pleasantly interrupted once or twice by carolers at my door. Silent in reflection, I gazed vacantly at the fire before me. Not noticing the gradual decline of the blaze, I was nudged from my reverie only when the flames had died completely. The clock in the corner reminded me that it was too late to trouble myself with additional kindling. Besides, I remarked with some amusement to myself, it would hardly be cordial to leave a fire burning should I have a visitor who might choose the chimney as his manner of entry!

I made the rounds of the lamps in the house, extinguishing each in turn. As I headed toward the stairs, I noticed through the bay window that the street was entirely dark. I, it seemed, was the last to bed on this Christmas Eve.

I had just begun to relax and doze when I thought I caught sight of something moving across the sky. The bedchamber curtains were thin, but lacy, and it was impossible to determine the exact shape or nature of the object. A shooting star, perhaps? No, it seemed much closer, almost as if directly above the roofs of the town slumbering unsuspectingly below.

I was about to dismiss the observation from my mind when I was jolted awake by a crashing noise on the roof above me. Sitting up bolt-straight in my bed, I waited anxiously, trying to decipher the jumble of sounds rapidly succeeding the initial shock of . . . landing? It seemed there were sounds as of someone dragging something, and perhaps bells or metal implements clattering together. Then I thought I heard the scuffing of animal hooves and the rapid thumping sounds of several feet dismounting from a vehicle. What on earth . . . ? Was I going mad?

I listened a few moments more as the noise quickly vanished from above me, only to begin to reappear *below*! But how? I heard nothing at any of the doors. My mind flashed back to the silly jest I had made to myself before retiring . . . the chimney! In the fright and excitement of the moment I could allow myself no time to reflect on the patent absurdity of what seemed to be happening around me. Instead, I slipped as quietly as I could out into the hall and down the back stairs. My eyes soon adjusted to the dim light and I was able to find my way through the kitchen, miraculously, without colliding with any of the clutter I had left strewn about from last evening's supper.

Attaining my desired vantage point, I peered, unseen I hoped, into the parlor. I could never have prepared myself for what I was about to behold. Instead of a troop of daring prowlers, the room was occupied by one large man in shapeless crimson robes and what appeared to be a number of small children. They seemed to be working from several large bags, rapidly transferring small items between the sacks and various parts of the room!

No *ordinary* thieves, then . . . but what *was* going on here?

I risked extending my head into the room just a little further to gain a better view. What was it they were leaving? To my horror, I could now see that they were scattering rocks, bits of excrement and filth, grimy machine parts . . . and what looked like segments of dismembered animals! And the large red-suited man . . . he foraged around in the embers of my fireplace until he found a blackened piece of wood, beginning then to write with it on the walls. I watched aghast as he scrawled obscenities and incoherent warnings to repent. Something about the polar caps melting and overcoming us all. No one had warned me of such a madman living in the town when I moved in . . .

I tried to step quietly away, hoping to exit the house and summon the police. But my foot slipped on something cast in that direction by one of the children. Small though the noise was, it was not lost on my visitors. Several sets of eyes turned quickly in my direction. Those faces . . . they weren't children at all! Rather more like midgets, perhaps. At any rate, they were upon me now, dozens of them it seemed, piling on top of me, nearly suffocating me. Like Gulliver, I was helplessly bound. The wordless silence which had prevailed until then was suddenly banished by the roaring cry of the large man, now striding toward me with a menacing look: "You think to interrupt Old Nick in his work? Hold him, imps! I will teach him his lesson!" As he turned his back, returning to the fireplace, thoughts began to tumble over each other in my mind. "Old Nick"?—Isn't he called "Saint Nick"—isn't "Old Nick" someone else? And did he call them "imps"? I thought I remembered it as "elves" . . . He had started the fire going again, very quickly somehow. And he seemed to be holding something in front of him. Hardly filling the Christmas stockings, I thought! Then I caught a glimpse . . . Oh no! He had taken a poker and was holding it over the flames. It was by now red-hot! My spine chilled to hear his malevolent chuckling as he turned toward me again. A mixture of fear and outrage gave me a surge of new strength. Throwing off most of the little fiends, I struggled to my feet and ran for the kitchen door, flinging behind me chairs, pans, any obstruction that lay ready to hand.

Outside now, I jumped from the porch into the back yard. The cold shock of the snow only gave me more energy to run, but the sheer depth and weight of the white blanket mocked my efforts at speed. How like a nightmare all this is, I thought! I sought refuge in a row of bushes at the edge of the lot. Feverishly I rummaged through a multitude of possible plans. Should I contact the neighbors? Seek better shelter? Surely the midgets would find me here if they fanned out across the yard looking for me. My sole hope was that the depth of the snow and their small height would make this impossible.

Minutes passed, their tense silence broken only by my labored breath. Then I saw a sight even more amazing than all the others of the macabre night. From the roof rose a large carriage or sleigh, born aloft by a team of some kind of horned abominations! If not for the irrefutable, grisly reality of the events about to transpire, I would yet swear that the whole adventure had been no more than a dream!

I noticed with a seizure of terror that streamers of brilliant light began to wave from the windows of the house! Flames licked at the structure like jackals on a carcass, appearing suddenly from everywhere! By now the strange craft had moved slightly in the night sky, and its passengers began to fling flaming missiles down among the homes below. Soon the whole neighborhood, the entire town, became a crackling inferno. Paralyzed with shock, I could but dumbly witness how the blaze had vanquished the natural darkness of the night. It was like midday, and indeed may well have been. I had lost track of the passage of time. Whether the conflagration took minutes or hours, I cannot tell.

As for the demon who had wrought the havoc, I thought I heard him exclaim something as he disappeared from sight, but it could scarcely be understood above the roar of the blaze. I am glad not to know what blasphemy he may have shrieked into the hellfire of his own making that morning. None of the townspeople had had a chance to save themselves. They perished in their sleep, roasted in their beds like so many Christmas turkeys. Their sudden, then quickly silenced screams filled my ears. What a grim mockery of the festive sounds of holiday singing I had heard only hours before. As the sun rose that Christmas morning, it must have been struck as I was by the stark contrast of the blackened ruins against the white snow. Bitterly, I thought of the old wives tale that naughty children would receive only ashes and coal for Christmas. The foul jest was not worth repeating even had there been anyone left alive to hear it. But as it was, not a creature was stirring.

–1976–

BENEATH THE TOMBSTONE

To eternal life are none but fools disposed.
The wise thirst instead for oblivion's repose.
The slumber of the tomb shall be thy rest,
A shield for thee from the unwelcome
guest.
If thy clay recline beneath the Elder Sigil,
Against the shambling foe it shall keep vigil.

—*The Book of Iod*

I.

I cannot say precisely why my eccentric Uncle Absalom had chosen me to inherit what remained of his worldly estate. God knows there were other surviving kin who had been closer to him than I, or at least I supposed there must have been. At any rate I had had little contact with him that I could remember since the family reunions of my childhood. What interest he could have taken in me I cannot readily imagine.

Nonetheless on the 5th of March I packed my belongings into my car (it was easy enough to do, there being so few of them), and set off for the old mansion amid the low hills of Lancaster County, Pennsylvania. Small towns had never been particularly to my liking, but times being what they were, I was not about to turn down a free house, no matter what shape it was in, nor how isolated it was.

The hamlet to which my uncle had retired was a bit difficult to find. Road maps did not list it, and even locals whom I stopped to ask did not seem to have heard of Tophet. Perhaps I was mispronouncing it. All I knew was that the name had a vaguely biblical ring to it, but then so did most of the towns and villages in this region. That fact became obvious as I drove aimlessly through several of them. If I had to be lost, Lancaster County was at least a picturesque place in which to lose oneself. But towards evening I did find Tophet with directions provided by the proprietor of a small general-store-and-gas-pump down the road.

It was tiny, a backwater really. Once there, it was not difficult to find Uncle Absalom's homestead. It was actually situated some miles away from the rest of the town, so that I wondered if it were technically included in the municipal jurisdiction. The old mansion rose in all its decadent grandeur amid the wild countryside. It was in fairly good repair, though gloomy in general aspect. The effect was rounded out by the series of chalked and painted hex-signs high up near the eaves. Of course, I had seen similar symbols and plaques all day, and appreciated them as true examples of folk art. But I had always wondered how seriously the Amish and Mennonite farmers of the region took their hex-icons. These pious folk were not ones for frivolous decorations, but surely their religion was equally unfriendly to superstitious belief in hexes and curses.

The key with which I had been supplied fit, despite the rusty disrepair of the lock, with a ready click, and I roamed the house trying to make its acquaintance. And quite a bit of roaming would be necessary even to cover the floor plan once. Passing from the front hall through the drawing room and study, I was quite impressed with the decor. There was oaken paneling in abundance which should have lent the interior a certain deep warmth, but somehow did not. Perhaps this was due to the neglect the elaborate woodwork had apparently suffered. In the brief time since my uncle's death, the finish could not have grown so dull unless it had been ignored long before. Uncle Absalom mustn't have shared the previous generation's fastidiousness. Perhaps he was, like many an eccentric recluse, altogether oblivious of things mundane, his mind being diverted to other channels. The corroded lock on the front door had already suggested his lack of care for minor repairs. In fact, the only housework with which he might have troubled himself was keeping the rug clean, and this I only noticed because the puzzling geometrical patterns in the rug-weave caught my eye. They would not have been so distinct if old Absalom had not groomed the rug periodically. Something in that odd weave seemed familiar, perhaps a coincidental resemblance to the hex-signs on the exterior of the house.

Well, no matter.

In the study my eyes wandered from the dull finish of the paneling to the well-stocked shelves, and finally to the framed portrait above the mantel. Of course it was Uncle Absalom himself. As I have said, I had not seen the man since my youth, yet the sight of the painting instantly filled in the holes the years had worn in my memory. That was he, all right. The skill of the painter had captured even the hint of bored irritation the old man must have evidenced as he sat for the portrait, a chore forced on him, no doubt, by some pestering relative. How must all of his relatives have annoyed this man who sought only silence, for him to have bypassed them, leaving his estate to me! At any rate, I was his beneficiary, and my uncle's bequest had been generous enough, despite his rather odd stipulation that I burn several listed volumes from his vast library and fill in the surprisingly large subcellar of the house.

I soon made ready to discharge the first of these obligations, starting a fire in the huge old hearth. I needed the warmth anyway, I reasoned, so why not take care of some business as well? The sooner my tasks were accomplished, the sooner the property would be legally mine.

It was not difficult to locate the books which my uncle had apparently hoped might follow him into whatever afterlife had claimed him. A few volumes were illustrated pornographic works of a quite spectacular character, exploring depths of perversion I had never even imagined. Into the flames they went. My glimpses of random pages had been enough to unsettle my stomach, so it was with relief that I turned to the rest of the books.

Several of the titles meant nothing to me, though languages had been a favorite interest of mine in college, and some of the strange tomes baited my curiosity. One called *The Book of Iod* was written in a scramble of Greek and Coptic, and seemed to be a Gnostic work of some kind. *The Cabala of Saboth* was apparently a treatise on angelology composed in a kind of barbarous Yiddish of which I could make little sense. Another volume, the *Confessions of the Mad Monk Clithanus*, was in readable but debased Latin. I dimly recalled having heard of it, an obscure specimen of the vast vision literature of the Middle Ages.

Might not some of these books be worthy of preservation or sale? They might be of real interest to an expert who knew what to make of them. Still, I did not want to violate the conditions of the will and risk losing my inheritance. Nothing, however, was preventing me from a leisurely perusal of the collection.

At last I came to a volume that intrigued me more than any of the others. My first reaction was one of mild revulsion, as its leathery binding seemed uncomfortably reminiscent of *human* hide. No less disorienting was the utterly unfamiliar tongue (transliterated into English characters) in which it was composed. The only discernible English word occurred in a partial translation of the title, penned in my uncle's handwriting on the title page—the *R'lyeh Text*. I tried my skill at enunciating a few underlined words on the page where a bookmark had been placed: "*mglw' nafh fhthagnngah cf 'ayak 'vulgtmm vugtlag'n . . ."* The words echoed in the large room, then were lost amid the crackling of the fireplace. And it was there, after all, that the books should be going, but the hour had grown late, and I decided to resume my duties in the morning. Preparing one of the beds upstairs, I turned in for the night. It had been a long day, and I soon fell asleep, disturbed only briefly by the abnormally loud chorus of frogs and whippoorwills in the woods at the edge of the lot. Yet perhaps they troubled my rest more than I realized at the time, for my dreams were shot through with visions of great forms, half saurian, half octopoid, ranged against backgrounds of forested slopes and carven masonry.

II.

Only partly rejuvenated by the night's sleep, I rose, prepared a light, cold breakfast, and carried my plate into the study where I began again to peruse the contents of the library. Uncle Absalom had made a file of clippings from local papers dealing with bizarre, yet seemingly unrelated matters. Several items from the *Lancaster Record* had to do with unexplained disappearances and cattle-mutilations. All of these clippings looked to have been filler material from the back pages. What Uncle Absalom could have found to interest him in these peculiar scraps was beyond me, yet already I had seen adequate proof of the old man's salacious and prurient tastes.

My reverie was interrupted by a knock at the door. The noise startled me, shattering as it did the silence which had encompassed me since the previous evening. Opening the front door I was greeted by the sight of a local police officer. The middle-aged patrolman was eyeing me suspiciously, but seemed to relax a bit as we talked. It seemed that during the night some local farmer's two prize bulls had disappeared. The officer was cruising about in search of any sign of the thieves when he noticed the smoke from my chimney. Knowing that Absalom Mueller had died a month or so earlier, he thought it best to investigate. When I introduced myself as old Absalom's nephew and heir William, he seemed satisfied and willing to leave to continue his search. Halfway down the steps, however, he turned to ask if I planned on settling down in Tophet. A natural enough question, to be sure, even a polite one under ordinary circumstances, but I could not help noticing a certain anxiety in his manner as I said that yes, I did hope to establish myself in the community.

Closing the door, I wondered what the policeman's question implied. A moment's thought suggested that Uncle Absalom might have acquired some kind of unsavory reputation among the townspeople, and this was not hard to imagine given their rural piety and his rather *outré* tastes. Who knew, or cared, what he had done to earn such ill repute; what worried me was that I might well have inherited my uncle's outcast status. And this was no way to start fresh in new surroundings. I decided that the books and papers could wait. Perhaps a visit to town would answer some of my questions.

I estimated that by the time I had made myself presentable and arrived on the main street of Tophet, most of the townspeople would be up and around, especially as this was primarily a community of small farmers who rose with the sun. True, most might be expected still to be busy with chores, but I hoped I might meet at least a few of my new neighbors. If I found no clues as to my (perhaps imaginary) mystery, still I might show myself to be no ogre and even make a few new acquaintances. With these calculations I set off for town.

But my hopes were disappointed. The friendliest response I could elicit from the few stragglers I accosted was a hurried "Nice to meet you," and I suspected that even those scant words were not meant. Was it that they feared me as Uncle Absalom's successor in some mischief? Or were they simply ignorant peasants who shrank from contact with any newcomer? The latter was not after all unlikely, since I believed I noticed enough similarity in the faces I saw to suspect inbreeding with the consequent mental decadence.

An idea occurred to me, and after picking up a few needed groceries, I returned to my car, heading for the roadside stand where yesterday I had gotten directions. The old fellow who ran the pumps there had at least known the location of Tophet, and he might know more. And not being a resident, he might be less tight-lipped than the others.

But here, too, I was disappointed. When I arrived at the station, the door to the cottage was locked and the blinds drawn. Fresh tire-marks in the dust and other small clues made me wonder if the little store were not occupied after all. The silence of the place seemed laden with anxious tension, as of someone hiding—almost as if the proprietor and his customers had seen me approach and frantically sought concealment. Baffled, I went back to the car to return home (for that is how I had already come to regard the old place). But as I pulled out into the road, I caught a glimpse of something that had eluded me before. Suddenly I noticed a makeshift hex sign, painted on a large circle of zinc, perhaps recently the bottom of a wash tub, and nailed onto the front wall of the store, above the door. Somehow I had omitted to notice it just minutes before, but my preoccupation would explain this. What I was fairly sure of was that no such sign had been present the day before!

By noon I had returned to the house more mystified than before. I decided my answer, if answer there were, must be hidden in my uncle's books, the very books I had almost consigned to the flames the previous night. There I read of fantastic entities with names like Leviathan, Demogorgon, Azathoth, and Zeernebooch. Somehow I knew it was of these very beings I had dreamt last night! Just what kind of researches had Uncle Absalom been engaged in? And, worse yet—what kind of *deeds*?

III.

Once more my thoughts were interrupted, this time by a strange sound . . . *below* me. The sub-cellar! In my absorption with my uncle's hellish books I had completely forgotten it. Following the sound as best I could (it was now dying away), I found my way down to the subterranean chamber. By now there were only ringing echoes, which might have been those of a beast's death agonies. But if the sound were no longer there to greet me, the sub-basement was filled with an equally horrifying *stench*, like that of a slaughterhouse. For scattered all about, almost concealing the traces of chalk circles and pentacles on the stone floor, were the carcasses of one or more cows, or . . . bulls?

The cover of night found me two miles further into the countryside, climbing over the rail fence of the Tophet Cemetery. You see, having returned to the pile of occult volumes in the study, I had searched them anew, doubly desperate for some clue. And in an underscored verse from *The Book of Iod*, I believed I had found it. If my conjectural translations were anywhere near the mark, I felt assured that the end of the whole horrific business lay here in my uncle's final resting place.

After some searching I found the grave and set to work, swallowing my own disgust and self-revulsion as I did so. Finally, the wood of the coffin came into view. With some surprise I noticed that the casket had been laid so that the grave marker rose directly over the middle of the box, not at its head, as was the usual arrangement. Thus, to unearth the whole length of the casket, I had to displace the gravestone. The stone itself was of curious design, having neither the basic rectangular shape nor that of a cross, but rather of a five-pointed star, with some sort of pattern carved upon it. With the marker thus out of the way, freeing the coffin was comparatively simple.

I paused, momentarily startled by a swelling crescendo of whippoorwills that seemed to explode out of nowhere. Regaining as much composure as the surroundings allowed, I made ready to uncover the corpse. But I was not prepared for the sight that greeted me upon opening the box. For my uncle's form was just as I had seen it in the portrait. He seemed not dead, certainly not decayed, but merely asleep. Yet I had but a glimpse of him in this state. The coffin lid had come open only with difficulty, and I was forced to wrench it free with one great effort. As the lid fell all the way to the ground, the hinges shattered, as did the star-shaped stone, upon which it fell. At this, my Uncle Absalom's eyes flew open in an expression of sheer terror, matched instantly by my own, as I beheld what followed. *For his formerly inert form began to erupt in bloody furrows, rent and mutilated by unseen talons!* The authorities at this place where I am now confined accuse me of desecrating the corpse, but I know only too well that *Uncle Absalom's dismemberment was the work of whatever eldritch entity my idle mouthing of an ancient incantation had released, and which my clumsiness had given access to my uncle's hitherto protected sleeping form!*

–1984–

Saucers from Yaddith

I.

Oh, I've little doubt that *you* will believe me, Mr. Turrow. And I suspect most of your readers will give my story credence as well. But to be perfectly frank, no *reputable* newspaper would listen to the first five words of my tale. Only a tabloid such as yours would even give it a second look. Now please do not misunderstand me, sir, I am no less grateful to you for this opportunity, but we are both adults, are we not? We both know how little commercial journalism need have to do with truth. So, even if you do *not* believe me, it is all the same. I can scarcely believe it myself. Perhaps it will take on a greater air of reality if I speak of it and get it out in the air between us, eh Mr. Turrow? Discussing something always seems to . . . Well, yes, I will get on with it.

I suppose one must place the beginning of the affair back merely a few weeks ago. My circle, ever dedicated to the expansion of its horizons, had applied itself with diligence to the study of this and that field of arcane knowledge. How well I can recall how old Elkhart, the artist among us, had experimented with Tibetan mandalas. His canvases were damnably suggestive of questions beyond mortal imagination—to frame, much less to answer. Our prolonged meditation on these windows to deeper recesses of the mind finally served but to increase our Faustian thirst to know what lay beyond.

Preus, ever the religious seeker himself, suggested that our grail of ultimate knowledge was obtainable only through certain doctrines and rites suppressed over the centuries by church authorities. In fact it was for the discovery and exposition of such gnostical fantasies that Preus himself had been first expelled from divinity school, then actually excommunicated many years before. But all of us had noticed only too readily the gleam one catches in the eye of the fanatic. It seemed an unspoken consensus that whatever hidden truths might lie down the paths Preus had trod, we would as soon pass them by. Expanding reality was one thing, after all, but leaving it behind was quite another. If Preus's proposal was received with a distinct coolness, Barlow's urgings to follow him into what he called the "left-handed path" of Tantric mysticism were

12

dispatched with all the speed that politeness allowed. For none of us were willing to throw over our inherited moral codes for the questionable pursuits which seemed so completely to have enthralled our friend. Seeing our reluctance, he quickly added that of course he only knew of such practices from his research.

Finally there was St. Joshua, whose philosophical views ran toward the mundane. An adherent of Russell, Ayer, and the positivists, he was merely tolerant of the rest of us, I suspect.

The group was, as you can see, heterogeneous, companions kept together by old school ties and overlapping interests here and there. All of us did share a thirst for knowledge, as well as an ache of frustration since none of us were any closer to our goal of enlightenment. At last I myself broached a suggestion.

I had of late taken a keen interest in the mind-expanding potential of certain drugs. The writings of Huxley about mescaline had intrigued me no little, and it was this avenue down which I would have our group turn. All seemed willing at least to consider it, if yet concerned to know what precautions might be taken for safety's sake. Such concerns were, of course, my own as well, and I assured my companions that I would attempt, as far as I might, to chart our probable course before we embarked in earnest. The conversation soon turned down other avenues. It seemed to me that the others felt only mild interest in my proposal, certainly nothing to compare with the excitement that I had begun to feel. Eventually the meeting adjourned, and I hurried home, lost in thought.

I decided I had best seek the advice of physicians. But given the controversial nature of our envisioned experiment, I would have to take especial care in choosing doctors whose confidence I could trust. At length I obtained the names of two local authorities. Their contributions to the medical journals implied that they might be sympathetic to the kind of exercise we were considering. In fact, as I read between the lines, I saw, or imagined I saw, reason to believe that one doctor had already tried such experiments himself. His allusions were so vague, yet so suggestive! Alas, this man, a Dr. Martin Rhadamanthus, was currently traveling abroad. His offices at the medical college where he taught were somewhat evasive as to either the exact location or duration of his sabbatical journeys. This I could well understand, however irksome the fact, since few professions are so harrowing and tiresome as his. He must need his solitude as much as he desired it. The other specialist I had chosen was not a teacher but an active practitioner, Dr. Phineas Whitmore by name. At length I succeeded in making an appointment with him. It was to be a simple physical examination, on the pretext that I feared I was evidencing initial signs of a particular nervous condition in which the doctor was known to specialize. Given his wide reputation, it was not surprising that the first available opening was yet two weeks away. I was assured that two weeks was in truth an unusually brief time to wait, and that normally one waited months to see Dr. Whitmore. I was appropriately, and genuinely, expansive in my thanks and hung up. Two weeks! Short enough by any usual reckoning, to be sure. Yet the thirst for knowledge which possessed me was now so consuming— and all the more since now a concrete possibility for its satisfaction seemed within reach—that two weeks seemed like as many years!

Before one week was out, I was ready to act impetuously. I would take a modicum of the drug myself, come what may. After all, Huxley and others had tried it, and with what risk? Surely, I had been overcautious up to this point, and would be merely foolish, even cowardly, to delay further. The very night of these deliberations witnessed my first experiment with the drug. I was charged with a sense of expectancy and, I do not mind admitting, a good deal of anxious apprehension.

Having taken a small dose I settled myself in a well-stuffed armchair, placed so as to face the large picture window. My thinking was that visual stimulation might serve as a catalyst for the, perceptual transformation I expected. And I was not disappointed! As Huxley had predicted, ordinary objects soon began to take on a kind of extraordinary aspect. They seemed to gain new depth and then to shine forth in hues only distantly akin to their mundane colors—somehow more vivid and brilliant. At the same time, all seemed fairly translucent, as if made of precious stones.

Though I had read several descriptions of this very experience, both in scientific journals and in the accounts of the mystics, none of my studies could have prepared me for the indescribable beauty of this panorama! How the most common things might be utterly transfigured!

Next I began to notice the auditory effects. Did I hear a subtle whistling or whirring? It sounded mechanical, yet musical. This sound was positively unearthly. In fact, it is puzzling that though I can recall it distinctly, I can in no wise imagine how to convey it by humming or whistling.

No sooner had the weird tones begun to sound than my attention was drawn to an indefinable disturbance of the air, just above the trees which divided my lot from the adjacent property. It was something like the sight of autumn leaves caught up for a few seconds in a whirlwind. Yet as far as I could see, nothing was being propelled in the wind. And, strictly speaking, there *was* no wind. As I said, it looked to be a disturbance, a spinning in the air itself. This motion centered about an expanse several yards across. I dimly recall wondering what natural phenomenon it might be that was so metamorphosed in my affected perception.

In less time than it has taken to describe my vague impressions, the spinning had commenced moving in my direction. I felt that I might be in danger, but that, given my present mental disorientation, this might be simply another hallucination. Being now able to view the uncanny phenomenon more clearly, I observed that the spinning seemed confined to a ring. Though the motion seemed rapid, incredibly rapid, it was not particularly violent or forceful. What might it be like at the center, I wondered?

So help me, with the thought itself, my perspective changed so that for the briefest instant I seemed actually to occupy the center of the whirling. I could see my house, my window, even my chair, *but the chair was empty!* Yet all these observations occupied but a moment until the scene changed yet again. Now I seemed to be lying prone atop a platform of some material and design quite unknown to me. The haunting sound was still discernible, but much more faintly now, and muffled in tone. At first I saw nothing, yet I did not fear any harm had been done to my sight, for such misty radiance was apparent as one "sees" in a darkened room. It was not the absolute blackness of space, the dark and complete oblivion of the blind.

A few moments passed in this manner, and I began to wonder if perhaps my metabolism had somehow dampened the effect of the drug so that I would remain under the present, rather unspectacular hallucination for the duration of the experiment. But I need have feared no such eventuality, for soon two shapes began to take form in the darkness, almost as if the dusk itself were gathering into a tangible aspect. As the outlines grew more and more distinct, my heart raced. For now, certainly, I was beginning to get what I had bargained for! Here were apparitions from beyond waking reality, albeit drug-conjured wraiths from the depths of my own mind. As tall as a man they were, the two creatures, yet anthropomorphic in no other respect at all. If I must employ the categories to which we are accustomed, let me say they were perhaps . . . insectoid. Even to designate them so is radically misleading, but let me not linger upon the point lest I rob my tale of whatever plausibility remains.

It was inevitably futile for me to try to discern the expressions that crossed faces of so alien a mien, but some intuition told me that the monsters were as startled by my appearance as I was by theirs. If anything, they seemed more agitated. As strange as it may sound, I did not feel

15

particularly alarmed. After all, I reasoned, this is my hallucination. It seemed to me as if I were the host, and they, the figments of my supercharged imagination, were my guests.

For some period of indeterminable length, I passed into an all but oblivious state. During this time, I had but the faintest sensations of what went on around me, or better, within me. In retrospect I would compare it to reports I had read of how a man under the influence of some drugs will gain a heightened sensitivity to his own heart rate and autonomic nerve functions. Yet that was not quite what I experienced in that pit of leaden torpor. Rather I felt that somehow I was being probed, even, yes, dissected and reconstructed; that parts of me were being removed and replaced, as one might adjust the parts of an automobile engine and replace its fuels and lubricants. Yet all these are but loose analogies that ill approximate my sensations. I seem to remember reflecting through the clouds of near unconsciousness whether this were what it felt like to die. Perhaps so, for just then I lapsed into thorough oblivion.

II.

When I came to myself, I noticed with a profound sense of relief that I was still in my chair, and had scarcely even shifted position. I was, I confess, a bit surprised that fully the whole night had passed. I had commenced my experiment an hour or two before sunset, and now the sun was just about to rise. Yet I had anticipated the possibility that my time perception might be affected, so I was not disturbed. I seemed otherwise to be quite unaffected. My only discomfort was my impatient and childish desire to tell someone, anyone, of my adventures of the night just past. The club would not meet again till the first of the month, and I had a week to wait before my appointment with Dr. Whitmore. How to contain my enthusiasm in the meantime? I was almost grateful to have the usual round of banal chores to occupy me for a few hours each day, and somehow I passed the week without exploding with my secret. How difficult it was, though, to pretend interest in the simple-minded matters I must discuss with my everyday acquaintances. How I wished to tell even them of my forbidden journeys into inner space, and of those weird denizens of my own subconscious! But I did not care to risk the odd stares and whispered remarks such words would prompt if spoken to the wrong people. Finally the day came for me to call upon Dr. Whitmore. As I sat vacantly leafing through one of the old books left on the waiting room table, I wondered how well I would be able to maintain the pretense of a nervous ailment. Could I keep it up long enough to detect some hint on Dr. Whitmore's part of his openness to discuss my hallucinatory experiences? The initial experiment had not been repeated, for the odd though illusory physical sensations I had undergone caused me to put off further attempts pending the physical examination for which I was now waiting. Indeed, what had originally served simply as the pretext for my visit was now a matter of real interest to me. I seemed in good, at least passable health, but mightn't the drug have had unexpected side effects? I would soon find out, as the door now opened, revealing the receptionist, dressed in a uniform so crisply white it almost seemed to shine. Responding to the call of my name, I rose and followed her down the hall to one of the examination rooms, where I would wait (but a moment, she assured me) for the doctor.

In surprisingly few moments, Dr. Whitmore himself arrived. He was a man of medium height, somewhat stooped, and bearing a bit of a paunch. Just past middle age, his hair and beard were well-grayed, but the lines of his face seemed to reflect more care than age. We exchanged a few pleasantries, and I began to lie as convincingly as I could about my invented symptoms. I spoke in generalities, and hoped I had the skill to phrase my data so it would sound more like the description of personal experiences than a list of textbook symptoms. Fortunately, he seemed satisfied after only a few questions, and began the tests. Some time later, I lay on the examination table waiting for him to return with a chart containing the results. Finally, Whitmore returned, still scanning the sheet as he stepped into the room. I sat up attentively and waited for him to show the mild puzzlement that all doctors evidence when their various probes yield nothing to justify the patient's complaints.

Sure enough, nothing seemed wrong with me physically. I was relieved at this news, but anxious, trying to hit upon a diplomatic way to reveal the true concern of my visit, to procure his advice, perhaps even his supervision, for further experiments by myself and my friends. But then he spoke again.

It seemed that the only ailment here was a typographical failure on my previous medical records. According to the files I had supplied him, my blood was listed as Type O, whereas the bloodwork he himself had done on me showed it to be Type A.

Had I not noticed this error myself? If so, why had I not had it corrected before now? It would certainly have caused some dangerous mischief had an accident rendered me unconscious and in need of a transfusion. But I was too overcome to answer him. I could only think back with frozen horror to the peculiar physical sensations of my . . . hallucination? For until now *my blood had been Type O!*

III.

It was with some puzzlement that Whitmore dismissed me, as might well be imagined, since my dumbfounded stupor seemed scarcely warranted by his mild rebuke. If I suffered further symptoms of my (pretended) malady, I was to let him know, but otherwise he could suggest nothing. How I longed more than ever to confide in the doctor—yet how impossible that had now become! Whatever his disposition regarding drug experimentation, Whitmore was after all an alienist and could hardly be expected to do other than take my fabulous tale as evidence of paranoid delusion on my part. And, indeed, might it *not* be? But, no, taking a moment to regain my composure after leaving the building, I satisfied myself that my memory and my sanity were alike intact. My blood type *had* formerly been as the records indicated, just as surely as it was now otherwise. Somehow the impossible had happened. Just how, I could not guess. Still less could I imagine what connection my hallucinatory experiment might have with the change, though certainly connection there was. And with this thought there rose anew in my soul the thrill of hope. Traumatic it had been, but was not the present mystery proof enough that somehow I had been right? Did I not hold at least the seeds that might yet blossom into that full occult knowledge that the club had sought, up till now, in vain? No doubt I did, and not even the instincts of foreboding caution which now stirred could make me pause.

With two weeks yet remaining before the next scheduled meeting of our circle, I considered two alternatives. It would be simple enough, of course, to call around and gather my colleagues for a special session. God, given what I might tell them, none of them would mind! Yet at this point there would actually be little to tell. There was but the bare experience itself, which still confounded me (though it had come to frighten me less since there seemed to be no damage to my health). My tale would cause no small stir, to be sure, but I felt I must be able to make it more intelligible, if I was to assure the circle that my course of investigation should be their own. I hoped I need not face further revelations alone. And so I decided upon the second alternative; I would use the remaining days to research as best I could the physiological marvel which had befallen me. I had little enough knowledge of medicine, but research into obscure byways was nothing new to me, and my brief study of the medical journals preparatory to my meeting with Dr. Whitmore had acquainted me with at least a few of the major periodicals in the field. With luck, I hoped to find some precedent or parallel to my own case. Whether connected to hallucinatory trance-states or no, had there been any reported cases of . . . how would it be designated . . . ? "Organic transposition"?

The day following my decision, I betook myself to the nearby university library and sought the help of the reference librarian. The self-assured competence of this fellow, a bespectacled graduate student in his late twenties, gave me hope that my search might at least be comprehensive if not fruitful. Yet under the guidance of the young man, I soon realized just how formidable was the task I had set myself. Truly the literature was vast and I hardly knew where to begin. It was difficult to make the subject of my interest adequately understood, but at length the young scholar grasped that I was concerned neither with organic degeneration due to inbreeding nor with ordinary deformation. Once he had some idea as to the goal of my curiosity he was, he said, inclined to discontinue the search. He was as good as certain that his indices and files of abstracts contained nothing on so outré a subject. However, an acquaintance of his was presently enrolled in the university's medical school, and he would try to prevail upon him to make a few inquiries.

I was quite grateful for this kind gesture, doubtful though I was that aught could come of it. Still, I gave the student my address and 'phone so that I might be reached in the unlikely event that something should turn up. Needless to say, I was duly amazed when but a few days later the call came. My surprise, my shock, was increased a hundredfold as I recognized the name of my caller. The medical student had related my request to none other than the same Dr. Martin Rhadamanthus whom I had believed to be on sabbatical abroad. It seemed rather that he had stayed secluded in the area, isolated from most social and professional contacts, in order to pursue some special researches normally precluded by the demands of his teaching. Nonetheless, the student, some sort of teaching assistant or apprentice I gathered, had been able to approach him with my strange inquiry, and he had taken an interest in it.

I considered myself fortunate to have so aroused his curiosity on so idiosyncratic a matter, though at the time I simply credited it to the polite generosity of the true professional, who feels bound to share what knowledge he has. Yet his very seclusion argued that such approachability was not his usual manner. If he had some personal interest in my case, I could not imagine its nature, nor did it then occur to me to do so.

At any rate, it seemed that Rhadamanthus's own research had once led him on a path of tangential cross-references which disclosed material relevant to what I had, he said, ingeniously named "organic transpositions." The account he had uncovered was contained in a seventeenth-century German work on, of all things, astronomy and astrology. It was entitled *Die Geschichte den Planeten,* or *The History of the Planets,* by a rather odd fellow named Eberhard Ketzer. He hailed from Schleswig-Holstein, and might have been a monk or perhaps a resident tutor in the Prussian court. No substantial biographical data had survived, save that derived from the book itself, to wit, that Ketzer claimed, like Johannes Kepler, to have heard the "music of the spheres." Only, unlike the more famous though equally eccentric Kepler, he had not liked what he had heard. Instead of the celestial harmony imagined by Dante and described by Kepler, Ketzer had ranted of a crashing cacophony as mad spheres rolled blindly on collision courses, veering crazily through overlapping planes and dimensions. The time must come, he said, when all would hear the screeching din, and when this time came, Doomsday, the final collision, would be at hand.

What had this lunacy to do with my quest? Simply that Ketzer had set down any curious reports that reached him if they seemed to his deranged mind to abet his theory, and the sheer strangeness of a report was liable to make it qualify.

The particular account to which Dr. Rhadamanthus had reference was the story of two brothers in Westphalen who claimed to have had an unusual "meeting" on their way back from Vespers one evening. They said they had been accosted on the path by shining "angels of God" who caused them to go to sleep, but a sleep filled with strange dreams. And when they awoke, they swore that they had shared one dream which seemed to have come true. The angels had removed and exchanged members of both brothers' bodies, so that each now possessed the hands and eyes of the other! They called on the village priest to bear witness that the odd change had in fact taken place. Their eyes, naturally, had been the same color from birth, so the hands must tell the story. Modern fingerprinting techniques would have made short work of the mystery, but an equally effective method was available. One brother was known to have lost a finger and the first joint of another in a recent woodworking mishap, yet this fellow's hands were newly whole, while his dismayed

20

brother now evidenced the other's mutilation! The finger and joint were missing, with no sign of recent injury.

Of course, Rhadamanthus averred, the historical value of such tales was nil, the verification standards of oral folk tradition being what they always have been. If one cared to look for them, even more spectacular episodes were to be found in literature from the same period, ranging from rainfalls of blood to apparitions of the Virgin, and all were alike fanciful. But he mentioned this one since it did come closer than any actual medical case history to the sort of phenomenon which interested me. In fact, I might study the legend for myself if I wished, since he himself had run across it in the university library not very long ago.

I thanked the good doctor effulgently, hanging up only after the gross temerity (I admit) of asking whether I might contact him again. To my surprise he was most willing, should the need arise. Of course, I still had in mind my original motive of seeking his counsel on my drug research.

I had by now concluded that Dr. Whitmore was quite innocent of the type of experience I had undergone. But fortune, I supposed, had guided me to the only remaining authority in this esoteric field.

Needless to say, I lost no time in returning to the library. The helpful fellow with whom I had previously spoken was not on duty, else I would have thanked him for his fruitful assistance. So I set to work locating the volume and securing a German to English dictionary. My study of the language lay many years in the past, and at any rate my merely conversational German would only get me started on what promised to be a difficult, rambling text.

Ketzer's work had been reprinted only a decade or so ago in an Oxford University Press series on the history of science. Gratified at this convenience, still I mused how odd a choice for inclusion in the series this tome of superstition seemed. The text was left untranslated, though modern typeface made it considerably easier to read than the original heavy black letter script would have been. And topical subdivisions were indicated by the editor's italics. This device made it fairly easy to locate my passage. Once I had found it, it turned out not to be too difficult to decipher, since Rhadamanthus had already summarized its contents fairly closely over the 'phone. But I noticed here and there an interesting detail— obscurities that any casual reader would neglect, but which assumed singular importance to me.

It seemed that the two peasants had not described their supramundane visitors in any detail, perhaps because they could not. Rather they had called them "angels" because their arrival was signaled by the appearance of a "halo in the air"! I looked up the appropriate end note, but the annotator was at a loss to explain this detail. In the manner of all unimaginative commentators, he suggested textual corruption or a printing error in the original edition. I, however, knew differently, for had I not seen such a "halo," or spinning circle, myself? Here it was, then; the same invisible craft containing visitors from . . . where?

Great mysteries remained; indeed, I had glimpsed, as it were, only the tip of the iceberg. Nonetheless, there was naught else to do now but break the news of my discoveries to the group, whose next meeting was only days away.

IV.

With old Elkhart's late arrival, our number was complete. Expectant faces all turned in my direction. My companions in esoterica sat about the spacious study: Barlow, Preus, St. Joshua, Elkhart. As was our custom, we rotated our place of meeting every month with the result that we now assembled in Barlow's home. Yet it was plain that I meant to take the lead this evening, and my demeanor gave me the aspect of host. Eagerly I recounted my experiment, my encounters with Drs. Whitmore and Rhadamanthus, and my research, occasionally doubling back to fill in a necessary detail or two. My friends were, as I had expected, quite astonished that things had proceeded so rapidly in the month gone by, when they had expected simply to hear whether I had secured any able supervisor, should any of us contemplate taking the drug. And here I had already taken it, without supervision, and with the most bizarre and unforeseen results! I half-suspected from the looks of one or two that they hardly knew whether to credit my strange tale.

Was I suggesting that the whole group embark on the voyage I had undertaken? Yes, I answered, I was, for did it not seem I had succeeded in making the first steps toward that goal of arcane knowledge that had so long eluded us? Further, I averred, I now felt sure that Rhadamanthus was our man, that he could be trusted to guide us and to take a scientific interest in our endeavors. With the group's permission I would approach him candidly with our proposal. With this suggestion all seemed in accord save the religious fanatic Preus, who was suddenly having second thoughts. For despite his wild flirtations with unorthodox mysticisms, he remained very much the Puritan in his behavior. And he could not, he said, countenance the use of drugs. Preus was obdurate in the face of our attempts to convince him, allowing himself at length to be won over by the reasoning of St. Joshua and myself. We pointed out that we would be using the drug in an almost medicinal manner, to reawaken dormant sense functions that evolution had atrophied. Henceforth Preus was willing, however reluctantly, to go along.

The next step was to be mine as I sought Rhadamanthus' help. We resolved to meet again the very next week, we hoped, with the doctor added to our number. The rest of the evening seemed anticlimactic as we tried to discuss books read in the last month. And conversation would return again and again to my vision and its aftermath. Impatient expectancy had consumed us all: we were like children on Christmas Eve.

The following day I telephoned Dr. Rhadamanthus. Assuming I would reach only his answering service, I was unprepared to hear his own voice on the line. Incredibly, he was quite willing to interrupt his work for a visit that very afternoon. I could call on him at his home, a large brownstone adjacent to the university campus.

His residence was easily located, and I pressed upon the doorbell about 4 o'clock that afternoon. Rhadamanthus himself met me at the door, another surprise since I imagined he must leave such chores to servants in order to concentrate on his sabbatical studies. Once inside, I removed hat and coat, draping them on the banister as my host indicated. I turned for my first good look at Dr. Rhadamanthus. He was a tall man, probably tending a bit to thinness, though his dressing gown obscured the details of his figure. His face, clean-shaven, had the almost fatherly aspect that serves doctors well in winning their patients' confidences. Indeed, his manner seemed a bit too paternal, almost patronizing, as he welcomed me and bade me follow him into his study.

The room was large and well-lit, with bookcases lining every wall, though not to a uniform height, since the cases did not match, having most likely been acquired and added one by one over the years as needed. But if the room lacked symmetry, still it was neat, every book in place, with papers and journals neatly stacked. If Dr. Rhadamanthus had been engaged in scholarly labors this afternoon, there was nothing to show it.

Seated behind his desk, he folded his hands in his lap and broke the silence. "What is it you want of me? And . . . oh, did you find the Ketzer volume?" I felt slightly embarrassed at his first words. I had interrupted him, one imposition already, and was making ready to ask yet another favor.

My intention, then, was obvious, so I reasoned I had best be as frank as he had been.

"Yes, Doctor, I have read it, and with much interest—more than you might guess, as a matter of fact. And to tell the truth, that is why I've taken the liberty to impose on your time in this fashion. Again, forgive me, but . . ."

"But you yourself have had such an experience as that described by the two peasants long ago, have you not?"

"Why, yes! Yes, indeed I *have*, Doctor . . . ," I stammered, considerably shocked by his prescience.

"Tell me, how did you bring about the . . . hallucination? Or did you? Did the experience perhaps come upon you uninvited?"

I replied that I had invited *something* by my use of the drug, but that I did not, could not have, expected the shocking physical aftermath of the experiment. Was it possible for mescaline to effect such a change in the body? Surely nothing I had read would lead one to think so, and it was hard to imagine . . .

"No, no, you are quite right; no *mere* drug of whatever kind could cause the change you have undergone. I see by your line of questioning that you did not read quite far enough in Ketzer. Yet I can see how you would miss it. The old astrologer's work lacked much in the way of organization. What of the name 'Yaddith'?" My blank stare was sufficient reply, and he continued. "Ketzer wrote in rather veiled fashion of certain distant realms, whether of outer or inner space he did not say, and I am no longer sure there is any ultimate difference. One of these realms he named 'Yaddith', all the more remarkably for the difficulty of rendering this word in German, where as you know, our 'th' sound is lacking." I wondered momentarily how he would know how the word was pronounced. Had he independent information? "Such realms are sometimes opened to men, to those who can make themselves ready by various means."

"But Doctor Rhadamanthus, surely not all those who have taken mescaline have experienced what I have experienced. If mere drug-taking were the key . . ." He waved his hand as if to brush aside my words like a cobweb.

"But you have prepared the ground by your various occult researches over the years, as have your friends, from what you tell me."

Little more would he say, but he had said quite enough for me to puzzle over. If nothing else, it was obvious that from our first contact he had known far more than he told me. Indeed he seemed to know *too* much, about the mystery itself as well as my involvement with it. Perhaps this fact should have alarmed me, but instead it fueled the fire of my excitement.

24

And with his last comment he had virtually asked my intended favor for me. "Yes, Doctor, the members of the group have, as you say, prepared themselves, and now they are willing to join me in plumbing whatever truth may lie in this direction." I outlined our plan to him, and he readily assented to supervise us, to my great relief. Time and place were set, and I departed, scarcely able to assimilate all I had heard that afternoon.

V.

I had still not sorted things out completely when the six of us gathered at my home the next week. But I felt sure all would soon enough be clear to me—both the mystery of Rhadamanthus himself and the deeper truths I had spent so many years in pursuit of. As things turned out, I was right.

Our chairs were arranged in a circle in the very same room from which I had embarked on my strange pilgrimage only a month earlier. All of us were excited, Preus perhaps a bit more apprehensive than the rest, Barlow the more eager, but we were all ready to begin. Doctor Rhadamanthus had supplied each of us with our own dose of the drug (or of *some* drug), which we should all take together on signal, so to facilitate a collective and simultaneous experience. Rhadamanthus himself, of course, took no mescaline and sat outside the circle, his chair against one wall, where he had a clear view both of the group and of the picture window. This last was my suggestion. I reasoned that only so could we know how much of whatever transpired was internal and how much external reality. If someone who had not taken the drug saw any of the phenomena I had seen through that window, then we would know for certain whether the drug-induced mental state acted as "bait" for some beings more real than hallucinatory fantasies.

What I refrained from telling the doctor was that I, too, intended to observe what happened without benefit of the drug. I would but pretend to take it and see for myself what transpired. Would I still see what the others saw?

The moment came, and with it a flash of guilty panic. What might I have recklessly led my companions into? Well, no matter—they had taken the dose and I could only wait to see what followed. In a matter of minutes, perhaps a quarter of an hour, it began. The unearthly, sibilant whistling . . . did I see it? Yes! The very air began to spin in a huge ring, this time above our heads. Then it was no hallucination, whatever else it must be called. Would to God it had been! Dare I risk a glance over toward where Rhadamanthus was seated? If he noticed, he would have to detect my subterfuge. Yet I supposed it did not really matter. I craned my neck to look, and . . . where but a moment before Rhadamanthus had sat in a posture of attentive concern, now there loomed one of the insectoid blasphemies I had seen in my vision last month! And this time I had taken no drug! God, I must rise and flee! But the strength had drained out of me, driven forth by the magnitude of my shock. As I felt myself fainting, I thought at least to turn back and catch a glimpse of my friends, but too late. Blackness swallowed me, this time the wholesome darkness of merciful unconsciousness.

When I came to myself, my first sight was of Rhadamanthus' now empty chair. Dreading what I should next see, I pulled myself to my knees and turned around to face a nightmare more hideous than any bred by fevered sleep. For amid scattered chairs and smears of blood stood abomination. To describe the indescribable the mind grasps wildly at the most improbable comparisons. What I saw resembled the cross-linked cage of a child's "jungle gym;" the revolting structure was a sagging composite of human limbs and trunks linked in a maze of insanity. Here a forearm ended at the wrist in another's chest, there a head sprouted from the small of a back; eyes stared out singly from shoulders or hands! Worse yet, no seam or breakage of skin was visible; the staggering castle of flesh looked as if it had grown as I now saw it! Dear Savior, if I could but tear from my memory the sight of the tortured faces of Elkhart, Preus, and the others, growing now from thighs and abdomens, staring blindly from empty sockets, screaming silently from mouths without vocal chords!

Reason fled my mind, as it must when reason has fled the world. All I knew was that this quivering miscegenation must outrage nature no longer. I half-ran, half-staggered from the room, down the stairs, and onto the porch where lay stacked wood for the fireplace, and . . . my axe! All I did, I did under instinct's dictates, pausing only later to contemplate my actions. Seizing the axe, I bounded back up into the room where the thing that had been my friends still tottered and flailed in agony. I determined that it should do so no longer. Poor Barlow, Preus, St. Joshua, Elkhart!

They should have peace, even if the peace of everlasting oblivion! So I swung the axe, again and again, hewing and hacking with a fury I had not believed myself capable of. But of course it was the strength of the mad, for that is what I was in that moment. Screams filled the air, but I now realize they must have been mine.

(Sit down, Mr. Turrow! I assure you my bloodlust has quite spent itself! All I ask is that you listen to the rest.)

When I had finished, I and everything in the room were virtually afloat in blood. But at least nothing indicated that a short time before the room had contained a *structure* of living flesh knitted somehow from four human bodies. Only pieces, small pieces, remained. Now I realize this to have been a mistake. For there is no longer any evidence of what really happened. One could prove no more than that a man went mad and butchered four men. But as I say, I was not thinking clearly then, not thinking at all. Nor was I when exhaustion bade me collapse on my bed in the next room.

The whole night I slumbered obliviously in the midst of that charnel house. When consciousness returned, so did the knowledge of what I had done. Perhaps all that saved me from final gibbering insanity was the detachment I felt, as if another had committed the atrocity, for as I have said, when I acted I was not myself. I sat up in bed and thought for quite some time. I resolved to complete two tasks that day, most likely to be my last day of freedom.

I dressed quickly, edged my way with tightly closed eyes through the next room, its air reeking of blood, and finally reached the door. Descending the stairs, I departed for the university library. I only hoped I might evade capture long enough to find some clue explaining the nightmare in which I now found myself.

Soon I had Ketzer's nefarious *History of the Planets* open before me once again. Sure enough, just as Rhadamanthus (or whatever he had been) told me, there was the mention of "Yaddith," and here was my answer, at least the beginning of it.

I replaced the book and left the campus, intent upon discharging my second errand, and that is when I came to see you, Mr. Turrow. My story must be aired, and from your paper's reputation I judged you the only one likely to air it. And I hope that you will. Now I have done all I may do, and can only await my fate. Perhaps the police will find me, but, more likely, *they* will. For you see, Mr. Turrow, this is what I read: that when a way had been opened to that other realm, contacts could be made, and truth sought and found. But openings might also be made *from the other side*, as presumably had happened in the case of the two German brothers. And in either case, those from Yaddith were just as curious as we. They, no less than we, were—*are*—inclined to . . . shall we say *experiment*? And now I, the seeker for truth, find myself in the position of a laboratory animal who through carelessness has escaped, and I believe they will not be long in finding me.

–1984–

27

BLACK EONS
With Robert E. Howard

"Vor dem Anfang der Historie, die erinnern Menschen sich, gibt es schwarze Äonen, denen ist es vielleicht besser nicht zu wissen."

"Before the beginning of the history men remember, there are black eons of which it is perhaps better not to know."

—Von Junzt, *Die Unaussprechlichen Kulten*

I. THE RIDDLE IN THE CRYPT

Beneath the glare of the sun, etched in the hot blue sky, native laborers sweated and toiled. The scene was a cameo of desolation—blue sky, amber sand stretching to the skyline in all directions, barely relieved by a fringe of palm trees that marked an oasis in the near distance. The men were like brown ants in that empty sun-washed immensity, pecking away at a queer gray dome half hidden in the sands. Their employers aided with directions and ready hands.

Allison was square-built and black bearded; Brill was tall, wiry, with a ginger-hued moustache and cold blue eyes. Both had the hard bronzed look of men who had spent most of their lives in the outlands. Allison knocked out the ashes from his pipe on his boot heel.

"Well, how about it?"

"You mean that fool bet?" Brill looked at him in surprise. "Do you mean it?"

"I do. I'll lay you my best six-shooter against your saddle that we don't find an Egyptian in this tomb."

"What do you expect to find?" asked Brill quizzically, "a local shaykh? Or maybe a Hyksos king? I'll admit it's different from anything of the sort I've ever seen before, but we know from its appearance of age that it antedates Turkish and Semitic control of Egypt—it's bound to go back further than the Hyksos, even. And before them, who was in Egypt?"

28

"I'll reckon we'll know after we've looted this tomb," answered Allison, with a certain grimness in his manner.

Brill laughed. "You mean to tell me you think there was a race here before the Egyptians, civilized enough to build such a tomb as this? I suppose you think they built the pyramids!"

"They did," was the imperturbable reply.

Brill laughed. "Now you're trying to pull my leg."

Allison looked at him curiously. "Did you ever read the *Unaussprechlichen Kulten?*"

"What the devil's that?"

"A book called *Nameless Cults*, by a crazy German named Von Junzt—at least they *said* he was crazy. Among other things, he wrote of an age which he swore he had discovered—an age undreamed of by moderns—a sort of historical blind spot. He called it the Hyborian Age. We have guessed what came before, and we know what came after, but that age itself has been a blank space—no legends, no chronicles, just a few scattered names that came to be applied in other senses.

"It's our lack of knowledge about this age that upsets our calculations and makes us put down Atlantis as a myth. This is what Von Junzt says: that when Atlantis, Lemuria and other nations of that age were destroyed by a violent cataclysm—except for scattered remnants here and there—the continent now known as Africa was untouched, though connected with the other continents. A tribe of savages fled to the Arctic Circle to escape the volcanoes, and eventually evolved into a race known as Hyborians. These reached a high stage of civilization and dominated the western part of the world, all expect this particular part. A pre-Cataclysmic race lived here, known as Stygians. It was from them that the Grecian legend of Stygia arose; the Nile was the Styx of the fables. The Hyborians were never able to invade Stygia, and at last they themselves were destroyed by waves of barbarians from the north—our own ancestors. In Stygia the ruling classes were pure-blooded, but the lower classes were mixed—Stygian, Semitic and Hyborian blood.

"In the southward drift of the barbarians, a tribe of red-haired Nordics fought their way south and overthrew the ancient Stygian regime. They destroyed or drove out the pure-blooded Stygians, and set themselves up as a ruling caste, eventually being absorbed by their subjects; from these adventurers and mixed mongrel lower classes came the Egyptians. It was the Stygians who built the pyramids and the Sphinx. And if I'm not mistaken, one of them lies in this pile of masonry." Brill laughed incredulously.

Allison resolved, then, to keep his conviction to himself, somehow as certain of what they would find as he was that the sun would soon be setting. And his certainty seemed almost like the certainty of memory.

It was not long before events vindicated him.

Both men rose and retreated into the merciful shade of the palms. Only an hour or so later, they were called back into the afternoon blaze by the excited shouts of the laboring *fellahin*. The ancient fastness had at last been breached. Allison knew that these native diggers felt none of his own excitement, the zeal of the searcher after antique mysteries and vestiges of the Elder world. Nay, he did not let himself imagine that in their mercenary single-mindedness they were even capable of it. The Aryan spirit of quest innate in his own stock could seek adventure down intellectual avenues when others were closed off, as physical heroics must ever be for Allison, having lost one leg in a youthful riding accident. But the Muhammedan craftiness of these jackals made the silver coin the only object of their quest. And now their joy came simply from the discovery that their job, for which they had been paid amply in advance, would be much shorter than anyone had anticipated.

All this occurred to Allison, almost unnoticed, as he ambled to the site, the slow but steady pace of his wooden leg belying the thrill of anticipation that charged him. He scarcely noticed the ill-concealed avarice in the eyes of the Egyptians, who hoped there might prove to be vast stores of golden treasure to divide, sell, and squander on hashish, so little did they understand their employers' motivations. Yet treasures—artifacts— were much on the minds of Brill and Allison, for they sought some evidence anchoring their find along the banks of Egypt's long flowing river of history.

The walls of the dome and the structure beneath it did not seem particularly thick, and it would have been simple enough to break through at any point along the considerable area already exposed. The diggers had suggested this, but Allison would have none of it. He was willing to risk damaging none of whatever artifacts might rest inside. Instead he had insisted they continue to clear away sand and rubble until the entrance portal could be found. As it happened, any more impatient course would have been foolish, as the door had been uncovered only an hour or so later.

As Brill and Allison joined the Egyptians, they were at the point of at last freeing the great slab of the door. The inrush of air spoiling the airtight vacuum of ages echoed the explorers' own hushed gasp of anticipation as they stepped through the aperture into the yawning

30

shadowed grayness.

Silence greeted them as they wended their way carefully along the newly opened corridor, their tread muffled by the gathered dust of uncounted millennia. The grandeur of the vast, dim mausoleum halls was not to be denied, but of gold and gems little was to be seen. There was but one singularly large translucent crystal sphere which sat upon a pedestal near a vacant, crumbling dais. Brill spoke for both when he mused aloud, "It almost seems like it wasn't a *royal* tomb at all, unless of course somebody got to it before *we* did." Robbers despoiling tombs and temples was the fear of all Egyptologists, Allison and Brill included.

"And there's really no sign of that," Allison continued Brill's thought for him. "No Bedouins who found a treasure trove would have taken the trouble to remove signs of entry. But you're overlooking the most obvious, in fact the most important, thing of all. As I told you, this tomb is *not* Egyptian! Yes, the general decorum of the place seems conventional enough, but I think you'll notice some significant differences here and there. Like the sarcophagus up there by the dais. Ever seen one like it?"

"One thing's for sure," Brill replied, "whatever his race or country, Egyptian or one of your hypothetical Stygians, this old boy *wasn't* a king." They had advanced to the dais. "This head-dress motif is all wrong for that. It's neither the triple-crown of a god nor the combined crown of Upper and Lower Egypt."

Allison joined him, locking his gaze onto that painted mummy-case. "And unless I miss my guess, not a true crown at all. I see your point, then. But what else? A priest? A vizier, like Joseph in the biblical tale? Or, if I'm right and the whole business is pre-Egyptian, we may have a whole new set of possibilities."

"Yes, and all of them unknown!" Brill sighed.

By this time the light had begun to fade, making it impossible to examine the relics in any kind of close detail, yet the two explorers only noticed the sudden fall of the desert night when the strains of Egyptian voices penetrated their reverie.

"*Effendi!* The twilight deepens, and it is not safe to linger further!"

"Very well," shouted Allison. Then, to Brill, "I'm itching to take a closer look at those hieroglyphs, and that odd statuary over there, but I don't think we've enough lights and wiring prepared to rig up tonight. It will have to wait for tomorrow, I guess." Brill sensed that Allison's frustration was keener than his own, as if he had some desperate need to unravel the mystery of the crypt. After all, there was his outlandish pre-Egyptian hypothesis, and he had his six-shooter riding on it.

"Cheer up, old man." Pointing to the mummy-case, now propped up against the wall, he laughed. "After all, this fellow's waited some thousands of years to divulge his secrets. Chances are they'll keep till we return in the morning."

II. ANCIENT DREAMS

Allison had expected he would not sleep that night for excitement, but surprisingly he soon fell asleep, and deeply. And, more, he dreamed. And dreaming, he knew that once he was Bane the Reaver, young member of a marauding tribe of Vanir, migrating like a flood-tide from the northern lands of their ancestry, seeking out new lands to conquer and settle. Down they had swept across the ruins of the once-proud Aquilonian empire, whelming the battle-weary Picts and Hyrkanians they met, taking them by surprise, their energies spent in craven scavenging among the debris of Hyborian civilization.

Amid the multi-hued and many-formed splendor of the collapsing Hyborian Age, still brilliant albeit with the glow of its own decay, the Vanir Bane was himself a wonder worthy of recounting. The men of his day were giants compared to the men of today, as evolution left them no option but to compete successfully with nature's monsters or perish. Feats of strength and endurance considered routine among them would be deemed fabulous among us. And indeed it is not improbable that those primeval warriors were the prototypes for the *Nephilim*, those 'giants', the 'men of renown' whose exploits loom so largely in the myths of the Near East.

And the tribe of the Vanir was by no means the least of the races of heroes. Like human snow bears they seemed, bred and trained by the brutal lessons of the arctic Nordlands. And Bane the Reaver was exceptional among even the Vanir. Approaching seven feet, his towering height was deceptive because of his massive build. Iron-thewed and ropy-sinewed was he, a brother to Hercules in an era before that name had first been uttered. And somehow this young frost-giant was one across the ages with the cripple James Allison, and with unknown dozens of lives in between. This Allison knew in his dream, though he knew not how it could be, nor did he scruple to wonder. For it seemed more that he had awakened from a dream, a dream of infirmity that had lasted much too long.

But now reality was the golden sunlight on his bare, sun-bronzed back as

Bane took the paved streets of the Stygian capital in long strides. Somehow as he surveyed the scene about him, all seemed to resonate inside his brain in a peculiar way. It was as if not his senses but his understanding had been heightened, for he saw everything with the eyes of James Allison as well as his own. But they *were* his own. All this, however, was lost on Bane the Reaver, as he sped past sparse knots of fighting and occasionally paused in his pace to sidestep the many corpses which littered the ground. Of this he noticed with no surprise that there were far more dead Stygians than Vanir.

As Bane's tribe had journeyed south they found that there really were no *new* lands to conquer. Nay, all these civilized lands seemed pathetically *old*. Even those like Aquilonia that might still give thought to military adventure, had long ago settled into the dribbling senility of civilization with its decadent and poisonous ways. And of no land was this more true than Stygia, the dark underworld of demons worshipped as gods. The red atrocities of the lunatic worship of Set the serpent had sent horrid whispers of Stygian piety everywhere. And rumors persisted that even more fiendish things were served in Stygia in the small hours of the night.

If the malignant sorcery of Stygia had for ages festered at the base of the Hyborian world, it was now to be cleansed by the fresh, arctic tide of Vanir steel. For the mutterings of wizards seemed little effective against the blades of Bane's people, as the quick victory of the Nordheimers in this, the chief Stygian city, made obvious. The penetration of the city walls was short work and the sacking of the city was almost complete already. There might be booty enough left for Bane to claim his share, but the young Vanir sought a different sort of prize—honor, and a name that would win renown and hold it, in campfire tales, in heroic lays, in future epics.

It was this lust that led the brash youth to dare what none of his compatriots had dared, though many were as brave as he in battle, and some were a good deal wiser. For love of fame, Bane headed now toward a district of the city so sunken in a spell of eerie silence that even the still-frequent noises of combat seemed unwilling to trespass. He neared the forecourt of the shunned temple of the dark god Gol-goroth which popular superstition made it blasphemy, even death, to enter. No Stygian, catechized by priests and frightened by mothers' bed-time whispers, would even think of setting foot in the sacred precincts. Thus far the grounds had been inviolate from Vanir profanation. Even in the short time since their capture of the city, the Northern folk's superstitious nature had rapidly picked up the weird scent and added Gol-goroth to their pantheon of terrors. Bane the Reaver had none of the rationalistic distrust of the supernatural possessed by his twentieth-century counterpart Allison. But neither did he lack the drive to conquer, and to be hailed as conqueror, that had ever driven the mightiest chiefs of his kind.

With the demon of fear thus exorcised, the impetuous barbarian faced the fane of Stygian darkness. The temple complex itself seemed surprisingly modest, a collection of small, fairly nondescript buildings, almost huts, adjacent to a dome built of blue-gray stone, and jutting out from a hill face. The structure boasted little ornamentation, save for a double row of black, monolithic slabs arranged along the paved path to the threshold. The coloration of the buildings themselves might have been chosen for the effect it had on the unsophisticated observer. To Bane's eyes the temple seemed to fade in and out with the lazy blue of the late afternoon sky, evoking the very spirits of the heavens to guard it, seeming to belong to the ethereal world of the gods.

The adventurer's ambitions soon got the better of that brief moment of hypnotic fixation, and he was busily calculating. He guessed that the dome hid the mouth of a network of tunnels and subterranean chambers. If so, he stood to find himself at a disadvantage; he was accustomed to the dazzling arcs of axes and claws in the arctic sunlight, else the desperate dance of the southern battlefield, which for all its menacing forest of enemy swords at least took place out in the open. How effective would even his skills be in some dark labyrinth shut off from the sun's vigilant watch? More than likely he would have to rely solely upon his instincts. Nothing to do, then, but start out. He walked forward, eyes sweeping left to right and back again for any signs of alarm or prevention. The black slabs he passed on either side stood too much exposed to afford hiding places for any guards, of which there seemed to be none anyway. The great rock faces were strangely carved, though it was beyond Bane's ken to take much notice.

Yet it did not escape his Allison-part, who even through the unreal haze of dream could marvel at the workmanship of Elder ages. Seeing what Bane the Reaver could not see and knowing what he could not know, he noted at once the utter alienness of the inscriptions. They were runes of queer design. They reminded him much less of Egyptian hieroglyphs than of certain strange characters he had seen on worn masonry in such far-flung spots as the jungles of Yucatan and certain wooded hillsides in the Balkans. And the Allison-self noticed something else—the graven glyphs on each stone seemed somehow to come alive with an inconceivable sentience as Bane passed each one.

34

III. MADNESS OF THE SECRET GOD

Though Bane saw no one as he advanced to the temple portal, his progress did not go unobserved. Within the structure he hoped soon to penetrate, eyes were fixed upon him—or upon his image, imprisoned in a crystal sphere. In the place where this bubble of magic sight rested, the air hung thickly with sickly-sweet incense. Occasional tapers smoldered, struggling to send forth a light that was as quickly swallowed up by the smoke-blackened tapestries that hid the walls. By far the greatest darkness in the chamber, however, was the psychic pall radiating from the lone figure stretched out on the dais, watching the tiny scene in the glass sphere. Like the cloud of ink ejected by a squid, the priest's black robes billowed out from his spare frame. The velvet luxuriance of his cassock clashed with the bony thinness of the man himself. His head was as a deathshead, his hands but claws, adorned with sigil-engraved ruby and sapphire rings. He seemed as a cadaver dressed up to mock the living, as if to show that all human finery serves in the end merely to decorate a corpse.

His was the face of the ascetic, the fanatic, lit now with the eager malevolence of the cobra, roused from its boredom by the intrusion of some new, unwary prey. Koth-Serapis, archimage and hierophant of Golgoroth, regarded Bane's furtive entry into the shrine. The hall was pitch-black, yet the scene was clearly visible to Koth-Serapis as he watched it in his crystal. Invisible to Bane (as to Allison), more of the dark stones hung from the walls, their strange markings somehow sensing the barbarian's moves and transmitting them into the translucent orb. Shrouded in the protective night of the temple, Koth-Serapis saw more clearly than did the Vanir himself that the young blasphemer had now unsheathed his battle-axe and held it before him, as much to grope through the blind gulf ahead of him as to protect himself.

Suddenly from every corner at once there seemed to gather a misty blue radiance which gave Bane for the first time a glimpse of the hall surrounding him. Tapestries lined the walls, but the light was too weak for their design to be visible. In such twilight the purpose of these hangings could scarcely be decorative. More likely they hid something, secret doorways perhaps, from which a man might be . . .

No sooner did the word "ambushed" come to his mind than Bane saw the tapestries on either side of him part, disclosing pits of darkness from which poured the temple guards he missed earlier. With impossible speed they fanned out, surrounding him on all sides. They were strangely silent, and strangely unlike the Stygian soldiers encountered in the city. Though what the difference was, he had no time to fathom, as rational thought surrendered to the red haze of battle fury.

"Ho!" cried the Vanir. "Jackals! You would deny me a fair fight, but I mean to make you pay heavily for your advantage!" So saying, he shifted his weight back onto his heels. Extending his axe as far as it would reach, he began to spin around, his blade blurring into a deadly silver arc that cut with little resistance through breastplate and flesh alike. His own attire, a scant leather harness, would give him little protection, so he knew his best defense lay in a blinding outburst to catch his foes off guard. Yet soon he might grow too dizzy to aim a blow once he stopped.

In a moment, three of the guards lay raggedly dismembered at his feet, afloat in their own steaming gore. Bane's axe had caught one of them neatly between the ribs, just as the Stygian had raised his weapon to strike. The blow had split him nearly asunder. Another's arm and head had been sheared off completely, the trunk tottering as if in surprised confusion before sagging into a reddening heap. The third, stepping backward, had not been quick enough and could not completely avoid the keen edge of Vanir steel as it struck him glancingly, neatly snipping the jugular. Not only so, but in his desperate effort to clear the deadly path of the axe, he had reeled drunkenly into the sword point of his fellow and taken it in the back.

It would have been hard to say which blow won the race to kill him.

Two guards remained, one on either side, and Bane knew he must choose one to attack first, leaving himself open to a blow, mayhap a lethal one, from the other. If the first be dispatched with sufficient speed, his partner would not be allowed a second blow. The young Vanir slowed, stopped, and somehow gained his bearings quickly enough to spring at his foe, who seemed almost to have been hypnotized by the death-dealing cyclone of steel. His unprotected back tingling with anticipation of an enemy blow, Bane raised his axe and brought it down on the flabbergasted Stygian, cleaving his skull to the jawbone. Blood sprayed Bane's back and shoulder as he ducked and turned, hoping to avoid the lunge of the last remaining guardsman. Had he been a split-second slower, he had died right there, his work of carnage mere preparation for his own crimson ruin. As it was, he felt the queer, electric coldness of what must have been an enchanted Stygian blade. It raked across his ribcage, leaving a thin trickle of blood, which shrank into a line of droplets, as if the sword had cauterized the wound even while making it.

But the momentum of the guardsman's charge carried him stumbling past the sidestepping form of the Northern interloper. The latter brought down the axe again, first hamstringing his attacker, then mauling him.

Bane allowed himself a moment to look round at the carcasses strewn about like dancers collapsed from exhaustion. He muttered, "By Ymir, I promise that whoever sent you will join you soon enough in hell." As he wiped the clotted brains and blood from the flat of his axe, his future self Allison half remembered, half observed the scene, and it occurred to him suddenly just what had seemed so strangely *different* about these Stygians. They were unlike the defenders of the city walls in that they looked slightly more like what Bane had *expected* Stygians to look like—a hint more menacing, dark, and sinister, more like devils masquerading as men. For all that, it had not helped them prevail against the lone Northerner. Still, Allison thought it (remembered it) a bit odd.

Bane turned to scrutinize the rest of the hallway. It had grown darker again, yet he could make out a faint greenish luminescence in the distance, around a corner far ahead. He felt for the Stygian blade that had grazed him, found it, and anchored it to his belt. In a place of nighted sorcery, a charmed blade might prove the best weapon. Starting out for the hint of radiance ahead, he felt puzzled, troubled by a peculiar sensation. Something seemed *wrong* about the ground-plan of the place. It did not seem to fit the shape of the temple compound as Bane had seen it from outside. Even allowing for the hillside into which, he had guessed, the temple was carved, the layout was just not right. To go on for this distance, the corridors must gradually slant downward and become ramps leading beneath the surface. Yet they did not. More sorcery, he concluded with the barbarian's pragmatism that caused him to take even the impossible for granted once encountered.

Thus pursuing his thoughts, Bane came at length to the corner around which the eerie lambency had shown. Stealthily he peeked around it only to find more hallways. This time the light had an identifiable source. Iron-bracketed torches flamed, or rather glowed, with the cold, slow light of fireflies. And in their dim haloes Bane could make out some sort of carvings placed higher up on the walls, so high that it was impossible to trace their outlines in any detail. Yet the twisting and turning of the shadows implied a series of bas-reliefs erratically jutting out at spots into real statuary. The archaeological imagination of Allison filled in gaps that Bane's outlander ignorance could not supply. The strange faces and forms half-visible below the line where penumbra lapsed into darkness must represent some of the animal-headed gods of Egypt, together with others unknown.

But his dreamer's glimpse was tantalizingly short, as Bane, caring little for the scholar's niceties, turned his gaze to the hall before him. What might await him there? Something did, for now he could pick out what appeared to be a blacker patch against the misty darkness of the corridor. Slowly he approached it, noting that these walls were bare of tapestries and so presumably empty of hidden guards as well. Still, there might be more than one kind of guard . . .

The object had remained stationary, its outlines difficult to grasp, and this did not change as one drew closer. It was a statue, and a massive one, yet its breadth was much greater than its height. In its strange lineaments could be traced rudimentary hints of long, ribbed wings, scaly folds of flesh, even tentacles wound together. It was as if some sculptor could not decide which kind of creature to depict in stone. Somehow Bane knew with a certainty whose source he could not name that it was meant to represent the secret god of Stygia, Gol-goroth. He stepped back to get a better look at the outlines of the thing as a whole, wondering what degenerate piety could revere such a god.

His nape-hairs prickled, his eyes widening—had he seen it *move*? In the half-light it was impossible to tell. Then sheer lunacy swept all doubts away as one tentacle, petrified no long longer, felled him heavily with a soggy, smacking blow. Bane rolled aside, yanking himself free of the stinging kisses of scores of questing suckers. His own blood trickled from scores of tiny matching wounds, flowing to mingle with that of the slain temple guards.

The shifting bulk of Gol-goroth was alive now, the extra-cosmic horrors that had been merely suggested in stone now writhing with hideous vitality. The shadowy halls echoed with its outraged roaring—the pained squealing as of a beached sea-beast. Tattered, membranous wings sought to enfold Bane like a spider's sticky web. Snaky tendrils dripping with strange venom crept toward him. Bane's eyes could not encompass it. His mind could not give it shape, this gelid horror from before the time of men.

The sword, blasphemously blessed with eldritch life—if Bane could gather his wits quickly enough, perhaps it could be turned against the very sorcery that had forged it. If he could just find the thing's vitals ... but it seemed to have none, not even any visible sense organs. The sword slashed and slashed, freeing bubbling handfuls of living slime which merely fell back against the unstable mass to be reabsorbed within it. Such a thing could not be.

Indeed, such a thing *could* not be, thought Allison, now convinced that he tossed and turned in the grip of nightmare. Or perhaps it was not *his* nightmare, but Bane's. Now random bits of insanity began to fall into a pattern. With the odd detachment of the dreamer, Allison was at once spectator and actor, and this gave him an opportunity his Bane-part could ill-afford, the chance to reason about the irrational situation facing him. So far, every innate fear of the simple barbarian had seemed literally to materialize. Armed men hiding behind the curtains, eerie shadows in the darkness, frightening idols coming to life. Mayhap the real sorcery in the fane of the secret god was the magic of the mind. Could it be that Bane strove against shades evoked by some evil force from his own primitive brain?

So far, the naked courage of the young barbarian had been enough to conquer these fears, but now he struggled in vain against a horror he could not name. Allison decided he must take a terrible risk; he must try to penetrate the seething mind of his alter ego, to reach across unimaginable ages and implant within that savage brain a thought of cool reason. He must make Bane know that which he himself had guessed—and he must hope dearly that he had guessed correctly. For he would try to convince Bane to cease struggling and see the illusion for what it was: a shambling phantom of the mind. If Allison had surmised falsely, his dawn-age self would fall unresisting prey to the god Gol-goroth, with who knew what effects on Allison's own yet-future existence?

Amid the hellish din of the flailing obscenity, Bane felt the intrusion of one thought like the tread of a creeping enemy. It was a thought of peace, a call from some deep recess of himself to have done with his fruitless combat. And strangely he listened, for somehow it seemed not a suicidal urge to yield (though how could it be otherwise?), but rather a faint inkling that this way lay victory. In this labyrinth of scarlet madness nothing was what it seemed. Perhaps, he listened more than thought, Gol-goroth was not what it seemed either. Perhaps even surrender would not be what it seemed.

Bane let his arms fall slack and released his grip on both sword and axe, watching both fall to the stone-flagged floor. As he half-waited for a crushing tentacle to end it all, he noticed distantly the clanging of only one of the weapons, his axe, on the floor. The sword had disappeared. Had it perhaps been mired and swallowed in the translucent blackness of the monster? But then where was the monster? The abysmal stench of it was suddenly absent, and the new silence of the corridor struck Bane's ears like deafening thunder. In truth, the god was gone. Nearby was only a low statue, about five feet long, that bore some resemblance to it.

IV. THE SORCERER'S CURSE

Perhaps the most surprising thing of all was the corridor itself—with the clouds of illusion dispelled from his mind, Bane could see that there was but a single hallway, straight and only a hundred yards or so in length. In truth he had walked but fifty feet since entering the portal! A quick glance about him revealed no bloodied bodies of temple guards, no eerily shimmering torches. Only something dimly visible up at the end of the hall—a dais with an indistinct figure seated upon it. The only light in that place flashed from what looked like a glass sphere, held atop an iron-wrought pedestal.

No sound was forthcoming from the dais. Bane started forward into the silence as if he were treading his way into the maw of a giant beast. Surely it was but a matter of time before the beast's jaws would snap shut upon him . . .

As he neared the platform he could discern the outlines of the shadowy figure poised there, and what he glimpsed he did not like. But his attention was drawn to the crystal beside the wizened and shrouded form. Now he could see that it contained a miniature image of the scene in which he found himself, not reflected head-on as in a mirror, but as if he were viewing the scene from behind and far above. How this could be, Bane knew not. He could give it no name but sorcery. But he did not pause to wonder long upon it. Suddenly a third tiny figure appeared in the crystal, behind him. An armed man, tall and wiry, padded silently but rapidly toward him from out of the gloom.

Turning to face him, the young barbarian noted in an instant his foeman's haughty demeanor, the bloodlust that enflamed him, and the striking black-and-gold garment he wore, something between the mail tunic of a temple guard and the sacerdotal vestments of a priest. The man must have been an attendant of the cultus, perhaps an offerer of human sacrifices.

With an inarticulate cry, the newcomer sliced the air with his upraised dagger. Bane just managed to sidestep the blow and began to calculate the course along which to direct his own weapon. Suddenly it occurred to him . . . "One more dream, then, sorcerer?" he called to the figure on the dais, who remained still, yet tensed with anticipation. Bane checked his blow, waiting for his attacker to fade into nothingness. Only instinct made him flinch at the last moment, and it was well for him that animal sense prevailed over the lessons of reason. He felt the hot sting as his blood spurted from a new cut just above his left eye! No sorcerous dream, then! Galvanized by the blow, Bane sprang in with the ancient battle-cry of his people. His brawny shoulder struck the would-be assassin, knocking him into the wall and driving the breath from him. As the Stygian hunched forward in pain, Bane's elbow smashed down on the base of his neck, breaking him to his knees. Loudly dragging in new air, the surprised priest-warrior swung weakly with his knife blade. Bane easily avoided the blow, then planted his feet for leverage, sending his axe toward his foe's midsection, as if aiming to fell a tree. The whistling of the blade cut through the musty air of the temple corridor until it ended in a sickening crunch. For an instant the Stygian hung pinned to the wall, then collapsed above and below the axe-blade. Bane had hewn him completely asunder like a slaughtered cow.

The Vanir tensed to pull his weapon free of the wall from which it jutted vibrating and dripping blood. Had he been able to glance at the dais whence the dark shape now hastily rose, he would have seen the first real signs of alarm on the priest's taut visage. For Koth-Serapis, his magic spent, knew what must come next.

"Come closer, barbarian," the wizard commanded his slayer. For the first time the dreaming Allison was aware that the words he heard were in no language he knew, neither ancient nor modern. Yet somehow he understood them. And so could Bane, though he had picked up but little of the Stygian tongue since entering the country.

"Mayhap I credit your apish kind too little. Have you indeed grasped my little puzzles, as I bade you take dreams for truth, and truth for a dream? Or are your wits simply too dull to play my games?" The black robes of KothSerapis belled with air as he stepped from behind the dais. He stood now only a few feet from Bane, regarding him with contempt, almost with mirth, from atop a short incline of cool marble steps. The light from the crystal sphere, now empty of any image, played oddly upon the diaphanous clouds of incense, seeming to fill the chamber with attentive ghosts.

"Look at you, and look at your fellows. Like a swarm of locusts you blindly destroy what is higher and better than yourselves. Everywhere across our land, your unreasoning herd tramples a world that was old and wise before ever your forbears staggered forth from the swamps. In a single day you extinguish the lamp of Elder wisdom. But do not think you can tweak the wick of the last candle without burning yourself, barbarian. For

41

you may take my life, but I shall take your death. The ages will hold no rest for you, poor savage. Your brutish soul will wander up and down the corridors of time, toiling from life to life till I come again to take my vengeance upon you."

Breaking off his gaze, the last of the Stygian sorcerer-priests sat down on the steps and began to laugh mockingly, enjoying a jest that Bane could not understand. Puzzled, he swung his axe one final time, to end the horrible cackle, turning it into a scarlet gurgling. He could not shake the strange feeling that the mage had given him permission to do it.

And in that moment James Allison awoke.

V. At Ages' End

He was astonished to find himself standing, barefoot and shirtless, in the newly excavated tomb. As he fought his way back to wakefulness, his mind was torn between the shock of having walked in his sleep, something he had never done before, and the dreadful fact of the *familiarity* of the place. He *expected* it to look as it did in every detail, as one expects his living room to look the same as it did when he left it. Yet he had entered the chamber only briefly with Brill that evening. He struggled against a whisper of realization that wanted to supply his answer, for somehow knowing would be more awful than the torment of wondering.

Then he caught sight of the crystal sphere, no longer dull and cloudy as it had been when he and Brill puzzled over it hours ago. Now it shone with a terrible sentience, and knowledge came flooding back to Allison. Of course, he now knew the crypt for the temple of Gol-goroth, the sarcophagus for that of Koth-Serapis, the priest whom he himself had killed ages (or did it seem just moments?) ago. And the sarcophagus . . . open!

Had he, could he have, opened it in his sleep? Inside it lay the mummy of Koth-Serapis, bound in swaths of black gauze, desiccated, but for all that looking much as he had in life. Even now he seemed more like a monarch on a throne than a lich in its box. The body was inert, though in this place of nightmares, Allison would not take even this much for granted. He moved over to study the face, and as he did so, he heard something move behind him.

A figure was stepping out of the shadows. In the feeble dawn radiance that had begun to penetrate the tomb, Allison could just make out that the figure was tall but thin, and wore a tunic of black with cloth-of-gold trim. And he caught the metallic glint of something else—the blade of a dagger clenched in whitened knuckles. The scene seemed unreal, a dream of a dream, until the tall form stepped far enough into the light for its face to be seen. Brill!

Then it had been he who came here before Allison, opening the mummy case. He must have found the costume of the ancient attendant of Koth-Serapis and been lured by his curiosity to try it on. But this last was an exceedingly uncharacteristic thing for a careful archaeologist to do. What if the moldering fabric should crumble? Frankly, Allison was surprised that it had not.

With these thoughts he began to return to some semblance of waking rationality. He allowed himself to feel for the first time the chill of the air in those wee hours. He made ready to say something about this to his partner when . . . Brill sprang!

With reflexes he had not believed he possessed since his accident many years before, Allison fell back. Still the taste of blood from the new gash in his cheek charged him less with pain than with an eerie sense of *déjà vu*. The identical trap had closed upon him only minutes, or ages, before. It was all true, then, and further, Allison had not traversed the course of lifetimes alone! Brill, too, must have been visited in the night with knowledge of his destiny. Allison-Bane had slain him once, and now he must even the score. The generations had diluted the blood in the veins of both, fading the black Stygian hair of the one, darkening the golden Nordic mane of the other. But across the ages they met again, and for the last time.

As Allison circled lamely to avoid his foe, he knew how it must end. The curse of Koth-Serapis had pursued him into a cul-de-sac. Brill knew Allison could not hope to escape, even to defend himself, with his handicap, and now he merely toyed with him. Still a combat instinct bred and honed over the span of countless lives would not let Allison simply give in. So he sent his eyes on a desperate search around the chamber, if possible, to find something usable as a weapon. If he only had his six-shooter! Sweeping the room, his gaze was dramatically arrested by the now-open eyes of the mummy! Though the corpse gave no other signs of animation, eyes which should no longer fill their sockets glared out at him. They glowed with a baleful hatred that had smoldered through black eons and now blazed forth out of control.

Allison knew he must escape the hypnotic spell of those eyes or be helplessly paralyzed, and butchered unresistingly. The scuffling sounds of Brill's rushing footsteps broke Allison's fixation, and he turned to meet him. The interior of the tomb-temple afforded no weapons, so Allison was empty-handed as he faced the man who had been his enemy, his friend, and finally his foe again. Allison had no lack of physical strength; after his crippling accident he had committed himself to a regimen of physical training that saved him from wasting away and equipped him for a career of travel and archaeological exploration. No, speed and coordination were his problem. Digging and fighting were two different things. Brill moved quickly, darting in with his dagger for a blow that should have disemboweled his victim. But Allison was as surprised as Brill when he slid past the oncoming arm, drawing himself around and behind his dumbfounded antagonist. Bracing himself on his sturdy oaken leg, he shot up with his arms under both of Brill's, clenching his fists as one at the nape of Brill's neck. A great squeeze brought a sharp cry from Brill, who nevertheless did not lose his grip on his knife. As if obeying commands from another brain than his own, Allison's body shifted its weight onto his one good leg, swinging the other like a club under Brill. At the same time he fell forward onto his opponent's back, sending him to the stone floor, and onto the point of his own blade.

Allison rolled aside, panting, his own torso wet from the widening stain of Brill's blood. Brill's fallen form writhed briefly, then was still. A small part of Allison felt grief for his dead friend, who after all was but a pawn in all this. But this emotion was outweighed by a strange yet familiar exultation over blood shed and victory won, victory against all odds. An almost animalistic howl of triumph struggled to escape him. And then, suddenly, the moment was gone, the alien mood vanishing as completely as the Hyborian Age Von Junzt had written of. For some reason he thought of Bane the Reaver and wondered if one could owe a debt to a dream.

He struggled to his feet, thought a moment, then stooped again to draw the crimsoned dagger from Brill's carcass. The hall echoed hollowly with his footsteps as he paced slowly to the sarcophagus of Koth-Serapis. The eyes were still open but seemed strangely blank and lifeless. Allison looked at them but a moment before he sank the long edge of the dagger into the mummy's shriveled throat. He heard the neck snap like a rotten tree branch. The head toppled down the length of the body, striking the rim of the sarcophagus, and then dropped to the floor, where it collapsed like a dried and dusty piece of fruit.

The glass globe seemed dull again, though the chamber had grown lighter with the encroaching morning outside, and perhaps that accounted for it. In any case, Allison did not take note of it, for with the end of Koth-

Serapis, his own sentence was fully served. He walked the few steps up to the dais, lay across it, and found a peace that had for millennia been denied him. James Allison drifted into a sleep from which he would never wake, ending a life no future self would remember.

−1985−

An Antique Coffin

I first chanced upon the shop as I hurriedly returned from my lunch along the crowded streets of the grey eastern city where I worked as an auditor. The time had escaped me, and I saw that I would not regain my office cubicle on time if I were to slowly shoulder my way, as I usually did, through the massed proletarian throng; so leaving the main avenue, I ventured down one of the side streets, the heaped and rotting squalor of which had always caused me to shun them. Perhaps I might make better time this way and avert a reprimand from my over-fastidious employer. I rushed as quickly as I dared, taking care even in my haste to thread my way through garbage cans and piles of empty crates that tilted at crazy angles along the cracked and oily sidewalks. Otherwise I would doubtless never have been sufficiently attentive to my surroundings to notice the newly hung sign betokening the opening of Ormsby's Antiques.

Here was a discovery capable of banishing any fear of an employer's ire. I have never been able easily to pass the open door of an antique dealer, since each seems to me an inviting portal to the past that I love. I have always considered myself as one born out of his time, a misanthrope among men who extol dull pragmatism and mechanistic mediocrity as the usurping gods of a decadent age. Antique furniture, whether elaborate or plain, polished or ill-kept, serves to link me with that treasured past I know from books and perhaps, I sometimes fancy, from some deeper recess of memory.

I tried the knob, but the door was locked, much to my surprise. A posted sheet, which I only now noticed, indicated that the shop opened in the late afternoon. The proprietor had neglected to note any hour of closing. All this seemed to me singularly poor business. I guessed, then, that the establishment might be merely a hobby, a pet project for some retired or wealthy person who did not have to depend on steady profits. I marked the times and resolved to try the store again the same evening after work let out, though I did not much fancy the prospect of revisiting the isolated and dingy alley in the dark. As it happened, I made it back to my desk only a minute or two late, and no one took any notice. My shortcut had worked. For the rest of the afternoon I found it difficult to concentrate on my assigned drudgery for the eager expectancy I felt. What

46

frustration awaited me, then, when I found I was compelled to work late. Some minor emergency had called an office mate away, and his work simply had to be finished. But so did my own, and the result was that I stayed hours longer than customary.

Naturally I assumed the little antique shop must long since have closed its doors again. Yet some odd instinct or hunch possessed me to pass by anyway, despite the imagined dangers of the late hour.

I was amazed to find Ormsby's Antiques open for business! The shop was dimly lit from within, and window displays were illumined by ornate table lamps that formed part of the merchandise. In my afternoon haste I had hardly noticed more than the sign featuring the name of the store and the sheet listing its business hours. Now I glowed with a kind of mixed wistfulness and vicarious pride: here were prime specimens of the taste and beauty of the beloved past. Their very existence seemed a rebuke to the tawdry and tedious modernity of the surrounding city block. An ornate hurricane lamp rested on a fine Empire pier table, whose ormolu mountings, marble top, and polished mahogany grain gleamed in the warm illumination. In the other window rested an ornately carved and plush fainting couch of the same period. I stood thus transfixed until I reminded myself that more such treasures awaited me within.

The tinny ring of the dangling shop bell announced my entrance, but the proprietor, Mr. Ormsby, was nowhere to be seen. No matter: there were many other new and beautiful acquaintances to be made. I had entered a wonderland of antique, yet timeless, beauty. I could almost feel that I had entered the lost era with which I felt such kinship. I wandered slowly from item to item, here an intricately carved bedstand, there an oak side-board with stained glass doors. Many of the pieces were truly remarkable, more like museum exhibits that one would never expect to see offered for sale, and certainly not at the surprisingly reasonable prices being asked here. The number of pristine and unique pieces, not only of furniture, but also finely bound books and various types of mementoes was truly astonishing.

As seemed somehow appropriate, I was no longer aware of the passage of time, so lost was I in contemplation and admiration; thus I do not remember how long it was before my host at last presented himself.

"I see you love old things, too," said an aged but firm voice which rang with charm and urbanity even in so short a sentence. I turned to face a slightly stooped, thin old man with silver white hair and a well-trimmed moustache of the same color. He wore a rumpled tweed suit, complete with vest and watchchain, and sported both bow tie and steel-rimmed spectacles. He looked more like an absent-minded professor than a merchant, but I suppose his business really had more in common with the former role than the latter.

Clearly he had been watching me from concealment (or perhaps I simply had not noticed him) for some minutes, enjoying my own enjoyment of his antique gallery. I could tell this as easily from his demeanor as from his words, and I extended my hand to return his greeting.

"Yes, indeed! You are Mr. Ormsby? I must tell you I have never seen the like of this in the many years I have puttered in antique stores. And I must say I am surprised, pleasantly of course, to find you open at this hour."

Ormsby seemed not to hear my last remark but responded readily enough to my first.

"Yes, yes. It all began as a hobby. Years ago, I inherited a good number of beautiful old pieces, and I just never could get enough of them. I had the means to buy what I wanted, and I'm afraid I overdid it. That's what my late wife used to say! And she was right, because I eventually ran out of space. That's when I got the idea for the store. I decided that I shouldn't keep all these precious things to myself. Even now, it's just a hobby. I want to share the beauty of the past."

So I had been correct about that part of it. It was not his livelihood. I pressed on.

"I somehow suspected that, Mr. Ormsby, but I doubted my theory once I saw the beautiful things you have here. They give every evidence that you trade with the best in the business. It hardly looks like the stock in trade of a dabbler. This marble bust of Charlemagne, for instance . . ." He cut me off with a smile and a modest wave of the hand.

""I told you, son, most of these things are from my own collection. Yes, there is quite a large stock, but I've been collecting for a *long* time. What about you, my young friend? Do you collect antiques?"

"Oh, a few pieces, but really nothing to mention. You see, I have only some small rooms in an apartment building not far from here, and between the usurious rent and the tiny space available, I barely have room for the few items that used to be in my grandfather's house. I suppose their value is more sentimental than anything else, but they do provide a tangible link with more pleasant times."

"Yes, but isn't that just the point of all antiques, my boy? Isn't that precisely why we love them, whatever their monetary value?"

I was by this time overjoyed at thus hearing my own long-cherished opinions spoken by another. Here was a kindred spirit who saw the

48

devotion to antiques as a real vocation, a man whose concern with them was not so much a mercantile or even an aesthetic affair as a *spiritual* one.

The hour had now grown very late indeed, and though old Ormsby showed no signs of preparing to doze, I had to take my leave. I promised I would soon return and headed for home. Both the day's fatigue and the unknown dangers of the city darkness were forgotten as I reflected that in Mr. Ormsby himself I seemed to have discovered a treasure of the past more precious than any in his shop.

In the weeks that followed, stretching into months, I visited Ormsby's Antiques often, and the old man and I rapidly became friends. He understood that I was in no position to be a real customer, though I did now and then buy the odd item whose charm I could not resist. But he seemed to value a friend to share his passion for "old things," as he called them, more than he would a regularly paying customer.

There were, alas, very few such customers that I ever saw; and no wonder, given those strange hours of business. I never questioned this, both because I was glad that the arrangement afforded me the chance to talk at length with him after work in such surroundings, and because I assumed he must have reasons of his own that were no business of mine. At first I wondered if Ormsby could be so inexperienced as not to realize the elementary fact that a business must be open when people are likely to be present to buy. Had an earlier life of independent means so sheltered him from even the most rudimentary rules of trade? But no, it soon came out that, though new to this location, he had been long in the antique business.

In fact, so much of a missionary calling did Ormsby deem his shop that he had for some time periodically moved it lock, stock, and barrel from one city and region to another. He felt he must continually move on and give new people a chance to enrich themselves with the beautiful artifacts he made available. He was always seeking others like myself to join him in cherishing and preserving the legacy of a finer time than that to which we found ourselves exiled by "progress." When he could not find receptive souls, he would shake the dust of the place from his feet and move his establishment elsewhere. Of course I assured him I hoped that day would be far distant, that he might even see fit to make this city his permanent location. And so I did hope, though I could plainly see that business was much too sporadic to merit his lingering here long.

49

We did not actually spend all our time (despite the impression I may have given you) in decrying the mawkish and soulless quality of the modern culture and its shoddy and tasteless products. Most of our long evenings were devoted to Ormsby's fascinating accounts of the history of each piece in the shop. To these entertaining disquisitions I listened in never diminishing rapt attention. Like individual persons, each chair, each bed, each mantel, each book, has its own colorful story, even its own personality. I found that even the physical beauty of each object seemed enhanced many fold by the knowledge of its unique history. Many of these stories were quite amusing, as that of one brass spittoon which had been put to many wholly unintended uses through the years.

Often I found myself wondering how on earth old Ormsby could possibly be familiar with such details, especially as he seemed cognizant of the most intimate facts concerning virtually every item in the shop. Naturally it occurred to me that the tales he told might be just that: tales conjured from his imagination during so many lonely hours in an empty shop that he could no longer distinguish memory from fancy. But it made no difference; the yarns he spun were no less enthralling in either case, and if they were not true then they should have been. Of his own life history, Ormsby never spoke. I guessed that past bereavements, such as that of his wife, to which he had once alluded, pained him too much to speak of them. Naturally I respected his reticence, no matter what its causes.

More baffling was the question of how the old man had come to possess some of these pieces in the first place. His stories seldom included the details of how he had acquired them. I never suspected anything improper, nor do I now, but the unexplained and unaccountable presence of some quite remarkable items lent a vague air of mystery to the quaint old shop.

Undoubtedly the strangest of the antiques to attract my notice was a fantastically ornate and highly polished mahogany coffin. The detail and extravagance of the thing, though not its actual design, reminded me of the sarcophagi of the ancient pharaohs. I came across it one evening just after arriving, as I waited for Ormsby to finish some errand.

The strangely beautiful box was not in plain view, its outlines obscured amid the lines of an intricately latticed Oriental dividing screen placed in front of it. It was while examining the screen that I first noticed the coffin. I stooped to examine the box. It had the shape of a conventional casket, but nothing else about it was at all conventional. There was no crest or coat of arms, but the lid was carved with elaborate scroll-work, the lines of

50

which, together with scattered inlays of some other wood I could not easily identify, suggested a swirl of autumn leaves. The motif extended to the edges of the lid, eventuating in beautiful raised scalloping, mimicking individual maple leaves hanging on the edges, as if about to blow away. It was quite beautiful, both as a piece of woodcarving and in its peaceful and natural, and I may add wholly nonreligious, symbolism for death.

My finger gently traced the carving on the silver handles on the sides of the box, and impetuously I lifted the lid and glimpsed the shiny white tufted velvet within. Something seemed queer, and it took me a moment to realize that, though the velvet inside looked rather worn, the finish of the wood outside did not. Well, perhaps the coffin had been used for displaying bodies in a mortuary, or perhaps the outside had simply been stripped and refinished without the inside having been reupholstered. At any rate, quite a beautiful piece, albeit bizarre.

When the opportunity presented itself later that evening, I could not resist asking my friend about the coffin. Clumsily I remarked on the oddity of expending such extraordinary workmanship on a coffin to be buried forever away from the sight of men. Lurking unvoiced was the twin question of how Ormsby had come by the relic. Certainly no wholesome or legitimate means came readily to mind, but of course for that very reason it would have been, to say the least, embarrassing for me to ask and for him to answer.

Fortunately old Ormsby seemed not at all discomfited by my transparently inquisitory remark, yet neither did he supply any real information: "Yes, how fortunate that its beauty was rescued from such oblivion, eh?" I laughed politely, perhaps a bit nervously. For this strangest of curiosities, then, he had none of his stories to tell. I had pressed a little farther than was proper, but no harm seemed to have been done. Our conversation moved on to other things, and finally it was time for me to be on my way home. My host showed me to the door, and with smiles and parting pleasantries we said goodbye for the last time, as it turned out.

As the end of the fiscal year rapidly approached, the work at my firm became more hectic and burdensome. Long hours of overtime were now the rule rather than the exception. During the ensuing weeks of mind-numbing tedium I found myself so exhausted at day's end that I fear I shamelessly neglected my friend and his dimly-lit shop. Now more than ever would I have relished our late-night sessions, yet less than ever could I afford them; with workdays ending long after sundown and beginning again at the crack of dawn, I simply had to get the sleep. Ormsby's store had no telephone (again that indifference to the rudimentary rules of business!), and at the end of every day I was so fatigued I could not summon the energy to delay my course homeward even long enough to drop by Ormsby's and explain my absence. I kept promising myself I would visit the shop briefly sometime the next week, but I never did.

Finally one afternoon I again found myself taking the short-cut back to the office and of course passing near the shop as I had that first day. I did not expect it to be open at this time of day, but neither did I expect what I saw. Outside in the street playing havoc with the traffic was a mover's truck! Burly workmen were loading huge crates containing, I knew, all the precious treasures of the old man. Dumbfounded, I rushed past them, and against their protests, into the shop. There I found more men carefully packing various items into crates. Ormsby himself was nowhere to be found. Directly the foreman stepped up to me and asked my business. I explained my connection with old Ormsby and expressed my surprise, my alarm, at this scene. I wondered both at the suddenness of the departure (at least it seemed sudden to me, though in fact I had not spoken with the old man for weeks) and that the shopkeeper himself should not be present to oversee the packing of his beloved "old things." What was amiss?

Of all this the foreman expressed his entire ignorance. All he knew was that arrangements had been made by mail and the key sent on ahead. He had to get back to the operation in progress. Apparently satisfied as to my harmless intentions, he left me standing amid the confusion as he stepped away to see to some chore.

I stood completely confused, amazed, and dismayed, all thought of returning promptly to work long since forgotten. Ormsby had as much as said he would sooner or later move on, and apparently the time had come. I was sad to lose my friend, as I now saw no chance of keeping in touch with him. The store's contents were being shipped to a warehouse for indefinite storage. Perhaps Ormsby was going ahead to his next destination to make arrangements in the meantime. I realized there was nothing to do but leave, and as I started for the door, I took a last lingering look at the few items not yet crated. Among them was the antique coffin with its unique autumn leaf pattern. I reached out to finger the intricate scroll work once more and found myself seized by a strange and pointless urge. Yielding to it, I grasped one of the silver handles and lifted, hoping none of the movers was watching me.

The coffin was now unaccountably *heavy*, with *what* I dared not guess. There was no lock, and it would have been easy to lift the lid a crack and glimpse the interior, as I had done once before, but, in spite of an almost desperate curiosity, I dared not open it. I feared for my peace of mind, for my very sanity, if I should see what lay within. Instead I let go the handle as if it were red hot and almost ran from the shop and down the street, oblivious of the puzzled stares and oaths of the workmen I jostled against in my stumbling flight.

Much later, it occurred to me that there were available quite ready means of tracing the whereabouts of the old man: trade listings, antique registries and the like, but somehow I never wanted to try, after that day in the deserted storefront. Perhaps surprisingly, I did eventually return to the place, for despite my unreasoning panic at the last, in the wake of my strange friend's departure, I loved the place for the shelter it had afforded me all those evenings as Ormsby and I shared our love for a bygone day and its relics. For those pleasant months, I had found refuge there from the soul-killing grind of my clerical work. And now, standing in the cold before the padlocked door, I made a decision.

For some years now a new sign has swung above the grimy sidewalks, and a new antique shop occupies the storefront. The business hours as well as the items for sale are far more conventional, as is, I dare say, the proprietor. It is my name on the sign, and it is my chosen calling, like my mysterious predecessor, to preserve the evidence of a more graceful past and to share the love of it with others.

–1987–

As by Lewis Theobald III

Wilbur Whateley Waiting

"Bug-shuggog . . ."

Wilbur Whateley's prayer had been heard. His last incantation had worked.

He had not chanted to free the unseen Thing from its confinement. He did not need to; time itself would effect that. As That in the farmhouse hungered and hungered in the absence of its brother, its keeper, it would instinctively burst forth, splintering the century-old hulk of the Whateley farmhouse, like a giant sea-turtle for some reason sloughing off its shell, and go forth to raven and to feed.

What its eventual fate might be, Wilbur Whateley had had no time to contemplate. It was his own immediate fate that concerned him. He troubled simply to get the alien syllables right, to sound them at the right pitch, a pitch which not even he could rightly hear, having too much of the human in him.

But it had worked. The greedy whippoorwills had abruptly ceased their gloating to flee in chaotic terror. His life rapidly ebbing on one plane, he succeeded in causing it to flow on, or onto, another. As his vast, mutilated bulk began to dematerialize, it would probably seem to leave but a viscous residue on the floor of the Miskatonic University Library, and soon that, too, would be gone. It would have gone to another dimension, that in which the blind and tenebrous Old Ones waited, that into which Wilbur Whateley, a servant of Their servants, had lately sought to recall the earth itself. Ironically, now he himself was going there alone. And like the Old Ones, he must now wait, mayhap for strange eons, until a Call should come. But in this decadent age, there might be none who knew how to issue it.

Time passed, generations of it, but not where Wilbur Whateley waited, dreaming, sending dreams. Receptive minds on the mortal plane were few, befogged as most were with what is called sanity. Here or there his transdimensional suggestions connected, registered. But none had the

54

knowledge to do what was needful. Some of these became murderers or maniacs, translating Wilbur Whateley's impulses into action as best they could, but in doing so they only dissipated the energy, and it did him no good. More time passed. Wilbur Whateley waited, and dreamed.

In Chorazin, New York, the crazy old man sweated and would have sworn, except that he knew too well not to add any stray syllables to the energy field he had created, which now charged the air in the dusty library in which he worked. He sweated from the effort, an elaborate ceremony now repeated for the twenty-first time, and to no apparent avail. It probably would make no difference if he swore, or, for that matter, if he sang the national anthem, since only his now-threadbare faith told him there was a psychic energy field present at all. Maybe he had made some simple error in his preparations. Or maybe his family had been correct and he was simply out of his mind. Well, nothing to do for it but to redraw the pentacle again, perhaps a different color this time. If this didn't work, he didn't quite know what he was going to do with That in the basement. He was trying to summon someone who would, who must, know what to do.

On the forty-third try, days later and still no sleep, it did work. First the shimmering white jelly in the middle of the chalk star. Then the stench and the interstellar cold, the sound as of a mighty rushing wind, though the air was still and dead. Then the jelly puffed and bulked. And color and shape entered it.

The librarian's description proved largely accurate. There were the tentacles streaming from the waist, above saurian legs, making the Thing look like a priapan hydra. There was the fur, dense and black and shaggy like a grizzly bear; there was the face which seemed almost accidentally human in aspect. It was all there.

The heap hesitated, as if struggling to return to sync with the rhythm of terrestrial time, and then the breathing began. Strange vein and artery nets began to quiver, and the beaded, reptilian skin began to change colors with the pulses of ichor through the body. And out of the body. The old man had to move quickly to stanch the open wounds of the giant he had called out of the sky. The job seemed simple enough, as the tissue damage

55

appeared trivial. Why such injuries should prove dangerous to such a titan was a mystery solvable only if one knew more about the workings of the fabulous alien physiology than the old man knew. But he did think he knew what to do with the wounds, if the old books were to be trusted. And the very presence of the creature indicated they were indeed to be trusted.

Wilbur Whateley began to stir. He had come back to the mortal plane from a state of consciousness so indescribably different from our own that to return from it was analogous to waking from sleep. There was simply too much of the human in him for him to retain his ability to conceptualize the Outer sphere once he had returned to the earth.

There seemed to be one of the little humans kneeling before him, for some reason, hands clasped in supplication. Shaking with reverence or fear, or more likely both, the old man spoke. "I bid you welcome, O Word of the Aeon, O Great Beast! Shall I . . . go on? I am your servant Ezekiel Prinn, and I have brought you back to finish the work you began. It is my work, as well, and the work of my family, of Abigail Prinn, and of Ludvig Prinn before her. Being human they all failed, and I have not even the knowledge they had—only these few books, I fear."

Fearing he had said too much, Ezekiel Prinn finished his welcoming speech with a wave of the hand indicating his small collection of moldering manuscripts and crudely-bound volumes. Through all this, the giant listened, if he listened, in silence. At length the goatish visage rose and the strange eyes met his.

"Yew dun well. Wut books?"

Prinn moved quickly aside, apologetically offering: "They weren't mine; I found them here, and there weren't many still readable." Wilbur Whateley slowly fingered the books and picked one up. The back cover fell away, sprinkling dust. Nervously Prinn continued.

"I only chanced to discover my heritage. Family tried for generations to cover it up. But I guess it was in the blood, and I got curious. I found out who I was, what my task was."

"Where is this?"

"We are in the old van der Heyl mansion in upstate New York. I read a diary published by the *Society for Psychical Research*. I don't know if you know what that is . . . Anyway, it told of a man who came here and contacted the Outside. The diary said there were books, and I knew I'd need them. But all that were left was what you . . . what my Lord sees. Not much. And I have these . . ."

"My letters." Puzzlement registered in the strange eyes as he took up one of the yellowed sheets. Here was one addressed to Wilbur Whateley's grandfather, the old wizard.

"*Frater Magnum Innominandum,*

Do what thou wilt shall be the whole of the law . . ." It proceeded to prescribe the very act of planetary sex magic which, with Lavinia Whateley's cooperation, had brought Wilbur into the world the first time, many years ago. It closed as strangely as it had opened: "*Love is the law, love under will. Your brother in Almonsin-Metraton, Frater Perdurabo.*"

Ezekiel Prinn waited, hoping the titan was not annoyed.

"From the wreck of your house. I visited there, too. Not much was left. Destroyed by the Thing." The nature of the unseen Thing Prinn could only guess, though he had surmised its purpose. Both tacitly assumed its destruction. Had it remained in the world, nothing else would have. The humans must somehow have defeated it.

"The meddlers from the University searched your house and they got most everything."

"The Book, too?" Wilbur Whateley mused. He had not been able to steal the Book from the humans, but they had stolen his copy. "Need it. Need more than that."

Ezekiel Prinn wore the look of a well-prepared pupil. "I have traveled widely, my Lord. I do have that Other of which you speak. You see, there was Another."

Surprise, definitely surprise, on the semi-human features.

"If you will follow me . . ." Prinn led his giant guest through cobweb-shrouded rooms, brushing aside hanging batwings of wallpaper, kicking aside unidentifiable debris, to the basement steps. The cellar was vast and dank and seemed to absorb the glow of the electric torch the old man held.

"I found It in a museum, of all places, in London some years ago. All thought it to be merely an odd bit of surrealist sculpture, but I knew it had been alive and would return to life with the proper Words."

The light now illumined, albeit dimly, a huge and strangely shaped sight. On a throne of stalagmites rested (Its anatomy would not allow one to say It *sat*) a globular body supported by six folded crab-like legs. The sphere was covered with puckered cilia and was surmounted by an elephantine snout and a collection of asymmetrical eyes. Something about it reminded

Prinn of Wilbur Whateley, though there was really no specific point of resemblance.

"It is Rhan-Tegoth, or so the sign said. Through it the Old Ones can return."

Wilbur Whateley nodded. Perhaps, presumably, he was satisfied. "The Words. Yew know them?"

"My Lord, I do not. They are in the Book, and I do not have the Book."

"Harvard? Miskatonic?"

"I have tried both, and others besides. They all . . . ah . . . learned their lesson. They have the Book but deny it exists. A legend, they say, or a fiction. But lately I have heard something that gives me cause to hope. South of here there is a place, as yet unmolested by the authorities, that is said to have the Book . . ."

"I will go. Clothes."

Ezekiel Prinn hastened to comply. He had intended to undertake the mission himself, but he was not about to argue. Evidently his Master felt the need to finish the task he had begun. This time he meant to return with the *Necronomicon*.

Hunched over in his seat because of the (to him) low ceiling, Wilbur Whateley found himself taken aback at the view from the train car. On the horizon lay fabled Kadath, or so it seemed. How could the tiny humans have reared the Cyclopean pylons he saw looming up before him? For all his knowledge of lost and elder universes, the human part of him was an isolated country bumpkin who had never glimpsed the like of New York City. It fascinated even him.

The train pulled in, and passengers began to disembark, scurrying off in a thousand directions through the huge cavern of the station. Wilbur Whateley consulted his elaborately written directions, comparing them with the large posted maps, the intricate and indecipherable colored lines of which reminded him of the cipher-scripts of far-distant worlds. Yet like most who consulted these charts, he could not afford to linger staring at them long enough to decipher whatever cryptic message might lie concealed there.

As he proceeded up the stairs, stepping over an unconscious human heap, he began to study the fleshy tide flowing around him. Most seemed to hover somewhere between soundness and decadence, but there was a diversity of faces and voices here that he had never encountered in rural New England. Like Darwin amazed at the variety of Galapagos finches, Wilbur Whateley was surprised that human beings could take such a multifarious range of hues and forms.

Some of the languages he heard sounded like they were not intended for human vocal apparatus. The loitering knots of youths, the outlandishly garbed eccentrics with their face paint and chopped, tufted hair, the carriers of noise boxes, those selling flowers or distributing leaflets: the rat-faced mongrel hordes repelled him, infesting like vermin the planet that rightly belonged to Those whom Wilbur Whateley served. If he had his way, They soon would have it back, and the metropolis surrounding him would be no more than a corpse-city. Yet amid this flood of loathsome humanity Wilbur Whateley was grateful for one thing: no one took the slightest notice of his goat-faced, seven-foot frame, swathed in tent-like garments. Where there is no normalcy, there is no abnormalcy either. For the first time in his earthly life, he need not hide.

He wandered the city streets for hours, wondering that if all went well, all this should be swept away to prepare for Those he served. At length he found his way to the district to which old Ezekiel had tried his best to direct him. The area seemed almost choked with bookshops large and small, these in turn choked with patrons. This surprised Wilbur Whateley, as reading had been an art lost or unknown in the rural backwater of Dunwich. He and his grandsire had been objects of suspicion as much because they owned and read books as because of their occult experiments.

The establishment he sought turned out to be one of the smallest and most squalid, tucked away mid-block on a side street. A human skeleton hung in the window along with some cheap plaster statuary of gargoyles and phallic witch-gods. On the door a hand-stenciled sign profanely warned away the merely curious and unsympathetic, and a larger sign hanging in the window gave the name of the shop as 'The Magickal Childe', which might after all have aptly described Wilbur himself.

He stooped and entered. He would have difficulty threading his way through the two narrow aisles, with his gargantuan bulk. Every inch of available space was stacked with occult paraphernalia, candles, bins of spices and herbs, all labeled according to their supposed curative or aphrodisiac properties. There was a case of jewelry, most crudely forged, all strange in design, some featuring glazed animal eyes as jewels. Wilbur Whateley marveled that such a place as this could flourish openly. Had it somehow escaped the notice of the authorities even in so close and crowded a city? Or had times changed so much in the nearly sixty years of his absence from this earth?

It seemed they had, for as he scanned the shelves, bypassing innumerable cheaply printed pamphlets on astrology and sexuality and whatnot, his strange eyes rested on the impossible.

Several copies of the Book itself!

And for sale in the open like any book might be! Instead of relief or joy, his reaction was one of profound disturbance. Yes, he now could procure the precious volume with no trouble—but so could any fool or dabbler! With the book of Alhazred in so many hands, how did the world still stand? Why did not the Old Ones rule already?

His puzzlement had only begun. Next he noticed that two very different editions were for sale. One featured the title *The Necronomicon, the Book of Dead Names* and purported to be a translation of the Dee text, or rather of a coded cipher-fragment of it. The other was larger and bore the one word *Necronomicon* in crude silver lettering embossed on black false leather. (Had he been familiar with such things, he might have thought to compare its binding to that of a high school annual.) This version was longer but not nearly the size of the ponderous thousand-page tome he had consulted sixty years before. It was the rendering of an ecclesiastic of occult leanings, one Simon.

Absorbed in mingled hope and unease, Wilbur Whateley extracted a roll of crumpled bills from his pocket and dropped several on the counter, scarcely hearing the polite chatter of the shopkeeper: "Oh, the *Necronomicon*—that's one of our most popular items. You know, we have classes on it every Sunday night after the Gnostic mass." He left, carrying both books under his arm.

After walking a few blocks under the increasingly clouded sky, he decided to stop in a place called Union Square Park. It was lined with benches, many of which were occupied by oblivious drug addicts and alcoholics. He chose a vacant bench under a lamppost and opened both volumes before him.

In vain he sought to collate the two disparate texts. After an hour or two of laborious plodding through leaden prose he concluded that the books had nothing in common except their title. At first he theorized that since manifestly neither book represented the complete text, he might have two independent fragments. His own copy, long since claimed by the authorities, had been the Dee translation but it was incomplete. Since this new Dee fragment seemed unfamiliar to him, he felt with a momentary thrill that he might have stumbled upon just the passage he had sorely needed. Yet the brief invocation of Yog-Sothoth turned out to be so much nonsense. One was to summon Yog-Sothoth merely to gain worldly wealth.

At this point a suspicion was born in his mind that matured upon closer examination of the other book which seemed to have been mistitled purely and simply. This was not the *Al Azif* of Abdul Alhazred but rather a collection of old Sumerian liturgical chants. Wilbur Whateley concluded he was the victim of a strange joke. He left the useless books on the bench and went in search of a telephone.

He could not squeeze himself into the tiny booths but soon found a telephone attached to a freestanding post. He dug out the paper containing the number of the telephone Ezekiel Prinn had lately had installed in the ancient van der Heyl mansion. He was relieved to see that the instrument had push-buttons as he would have had trouble fitting his huge fingers into the tiny holes in a dial. Still, he had trouble not pushing three buttons at once.

Prinn did not answer, not on the fiftieth ring. This boded complications, trouble. Wilbur Whateley would try to reach him again, but now he wanted to be away and pursuing his changed plans, the plans of which he had meant to inform the old man.

Luckily he had not purchased a round-trip ticket, since he had decided not to return to his point of departure. Instead he would ride the train to the Upper Miskatonic Valley. His next stop was Arkham, Massachusetts.

He was able to ride directly from New York to Boston, but there he had to wait for the ever-delayed Boston-Arkham Local. North Station was tiny by comparison to Grand Central. People rushed through it just as fast, though fewer of them, impatient to be somewhere else. All, like ants in an anthill, were frantically busy at tasks to which Wilbur Whateley hoped soon to put an end, though his increasing sense of foreboding made him doubt his ultimate success. Suppose he could not manage to wipe this world clean: could he stand to live in it as it was?

Finally the train pulled in and he was underway again. The trip was not overly long, though much time was wasted simply because the route did not cut across country even where this was possible, following instead the crazy, winding path of the Miskatonic River itself. This must be because the track had been laid to connect the various small towns dotting the banks of the river, built there when immediate access to the water was necessary for trade. The train began to slow as it entered the ancient, picturesque town. Wilbur Whateley could make out street names. There were Derby, Hyde, and West Streets, and finally the B & M Station at the corner of High Lane and Garrison Street. He got off the train car and walked across the old brick platform, quaint but in need of repair (like most of the town), to the nearby telephone. He tried to call Ezekiel Prinn. Again there was no answer, and Wilbur now knew something had to be amiss.

Returning the receiver to its cradle, he turned and scanned his immediate surroundings. He had not seen this place for nearly sixty years. He had not felt the passage of time, occulted as he was in another reality; his memories were as if he had visited only weeks ago, but sixty years had wrought many changes. Some of these buildings had been decaying even then. Sometime since, they had been refinished in the Victorian Gothic style, something that looked strange even to Wilbur Whateley. He decided to take a circuitous route to see more of the campus, for it was of course Miskatonic University he had come to visit.

He turned right from the station and strode down High Lane, turned left onto West Street and crossed the bridge over the River, passing an island famous for its ancient menhir which had fabulous and dubious associations. Wilbur knew the truth behind these legends. How much, in fact, he could tell the professors in Miskatonic's Anthropology Department were he so inclined.

He then crossed River Street with its ancient row of warehouses, many of them apparently still in use, though a sign indicated one had been made over into an artists' colony. He proceeded down West past Main to the next corner where he turned left onto Church Street. This had once been Arkham's main business district, but most shopping had shifted a block northward to Main Street or to the large shopping centers outside the town on the highways. The University faced Church Street on one side and had some years previously bought up the other side as well. Over the protests of many in the community, the mostly bankrupt and abandoned shops had been razed and replaced with new houses, built in the old style (which somewhat mollified the irate antiquarians) for the use of the fraternities. As Wilbur walked down Fraternity Row, he noted a few of the signs posted in front of the gambrel-roofed houses. There were Lam Kha Alif, Kaf Dhal Waw, and others. He did not know what fraternities were, his own education having been restricted to home.

He turned right onto Garrison Street. The first building he came to was the University Spa on his left, but his attention was immediately attracted by the massive new Administration building across the street. But his business was not here. Down the block was the Library, familiar to him, all too familiar, from previous visits. Here, logically, should be the goal of his quest. Yet it occurred to him at once that the Book might no longer be housed here. Certainly, from what old Prinn had told him, it would no longer be available for casual perusal.

He decided to take the direct approach and walked up the great stone steps into the building. He paused at the circulation desk and waited. A figure of his proportions and demeanor is difficult not to notice, and within moments a prim and intimidated librarian was asking if she might help him.

"I hope yew kin, Miz. I need to see a book I hear tell yew got, call't th' *Necronomicon*."

"That book doesn't exist, sir. It's just fiction, you know. You know, you're about the tenth person who's come in asking about this book since I've worked here. All I can say is, whoever writes those stories must make it pretty convincing, but it's only just fiction. Why we've actually had practical jokers come in here and stick phony cards for that title in the card catalogue . . ."

Wilbur could tell she believed this. Of course, as a subordinate she would. No one would have told her the truth.

"But I have to do some research on't. Cud'n't yew tell me who *cud* tell me su'thin' more?"

"Well, maybe one of the Literature Department people, or you might try the Foundation. Yes, they might know something. You can find them out the door, to the right, down to the corner, then turn left. You can hardly miss it, it's right past the Pickman Nuclear Lab."

It did prove easy to find. A plaque in the lobby indicated that the new and sparkling building housed a Foundation named for a retired University folklorist, now dead, yet the work of the Foundation was described in vague terms suggesting experimental work in parapsychology. Wilbur surmised that this obscurity was intentional—that it denoted that during the years of his absence the humans had learned quite a bit about Those he served and did not want the public to know too much that might be disturbing.

There seemed to be no one in evidence, so he decided to explore as far as he could before he might be detected. Presumably as a part of the University, the place was open to the public. Voices down the hall indicated that classes were held in the building. He paused outside a door to listen.

"My young friends, these stones, originally the product of an ancient science predating even the Druids, are our greatest technical achievement. We can now reproduce them in our kilns, and like their prototypes, they act simultaneously as a kind of detector device as well as a safety shield. If one of the CCD or their minions were within miles of us, whether in a lateral radius or below, we would both know it and be protected by a shield of psychic force keeping the enemy at a healthy distance . . ."

Wilbur could make nothing of this, but as he mused on it, he felt a hand at his elbow.

"Sir, I'm afraid you're in a restricted area. This whole building is restricted, I'm afraid. You'll have to leave." This man was armed, a helmeted security guard. Others now appeared from further down the hall. He apologized and left peaceably.

This had to be the place. If the Book were anywhere on campus it must be here. But instead of filling him with hope, this certainty turned his foreboding into resignation. What could he do now? He did not know where in this vast complex the Book might be secreted. Perhaps they had even destroyed it, as the authorities had done in ages past. And if he had nearly met his doom at the jaws of snarling Dobermans once, what could he do against armed guards? The Book was now beyond his grasp.

In Union Square Park a furtive figure in a ratty, urine-smelling overcoat stooped over in mild curiosity to examine a book, two books it turned out, illumined by the lamp light. The one on top looked like a high school yearbook, and that's what he thought it was at first, even though he had never been to high school. He flipped it open and saw lists of strange-looking sentences. He studied it for a few moments and began to piece together what, more or less, it was supposed to be. An impulse seized him, and playfully he took up the book; he looked around, and his gaze fastened on a drunk sleeping on a bench a couple of yards away. He began to repeat some of the sentences aloud while pointing to the drunk. He felt silly, but it was kind of fun.

Suddenly his eyes closed against a terrific flash that singed his face. Shading his eyes with one hand and holding the now-closed book in the other, he saw (and heard) that the bum had burst into flame. Not even screaming, the derelict lay there roasting on the bench, the alcohol he had absorbed making his funeral pyre burn brighter.

Before he left Arkham, Wilbur Whateley tried to telephone Ezekiel Prinn one more time. There was still no answer. The reason for this was simple: Prinn lay, drained of blood, in the cobwebs of the van der Heyl mansion and, naturally, could not hear anything. A day before, eager to further the plan, he had sought to vivify the Thing called Rhan-Tegoth. It turned out that the manuscripts available to him did indeed contain the Words he needed, though at first he had misconstrued the reference. Prinn suddenly discovered the purpose of the long proboscis and the thousands of sucker-tipped cilia coating the Thing. He had misconstrued these, too. It was something of this kind that Wilbur Whateley imagined must have occurred. But he never returned to Chorazin, New York. Rhan-Tegoth waited on its stalagmite throne for a priest to bring it new sacrifices, but none did.

There was no bus to Dunwich, not even any signs directing Wilbur Whateley to his destination as he set out on foot down the Aylesbury Pike. All he knew to do now was to head for his only earthly home, or what might be left of it. He reached Dean's Corners late in the afternoon as the sun was beginning to set. He reached the fork where the route to Dunwich branched off. Though all signs had been taken down since 1928, the path was clearly designated by its state of neglect and decrepitude. The moon rose as he trudged on, and by its gleam he saw the familiar stone walls so close against the roadside that they made the road seem almost like an interior hall in some great castle. There was no shoulder of the road to walk on here, but Wilbur feared no automobile suddenly overtaking him. The road had not been used for decades. Frequently individual blocks or whole sections of masonry had fallen out of the bordering walls into the road. It had never been cleared, nor had the walls been repaired. Most houses in sight were total ruins, their gray boards falling to dust, a few broken planks still held together only by intertwining vines.

The peculiarly domed hills with their crowning circles of monoliths, now mostly fallen, seemed alive with memories from Wilbur's childhood. He reached the covered bridge and found to his dismay that the bottom had fallen out of it. In the ravine below he thought he could see the rusty remnants of an old automobile. There was nothing to be done about it but to climb down the side and swim the river. He could do that.

Dripping wet, Wilbur Whateley arrived in the town of Dunwich some hours later, near dawn. Despite being cold and wet he felt no discomfort. With his inhuman senses, he could not feel discomfort, at least not from such a source.

The main street dead-ended abruptly at an open field. The end of the road was marked by the fungus-covered, splintering stump of the centuried oak from which the corpse of Wilbur's great-grandfather Oliver Whateley had once dangled, lynched by the villagers, forgotten scores of years ago. Wilbur passed by, not sparing it a glance as if not welcoming the silent reminder of another Whateley failure.

The crossroads was falling into ruins like the rest of the village, but the people of Dunwich had never had what one might call civic pride, and it was difficult to discern whether anyone still lived here. At this hour no one would have been out and about anyway.

He continued through the town, only a few minutes' walk. He was headed further into the countryside, to the old Whateley farm. He did not expect to find much left standing on the property.

The first rays of dawn revealed the ancient granite hillside against which the farmhouse had once stood. Of this all that remained were some fallen bricks from the chimney. The great wooden structure that had housed the unseen creature had vanished utterly, the shattered boards and beams having long since rotted completely away.

He was pleased to see that the various outbuildings still stood in some fair state of repair. These had been his final quarters once he had devoted the whole of the farmhouse to his unhuman charge. The shabby sheds had been roughly maintained for a few years by some of the poorer Whateleys who had claimed Wilbur's property after his apparent death. Their legal claim having failed, they moved in as squatters, living undetected for years while the inheritance was being slowly settled. Though they were finally driven out, no one ever moved in to replace them. Thus the emptiness, and the desolation, of the place on Wilbur's arrival.

He would stay here and decide what to do next, if anything.

Weeks passed as Wilbur Whateley waited and considered. All his grandfather's books were gone, appropriated no doubt by the University or the Foundation, the humans at any rate. He had accepted defeat; without the requisite formulae he, even he, was quite powerless. He felt doubly the outsider: if his alien appearance were not enough to isolate him from the ordinary run of mankind, his very reason for being set him utterly at odds with his surroundings. Not even the product of this planet's evolution, he had been bred in the outer spheres for no other purpose than to open the flood-gates of the world to the tide of its destruction. If these gates were forever closed, he was trapped inside.

He spent much of his time these days atop Sentinel Hill, sitting on the forlorn heap of stones that had once formed the forbidden altar and menhir, looking out on the rounded hills, steep valleys, and thick foliage now reclaiming more and more of the depopulated region. His strange mind was filled with unearthly memories and dreams. For the first time in his unnatural life he knew melancholy.

One afternoon, Wilbur Whateley risked hiking back to the town of Dunwich. He found that some hardy rustics did after all remain in the village. From then on, he took to entering Dunwich from time to time, visiting Osborn's General Store for what few physical needs he had. Even in Dunwich no one showed him the slightest suspicion. Most of them had been born since the Dunwich Horror of 1928, and none, it seemed, had even heard of it. None, that is, except old Luther Brown, who had been a youngster at the time. And he never mentioned it, probably having learned his lesson from years of facing the skeptical mockery of the younger Dunwich villagers. Luther himself was no longer certain the whole business had not been a childhood nightmare.

As time passed, Wilbur became less of a recluse and would make the trip down to the village more often than he actually needed to. In fact it was not much longer before he became one of the regulars at Osborn's store. Even his great size and odd proportions excited no fearful comments: after so many years of absolute isolation from the outside world, the people of Dunwich had become so freakishly inbred and mentally degenerate that some saw nothing physically out of the ordinary about Wilbur in comparison with their own relatives, while others simply could not recognize the unearthly when they saw it.

Years passed, and still Wilbur Whateley waited, he knew not for what. But he began to fill his time with walks through large tracts of countryside. On these occasions he was more and more lost in memories of his youth, those days when his purpose, his messianic mission, had absorbed every thought and effort. He wondered and wondered again how things might have been different, what he might have done instead of what he did do. If only there were some way for him to have a second chance, he would not fail.

One fading afternoon as the setting sun cast a peculiar golden light on the landscape before him, reminding him of that bright dimension into which he had once hoped to recall a transfigured earth, Wilbur found himself even further than usual from Dunwich and home. As he returned from reverie, he noticed that he was scaling a hill thickly mantled with elms, a hill overlooking a fallen cottage below. Through the trees he came upon a collection of megaliths, encrusted with lichen and draped with moss, somehow reminiscent of the hilltop stone circles he had so often visited in his childhood. But whereas the Dunwich stones had been artificial, these seemed natural, as if the former were the imitation of these latter, as if these stones somehow embodied certain cryptical secrets inherent in the universe, jealously guarded from humanity, yet left enciphered here to taunt the mortal seeker. Wilbur paused to study them, and on a level of consciousness deeper or higher or other than the human part of him, he seemed to understand something of their message.

He set off again, crossing a dried-up stream bed, all the while in the tightening grip of a sense of mysterious expectancy, at last coming upon the mouth of a large cave. Entering, he ran his huge hands along the rough walls to guide him while his eyes took longer than ours would take to adjust to the gloom. The ceiling of the cave was sloping rapidly downward, and even stooping lower and lower he could not avoid frequently bumping his slope-browed head.

At last he was crawling as the cave shrank to a mere shaft's height and width. Despite his giant size he could navigate the small tunnel without much difficulty because of the remarkable elasticity afforded by his alien, almost boneless, anatomy. He pressed on, oozed further, because some secret instinct told him something awaited him in a place beyond the darkness and slime and crayfish.

He had not long to wait before the narrow fissure began to grow again, and soon he was standing free in an imposingly large vaulted chamber. Here and there appeared possible signs of workmanship, though if this place had ever known the workman's chisel, centuries or millennia of dripping niter and water erosion had returned the cavern to its primordial state. Yet as Wilbur Whateley scanned the rock face, looking for something, he knew not what, he imagined he caught sight of a faint glimmer, reflecting dim radiance from some unknown source, perhaps from the luminescent fungi that thinly coated patches of the walls.

Stepping closer, his splashing pad-like feet disturbing the peaceful pool-world of the translucent eyeless fish, Wilbur saw a metal ring protruding from the black and porous wall. Upon examining it more closely, he could see it to be the circular handle of a huge key. Its tarnished surface was minutely carved with cryptic symbols, many of them familiar to him through his childhood studies. Suddenly a whole hitherto obscure chapter of the Book made new sense to him.

Unhesitatingly he reached out his hand and grasped the key with two huge fingers (all that would fit through the handle). Despite the dank cold of the dreadful place, the key seemed to glow with an inner warmth, and even to vibrate slightly. He did not try to turn it, nor did any unseen crack widen into a hidden door.

It was Halloween, and soon the fires would be lit. This night was a happy and exciting one for all children, but for none more than Wilbur Whateley who unlike most youths knew why he was born and what great thing he would achieve when he grew up. With the boy's uncanny gift of presentiment, his proud mother and grandfather were sure nothing would ever stand in the way of his destined accomplishments. But for now, there was the celebration to get ready. The boy and his mother were both aware of the night air's chill, but soon the raging fires would warm them. Below, a spark, perhaps of lamplight, hinted that down the hill someone might have seen them.

−1987−

ASHES TO ASHES

Gilbert Richfield, the young rector of St. Rumwald's Church, an old parish, found himself a good deal busier than he might have expected this Shrove Tuesday. What with customary parish suppers and whatnot, the day and its evening were bustling ones in most churches, but St. Rumwald's was not ordinarily what one might call bustling. It shared the fate of many old, urban parishes, and that is that the majority of its members now resided just outside in the churchyard. Closer to the house of God, it is true, but hardly active congregants. This irony had not escaped Mr. Richfield, we may be sure, since he was in the habit of referring, when exchanging shop talk with brother clergy, to his "parish of the perished." Perhaps his superiors reasoned that the recent seminary graduate could do little harm to a shrinking congregation already in its collective dotage. The match was not a perfect one because, as may be imagined, a church such as St. Rumwald's will be steeped in tradition; tradition hung about its Gothic lineaments like a tangible cloud of the incense that had graced each service until the arrival of the reforming Mr. Richfield. He had managed rather quickly to alienate some of the old "sticks in the mud" as he called them.

Let it not be imagined, however, that our rector was wholly unappreciative of the benefits of tradition; St. Rumwald's did after all accord a certain dignity to its shepherd by virtue of its rather special congregation, that silent majority in the graveyard. It happened that this old church was the traditional burial place for the bishops of the diocese. At times the realization haunted Mr. Richfield that he was less a pastor of Christ's flock than a custodian of a cemetery. But the young man's vanity allowed him to choose the most flattering reading of the situation, and he was content to see his position at St. Rumwald's as a reward granted him by perceptive superiors who saw a promising young priest and placed in his hands an important trust.

Such thoughts were much on Mr. Richfield's mind this Shrove Tuesday evening, and inevitably so, since he had just finished performing the funeral of another bishop, soon to join the ranks of that "democracy of the dead," as Chesterton called it, just outside. The dark nave had been filled with ecclesiastical dignitaries, most from this state but a surprising

70

number from far points in the country. One even from England. The late Bishop Humphries had had a long life in the church and had discharged many different offices.

As the pews, then the aisle, began to empty amid many handshakes and subdued voices exchanging griefs and comforts, Mr. Richfield hastened to the rear door to greet as many as possible, and we may suspect, to be seen and remembered by these dignitaries.

As it happened, the priest's parting words to the mourners were more than the polite generalities that might be expected in such a situation, because, though only recently ordained and installed, Mr. Richfield and the late Bishop Humphries had already had a long association. At least it seemed long in Mr. Richfield's mind for it had not been a very pleasant association. And for this reason, we cannot say the young rector was himself truly much of a mourner that Shrove Tuesday.

Allan Humphries had actually had a shorter tenure as a bishop than Gilbert Richfield had as a priest. Until very recently the older man had served as Professor of Liturgics at St. Anselm's Seminary, where, you have guessed, our Mr. Richfield studied. Gilbert could not seem to escape the tutelage of then Professor Humphries in a whole series of required courses. Professor Humphries embodied both the stricter academic standards of an earlier day and an almost Puseyan high churchmanship that did not take kindly to the sort of casual, low-church modernism which young Richfield espoused. The truth is that ritual of any kind held little appeal for the pragmatic young Gilbert as for many of his contemporaries who saw much more value in "group dynamics," "educational methodology," and social reform. His position regarding liturgy, if such it might be called, was "the less the better." But no Episcopalian priest could escape liturgy (save perhaps through the gradual erosion of Prayerbook revision), and in his classes the troublesome Professor Humphries insisted that his young men and women get it right. His favorite and oft-repeated warning was "Remember Nadab and Abihu!" (You will not need to be reminded of the fate of those two Old Testament priests, struck down for "offering strange fire.")

When Gilbert graduated he was glad to be rid of the old man and his pesterings. And when only two years later, while serving as assistant rector in a suburban parish not far from this one, he had heard of the Professor's retirement from the classroom and elevation to the bishop's chair, he was vicariously relieved—glad, with Christian compassion, he assured himself, to know that the old Pharisee would no longer be terrorizing intimidated and forward-looking seminarians like himself. Imagine his dismay, then, when Gilbert Richfield soon discovered that *Bishop* Humphries would replace the retiring Bishop Anderson in his own diocese!

Sure enough, the familiar pattern had quickly begun to repeat itself. Mr. Richfield's appointment as rector of St. Rumwald's had brought him to the new bishop's unwelcome attention. Bishop Humphries was anything but lax in the supervision of his flock, and little escaped him. He lent a ready ear to the complaints of St. Rumwald's offended parishioners, their reports of young Richfield's flippant irregularities and ill-considered innovations. There was much grumbling among the Vestry about "Methodism." You may be sure the Bishop let his displeasure be known, but the old man was ever the teacher, never the tyrant, so did not actually intervene, hoping that his young rector might yet learn maturity and to venerate his great liturgical heritage.

But Bishop Humphries, alas, did not live to see whether his patience, and that which he urged on the congregation of St. Rumwald's, was justified. Some ailment took him as takes the old, and he died just before the Lenten season was to begin. His will had mandated cremation in the purifying flames.

"Purifying flames indeed," thought Mr. Richfield with less-than-Christian condescension when informed of the Bishop's wishes. "He probably believed in Purgatory, too, the old papist." It was in such a spirit, not unmixed with glee, that the rector conducted the Service for the Dead late that Shrove Tuesday afternoon. Bishop Humphries was now free of mortal ills, but more importantly Gilbert Richfield was at last free of his old nemesis. That was something to thank God for, and this feeling lent what element of feeling there was to his prayers that evening. And, he considered with some irony, he had handled the funeral liturgy so expertly that even Bishop Humphries would have found no quibble.

The service had indeed gone well, well enough at any rate, but he could not relax yet. The Bishop *would* have to die during one of the busiest seasons of the Church Year. Tomorrow was, of course, Ash Wednesday, and he would have to see to the proper interment of the Bishop's urn in the morning and get back to the church in time for the noon service. This, the great day of penitence, seemed to play especially upon the consciences of parishioners who seldom darkened the door of a church otherwise. They seemed to come out of the woodwork to receive the customary imposition of ashes. Perhaps secretly they felt their smudged foreheads proved to others their religiosity in case their absence from church might indicate otherwise.

As he changed out of his vestments, Mr. Richfield considered what chore to take up next so he could most quickly be done and at his long-delayed supper. First, the urn would have to be put in a safe place. Then he needed to make ready for the next day's service, which, given his normal rising time (he had dispensed with the Morning Office, much to the displeasure of the few elderly ladies who had attended it), would allow him little enough time for the interment. There was, he prudently reminded himself, no reason to cut things closer than necessary. All right, now where were those palm fronds from last year's Palm Sunday procession? He hoped he hadn't misplaced them or thrown them out during the year, since the rubric demanded they be burnt for the following year's Lent. Though what difference it made, Mr. Richfield's pragmatic and modernist mind could not see. Ashes, after all, were ashes. At least, thought the rector, the old man was not here to rebuke his disorganization!

A full hour of searching turned up nothing. Tired and hungry, Mr. Richfield decided to dispense with legalism. Besides, come to think of it, there *were* ashes ready to hand. And who would know?

Ash Wednesday began gray and rainy, appropriately enough, Mr. Richfield supposed, though his grief that morning was mainly over the nuisance of having to carry out his funeral duties in muddy discomfort. Yet it was all over soon enough, and he had taken his place in the chancel right on schedule and was now facing the congregation, every bit as uncharacteristically large as he had expected, ready to begin the Ash Wednesday service.

He began to drone the Collect for Ash Wednesday: "Create and make in us new and contrite hearts, that we, worthily lamenting our sins and acknowledging our wretchedness, may obtain of you, God of all mercy, perfect remission and forgiveness . . ."

Next, old Mr. Parks, the Lay Reader, took the scripture passages, leading the Psalm antiphonally and concluding with the text from the Sermon on the Mount which, paradoxically given the occasion, exhorts its readers to wash their faces and anoint themselves when they fast so that no one but the Heavenly Father will know.

The rector waited for the congregational response, "Praise to you, Lord Christ," and took this as his cue to rise from his seat and return to the center of the chancel, where he would start to deliver a brief, half-impromptu homily. He caught a few restive glances toward the empty pulpit. Traditionally the priest was to preach from the pulpit off to the side on the assumption that the Eucharistic altar was central and nothing

73

or no one should ever obscure it, but Mr. Richfield felt it was more important to be informal, closer to the people, whether they liked it or not.

The homily over, all stood again to hear the rector continue the prescribed liturgy: "I invite you, in the name of the Church, to the observance of a holy Lent, by self-examination and repentance; by prayer, fasting, and self-denial; and by reading and meditating on God's holy Word. And, to make a right beginning of repentance, and as a mark of our mortal nature, let us kneel before the Lord, our maker and redeemer."

Joints and pews creaked in unison as fumbling hands lowered padded kneelers and rested bent knees on them. Now only the rector stood, though he had descended the three chancel steps and was now standing at the head of the aisle, silently making ready for the next stage of the ceremony.

"Almighty God, you have created us out of the dust of the earth: Grant that these ashes may be to us a sign of our mortality and penitence, that we may remember that it is only by your gracious gift that we are given everlasting life; through Jesus Christ our Savior."

With a collective "Amen," all settled back into the relative comfort of their pews, except for the frontmost pew, whose occupants began to file out and up to receive the imposition of ashes. As each row slowly emptied and shuffled forward, Mr. Richfield carefully reached for the shallow basin and dipped his first two fingers, then looked into the face of each bowed head and smeared the rough sign of the cross. Again and again he intoned, "Remember that you are dust," he would pause, "and to dust you shall return."

Soon he could see that the line was short; only a few remained, and mentally he made ready to lead the reading of Psalm 51, which would lead into the last series of prayers, the Litany of Penitence. And then lunch.

Here was the last of them. His peripheral vision registered that the last man in line wore clothing of off-white. The rector repeated, "From dust you were created . . . ," as he lifted his ash-besmudged fingers, and with them his eyes, to gaze directly into a too-familiar scowling face. The figure before him then raised his own finger to the stunned rector's forehead and finished the hanging sentence for the speechless young man: ". . . and to dust you shall return."

The seated congregation looked with puzzlement on what they could see of this last. Why did the priest pantomime the motions of imposing the ashes when there was no longer anyone standing before him? Was this, too, some silly liturgical innovation? But such thoughts were extinguished when having said only half of the formula, Mr. Richfield collapsed to the ground, dead, as hasty examination showed.

–1988–

MIDNIGHT MASS

I had started to doze again but was abruptly awakened when the driver failed to avoid a particularly bad rut in the road. So I shifted my weight in the seat and resigned myself to more vacant gazing into the night. The four of us had set out hours earlier for a weekend conference on the liturgy sponsored by our denomination. My wife Cheryl and I and our friends Alvin and Karen Thorsson had volunteered to be official delegates from our parish, Saint Alban's Church, a small but old and venerable congregation tucked away in the little North Carolina town of Silverton. The convention was over the border in Virginia, and we welcomed the opportunity both to see new sights and to hear some of the most renowned scholars of the church expound on the Liturgy of the 1979 *Book of Common Prayer*. The latter held special interest for us because our parish was having more trouble than most adjusting to the new prayer book. Though fully eight years had passed since its introduction, many in our church were adamant in their loyalty to the old ways. We were not, and we felt the conference to which we were headed might furnish some insights into our church's difficulties.

Only now it looked very much as if we were never going to make the conference. Alvin had managed to get us quite lost, insisting hours ago that he knew the way despite our doubts. The now useless map languished at my feet in the passenger side as the car sped on further into terra incognita, racing down unmarked and unlighted, and at last unpaved, country roads. We tacitly awaited the inevitable and were not at all surprised when the car coughed in meek surrender and coasted to a halt.

As we wearily piled out of the inert heap, I thought I heard our driver mutter, "I still say we have gas; something else must be wrong with the car." His wife Karen said nothing but dutifully took his arm and we all began hiking into the night. It may seem strange to hear that we continued further in the same direction, but we knew well there was nothing, absolutely nothing, for miles in the direction we had come from. I was tired past feeling annoyance and Cheryl suffered in silence since her shoes were not designed for the service they now had to render. Our one consolation was that the full moon had risen, and its light lent a certain

76

strange beauty to the wild countryside around us.

About an hour later, Cheryl's voice rang out with the fervor of a desert wanderer who has spotted a mirage: "Look! A house!"

Indeed it was. In our present state of mind it seemed like golden Eldorado, but even in ordinary circumstances it would have been worth remarking. Against a hillside it stood, a small two-story affair with three steep gables protruding from a slanting *Italianate* roof. At one time an elaborate lattice of gingerbread must have bedecked the porch, though much of it had since fallen away. The symmetry of the structure had been disturbed by the addition of an extra room or two, but the whole aspect of the place was not atypical of nineteenth-century eclectic Victoriana. Most of the paint had peeled away, an effect which often gives old roadside houses a deceiving look of desertion; a closer look revealed that there was very little of disrepair about the place. I hoped this meant some Samaritan still lived there who might be able to help us.

Our vigorous knocking soon elicited sounds of stirring within. In a few moments a porch light came on, and the door creaked open to reveal a small but sturdy-looking old woman with well-kept silver hair and rimless glasses, her lined face alert with friendliness and intelligence.

"Yes? Can I help you young people?"

"Ma'am," I began, "we hate to disturb you, but our car has broken down, and on top of that we're lost. Do you have a telephone we might use to call for help?"

She frowned with motherly concern. "I have a telephone, but I'm afraid it hasn't worked for some years now. The company never seems to get out here to fix it."

"That's just like the phone company," growled Cheryl, whose tolerance for professional incompetence is low.

"Oh, I don't really mind so much, dear. You see, I'm quite old now, ninety-three actually, and there's no one much for me to call any more. But what about *your* problem? Well, do come in while we decide what to do next."

As she motioned us into her foyer, we exchanged impressed glances: this spry and good-humored woman was ninety-three years old? Would that I could live so long in half as good condition!

We took seats in her parlor, a museum piece of the Victorian period, singularly free alike of dust and of any vestige of modernity. I had entirely forgotten any feeling of inconvenience or fatigue, thoroughly enchanted by my surroundings. I knew my wife must be embarrassed by my childish gawking, but I could not refrain from scanning each finely carved chair or end table, each framed photo or motto, each polished mirror or ceramic curio. It was an antique lover's paradise.

When I came back to reality I gathered from the half-hearted protests of my companions that our hostess had insisted we stay the night. Cheryl and Karen volunteered to help prepare the long unused bedrooms, once children's rooms, upstairs. I turned to Alvin and said, "I owe you an apology, old man. Looks like you knew just what you were doing after all. This promises to be much more charming than any stuffy old convention." He laughed.

Alvin and I busied ourselves with idle male chitchat until the three women returned. "Oh, Alvin," bubbled Karen, "wait till you see the upstairs! It's just like my grandmum's home in Sussex!"

Our hostess, Violet Higgins as she told us, seemed silently delighted to have admiring guests. I'm sure she had lived alone in this house for many, many years, and now it must seem like a houseful of family had come to visit her.

"Will you join me for a late supper, children? Oh, don't worry, there's plenty for all. I've just had my visit from the village grocer's boy and everything's well-stocked."

This time we could not even muster the polite hypocrisy to say no, as we were all ravenous from hours on the road.

Her dining room was another humble wonder, with its mahogany sideboard, table, and china cabinet. Between the decor and the conversation, I took insufficient note of the dinner fare to tell you what it was, though I recall enjoying it.

"Violet," Alvin spoke up between bites, "you said there was a village not far from here." She gave its name, which again I cannot recall, but I do remember that it struck no note of familiarity despite my desperate study of the road map hours before. It proved that we were indeed hopelessly lost. Perhaps we might make our way to the village for help and directions the next day, though I held out little hope of finding an open service station as tomorrow was Sunday, the second and last day of the liturgical conference which it was now clear we had missed.

Dinner conversation was stimulating, ranging between various topics, and refreshingly avoiding the superficiality usually shared by new acquaintances. Violet, it turned out, was a fellow-Episcopalian. This was not surprising; we are not exactly a rare species in Virginia, given the long history and firm entrenchment of the Episcopal Church in the state. We discussed various religious issues of concern to us. I shared my rather liberal interpretation of the Episcopal creed without much comment by our hostess, but this led Karen to voice her dissatisfaction with my stated view.

"But Robert, if you look at it that way, how can you trust *any* of the creed's statements—for instance eternal life? If we don't take that literally, where are we? Like Saint Paul says, 'We are without hope, of all men most miserable.' Don't you think so, Violet?"

"At my age, I've had good reason to think long and hard on the matter, my dear. And I should tell you I have no doubts at all. I just don't see any room for any." She spoke not with the confidence of fanaticism, of which I have seen plenty, but rather somehow with a deeper serenity. Perhaps the peaceful deaths of friends or family members had convinced her. I have known others to be much encouraged by that means.

Finally Violet inquired about the reason for our trip. We briefly explained the nature of the conference and our reason for attending. It developed that our hostess was not in sympathy with the "new-fangled" service. She would have gotten along well with the intransigent conservatives of Saint Alban's vestry! Someone Violet's age might readily be expected to resist changes; what surprised me was that her whole church felt the same and in fact still did things the old way!

"Violet, you mean you belong to a schismatic church? I'm sorry, I realize that's a loaded term. I mean, has your church left the denomination?" I knew that many congregations had left in the late 1970s to form the Anglican Orthodox Church, outraged not only by the new liturgy but by the ordination of women to the priesthood.

"Oh, heavens, no." She laughed. "We just never took to the new prayer book and the new way of doing things."

How interesting. Here in an isolated backwater of Virginia was a forgotten little congregation blithely ignoring the official canons of the national church! Though I favored the 1979 prayer book, I was enough of an antiquarian to appreciate such a living relic of our church's past.

"Would you like to see it for yourselves?" she asked, looking over at the mantel clock. "There's a midnight mass tonight, though I was planning to stay here to look after you all. But if you're interested, we could still make it with time to spare."

"That would be wonderful, Violet," I said, reading agreement in the eager expressions of my companions, "but it must be quite a little walk to the village, and so late at night . . . ?"

"Oh, no—it's nothing really. You see, this house used to be the rectory. My grandfather was the priest long ago, and the church is just over the hill. It's just a little country church, but the people are still very dedicated, and even at this hour there should be a good crowd."

Silently I wondered at there being a midnight mass when I could think of no liturgical occasion to warrant one. Surely it must be some saint's day, there were enough of them, but hardly one of sufficient importance. Well, one had to take into account local traditions.

"I say 'midnight,' but actually it starts at eleven and *ends* at midnight, so if you want to go we should get ready soon, I suppose."

We quickly finished our meal and retreated to our rooms to freshen up. I hurried Cheryl, contrary to my usual habits, since I am always the one late to every appointment. Soon we were all ready to go, and we followed our still-energetic hostess down the path at a brisk pace and over the rise, and there it was: a small church, a chapel really, that lay nestled amid the trees on the other side of the little hill.

The church, Saint Dunstan's it was called, represented the same period of architecture as the house, but it was not nearly so well kept up. This was quite odd, since one would imagine that a whole congregation, however small, would be better able to care for a building than a lone ninety-three year old woman, yet Violet's house was in much better condition. Still, in its very dilapidation the place had a kind of rustic romanticism.

As we neared the small building, I could see that the begrimed stained glass windows were missing panes here and there, an especial shame considering the value and workmanship of stained glass from that period. But when we entered the cozy little sanctuary, I could see I had too hastily judged the congregation, for the interior of the place seemed virtually in pristine condition! The elaborately carved screens and chancel furnishings were spotlessly polished and shining. So were the windows, the scenes of which glowed with an ethereal lambency due to the strong moonlight. And strangely, I could no longer find the places where, viewed from outside, panes seemed to be lacking.

The chapel was quite full, a marvel at such an hour, and the pious throng kept a reverent silence like I had never before encountered in more modern churches where the true solemnity of worship has largely been lost.

The sanctuary was only candlelit, and it was difficult to make out individual faces and forms. But generally I gained the impression of a congregation of devout elderly people, who perhaps in their winter years looked toward heaven with more expectation than others might.

Violet found an empty pew and signaled us to follow. We settled down and imitated her as she pulled down the padded kneeler bar to pray. Less spiritually minded, I suppose, I couldn't help noticing the really fine velvet with which both pew and kneeler were upholstered. How stark a contrast between the slovenly exterior and the exquisitely preserved interior!

It was clear that our rushing had been wise because scarcely had we arrived when the service began with a softly chiming bell. We rose and sang a hymn, or I should say the congregation did. I saw no hymnals and did not know the hymn, nor did Cheryl or the Thorssons. We all looked at each other with a smile. This was indeed an extraordinary evening!

The procession, the priest in his surplice and two acolytes, one bearing the cross, passed us silently and filed into the chancel. I looked in vain for a prayer book. There were none of these in the pews either. Apparently these people no longer needed them, having learned their beloved litanies by heart through years of repetition. The service began with the Lord's Prayer and proceeded through the collect. I expected the whole procedure to be a bit foreign to me, accustomed as I was to the 1979 order of service, but I was soon surprised at just how subtly alien everything seemed. Then it struck me: this was not the prayer book liturgy of 1928 as I had assumed, but rather that of 1789!

As I was pondering this wholly unexpected development, the service had come round to the Holy Communion. The forward pews began to empty, their occupants filing up the narrow aisle to receive the body and blood of Christ. Here I was at sea. The 1979 prayer book allowed all baptized Christians to partake, but the 1928 rubric was that only the confirmed might do so. Karen, Alvin, and I had been confirmed, but Cheryl had not. What was the 1789 rubric?

The row in front of us had just stood. I was about to do the same when Violet, who sat beside me, leaned over and whispered, with the staying touch of her hand, "No, we mustn't. I am only an associate member." We weren't even that, so we remained seated as the silent throng finished communing and returned to their pews. All the while I puzzled more and more: what could it mean to be an "associate member"? I was rusty on the older canons of the Church, but I knew of no such status in the Episcopal tradition.

The service hastened toward conclusion, right on schedule, I thought, as I peeked at my watch through the semidarkness.

The old priest had about finished chanting his final prayer, having just managed to say, ". . . very members incorporate in the mystical body of Thy Son . . . ," when the bell again chimed with a hollow echo, marking the striking of midnight. I had been kneeling, the required posture at this juncture, following along with the prayer with eyes closed. But his words

81

did not resume after the chiming of the bell. Seconds passed; finally I looked up. Violet remained at prayer, while Cheryl, Alvin, and Karen had not waited as long as I. Now all four of us looked about in astonishment at a sanctuary suddenly and impossibly empty of all but us and our hostess!

It took another few seconds for another fact to register: the inside of the chapel was now fully as decrepit as the outside! The roof sagged, dust thickly caked the rotten wood, windows were missing panes after all.

When Violet had finished her prayers, she found all four pairs of eyes fixed urgently upon her.

"We love the old ways here," she said with a smile. "I suppose it's not for everyone, not for young folks like you. But I'm quite old now. Soon I'll be a full communicant."

–1988–

THE DEPROGRAMMER

". . . and we'll appreciate *anything* you can do for Ginny, Mr. Brigham." You would think she was talking to her minister, thought Ted Brigham as he hung up the phone. Let her talk any way she wanted as long as she came through with his check. Swiveling in his chair, Brigham took one last glance at the thought before letting it slip away. Her minister! Here he was doing the job her minister couldn't do. Doing the job that probably nobody would be doing if it weren't for naïve ministers opening doors they couldn't lock again. Filling kids' heads with beliefs they'd take more seriously than their mealy-mouthed parsons ever thought of doing. Ted Brigham was no minister, not much of a believer either. Yet religion *was* his business. He was a deprogrammer. Upper middle-class parents paid him (and *boy* did they pay him) to catch their precious kids after they'd flown the gilded coop.

In the old days, Brigham's days, they'd just up and run away. In the 60s they grew their hair long, stopped bathing, and became hippies. Now the fad was religious cults. Little junior's been fed heaven and hell in Sunday School till he's got catechism coming out of his ears. He goes away to college, majors in business or poly sci, and sets to work on a sheepskin passport. Destination: the great American middle class, just like Mom and Dad. Almost like a homing instinct. But sometimes something goes wrong. All that religious tranquilizer they fed the kid Sunday mornings suddenly ferments. The opium of the people turns into LSD, and junior takes a running jump into the Moonies, the Krishnas, or God knows what crazyhouse. That's when the folks back home call in Ted Brigham or one of his many competitors.

You should hear them explain, almost apologize, as if instead of a deprogrammer, Mom and Dad were talking to God. "Really, he was always so happy at home. We got along fine, didn't we, hon? And he was just the model student—head of the yearbook staff, A's in all his classes. But now he's quit school mid-semester and never even contacts us anymore. We don't know what we did wrong—did we do anything wrong? We're pretty religious. You're on the board of deacons, aren't you, hon? We just can't figure it out."

Brigham could never understand why they even tried. Look, who can figure *anything* out when it comes right down to it? The thing that matters now, he would always assure them, was to get their pride and joy out of the clutches of the cult (and back into *their* clutches)—by the hair if necessary. And it usually *was* necessary. These cults knew what they were doing. You don't invite desertion by letting recruits visit home sweet home in the heat of combat. If you *ever* saw your kid again, you were lucky. And then you'd wish you hadn't. The glassy eyes and stereotyped script ("Hi! Life is so exciting when you're giving your all for God! And that's just what Reverend Moon/Moses David/Guru Maharaj Ji is showing me how to do!").

No, junior wasn't about to stop in for a casual chat. You had to fight fire with fire. So you call up Cult HQ and ask to speak to junior: "It's an emergency." You tell the little robot that a relative's died or something. By now he's been hammered into a mental state where he's liable to believe anything with a little prodding, so he's not hard to convince. Won't he just come home for the funeral? It would mean so much to everyone, and it would be an opportunity for them to try and understand his new faith . . . Amazingly, more often than not junior actually walks wide-eyed into the trap! (They'd have to start wising up soon, though, so Ted and his sharper competitors were already trying new strategies.) Once the family meets the kid-saint and they exchange uneasy hugs, it's into the car. It isn't too long before the poor sap notices the car isn't headed over the river and through the woods to Grandmother's house. No, the car's taking him to the last place he wanted to see—the real world.

The parents usually have a hard time with the idea of their baby being tied to a chair and verbally barraged for days on end. Because of this Ted would wait till they actually got to the hotel room to break the news. By this time, they'd feel more foolish for backing down than they'd feel guilty for putting junior though it. And, Ted would assure them, no harm would come to him. Brigham was just going to talk some sense into him. And God knows these brain-washed zombies aren't going to listen to it unless you literally tie them to the chair.

Ted Brigham had gone through the whole routine scores of times since he'd gotten into deprogramming. And he seemed to have a knack for it. His success rate was one of the best. Scarcely any of the ones he deprogrammed ever "reverted" and rejoined their cult. Maybe Ted's secret was his earnestness. The kids could see it in his eyes. They could tell he was really on *their* side; he had *their* best interests at heart after all. Too many deprogrammers made it into a contest. The kid would be admitting personal defeat if he finally gave in to the treatment. Not with Brigham. He realized that you had to make the kid think that chucking this religious hysteria was *his* idea. That all the deprogrammer had done was to prompt a little thought.

But no matter how winning your bedside manner, nothing would happen if you didn't know the questions to ask. So Brigham set to work immediately. He stepped over to his bookcase to begin his research into the cult Ginny Salamone had joined. He couldn't afford to waste time since they were shooting for the first session tomorrow night. And when Mrs. Salamone mentioned the name of the cult, Brigham had drawn a blank. He'd said, "Sure, I know all about 'em. Dealt with 'em many a time." But he hadn't. In fact he wasn't completely sure he'd even heard of them, but he couldn't tell the old lady that. No sense risking losing the job to a big outfit like the Freedom of Thought Foundation.

What had she called it? The . . . um, Starry Wisdom Sect. Brigham reached for Martin's *Kingdom of the Cults*. He opened it to the table of contents and scanned it. Jehovah's Witnesses, Mormons, Black Muslims . . . . zilch. Hell, Martin didn't even cover the Moonies or the Children of God. Ted needed something more up to date. How about Melton's *Encyclopedic Handbook of Cults in America*? That had helped him before. But no.

Twenty minutes of paging through similar volumes turned up nothing. Next he tried the case books. A couple of years back, deprogrammers had started compiling reports of representative cases so everybody wouldn't have to learn it all from scratch. But recently the field had gotten more crowded, and tricks of the trade became trade secrets. Nobody would share. So the case books only went up to last year, and the index showed nothing about any "Starry Wisdom" group.

Okay, the name sounded like it might have something to do with astrology. It was a long-shot, but there might be some connection. Hadn't there been some kook in New York a few years back who did horoscopes for actors and celebrities? One day the cops broke in and found the guy leading a prayer-vigil around a week-old corpse. They were trying to resurrect the poor stiff, and after a while the neighbors couldn't stand the smell. The guru jumped out the window and died. Wonder if his own horoscope had said "Watch out for cops and corpses today?"

No, that was the only real astrological cult. If he didn't find some lead soon, he'd have to call the Salamones back and tell them to forget it. But that thought didn't sit too well with his wallet. Only one thing left to try—

the clipping file. There was the usual sheaf about the Moonies, their being sued and suing back, then the Children of God getting arrested for religious prostitution, and of course Jonestown. Brigham flipped past the file on the feuding polygamists in Utah, past the bank-robbing Black Muslim splinter groups. Fortunately nobody had ever asked him to snatch somebody from *those* bastards! So far his biggest risks were little more than a kick or a bite from an enraged Krishna.

Toward the back of the file, right before the folder on Manson, he hit pay dirt. It wasn't much, but it was something. Starry Wisdom was the subject of a brief newspaper item from six months before: "City Plans Probe into Cult Fundraising Practices." The story was so typical it hadn't stuck in his memory. He was surprised in retrospect that he'd even bothered to clip the article. One cult was like the next when it came to money—always trying to con you into giving to this nonexistent charity or that phony front organization. Come to think of it, that's why he'd clipped the item; he himself had been approached by someone from the Starry Wisdom Sect with a typical pitch, and he'd seen this story in the paper the next week. Standard accusations—kids kidnapped and brainwashed, working all hours, handing the money over to the leader of the cult, one Enoch Bowen.

It seemed that the sect claimed to be in communication with extraterrestrial beings. Of *course*—UFO nuts. Now it was falling into place. These flying saucer fruitcakes had traditionally kept to themselves, but back in 1976, a couple of fanatics in the Southwest said they were reincarnated spacemen and got a hell of a lot of people to just walk off their jobs and follow them into the desert. The story was that they were going to meet the "mother ship" that would take them all to planet X or wherever. From then on UFO groups began to enter the marketplace with the rest of the cults. Starry Wisdom must be one of them. And that explained the obviously phony name of the leader—"Enoch." That was the name of the wise man in the Bible whom God took straight up into heaven. No doubt that's what the Reverend Bowen predicted for himself and his followers. They'd pass through the pearly gates aboard a spaceship. Captain Kirk, move over.

Who knew what the hell they we're doing with the money they collected? More likely than not, Bowen was putting it toward some paradise here on earth, far enough away that when he skipped the country his followers would believe he'd gone to the great beyond. All these guys were the same. The regular Sunday ministers, too, though few of them had the guts to pull the sort of scam Bowen was pulling. They were all in religion for the bucks. Ted Brigham sure was, so he really couldn't blame them. He still didn't know quite enough to give Ginny Salamone a good run for her fanaticism. Maybe one more lead, after all. Brigham opened a drawer and pulled out his address-and-number book. The binding was cracked. He'd either have to start memorizing numbers or invest in a more expensive book. Soon he thumbed his way to the listing for "Horizon House." The name was a cute pun. The horizon is halfway between heaven and earth, right? Well, the operation was a sort of halfway-house run by the local council of churches for kids who had quit or been deprogrammed from cults. Maybe they would know something more about Starry Wisdom.

It took a few seconds to hunt through the scratched-out numbers and find the latest one. Horizon House was periodically forced to change its number because of crank calls and threats. Unbelievable; what a line of work.

On the fourth ring, somebody picked up. "Horizon House. May I help you?" Ted recognized the voice of Mitch Ames. His "Father Flanigan of Boystown" impression was up to par.

"I *hope* you can help me, Mitch. I've got a job tomorrow night, and not much ammo."

"Well, saints preserve us—it's 'Brigham Back Alive!'"

"Come on, knock it off with that crap, Mitch." He added with a note of false gravity, "I've got a matter of spiritual life or death here! You ought to be able to appreciate that!"

"Sure, Ted. What's up?"

"Mitch, have you ever put up anybody from something called the 'Starry Wisdom Sect'? Have you heard of it?"

"Actually, I have heard of it, but you probably already know more about it than I do. I got to thinking once that it's kind of odd we *haven't* had anybody here from that cult. I even got curious enough to ask a few of your esteemed colleagues about it. How come they seemed to dig up every other garden variety but never brought us anyone from this Starry Wisdom cult?"

"Yeah, so?" Ted's interest was beginning to grow, along with a hint of unease. "What'd they say?"

"Mostly shrugs. But one seemed to know something he didn't say. I just got the impression there was some good reason. But as to *what*—beats me."

"Maybe the jerk's on their payroll, huh? It's probably just chance. Don't worry, pal. If this job comes off as planned, you'll have a 'Starry Wisdom' specimen for your collection. After I deprogram their precious daughter, Mom and Dad'll jump at any advice I give them. And what could be better than a relaxing convalescence at Horizon House, right?"

"You're good to me, Ted. I'm sorry I can't be more help to you this time."

"No problem, Mitch. I'll collect another time."

"Oh say, Ted—one more thing. You'll be glad to know that we're thinking of starting a retirement home for over-the-hill deprogrammers, and I'm reserving an oxygen tent just for you."

"Yeah. Thanks a lot, pal. I may need it after a few more of these jokes."

Brigham decided he'd take off for a seminary library. Maybe that would yield some new information. In the meantime, he'd phone up O'Rourke and Graves. They were a couple of husky ex-college football players he'd deprogrammed a year before. They were so grateful to Brigham for helping them "see the light" (or maybe *stop* seeing it), that they were happy to help him snatch other cultists. In fact, their zeal was almost religious. The poor dopes couldn't see they were just doing the same thing as before, only playing for the other team. Who cares? They were willing to donate their time and energy for only a fraction of what they were worth. And now Brigham needed them to ride along behind the Salamones' car to make sure the meeting with Ginny went off all right.

The next day was overcast, and it had begun to rain lightly as Brigham turned off the interstate. He clicked on the wipers, then stepped on the brakes softly to slow his pace earlier than usual. Even with a sprinkle like this, the ramp might be slippery. No use taking chances, he thought.

A couple of minutes later, he pulled into the Holiday Inn parking lot. Sure enough, there was O'Rourke's van. The Lincoln beside it must belong to the Salamones. They'd be expecting him. He never minded being a little late; it gave the "patient" a chance to work up a little . . . anticipation. By the time they'd had a chance to sweat a bit, they'd have lent Brigham's entrance twice as much dramatic effect as it deserved. They'd be so sure he was a vampire come to suck out their little souls, that they'd be downright grateful when they saw how regular a guy he was. They'd usually be so relieved that their defenses would fall noticeably. It would be much easier to get them to listen to reason.

The only thing that had Brigham the slightest bit worried was that he hadn't been able to come up with much more background information. But that was probably okay. He'd just throw a mishmash of the same charges he always made against Moon or other gurus. Then he'd shift gears and remind Ginny how good it had been to be free and on her own—to make up her own mind what she wanted to do, where she wanted to go, what to do with her money. And ultimately it didn't matter *what* you said. The important thing was to wear them down. They'd give in. And if it took hours, even days, so much the better. His fee would be that much higher.

His shoes crunched on the gravel of the parking lot as he headed for room 18. They used to excuse this stuff by claiming they were saving the money on their low room-rates. At 60 to 70 bucks a night, he wondered what their excuse was now. Well, he wasn't paying for the suite today. It was unlocked. Brigham had told them to make sure it was a suite since they'd want one room to wait in, and another for the deprogramming.

That must be the Salamones. Dad had on, of all things, an orange leisure suit. That alone might send you off to join a cult, or make you think the old guy was in one himself. Not letting his contempt show, he shook hands with Salamone. As he introduced himself, Mom walked over, having finished reassuring O'Rourke that there was to be no unnecessary force. It was probably the third time in twenty minutes.

Brigham found himself almost embarrassed at the respect, even the awe, they showed him. "She's in your hands now, Mr. Brigham." As if he were a doctor about to give their daughter brain surgery. Come to think of it, that wasn't a bad way to put it . . .

"You don't need to worry, Mr. and Mrs. Salamone. Ginny is an intelligent girl. All she needs is for somebody to put things in perspective for her. That's all. We might as well get right at it."

As he stepped into the adjoining room, he recognized Graves's large frame silhouetted against the window. The girl must not be too talkative. Her back was toward him as he came through the door. Her hands were tied behind her.

"Hey, why no lights?" Ted said with mock surprise as he clicked them on. Of course, he had ordered them shut off, just for the atmosphere. The idea was to give the "patient" that sense of relief when he turned the lights back on. ("Hey this guy's not so bad after all; maybe I'll trust him.")

He stepped around to face her. Not much of an expression, but what a face! She didn't get it from Mom, that's for sure. And from the looks of it she was trying not to keep it. She was very pretty, not quite beautiful, though almost. She had begun to look pale and drawn. No doubt all those hours of work, little sleep, and starchy meals. Bowen's mission must be more important than their health. Stupid kids just couldn't see when they were being exploited, any more than O'Rourke and Graves could.

What galled Brigham the most sometimes was the way these cults screwed up kids who had a lot going for them, like Ginny. Kind of like you convinced Miss August to enter a convent. As if they were punishing themselves for being talented, sexy, or whatever. He almost felt like saying "What's a nice girl like you doing in a place like this?"

He sat down opposite her and waved for Graves to leave them alone. At this she seemed to stiffen with apprehension. "Nothing to worry about, Ginny. I'm Ted, and I just want to talk. You can guess what about." He waited, giving her a chance to spit a couple of remarks at him. Might as well let her put her cards on the table, he thought. But she said nothing. Well, then . . .

"I guess you know your parents are pretty worried about this group you've joined, Ginny. Maybe you think they're just misguided. Like, they love you but they just don't understand. But maybe they understand better than you think, Ginny. Isn't there something strange about a group that won't let you answer letters from your own family? Doesn't it sound like they don't want you to think for yourself? I just want you to think about that, Ginny. And to tell me *what* you think."

She was silent for a moment. Then she began to speak, but in low tones, and in a language Brigham didn't recognize. It was some kind of chant, like the one the Krishnas use. Through clenched teeth, Ginny began to repeat pure gibberish: "*Iä . . . ngai . . . Ygg . . . b'gg-sh'ggai . . . shigama hondai . . . oliorashimi . . . k'thun f'taghn . . .*"

Brigham tried to interrupt. By now she was repeating the same thing over and over again, and there was no point in listening to any more of it. "C'mon, Ginny. You're not going to pull that one on me, are you? Don't you see that the sooner we can talk this thing out, the sooner we'll all be able to leave?" He had almost said "the sooner we'll be able to go back home," which would have been a mistake, because that's the last place she wanted to go.

In the next hour, he tried everything to goad her into responding, but Ginny just kept chanting, never so much as stumbling over a syllable, any one of which sounded like a tongue-twister. Ted was getting a bit nervous now. He had run through all he knew or even surmised about the Starry Wisdom sect or Reverend Enoch Bowen. If she'd even tried to rebut his accusations, her replies would have given him more material to work with. But nothing. And it was unsettling pretending you were talking to someone who just ignored you and chanted. "Okay, Ginny, I'm gonna go out for a cup of coffee . . ."

". . . *Iä ngai* . . ."

"I'll send my friend back in here with some . . ."

". . . *ygg b'gg–sh"ggai* . . ."

". . . lunch for you. If you change your mind and decide to talk . . ."

"*Shigamahondai* "

". . . I'm sure you'll find Stan Graves is a good listener."

". . . *oliorashimi k'thun f'taghn* . . ."

What a psycho! After conveying to the Salamones a little of the assurance that he wished he felt, Brigham left them and O'Rourke to the idiotic game show they were watching. As he strolled down to the motel coffee shop, he wondered just what tactic he should try next. Would she get tired of chanting, and talk? Should he pretend to be open to her side of the story? Should he maybe slap her around just a bit? No, that only tended to reinforce their martyr-complex and convince them you were the devil himself.

He had just ordered when a well-scrubbed but slightly threadbare fellow sat down on the stool beside him. Brigham noticed he had a worn-looking Bible with him which he laid on the counter, carefully placing it on top of his newspaper. Having all the crazies he needed already, Brigham tried to ignore the man. But he would not be ignored. Inevitably, he tried to strike up a conversation.

"I must say *you* appear to be deep in thought, my friend!" Why hedge? thought Brigham. It'll take more imagination than I've got left to be evasive.

"Yeah . . . deep in thought's what I am, all right. I got a friend I'm trying to talk some sense into. She's joined some wacko bunch that believes in flying saucers and little green men."

"Don't be too quick to scoff, my friend." Picking up his Bible, the old man went on: "Scripture says not to sit in the seat of the scorner." *What kind of a can of worms have I opened up here?* Brigham moaned mentally. Probably the old geezer had been just waiting for something like this to set him off.

"But wait a minute, pal, I didn't think you Bible-thumpers believed in UFO's. I thought that was somebody else's trip."

"Well, I only know what the Word of God says, and in Revelations chapter one and verse twenty, it says 'The mystery of the seven stars which thou sawest in my right hand is this: The seven stars are the angels of the seven churches.' And in the original language, that word 'angel,' why, it just means 'messenger.' So who's to say there aren't people coming down to see us from the stars?"

Where'd he get this? Garner Ted Armstrong? He felt like saying "Listen buddy, I'd like to start a file on you, maybe even deprogram you if I had the time, but I gotta get back to another nut!" Instead he said simply, "I guess so; that's one way to look at it. Gee, mister, I don't want to be rude but I'm pressed for time, and I'd like to plan what to do next."

"Sure, son. Just don't be too quick to mock what you may not understand." He patted Brigham on the back and walked out. *He didn't even order anything,* Brigham thought. It might have struck him even stranger if he'd had time to let it. But back to the business at hand. By the time he'd finished his Danish, he had about decided to fall back on a general refutation of flying saucer myths. If she still wanted to chant, he'd just have to speak over it. He'd run down several cases of groups who thought they'd been contacted by extraterrestrials, groups like the Aetherius Society, the Solar Light Center, the Friends of Venus, and more. And how every last one of them made awful fools of themselves when D-Day came, but no flying saucers. And what made her think her cult was any different? Maybe that would budge her a little, if only to get her to defend her cult. That would at least be something. If she'd just start to talk, real words that is.

He paid, got up, and started back down the sidewalk to the room. Something made him give a quick thought to the old man. Sometimes he wondered if the sane people were actually in the minority. If it were true, he just hoped he stayed in the minority. He remembered reading once how some agnostic used to look at religious nuts and say, "There, but for the *lack* of the grace of God, go I." Amen to *that.*

Brigham was only a few yards from the door when he heard the commotion. First there was something like a wrenching crash, followed by screaming, suddenly choked off. Then another sound less easy to identify. As he sprinted the rest of the way, he thought to himself, *What the hell can Graves be doing to the girl? Has he gone crazy?* As he stumbled into the room he saw the Salamones and O'Rourke all trying to force the door to the other room. Apparently, it had jammed, or else with all the confusion they couldn't figure out the lock.

92

Mrs. Salamone was yelling "I told them not to hurt her! I told them to be careful!" O'Rourke pushed the Salamones away and got the door unlocked. One glimpse inside, and he turned to push them away, across the room in fact. Brigham took the opportunity to step into the next room. As he did so, he felt he had walked face-first into a wall. The shock and the smell combined to send him reeling. At first it seemed the room, though a mess, was empty. The windows were still secured, there were no other doors, yet no one was there. Glancing at the chair that had held the defiant Ginny, all Brigham saw were severed ropes. Then he noticed that the room wasn't completely deserted after all. For though Ginny was indeed nowhere to be found, poor Graves was still there. In fact, here, there, and everywhere. He had been splattered all over the room.

He sat, pensive for the moment, on Mitch's couch.

"What's wrong, Ted—coffee no good?" Mitch had dispatched the innocuous probe, hoping to elicit some clue about his friend's deliberations. At least he hoped they were deliberations. The same intermittent lapses into silence often marked shock trauma in some of the young people that came to Horizon House.

The comment worked, dissipating momentarily Ted Brigham's bemused fog. "No, no, the coffee's fine, Mitch; it's your advice that doesn't taste right for some reason. And I'm not sure why—it's usually as good as your coffee. Look, you know and I know it's not safe for me around here. Sometimes if you blow a deprogramming and the kid escapes, he'll get his cult to sue you, maybe even arrest you for kidnapping. It's happened. But that's not what I'm worried about. I've got a feeling that somebody's got something a lot worse planned for me. You're right; the cops don't consider me under suspicion for . . . the, uh, mess with Graves. So I *could* take off; nothing's stopping me. But the way it all happened . . . I just can't imagine there's much I could do to be safe from who or whatever could do *that*. If they *wanted* me, no precautions I could take would stop them from *getting* me."

"So . . . ?"

"This is just a hunch, and probably a suicidal one at that, but I'm going to try and get into this thing a little *deeper*." Mitch's eyes widened, despite his discipline of keeping a poker face during counseling sessions.

"Okay, I know you think I've been pushed over the edge by what I saw, but I haven't. I'm not that squeamish. You're forgetting some of the other things I did before I got into deprogramming. Listen to my reasoning for a second. I figure it this way: If I can find out anything about these Starry Wisdom cultists, maybe that'll give me some sort of clue as to what to expect—say, whether they'd even be interested in catching up with me, and what they'd do to me if they did."

Mitch conceded. "Ted, you obviously don't need my permission, but maybe you could use my cooperation. I don't know, maybe a crazy course of action *is* the only right one in a crazy situation. Will you keep in touch while you're . . . looking around?"

Brigham thought for a second. "No, Mitch, because that could very easily pull you down into any hole I wind up in. It's best that I sink just myself on this one. But here's a deal for you . . . I *will* give you any information I come up with after it's over. How's that?"

After he'd decided that his nerves had settled as much as they were likely to, Brigham took off. The first thing he did back at the office was to clear his schedule. Several moms and dads would have to check out some other professional savior, and Ted knew several to recommend, hoping they'd return the favor sometime.

Nearly a month passed before anything occurred to him. And when it did, it practically wasn't his own idea. And that made him just a tiny bit uneasy. It was, quite literally, handed to him. The leaflet read like the advance promo for a new science-fiction film: "The Space-Flight Ministry." Sure enough, it was publicity for some kind of evangelistic crusade run by none other than the Starry Wisdom sect.

Brigham hoped he looked no more the likely target than most people, but he invariably wound up receiving more tracts and pamphlets than your average passerby. After all, it was his business to keep up with this kind of thing. So whenever he saw somebody handing out slips of paper on the street corner, he'd take a second look.

Most people would spot the lone figure standing at the center of his circle of obnoxiousness. Some nameless zealot mechanically handing out—what would it be? A coupon for a free stomach pump at a fast food dive? A ticket to "the works" at the local massage parlor? Or a cheaply mimeographed message of salvation? Most people altered their trajectory slightly, so as to avoid the sidewalk pest without seeming too abrupt. Few wanted to get involved even to the extent of saying "Outta my way." Any who did allow the leaflet to be stuffed into their hands tossed them in the gutter not two yards further down the walk.

But with Ted Brigham, it was just the reverse. He'd veer ever so slightly *toward* the pedestrian prophet. He'd reach out and grab the tract as noncommittally as possible. Then he'd look at it after rounding the corner. If it promised some new material for his file, he'd not only keep it; he might even go back and feign the interest of a wide-eyed seeker, hungry for spiritual truth. If it turned out to be a flyer for "a good time," well, that, too, had its uses.

Ted's eyes fairly bulged this time, when he saw it was the Starry Wisdom sect he had encountered. But for the same reason, he didn't want to risk going back to talk with the cultist. That would be too close for comfort—for all he knew, the cult had everyone watching out for him. Maybe this cultist had even recognized him. No, he'd wait and march into the lion's den next week at the rally. Perhaps, suicidally, that's what he'd decided to do.

The meeting wasn't hard to find; somehow this obscure sect had managed to rent out the largest auditorium in the city. From the crowd pouring in, you'd think they were here for God's first press conference in two thousand years. Of course, maybe they thought they were; now that he thought of it, Ted surmised most of them were cultists, sent in to pack the audience to impress the outsiders, like himself. And he *was* impressed. Even though he saw through the ruse, it said something that Starry Wisdom had this many people in the area. You wouldn't have thought so. From the look of it, they were probably giving the Methodists a run for their money.

As he filed slowly down along the packed aisle and down between the rows of seats, he had time to study the set-up of the place. It was hard to miss the huge kindergarten-style banners, the colored felt jobs with cut-out letters that had become the rage in most churches in recent years. Ted always suspected that churches were places where you could return to the toyland of yesteryear, so at least this was appropriate décor. At least the big banners were easy to read, with their yellow letters on a bright green background. But understanding them was a different story. Here was one announcing, WE SHALL ALL BE CHANGED IN THE TWINKLING OF AN EYE (I COR. 15:51-52). Over there one said, OUT OF EGYPT I HAVE CALLED MY SON (MATT. 2:15). Ted was reminded of just how much he didn't know about the Starry Wisdom Church.

His eyes wandered to the platform, where sprawled a massive pile of electronic equipment; speakers, screens and things harder to identify. Well, he had come expecting a show, and it looked like he wasn't going to be disappointed. But you couldn't really expect to escape being preached at, and sure enough, there was the lectern. Who would it be? If he was lucky, maybe he would finally get a look at the evasive Reverend Enoch Bowen.

His gaze swept out over the rest of the audience, partly to kill time till the crusade got under way, partly out of wariness. After all, *somebody* must know he was here by now. Here and there you could pick out pockets of cultists who didn't bother to hide it, P/R or no P/R. A few rows down, there was a little group singing and clapping some jaunty chorus, but Brigham couldn't make out the words through the general buzz of the crowd. Across in the next section there were a few kids, hands raised, eyes half-closed, speaking in tongues. Even if you *could* make out the words, it wouldn't help. Then a couple of smiling ushers passing out leaflets. He'd have to get one of those, he mentally noted. Pretty empty stuff, most likely—just beaming faces and testimonies of a few satisfied converts—but anything to fatten his new "Starry Wisdom" file would help. He didn't want to get caught short again. But listen to him . . . he couldn't be sure he and his ass were ever going to be healthy enough to do any deprogramming again. No, he might wind up learning a lot more about this cult than he ever wanted to know. But why worry about that at the moment? There's less to worry about if you stay alert, so back to the crowd. Brigham noticed the typical longhaired "seekers," the kids that seemed to try on any new creed like a new shirt and then discard it. These clowns were so fickle that even most of the cults weren't interested in them. Neither were most deprogrammers. Since, given time, they'd probably drop out of any group with no outside prompting, grabbing and trying to deprogram them was usually counterproductive. You were just challenging them and giving them more reason than ever to stay *in* it. Then they were likely to become true believers like . . .

Ginny Salamone! Good God, there she *was*! And her parents with her! They had seen him before he had seen them, and they were moving across the auditorium toward him. Brigham's heart began to pound, probably just from acute confusion. What did this mean, seeing her with them? He had never been completely sure she hadn't been obliterated in that motel room along with poor Graves, almost hoped she *had* been, though all the recoverable remains seemed to be Graves's. But here she was in the flesh, and that meant trouble. Or *did* it? After all, she *was* with her folks, and didn't seem upset about it. Had the experience, whatever the hell it was, been too much for her, shocked her back into reality, and into Mom and Dad's arms? One little flaw in that theory—they weren't just together, they were together *here*, at a Starry Wisdom Crusade. And that meant . . . Here they were.

"Mr. Brigham! How wonderful to *see* you!" said Mrs. Salamone as she grabbed and pumped his hand a trifle over-enthusiastically.

"Yes, we'd wondered what had happened to you!" echoed Dad.

"It's . . . uh . . . quite a surprise to see all of *you*, especially you, Ginny," Ted stammered mechanically. It was like they had all come back from the dead, and Brigham was utterly dumbfounded. *They* wondered what had happened to *him*? Little Ginny had vanished out of a locked room at the same moment a man was blown to bits there, and by what? And you'd think everybody just got separated in a train station! The sheer enormity of the questions made it impossible to ask them. So how about a smaller but just as puzzling one—"Pardon my asking, but what are you folks doing here?" He expected, then realized he desperately hoped, Ginny would answer, but she didn't. She just stood beside Mom and Dad watching Brigham's face, radiating self-assurance, speaking through her parents. It was a strange reversal of roles, as if *she* were the deprogrammer, and *he* was squirming in the chair. He didn't like it.

"Well, Mr. Brigham, as you can see, there's no more trouble between us." Mom moved to cut Dad off: "When we saw how her faith helped her though her . . . ordeal, we thought there might be something to it." Ordeal? Did she mean the slaughter of Graves, and if so, did she know how Ginny escaped? Or did she mean the deprogramming itself, which would make Brigham the villain?

"She's been a great comfort to us, and she was willing to meet us halfway. Which was more than we were willing to do at first, when we called you, I mean." (She *did* consider him the villain.)

"And we thought her new faith deserved a second look. After all, we've been sort of cool on our own Presbyterian Church ever since they got so involved in *social* questions. Mr. Brigham, do you remember when they gave all that money to Angela Davis?"

"Yeah, uh yeah, Mrs. Salamone. I sure do. I've never been too hot on the Presbyterians myself." Damn it, he couldn't keep his eyes away from Ginny's even when he was answering the old bag. He hated to show a breach in his defenses this way—she must know he was shaken. Well, he couldn't get her to say a word to him before, but maybe on her own ground she'd feel more like talking. It was worth a try.

"Hey Ginny, are we going to get to see Bow . . . Reverend Bowen?"

She laughed, as if at an absurdity spoken by a child. "Oh, no one *sees*

Reverend Bowen anymore." She must have meant he had gone into seclusion, maybe to that real estate Ted suspected he had in some tropical clime. Still she had emphasized her words in an odd way, and Ted felt disturbed.

"Looks like things are about ready to start. I'm . . . uh, glad you've all settled your troubles. And, Ginny, I hope there's no hard feelings . . ." Ted *desperately* hoped this. "If your parents have no more problems with your beliefs, then I sure don't either. It's just my job, you understand . . ."

Ginny and her folks were already turning to leave. She gave him one more look that said she *did* understand. At least there was *something* she understood very well. They left to find their seats, closer to the front than his. Ginny, after all, was a member, probably even a candidate for sainthood after the deprogramming fiasco.

The evening's speaker had assumed his position behind the pulpit. As with most cultists and fanatics, his body language suggested that he viewed the lectern as a kind of command center or control panel from which he was about to launch a psychological assault on his audience. When Ted got a good look at his face, he was somehow not surprised to find that the preacher was the very same Bible-toting pest he had brushed off in the Holiday Inn coffee shop! This meant one ominous thing to Brigham. This guy was obviously a big gun with the cult, and for him to get personally involved distracting Ted while Ginny made her escape meant that Ginny was somehow pretty important to them. This, in turn, meant that they probably weren't going to let Ted off that easy. Judging by the condition they found Graves in, the Starry Wisdom sect was not big on turning the other cheek.

The preachy sing-song tone sounded familiar as the man introduced himself as Reverend Baruch Rowley and began his presentation. "If you're like me, your heart is grieved today when you look to the right and see young people enslaved in the bonds of drug addiction, and you look to the left and see their parents caught up in the rat-race of materialism. Both generations are equally at fault, Amen?"

A few scattered "amens" obediently echoed, punctuating Rowley's run-on sentences with affirmation. If what he was saying lacked any inherent power to convince, maybe this sort of cheer-leading would make up the lack. Ted had heard the same tricks, and the same claptrap, before.

"I tell you, my friends, that everywhere you turn in this old world, you see folks that are part of the problem, not part of the solution! And, mind you, that's why the prophet Isaiah said 'We all like sheep have gone astray. We are turned everyone unto his own way.' And that's why today we need a salvation that's not from this world. That's why today whatever deliverance is going to come, is going to come from *out there!*" At this, Rowley swept his arm skyward, following with his eyes, apparently hoping to lead everyone else's glance along behind.

"You know, that's not just Baruch Rowley's belief, and that's not just the belief of this fine-looking group of young people that invited you here tonight. No sir, and no ma'am, that's what the Word of *God* says, I'm here to tell you. But maybe you've read the Scriptures, and you don't seem to recall ever reading anything like that. Well, let me ask you, didn't David pray, 'Open mine eyes, that I may behold wondrous things from Thy Word'? Yes, he did. And I bear witness that the Lord sent someone to open *my* eyes to some of those wondrous things. And that man was the Reverend Enoch Bowen, God's man for this day and age."

Many "amens" this time, full of spontaneous enthusiasm. Was Bowen going to appear to this accolade of his fans? From what Ginny said, Brigham didn't think so, yet he felt sure Rowley was leading up to something. That weird bunch of equipment wasn't piled up on stage just to amplify the old windbag's voice. He practically didn't even need the microphone anyway.

"Reverend Bowen opened the Scriptures to reveal the meaning of Saint Paul's words in First Corinthians, chapter 15, 'I show you a mystery. We shall not all sleep, but we shall all be changed in a moment, in the twinkling of an eye. These mortal bodies must put on immortality. For I tell you, brethren, flesh and blood shall not inherit the Kingdom of God, neither shall the perishable inherit the imperishable'! But even Saint Paul said it was a mystery. Even *he* didn't know just *how* this grand resurrection would come to pass. But as the time draws near at hand, God has sent that answer to his servant Enoch Bowen, so that the rest of us might prepare ourselves for that glorious day. 'For as we have borne the image of the earthly man, so we must bear the image of the heavenly man.' Why, that word 'heaven' doesn't mean anything but *sky! Space!* And that's where our salvation's due to come from.

"But you've listened to me enough! You good folks didn't come here tonight to listen to an old man like *me.* No, you were told this would be an *experience,* and it will be. We've got a program rigged up that will *show* you what I'm talking about. And I'd better just get out of the way and let you see for yourselves. Lights!"

Suddenly finding himself in darkness made Brigham feel more than a trifle uneasy. But then, at least a good many of these people must be outsiders like himself, and probably the cultists wouldn't risk the commotion of trying to take him right then. Still on his guard, he began to watch.

But soon his apprehensions began to slip away, crowded out by the wonderment he felt at what he was seeing. Just from the standpoint of technology, he wondered how they could do it. With some gimmick George Lucas would probably give a couple of *Star Wars* of profits for, they had been able to create a sensory illusion of being completely surrounded by images. You lost sight of the rest of the audience and seemed to be just hanging like a disembodied observer in the middle of the scene. He had once read of a French filmmaker who experimented with rear-projection above, below, and around the audience, and maybe this was the same thing, though Brigham couldn't imagine how this auditorium could have been fitted for this kind of set-up.

Just as spectacular was the series of images that you . . . saw? . . . that you almost felt a part of. If these people could conjure special effects like this, some cultist was missing his calling. Vistas of planets and suns opened up before the viewer. Hard-to-describe beings shot through the sky, gesturing as if to communicate. And, strangest of all, the viewing perspective seemed to suggest that you might be one of them.

Vast leagues of space were traversed somehow, and the earth came into view, rapidly expanding from a dully glowing blue dot in space to a horizon-filling disk of clouds, oceans, and continents. Then Doomsday seemed to have arrived, with mountains splitting down the middle and lava pouring out, cities falling into opened crevasses like collapsing sand-castles. The seas churned as if they were boiling, and the ruins of ancient castles stood exposed where ocean beds had emptied. Everything was chaos. And over everything stood a lurid glow of a spectrum in which the wrong colors seemed to fade into each other. The odd umbras narrowly slipped away from the mind's attempt to grasp them.

Through all this Brigham could hardly keep any sense of where he really was. All he could think was how fantastic it was. And how very dreadful, for it seemed as if it were really happening, like a good movie that could draw you in and make you forget it was only a movie. And actually, Ted had begun to wonder if it really *was* just a movie. Was it possible they were pumping some kind of drug into the place? He had always heard that some cults used drugs to snare kids—sort of an instant-conversion technique. But there had never been any documented cases of it, and this probably wasn't one either, but it seemed so real . . .

The film, or whatever it was, went on and on until . . . Brigham didn't know when. Eventually Rowley came back and said something, maybe a prayer, to dismiss the meeting. Ted didn't catch what it was. It didn't even occur to him to check his watch as he left the building and headed for the subway. He was too blown away. But at least now he *knew*. He had his answers, and he knew what to do next.

Weeks went by, business pretty much as usual, except that he didn't get in touch with Mitch Ames as he'd promised. At first he was too busy; later he was kind of embarrassed. He had found a better place to refer his newly deprogrammed charges, and he didn't quite know how to break it to old Mitch. He'd figure a way soon enough though. You couldn't just drop a friend.

And there was plenty of business. Mostly the usual cults—Moonies, Rajneesh, Forever Family. Not much of a challenge after that brush with Starry Wisdom, but Ted wasn't of a mind to complain. Today's reluctant client was one Bill Jenkins, or as he now preferred to be known, "Ananda Isopanishad." Brother; how could they take it seriously themselves? It was too bad these brats couldn't see that for all their gullible idealism, their fanaticism was just adding to all the chaos in the world. Ted shrugged at the thought as he closed the door of the Ramada Inn room behind him.

"Hey, why no lights?" he began according to his accustomed script. "Bill, my friend, the name's Ted Brigham." It would probably have been more diplomatic to play the kid's game at first and call him "Ananda," but Ted just couldn't bring himself to do it. He would have sounded just too foolish. He saw the familiar mixed look of defiance and ill-concealed fear on the kid's face. The smear of brown paint up and down his forehead didn't change that. They all tended to react pretty much the same way.

"I can imagine what you've heard about me, but I think you'll find it's not true. Unless they've told you I'm just a guy who wants to talk with you and set a few things straight." Still the look of hostile suspicion. It would be a while before any cracks of vulnerability became visible. It always was.

"Bill, let me ask you . . . you and I both know there's an awful lot wrong with this world. No disagreement there, right? But do you really think it'll do much to help for you to wear that get up and shave your head? I mean it's your business, and really I'm not laughing at you. It just seems to me it's a futile gesture. I think if you'd stop and think about it you'd agree

101

that all this is no answer," Ted said, indicating the saffron robes. "I'm afraid we're going to have to stay here until you realize that. Look, you probably think I want to make you run back to your mother's apron-strings or become an accountant like your old man. No, listen, I agree with you that that's just a dead end." You could see some genuine curiosity in the kid's eyes at that, just as you could see he was trying to hide it. Maybe he was beginning to feel Ted was in his corner after all.

"Bill, the world *does* need salvation, any fool can see that. I see it, you see it. But I'll be blunt with you, Bill, chanting 'Hare Krishna' isn't going to do anything about it. You see, the real salvation is going to come from *out there*." As his hand swept out and upward, he just missed the lampshade.

–1989–

A THOUSAND YOUNG

Sex was my god. I do not blush to admit it. Indeed I have always been at a loss to fathom how anyone could seek any other altar. For what besides sex holds the keys both to life's generation and to its uttermost ecstasies? The knowledge of my vocation has been life-long, passionately felt, though at times dimly understood.

My early years witnessed no especial circumstances or experiences to set me off from other boys, save in this one respect: that I was positively more religious than most, certainly more so even than my parents, to whom my catechism was a mere custodial duty no different in kind than enrolling me in grade school. So no excesses of churchly zeal or over-active conscience were ever forced upon me. I note this lest anyone interpret my eroticism as childish reaction against repression, as was the case with other lustful luminaries such as the puzzling Aleister Crowley.

No, my awakening adolescent sexuality caused no trauma, and did not even find occasion to affront my deeply-felt religious convictions. My faith, did, however, cause me to resolve to defer full sexual gratification until marriage would one day make it legitimate in the eyes of the Almighty. But until then, I could wait. And, of course, masturbate. No text could I find in Sacred Scripture to forbid the practice, imaginary commandments against "Onanism" notwithstanding. Even then I was astute enough to realize that natural exegesis erected no barrier to natural self-expression.

But from what I have said it becomes obvious that I had privately begun to interpret my creed for myself (since my peers in piety would certainly never have endorsed the opinions I have here expressed). And it was this intellectual inquisitiveness that led me during college years to slough off conventional dogma altogether. Once again, however, this transition necessitated no violent break. Rather, I bade my youthful faith a fond goodbye, seeing in the parting no more than Saint Paul himself had described as a "putting away of childish things."

Once one has been singed with the fire of religious zeal, one can never quite get beyond its influence, no matter what intellectual permutations one undergoes. And so with me. My instinctive questioning after the cosmos and its ultimate meaning simply pursued new and different channels. And, needless to say, so did my sexuality, now free from what
103

strictures even my own theology had imposed. I sampled new philosophies and new flesh with equal relish, and though grateful for the savor of each successive encounter, intellectual and physical, I never could rest content.

In pursuit of the sexual quest one hears of many, I suspect, less imaginative souls who become quickly jaded, failing finally to become aroused by whatever previously titillated them. I confess my inability to understand this unfortunate course, except to liken it to drug addiction and its diminishing returns. It was not my experience, for I continued to take the same delight in the tenth virgin as I did in the first. Every breast and buttock was as sweet as the last to me. I sought to expand my libidinous repertoire only because it seemed the natural path of growth. And the sense of dissatisfaction I eventually came to feel arose not so much from weariness with what I had experienced, as from curiosity about what I had not.

I have said that my quest of spirit kept pace with my sexual adventuring during this period. But here the picture was somewhat different. For unless one be a pure dilettante, one cannot simply sample philosophies and worldviews as at a buffet. When one moves from one system to the next, one does so in rejection of the first. And it did not take me overlong to progress through several schools of opinion in this manner.

The Logical Positivists seemed to me to have created a singularly depressing cell in which to imprison the human mind, disdaining all the concerns of classical philosophy that did not lend themselves to the neat solution of a mathematical problem. A sympathetic attempt to acquaint myself with their tenets assured me that Positivism, or any other myopic strain of Materialism, was not to be my home.

Surely, given my more mystical predilections, Idealism was more convivial to me, yet I could not help but feel that the great spokesmen for this school—Plato, Bishop Berkeley, Hegel—were missing something, as if they had left some important tract of ground uncovered. There *was* a Reality transcending humanity and its mundane grind, or at least I felt sure of it, but what was its nature? "The Absolute Spirit"? "The Form of the Good"? With all such abstractions I was dissatisfied, all the more since each philosopher superimposed his own version of that transcendental realm as an eternal *imprimatur* on the temporal establishment to which he belonged: Hegel to the German monarchy, Berkeley to the Church of Ireland, Plato to the totalitarian "Republic" he longed for. I, the reader will recall, was no friend to conformity and demanded to think, and act, for myself.

As so often happens (so often, in fact, that we really should cease to be surprised at it), my answer came to me serendipitously. Though my philosophical studies demanded most of my time in college and university years (necessarily so, since it was to be my professional field), I occasionally relaxed with other reading. I became an aficionado, even a connoisseur, of pornography. I began to read such material for the same reason that anyone does: for the vicarious sexual thrill of it. Only I found that most of the modern works were so shoddily written—little better than toilet graffiti, actually—that only morons might be seduced by them. So I concentrated on and began to collect the classics of the genre. It was my great fortune to stumble across a copy of Pisanus Fraxi's nearly unobtainable *Index Librorum Prohibitorum*. This was a nineteenth-century work which, while posing as a pious syllabus of errors cataloguing unwholesome books, slyly sought to aid the salacious collector in tracking down and amassing a pornographic library. And that was precisely the use to which I put it.

It was through such enjoyable researches that I finally chanced upon what seemed the object of both my intellectual and erotic searchings. For there in the pages of the Marquis de Sade I discovered the delicious and daring philosophy of Libertinage, the "Philosophy of the Boudoir," as he himself had put it. There I read of the "sodalities" and societies of kindred spirits, yea, damned souls, who sought to flout the world's norms in every conceivable way—and in some ways, I might add, which I had never conceived! To rend the fabric of reality was their goal, by subverting every established convention and ethic. Sex, of course, was their chosen focus of attack in their assault: what facet of life is so volatile, so powerful, and therefore the object of such meticulous rule-weaving? In the words of Saint Paul, my old mentor, "their glory was their shame." And *what* shame! And what *glory!*

Yet Sade himself had written only from his own blasphemous fantasies. An outcast from society he was, as one might guess, but for fairly trivial reasons. His own character Juliette, mistress of poisoners and fiends, would have scorned the petty perversity for which Sade was incarcerated: pouring hot wax into the cuts and scratches of a harlot he had whipped. Alas, Sade's corrupt monasteries and secret societies existed only in his mind. Certainly my own erotic pilgrimage had never brought me in contact with any of them. Oh, it was not difficult to gain admission to sexual retreats and partner-swapping groups. But the sad and base individuals who populated such gatherings had no real inkling of why they should be doing what they did. None of these fools grasped, as I now did, that the key to the ultimate erotic experience lay not first and foremost in

105

the flesh but in the *spirit*! Perversion is nothing without blasphemy, transgression! The secret was that, paradoxically, sexuality is fulfilled only when it is instrumental to *something else*—the utter repudiation of the world and the standards to which it imperiously requires conformity.

Eagerly I plumbed my new-found knowledge in the pages of the various forbidden books which now occupied the place that Holy Scripture had once held with me. But I must share these secrets only with myself, for nowhere was I likely to find what I so desperately craved, an orgiastic fellowship in the midst of which to consummate that urge toward true enlightenment.

II.

In this manner I passed many months, my fervor waxing and waning as all but the most obsessive passions must, but never losing my longing for fulfillment. My usual round both of academic and sexual activities continued unabated, as did the part-time work with which I supplemented my tuition scholarship. My acquaintances little suspected the nature of the preoccupation I sometimes could not hide. Instead they ascribed it with a laugh to my being "a philosopher," an epithet equivalent in their minds to "dreamer." This mild spoofing, naturally, did not bother me, and I was grateful for it since it prevented closer scrutiny. Actually, during the past years of sexual adventure, I had found it eminently simple to hide my activities from even fairly close associates. People seem to be remarkably incapable of imagining that anyone might occupy himself with interests they themselves do not share. So be it.

This was true even of my fiancée. A word, perhaps, should be said of her. I had met Marilyn in college, in the philosophy department as a matter of fact. We got along splendidly from the beginning. I was pleased to discover early on that she was not particularly inhibited sexually, and we became close friends, casual lovers. Ours was an attachment that required no exclusivity, as romantic love was not the heart of it, and probably did not enter it at all.

But Marilyn had begun to show a need for security in recent months and suggested that we make our relationship a permanent one. I concurred, but for reasons she could scarcely suspect. Since the secret, the forbidden, had become a spice my sexual appetite could not resist, I felt that Marilyn's love would be most satisfying to me insofar as I betrayed it. This I deemed superior to initiating her into the mysteries of Libertinage, since I doubted that she could fully appreciate either its philosophical subtleties or its sexual ravages. I recall the night we announced our engagement to a small gathering of relatives and friends; several hours later, I was announcing it to the laughter of the prostitutes locked together with me in an embrace difficult to describe. I do not mean to give a false estimate of her intelligence; Marilyn probably suspected that I was not completely faithful to her. After all, as I have said, our previous arrangement had not been entirely monogamous, nor had it been expected that it should be. From her perspective, this last had quite likely changed, but she like many women no doubt felt it best to compromise silently. So of my infidelity she could not have been altogether oblivious. It was just that it was not in her head to guess just *what* I was up to, or with whom.

I derived my usual amusement, then, from my varied pursuits during those months, my joy sullied only by the regret that my ideal was likely to remain unrealized, unless perhaps I were to try and organize a Libertine cell myself. But this I knew, without having seriously to consider it, would be too dangerous a thing to attempt, professionally, and perhaps legally as well. Remember poor Sade!

New hope was forthcoming, once again, from an unsuspected quarter. It was the middle of March, and I found myself across the country for an academic convention, some philosophical seminar as I remember. After I had bade my colleagues goodbye for the evening, I headed for the seamier section of the city. I little doubted that my recent companions were seeking similar entertainment, but I suspected that they had tamer pursuits in mind. After some leisurely perusal of the merchandise, I settled upon a buy. Approaching a leather-clad strumpet with a particularly suggestive look on her face, I confirmed that her specialties were as I had surmised and negotiated a fee. Her "studio" was not far away, and we soon were busy. I will not bother to describe our activities, as the reader may imagine them readily enough.

An hour or so later (I had paid her well for her time), I noticed a curious thing: one of her nipples seemed to have been either surgically removed or perhaps . . . bitten off? It may seem odd that till now I had not noticed this singular fact, but her intricate costuming and our no less intricate positions had prevented me from catching this detail. Upon my asking she admitted that my second guess was correct. Her injury had been incurred a year before, during a job for a religious "cult" on the coast. This bit of news excited me no little. True, she had given me no solid information; a "cult" might denote any unfamiliar religious group. But how many

107

religious groups of whatever kind would engage the services of prostitutes? Instinct told me that I might be close to the realization of my dream. Were they Satanists? I hoped not, for I had no interest in that band of childish neurotics. Her surprise at my interest in this aspect of the matter implied that most clients were as intellectually uncurious as she herself was. When I persisted, she said she didn't think so, since the orgy took place in a church! She mumbled something about how all religious people were hypocrites, but I interrupted her with more questions that puzzled her for their seeming irrelevance. Soon I rose, cleaned myself off as best I could, and prepared to leave, again to my hostess' astonishment, since my expensively purchased time had not expired.

III.

Fully a year and a half were to elapse before the hints supplied by the slut would come to fruition. She had taken so many sexual assignments in the months previous to our meeting that she could sort out details only with difficulty. And my various duties took their large share of time, so that it was quite a while before I made any progress. But connections were made, and one day I found myself wandering through a rather depressed and decayed section of the inner city, casting nervous glances this way and that, lest one of the troglodytic inhabitants take undue interest in my prowling. Common sense dictated that one proceed with an air of assurance, since street felons would not hesitate to spot and swoop down on strangers who made themselves known by their air of disorientation. I was not quite sure of my way, but at last I did manage to find my destination without incident.

To my delight, the address with which I had been supplied was an old Episcopal church, perhaps the very one the whore had described. It was almost like a cathedral in design, if not size. The structure was in a state of some disrepair, but not nearly what one might expect under the circumstances. It was no burnt-out hulk, but seemed to have suffered only such minor vandalism as was not deemed worth troubling to repair. Mayhap it was maintained by the diocese as a rescue mission or community center of some kind, kept open only to salve the consciences of affluent former-congregants who had long since moved to the suburbs and now hoped to associate only vicariously with the publicans and sinners.

None of this mattered much to me, however. If my leads were correct, and if the voice with whom I had recently spoken by phone were not having a joke at my expense, the church before me was the secret sanctuary of the Libertine sect I sought. If so, it had been chosen with perfect sacrilegious intent. What desecrations might be wrought on the very altar of propriety!

The door was unlocked, quite a risk to take in these parts, I thought, but perhaps a sign that I was expected. I stepped as quietly as I could through the narthex and into the sanctuary proper. The dimness inside made it difficult to see in what condition the interior lay. But at the same time it made it easy to find my direction, since through the gloom shone clearly if hesitantly a gleam of light. It came from under the door behind and to the side of the altar, probably the choir entrance. I reached it, knocked lightly, and thought I caught the sound of movements somewhere within, though no answer to my knock. I entered anyway, hoping I would not find some street thug who had gained entry as simply as I and now waited to ambush me.

Beyond the door was a narrow passage, lit with a naked and faltering bulb, but vacant. Where was the one I came here to meet? By the dim radiance, I could barely make out an office door at the top of some stairs. As I ascended the short staircase, announcing my presence by the creaking of the boards beneath my feet, I wondered if in fact the very pastor of the church were a clandestine Libertine? Hesitantly I pushed open the door which already stood slightly ajar.

He stood with his back turned, though apparently awaiting me. The tiny office was not lighted, and I had trouble tracing his form, which at first seemed to shift amorphously. My eyes were now rapidly growing accustomed to the shadows, and soon I noticed that the man, who still had not spoken, wore a billowing leathern robe of unusual design. I would have expected clerical garb, but was not unduly surprised since the wearing of leather was naturally quite common in the circles I frequented. The wholly unconventional pattern of seaming I confess I found vaguely troubling, but there was no time to dwell upon trifles.

The man smiled and motioned me to be seated. He never gave his name, understandably, and I had to deduce what I could from his general aspect. At a glance I could see that his face, well into middle-age, was lined and creased. To Episcopal parishioners it would no doubt seem he was careworn with pious duties, but I believed I could guess the quite different acts of devotion that had taken their toll. His ample jowls indicated indulgence in fine food and wines, a taste which is famously no less common to Anglican clergy than to Libertines.

I introduced myself and allowed my eyes to stray momentarily to the shelf of books above his desk. And in that moment I knew I had attained my objective, come home as it were. For there next to his Bible and Book of Common Prayer, were some of the very same titles I myself had come to treasure: Marquis de Sade's *One-Hundred and Twenty Days of Sodom*, Comte d'Erlette's *Cultes des Goules*, Gilles de Rais's *Concubinage to Satan*.

IV.

Of that interview I need offer few details save that a certain list of initiatory tests was agreed upon. Some of these tasks I found a bit startling, but this, I was made to understand, was precisely their intent. Just as the Zen master assigns the novice a *koan*, or enigmatic riddle, in order to wean him from the accustomed structures of rational thought, my list of labors was designed to deaden me to the last twinge of conventional moral conscience. I must steel myself to commit the most intolerable and bestial outrage and so emerge as a true Libertine, caring naught for the laws of God and man, but to tread them underfoot.

How can I describe my mixed jumble of emotions as I left the dark church, all but oblivious to those dubious surroundings which had so intimidated me but a short time before? Along with the anxiety and, I admit it, a degree of disgust at what lay ahead of me, I felt spiritual elation, sexual arousal, and perhaps surprisingly a dash of amusement that made me chuckle aloud. You see, I had eventually gotten around to asking the priest about his unusually cut robe, and his answer was unexpected. It had been stitched together, so he claimed, from the flayed skins of previous leaders of the cult!

This I knew immediately to be hokum, but it was a type of imposture I could appreciate. Role-playing is an integral element of truly epicurean eroticism, and what is more needful than befitting costumes and props? So I was willing to go along with the fiction and did not press him further. It was all part of the game, and so delicious a touch that thinking of it again now brought pleased laughter to my lips.

The next several weeks afforded little opportunity to begin fulfilling my list of assignments. Professional obligations, committee work, and increased dissertation research left me with little time to spare. But I did make good use of what rare moments offered themselves, planning just where and how to discharge my new duties. First on the agenda was the matter of homosexual encounter. In my sexual career up to this point I had never felt particularly inclined in this direction, so had never indulged, but neither was the prospect repugnant.

Now what, the reader may ask, could have required so much planning to arrange a homosexual tryst? One might think a university setting ideal for such liaisons. And, yes, there was a sizeable and burgeoning homophile underground (and barely underground at that) at my institution. But I knew that to enter it even briefly would expose me to the ostracism of some and to the amorous attentions *of* others, and I did not wish the entanglements that were sure to follow. No, a casual liaison someplace where I would not be recognized was preferable.

My first attempt was careless. I sought out a homosexual prostitute on a weekend trip into the city. He was agreeable enough, though with that air of contemptuous aloofness that actually appeals to some customers. But when he ushered me into a nearby public restroom, I began to have second thoughts. I told him so, but soon found out that I had even less say in the matter than I supposed, as he cut off my words, and my breath, with a rough push to the wall, jackknifing my arm behind me in a painful grip. Had I mistakenly picked up a sadist, or was I being robbed? I never found out, since the sound of rushing footsteps somewhere down the hall seized my assailant's attention, causing him to wheel, exit the restroom, and speed down the hall in the opposite direction. His trouble, whatever it might be, was my fortune, and I lost no time quitting the place. Having hailed a taxicab, I nursed my aching arm and wiped the slimy residue of the restroom tiles from my cheek as I planned an alternative course. As it turned out, I needed search no further, for the driver himself was able to oblige me nicely, and soon I was considering how to tackle the next items on the list.

Some of these looked to be more logistically difficult. I was finally forced to ask the help of the priest in arranging them. Initially I hesitated to do this, fearing that it might count against me, but I was reassured that it would not, since the objective was to recondition me morally, not to test my ingenuity. I discovered that for modest sums certain favors might be obtained from veterinarians and even funeral directors. In such dealings, as in politics and other such behind-the-scenes work, one quickly comes to realize how intricately the world of appearance is honeycombed with the unexpected!

But this was not my only discovery, as I learned the pleasures of strange flesh, eschewing distinctions of species or preservation. Freud was entirely correct; he had written of "polymorphous perversity" whereby one experiences each touch, every bodily part as erotic. He had compared it to religious mysticism in that both were attempts to return to the blessed warmth and cosmic oneness of the womb. And if both paths, mysticism and perversion, alike led to the same place, was it not evident that there was in reality but *one* path? Through my initiatory exercise I came to know that flesh and spirit are one, that when mysticism "denies the flesh," it simply means to deny that the flesh is a department separated off from the soul. Man's sensuous part hampers his soul's flight only when he fails to see that it shares the same destination. Both together must reach the orgasmic release of salvation, or neither can.

All this and more did my secret mentor teach me. And as I passed through one degree after another, I was shown deeper levels of the life of the sect. I met various brothers and sisters in the Libertine path; bound myself to them with mutual oaths of pleasure and pain; was permitted to watch as they performed acts which hitherto I would have deemed impossible, unimaginable. With eager anticipation did I greet the promise that I, too, should learn the secrets of such ecstasy!

After some time I attended my first meeting of the whole membership. The clandestine convocation took place in the church I had first visited. I was strictly charged to arrive after things were underway and, alas, only to observe, for my novitiate was not yet quite complete. Obediently I complied, arriving at 2 a.m. on the designated date. Even from the street the raucous roar from within was plainly audible; so that I wondered that no one ever called the police. But the area, as I have said, was blighted, and its inhabitants did not seem the type to regard any noise as untoward.

I entered the church, straining to see through the deep gloom into the mass of wriggling forms, but, advancing no closer than I had been told. Need I say that the sight, what I could see of it, was sublime? I had never dreamed that the group had so huge a membership. The pews, being of the detachable variety, had been cleared away, and before the altar there seemed to be a mountainous pile of bodies, heaving and swaying with wild abandon. Groans of ardor filled my ears; the crack of the lash could be heard, and the accompanying gales of laughter and tears; oils, blood, and other fluids arched through the air to splash on flesh and stone. Oh, that I might be a part of it! I thought to masturbate but lacked the chance, as erection had already come unsummoned and ejaculation followed in its wake. In the wonder of it all I nearly lost track of the time. Happening to

112

catch a glimpse of my wristwatch I realized it was time for me to be away. For I had been warned not to stay for the full duration. This was not explained to me, but I imagined that at the conclusion of the festivity, the lights should come up, and the participants would not wish to risk being identified by anyone not yet fully initiated and committed to the sect. So with reluctance I departed, all the more eager now to complete my tutelage and to participate in the next celebration.

V.

My final task was rape. I was grateful that up till now none of my sexual assignments required the unwilling involvement of others, since legal risks were not to my liking. Of course it was in the interests of the sect to avoid them as well, and this was no doubt why certain other crimes were not mandated. But this one was deemed important enough. If I had lain out my plans carefully before, I was doubly meticulous now. I believed I saw how I could carry it off undetected, and right on my own campus to boot.

Marilyn was to be my victim. And if all went according to plan, she would never learn the identity of her attacker. One of the major fraternities was sponsoring a semester's end costume gala not very many days hence. I knew that on the appointed night, Marilyn would be in the same area of the campus, returning to her apartment from the office where she did part-time secretarial work. I knew the route well, as I sometimes accompanied her.

It was a simple matter to inquire at the local costume shop as to which outfits were most in demand. Ascertaining that several young men had already rented pirate regalia, I did the same, choosing a silken bandana large enough to cover my face. I planned to be long gone by unmasking time, and there would be several other pirates from which to choose a culprit. Any of the drunken fraternity members would be a plausible suspect.

On the night of the party, I stepped into the fraternity house long enough to make sure that there were a number of other bogus buccaneers present and then returned to set my vigil. Right on schedule my fiancée took her customary short-cut through the bushes. I sprang upon her, knocking her to the ground and silencing her with a sharp blow to the back of her head. She was stunned and could marshal no resistance. Let me say simply that I hiked up her skirt and sodomized her. She groaned incoherently, vomited, and then fainted mercifully away. As it happened, she could never have seen me straight on, costume or no costume.

Later I learned that she had been discovered soon after by campus security, shaken and disoriented as might well be imagined. She took an academic furlough for the rest of the year and returned home. Naturally I have written her letters of sympathy and support.

My course of preparation finished, I now waited for the next assemblage, where I would at long last know the joy of fellowship with those to whom I would be joined in body as well as soul. For this, my first participation, there was set but one final restriction. I must still arrive after things had commenced, though this time I might remain through the finale. I was happy to oblige.

Walking the now familiar pathway through dilapidated tenements and reeking garbage cans, I neared the old church as Bunyan's Pilgrim neared the Celestial City. The muted clamor of voices within stirred my soul and thrilled my loins. Inside, all was again dark, but I knew the floor plan of the place well enough by now that I did not miss a step. Flinging aside my clothes, I ran to take my place at last amid the passion-crazed mob that once more formed a veritable hill of bodies before the desecrated altar. Atop the altar itself stood the leather-robed priest, intoning some barbaric litany whose significance I could not guess. The din of the mass beneath him made it quite impossible to distinguish more than random phrases. But this was hardly of concern to me then. In the moment itself I was cognizant only of the press of flesh to every side. I sought entry wherever I could, making no distinction in that shadowy place as to color or gender. That around me were veterans of the sexual combat I could tell by the variety of scars and scratches that could be seen close up, along with other reddish welts less easily identifiable.

The night passed in this way, bereft of time, bereft of reason. I found myself lulled by fatigue and by the priest's droning chant, of which I once believed I caught the nonsense syllables "Iä! Shub-Niggurath!" Indeed he was fairly screaming it toward morning, near the crescendo of that ceremony of debauch, when the lights finally came up.

And then it was that I, too, began to scream. For the sight I saw then sent me fleeing mad and naked into the cold dawn air. Though I was not conscious of anyone pursuing me, I sped down the littered streets, oblivious alike to the damp chill and to the glass and metal fragments upon which I trod. At that early hour there was yet no one about on the streets to stare at the strange and ridiculous spectacle I made. Finally, my exhaustion from the night's revelry overtook the new strength my terror

114

had lent me, and I collapsed, nauseous and bleeding, in an alley many blocks from the church.

How long I remained unconscious I cannot say, but eventually some police patrolling the area found me lying in my own vomit among the heaps of trash, and retrieved me. How did I come to be in this rather remarkable position? I was now actually feeling the cold for the first time, my nerves having recovered somewhat, and this new shock made it difficult to think. Fortunately I stumbled upon this lie: I said I had been set upon by muggers and been completely stripped and beaten. Given my several bruises and cuts, both from my night's debauchery and my subsequent flight, this must have seemed plausible enough, albeit strange. At any rate, the patrolmen appeared more or less satisfied. They kindly provided a rough blanket to cover my nakedness and drove me home.

And it was there I remained, disoriented, confused, unresponsive to communication, and unable to meet my responsibilities. It has been all I could do to recapture my wits sufficiently to reflect and re-evaluate. I have come at last to repent of my ways and to renounce my former pursuits. I imagined that no perversion, however loathsome, could cause me to turn back, yet now I am resolved to celibacy and wish I had always been so.

I had expected to behold the beatific vision in the profaned sanctuary that morning, but what I saw has instead robbed me of any further desire for sex. For there, revealed by the glare of the lights, was no solid heap of swaying orgiasts, but rather chains of bodies spread over the pulsing and gelatinous surface of a tentacled, amoeboid horror, the revelers grotesquely arrayed like suckling whelps as the thing fed greedily on their sexual vitality through the questing pseudopodic phalluses, teats, and vulvas it sent forth!

−1989−

THE DWELLER IN THE POT

Or The Pasta Out of Space Eaters

Since my friend and long-time correspondent Howard had moved to that "Babylonish Burg" New York City, a relocation, he had sworn months before when the proposition was merely theoretical, he could never be constrained to make under the direst circumstances, it was not uncommon for me to pick up the ringing telephone at well-nigh any hour and hear his high-pitched tones at the other end of the line, summoning me either to a barely affordable expedition through the city's bookstalls or to some adventure in gluttony (this latter may surprise the reader in view of Howard's well-known stature: tall, somewhat stooped—and almost cadaverously thin). On the particular afternoon of which I will write, it was the latter to which Howard's excited, nasal tones beckoned me.

I see I have neglected to tell you how my remarkable friend had chanced to move to the "pest zone," as he fondly called it. What could have motivated this staunch Novanglian Yankee to leave his beloved Providence to plunge into New York's "sewer of ethnic excretions," to swim upstream against the "foetid tides of rat-faced mongrel hordes," as he lightheartedly called them? In fact it was the non-Aryan charms of a colleague in amateur journalism, his beloved Sonya. Having somehow managed to prompt Howard to break his once-adamantine bond to bachelorhood, she went on to dissolve his tie to his native Providence as well.

It seemed that just now, Sonia was out of town on a buying trip for her fledgling hat business, and Howard found himself left for a week to function in his old bachelor mode. As if to celebrate "the cat's being away," Howard intended to splurge with a big pot full of his favorite spaghetti. This preference in food was itself surprising in view of Howard's aforementioned distaste for any racial group that hailed from without the radius of Northwestern Europe. As the temperature of one's homeland rose, so proportionately did Howard's esteem for one's pedigree plummet. In fact, Howard did not hesitate to broadcast his racialist sentiments, wholly unmoved by my attempts at moderation, at every opportunity. True, he rarely wore his immaculately lettered INFERIOR RACES GO

HOME sandwich board in public, but other avenues for propaganda were ready to hand, amateur journalism being one. Though few readers will be aware of the fact, equally few will be surprised to learn that the title of Howard's famous tale "Dagon" had been shorter by one letter (I leave the reader to imagine which one) and in its first draft depicted the fevered reactions of a shipwrecked mariner beached on the Italian mainland as he witnesses a stout native emerging from the sea to hug the Leaning Tower of Pisa. Here I was able to persuade my friend to a greater degree of subtlety in a second and better known draft.

But let me cease to linger and press on to linguini. No doubt I hesitate to face the memory of the eldritch events of that evening of eating.

It was with a distinct foreboding that I wended my way with many an over-the-shoulder glance, through the squalid Red Hook section of Brooklyn where Howard lived. I had once wagered that even Howard's febrile imagination could not wrest a truly cosmic spectral tale from what I then viewed as the purely mundane urban decay that formed the environs of his Clinton Street address. Now I was not so sure.

I breathed easier as Howard opened promptly to my customary three-two knock.

"Chimesleepius!" he greeted me, simultaneously pumping my hand and patting me on the back, as might a doting grandfather welcoming back his prodigal grandson not seen for years. In fact Howard's proprietary interest in my writing career was genuinely parental though he was only a handful of years my elder.

"Just let your olfactories partake of the bewitching aroma that your old Grandpa has conjured! I make bold to guarantee they've never sniffed the like!"

Indeed they had not. Though I had been party to many of Howard's spaghetti feasts in the past months, this collection of smells was unprecedented. Neither unpleasant nor altogether inviting, the fumes of the bubbling pot seemed almost to awaken a hitherto-dormant sense that nature in her wisdom had long since judged best to breed out of the race. It was only by analogy that it could be called a smell at all.

As Howard doffed his bulbous chef's hat, so disturbingly reminiscent of some bloated, detestable fungus, and his KISS THE COOK apron, he motioned me to take a seat. I complied, rapidly becoming aware of some disquieting sense of cosmic dislocation in the close quarters of the scent-filled apartment. Did I catch the haunting tones of cracked flutes wailing some malignant dirge as if gloating over the impending heat-death of the

117

universe? But then the common sense of the self-blinded earth-gazer reasserted itself, and I recognized the music as proceeding from Howard's much bemoaned Syrian neighbor upstairs.

Howard ladled out a clenched mass of pasta tendrils, dumping them in a smoking heap on the plate in front of me. As I reached for the meat sauce, he strode over to the kitchen counter and took up a large black volume. Holding the folio-sized tome propped against his chest for my perusal, he announced triumphantly, "The recipe comes from this curious cookbook I discovered last evening when some whim moved me to take a late stroll down toward the harbors. When the old Levite who ran the shop saw my interest in gustatory antiquarianism he parted with the volume for a ridiculously small sum. Yes, don't strain yourself, Chimesleepius, it's in Latin all right, but the ingredients are readily enough decipherable for one of my classical erudition."

I could barely make out the faded lettering imprinted on the spine: *De Vermicelli Mysteriis*. I shuddered involuntarily, and my amply laden fork hesitated in its progress to my mouth. Yet offend my enthusiastic host I dared not. I chewed in silence for some moments, considering whether to identify the peculiar taste as surpassingly delicious or unspeakably repugnant. Howard in the meantime had fallen to with gusto. The quizzical look written across his grotesque lantern-jawed visage, now stuffed with pasta and tomato sauce, made clear that he harbored the same cryptical doubts as I.

Howard dished up another platter of the seething stuff, while I reached for coffee (my tee-totaling friend would not stock wine even for such an occasion as this) to wash it down.

It seemed that Howard had decided what he thought of the doubtful dish and was about to make some pronouncement to that effect—*when suddenly silenced by one whipping tendril of spaghetti* which unreeled from the spoonful he held ready and wound itself with lightning speed around his head like a gag stopping his open mouth! His eyes started from their sockets; his bony arms began to flail like the wings of a windmill. His chair legs scraped across the floor; momentarily I thought he had leapt back from the table in a gesture of escape. In fact, his gaunt form was being repelled from the table by more animate tentacles seeking to defend themselves against this human devourer.

Myself, I had lost no time in leaping clear of the table, now become an interdimensional gate for trans-cosmic forces so reminiscent of Howard's famous tale "The Call of Calimari." The narrow dimensions of the room afforded little refuge, especially as Howard had cooked up a great mass of

118

the stuff, unwittingly providing more than enough rope to hang himself—and me!

It was clear by now that we were dealing with no recipe ever devised by sane mortals. Poor strangling Howard began to turn purple; I had bare moments to think as I dodged the snapping feelers of extra-cosmic spaghetti. From the corner of my eye I spotted the worm-eaten binding of the cookbook which had become the source not merely of a meal but now, as it seemed, our soul-blasting doom. With a sidewise lunge, I snatched up the evil volume and let it fall open to the place Howard had last opened it.

Holding the place with my finger and trying not to stain the page with sauce (I knew how particular Howard was about the condition of his books), I sought egress via the window and climbed out onto the rusting grate of the fire escape. Slamming the window on a fugitive strand of the evilly sentient pasta, I was revolted to see the severed stalk wiggle like a maggot and fall into the alley below.

I stood shaking with exertion, newly aware of the dropping night temperature, my threadbare overcoat lying useless inside the apartment. I fumbled the book open again, and my eye scanned the page. A quick glance back inside revealed Howard, somehow having freed himself from the gag, perhaps by taking a vicious bite, fencing with his salad fork, in retreat from the questing bands of that amoeboid cluster of living pasta.

My Latin was none too proficient, but I dared hope I might chance to discover some antidote, some counter-recipe that might send the malevolent meal back into its harmless components. Alas, with mocking conciseness the relevant page closed with the epigram, roughly translated. "Do not cook up what you cannot keep down."

I cast the useless volume aside as another idea came to me: Where one book did not serve, another might. As Howard had said between mouthfuls, he was something of an authority on ancient cookery, and more than likely his study contained other volumes which might yield the secret that alone could save us from being ourselves the main course for the ravaging noodles from beyond. I dashed across the fire escape to where it extended under the next window, which opened upon Howard's makeshift study. Kicking in the glass, I fell heavily into the room, sending the book-laden ottomans and end tables flying. As Howard had often generously pressed upon me the use of his private library for my youthful studies, I had a fair idea of the lay of the land. As my eyes adjusted to the gloom, I quickly found the shelf of cookbooks and squinted at their spines. I knew that Miss Murray's *The Sandwich Cult in Western Europe* would be of little use, as would *Cultes des Goulash*. With but a glance at the all-but-unreadable blackletter pages of the *Unaussprechlichen Kuchen*, I hastened to the one volume that might hold my answer—the abhorred *Home Economicon*.

The sounds of crashing vases and toppling furniture assured me that in the next room Howard continued his valiant struggle, but I knew that unless my own efforts bore fruit very soon, all would be lost.

Luck was with me! Thumbing through the musty pages feverishly, I quickly determined that Howard had used a most potent ingredient, the Cheese of the Goat with a Thousand Young. But, thank God! the solution was a simple one! So simple in fact, that I cursed my stupidity for not thinking of it as soon as I had noticed the lack of a customary ingredient in any Italian recipe. The text, again roughly translated, ran as follows: "Garlic is not a passive agent, but has oft-times appeared in belches in the midst of our covens, scattering all present with its power." If it worked on vampires, why not on sentient spaghetti? I slammed the book shut.

Now, of course, the challenge was to reach Howard's spice cabinet across the room in which he fought tooth and nail with the vague cloud of spaghetti-tentacles. As I cocked my ear to listen for the direction of the struggle, better to aim the headlong plunge for which I had already begun bracing myself, I noticed the sudden echo of silence.

Dread crushed me like a *Weird Tales* rejection slip. Surely my beloved mentor was dead, flayed to a crimson ruin by the threshing stalks of the pasta out of space!

I began to weep, dropping to my knees, cushioning my forehead against my folded arms. Then I heard—and *smelled*—the belch! Of course! Howard must have known the contents of his own library! He must instantly have inferred what I had had to discover.

As I rose and entered the kitchen, my suspicions were thankfully confirmed. The struggle had in fact been one rather more of tooth than nail! A bloated Howard, half-empty garlic can in hand, stood by the emptied vessels of a hasty and desperate feast. His apology punctuated by a series of scarcely diminishing gastric explosions, Howard wiped sauce from his mouth and shrugged, "Well, Chimesleepius, one can't *always* play the gentleman!"

The Dweller in the Pot was vanquished, the pasta out of space consumed. Howard broke out the ice cream.

–1990–

As by Frank Chimesleep Short

EXHAM PRIORY
FROM THE PAPERS OF SIR WILLIAM BRINTON

On August 15, 1923, Thomas Delapore, or de la Poer, to use the older form of his family name he had affected in late months, was incarcerated in a barred and padded cell in the asylum for the mad at Hanwell. De la Poer, an expatriate Englishman and last scion of an ancient if not venerable baronial line, had only recently arrived from America to take up residence in the newly reappointed seat of the de la Poers, Exham Priory. He had resolved, all other worldly interests spent, to live out his remaining days in the centuried halls of his forbears. Yet a fate decreed beforehand by his tainted bloodline, an hereditary madness lurking latent only to be nudged to full wakefulness with the proper surroundings as catalyst, assigned him rather different lodgings in which to spend what days remained to him. Padding replaced the black oak paneling and polished wainscoting on the walls around him, though I am told by Dr. Pettijohn that at the last poor de la Poer no longer knew the difference, having sought refuge in the delusion that he dwelt after all in an unsullied Exham about which hovered legends that were no more than legends and could be easily dismissed. His ghostly rats had left him, or rather they had driven his mind into a retreat in which their spectral echoes could no longer be heard. Thus one paranoiac fancy replaced another, and at length he died in peace, two years ago, I believe.

His strange case, however, would not be put to rest as easily. For none of the survivors of the party of seven who had accompanied him on his descent into the Stygian recesses below the Priory could easily forget what we had seen, nor yet the beguiling yet maddening suggestions of what we had *not* seen: those lightless caverns and abysses that yawned *below*. All of us sought as best we could to retreat into the numbing comfort of mundane pursuits and wholesome scholarly activities. I now think that de la Poer in his flight into madness had chosen the wiser course, as his delusion shielded him from a reality far more insane, a reality the rest of us would seek to face again. We had not sought to stay in contact after the affair of Exham Priory, indeed had sought not to, as if never again to discuss it would lend it the aspect of unreality. One cannot easily dismiss

121

as nightmare what several acquaintances recall in common. All of us were specialists representing different fields, each chosen by de la Poer and his ill-fated companion Norrys based on our reputations. No two of us had natural professional acquaintance, so it was easy, by unspoken agreement, to part company and keep quiet.

So things remained until we all received copies of a letter from Dr. Randolf Holmes Pettijohn, one of the original party and an alienist recruited for the adventure by de la Poer whose recent dreams and apparent auditory hallucinations had led him to suspect his own sanity, rightly as I once thought. After the tragedy, the murder of Norrys, Pettijohn had immediately taken charge of de la Poer and had arranged his committal to Hanwell. The case was so spectacular, from a clinical as well as journalistic standpoint, that Pettijohn had made it his business to delve into de la Poer's family origins as fully and deeply as time allowed. None of the rest of us knew even this much until the arrival of his letter so informed us. He had at last, he said, made a discovery that shed unexpected light not only upon de la Poer's case but on our common subterranean adventure as well. Pettijohn was urgent in his insistence that the exploration party regather to hear his findings. After some deliberation, I replied in the affirmative though my reluctance and foreboding colored every sentence of my reply.

On the appointed day we gathered in the London rooms of Dr. Pettijohn; besides myself and the alienist there was, to my surprise, only one other present, the anthropologist Francis Abelard Trask. My initial surprise was mitigated as soon as I recalled that of the original seven, Norrys and de la Poer were both now dead, and the unstable psychic Thornton had accompanied de la Poer to Hanwell, never to emerge. To tell the truth, I could no longer recall the seventh member, a man I had only met briefly on that occasion. I now assumed he had judged sleeping dogs better left to lie and had declined to appear. This was not the meaning attached to the man's absence by Dr. Pettijohn, however, who had for purposes of his inquest secured and maintained information on each of the seven. The absent man was Andrew Powys Thayer, a folklorist expert in the local Anchester legendry concerning Exham Priory. De la Poer had often consulted Thayer as to local folk belief attached to his family seat and had felt the man's detailed knowledge of the Priory and its history might prove invaluable in the exploration of its catacombs.

Professor Thayer had indeed received the identical letter that had summoned Trask and myself, but as Pettijohn expected, it had gone unanswered. Thayer, a recluse since his retirement from teaching, was often unavailable or unresponsive, but Pettijohn had recently had to conclude that more than this was involved. Upon revisiting Anchester to interview some of the local workmen and townspeople in connection with the de la Poer case, Pettijohn had learned that he was not the first to return there. Thayer, too, had been on the scene with unwelcome inquiries, once even asking after hidden entrances to the Priory's interior through unseen crevices in the cliff-face.

For indeed Exham Priory still stood. Pettijohn had thought it best to deceive de la Poer on the matter, informing him of its supposed demolition and hoping that with the focus of his delusions thus "removed," the poor madman might give up his dangerous ancestral fixations. But very soon the Priory would be destroyed in truth, and at the frenzied petitioning of the people of Anchester.

Pettijohn's alarm came from his conviction, unprovable to the authorities, that the eccentric Thayer lurked somewhere, perhaps injured, within the walls of Exham Priory. If indeed he were trapped there, there would be no better search party than the three of us who had shared his experience and were familiar with the lay of the land. With this Trask and I had to concur. Besides, the only concrete physical danger faced on our previous descent was that from the mad de la Poer himself.

But what, I asked, of this discovery that so excited Pettijohn? Here his demeanor changed: the severity of concern he felt for the missing Thayer fell away as the gleam of professional, scholarly discovery lit his face. He told us how, judging from the confession of de la Poer, much of his self-appointed task of reclaiming his ancestral manner was in truth an unconscious quest to cure himself of a kind of family amnesia, knowledge of his line that had been lost in the burning of Carfax Plantation during the War Between the States. Until then some great secret had been passed in a sealed envelope in a spidery hand of ancestor Walter de la Poer from each father on his deathbed to his eldest son. This rite of full manhood included not merely the inheritance of the burden of family responsibility, but a burden of self-knowledge, too; some secret without knowledge of which one could never know what it was to be a de la Poer. Shameful or frightful though the secret might be, ignorance of it might seem worse to a curious mind forever tantalized by its irretrievable absence. De la Poer, in the alienist Pettijohn's professional judgment, had been in all his efforts trying to regain that lost knowledge. Apparently he had succeeded, or thought he had, his fevered mind supplying a mad revelation perhaps much worse than any the lost envelope might have contained.

123

Of course the very existence of the bone-choked Tartarus we seven had stumbled upon beneath Exham Priority lent an undeniable element of the fantastic to de la Poer's family history. But who could say if old Walter de la Poer, who fled England for American shores, had known of the caverns? Only the flame-obliterated record once sealed in that mysterious envelope might answer that question.

Pettijohn's news was that the envelope had in fact come to light! Following the most improbable of hunches, Pettijohn had gambled upon the notorious rapacious tendencies of Federal soldiers during the War. Seldom did they fire a plantation home without sacking it first. Suppose Carfax had been thus ransacked by the Yankees before they torched it? And suppose they had discovered a lockbox they were unable to open? Might not a determined and greedy man have borne his stubborn prize away for further attention later? And, minus money and valuables, might not the personal effects, including the sealed letter, have made their way into some closet where with the passage of decades they would accumulate a certain antiquarian interest? And might they not have passed thence into the hands of one of the many dealers in such artifacts?

It was all improbable to say the least, absurdly improbable really, but it would cost the determined researcher little in either money or time to set in motion the necessary inquiries. The trail led at length to a historian on the faculty of one of the Border State universities. Astonishingly, the Delapore papers had actually come to rest in the University archives. Pettijohn lost no time in acquiring photostatic copies of the relevant material.

What the rediscovered epistle contained was almost as mysterious as it was revealing. Indeed, it was only the experience beneath Exham Priory that enabled Pettijohn to penetrate the cryptic reluctance of the missive. Without such knowledge various sinister allusions must almost certainly have escaped the American Delapore heirs. There were pathetic confessions of miscegenation and murder, of incest and insanity, of outrage against nature and blasphemy against God. There were hopeless intimations of a taint that could not be expunged. Most likely the confused young Delapores must have inferred that their veins harbored forbidden Negro blood with a furtive hint of something more. Dalliances between white master and black slave were not uncommon, though usually kept out of the line of inheritance, and presumably the unsuspected octoroon taint was enough of a scandal to keep hushed up, especially if it occasionally burst through the surface in a reversion to type as it had in the case of young Randolph Delapore who had abandoned

124

white society for the slave quarters where he became an Obeah shaman, much as one occasionally now saw whites adopting Negro style and manner in the Harlem jazz clubs of America. Such outlawed cult-worship was nothing new in the Delapore lineage, the letter made clear with evasive penitence, but again the warning must have been lost on the Virginia Episcopalians who read it without the key of unstated knowledge.

Pettijohn felt that the riddle of the Delapores, or de la Poers, might finally be solved by a return trip to the caverns beneath Exham Priory. What difference did it make, Thomas de la Poer being dead two years? Neither Trask nor I asked this question. The de la Poer madness was so singular, opening up new lines of inquiry into the much-debated question of ancestral memory, that no men of the psychological sciences could in good conscience fail to try to resolve it. And in no better conscience could Trask, an anthropologist, and I, an archaeologist, continue to pretend deafness to the sirens of lost knowledge that had tempted us since that initial descent. We would return, come what may. With luck we would find our colleague. As men we could hope no less. But as scientists we could hope for a great deal more.

The initial entry into Exham Priory was not half the obstacle we had anticipated. Though I am loathe to trade on the modest fame my work has earned me, the rehearsing of my credentials, plus the implication by Dr. Pettijohn that his investigations were aimed at the final extirpation of the de la Poer blight, proved sufficient to gain the limited cooperation of the local authorities as the missing folklorist Thayer had been unable to do. We retraced our steps with a shiver of *déjà vu*, recalling too vividly our first expedition with Thomas de la Poer. The series of sub-cellars reminded me of the circles of Dante's Hell, but I knew we traversed but the antechamber of Hell. The cleverly hidden altar stone designed to mask the netherworld of the de la Poers still stood tipped open. None of us had thought to restore it to its original position in our precipitous departure nearly a year before. As we crouched to pass this portal into Pandemonium, I understood another piece of the Priory's puzzle. Local lore spoke of an "inner cult" to which only certain even of the tainted de la Poers would be initiated. I now knew that whatever blasphemous revels of defilement occupied the demented clan as a whole, they must have been restricted to the Roman-era chambers we were now quitting. Only the inner initiates would be informed of the twilit grotto below—else why disguise the doorway to it beneath a secret altar stone which none outside the family might see in the first place? Had the parricide Walter de la Poer

125

known of the secret cult and its netherworld? No doubt the "outer" Attys and Cybele cultus with its orgies of castration and infanticide would have been enough to provoke his desperate act. But we were going deeper, to those levels of nightmare the visitation of which had driven Thomas de la Poer to cannibalistic insanity.

Beneath us stretched away the skeleton-scattered plain dotted with architectural stragglers from Roman, Celtic, Saxon and Jacobean times. All this we had seen, and despite our best efforts, we had all of us failed to forget a single detail of it. Trask and I had come prepared with cameras and as many photographic plates as we might accommodate in our rucksacks, hoping to gather enough evidence to persuade the government authorities, in the name of science, to delay the planned destruction of so singular a site. So we paused to record as much of the unearthly scene as we might, then· headed for *terra incognita*. On our first trip we had not dared to penetrate the deeper recesses of the place as we had nothing approaching adequate lighting. The dim twilight of the place was supplied by the unseen cliff fissures that let in the cool breezes that alone made the place sufferable. But out of range of that faint luminescence we had not dared explore further. This time we were prepared. High intensity chemical torches, plus an ample supply of matches, should more secretive illumination prove advisable, now made further descent practicable.

I will not tax the patience of readers who may not share my own scholarly pedantry with all the details of our exploration. These may be found in the official reports. Suffice it to say that we found a *series* of once-inhabited caverns, all connected by well-worn, sometimes almost-effaced stone steps. Given the curious mix of architectural styles evident on the topmost layer we did not know what to expect below. If I had had to guess, I would have predicted that the structures on the lower levels would have been of more recent design the deeper one went. The variety of styles up top would have reflected the continuous use of the area through the ages, with the lower levels reflecting a gradual tunneling descent as more space became necessary (for whatever blasphemous ends). Hence, each lower level ought to show more recent style. In fact, though the evidence was not altogether unequivocal, the very opposite seemed to be the case! The further down one went, the earlier in style the structures, or their ruins, became!

This finding comported well with my tentative observation on our initial exploration, that the tunneling seemed to evidence stroke-marks from *below*. At that time I assumed the unusual effect to be the result of some

126

ancient and inefficient constructional technique. Now I began to see the evidence in a bewildering new light.

Stranger still were the apparently contradictory indications of more decadent, secondary workmanship that became more inept, almost appearing hurried and careless, as one descended. The secondary character of what seemed to be renovations was evident from the plain contrast with the finer work that prevailed generally on every level. My only guess was that the more recent reworking reflected a route of *retreat back underground*. Stray relics such as cups and utensils anachronistically scattered on the "wrong" levels tended to confirm this hypothesis. Actually the general interpretation of the data seemed fairly clear, but the tendency of it equally seemed scarcely capable of belief. From whence could these ancient tunnelers have come?

Often we came upon stretches of tunnel wall that had once, I am sure, been hung with tapestries. All that now remained, thanks to the corrosive effects of the salt sea air that penetrated the cliffs, were discolored shreds. Yet it could be seen that the intricately woven arras had once borne complex and detailed scenes which presumably enshrined stories important to and informative of the weavers, whoever they may have been.

Trask had stayed behind attempting to catalogue some of the queer semihuman skeletons and skeleton-fragments that thickly littered the topmost cavern floor. Now, sketches and photographic plates tucked away, he caught up with Pettijohn and myself. Without living subjects to interview, poor Pettijohn had had no research with which to busy himself while Trask worked on his skeletons and I studied the various ruins and artifacts. But soon his patience was rewarded.

At first the three of us thought we were becoming the prey of de la Poer's auditory hallucinations: we seemed to hear the scuffling of animal feet from further down the tunnel. We gave our lights a rest, following the ghostly radiance of phosphorescent fungi which coated the nitred walls on this level. If such plant life existed here, it was not inconceivable that there were animals of some sort as well. After assuring each other that we all heard the sounds, unlike the case of poor de la Poer whose rats only he could hear, we agreed to creep slowly forward to spy whatever animal might be grazing on the fungi.

We were not quiet enough, for instantly we heard the confusion of a group of apparently clumsy animals lumbering away out of sight. *But their herdsman remained.*

Directly before us, half-turned as if to follow his fleeing charges, stood a stooped and skeletal figure. His dirty white hair hung in strings from face and head, penetrated by the startled gaze of red-rimmed eyes. The clothes were filthy rags that hung precariously from his spare frame, and his shepherd's crook was a walking stick that revealed him to be, like ourselves, a visitor from the upper world. His pallid, almost translucent skin implied he had been here much longer than we, however. He looked alarmed, but more than that he stared in disbelief. He made no move.

I spread my hands to show I meant no harm and began to speak. I hardly knew where to begin. Could he have been a shepherd in the Anchester area who followed lost animals through one of the hypothetical hidden entrances to the caves? But how to account for his apparent at-home-ness here? I thought it better to explain our presence first and let him react to that.

I told him that a family called the de la Poers had once lived here, or above here, intending to tell him of our former and present missions here. But at the mention of the syllables "de la Poer," the ancient herdsman's rheumy eyes widened fully to perfect circles, and spewing spittle he unbottled a verbal torrent.

"*Used* ta live 'ere, ye say? Hee hee hee! Ye don' know the 'alf of it, ye don'! Why, I knows all *about* them de la Poers, knows *too* much, I do! More'n ye might expec', f'm the look o' me! Them devils been stealin' babies and young girls f 'centuries hereabouts! And ain't nobody don' know that! But *I* (here he tapped his head and squinted one eye) knows plenty more'n *that*, I does! I knows what they did aforetime in these 'ere caves, all the breedin', and the *killin'*, and the *victualizin'*! Regular epicures, them de la Poers!" (I noted mentally how the mad oldster had begun to use words with which I would not have thought him familiar given his crude and wild demeanor.)

"I knows all about the *livestock* they raised in them pens up there! And they'd go betimes t' *fatten* that herd! And I knows what they begat on the village girlies. I does! An' *rats*! Knows all about 'em, I does!"

Here the tottering graybeard began to prance erratically from foot to foot, breaking forth into a child's ditty I had heard for years concerning one Bishop Hatto who in a time of famine had invited the poor into his huge barn ostensibly to distribute provisions while actually luring them into a deathtrap. Locking them in, his grace set fire to the barn.

> "Then, when he saw it could hold no more,
> Bishop Hatto made fast the door,

And while for mercy on Christ they call,
He set fire to the barn, and burnt them all."

Soon after, divine justice overtook the wicked bishop in the form of a plague of famine-starved rats which swept down upon his estates and devoured all in their path, pointedly including Bishop Hatto.

"They have whetted their teeth against the stones,
And now they pick the bishop's bones;
They gnawed the flesh from every limb,
For they were sent to do judgment on him."

"No fairy-tale, me kind sirs! It *'appened!* Roight 'ere! But that bishop weren't no *Christian* bishop, *no* sir! Served the Old Gods, 'e did! A *de la Poer!* He roasted them people right enough! But *one by one* . . . f *'supper!*"

In his delvings the unfortunate Thomas de la Poer had become acquainted with a whole cycle of legends concerning the rat-plague and had informed me of these when initially recruiting my efforts. The gnaw-marks we found on the skeletons on the topmost level seemed conclusive evidence of a link between the story of the rats and the evil of Exham Priory. But how could this senile old rustic be expected to make such a connection? Trask, Pettijohn, and I were all too amazed to think of interrupting the crazed old swineherd.

"But the worst 'orror is wot most folk don' know—but *I* knows!—Them devil de la Poers *still live* 'ere! They never died—just went back underground after young Walter's deed back in 1610. 'E killed the sire, an' his *legal* family, but them devils bred like rats . . . bred *with* rats of a kind! And they wuz plenty of 'em as had never seen th' outside o' the Priory. Just went down below, 'n they been goin' *deeper* ev'ry generation.

"But 'taint really the de la Poers, y'know! Any more'n it was the Romans! They jus' got sucked inter it, like all the res'."

I could resist no longer: "*Who,* then? Who *was* it . . . that tunneled up from below, that built this place?"

The old man paused, savoring my rapt attention, as if considering whether to divulge this bit of information for free.

"They wuz the *Little People,* the Old Ones o' the hills!"

129

Trask broke in: "Of course! Miss Murray speaks of them in *The Witch Cult in Western Europe*! Most anthropologists dismiss her theories as wild conjectures, but . . ."

"But," finished the mad old herdsman, "she's *right*, *ain't* she, Doctor Trask? Hee, hee, hee!"

Our jaws dropped as one. We had found Andrew Powys Thayer, retired professor of folklore studies, University of Sheffield. In his seeming insanity he had reverted to the plebian accents of his childhood but the filth-clad old spectre's memory still served him. Of the long conversation which followed let me report only the gist.

Thayer hailed originally from the Anchester countryside himself and despite his later intellectual achievements had never quite forgotten his humble origins. Indeed it was the rich if frightening lore of his village that had first interested him in the science of comparative folklore. Mastering the tools of the discipline he had returned to the massed mythology of his home region and had actually founded his academic career on the Anchester-Exham legendry, systematizing and cataloguing it in a dissertation still regarded as a classic in the field. No wonder Thomas de la Poer had found him so inexhaustible a source of information, albeit disturbing, about his ancestral past.

Hearing, as we had, of the impending demolition of the Priory, Thayer had resolved to get a second, closer look at the caverns below it. He realized that the wealth of local legends to which he had dedicated his professional life was but the tip of the iceberg. Once inside the cliff-face and its caverns, he had taken pretty much the same path we had mere hours before. He had found what he sought, but much more as well. For the de la Poer clan, as he now mumbled, still lived, more degenerate, more terrible, and more secretive than ever.

When Thayer had penetrated into their lair he had first been seized and bound in one of the butcher's sheds which were familiar to him from our first, common descent in the company of de la Poer and Norrys. Weeks passed in this captivity before (as he supposed) the stock of flabby albino anthropoids ran thin and the swathed and hooded butcher picked him to die. He was rudely stripped and tied to the block, dull-bladed axe about to descend on his scrawny turkey-neck, when the downward arc abruptly halted and the muffled tones of the butcher grunted something in a semicoherent decadent patois. Hastily led into the presence of several other carefully shaded and mantled figures, Thayer's spare, nude form was inspected with rude jabs and close peering through masked eyes.

130

After much whispering and grunting, the dazed Thayer was at length made to understand that through the presence of some obscure birthmark or anatomical configuration, the furtive figures had recognized him as a distant relation! In his own veins flowed a sluggish stream of impure de la Poer blood, impure with the infection of unguessable, doubtfully human ancestors. Instead of a livestock pen he was given his own dwelling.

Thayer had adjusted with difficulty to his new aristocratic status in the unsuspected underground realm. Communicate with his newfound kin he could not, as their speech had decayed beyond any surface dweller's grasp. Nor would his hosts unveil themselves in his presence. He received the impression, from what seemed intimate scenes stumbled upon, that the netherworlders neither uncovered themselves in each other's presence. Whatever deformity resulted from centuries of inbreeding, perhaps the reemergence of the recessive traits of prehuman ancestry, it seemed to be shared by all, yet universally regarded with a repugnance that must be the only surviving vestige of surface, human existence.

Anthropologist Trask listened with renewed fascination as Thayer began disjointedly to explain what he had been able to understand of the social structure of the cavern world. It was a system of class privilege, but not of law. It was apparently a fairly small society, though even Thayer had not had occasion to find out the full extent of the subterranean world. The concept of prescriptive law had been alien to the original founders of the mysterious race. They, it appeared, lived in harmony with the inner laws of their species, these natural laws forming the basis of custom and ritual. However these customs of incest and cannibalism might clash, had clashed, with the mores of surface dwellers whether Cymric, Roman, Saxon, or English, they were deemed wholly natural and invariable by the denizens below Exham Priory. The tiers of this society were organized on the basis of racial purity. The more direct one's descent from the founders, the higher the status one held. Those whose blood contained more or less admixture with various races assimilated over the millennia were more or less inferior in the social scale. Class privilege was largely a matter of initiation into inner circles of the cult.

Only the outermost fringe of the concentric initiation system was visible in the affairs of the surface-dwelling de la Poers. The first level involved nameless feasts of human and semi-human flesh, that of the flabby beasts nourished on the coarse vegetation harvested from the gardens of the Priory. It was "merely" this that had spurred Walter de la Poer to murder his accessible family and flee to America in 1610. These feasts, with their

131

orgies of mutilation and carousal had been preceded by rites and liturgies in the Attys temple below the Priory.

The second level involved not just the slaughter of, but the blasphemous interbreeding with the awful fungous beasts in the twilit grotto below. The innermost circle of the cult known to Thayer involved the consumption of the well-preserved and *seasoned* corpses of the mummified progenitors of the cult (here even Pettijohn, inured as he was to the aberrations of the insane, blanched and nearly fainted). In some vague way this process was held to reincarnate the original Elder Ones. Of these, only one remained in the flesh. It was called the Faceless God.

Thayer had glimpsed this entity but once during a high festival when it appeared for a moment upon its dais flanked by two of the mindless, flabby subhumans which had somehow been trained to play what must have passed for melodies on two cracked, shrill flutes. The Faceless God derived its title from the bulging mask of yellow silk it wore, which, from the asymmetrical protrusions beneath it, must have veiled a physiognomy not only inhuman but positively non-Euclidean in its dimensions. To the presence of this numinous monarch the only response was immediate prostration, so the awed Thayer had caught only a glimpse before the indescribable form retreated again into occultation.

Thayer had clearly been transfigured by his experience. He seemed to view it now as an exaltation never experienced by lesser mortals, now as equally unparalleled degradation, depending upon the random mood of the moment. In any case, he refused to leave his "sacred duties" as a herdsman of the fungus-fattened cattle. Besides, if he tried, he would surely be found by agents of the cult who still foraged on certain nights among the young females of Anchester, and terribly killed. He would take his chances with the dynamiting of the Priory, feeling confident that no harm would come to those who lived so far beneath the surface.

Pettijohn, Trask, and myself, however, he admonished to leave now and not come back. This warning put the three of us in a quandary. On the one hand, we had accomplished our humanitarian goal of finding the missing Thayer; if he wanted to stay where he was, even if it was in a hell inconceivable to some minds, that was his decision. On the other hand, how could we turn back without verifying even a little of the wild tale Thayer had told us? Yet if it were even half true, we would be placing ourselves in extreme danger if we explored further. Thayer assured us he would not try to stop us, but it would be on our own heads.

The tattered form turned down the passageway into which the fungoid flock had lately vanished. We took the other path. After another mile or so of gradually sloping descent we began to notice certain changes in the environment. There appeared to be no fungus growing here (hence no ghostly illumination, so we reluctantly reactivated our torches), probably because it had grown less moist. I began to think I could discern the echoes of faint and distant piping. In view of Thayer's mad ramblings, I was not eager to happen upon the echoes' possible source. At the same time the darkness began to lighten almost imperceptibly with a misty purplish radiance. Surely we must be nearing another level of the underground labyrinth.

Soon we exhausted the supply of steps. A cave mouth yawned before us. Tentatively we crept to its rim and looked out. What I saw gave credence to the whispered legends of a flight of seven thousand onyx steps that led to the gate of deeper nightmare. For there stretched out what seemed to be a featureless, windowless city of black basalt, a collection of weed-grown terraces, collapsing towers, crumbling minarets, cracked domes, and tenuous bridges suspended over oily black rivers of unwholesome ooze. This could be none other than the primal and ultimate citadel of the awful entities from whose evil roots the poisonous mushroom of Exham Priory had sprouted.

As none of the inhabitants seemed to be in evidence, we bade prudence goodbye, yielding to Pandoran curiosity as we made for the nearest building.

Of furniture the place had none, so it was difficult to assess whether it was momentarily or permanently untenanted. The sole decoration in the rather large domed hall was a huge mural tapestry which I judged to correspond to that whose mere shreds I had discovered earlier in the day (or on the previous day?). By our flickering light the three of us studied the scenes, trying to make sense of the images which reflected no known culture's artistic style. The reader will recall that my professional judgment on such a matter, however extravagant it may sound, is to be accepted. To my bafflement was added the disturbing insight of Dr. Pettijohn, whose analytical techniques include the inference of personality type and psychic health from a patient's drawings. He whispered that some subtle aberration in the style suggested a characteristic state of mind wholly without parallel among the common run of mankind. His judgment is all the more unsettling when it is recalled that what we were viewing was apparently a conventionalized representational style, not the idiosyncratic manner of an individual.

Dr. Trask, too, was hard-pressed to make sense of the physical forms represented in the arras before him. Not only were they but vaguely suggestive of Homo Sapiens, they could scarcely be placed at any conjectural point in the known cycle of terrestrial evolution.

At last we came upon another tapestry which suggested unavoidably the answers our minds had tired themselves in suppressing. I believe that what we saw depicted the arrival at some time in the remote dawn-era of our planet of these Elder Ones, the parent stock of the hellish de la Poers, from another world altogether. By piercing together various equivocal hints from this and that scene we inferred that these beings' home world had been slowly rendered uninhabitable. First the surface grew contaminated in some unspecified way, whereupon all survivors took refuge underground. Thus began their troglodyte existence. When this shelter, too, became unlivable some years or epochs later, they had gained the capacity to travel through space. This earth was their destination. Though the surface of the planet would have accommodated them, they had grown so accustomed to underground life that they shunned the clean sunlight for the inner darkness.

There was more, much more, recorded in that arras, which I supposed must be a standard household relic, much as a crucifix or religious statue is in many of our familiar households. We had time to decipher but a small fraction of the mad revelations, indeed I suspect far madder than the little we could interpret. But inevitably we were interrupted. I should have realized we were left unmolested only as long as our unseen hosts chose to study us from concealment. For suddenly a rustling behind a section of tapestry indicated the rush of air from a hidden door swiftly opening.

Thayer, the daemonic swineherd, had returned with his flock. I received my first glimpse of those scabrous, rugose beasts as they sprang with unexpected speed upon my two companions, ripping at their slackjawed throats with dirty, yellowed clawlike nails. Their squealing forms were a blasphemous parody on the human figure, but the resemblance, the kinship, was undeniable.

With a burst of insane adrenaline, I acted before I thought. Igniting one of the remaining chemical lamps, I hurled it full in Thayer's gloating, bleating face. As he crumpled, the blazing torch rebounded to the floor, spraying the beasts with sparks and igniting the tapestry. I made for the nearby cave mouth and began in a frenzy to retrace my path to the surface. I heard the sounds of half-hearted pursuit as I began to stumble hurriedly up the worn stairway. Clearly the cave-dwellers had hoped to finish us

134

there and did not relish coming up any closer to the surface. As a few brave souls began pursuit, I opened my rucksack and in a moment laid my hand on the revolver I had brought. A few wild shots in the direction I came from silenced the dragging, clumping steps.

My ascent was slow; I am an old man. Though kept in sound physical health by my many archaeological delvings, my energy is quickly spent, and I had pressed on far too long in this day's mad quest. On my Orphean ascent I was overcome once or twice by sleep, hoping resignedly that the devils from below would not decide after all to pursue me. Obviously they did not. But the knowledge I gained below Exham Priory has pursued me like an avenging spirit, like de la Poer's ghostly rats, and who knows that it will not succeed in hounding me finally to death? For the pictographs I saw in that daemonic tapestry in the last moments before the renegade Thayer burst in upon us made rather too clear the *nature* of the resemblance I discerned in the too-familiar lineaments of the flabby beasts. What the arras showed unmistakably was not a devolution from humanity's true eidolon to the quadrupedic, slope-browed imbecility of the fungous beasts. Rather it indicated that unspeakable miscegenation between the Elder Ones from the stars and their vaguely humanoid livestock was no innovation of the de la Poers. No, it was by such soul-upheaving bestiality that the first human beings were created in earth's dawn age.

-1990-

THE ROUND TOWER

BEING THE NARRATIVE OF ARMITAGE HARPER

Author's Note: August Derleth's *The Lurker at the Threshold* has always been my favorite among that author's weird fiction, and one of my favorites among post-Lovecraft Cthulhu Mythos tales generally—or at least the first two-thirds of it, the segments entitled "Billington's Wood" and "Manuscript of Stephen Bates." More than any others of his "posthumous collaborations" with Lovecraft, really pastiches based on a handful of notes from HPL, these chapters managed to convey, to me, much of the eerie quality of Lovecraft's New England tales, and with just the right amount of narrative restraint. But my love for the first two episodes has made my disappointment with the last section, the "Narrative of Winfield Phillips" all the more drastic. For at this point the story nosedives. The book suddenly becomes one of Derleth's hokey "Mythos investigator" tales like those in *The Trail of Cthulhu*, only the psychic detective is named Seneca Lapham instead of Laban Shrewsbury. The abrupt genre-jump is accompanied by Derleth's inexplicable abandonment of any suggestive restraint; all is cold, explicit, and cut-and-dried. Not only that, significant plot threads, crucial to the story's development, are cut; intriguing characters, of whom we cannot believe we have seen the last, are rudely dropped; and the superfluous Dr. Lapham and his Watsonian scribe Phillips are forced upon us. Lapham's prolix pontifications and his Gordian "resolution" of the mystery of Billington's Wood make us wonder whether the author of the previous two chapters has been psychically supplanted, like Ambrose Dewart, by some malign intelligence intent on ruining a good story. With unprecedented hubris, I have here attempted a "posthumous collaboration" with August Derleth. Whereas he sought to finish what Lovecraft left in fragments, I have dared to try to improve upon what Derleth left complete. I have chosen to disregard the ill-fitting "Narrative of Winfield Phillips" and to write the conclusion to which I believe Derleth's splendid beginning properly led. Any readers who have

136

been similarly disappointed by the conclusion of *The Lurker at the Threshold* are hereby invited to re-read the first and second sections, then lay the book aside and begin reading what follows.

On the seventh of April, 1924, I received a visitor, unheralded by telephone, in my upper-story office at the Abner Hoag Library of Miskatonic University. The unannounced visitor was my acquaintance Mr. Stephen Bates, a colleague from nearby Boston and a fellow specialist in matters of Commonwealth history, though it was not from Boston that he had now arrived. I had last seen Mr. Bates during his prolonged stay with his troubled cousin Ambrose Dewart at the latter's secluded property the previous autumn. Bates had returned there with his cousin, whom he had persuaded, at my own suggestion, to winter with him in Boston, a healthy distance away from Dewart's recently repossessed ancestral home at Billington's Wood. Now both men had returned, and though I had laid eyes upon Stephen Bates but a few months previously, I was now startled, I hoped not visibly, at the subtle alteration of his appearance. The slanting rays of the afternoon sun through my study skylight revealed new lines in his hardy, forty-odd year old face, and where his still-fulsome hair had before evinced but the merest shadings of encroaching gray, now that process seemed well-advanced. I had neither to ask nor to wait long for the explanation of these developments, nor for the reason of his visit.

Last fall, Bates had come asking my advice about his cousin, the enigmatic Dewart, whom Bates feared was manifesting early signs of incipient paranoid schizophrenia, namely puzzling shifts of personality, surly and evasive one moment, accommodating and friendly the next. Connected with these untoward alterations, Bates had noted, was a near-obsession with the matter of his ancestors Richard and Alijah Billington, whom local legend made the veriest warlocks and rogues. Dewart's own genealogical delvings in the study of his inherited family seat lent seeming confirmation, however evocative of deeper mysteries, to these rumors, and it was this historical aspect of the trouble that had led his cousin Bates to seek my advice in the first instance rather than that of an alienist.

On the occasion of that first visit, I sought to assure Bates that while it was altogether possible that the Billingtons had taken to themselves the shunned practices of certain ancient cults still surviving in remote areas of the countryside, and that Dewart's fixation might be no more than the fascination exerted upon the antiquarian mind by such, in this case morbid, matters, I suspected that Dewart might have fallen victim to some lingering psychic malaise, an ectoplasmic residue of the perversions once practiced at Billington House by the former residents. Only so far was I then willing to venture beyond the vagaries of conventional psychology.

Now, seeing Bates's singularly agitated state, I had to wonder whether he, too, had exposed himself too long to the unwholesome atmosphere of Billington's Wood. It was a suspicion he shared, and in fact he was the first to voice it. What made poor Bates begin to question his own sanity was the sudden and nocturnal acquisition by his strangely transformed cousin of a very remarkable servant, a Narragansett Indian factotum named, of all things, Quamis. Of course, as Dewart knew he would, Bates instantly recognized the name as that of the Indian servant of old Alijah Billington, recorded in his son Laban's daybook. Given the scarcity of Indians in present-day Massachusetts, it was too much to believe that Dewart's new companion happened simply to bear the same name. Yet the implication, which Bates seemed reticent to vocalize, was too much for a sane mind to entertain. Bates had now resolved that the preservation or, as it might be, recovery of his own mental balance necessitated the abandonment, at least for the present, of his efforts to reclaim Ambrose Dewart from the latter's increasingly serious delusions. If nothing else, the trouble taken to secure an Indian for employment, and the forcing upon him of the pseudonym Quamis (if, as I suggested, that alone had happened), indicated that Dewart had come to view himself as Alijah Billington *redivivus*. But Stephen Bates would be of no use to poor Dewart if he found his own sanity threatened. Better to beat a tactful retreat.

Bates hardly needed my counsel on that point; he had in the early hours of dawn packed his valise and upon some flimsy pretext announced his departure to Dewart and his new, impassive companion. Dewart seemed glad enough to hear the news, not even bothering to see his once-beloved cousin to his automobile. Instead he sent Quamis to whistle up yet another new servant, one whose employment, like his identity, was a surprise to poor Bates, for it proved to be a young Dunwich local whom Bates had chanced to apprehend spying from concealment only days before, one Lem Whateley. The youth seemed cowed, obsequious, truly afraid of his employer, as if the employer-employee relation were not the true nature of the bond between them. This lad Dewart dispatched to drive Bates to the Arkham train depot. With scarcely a word of farewell, Dewart and the Indian turned away and began to walk in the direction of the ancient tower and circle of stones about which the great mystery seemed somehow to revolve.

Young Lem loaded Bates's few belongings into his master's Packard and climbed into the driver's seat. Given his low estimate of the mental level of the natives of nearby Dunwich, Bates was not sure he trusted his driver's motoring skills, but greater was his fear of the man, now the men, he was leaving behind. Attempts at interrogating the tight-lipped boy proved fruitless. If possible, young Whateley seemed more frightened, even terrified, than his passenger. Bates could only guess that he had been caught spying again, this time by Dewart or his mysterious Indian companion. Perhaps threats of unguessable punishments had bent the lad to Dewart's service. But Bates recalled how all the degenerate folk of Dunwich seemed to hold the heir of the Billingtons in a kind of near-religious veneration, even as they seemed to hate and fear him. It was possible, then, that Lem Whateley had simply been pressed into service and dared not decline. At any rate, as no information seemed to be forthcoming, Bates settled down to endure the drive on the yet-unpaved road his cousin had caused to be run from Arkham to his property some months before. His occasional glances at the driver beside him revealed little more than the latter's hands, whiteknuckled, clenching the steering wheel. And though it was difficult to be sure, with the youth's fingers thus wrapped around the wheel, Bates felt sure that the digits were webbed together for an inch's width, another of the repugnant marks of degeneracy among the isolated and inbred Dunwich population.

Gladly leaving his companion at the station, Bates waited until the automobile was out of sight and hailed a taxicab for the Miskatonic University campus. Thus he came to me. After relating the most recent episodes of his adventure much as I have related them to you, Bates deposited with me a sheaf of manuscript pages chronicling his involvement in the Ambrose Dewart business, together with copies of some of his cousin's documents and clippings. He said he felt a strange foreboding, that Ambrose, or Alijah, or whatever name now seemed most appropriate, had let him go rather too easily, given how much he already knew. In the event anything should happen to him, he wanted me to have his papers. I tried my best to reassure him, insisting that once beyond the sinister radius of Billington's Wood, back home safe in Boston, the shadow would be lifted from his spirits. He seemed mildly heartened by my words of bland optimism. In the meantime, I suggested, since the day was far spent, why not avail himself of such modest accommodations as I could offer? I would return to my small apartment a few blocks from the campus, and he was welcome to make use of the comfortable cot and toiletries I maintained here in my office rooms for those occasions when my research so absorbed me that I did not bother leaving the campus for the night. And if he still felt too agitated for sleep, he might compose his nerves by writing up an account of his cousin's delvings before summoning Bates to join him. Bates had said that during the periods when his cousin seemed to be "his old self" he confided these matters in great detail, and that time constraints had forbidden him to relate more than the highlights to me during our previous interview last autumn. But if I were now to try to take up Bates's efforts toward the reclamation of Ambrose Dewart where Bates had been forced to leave them off, I had best be as near fully informed as possible. Bates thought this advisable, and judging by the length of his report, which I have given the heading "Billington's Wood" and appended, along with his own first-person account, to the present narrative, I imagine he must have slept very little that night after all. Yet he did seem calmer, relieved or perhaps resigned, the next morning when I called upon him again. Promising to telephone him with any new developments or theories, I drove him to meet his train and saw him off to Boston. I was never to lay eyes on him again.

That afternoon I began to work my way through the pile of manuscript, cross-referring to the various copied documents. As I read, the feeling increasingly took hold of me that the mystery was far greater, much more enigmatic and all-encompassing than even the perceptive Bates had come to realize. Strangest of all, I began to think that somehow the danger was not confined to the mad Ambrose Dewart, nor even to any threat he might pose his cousin, nor yet even to me as Bates's successor in the investigation. Perhaps I thought vaguely of the repeated cases of mysterious disappearances and the subsequent discoveries of unaccountably mutilated bodies. Or was there something *more*, on a vaster, even cosmic scale?

Most intriguing from a purely scholarly standpoint were the frequent references in Bates' manuscripts to certain arcane formulae, tongue-twisting names, and ancient forbidden books. It was of course such details that had caused our first conversation to turn to the subject of obsolete religions and suppressed, though still-surviving, cults. Then I thought them merely the accoutrements of Ambrose Dewart's delusions; now I was not so sure. Possibly these peculiar references might prove more central to the puzzle and its solution. And here I had a considerable advantage over Stephen Bates, namely free access to the volumes in question. Where the Billington study contained fragmentary and in some cases unreadable copies of some of the books, I now quite literally sat on top of one of the fullest collections of such *outré* literature in the Western Hemisphere. And while Dewart's encroaching madness had more and more restricted the prying Bates's access to the Billington collection, I had full authorization to make such use of Miskatonic's locked stacks as I chose.

Taking only a notepad marked with a few bibliographical citations, derived from Bates's manuscript, I made my way downstairs and to the Rare Books room, where a few words passed between the circulation clerk and myself ushered me into the otherwise-empty room. I paused to glance with some pride over the authentic Shakespeare folio and the little-known fourth-century vellum biblical manuscript *Codex Miskatoniencis* with its remarkable textual variants which church authorities had judged best concealed from the ecclesiastical public. Then I hastened to extract the volumes I would require for what promised to be a wearying and disturbing afternoon of research.

I thought it most advisable to begin with those works present in the Billington study, many of them medieval magic books of dubious reputation. From the colonial Americana section I drew forth two volumes. The first was old Abijah Hoadley's *Of Evill Sorceries done in New-England of Daemons in no Humane Shape*. Famous in its day, this huge tome, printed in eye-torturing miniscule, rivaled the contemporary *Magnalia Christi Americana* of Cotton Mather as a compendium of superstitious lore. Even less creditable was a smaller polemical tract entitled *Thaumaturgical Prodigies in the New-English Canaan* by a Baptist parson here in Arkham, a Reverend Ward Phillips. Hitherto I, like many moderns, had been in the habit of derisively dismissing the beliefs and fears of these colonial clerics as the product of an unhealthy mix of puritanical repression and the harsh siege of Novanglian winter elements. I now had the uneasy feeling that I would soon be in a better position to appreciate the warnings of the old Calvinist savants.

Gradually a strange pattern of peculiar hints began to emerge from my studies. It became clear that Richard and Alijah Billington had conjured some entity known in the dialect of the Wampanaug Indians as Ossadogowah, or the Son of Sadoquae. The grisly deaths of the enemies of both men had been interpreted by them as the vengeance wrought by this demon once unleashed. It occurred to me as possible that the deaths might have been effected by more earthly means, yet attributed to the legendary Son of Sadoquae for the value this would have in preying upon the superstitious fears of the populace. Perhaps both Billingtons judged this the best method of intimidation in order to protect their privacy. If

141

there had been more to it than this, however, I was in for a major realignment of my views of what the universe could accommodate. Yet, is not openness to such possibilities the most basic precondition for the advancement of learning? Besides, I felt my own safety might now depend upon taking a broader view of these matters.

The resemblance of the name "Ossadogowah" in the pages of *Evill Sorceries* and that of "Tsathoggua" in one of Bates's excerpts from the volume he called *Al Azif, ye Booke of ye Arab,* and which I suspected might be the same as the infamous *Necronomicon,* a volume I had never been particularly inclined to examine, opened up a new line of my investigation that took me ultimately to Philippus Faber's edition of the *Liber Ivonis,* a confusing collection of legends and myths purporting to stem from a vanished civilization within the Arctic Circle, perhaps that hinted of in the ancient Greek legends of Hyperborea. As the hours passed, I came to find much cognate material in the pages of the *Pnakotic Manuscripts,* which to consult was no easy task: each crumbling parchment page had long ago been preserved between large glass plates to stave off further deterioration. I thought it best to consult the originals since the Miskatonic's Hoag Library has them, rather than the conjecturally restored print versions.

I concluded, long after all the patrons and most staff had retired for the night, that the "Sadoquae" of Hoadley's *Evill Sorceries* could be none other than the Hyperborean deity Tsathoggua whose myths loomed large in the *Liber Ivonis.* This Tsathoggua, the legends said, had come down from the stars in earth's primordial past. He had taken up residence in a subterranean realm called N'kai, and been worshipped in the polar regions under the form of a repellent totem combining the features both of a bat and of a toad. Whether extraterrestrial or not, this Tsathoggua cult must have been of foreign origin, since neither frogs nor bats are known that far north. Perhaps it belonged to the myth-patterns of Asia, where both species are common in folklore and religious symbolism. The identity of "Tsathoggua" and "Sadoquae" seemed beyond dispute, especially in view of the latter's toad-like appearances according to Indian descriptions recorded by Hoadley.

These conjectures coincided with others yielded by my reading, namely that in Hoadley's time, some two centuries ago, there was current among the Wampanaug savages the belief that their tribal origins lay far to the north, that they had in fact descended, with some strange admixture only hinted at in his text, from the extinct tribe of "Lamah," which I took to be the exceedingly ancient kingdom of Lomar chronicled in the *Pnakotic*

142

Manuscripts, perhaps identical with Hyperborea. I recalled that old Mrs. Bishop, interviewed with meager results by both Dewart and Bates, was of half-caste blood, her ancestry containing at least a measure of the Wampanaug. And hadn't Bates quoted her as telling his cousin that this tribe were "more than Indians"? Perhaps the centuried tribal legends survived in her memory. At length I coaxed from this assortment of equivocal texts the disturbing suggestion that the Wampanaugs had not been entirely *human*, that the notorious powers of their medicine-men, the famous Misquamacus being the chief recent example, were a result of the fertilization of their line by some ancient blasphemous intercourse with the batrachian-bat entity Tsathoggua; that "Ossadogowah," precisely in his aspect as Tsathoggua's *son*, was the tribe's secret totem, the symbolism of which now took on a whole new meaning.

Oddly enough, the more bizarre and outlandish the results of my research became, the greater grew the disquieting sense of conviction that more than obscure ancient mythology was involved here. Was the Billington madness beginning to affect me, too? At any rate, I could now sympathize with poor Dewart's enthrallment with these matters. And lacking the scholarly resources of Miskatonic's Abner Hoag Library, the fascination of both Dewart and Bates with the mystery must have grown all the greater with their frustration at not being able to delve more deeply into it. The Tsathoggua lore might have made poor Bates's alarm even more acute had he discerned the symbolic significance of the *toad-like* creatures he thought he had seen through the Rose Window of the study.

Recognizing this for one of those nights I must pass in my office upstairs, I retired there, my overfilled brain still roiling with recondite information and disturbing implications. Bates's reports of old Mrs. Bishop, seemingly confined to her rocker, whispering in darkness, kept returning to haunt me, as if there were some facet of this great enigma that she only seemed to conceal, but actually revealed if only one possessed the key to decipher her cryptic cacklings. Neither Dewart nor Bates had possessed it, yet the interviews Bates had recorded might still yield some clue. I must reread them on the morrow and, if necessary, make the trip to Dunwich to interview her myself.

I lay awake on my cot for an hour or two as the campus tower marked them off. My eyes sought the view of the starry heavens through the skylight. I saw the familiar constellations as never before. For the first time in my life, they seemed to me almost to take on the malignant aspect of a threatening void of blackness from which untold horrors might one day

143

descend, or have already descended, to plague mankind. I fancied I heard, at the edge of consciousness, the exaggerated croakings of some batrachian chorus from Euripides. Then I slept.

I rose early, breakfasted at the faculty club, and after a telephone call to Bates which went unanswered, I headed for my apartment. I had awakened with the conviction that I must in fact visit Dunwich to call upon Mrs. Bishop. I spent the morning rereading the transcript of her words, feeling that some clue lay in Bates's description of her, something that should somehow be obvious, yet which would so baffle reason that the mind suppressed the recognition of it. This reading and pondering were done in my rooms, for while my library office might have been a more appropriate or even convenient setting, I had to abandon it temporarily to make way for the University carpenters together with a local Arkham glazier; I had arranged at very short notice some alteration work which suggested itself to me after the last evening's scrutiny of my study skylight. I had business to settle elsewhere on campus, though, and after rereading the manuscript, I paid several calls, arranging with my secretary to cancel appointments, rechecking a few items in the Rare Book collection, and stopping for a visit with the curator of the University's Shrewsbury Collection of antiquities. For so strange a trip as my drive to Dunwich promised to be, one must needs make some rather unusual preparations.

At several points during my busy day I paused to try and contact Stephen Bates, but could never seem to get an answer. I verified his number and tried again, but to no avail. I felt a sense of foreboding at this failure to reach him, yet I reasoned that he was likely out seeking fresh air and convivial company. Then I realized any call of mine would only remind him of his unpleasant visit to the Billington estate, so I resolved not to try him again until I should make some real progress toward a solution.

My age is not so advanced to prohibit a day full of activities—indeed I am perhaps unusually hale for my years—but it is quite sufficient to make me long for rest at the close of such a day. Back in my quiet Arkham apartment, I had not the slightest difficulty surrendering to Morpheus. The croaking of marsh frogs, only to be expected this time of year, together with the gentle call of the whippoorwills in the nearby hills, only served to lull me all the more peacefully to sleep. Yet I confess to a night of uncharacteristic dreams, undoubtedly the psychic echo of my outré reading over the previous days. In one dream, I seemed to be ever in shadow, and no matter how or where I ran, I could do naught to escape its

144

confines. Above me sounded the muffled beating of mighty wings, while I seemed to sense rather than hear the upheaval of huge footsteps below the very ground on which I stood. Most vivid and most disturbing of all, however, was the far-off plaintive wailing of a familiar voice. All the stranger was the fact that I seemed to hear the voice in periods of wakefulness between the other nightmares, yet I later concluded I had not wakened at all, but still dreamt, as one often does after dreaming that one is dreaming! The identity of the owner of that voice eluded me until daybreak, finally disclosing itself just as I shook off slumber. And then just as quickly it abandoned me.

Despite my troubled sleep, I felt fit for the long drive into the lonely Dunwich country. Given the usual spring thaws and April rains, the roads of rural Massachusetts can be treacherous, but those leading beyond Dean's Corners to the Dunwich countryside proved to be doubly difficult because of their poor state of repair. Driving was made yet more mentally exhausting by reason of poor visibility. The Dunwich area is peculiarly hilly, the rounded domes of the hills rising abruptly almost from the very edges of the roads. One rounds every bend with a prayer that one may not collide with a less vigilant motorist. At length I attained Dunwich, a more slovenly hamlet than even my own research into Commonwealth history had led me to anticipate. Stopping for directions at a tenuous collection of weathered boards dignifying itself with the name OSBORNE'S GENERAL STORE, I ascertained from the muddled-looking shopkeeper the detailed route to Mrs. Bishop's house. Though the inbred region abounded in Bishops, my informant had heard the recent gossip concerning the much-visited Huldah Bishop, as I now discovered she was called, so he knew readily whom I sought. As I climbed back into my waiting Essex, I noted mentally the same abnormality described by Stephen Bates: the shopkeeper had the same goggle-eyes and strangely flaring ears, doubtless the ravages of inbreeding. As I passed through the squalid streets of the town center, I noted with a subtle shock that virtually every individual I saw, whether elderly lounger or cavorting ragamuffin, possessed the same peculiarity, what I began to think of, uncharitably, as the "Dunwich look."

I found Huldah Bishop's house, or to be plain about it, her shack, with little trouble. There, as Bates had described it, was the post with BISHOP traced on it so crudely that it seemed the painter had copied letters of which he had no familiar command, as if I should try to copy an inscription in Mandarin Chinese. My creaking footsteps on the precarious porch boards announced my presence, calling forth a wary voice from within. "What business have ye, stranger?" The voice sounded oddly flat, or hollow, in tone.

"Huldah Bishop?" I inquired politely, but with a tone of official directness, eliciting no answer this time. I thought it best to continue. "I am Dr. Armitage Harper of the Miskatonic University in Arkham. I am an historian of rural Massachusetts, and my colleague Mr. Stephen Bates, with whom you recently spoke, has told me what a treasure house of local tradition you are. I wonder if you might be kind enough to humor still another old scholar in search of curiosities."

A few moments' silence ensued in which I felt she might be consulting someone with her in the unlit interior. Finally she croaked, "Come on in. Never thought yew college fellers 'ud keer much whut an old Dunnich hag'd haf' t' say." This she found amusing and burst into the phlegmy chuckle Bates had described as an almost bat-like chittering. Not so much the sound she made as the aptness of Bates's description of it made me shudder involuntarily as I stepped into the darkened, shaded room and pulled up a chair opposite hers.

I had expected, from the accounts of the two earlier visits, that the room would be swathed in shadows, but I had supposed that window shades would be drawn against the unwanted daylight. Now I was startled to see from the telltale pattern of what little light managed to gain entrance that all the windows of the house had been *boarded up*. In the all-encompassing gloom I could hear but the sounds of the rocking chair and occasional feline purring. Soon my old eyes adjusted somewhat to the darkness, and I could make out the stooped silhouette of the old lady hunched over in her chair. Only the dim reflection of vagrant light revealed her hair to have a silver sheen. Of her face I could see nothing, of her form scarcely more.

"Mrs. Bishop, I hope you will bear with a few questions that may seem childish to one of your obvious knowledge in . . . ancient matters. Over the past few days I have been reading in some old colonial records as well as various books of magic and legend we keep at the Library. They treat of certain questions that Mr. Bates said you know much about. The name 'Ossadogowah,' for example . . ."

"Tsathoggua," she croaked, anticipating my question with a startling prescience. "Same as Tsathoggua whereof Eibon telleth. My people, the Narragansetts, an' before them the Wampanaugs, did traffick with

146

Tsathoggua an' his son of old. Misquamacus knew him, talked ter him face ter face as a man talketh with his friend."

"Clearly, Mrs. Bishop, I am asking the right person! Now am I correct in thinking the tribes you mention believed themselves somehow to be descendants of this toad deity?"

"'Believed'? Why stranger, they *knowed* it right enough! 'Cause it weren't no 'myth' as yew city folk 'ud like folks ter think."

Instantly I understood her implication, or thought I did.

"Do you mean the famous story of Goodwife Doten and the . . . creature she bore?"

"Yer beginnin' tew ketch on, mister. That wuz one setch, back in '87, but not near an' about th' only setch. They bin *mixin'* with folk hereabout s' long as Master sought to come back."

I knew "Master" was the legendary Richard Billington, whom to judge from the conversations with Bates and Dewart, Mrs. Bishop believed to be periodically reincarnated. I expected "Master" would come into the discussion sooner rather than later.

"Mrs. Bishop, why is it you refer to Richard Billington, or his wandering spirit, as 'Master'? It was my understanding that you owe him no fealty, that you are a Christian believer."

"That I am, that I am, but so wuz that nosy Ward Phillips, and the good Lord didn't pertekt him none when he got to stickin' his nose where't didn't belong. And the fact is, he is due to be called Master who kin command the Sons of Tsathoggua."

At first the plural gave me pause, until I recalled that in the earlier interviews she had spoken of "Them Things," and that Bates himself had seen at least two of the bat-winged toad-like horrors in his Rose Window hallucination—if that is truly what it was.

"And those are the things that Alijah let in, and that you fear Ambrose Dewart will let in?"

"*Did* let in, mister, *did* let in. I know it, 'cause they're at it agin, a' swoopin' an' a' rippin. They took yer friend Bates. I heered him only last night, though he weren't a' speakin' any words you'd recognize."

I must have been visibly shaken. For it came upon me in a flood of realization whose voice it had been that I heard in what I had imagined were my dreams the night before! In my repeated failure to contact Bates, I suppose I had feared something like this, as had Bates himself before he left me. But still, as far as I knew, no corpse had been discovered, and I could yet hold out the hope that the old woman, too, had been dreaming, and that our dreams had simply chanced to coincide. This rationalization sounded hollow even as I sought to use it to dampen down the rising sense of panic I was beginning to feel. Yet I must proceed as calmly as possible. If things were taking as sinister a direction as the old hag's words implied, it was now more important than ever that I learn all I could, for my own protection, Ambrose Dewart notwithstanding.

"I hope you are wrong about Bates, Mrs. Bishop. He was a good man, is a good man, who sought only to help his cousin." Her chittering cackle mocked my naiveté.

"D'yer think Master keers abaout thet? All he keers abaout is his plans, plans delayed so long now, and he ain't abaout ter let meddlin' fools git in his way. He let my grandsire Jonathan Bishop lie in his own bed onct he laid it, an' Bates was no different."

"Let me ask about your grandfather, Mrs. Bishop," I interjected, seeking to turn the flow of conversation into what I hoped might be a less alarming channel. "What precisely was he up to? Was he using the Old Ones to enrich himself?"

Again the cackling: "No man uses Them Ones, though some thinks they do. Setch finds they themselves been used. But Jonathan wuz a faithful servant by his lights. He finally got in too deep, an' got careless, but his task was to aid in the *mixin'*."

"Mixing? Of what?"

She shifted in her rocker. For the first time I noticed that she seemed to hold in her lap a half-spread Oriental fan, though she made no motion to stir the air in the clammy closeness of the dark room. "Th' Old Ones can't come back unless they have their children hidin' behind human faces to make ready Their return. Old Jonathan sought to prepare the way. He used the rites to cause the Things to breed in the unseen spheres. He got whut girls from Dunnich an' Duxbury as he kud to help. He called up gold now 'n agin, but just setch as he needed t' make the girls an' their fathers willin'. Them that helped special 'ud git special rewards when things changed an' the Sons of Sadogowah ruled, as wuz their right."

I thought of the mad staring visages of the poor Dunwich yokels and began to wonder if inbreeding were after all the cause of their deformities. *Their semblance no man can know, save seldom in the features of those They have begotten on mankind, which are awful to behold.* Sons of Tsathoggua . . .

"Did you ever see any of these activities? Are you sure . . . ?"

"No, I didn't, I didn't at thet!" Inexplicable tittering, knowing laughter, punctuated her words. "But my old mother did! She saw it up close!" My scalp began to prickle, my heartbeat to speed up. "D' yew have a match on yew, Mister Harper? Good, well, go ahead, strike it."

Huldah Bishop held no half-spread fan. The radiance of the match revealed her hand lying across her lap, a hand with inordinately long, pencil-thin fingers, each pair webbed from the tip with a satiny-black membrane! I dropped the match; I had seen enough.

I rose to leave, and as I did so, I heard the door behind me creak open all the way. Even so, little daylight entered the room as the doorway seemed packed with bodies. In the twilight I could see the broad faces, the wide gash-mouths, the unblinking eyes, the flaring ears, some, I would swear, pointed at the ends. The whole population of Dunwich must have been gathered there. One or two fists holding aloft menacing rakes or chair legs seemed to bear the tell-tale finger-webbing.

I faced the shadowed, grunting mob. Their relative silence implied they awaited further words from the crone who sat behind me. They were not long in coming.

"Master came, an' it wuz right. But then the Bates feller came a' pryin' and he got his due. Yew got no business here neither, and we ain't lettin' yew take word of us 'n our affairs back aout o' th' Dunnich hills." The crowd began to poise themselves, in their palsied way, like hunting dogs barely restrained by the leash. I fought down blind panic, and reached deliberately into my coat pocket. I cleared my fear-constricted throat and spoke hoarsely.

"But I have the Sign," I said, and held aloft the grey-green stone I had contrived to borrow from the Shrewsbury collection. I struck another match and held it beside the star-shaped object so they could better make out the crude tracing of a lozenge-shape with a pillar of fire within it. "The Sign of protection. You have to let me pass."

Next I would have tried the elaborate finger-sign also mentioned in the old repositories of forbidden lore. I had been reasonably sure one or the other had to be the Elder Sign before which the Old Ones' servants had to yield. Luckily my first guess was correct. Every head bowed in apparent reverence, every eye lowered to the floor. The now-quiescent mob parted at my approach, bodies elbowing and stumbling over one another in haste to clear my path, to be out of the wake of the Sign as it passed. Behind me I heard only the renewed sound of rocker treads wearing on the floorboards.

❖

Heaven be thanked none of the dull-witted Dunwichers had thought to disable my motor car, which would have been easily enough accomplished. As I retraced my route through the filth-strewn village streets, I noticed how several houses had windows boarded shut, and I shivered with the thought of what might be hidden away within them. I raced back to Dean's Corners, and finally into familiar ivy-covered Arkham at immoderate speed. No mud-choked, hill-locked roads could retard my pace this time! I drove directly onto the Miskatonic campus, then to the Library and hastened up the staircase to my office.

Setting down my valise and tossing my hat and coat onto the sofa, I lifted my eyes to the skylight. It now bore a rudimentary Elder Sign device executed in bars of stained glass soldered onto the original work. (I had told the workmen that the curious design represented a Masonic emblem.) Aesthetically questionable, perhaps, but I felt the addition might prove wise. In view of my late experience in Dunwich, I now felt I had been especially prudent. Whatever had claimed Stephen Bates (I no longer doubted the truth of Huldah Bishop's words) would very shortly be coming for me. Repeating to myself the Arab's phrase "powerless to touch ye Elder Sign and fearful of its great power" as another man might silently chant the Twenty-Third Psalm, I readied myself to retire for the night. I placed the cot directly beneath the skylight and stretched my spare, tired form out upon it.

I think I slept that night, but at some point I dreamt that I roused at the sound of beating wings above me. Reluctantly I opened my eyes and saw through the skylight two hovering cloudy forms, recalling those Stephen Bates had described. They were vaguely toad-like in outline, but winged, and with a roiling mass of feelers where one might expect a face. The great behemoths were partly translucent, and through their shifting bulks I could catch glimpses of an altogether unfamiliar night sky sprinkled with unknown stellar configurations and nebulae. And suddenly all was as it should be: the monstrous forms had vanished and familiar Orion with his brother constellations smiled down like old friends. Remarkably enough, it was not the insane extravagance of what I had seen but rather my calmness in beholding it that gave me to think I must have been dreaming at the time.

I rose with the sun, feeling much refreshed. Where I suppose I should have been daunted by my visions in the night, instead I actually felt oddly braced and confident. The dream had served to confirm the wild truth to which my delvings, with those of poor Bates, had led me. Having at last the sure sense that I was not simply boxing at shadows, I rose in full force to meet the challenge. First I made notes of my abruptly-concluded interview with Huldah Bishop, setting down all as accurately as I could. Why bother with such trifles in such a situation? I realized all too well that Bates's fate might yet overtake me, and I felt I owed it to any future investigator who might take up the trail to provide for him what clues I could toward the resolution of the mystery of Ambrose Dewart.

Now I glanced back over Bates's manuscripts, in search of any possible defensive tactics which might suggest themselves. True, I had for the moment managed to gain sanctuary from the Outside entities who sought my doom, but I could scarcely spend the rest of my days under the skylight, clutching the stone relic! I felt I had some genuine chance at saving myself simply because it had been done before. As Mrs. Bishop told Bates, "only Alijah outsmarted Master." How had he done it? Alijah Billington's accumulated occult knowledge was past recovery, I knew, but surely the key must lie in the instructions bequeathed to his heirs never to disturb the tower, the stream surrounding it, or the chorus of frogs and whippoorwills that guarded it.

Bates had recorded that Dewart once speculated about exterminating the frogs, but that was moot; their only function was to mark the coming of the Things from Outside, and it was clearly too late for that to matter much. The tower capstone, engraved as my skylight now was, had made the Things' entry impossible—until Dewart, under Master's influence, had disastrously removed it. The last thing to do now was to replace the stone, even if it were possible, since its presence might for all I knew prevent exit as well as entry! No, the more I read, the more I became convinced that the dried-up river surrounding the islet of the round tower was the key. According to the relevant passage in Hoadley's *Evill Sorceries*, the medicine man Misquamacus had managed to imprison Ossadagowah, presumably in the tower. But in what did this imprisonment consist? Had the Indian been responsible for the capstone? That seemed far more likely to be the work of the owner of the property, Alijah Billington. What Misquamacus must have done was to confine the demon to the islet by somehow enchanting the flowing water which encircled it. This I felt certain was the case because of a detail recorded by Stephen Bates, who was sufficiently observant to notice it, but not quite perceptive enough to grasp its significance: in an unguarded moment, his cousin, possessed of the Richard Billington persona, let slip that this minor tributary of the Miskatonic had been called "the Misquamacus," though no modern map retained the name. Local legend must have provided the name in memory of the Wampanaug sorcerer whose incantation accounted for its being important enough to *have* a name. To call it the Misquamacus was as good as to remind oneself that only its circumfluence of the island separated the local populace from their supernatural nemesis. Of course, some years before Dewart's ill-advised arrival on the property the stream had dried up. But in its absence, the graven capstone prevented the return of Those from Outside.

A few calls to the state geological survey division revealed that the stream was believed simply to have altered its course due to soil erosion some miles upstream, and that these days only unusually heavy spring rains ever caused the stream bed to flow at all down in the vicinity of Billington's Wood, though few surveyors had ever ventured into that region to be sure. By late afternoon I had come to think I might have the answer: if the Misquamacus could somehow be restored to its old course, its waters might once again perform their old protective service.

During all these deliberations, I could not keep my eyes from wandering again and again up to the skylight with its new heraldry. I really did not expect any overt move on the part of Billington (as I had now begun to think of him who bore the face and form of Ambrose Dewart), at least not through the more spectacular means open to him, while daylight left his actions open to public witness. But might he not, now that I considered the matter, attempt something through more mundane means? There was no doubting, since my visit with Mrs. Bishop, that I must have become at least as unwelcome an object of his attention as the ill-fated Stephen Bates had been. Knowing that my actions must seem increasingly eccentric, I telephoned the campus security office and requested that a patrol of guard dogs be dispatched to the University Library. This request they seemed to regard as most unseemly and were willing to put the dogs in place only after the Library had closed its doors for the evening.

But I had not finished placing my credibility at risk. Now I asked the campus operator to put me through to the Dean, an old schoolmate of mine. I sought his permission to approach the office of the Governor of the Commonwealth on behalf of a group of the history and geology faculty with the unusual request that men be detailed with picks, shovels, and earth moving equipment to redirect the flow of a certain tributary of the Miskatonic. Actually such a case was not at all difficult to make, since credible appeal could be made to the benefits accruing to local farmers as well as to the preservation of certain historic topography soon to be threatened irreparably with erosion if the course of the stream remained unaltered. It was less easy to account for the rapidity with which I felt the work ought to be done, but the job was not really complicated and would require few men. In the end, I suspect it was the school loyalty of the Governor, a Miskatonic alumnus himself, that made him accede to the Dean's wishes. In turn it must have been personal loyalty to me, his senile-seeming friend, that led the Dean to grant my peculiar request. In the end, the authorities sent a chain-gang from the county prison farm to do the work under the direction of one of our senior geology students.

The reason for the urgency of the work, which I could not confide to my colleagues, was not simply my concern for my own safety. Rather it was the dreadful sense of certainty I had come to feel from further researches in the old books Bates had seen in the Billington study. I was now convinced that Billington and his Indian assistant meant to open the dimensional gates to the influx of those beings called by the old scribes the Ancient Ones, or Great Old Ones, who individually bore the names of Tsathoggua, Yogge-Sothothe, Lloigor, and others. To what realities these strange names might or might not correspond I did not care to speculate, but the evidence of the recent Billington-related deaths convinced me that this sorcerous enterprise was dangerous enough to be stopped, if possible, forthwith. But whence the urgency? All the ancient books agreed that May Eve, or Roodmas, was the prime occasion for such blasphemous doings. And Roodmas was now scarcely a fortnight hence.

I hoped that, essentially, once the work of restoring the Misquamacus to its ancient path was done, nature would take its course. The work was being done far enough upstream as to escape the notice of Billington and his confederates until it was too late, or so I hoped. The same impenetrable blanketing of the ancient woods that hid his doings from the eyes of outsiders would presumably serve to hide outside doings from Billington's scrutiny as well. I could only imagine his surprise when, any day now, the water made its irresistible way down its old stream bed and sealed off the islet, with its tower, from the surrounding property. If the waters had not lost their ancient efficacy, I judged that Billington would be cut off from the source of his power. Then, I hoped, he would be no more difficult to deal with than any madman who believed himself to be a remote ancestor reincarnated.

❖

During the few days in which all I could do was wait and conserve my energy for whatever contest might come, my sleep was again troubled by auditions of what I now recognized as the tortured voice of Stephen Bates. His cries seemed at one moment to emanate from only inches away, then to be heard with impossible distinctness from miles and miles *above*. The voice wept, then laughed, then chanted in accents scarcely compatible with the human vocal apparatus. "*Iä! Iä! Hastur! Hastur cf'ayak 'vulgtmm, vultlagln, vulgtmm!*"

On one such night I was gratefully aroused from my sheet-wringing slumbers by the sudden explosion of canine chaos on the floor below me. The German shepherds, lips retracted in fearsome growls, had cornered a young and ungainly intruder, Lem Whateley, as later interrogation would prove. From his hand dangled a butcher knife. I had a fairly good idea of whom the dull-witted youth had intended for his victim. My eyes strained to capture the details of a second figure who stood just outside the reach of the lamplight filtering in through the stained-glass Library window. I felt sure I could discern the prominent cheekbones and aquiline nose of an Indian, but as soon as the night watchman stumbled through the door and turned the lights on, the near-blinding illumination revealed no intruder besides young Whateley, who was soon in custody. Either the old Indian was surprisingly fleet of foot, or I had not shaken off the last vestiges of dream. Or perhaps there were other possibilities that evade rational explanation. At any rate, the wisdom of maintaining a canine patrol at the Library was no more questioned and has continued till the present.

It was April 29, and I knew the denouement of events must come quickly now. The detail of convicts had finished their work on the previous afternoon, and I meant to be present at Billington's Wood, accompanied by a detachment of Arkham and Dean's Corners police, to witness whatever would transpire. My nagging sense of reluctance to leave my second-floor sanctuary was dispelled quite dramatically an hour before dawn. Some sixth sense had aroused me from disturbing dreams which, mercifully, I could not remember. As I lifted my age-stiffened frame from off my cot, the silence of the night was banished by the crash of a heavy object hurtling through my skylight! So great was the momentum with which it struck, actually cracking the floor beneath it, that it seemed not to have fallen but to have been *thrown* from above. It took a few moments' examination to be sure, but at length no question remained: the torn and peculiarly *weathered* body of Stephen Bates now lay sprawled at anatomically crazy angles on the floor of my office quarters. I did not even try explaining the situation to the puzzled night watchman, whose duties had in the last week become so much more troublesome. And what, really, did I know? Simply that poor Bates had been Outside.

I spent much of the day in the company of the police captain, apprising him as best I could of what would transpire out at the Billington place about sunset. Of course I had to choose my words carefully, to conceal the real horrors that I myself could only vaguely picture. The police could hardly be expected to send a substantial force of men merely to humor the delusions of a lunatic, even a lunatic on the faculty of Miskatonic University; and a lunatic I must seem should I tell them more than that a potentially dangerous mob of cultists would gather for mischief and moonshine.

About mid-afternoon, several carloads of officers set out from the Arkham police headquarters to rendezvous with a comparable group from Dean's Corners. I noted the presence of a small group from the Essex County force as well. We formed an impressive caravan, traveling, of course, without sirens out along the rude stretch of road built the previous year at the direction of Ambrose Dewart. Our convoy stopped some hundreds of yards away from the vicinity of the Billington grounds and continued on foot, hoping to maintain secrecy to the last. A collection of junk automobiles confirmed my expectation that a large contingent of Dunwich folk would be present to welcome their Master and Those he served.

The thick foliage of the area provided ample cover for our numbers, and the sounds made by the large number of men were easily drowned out by the startlingly loud chorus of the frogs and whippoorwills, which it seemed Billington had not bothered to eradicate after all. The day had been overcast, ever threatening rain, and now we could hear the rumbling of thunder far off. The incoming thunderclouds made the dusk hour prematurely dark. We filtered slowly through the undergrowth to what we judged a safe distance for concealment.

From our hidden vantage point we could see a gathering of roughly eighty or ninety slovenly-looking Dunwich hill folk, most milling aimlessly, waiting, as we were, for something to happen. A few busied themselves readying large bonfires. The stream was flowing, but it was impossible to tell if it would make any difference, or if any of the gathered congregation thought the fact remarkable. The visitors from Dunwich stood on the near side of the stream, while two distinctive figures stood on the islet before one of the colonnade arches of the cylindrical tower.

For a time nothing happened, save that the bonfires were lit, the cultists unwittingly making our covert observation easier. During this interval, the thunderheads moved closer, finally directly overhead, their cymbal-clashing music growing ever louder, lightning occasionally illuminating the night sky, but as yet without rain. Billington had disappeared within the tower, while the other figure, a stooped man dressed in the distinctive costume of the Narragansett Indians, said something to the crowd gathered opposite him. They in turn began a chant which sounded something like "*Ngai, n'gha'ghaa, y'hah-Yog-Sothoth! Ai! Ai! Nyarlathotep! Phn'glui mglw'nafh Tsathoggua N'kai wgah'nagl fhtagn!*"

After some minutes of this, during which I observed how the agitation of the hidden police officers gradually heightened, as did the ranting of the cultists, Billington emerged from the tower, swathed in black robes embroidered in gold. Though distance and the unsteady quality of the light made it difficult to be sure, I thought his vestments were decorated with the traditional astrological symbols of the sorcerer. He spoke some words, apparently in archaic English, and I believe I caught the phrase "the million favored ones." He turned to face the tower and began to gesticulate in seemingly random patterns. At this, oddly, my eyes began to ache, and I noticed that when I closed them I saw peculiar after-images as of jetting arcs of flame or lightning erupting from Billington's outstretched hands. But when I opened my eyes again, there was nothing to be seen but the strangely waving hands, the hands it hurt to look upon. Involuntarily I averted my glance. But I listened intently and began to recognize syllables of debased Latin: "*Tibi, Magnum Innominandum, signa stellarum nigrarum et bufaniformis Sadoquae sigillum . . .*"

The chanting continued, as did the crash of thunder overhead, until finally it seemed, preposterously, to be *answered* by a great cracking beneath the very earth, almost as if a slumbering giant were rousing. More than a few of the police had drawn their revolvers and made as if to rise and throw off their concealment, but I bade the captain to call for his men to maintain their position a little longer. I knew the most astonishing developments had yet to appear. But we had not long to wait.

At once the chanting and gibbering of the Dunwich folk fell silent, and we, too, involuntarily caught our breaths, as a column of queer greenish-blue light poured up through the tower into the night sky, eerily illuminating the lowering cloud bank that obscured the heavens. How had Billington contrived such a marvelous effect, I wondered dazedly, and what was its purpose? To serve as a beacon for Something whose advent he and his flock awaited?

As we watched, hypnotically transfixed, it seemed that a fragment of the storm cloud dropped lower and detached itself. In the midst of the cloud, vague motion could be seen, as of wildly flailing ropes or tendrils. It came down to meet the crest of the roofless structure and settled about the mouth of the cylinder. The still-flowing light momentarily caused the interior of the pulsating mass to glow hollowly; then the shaft of illumination ceased altogether, and the amorphous mass seemed to be sucked into the tower opening, condensing as it fell.

By the lesser light of the bonfires on the near side of the stream, the form of Ambrose Dewart or Richard Billington could now be seen slowly walking backwards out of one of the tower's arches. Still within the ancient masonry structure was a solid mass of confused outline. It seemed to have huge, folded batrachian hind legs, and to hop obscenely, yet to cover little ground with each movement. After some moments, as Billington and his Indian assistant, both gesturing, took refuge behind two of the encircling menhir stones, the great Thing cleared the tower and waddled into view. It had neither head nor forelimbs that I could see, when I dared look, but only a mass of writhing feelers and sucker-tipped tentacles. It extended great membranous wings that glistened greasily in the firelight.

By now the apish Dunwich throng had thrown themselves prostrate and wallowed in primitive genuflection. Some shouted one thing and some another, none of it intelligible. I glanced to either side of me to see faces frozen in wide-eyed astonishment. The sudden sound of crashing here and there amid the bushes told me that a few of our party of stolid veterans had fainted. I could not blame them, myself saved from the same reaction only by my previous dream-visions of similar entities. No one now made the slightest movement. The night's task had quite suddenly taken on an altogether different coloring.

Now Billington's waving arms seemed to pantomime directions for his hideous visitor to be off and to wing its way skyward again, no doubt for yet another mission of demon-sent vengeance such as had consumed poor Bates. I noted with icy terror that Billington was indicating the very area in which we crouched in apparently futile concealment! He had seen us!

157

Billington's composure left him abruptly and he began to rave as his entreaties did not meet with the expected compliance. He turned to the Indian who said nothing but simply pointed to the flowing stream, seeming neither surprised nor eager to venture undoing the enchantment wrought long ago by the ancient wonder-worker Misquamacus. And as Billington turned back to his uncooperative familiar, his Indian companion suddenly plunged into the stream and stumbled across it, making for the side opposite that where the cultists clustered. He disappeared into the black depths of Billington's Wood.

Clearly, my guesses had proven out! The flowing stream retained the mystic potency of its namesake: the charmed circle of water imprisoned the Thing from Outside, presumably in the same way old Alijah had done more than a century earlier. Apparently Master's overweening hubris had led him to disregard the fact, though his Indian servant had known, or suspected, better. What might now happen, however, was beyond prediction. But had not the old books indicated that, once summoned, the Son of Sadoquae would not return to its proper realm without the appeasement of sacrifice? And if the Thing could not escape the confines of the islet, must it not seek some sacrifice *there*, else be confined there as the old wizard Misquamacus had once confined it?

In the twinkling of an eye, the lifted hands of Master Billington ceased from their cabbalistic signings as they were each held fast in the coil of a whipping tentacle from the Medusa-like creature before it. Another prehensile limb embraced him stickily, then another, and another, till his form could scarcely be seen.

The effect of this spectacle, so contrary to the fervent expectations of the Dunwich crowd, panicked them as the sudden pounce of a fox will scatter the hens in a barnyard. As the terrified mob took to their heels, some loping with animal speed, others unsteadily shambling back toward their automobiles, the police officers manfully shook off their momentary paralysis and broke from concealment, pursuing the fleeing miscreants, and trying to round them up with a series of warning shots in the air above their heads.

Waiting till the general melee, punctured with wild shouts, meek whimperings, and occasional cries where more than a warning shot had been necessary, passed me by, I headed in the opposite direction, making for the stone-circled islet.

All had changed in an instant. The nightmare creature which had enveloped Billington in a cocoon of gelatinous tendrils only moments before, was now nowhere to be seen. But prone on the ground between the tower and one of the standing stones was the inert form of Billington. For a moment I expected to find his body a mutilated shambles like that of Stephen Bates, but as he had not been propelled groundward from a precipitous height, I found him intact. The surprise was instead that he yet lived! I stooped and cradled the unconscious form of Billington, or as I should say, of Ambrose Dewart, for again it was he as I later determined, freed at last of the malefic influence of Richard Billington's shadow. Old Mrs. Bishop, after all, had said that the entity from Outside consumed not the flesh but the life-energy of its victims, and this time it had feasted upon the essence of Master himself, leaving the physical shell vacant again for its proper occupant, Ambrose Dewart, to inhabit.

I write some weeks later, when things have been more or less resolved. Ambrose Dewart, his memory mercifully wiped clean of most of the strange events that occurred since his arrival at the old Billington estate, is recovering nicely in Arkham's Mercy Hospital. When he has regained his strength, he intends, wisely in my opinion, to abandon our shores to return to his native England. The tower on his property has, with his permission, been dynamited, though he does not know why and seems happy enough to remain in ignorance. The degenerate Dunwich villagers were hastily moved to a government internment camp in the South, where they are to be examined by a team of mystified doctors and ethnologists. There were few complaints from their relatives back in Dunwich who appear to regard themselves as well rid of their decayed kinfolk. Old Huldah Bishop remains in her chosen seclusion which her neighbors apparently know better than to disturb. Nothing more has been seen of the elusive old Indian, and I am inclined on that matter to leave well enough alone.

I believe I should wait a while to inform Mr. Dewart of the tragic death of his cousin from, as I shall tell him, a mountaineering accident. And I am not sure I shall ever inform him of another item, namely that the workmen who dynamited the round tower discovered that the structure seemed to be but a minor above-ground extension, a turret really, of a vast subterranean structure, the depth of which no line of theirs could sound.

–1990–

THE STRANGE FATE OF ALONZO TYPER

[*Editor's Note:* In the previous number of the *Annals of the Society for Psychical Research* we published the contents of the recently authenticated diary of Alonzo Hasbrouch Typer, a distinguished, if estranged, former member of the Society. The present document is closely linked to the diary, though stemming from a different source, namely the late medium Edgar Dowling. The Reverend Dowling's name will of course be readily recognized from his famous trance-state "readings" of the Akashic Records. His ability to read in the cosmic æther the recorded vibrations of all past thoughts, memories, and events has furnished guidance for hundreds of grateful seekers, in the process providing valuable glimpses into life in ancient Atlantis and Lemuria. As if Reverend Dowling's reputation alone were not sufficient to put suspicion to rest, we need only note here that the present transcript, the last before his untimely passing, was taken down by his secretary in April of 1928, fully two years *before* the recovery of Dr. Typer's diary. This reading from the Akashic Records, in fact, was seen to make full sense only after the discovery of the diary. As any unbiased reader will admit, the diary and the Akashic reading confirm one another in striking fashion. (Ellipses in the text indicate a pause by Reverend Dowling to rest and regather concentration.)]

As the thunder outside and the saurian roaring below race one another to reach crescendo, the black paws beckon, and I feel myself dragged toward the cellar by a compulsion of the will that I cannot resist. I have already dropped pen and paper and find my hand groping as with a life of its own toward old Claes' manuscript book, lying on the desk. Clutching it in one hand and the glowing strangely-carved Key in the other, I march with wooden pace down the hall, down the stairs . . . and to the cellar door. There are no lights now, but I find I do not need them. That which draws me knows where it means to take me . . .

Transferring the old book into the crook of one arm, I manage to descend the ladder, from which I jump the last two rungs to the flag-stoned floor, raising a swirl of almost sentient-seeming dust. Facing the awful portal, my face and hands reflect the twin luminescence of the hellish Key and lock. An impatient magnetism draws the former to the latter in a motion of my hand I know I did not initiate. Amid the gathering and oppressive sense of doom I feel a distinct note of surprise that, despite the antediluvian age of the lock, the Key meshes and sets the tumblers to life as if the mechanism had been recently oiled.

The vast slab of the door swings ponderously inward, and I do not—I cannot—hesitate to enter. Once inside the nighted crypt, I cannot help but notice how the curtailed light is replaced by heightened sound, for the strains of the frenzied sabbat orgy on the hill have grown plainly audible, their echoes magnified by the walls of what I now know to be the tunnel leading from beneath the cursed van der Heyl house out and up to the hilltop cromlech. This, I feel sure, is shortly to be my destination. But first, what of the Nameless Thing I am surely here to meet?

. . . As my eyes adjust to what at first seemed Stygian darkness, I can trace dim outlines by the ghostly radiance of the decaying fungi encrusting the walls. And by that light that is worse than darkness, I discern that the taunting, teasing black talons have not deserted me. They beckon still, only now I see the *extent* of that to which they belong! Great God! I at last *know* that snouted, simian *thing* with whose like the van der Heyls interbred!

But the greater horror is that I know this is not that Ancient One I must at length face. Whatever species of fiend this may be, it is loathsome enough, and I will seek to dispatch it. Pathetically, I think of my abandoned electric torch—this time it would scarce suffice to dissipate that which prods and toys with me. But am I not master of the Seven Lost Signs of Terror? With nervous haste I mumble the syllables and perform the gestures with hands suddenly free of mesmeric restraint. And the chant works, or seems to; with a hint of bestial chuckling, my unwelcome companion fades into the shadows, leaving me to tread a path whose direction is evident enough, winding ominously deeper into the hillside.

The weathered stones beneath my feet show an antique and intricate workmanship, but in many places wide expanses of the stone paving have been worn away, merging imperceptibly into the naked rock beneath. Clearly some vast armored bulk has eroded the solid stone over unguessable eons of slow passage. And I am ineluctably progressing toward its den . . .

It has not been long since I reached my destination. I stand before a shadowed, pulsing entity which has no shape I can yet distinguish. It is coiled in and over upon itself in a nightmarish way which can only betoken a system of folding joints and ligaments unlike any form of life spawned by sane evolution. Yet I think or fear I can discern hints of a form akin to that obscene drawing inserted by Claes van der Heyl into his manuscript, which volume I now hold open to a certain formula in horrid anticipation. For I cannot deny that even now I feel a forbidden glee that my prayers to the Dark Gods may be close to fulfillment!

. . . The Thing has roused. It is the octopus-dragon depicted with devilish skill in the color sketch. Why am I not more terrified? Perhaps I feel a certain . . . recognition. Surely with these eyes I have never seen the remotest like of it, but then old Claes could never have seen it either . . . could he?

The Chant—its sibilant words and weird intonations seem to take shape of themselves, as if my tongue were moved by another. Perhaps I am to be a mere pawn in some titanic game, chosen for the role simply on account of that strain of tainted van der Heyl blood that oozes unbidden through my veins. So be it!

As awful as the Thing is now, what must it be like . . . transfigured? It seems I have not long to wait, nor much longer before the Sepulchered Guide at last shows me the Gateway I seek, or that something seeks through me . . .

As the mouse is charmed by the snake, as the fly is hypnotized by the fly-trap plant, I can only watch, clasped in a vice of futility as the Thing, now translucent and glowing the sickly verdigris green that has become so familiar, turns toward me, its clawtipped facial tentacles opening, circling, grasping me, and drawing me toward its beaked maw. Am I thus to perish on the very threshold of my goal? Or is *this* . . . ?

All sense of weight is absent as I seem to float within the shimmering, shifting outline of the Thing, like Jonah inside the whale. Involuntarily, my knees rise to my chest, my head sinks to rest on them, and my arms clutch the moldering grimoire to my breast. I rest thus curled like a passive embryo, waiting. The Thing is in motion, perhaps moving along the tunnel, and up to the surface! Bursting forth from the well-mouth in a volcanic spew of vomit from the bowels of the inner earth, filling the charged night air above the upraised heads of the degenerate villagers gathered there in loping, hopping worship! Thunderclaps now resound in such preternaturally rapid succession as to sound like a celestial cannonade. The nauseous green glow of the standing stones, suddenly increased a thousand-fold by the blinding abomination from the vault, illumines the blank faces of the ape-like cultists and casts a hundred clashing shadows at their tripping, panicking feet. They collapse and wither like grass in the desert sun, allowed scant moments to wonder in terror that they have invoked their own doom, even as I have . . .

After seconds or eons, I regain the consciousness I was not even aware of losing (how surreal has my adventure become!), and I am at rest again, upon a cold stone floor. About me all is darkness. As to my whereabouts, I can make no conjecture, until the levelness of the floor and the absence of moisture from the air tell me that at least I am not back in the infernal cellar-catacomb of the van der Heyl house. As I begin to stir and rise cautiously to my knees, then my feet, the slight sounds I make echo oddly, seeming somehow to reverberate doubly, as if my enclosure were itself enclosed.

Again my eyes become accustomed to the semi-darkness, but this time the feeble radiance does not stem from nitrous growth on the walls (as it is too dry for that), but rather—now I see it—from the crack of a door. My limbs are fairly palsied with shock greater than mortals ought to endure, and it is with difficulty that I shoulder the low stone door outward on its corroded metal hinges.

As I surmised, I find myself inside a greater stone chamber, so vast, indeed, that the dim light will not allow me to gauge the full height of the vaulted ceiling. When I have taken a few halting steps away, I turn to see the shape of my erstwhile cell. Yes . . . it is a twenty-foot high, hollow stone statue roughly approximating that immemorial Thing I had awakened. So it was itself the Gate, and not merely the Guardian of the Gate. But why am I here? And where *am* I? I suspect already.

The great cyclopean room is lit by a disquieting radiance with no visible source. By it I am guided to the nearest wall, and to examine the mural carved in relief upon it. From the mad scenes engraved thereupon I catch repellent hints, nay certainties. Almost oblivious of the fact till now, I abruptly realize that I still grasp tightly the manuscript of the warlock van der Heyl. With its aid, no doubt, I could fully decipher the hieroglyphs lining the bas-relief, but the mural is more than articulate by itself. The warm pulse that beats through living stone, the impossible reptilian texture of the rock: these only reinforce the significance of the carven vista. There are the thousand rivers, the thousand bridges, and that throne atop which broods a Hooded Thing of not-quite-human outlines. In the flesh of this body, I have come to Yian-Ho; it can be no other.

And with equal certitude an inner voice commands that if I would learn the final secret of the doomed van der Heyl line, of which I now know myself to be a part, I must again open the book. Here on the wall are the ideographs to complete certain puzzles and fragmentary mandalas which had baffled me hitherto . . .

Collating the references in the manuscript with those on the walls of the vault has taken some time. I am amazed at the exact correspondences and can only conclude that old Claes actually composed his abominable testament in the very halls in which I stand. How he managed to come to Yian-Ho is a mystery to me, since by his own testimony, he had never done what I have— completed the Chant of Transfiguration. Yet how else did he penetrate to the city between the magnetic poles? There is much I do not comprehend about this unholy business.

. . . But one thing I fear I *am* beginning to understand, however reluctantly. My deciphering of the hieroglyphic mural has directed me down a mile-long stair into yet another chamber, one of unthinkable dimensions. As far as vision extends there are walls into which have been carved innumerable niches. These in turn bear small, stoppered urns or bottles of alien workmanship, the designs seeming to vary only by age and successive cultural period, all being of more or less the same style. It does not surprise me to find them made of the same eerily iridescent greenish metal as the Key.

It is writ that in this chamber, which in reality as in appearance, has no end, are stored all the souls of the dead, each shut up unto the particular torments befitting its sins. Claes van der Heyl and his clan could no more hope to avoid their fate here than anyone else, though their unique blasphemies must have made them more zealous than most to try. What they *had* been able to do, through generations of sorcerous endeavor, was to keep open a kind of portal between life and death, whereby they might one day escape perdition. All too clearly do I understand that grimy gallery of leering visages that haunted the van der Heyl house!

Only the last of their own adulterated blood might perform the ritual and cause them to materialize again in mortal (or immortal?) flesh, free to walk the earth once more. But the manuscript speaks of an "atonement." What is its nature? And must I be the one to pay it? No matter; I am what I am, and cannot turn aside from my destiny.

I have located the proper section of the wall. There must be forty or fifty urns, glowing as if in gloating anticipation. Again as in the old house, I feel the presence of malignant intelligences. Where is it . . . the variant version of the Third Aklo Formula—I can see why the old man made the changes in it he did . . . Who could have suspected?

. . . Hours later and it is done. Will there be any sign? I can only wait . . .

Yes! They glow more brightly—I throw my arms up to shield first against the blinding brilliance, then from the flying shards, as scores of the jars shatter! The very air is filled with rustling presences. Echoes magnify the gales of cacodaemoniacal laughter! I am glad I am not back in the ancient house now to see the centuries-old devils stepping forth from their mildewed picture frames, as I am intuitively certain they are doing.

But what is to be *my* fate? Am I not a van der Heyl? In truth I am, and all too late do I see the terrible implication; for one lone urn stands in the midst of the wreckage, and its stopper is not yet in place. I am a van der Heyl, but were I not, I would still have much to answer for. All my life I have sought out abominations, and I fear I shall presently have what I have sought.

[*Editorial Postscript:* At this point, of course, the reading terminated with the fatal heart attack of Reverend Dowling at 2:30 a.m. The witnesses and Reverend Dowling's secretary proved unable to aid him. Whether more of the Akashic reading would have followed is naturally unknown. One final point, of questionable relevance but perhaps worth noting, is that subsequent to the publication of Dr. Typer's diary, some curiosity-seekers visiting the gallery in the Society's headquarters claimed that Dr. Typer's portrait can be observed to glow with a greenish, mottled sheen on certain nights of the year.]

–1991–

BEHOLD, I STAND AT THE DOOR AND KNOCK

Sid nearly didn't hear the knock at the door, what with his favorite CD of Fried Spiders blasting on the box. But whoever it was, he was so bloody persistent that he was still knocking at the pause between songs, and that's when Sid got up out of the lotus position, back aching, to answer the door. He just turned the volume down instead of turning the thing off, since the little gizmo that should have allowed him to locate the cut he wanted after turning the machine back on was broken. He wanted to hear the rest of the album, and he hoped he could get rid of this pest quickly.

As he stuffed his black concert T-shirt into his jeans, he hoped it wasn't another bloody bill-collector. He had them all paid up this time, he thought.

In the doorway stood a man in his 40s, Sid judged, with the look that all door-to-door salesmen have: they had been neat as a pin in the morning, but by the time they got to you, the day's mileage showed in skewed tie, rumpled jacket, and dog-bitten pants. How did these blokes make enough to keep themselves in pants?, he wondered with redoubled annoyance now that he saw who, or what, it was.

The man extended a hand, saw it was the wrong one, shifted his sample case to the left, and put out the right for a shake. Sid hated this intrusion of privacy as well as of personal space. He didn't want to shake like a friend with a man he'd as soon kick off the stoop. But he shook, kind of a jellyfish shake, all he could muster at the moment.

"Good day, Mr. Hingley. I wonder if you'd allow me to take a few moments of your time this afternoon. I'm sure you'll find them an investment well spent."

Sid glanced at the huge case, which looked less like a suitcase and more like a foot locker with a handle. Imagine carrying that bloody burden around all day. Poor joker must need the money. Of course Sid needed it, too, but it was tough making a paying career out of interests like his. So he read his books, listened to his albums, and stayed in contact with a few other like minds, while by night he washed dishes in a local Brichester pub and by day he passed out leaflets for a Mercy Hill massage parlor. But this

166

he'd never stoop to, God help him.

"Say, how d'you know my name, anyway?"

"Oh, rest assured, you're on the list, Mr. Hingley. Now if you'd just let me show you . . ."

As the salesman began unsnapping the case, Sid glimpsed the spines of a set of well-bound books.

"I can see you're no stranger to books and reading. That's good," the salesman said, his hand motioning around the tiny room, one of the two Sid could afford in this low-rent block of red brick flats in the worst section of the old town. And books there were in some profusion, scattered here and there in inelegant cinder block and board shelves. There was Colin Wilson's *The Occult*, the book that had started it all for Sid Hingley, plus a Kenneth Grant or two, some Panther reprints of work by Norman Owen and Ronald Shea, even a few odd volumes of a cheaply produced reprint set of *The Equinox*.

"Yeh, that's right, but you can see for yourself I'm no *Britannica* man, so you're wasting your time. Last time I used it was in school. Cribbed from it for a paper. Failed it—must have used the wrong set. Micropaedia instead of Macro. Not long enough."

"Not so fast, Mr. Hingley; you misjudge me. Shouldn't judge a book by its cover, as they say. I think you may find our product interests you after all. If you'll just take a look."

Bloody record was ending. With visible irritation, Sid grabbed the book and, ignoring the engraving on the spine, he opened to the title page for a quick look. He wouldn't be much more interested in The World's Classics than he would be in a set of encyclopedias. But the page announced:

THE REVELATIONS OF GLAAKI

Sid's inner gears shifted. Suddenly the man and his books moved from the periphery to the center of things. Sid's irritation vanished. He had heard of this book, or set of books. He'd even tried to get a look at a copy a few years ago. He'd felt sure the library over at Brichester University would have it, but he was told the set had disappeared. This was back in the days of the local flap about somebody named Franklyn and a secret cult of homosexuals. The University curators suspected the queers of stealing the books, but they never had any proof. The *Revelations* purported to have been channeled by the worshippers of some god that lived in a lake, one more local Nessie. The contents, as far as Sid knew,

167

were a jumble of strange facts, almost an almanac of occult oddities, written in fragments by different members of the group. It was almost as if a bunch of people had gone into a library at random and each copied odd passages out of totally different books. Or that was the rumor. He had liked what he'd heard.

So, yes, he was much interested in the salesman's product. He just couldn't believe the books were now mass-published . . . let's see, by Ultimate Press. Hadn't they become an imprint of Collins or something? "How many volumes to the whole thing? One, two . . ."

"I have twelve here, but there are more in the works. It's not exactly a definitive edition, y'see. More of a work in progress."

"Well, it's sure not the *Britannica*, you're right there. How much would the whole set cost me? I haven't much to spare just now. But I would enjoy having the books, Mr. . . . ?"

"Undercliffe, Errol Undercliffe."

"Mr. Undercliffe, I really am interested. But . . ."

"We offer the books on a subscription plan. Why don't you keep the first one on a trial basis for a week? See how the book suits you. I'll be back then, and we can discuss terms."

Sid shrugged. Sounded more like a drug dealer than a book salesman. But he had no objection. And in any event, there were always ways of getting some extra money in Lower Brichester.

Undercliffe left him his calling card and retreated down the weed-grown front path. Sid watched him for a moment. The man did not turn down the next walk, nor the next. He rounded the corner and was gone.

He would have liked to examine the book at greater length then and there, but it was nearly time to head downtown to the pub, the Black Goat. He hadn't to dress up much for the job since he entered through the alley to work in the kitchen, but he fixed himself up a bit just the same, because there was that new barmaid, Jill, who had paid him some attention last week. So he was off.

As it happened, he wished he'd called in sick. The first sight he caught of Jill was of her coming on to one of the Rugby men from the University team. Bitch. He turned to his pile of dishes and mugs (how the hell did that tart get in with them?), and he began to think about the book.

He felt he might be on to something, finally. Not just paperback *Necronomicons* from Corgi Press this time (though he hadn't been above trying one or two of the spells given there for love and money).

He remembered how his dad had thrown him out of the house a year ago when he'd seen Sid ready to board the Underground wearing his O.T.O. robe and carrying his ceremonial blade for the Gnostic Mass. "Oh, for Christ's sake, Sid, you're not going out in public with a bloody knife . . . !" And when the old man snooped into it more, he'd accused him of going just so he could see the naked girl they used for an altar. "Be like normal people, Sid, go to an effin' peep show or something!" It was only a month later he was told to leave, his mother blinking back tears on the doorstep as she watched him sullenly leave the nest.

Suppose he *was* on to something. Suppose the *Revelations* really had something. That would go a long way to vindicating him. Yes, it was worth a try.

That evening he set the Spiders to spinning again, and a bit of pot didn't hurt either, though after a while he found it hard to keep his mind on the confusing text before him. Next noon he would find it impossible to tell at just what point he had dozed off. But somewhere during his reading, he began having visions.

He received an engraved invitation (who gave it to him? Someone at the door, as if it were a telegram. Was it Mr. Undercliffe? He couldn't be sure. But it was inviting him to something called the Feast of Eihort. In the dream he had gone to his closet to don a tuxedo, as if he'd own one. Once he had taken it off the hanger he saw that hanging there it had concealed a trapdoor in the closet floor that he had not known was there. Storage space?

Once the tux was on him, he stooped down and managed to claw the wooden plywood panel upward. Dimly lit below was a decline of many yards. He knew his path lay here if he was to go to the feast. A few unpainted plank-steps soon gave out, as did all but the faintest radiance coming from somewhere in the distance, and he had to feel his way onward through a squirming tunnel-surface of wet mould and fungi, punctuated by the occasional salamander or insect.

After a vague period of this blind trudging, he reached an opening into a large dining hall. And now it seemed that the entrance through which he stepped was at the end of a long and elegantly appointed foyer, like a huge restaurant. Looking down at his pants, which he felt must be caked with revolting filth, he was surprised to find them as crisp and clean as they had been in his closet.

A soft-spoken maitre d' took his elbow and guided the nonplussed Sid to a dining room specially reserved away from the general clamor of the dining throng. He accompanied his guide through several winding hallways and through a medieval-looking oaken door. Inside there was a great company of feasters. On a second look, these figures threw a start into him, for each was a duplicate of the other, all swathed in blue-black robes and cowls.

Their baggy clothing seemed to bulge and bend in unaccustomed places, but Sid scarcely noticed this as he took his designated seat. He fumbled with his napkin, feeling uncomfortable in his tuxedo. For though he had never been in less danger of under-dressing for an occasion (something his parents always berated him for), he felt positively out of place without a robe like theirs.

He looked around at his silent dining companions, whose occasional expansive gestures and pats on the back implied merriment, but whose voices he could not hear at all.

In all the confusion it took him a moment to notice just what constituted the main course for the evening. There was a huge meat platter on the large banqueting board, and some great beast had been laid out, cooked, upon it. With a start, and a bit of nausea, he saw that it was a plump human shape, though by now an arm and the best part of two legs were missing. But the light was dim, the fickle product of bracketed tapirs set into the great stone block walls.

It was only once the chef emerged from what might have been the kitchen door and served Sid the head on a platter, with an apple in its mouth, that Sid saw plainly that the head was his own.

He awoke, apparently straightway out of the dream, on the floor of the tiny bathroom, heaving into the toilet. Lucky he hadn't puked lying down and choked on his own vomit. He rested the remainder of the afternoon, pondering what he had dreamed. And then it was time to go to the designated corner with his leaflets.

Each leaflet was a little bit of pornography, showing a poor color photograph of two women, neither your top-grade model, not even by industry standards, giving sexual service to the same man. One sucked him, the other squatted on his face. Better to imagine your own face there, he supposed . . . Still, his was not to reason why.

He took the stance of the pamphleteer, leaflet at the ready, held out tentatively so as not to seem too pushy, never meeting the eyes of a prospective customer unless he seemed to slow down. He would mumble some inanity, it didn't much matter what. He wasn't particularly eager for anyone he knew to recognize him. It was a pitiful line of work and paid a pittance. Still it did add to his washer's income and kept most of his day free for studies and sleep.

170

And there were the side benefits. One or two of the Asian girls would give him the five minutes he needed occasionally, especially when he did favors for them. Their English was not so good. After the way Jill had spurned him (had he only imagined her initial interest?), he felt like taking a bit of comfort. So he arranged things with Benazir for closing time.

At the Goat nothing much was happening. No Jill to be seen. Maybe she'd married her University man and he'd taken her away from all this. Time dragged by, and he tried not to give much thought to his dream. But he couldn't let it go. He didn't know what to make of it except that it had coincided with reading the *Revelations*, and it made him think things were beginning to spark. Time to go. Benazir was waiting, he hoped.

He hadn't seen her in recent weeks. Arrested in a recent raid, which was always a danger, though little more than a formality, an occasion for the Brichester police to get their cut, he guessed. But the girls would be tested on such occasions, and there was some merit in that.

He entered through the back door of the establishment, wanting to avoid the tangle of a couple of drunken underage teenagers being shown the door by the bouncer in a rare display of scruples. He passed the bar and went right into Benazir's "dressing room," as they called them. She was wiping herself from another of the teenagers who had proved too drunk to aim himself properly. He was passed out on the couch, from which Sid dumped him unceremoniously into the hallway.

"It is good you are here to help me, Sid. I am wanting to be rid of this bastard."

"Yeah, I'll see they don't let him in again" (sure, as if Sid had any kind of authority in the matter).

As he unzipped his pants, his erection already making him zip carefully to one side, he said, "Get the gag, OK? You know how I like it."

She let him chain her to the bedposts, waiting for it to be over, with the eternal resignation of the women of the East. She knew there was nothing to fear, that it was this ritual symbolism of power more than anything else that was important to men like Sid.

He mounted her and began to ride, feeling himself get stiffer and longer. His hands rested a moment on her rib cage, his sweat falling like raindrops on her stomach, collecting like a rain pool in her navel. He looked at her full breasts and licked his dry lips. He made to grab her and squeeze, but his eager hands went numb as her breasts began to elongate fantastically, forming a pair of squid-like tentacles. These caught him in a cloying embrace. Each was lined with a double row of suckers, but Sid could see,

171

and more to the point, feel that the suckers were shaped and worked like human lips, kissing him everywhere at once. He began to feel a kind of lust he had never known, a lust for things he had never known were possible. He was almost able for the first time to give a name to urges he could never before identify, much less fulfill.

He was floating in a cloud of heady ecstasy, even though the illusion passed quickly. But now something else seemed to be happening. Was this possible? He seemed to go right on growing, reaching the maximum dimensions of the biggest erection he'd ever had. Benazir could tell the difference, too, as her eyes widened in interest, then, it seemed, in panic. For it kept growing, like a python expanding within her.

The thrill of it was almost too much for Sid, who was now sure it was another of those strange dreams. He was about to faint with the painful pleasure of it. Benazir was flopping like a fish now, desperate to get out of the straps and off the bed, to get Sid out of her. The gag stifled her screams effectively, but the cuffs were cheap stages props, and she soon had shaken one of them off. But before she could go further, she stiffened, back straight.

Sid's back arched, and at first he only heard and did not see the impact against the headboard as his living club of a penis, having penetrated her entrails, ripped resistlessly through her esophagus and tore her head three quarters away from her shoulders. It was the splash of blood which brought him out of it.

There he squatted, astride the mutilated form of a Pakistani whore, the both of them soaked in blood. He stumbled off her, off the bed, and grabbed a towel. A few moments later he tried to listen, then ventured a look out in the hall. The place was deserted. How long had he been at it?

He looked himself over. He seemed physically normal. He would have sworn it was all one of those crazy dreams, but the carcass on the bed gave the lie to that. Unless he was maybe still dreaming. For now he'd best assume it was all real.

He felt no grief; the girl was merely an instrument to him. And with the clarity that emergency lends, Sid went back over things in his mind. Who had seen him go in? He didn't think the bouncer had noticed him. Most patrons had left.

Well, there was no way to clean this up, that was for sure. He just hoped no one would think to suspect him. And from the type and especially the extent of the damage, he wasn't even sure they'd be looking for a single assailant, maybe not even a human one.

So with a surprising air of casual nonchalance, Sid quietly locked the body into what had now become a meat locker, and made for his flat. He had a quiet confidence that in the last analysis no facts could justify, that he would not be caught. He somehow felt that someone or something was watching over him. And he wondered just what would happen next time he felt in the mood.

What followed was a night of lamplight reading of the *Revelations*. Despite the crudity of the writing in many places, it was something Sid just couldn't put down. Much of it, too, was apparently providing the answers to questions he couldn't even understand. What the f— was the Zone of the Colossi anyway? He was in way over his head. But he'd take it slow, find an entry point somewhere, and then he was sure things would start making more sense. But it was bloody interesting anyway. He suspected that if he did get to understand it better it wouldn't be as interesting. Less of a sense of mystery.

He dreamed again. This time he was in a slaughter house. He stood beside a man wearing a bloodstained apron. He was working over a side of beef. But suddenly the man seemed to be a doctor, and Sid dimly realized he was playing the role of the man's assistant. And the side of beef was now the body of an obese man. It was a relief to see that this time it was not his own.

The doctor/butcher reached down to the side of the slab table on which he was working to hoist up another meaty mass. It was a different color, pale blue-green. And the texture didn't quite match either. Sid looked closely and was surprised to see it was a whole octopus. The doctor handed it to him and, though inert, it was still unwieldy, and he came close to dropping it.

While he held the reeking thing, he watched the doctor neatly saw off the head of the corpse before him. Dropping this heedlessly on the floor, he motioned for Sid to hand him the dead octopus. This he somehow proceeded to sew in position where the man's head had been. He injected some fluid at several points on the hybrid form.

The tentacles began to stir, at first slowly. As they parted, Sid could see the beak of the octopus, but then the feelers parted again, and the beak had been replaced by a set of human lips. And they were forming words. He bent close to hear, his curiosity overcoming his natural repugnance for the nightmare before him. He heard gibberish: *Ph'nglui mglw'nafh Cthulhu R'lyeh wgah'nagl fhtagn* . . . He had no idea what it meant but instantly his heart began to pound, and he awoke. He was shaken. And yet there was a whisper of a desire for more.

And there was more. Two days later he returned to Mercy Massage, and there was Benazir, her cherry lipstick almost purple against her natural swarthiness, just as alive and tawdry as ever. It had been a dream, then. So, just to see what would happen, he got her to let him tie her to the bed frame again—and the same thing happened. And just before she started to scream, or to try to, there seemed to come into her shaded eyes a strange look, as if she knew what was coming, as if she remembered it.

He found himself the next night facing a lonely row of a half-dozen dilapidated houses that leaned crazily in all directions, seeming to support one another like a group of drunks staggering together down the street till they all fall in a heap. It must have been two in the morning, and he didn't know how he had come to be here. The wind whistled off a lake behind him. It chilled him to the bone. Then he noticed he was naked, and that some kabalistic designs had been painted on his body. Hmm, had he done it? He couldn't remember.

He took a few steps closer and looked at one of the houses. Dimly visible through a large front window was a gaunt man, peering, he supposed, at him. He could make out no features except that he was sure that the man had a full beard, which, unless the dusty shadows lied, moved like a nest of serpents. He stepped forward, up onto the rotting porch, and stared straight into the window where the man was.

He couldn't have been more than six inches from the face that he still could not quite see, except for the fact that, yes, those locks of beard—if that's what they were, were moving. There was a thick coating of grimy fingerprints and caked dust. Just couldn't see through the window glass even at this range.

And there was a sudden conviction that he was missing something, like a punch line of a joke that left him feeling stupid, not getting it. He knew in a moment, though he knew not why, that what he must do was to recite the Daoloth formula. He had read it in the *Revelations* and seemed to know it well, though he didn't recall bothering to memorize it. There was much here unseen, and he wanted to see it. The words came unbidden to mind.

It was pitch black, but a geyser of light now seemed to erupt from behind him in the direction of the lake. And in that light, things were transmogrified. There were no more six crazily leaning houses before him, but rather six huge, high heaps of living stuff. From the top of each waved three primitive eye-stalks, and from the sides emerged a forest of

174

porcupinish spines, giving the things the improbable appearance of titan, living haystacks.

And then Sid flexed one of his eye-stalks and beheld that he no longer faced the houses, or the Colossi, but was instead one of their company, the one on the extreme left.

The visions and hallucinations went on all week. By the middle of the week, he had called in sick at the pub, just stopped showing up at the massage parlor.

The knock came again. This time no CD spun on the player. Sid Hingley lay, naked, in the middle of the floor, dry mouth and bloodshot eyes wide open.

"I see the door's not locked. I trust you are well, Mr. Hingley? I see you've made full use of the book. Remember, it's just the first in the set. Wait till you get to the one I wrote, that's number fifteen. It's at the printer's now, they tell me. Can I sign you up?" Sid had risen with difficulty to a sitting position. He fingered his crotch with one hand and rubbed his reddened face with the other.

"Yeh," he muttered, "it's really great . . . I didn't suspect . . . But how much? What price to pay?"

He began to manifest the drunk's belligerence. He rose unsteadily and tried to grasp Mr. Undercliffe's lapel.

"Y' bastard! It's too much, ain't it? More than somebody like me could pay in a lifetime, idn' it? Why? Why'd y' torment me wi' it, then?"

Straightening his jacket, Undercliffe tried to reassure his star customer. "You don't understand, Mr. Hingley. We don't want money. We're simply concerned that this important truth be propagated. We'll give you the books. I suppose it's really like winning a sweepstakes. We wanted to see if you were the man for the job. And you've acquitted yourself well. Don't think we haven't been watching the past several days."

"Unh?"

"Let me put it this way, Mr. Hingley. In every age the world has need of a Mighty Messenger. I feel that from your studies that name will mean something to you. Over the years, the centuries, really, special individuals have been chosen to transcend the limits of the mundane and to carry out that special task. It is a path of glory and knowledge untold. You have tasted a sample of it. The rest of the books will fully fit you for that task. I am in the position to offer you this high privilege."

Sid was speechless, but the dimensions of what he was hearing were quickly pulling his mind together. He was beginning to understand what was being offered him.

175

"Now, I don't want you to tell me anything now. I know it's a big move. A life change. Nothing will ever be the same again. Sleep on it, Mr. Hingley, and I'll call on you again tomorrow. Is this a good time?"

The door shut. Sid dragged his naked form, which he now realized, with acute embarrassment, he had shamelessly displayed in front of the officious Mr. Undercliffe, into the shower. The cold water helped bring him farther along the way to normal waking consciousness. It was really funny, he thought underneath the pressure of a now-blinding headache, how the after-effects of a mystical trance were so similar to those of a drunk.

Coffee helped him even more. In the cold light of early afternoon, by the slanting of declining sun rays against the wall, illuminating his posters of Fried Spiders and the Whisperers, he found himself considering his position. Here in these familiar and, he admitted it, depressing, surroundings, he faced two possible futures. One was as a worthless ne'er-do-well, bearing the scorn of family and employers, his pretensions of esoteric knowledge and a higher purpose revealed as a pathetic defense against an adult world for which he was unsuited.

The other meant confusion, to be sure, even horror, but that was just the acclamation of the worldly mind to the glories beyond. He had seen enough to know that firsthand. And though it meant the end, really, of human life as he knew it, the end of any hope of a normal existence . . . what choice did he have? He knew too much.

And to go in one big jump from being one more nothing from Lower Brichester to being the Mighty Messenger, winging across the void bearing forbidden knowledge . . . visions of Hermes Trismegistus and Thoth, Crowley and his Aiwass, the Word of the Eon. It could be his. He would do it.

Some weeks later, the Mighty Messenger was hard at the job. But things weren't quite as he had imagined them. For one thing, no matter how much of the *Revelations* he might read, the wild visionary splendors were a thing of the past. Unless he tried for a day to shirk his duties—then visions came, came with a vengeance! Like the one in which he played the role of a supine Benazir strapped to the bed and torn apart in unspeakable ways. Yeah, those visions came easily enough.

Thus muttered the great Revealer, the Mighty Messenger, as he pounded the pavement of Temphill one hot August afternoon, looking for the next address on his list, his neck-tie chafing him, dragging along that bloody suitcase full of books.

–1994–

THE BEARD OF BYATIS

The blustery autumn afternoon found Mr. Batchel on one of his rare trips away from his accustomed Stoneground parish. Clerical colleagues had often joked how that when Mr. Batchel was installed as rector of the parish the bishop had used screws and bolts. And thus he considered it something of a quiet victory whenever he ranged any distance from home. In this instance his holiday coincided with an archaeological conference held at the venerable Brichester University in the Severn Valley. An amateur expert in the archaeology of his own beloved Stoneground region, he had been invited to speak on avocational archaeology in one of the morning sessions. He had amply demonstrated, he hoped, that one might yet be a scholar without holding a professional post in the field. He could not deny that the occasion to address an audience mostly composed of young students in the department, budding scholars who might well already exceed his own knowledge, was more than a little daunting. He caught himself feeling once or twice that he was in the position of defending his amateur status before a skeptical audience, though in fact the subsequent question period revealed no such thing.

At any rate, now, after a hardy lunch in the University Commons, he felt nicely relaxed. Strolling about the stately grounds with young Mr. Barlowe, a seminarian in the Divinity School of the University, and as it happened his own temporary assistant, Mr. Batchel held his program leaflet close before his eyes and deliberated aloud as to which of the afternoon symposia he might choose. Young Barlowe persisted in interrupting the older man's concentration as he seemingly felt compelled to play the tourist guide and indicate every point of interest on the grounds of the Divinity College.

"Now there's a difficult choice! 'Recent Excavations of Megiddo' simultaneous with the report of the Prussian Palestine Exploration Fund. How's the knowledge-hungry scholar to decide? Eh? What's that, Barlowe? Yes, of course. I've seen it more than once, y'know. Didn't I tell you I'm no stranger to your campus? Past years have brought me to Brichester on more than one occasion. I might even be able to fill *you* in on a detail or two. But back to the matter at hand. What do you think of this lecture on the Assyrian Monuments and the Old Testament? After all, it's to be given by one of your Old Testament men. Do you know him? I'm afraid most of the faculty these days are new to me."

Barlowe knew him all right. "Oh him! The story is that Professor Thistleton's primary qualification for his post is that he's quite the fossil himself! It's said he's able to take the most interesting topic and give it all the excitement of a sealed tomb."

"I see . . . ," mused Mr. Batchel, trying to seem disapproving of such levity at the expense of an esteemed scholar, yet scarcely able to repress a grin in memory of the jokes he himself had long ago circulated concerning his own divinity professors. "Then how about the presentation on 'Near Eastern Numismatics and the Gospels'? Is Professor Lampton any more inspiring? Seems I may be acquainted with one or another of his books . . ."

When no quip was forthcoming from the garrulous Barlowe, Mr. Batchel looked up from his creased brochure to discover that he was alone. He had left his assistant a yard or two behind. There he stood transfixed before a niched statue. Catching "up" to him, Reverend Batchel registered recognition as he, too, saw the statue's unusual aspect. The subject depicted appeared to have posed in an attitude of complete startlement, a highly unconventional design to say the least.

"I see they've moved it again," he mumbled.

Barlowe's eyes had now transferred themselves to his mentor. "So you know it, do you? I can't imagine why I've never seen it before now."

"That doesn't surprise me, my young friend. It's never been one of the proudest possessions of the school, I'm afraid, yet in view of certain factors, the administration have never felt free to dispense with it altogether. There are few left who even remember Professor Ashdod. I fear I am one of them." He knew he was now in for a bit of explaining, so he took the younger man's arm and guided him to a bench in the shade of a nearby oak.

"Many years ago, when I was fresh out of Cambridge, my interest in archaeology already keen, I took the opportunity to come over to Brichester for a symposium I'd read of in the *Ecclesiastical Circular*. The subject was the myth of the Gorgon and new light brought to bear by Mycenaean excavations. I'd heard of the great Dr. Ashdod during my days at Cambridge and had read an article or two he had written. So I felt I couldn't pass up the opportunity. The statue, as peculiar as it is, represents him at just that time, which also happens to be the time he disappeared."

179

"So there's a mystery attached to it, is there?" asked Mr. Barlowe, whose startled curiosity of a moment before had now passed into genuine interest. "Was there foul play? Some professional rivalry? A jealous colleague did him in? It wouldn't be the first time, from what I've heard."

Shaking his hoary head in distaste at such a blatant display of salaciousness, Mr. Batchel replied, "Not a bit of it, young man! And yet now I suppose I must tell you the whole story." With a sidewise look at his companion, as if sizing him up, he continued, "But I can't say I'm persuaded you are, as the Writer to the Hebrews says, mature enough to graduate from milk to solid food."

"Why, what can you mean, Mr. Batchel?" came back the stung reply.

"If I am not mistaken, young Barlowe, you confess yourself under the baneful influence of the Rationalist critics of the Continent, do you not?"

Here the younger man drew himself up straight and ventured, "I am not ashamed to say I have read Strauss and Baur, a bit of Kuenen and Schleiermacher. I find in them many things that are praiseworthy. I like to think I am forward-looking in my sympathies, yes."

"As I thought. Let me remind you, young man, one must have one's bearings straight before one will know where 'forward' points. Well, I am going to tell you a tale that your German pundits would scorn, and I can only hope you will be more open to certain possibilities than they. 'More things in heaven and earth,' you know.

"This will seem a digression, but bear with me. I well remember my anticipation on the morning of that lecture, filing into one of the great auditoriums, Handley Hall, I believe it was, borrowed from the Chemistry Department for the day. Professor Ashdod was putting his papers and charts in order with the care of a Hindu priest preparing the grass square for his Vedic mummery. He seemed visibly annoyed at having to work around the collection of nozzles and spouts built into the lab lectern he had been assigned. I quickly made my way to the front and greeted the great man, mentioning how I had been intrigued with his work. This he seemed to appreciate. I noticed how in the presentation which followed that he often appeared to be directing himself to me, as if he were unsure of more than one interested listener.

"His thesis was a fascinating one. He ventured the singular theory that the legendary Medusa was at first a sun symbol, a symbol for the eclipse, at which one dare not look straight on. Her snaky locks, of course, were the rays of the sun, as in the Ninety-first Psalm. The noonday devil, you know. And behind this lay a deeper significance, that of the terrible power of the divine whom none may see and live. These symbols came to be coarsened

180

and ill-understood until all that remained was the nursery-tale of a woman whose visage could turn the viewer to stone.

"All this was quite ingenious. But the most exciting thing was what he had pieced together from his extensive digging in these English hills. Various remains, barrow carvings, a ritual artifact or two, a fragmentary bas-relief, of which he proceeded to circulate rubbings and photographs, had led him to the conviction that the Gorgon cult had reached these shores, perhaps on the fabled trading ships of Tarshish, and that the worship of Medusa had survived longer here than anywhere else. The data allowed for a hypothetical reconstruction of a further stage of mythic evolution than had been traceable in Classical sources. It seemed that in Britain, Medusa's cult had been combined with that of a local fertility god, one of Frazer's 'corn-kings,' if you will, called 'Byatis.' Medusa was made his consort, no doubt because of the familiar pattern of the widespread Phrygian Mysteries of Mother Cybele and her consort Attis, of whom Professor Ashdod judged Byatis to be a local variant. I'm sure you are aware of the rumored practice of the grim rites of Cybele in nearby Anchester, for instance.

"This Byatis began to be assimilated to his new bride, taking on some of her traditional iconography. For instance, where Medusa possessed a mane of serpents, Byatis sported a full beard of the revolting creatures. And, like his better half, the old man's gaze was petrifying. There was more, but this will suffice for our purposes.

"Well, I can tell you, as a budding archaeologist I sat spellbound. After the lecture I made my way again to the front of the hall and waited impatiently as others asked their questions. As they gradually dispersed, Professor Ashdod recognized me and seemed pleased to see me. As I would soon learn, he had no living family, and preoccupation with his researches had permitted him little in the way of a social circle. He was a lonely man. I could sense this and so summoned the great effrontery, youngster that I was, about your age, as I say, to invite him out to a local pub to continue our discussion. This he seemed gratified to do.

"We repaired to a private table and the Professor bore with my eager queries. It is not often one has the opportunity to speak with a genuine authority, much less to share the personal speculations he hesitates to commit to paper. At length, Dr. Ashdod, seeming somehow satisfied, as if I had managed to pass some test I was unaware of taking, gave me the greatest surprise of the afternoon when he invited me to join a local dig he was planning to mount in the nearby Berkeley-Camside area.

"'There are ruins there, young sir, that I believe may well have a connection with the worship of Medusa and Byatis. They seem relatively undisturbed, mainly because, if I am correct, the exposed section appears to be the covering of an underground tomb, and your casual delver hasn't the fortitude to move the massive slabs. To the untrained eye it probably looks like no more than a Roman foundation stone, and there are plenty enough of those around. Actually it was a cycle of local legends that first put me on to the place. As confused as they were, the stories suggested at least that there might be something under the visible stonework.

"'And there was the serpent motif. That's what makes it a bit more than a hunch. But I admit it's speculative. I'm asking you because so far I've been able to hire only manual labor to move the outer stonework. We've surveyed the site. The next step is to gather a small group of educated colleagues such as yourself. You see, young Mr. Batchel, I need people who have some idea of what we're looking for, and with a sensitivity to the careful nature of what we're doing. Not just diggers.'

"I can only say I was speechless. But at length I assured the savant that I was certain I could take the time from my new parish duties (meanwhile hoping it was so!) and learned from him the details of date, place, and necessary preparations. That night on the train home I had much to consider.

"At that time I was a young apprentice as you are now, and it was fortunate for me that I served under a man with scholarly interests of his own. He understood something of the importance of the mission I sought to undertake, at least that it was important to me, and he gladly agreed to excuse me from my parish rounds for a week, longer if necessary. Thus it was that with a clean conscience I found myself packed and eager to join Professor Ashdod and to meet the small coterie of students he would have assembled.

"My train pulled into the Camside station in the late afternoon. I found the Professor in the tap room of the local inn where we would be staying. I sat down as we exchanged pleasantries, and soon we were joined in the cool darkness by three other young men, graduate students from Brichester University, as I was soon made to understand, each engaged in thesis work under Dr. Ashdod's supervision. I have followed the careers of those young men in the intervening years, and each has repaid his mentor's faith in them.

"With all of us assembled, the Professor shared the dismaying news that the workmen we expected to aid us had missed their train and that no locals sufficiently familiar with the requisite equipment might be found on short notice. We would be unable to start work till sometime on the morrow. This, however, was no serious blow to any of us, as it was unseasonably warm for the late spring afternoon, and we were as happy to pass the time in convivial company.

"It was not long before our discussion left trivial matters and focused on our common task. The Professor had gathered a modicum of fresh information from the morning's informal scrutiny of the surface masonry, as well as from conversation among the Camside villagers he chanced to encounter while making arrangements and securing the necessary permissions for digging. It seemed that our purpose was known to the local rumor mill. The usually tepid business of archaeology, of interest only to the specialist, was here attracting a good deal of popular attention. Dr. Ashdod was everywhere met with suspicious questions and mumbled replies. About all he could extract by way of explanation was a muttered 'Best to let sleeping dogs lie.' This riddle he presented for our exegesis, but no solution was forthcoming from our amused company of smug sophisticates.

"But someone else in the smoky recesses of the tap room must have heard him. Over shuffled an aged form, carrying something in one hand. Without looking, without really noticing at the moment, I assumed he held a pint as we did. Later I had cause to wonder whether it were perhaps something else. At any rate the wizened form looked down at us with blazing eyes, so intimidating that we by tacit consent thought it best not to offer him a seat in our circle. He said, in accents I cannot now repeat, a dialect I knew must be peculiar even in rural Camside, something to this effect: '"He catcheth the clever man in his cleverness," saith the scripture. Ye with your vaunted science are wise in your own conceit. Take care what ye will do!' And with that the man turned like a soldier on his heel and strode back into the obscurity of the tavern. And at the last moment it occurred to me that his dark dress, which seemed to merge with the shadows of the place, looked for all the world like a clerical habit of an earlier generation.

"My companions had a good laugh over this intrusion, but I will confess that I found myself strangely sobered by it. And then, I need not tell you, the others had a second laugh at my expense. I joined them in the merriment then, as several of us took out our pipes and began to pack them.

"The long afternoon drifted imperceptibly on into evening, and I begged to be excused and made for my room for a bath and a quiet evening of reading. As I finally dozed off I reflected how lucky I was to have a rector of enlightened temper and not one of the sort who had rebuked our party earlier.

"We were up early and gathered at the site to await our workmen, who were not long in arriving. I noticed a local man or two drifting about the periphery of the site for the first half hour, but after that we were left to our business. As the sun rose, it became uncomfortably warm. Some removed their shirts, others made a makeshift head dress from their handkerchiefs. Now, I remember thinking, we looked the part indeed. One might have transferred us bodily to the sands of Egypt or the plains of Sumer with no incongruity. So again we waited as the powerful winches lifted the hindering stonework out of the way. In all this Professor Ashdod let nothing escape his supervision as the stonework itself was something of a relic even if it paled by comparison to what we hoped to find. And what was that? I don't suppose any of us, except perhaps the Professor, had any specific notion.

"At length the path was clear. It was by now no surprise that the slabs had indeed covered a passage underground. It was, however, quite a relief to see that the passage itself was not seriously clogged by boulders or collapsed masonry. And yet the danger existed that our very efforts might be the cause of a collapse, so we proceeded carefully, the Professor of course in the lead. There was precious little leeway to navigate the shaft, so one of the students stooped at Dr. Ashdod's side as he sought with lamp and magnifier to decipher what carving remained on the striated wall surfaces. The rest of us busied ourselves with examining the now-revealed underside of the cover slabs. These held little of interest, one or two fossils trapped in the limestone, signs of chisel-work here and there. We grew anxious for news of whatever the Professor might be discovering and perked up at each morsel he or his assistant might call back to us.

"As the sun sank, we could see that the two of them had made a great deal of patient progress toward the inner recess. There was no sign that the chamber would prove to be very deep, and we all knew it might have been breached in a single hour or two, but the Professor had over many years and many expeditions learned that painstaking work is least likely to damage what is not at first seen.

"He now called in the rest of us to see what little we might of an inner door, which might be expected to open upon the tomb proper, if that should indeed be what it was. The sun was by now faint, and the lamp light was insufficient to gain more than a hint of the outlines of an inscription. So, like children sent to bed on Christmas Eve, we reluctantly

184

packed up and returned to the town, leaving behind our crew of workmen who doubled as a night watch team, happy to do it for the generous compensation Professor Ashdod offered.

"Hot and tired, we all made for the comfortable tap room again, abuzz with excitement, eager to hear from the Professor's own lips what finds he had made. He seemed as ready to tell as we were to hear. He opened a nap sack and began to spread out for our examination a collection of small broken artifacts he had recovered from the scattered rubble of the shaft. Our eyes strained for details in the cozy but frustrating gloom of the place. He took up each one as he explained what he made of it. I knew we were getting the oral version of what would be a major scholarly paper, and my ears missed nothing. The inside of the pub had become a seminar room.

"In short, it seemed the Professor had already found ample corroboration of his theories at several points. The walls of the shaft harbored votive tablets dedicated to the divine pair Medusa and Byatis. Of these two worthies themselves no likeness was found, though perhaps this was because of the legendary danger of seeing their visages. Might the superstitious mind (as we then viewed it) not fear that even the second-hand depiction of the pair could prove petrifying in its own right? There were new relics, also some which paralleled the evidence already collected from other British sites, a few of which confirmed his conjectural restorations of fragmentary earlier items. The few inscriptions, mostly the prayers inscribed on votive plaques, were in Koine Greek or monkish Latin. It would be difficult to date the find, but this linguistic evidence suggested a date somewhere in Late Antiquity.

"From these scholarly ruminations we were rudely recalled by the sudden reappearance of yesterday's dour intruder. This time none of us had even noticed his approach, so preoccupied were we. His peculiarly accented declamation was punctuated by the flashing of his eyes in the lamplight: 'Woe to them that heed not even after the second warning! Their conscience is seared, and they wot not the evil that they do!' With that, his knobby hand, protruding from the black sleeve of his cassock, made to descend like a hammer on our table. I braced for the clatter sure to result, but there was no impact, no sound. My eyes had strayed for an instant to the alarmed face of Professor Ashdod who little fancied this old man scattering his precious relics by a clumsy blow. When I looked back, the old priest was gone.

"The Professor was the first to speak: 'Science must always make its way in the face of superstition, gentlemen. Let us hope our watchmen are alert against this man's compatriots. Let us turn in so as to be ready for a great day tomorrow. We will see what awaits us within.' With that he drained his mug and began to collect the artifacts he had spread out on the table, rather like, I thought, a player at cards cradling his winnings.

"I saw one item he had neglected, gingerly lifted it by a corner, and passed it to him. I was surprised at his reply. 'Not one of ours, Mr. Batchel. Keep it for a souvenir.' I did just that and have always carried the stonework fragment upon my person as a keepsake to this day.

"The night was full of dreams, some ominous, anticipations no doubt of what ancient heathen remains we might discover on the morrow, others depicting our own imagined future fame as partners in a great discovery. Quite silly in retrospect.

"The morning began with a surprise. Doctor Ashdod did not appear to meet us in the breakfast room, nor did he answer to a knock at his door. Growing worried, we finally decided he must have risen earlier than the rest of us and preceded us to the dig. It was a relief when this surmise proved out. As we approached the site over the clover fields separating it from the town, followed again by suspicious village eyes, we were relieved to see Professor Ashdod emerging from the shaded mouth of the shaft.

"'Welcome, young men! To tell the truth, I just couldn't wait. I never managed to fall asleep, so I decided to be up before dawn and ready at the first light. The workmen were surprised to see me,' he chuckled, 'and I found a rifle barrel greeting me as I approached. But soon the men recognized me. They reported no trouble. I half feared some of the locals might try to close up or damage the site, though I still haven't the faintest idea why.

"'But here's the news: I've managed to pry loose the barrier. You'll find it propped against that rise.'

"We gathered round the stained slab, the workmen moving back from their surveillance as we did so. It was they who had deposited it there after the Professor had dug round the buried edges so as not to damage the thing. We studied it in silence for a moment, and I don't mind admitting I was the first to venture a translation. It was ecclesiastical Latin, and it was the Vulgate text of Exodus 33:20, 'Ye cannot see my face, for man shall not see me and live.'

"'Obviously,' someone pontificated, 'it wasn't placed there by the worshippers of the god. It's a warning to stay away. Perhaps placed there by church authorities after having closed down the shrine and persecuted the devotees. What do you think, Professor?'

186

"'Likely enough, Mr. Bainbridge, but don't forget that some of yesterday's inscriptions were rendered in the same Latin. We shouldn't be too quick to rule out a secret worship of pagan deities by nominal Christians. It wouldn't be unparalleled. And even they would have sufficient reason to warn people away from looking at their gods, given what they believed about their deadly powers. Anyway, I'm going in. I want the rest of you to wait out here. Oh, don't worry, you'll soon enough have your turn. Shipley, be a good lad and fix me up a couple of torches. The sun doesn't help much in there. The shaft seems to turn a corner and to open into a small grotto, much like a Mithraeum.

"'I can tell from the echoes, that we've not been so lucky here as in the shaft: much of the inside must have collapsed long ago. So quarters are tight, and until I see for myself what's in there, my clumsy feet are the only ones that will be trampling the floor, understand?'

"We all saw his wisdom, though that hardly lightened the burden of frustration. Shipley tied handkerchiefs onto a couple of fallen branches, dipped them into our lamp oil and set them ablaze. He passed them one by one to the professor who must have hollowed out makeshift brackets or holes for them. Then all alike, we waited and listened.

"His familiar voice began to take on an eerie quality as he passed further along the hidden recesses of the underground structure. No obstruction so far, that was obvious. His voice drifted up as if from the underworld.

"'I'm able to stand erect here, and I believe I've reached what was the altar area. What luck that it survived the centuries! And this . . . Good Lord! It must be the likeness of Byatis himself!' He laughed in exultation. His efforts were now rewarded, his theories confirmed, his lasting fame assured. Back on the surface we began to applaud him. Our excitement rose like a fever as we awaited his momentary reappearance and our own turns to retrace his path one by one. But there was no sound of bootfalls, no further word of discovery. Was he so lost in deciphering some inscriptions? We called, but still there was no answer.

"Genuinely worried for our mentor for the second time that morning, we argued over who ought to go in after him. These deliberations were cut short by the sudden eruption of a figure from the mouth of the shaft. He sped into us, knocking us aside like so many ninepins. What could have so panicked the Professor?

"As we picked ourselves up we were dumbfounded to see the figure, now clearly naked, run with blinding speed past us and on into the hills opposite the village. This could hardly be the sturdy but middle-aged form

187

of Professor Ashdod! Frankly I doubt that any of us, hardy young specimens as we were, could have caught up with the fleeing figure, but none of us thought of that just then. Once we realized our leader must still be inside the tomb, more than likely injured by this lurking enemy, we decided we must throw caution to the wind. Shipley shouldered the rest of us aside and began to crawl inside.

"Fearing more mischief, we waited with bated breath. Only a moment later, Shipley's voice came up: 'Rum thing! He's not here! And I can't see any image he might have been describing, either! Wait, here's something . . . No!'

"Our blood chilling, we looked at one another, and this time it was Bainbridge who took the plunge. Moments later, his voice came back, rather too calmly: 'Listen chaps, there's enough room on this end. Come on down. But get a grip on yourselves first.'

"With the help of our stolid workmen we were able, an hour or so later, to trundle into a borrowed wagon what we had found in the shrine of Byatis. We knew we would have to remain in Camside long enough to arrange to have the thing shipped back to the University. That much was easy to figure out. The difficult thing was trying to come up with a tale to tell the University authorities, one that they might believe. What we finally decided on was this: poor Professor Ashdod, on the eve of our planned excavation, sought relief from the unusual heat with a dip in the River Cam. From this seemingly innocent amusement he had not returned, overcome with a cramp and drowning before any of us understood his peril. Nor was his body to be found. We would say we had commissioned the statue of the Professor as a commemoration of our beloved mentor and donated it to the University. Once we returned to the campus, we waited a plausible length of time before presenting the statue, and there it stands today."

The patient Mr. Barlowe seemed at first not to understand that Mr. Batchel had concluded his story. Then: "But, if you please, what *did* happen to the Professor? And what was it you shipped back to the University from Camside? Surely not the statue?"

"I had thought you took my meaning, Barlowe. Don't you see, it was no statue, but the Professor himself. The ancient power of Byatis had not faded with the ages."

The younger man was silent in disbelief. He stared at Mr. Batchel as if the latter had suddenly sprouted a second bald head. "Surely you don't mean to tell me that he was turned to stone by the statue of a Gorgon? You're *not*, are you?"

"I needn't. To quote our Lord, thou hast said it. But I don't expect it to sink in all at once. No indeed. It took me some years of further investigation to come to the conclusions I now hold on the matter. One of those conclusions is that the stone image of Byatis which the Professor stumbled upon was no more a true statue than the one we have just seen. Think back to the naked running figure. My first thought was that he must be one of the hostile Camside villagers who had lain in wait for the Professor to do him ill. But the more I considered it the more mysterious the matter became: how could such a one have entered the sealed tomb ahead of us and contrived to re-seal it from within? Were the workmen, too, in on the scheme? They weren't even native to the area. At length our naked runner seemed fully as puzzling as the naked man who fled away when our Lord was arrested in Gethsemane. But in recent months I have, shall we say, formed a hypothesis. And I want you to help me test it."

"Me?" protested the nonplussed Mr. Barlowe, as if afraid he was being reeled in like a fish on the older man's mad hook. "Really, it's fine for you to believe whatever you please, but . . ."

"Why, Mr. Barlowe! You disappoint me! I should think a rationalist like yourself would welcome the opportunity to debunk the supernaturalist delusions of a medieval relic like me. I was so sure you would rise to my challenge that I invited you along for this conference in the first place. You see, it was no accident that we ran across the 'statue.' I knew we should sooner or later, and I counted on your healthy curiosity. It did not fail me. I hope it will not fail me now."

After a few moments, the two men rose and returned to the Refectory. The afternoon seminars had passed without benefit of their attendance. They chose a table and continued their conversation, employing hushed tones as the seats around them began to fill.

"There is a man here at Brichester I wish to question. He is a faculty member, in the Classics Department. Perhaps you know him or have studied with him." Here Mr. Batchel mentioned a name that is perhaps best withheld. "I believe he may hold our answer. You say that you do know him? Good. What I wish is that you may request an appointment to see him. Say that you wish to introduce me, that I wish to pursue the possibility of offering a lecture course at Brichester. It will not sound outlandish; you may know that I am retained by my own alma mater to examine prospective graduates."

Still looking as if he had been made the dupe of a joke that had not finished tightening its bands about him, young Barlowe stammered his

189

agreement. "I suppose that couldn't do any harm. But please remember, Mr. Batchel, I am not yet through this institution. I will trust you not to say anything that might prejudice the faculty against me."

Mr. Batchel smiled and took his assistant by the shoulder. "Rest assured, my young friend, you will have nothing to regret. And soon all things shall be made clear. It's been a long day. Let us retire."

As the professor in question was himself participating in the archaeological conference, it was no great matter for Barlowe to locate and arrange to see him in his office the following afternoon. The baffled divinity student stayed close to Mr. Batchel for the duration of the morning and afternoon, attending this and that lecture, but retaining little of what he heard. He could not cease turning over Mr. Batchel's cryptic half-explanations in his mind. And still no light came.

Beside him his older comrade rose and clapped. As they made their way through the thick crowd of those filing out of the lecture hall, Mr. Batchel exclaimed, "Well, it seems that even I am not yet too old to learn. But I do wonder how those Aztecs and Incas are to be reconciled with the Table of Nations in Genesis chapter 10. Leave it to the theologians, I suppose. They'll come up with something. They always do. Why, what troubles you, Mr. Barlowe? Oh yes, of course, we have an appointment across campus, don't we? No time for tea. We'd best hurry along."

The secretary was waiting for them in a thickly carpeted, well appointed office. "I believe you are the Professor's last appointment for the afternoon. Please do try to keep in mind he has had a busy day with the conference. You may go on in. He's expecting you."

It was quite a study, a private library to envy. Mr. Batchel could scarcely keep himself from devouring the exotic rows of bindings with covetous eyes. Young Mr. Barlowe could not hide his timidity as he addressed the imposing figure before him. Though he had been a student in one of the professor's classes only the previous year, he knew it was not likely he would be remembered among scores of university and seminary students. After a few fumbling words, Barlowe introduced Mr. Batchel to the professor. The tall, broad, bearded man would, save for the cut of his suit, have suggested more the successful London financier than the erudite academic. He greeted Mr. Batchel, though he made no move to shake hands. Nor did the smiling Mr. Batchel. All three sat down, as if on signal.

"Yes, Professor, it is just as our young friend has said. I would much enjoy piloting a lecture course in some upcoming term. Local archaeology
190

has long been a specialty of mine, and I should like to develop some of the theories of one of Brichester's own esteemed faculty, now sadly deceased. He had certain speculations, not unsupported by evidence of a striking character, as to the immigration of the cult of Medusa to these very shores, and the fusion of that cult with a local mystery religion, the religion of . . ."

The deep, vaguely accented voice interrupted him: "Yes, I have heard of the work of the man you speak of, a Professor Ashdod, I believe. I regret to have to tell you that his work has been long ago surpassed, discredited really. I am afraid some of the most recent work in the field may have escaped your notice, busy as you must be with parish duties. And yet I do not mean to denigrate your scholarly gifts, sir. I attended your own lecture yesterday morning and was quite impressed. I take a dim view of this Medusa business, but it is not impossible we might be able to arrange something for you in the next spring term on some other subject." He rose to signal the interview was at an end.

The Stoneground rector and his apprentice made for the door and were called back a moment later. The study door was now closed, but the secretary hailed them. "The Professor has asked me to have you meet him tonight after the final convocation behind the main Library building. By then he may have had the opportunity to speak to the Dean about the matter you discussed."

"*Splendid!*" said Mr. Batchel. Young Barlowe's eye's remained empty and expectant. As the two men left the building, their long shadows pouring down the steps they slowly descended, Barlowe could contain himself no longer.

"I'm sorry that proved a cul-de-sac, though you may get your lecture course."

"Tush tush, my boy. My duties at Stoneground would never allow it. And your professor may yet have our answer for us. We must be patient. As Professor Ashdod knew, that is the only way not to overlook crucial bits of evidence."

"But he never even let you finish your question about Medusa and Attis! That can hardly be what he wants to discuss with you!"

"The trained archaeologist learns how to read even the smallest and least obvious signs. And I believe you mean 'Byatis.'" At this, Barlowe gave up and resigned himself to wait for the outcome later that night. He only thought it odd that the Professor should choose so recondite a meeting place. Perhaps he simply thought it best to avoid the crowd of those attending the convocation.

The convocation came and went, ringing down the curtain on another scholarly conference, each enough like the others that Mr. Batchel invariably found them assuming the monotony of a stack of old neglected journals on the dusty shelf of memory. But each in its hour was conducted with the pomp of a state occasion. As one of the conference speakers this time he himself was entitled to don his academic regalia and join the processional. From the front line of pews in the Brichester University Chapel, he had one of the best seats in the house for the seemingly endless round of invocations, testimonials and finally the keynote address.

Later he could not recall the identity of that final speaker or even his theme. He was busy reviewing in his mind what he might have to say an hour or two later when he had his much anticipated meeting with the Professor. The Professor himself Mr. Batchel noticed up ahead in the line of march and marked it when the man briefly ascended the dais to introduce one of the speakers who was to introduce yet another speaker.

The moment finally came to march back out of the Chapel and disperse. As he again took his place among the grandly vested faculty and visiting scholars, Mr. Batchel could not help but reflect how one might be inclined to have a bit of sympathy after all for those old scribes and Pharisees whom our Lord rebuked for lengthening their tassels for acclaim among men. But enough of that. There was young Mr. Barlowe waiting for him.

After a brief return to their assigned rooms to shed his academic gown, Mr. Batchel led the way to the appointed meeting place. Many hours had passed and the moon was high, and by its light they had no difficulty finding their way to the main Library, then circling its vast girth. The rear of this building was whiskered with rows of trees and hedges, and the Professor's presence among all these standing shapes was not immediately apparent.

"Professor?" called Mr. Barlowe hopefully, yet not without a note of intimidation. Almost like a distant bird call came the response at once.

"Here, gentlemen."

The two companions followed the voice, arriving in a few moments' time at what seemed an artfully contrived portico of ivied arches rising from a thick bank of shrubs. Within one arch stood the shadowed form of the one whom they sought. His silhouette was vague, almost shapeless, implying he had not taken time to doff his voluminous academic regalia.

192

"Ah, the Reverend Batchel, and of course, Mr. Barlowe. I trust you enjoyed the convocation. Always a great stimulation for scholars to gather for their mutual enlightenment, don't you think? And now to the matter at hand. I must confess that I have had cause to give your unique theories further consideration. And it may surprise you to hear that I have experienced something of a change of heart on the question. Indeed, I now find myself very much convinced that you and your late friend Ashdod were correct. Further, I would like to supply you with an irrefutable bit of evidence . . ."

Drifting clouds slid off the face of the full moon, and by its light Mr. Batchel believed he could behold an odd *shifting* among the hair of the Professor's full beard. As the clergyman's hand went to his pocket, his gaze remained fixed and he believed he saw, as he had expected to see, the slow emergence from that stirring hair of something like slugs, their tips sickly white in the moonlight.

"Barlowe! Look away, if you value your soul!" exclaimed the Reverend Batchel with uncharacteristic urgency. Withal did he close his own eyes, flinging toward the third man some object he had palmed a moment before.

As the frightened and obedient Barlowe swung round, his eyes caught sight for a brief moment of that which his mentor made ready to pitch at their enemy. It was a stone star-shape, possibly bearing a central sigil of some sort. But then he clenched his eyes as if he planned never to open them again and he dropped to the ground.

"Now I believe it will be safe to look," came Mr. Batchel's again unperturbed tones. "More than likely the University will have to find space for another commemorative statue."

But Barlowe was not looking where the Professor had been standing. Rather his eyes followed a small shape scuttling crab-like into the cover of the shrubbery. He thought it resembled a living starfish, though fleshy in texture, surmounted by a single, disproportionately large, unblinking eye. But then it was gone, and who could say?

For the first time Mr. Barlowe found himself greatly relieved to be leaving the rare atmosphere of the University and returning to the provincial gravel-ground parish. At length he ventured to interrupt Mr. Batchel, sitting opposite him in the train car, absorbed in a biblical monograph he had purchased at Brichester University two days before.

"Mr. Batchel, I really must ask you something."

193

"Yes, my young friend? Some theological matter? Or archaeology perhaps?"

"Neither, or perhaps both! You must tell me what happened at the last. How did you dispatch the Professor? And, well, *why?*"

Closing his book, Mr. Batchel leaned forward and said, "Now I should have thought that obvious. But perhaps a word of explanation might be in order. Let me take you back to that tragic day many years ago, after the loss of Professor Ashdod, as we, his young protégés, were on the point of dispersing. One evening, as I strove to make sense of all that had transpired, rather in your state of mind at the present, come to think of it, I took a long walk. I found myself on the road leading from Camside to the nearby village of Severnford. As I looked up, my eye fell upon a quaint chapel. At once I veered from my path to seek a place of prayer within.

"As I trod the moss-covered pathway and passed between a pair of blackened pillars, I could not help but notice, with my eye for rare church architecture, a striking piece of stonework adorning the arch over the gate. It depicted something I first took for the familiar St. George and the Dragon motif, but a closer scrutiny revealed an unusual variation on that theme. The dragon had more the shape of a gargoyle and seemed too bearded, a detail found on Chinese dragon sculptures, but never on their European cousins. And its nemesis was a winged angel holding aloft no conventional cross or sword, but a great five-pointed star from which the monster seemed to recoil. I entered the church with renewed interest but found no one of whom I might inquire. Hoping someone might yet appear, I resolved to pursue my first design of quiet prayer amid the empty pews.

"It was not long before a worried-looking verger appeared, hoping it was not a prowler whose tread he had heard and relieved to see that it wasn't. I rose and followed him down the nave, as he had generously agreed to give me a brief tour. I am, as you know, always curious to see the nooks and crannies of country churches for whatever antique wonders they may afford, but that day I was really only concerned to know of the peculiar stonework piece. And yet that fled my thoughts completely once I laid eyes on the first framed portrait we passed. It was the likeness of the old priest who had accosted us in the taproom!

"'Is this your present rector?' I asked, as nonchalantly as I could. Here the man chuckled and replied, 'Hardly! This is old Doctor Raines, and him a century gone!'

"I cut the tour short at that point, for I knew then what I needed to know. I knew who had visited us in the inn, and, recalling the star held aloft by the carven angel, I also knew what he had brought us. The extra relic on the taproom table had been a miniature replica of that star, and it was that which I learned too late could counter the baleful influence of Byatis, who escapes his stony confinement by luring the unwary to take his place. But as you saw last evening, the star retained its power."

Mr. Barlowe did not again disturb the silence which recaptured the compartment. For the rest of the rail journey only the chugging of the train was to be heard. We will not follow either the train or Mr. Barlowe further, save to mention that his remarkable experience was not without its effect upon his developing theological convictions. From that day forward there existed a greater commonality of spirit between him and his mentor. And it may not be out of place to divulge the fact that many years later, when Mr. Batchel went on to his reward, it was none other than Reverend Barlowe who succeeded him in the pulpit of Stoneground Church, which he served well. Nor would it be unduly surprising if, on some future visit to his old divinity school, he should pause with a curious seminarian before a peculiar statue depicting a robed and bearded scholar. One might speculate whether Mr. Barlowe would venture any sort of explanation.

–1995–

DOWN IN LIMBO

DEDICATED TO JAMES WADE

Larry's eyes scanned the menu and paused at "squid"—then moved on. The University dining room was staffed by culinary students from a nearby community college, and he wasn't exactly sure he trusted their expertise in seafood. That poor mollusk might take its revenge!

He finally decided to play the gentleman and order a second plate of whatever Barb was having. It wouldn't be too much of a risk, he reasoned, since one of the things that had made him like her so much so quickly was the uncanny way she shared his likes and dislikes.

Larry was a teaching assistant finishing his doctorate across the campus and down the block at the Sanbourne Institute, which had been absorbed by the University only a year ago. The underpopulated field of Undersea Archaeology was his real passion, and to make any money from it, at least in the short run, he found himself teaching an improbable hybrid slate of courses in ancient languages and oceanography. Barbara Gilbert was a student in a Marine Biology section he taught. She was a nut on the subject, it turned out. And it didn't take long before Barbara was Larry's real passion.

He liked just about everything about her. He'd had other relationships, abortive ones, where it turned out he was more the object of hero worship than affection. But between him and Barb there was not only the link of mutual admiration, but mutual desire as well. And, like positive and negative poles in electricity, you had to have both.

After she ordered, Barb handed over the menu and quizzed her pensive partner, "How's the dissertation going? Near the home stretch yet?"

"No, I only wish I were. It's a long haul, and yet I do feel that perhaps I'm near some kind of a breakthrough. Today I finally got those rubbings of the glyphs they found last year on the Bimini Wall. Nobody suspected there was anything there till some surveyors picked up something strange with infrared photography, all purely by accident. At first they thought it was just scoring, maybe trails left by some form of sea-life."

Barb's pretty green eyes widened as she listened. Larry warmed to his topic. It was great to have a listener who didn't have to feign interest.

196

"Anyway, it turned out to be real writing, though not at all clear. And bigger than you'd think would be necessary."

Barbara took his hand and spoke with real enthusiasm. "And you're sure no one's done anything with these inscriptions before? Are you having to translate from scratch?"

"Well, actually, Professor Maitland did the earliest work on it, and that's how I knew about it to begin with. There hasn't been much in the way of real publicity, not even in the journals. The discussion has focused mainly on a real strange puzzle. Somehow they can tell that the Bimini Glyphs— that's what they're calling them—were carved *while they were submerged*. Up to now everybody figured that the blocks formed part of a structure that was overwhelmed and covered when the coastline changed. But apparently not. And then you have to ask why the hell anyone would have carved those words into underwater masonry. For the fish to read?"

His dinner companion laughed brightly, and the food came. What do you know, fish after all? Well, live dangerously.

After a few mouthfuls that boded well enough, Barb asked him, "What *did* they say? The carvings. *Was* it some message to fish?"

"Ha! No, not exactly. Really, it's still pretty conjectural. Seems to be a warning of some kind. It's just possible that it was a sign alerting people not to disturb some undersea patch of vegetation or coral, maybe a fishery or hatchery. But those are just guesses. There really isn't enough left to say for sure."

"But you're not doing your thesis on that."

"No, you're right. But I'm full of it just now, because there's something in the shape of the characters of the inscription ~ they seem to be pictograms of some kind ~ that gives me a clue to what I *am* working on."

"*The Reliant Text*? Is that it? I still can't get it right." She brushed back a strand of dark brown hair.

"Who knows? Maybe you are right, sweetheart. Nobody knows much better, that's for sure. But the accepted way to say it is the *Ril-Yay Text*. Ever since that old Yankee trader Hoag brought it back from one of his voyages, scholars have scratched their heads over the thing. There's never been a real translation of it, though once some hoaxers passed off what they said was a translated version of it . . . filled a whole paperback book. There's not nearly enough text for that.

"In fact, that's how I first heard of it. When I was a pimply junior high nerd, and as you will note, I'm now a well-groomed nerd with a clear complexion, I was reading all these stupid books like Churchward's *Lost*

Continent of Mu, and I think he mentioned it."

Quietly munching through this speech, Barb now began to giggle, spraying a fish bone or two.

"Oh yes! I read that one, too! I kept hoping Nancy Drew would make a trip to Mu! I thought it was like Oz."

"You were right the first time, Barb. Churchward was debunked as a faker long ago. Copeland, too. The worst of these guys was Shrewsbury, if you can even believe he was named that!"

"One thing's for sure: you must have read them all."

"Yeah, I did, as a matter of fact. And if you want to know the truth, that's where I got the idea to go into this crazy field I'm in. When I got old enough to take the relevant science courses, I got a big dash of cold water. That's when I learned these guys were all either con men or just didn't know their stuff. I decided I'd be for real, what these old guys were supposed to be, you know, do something to deserve the honors one or two of them got. You must have seen Copeland's portrait in the entrance hall at Sanbourne. He was what passed for a scientist in those days. But he didn't know a pictograph from an ideograph."

"Neither did I, remember? In fact, I think that was my excuse for coming to see you that first time. You mentioned both in a lecture and I figured I'd as soon get private tutoring on that as anything else!"

"See? Even trivia has its uses!" Larry pushed away the empty plates and sidled around to sit beside Barb, putting his arm around her shoulder. "I guess you're sick of the tutoring you're getting tonight, though. Let's talk about something else."

"Okay, Larry, I did want to tell you something. I know you'll think I'm being 'unscientific' and all, but I went with my roommate to see this channeler the other night . . ."

Larry Stanton, inflexible rationalist, stifled a groan a moment too late. But Barb just smiled and went on. "You can laugh at it if you want to, but I was just curious. And besides, it sounded like fun."

"I bet it was *loads* of fun when they started sacrificing chickens. I know all about this stuff, remember. I watched *The Devil Rides Out* and *The Exorcist* and plenty of others in my day."

"Oh, no!" She laughed, "It's nothing like that! More like a church service, actually. We all sat down quietly and waited about ten minutes till the channeler came in. It was in one of the big meeting rooms in the University Center. I think we heard Carl Sagan there once. Anyway, they had these great lighting effects, deep greens and blues, like in some seafood restaurants. You felt like you were underwater. Come to think of it, you'd feel right at home!"

"Maybe I would. This is starting to get interesting. Go on. Say, seems like I once heard of some guy whose specialty was to channel the thoughts, or was it the vibes, of dolphins. And not the Miami kind either. Though I don't think those guys *have* thoughts. Maybe we can order one for the Anthro Lab and find out . . ."

"Listen, Larry, you can laugh your ass off if you want to, but let me finish the story, okay?"

"Sorry. I'm duly chastened. You may continue. Just don't say he was broadcasting from ancient Atlantis or something."

"Well, he was."

"And? I'm trying to be serious here. I promise I'll take whatever you say seriously."

"He did past life regressions."

"Figures. And?"

"I had him do mine," she said and paused to wait for the explosion. But it didn't come. She felt almost annoyed at this, for some reason, and asked why.

"This *is* getting interesting! Actually, I'm not quite as down on this stuff as I give out. Of course it's hokum on one level. But I'm willing to admit that these people can get in touch with their subconscious, both the medium and the person who gets regressed. Reincarnation's bullshit, of course, but regression is an interesting free-association sort of exercise. Psychodrama, I guess."

"Coming from you, that's almost a profession of faith!"

"Don't make too much out of it. I'm going out of my way to be tolerant."

"I can see that, Larry. But y'know what I think? I think you're still so stung from being fooled by Churchward and those old frauds that you're being skeptical as a defense mechanism. But you have to be open to new experiences."

"I suppose so. That's why I want you to tell me what happened when you were regressed."

"OK, back to our story. Maybe you're right and it was pure power of suggestion. But I felt that I was a priestess in ancient Atlantis, or at least some sunken civilization."

Larry had imperceptibly moved away from her again. He wanted to look into her eyes as she talked. He had done this unconsciously. It was just that when they were on the same wavelength, they almost seemed to merge into one, like a set of twins. But when, as now, they differed, his body language reflected it. He faced her as an object of scrutiny, almost like one of his strange marine life-forms. And now he held up a finger to flag another interruption.

"Y'know, you *were* in a sunken continent, the kingdom of the subconscious. Jung knew it well. Seriously. Now, go ahead."

Barb continued, "At first I didn't think it had worked, the hypnosis or whatever it was. Because the light was the same as in the meeting room, all dark blue and green. I know that's just dream imagery, right? Borrowing the background from waking life." Larry nodded.

"But this couldn't have been taken from waking life. I had the most vivid sense of breathing water! This wasn't Atlantis before it sank! It was *already* sunk, and we lived in it! That's why I'm mentioning this! It's just like your Bimini Wall!"

"Damned if it isn't!"

"I was naked, I know, because there was no place I couldn't feel the water on me. And I was walking in line with a whole group of women. Or . . . I'm not sure of that. They were all naked, and none of them had anything between their legs. And, uh, we were all . . . bald . . . ! I had forgotten that till now."

Larry's analytical mood had passed. He was back at her side again, holding her. It was as if she were a child having a bad dream, or someone having a bad trip. And he was extending a hand to keep her in the real world.

"Where were you all going? What were you doing? Did you feel like you were drowning?"

"No, I'm sure it wasn't that, because once when I was ten I nearly *did* drown. There was none of the panic, the clutching, the blacking out. It felt as natural as . . . a fish in water!

"And we were walking up, kind of gliding, really, along a beautiful coral reef, you know, like you see when you go snorkeling: everything is absolutely brilliant and glowing. It overcomes you, and you feel like you're trespassing in someone else's world.

"Anyway, we got to where we were going, and this is the hard part. We seemed to be crawling down a hill, a big tilted plane, really, and we had to be careful not to lose our balance, but when we made it there, we were at the *top* of the thing!"

"What thing?"

"Something like a huge garage door, or those shutter doors behind a house, leading down into a basement. Some kind of stuff was coming up from a narrow crack of an opening, and it was, like, smoking up through the water. And then we stopped and we looked down at the crack, and we all just stood there, as if we were waiting for something to happen, and it never did. I had the feeling I wanted to sing something—under water! But I didn't know the words. That's when I woke up."

"Barb, I'm sorry; I can see this thing really moved you. I don't mean to make light of it. Are you feeling okay? Are you—?"

"Larry, I'm fine! It wasn't scary at all. I guess I speak of it with a kind of amazement, that's all. In fact, I don't think I'd mind going through it again."

"If you do, promise you'll tell me what happens. I promise, next time no smartass remarks."

"Sure, Larry, sure I will. And maybe you can come along. I think the channeler has regular meetings, or performances, or whatever, at a New Age store with an auditorium downtown. It would be something fun to do together. And besides, you could use a break from your work."

"I could, that's true. But I better wait till the Midterms are over. I'll have piles of papers and exams to slog through—like sea-floor ooze!"

Larry paid the check and they headed to the off-campus housing complex. Barb's roommate was away, so they passed the night there. Larry forgot to set the clock and got to class the next morning just in the nick of time. He'd had little chance to prepare for his lecture, but luckily most of the students wanted to ask questions about the Lab two days before. For once he was grateful they were so obtuse.

When that was over, he shuffled out of the building and down the block to his office at Sanbourne. The pebble-glass door was ajar. This did not alarm him, since it was a cubbyhole shared with two other part-timers. Either of them might have been there. But neither was.

Instead it was the tweed-clad form of the gaunt Professor Maitland. Typically he was standing, not sitting, holding up a sheaf of papers to the window.

"Sorry, Stanton, I was just impatient to see what progress you'd made on the *Text* in light of the Bimini evidence. Not much, I see. Too deeply submerged with that young lady."

201

Tossing his jacket like a shapeless bag over the top of the coat rack, Larry replied, "I guess you're right, Professor, but I can't be a cold fish *all* the time. But the Glyphs are a big help. Almost like a Rosetta Stone. I guess you expected that. I swear I'll have it done by the end of the semester, at least in draft. The *Text* isn't long, and it should progress pretty rapidly from here on in."

Professor Maitland handed him the stack of notes, restored to their folder, and headed for the door. With a backward glance, he reminded his apprentice: "Just see to it that you have something in shape to present when the Academy meets in February. My reputation, not just yours, is riding on this, remember!"

Larry sat down to get to work. He smiled at the gruff exterior of the old man. Larry had become almost like a son to the bachelor professor, who had never expected to find anyone to share, much less carry on, his obscure work. He had, he once told young Stanton, never expected to live long enough to see certain puzzles solved, but the arrival of the promising young student had given him new hope that he might see their solution after all. It would be worth the wait.

An hour into it, Larry found that his words to his mentor had been no exaggeration. The Bimini Glyphs plugged right into the *R'lyeh Text*. It was going surprisingly well. The way it was shaping up, the *Text* seemed to be a cultic text, possibly something of a cross between an apocalypse and a litany.

The Bimini inscriptions were a boon all right, but Larry found little of it would have made any sense at all without an extensive knowledge of the myth-patterns of the South Pacific. And there his predecessors *had* done some valuable work. Whatever else one might say about them, Shrewsbury and Copeland had set down and systematized a lot of esoteric stuff from the Trobriand Islanders, even some retrograde Ponape cultures, the very existence of which had gone unsuspected by previous anthropologists.

Much of it was colored by the Victorian biases of the nineteenth and early twentieth century ethnographers, but you could pretty well strain out distortions like that. There was no retracing their steps, because the global culture, together with missionary expansion, had largely obliterated any trace of the really ancient traditions. The only things the natives seemed to remember nowadays was the recycled stuff the tourist guide books told you anyway.

But the myth-patterns of the region, especially the real inner-circle stuff that Copeland had somehow gotten certain chiefs and shaman-priests to share, was proving invaluable. There were kindred myth-associations and even names, though they were a mouthful even in transliteration. "Ghatanothoa," "Ythogtha," and others even less comprehensible. Even worse than the names of the Aztec deities!

Midterms passed, and so did most of the students, though just barely. He was beginning to see Professor Maitland's urgency. You just couldn't bank on the future generations of students to be worth a damn. What would happen to scholarly discovery when people like these were in charge of it?

Early one evening in November, Barbara reminded her increasingly serious boyfriend of their date at the channeler's. They found the address of the New Age Center in downtown Santiago and called first to make sure there'd be a meeting that night. Sure enough, Dr. Waite, the channeler, whose name Barb hadn't been able to recall, would be there. They set off on foot for the address, shunning a cab, given the balmy California climate even so late in the fall.

Maybe they should have hailed a cab after all, because when they arrived it was about time to start, and the place was packed. Dr. Waite, an impressive-looking man in a sea-green turtle-neck, settled his considerable girth into a leather chair. Larry recognized the face from the poster in the lobby as well as from the numerous paperback books and cassette tape boxes on the display tables. Waite was perfectly bald but sported a luxurious beard of curling locks that spread out on his chest like a nest of writhing serpents.

As he sat there, he began to twitch, a common mannerism of channelers, part of the act. His posture became suddenly different, subtly animated by a sense of regal pride and authoritativeness. And then the blue and green lights came on. It was hard to say where they were coming from. It was an impressive effect. Must have cost some money.

"I bring to you the greetings of the Great Ones, who in Their grace retired from before the coming of men, so that men might have an hour upon the world-stage. One day, when men have spent their childish imaginations, the Great Ones will take again what is theirs. But for the present, they are content to speak in dreams, even as I now do. I speak to you from the depths of—"

Larry Stanton virtually jumped from his seat, Barb grasping his arm as if to keep him from ascending into the sky, glaring at him in shock.

"Larry, what *is* it? What's *wrong?*"

He sank back and whispered in her ear, "Didn't you hear what he *said?* He says he's from, he's transmitting from *R'lyeh!* Only that's not how he pronounced it. Maybe that's why you didn't recognize it before."

"So what? Didn't you tell me it was common knowledge in the occultist paperbacks? Maybe he's read his Churchward, that's all. Now calm down."

"Sure, sure, you must be right. I don't know what got into me. Working too late, I guess. But he did say it with almost a South Sea Islander's pronunciation. I'd still like to know . . ."

"Shhhh! He's having people come up to the mike. I'm getting in line! You can come, too, or wait for me." And she was gone.

Larry waited in his seat, his momentary surprise replaced by a mixture of pity and disgust. What he was seeing was little more than one of those pathetic healing lines in an evangelist's tent show. People would kneel before the channeler, muttering some formula he told them.

Then, as Edgar Cayce and a hundred others had done, Dr. Waite would take them back in their imagination to some previous life, more likely some Walter Mitty secret life of their fantasies. They would ask a question, about a loved one or a problem. And they would learn that they were overweight because they were compensating for having starved to death in the Irish Potato famine, or they were attracted to a new lover because they had been together in a previous incarnation. Most of it had the profundity of a newspaper horoscope, and Larry found himself feeling ashamed of Barb for taking it seriously.

But then it was Barb's turn. She knelt, like the rest, for the channeler's blessing. He cupped his quite large hands over her forehead and muttered something *sotto voce*. Larry couldn't make out what it was. Until Barb repeated it: *Ph'nglui mglw'nafh Cthulhu R'lyeh wqah'nagl fhatgn.*

At this, Larry jumped to his feet and shoved others aside in his rush to reach the foot of the stage. He didn't want to miss anything. For what he heard sounded for all the world like a passable vocalization of one of the more difficult lines from the fragmentary *R'lyeh Text*. And the channeler couldn't have got *this* from Churchward.

The rest was in English. Barb's eyes were opened. She had turned and now faced the audience. She dreamily recounted a scene similar to the one she had repeated to Larry weeks before in the restaurant.

204

"I am joined to the company of those who make ready for His Returning. We drift like minnows across the vast face of the Great Seal. All that dwell below the watery firmament gaze with expectation. We assume our positions and make as if to sing forth. But we have forgotten what we are to sing. It is withheld from us. We wait and wait and then we return home again. How long? How long, O Mother Hydra? How long must we wait for the Great Betrothal?"

At this, her eyes fell shut again. She had actually been in a trance, then, not just letting her mind wander like the rest seemed to be doing. Only instead of waking up, she seemed to have fallen into a deeper sleep. Her form crumpled and she fell from the stage like a sack of potatoes.

The channeler had apparently not expected this, and made only a feeble effort to hoist his bulk from the seat where he was installed. Luckily, though, Larry's curiosity had driven him to within a few feet of where Barb had been standing, so at the crucial moment he found himself directly beneath her and poised for the catch.

Sparing not a look toward the stage or the vacantly curious crowd, Larry returned Barb to her seat, massaged her wrists, and told her to stay still while he got their coats. When he returned from the lobby she could stand again, and the audience had lost their momentary interest, returning their gaze stageward, where the unflappable Dr. Waite was already at work regressing another inquirer. They left.

Back at Larry's apartment, the couple strove in vain to make some sense of the experiences of the evening. Both had been affected, though Barb's hypnotic trance and fall so overshadowed Larry's momentary panic that they both nearly forgot how shaken he had been over the channeler's mention of the name R'lyeh.

"Larry," she said, "you're so sweet to worry over me like this, but really I'm all right. I'm more worried about *you*."

"Yes, I can see you're fine now, Barb, though I'm steamed at that Waite bastard for not taking any precautions. He's been at this game a long time now. He must know what can happen. But even that's not what has me so spaced."

"What *is* it, then?" she asked, brushing his sweat-greased strands of hair off his forehead.

"It's what you said in that trance, Barb. Do you remember any of it? Doesn't matter much, I guess, because I'm not liable to forget it. I know this sounds crazy, but do you remember me reading you any of the translation I've been working on?"

205

"No, I know you haven't, because, remember, I asked you to once or twice and you said it was too rough and I wouldn't be able to make any sense of it anyway. Why? What on earth does that have to do with what happened tonight?"

"Just this—" he turned and stared out the window into the empty parking lot outside. In the wan moonlight he could see, even at this distance, crisp, curled autumn leaves floating in rain pools in the cratered blacktop, barques on the River Styx.

"You were chanting some of the words from the *Text* as I've translated it. In fact, your version's better than mine."

"I . . . Larry, I don't even remember what I said. In the dream I seemed to understand it, but when I woke up it was all just gibberish, and I forgot it. What is it that you seem to be afraid of, Larry? Do you think someone's sneaking a look at your work, planning to pirate it or something like that?"

"I can't say. It's like I'm looking at something so huge I can't put any shape to it yet. Listen, I better walk you home."

"Okay, *mein Docktorvater*, it's done. I wanted you to be the first to take a gander at it." Professor Maitland rose from where he had been ensconced, seemingly forever, among his clutter of open books, scattered papers, and artifact paperweights. It was almost like seeing one of the figures in a museum display of ancient Egypt walk out of the diorama. He picked his ribbon-strung pince-nez off his vest and secured them on his thin nose bridge with one hand as he reached out to grasp the sheaf of smudged and interlineated pages with the other.

"Of course, it's far from the final typed perfection demanded by the rules of the Institute, and the footnotes are going to take a while . . ."

Larry's tired voice trailed off as his old mentor brushed the words away as a distraction. "This is a great day, my boy," the old scholar said, not once lifting his eyes off the page before him. "I had thought I never would live long enough to see the riddle of the *Text* unraveled. I failed myself, but it took new blood, a fresh mind, to find a new approach . . ." His voice, beginning to constrict with emotion, faded into silence.

"Here, Professor, let me show you something about one of the charts. I think . . ."

"Never mind, Mr. Stanton; I may not have proven capable of deciphering the *R'lyeh Text*, but I'm quite confident I can decode anything *you* wrote! Run along, now. The faster I can get to it, the sooner I'll have my suggestions for revision to you." He was slowly returning to his seat, eyes on the second page, posterior following its own guidance system back to its point of origin. "Hmmm . . . Yes . . ."

Speaking more to himself than to the other, Larry replied, "Yes, I'd best be on my way. There's another little mystery I have to clear up. I'll see you later, Professor." He pulled the glass door shut and left a trail of hollow echoes down the hall of the Sanbourne Institute of Pacific Antiquities. From there he turned into the too-brightly lit mid-day streets of Santiago. Intermittently shaded by the waving palms, he strode single-mindedly downtown to the New Age Center where, a couple of weeks earlier, he and Barb had attended the peculiar channeling show.

He had to talk to the mysterious Dr. Waite. He felt sure that if Waite were any more than a fancy charlatan, he would talk to him, be willing to explain how he apparently knew so much of the *R'lyeh Text*.

Back in Professor Maitland's cluttered office, the pages turned rapidly. The old man's eagerness to learn the long-kept secrets of the enigmatic text had been gradually supplanted by the fatherly pride he felt at the accomplishment of his star pupil.

But minutes ago, that feeling, too, had passed. The more he read of the translation, the more uneasy he became. A pattern was beginning to form. He began to see certain damnable connections between the rough rendering before him and other, nearly forgotten, scraps of what he had once, perhaps too hastily, dismissed as quack pseudo-science.

At first his rising sense of unease brought a flush of embarrassment to his wrinkled cheeks, as if what he feared was having to eat crow and admit that certain long-discredited names might after all have somehow anticipated the results of modern linguistic scholarship and thus might be due an apology, posthumous vindication, like poor Galileo finally forgiven by the Pope.

But he realized almost as quickly that this was not the source of his keen discomfort. He could not so fool himself. Professor Maitland began to realize he was one of those unfortunates who knew enough to know that he knew too much. He had reached the end of the document already. For all the months of work that went into translating it, the *R'lyeh Text* was actually quite short. And concise. And clear, *too* clear in its implications.

His face now drained of blood, the old scholar sat a moment deliberating until his course seemed clear. And as if it were all perfectly routine, he gathered the pages of his student's draft translation, made sure they were all there, tapped the edges to make a square pile, and walked down the hall to one of the lab rooms. There he locked the door, dropped the stack of sheets into the insulated sink, and lit a match.

After the manuscript was no more than a pile of ashes, Professor Maitland, with his customary precision, turned the handle on one of the nozzles, making the ash into grey muck. This he disposed of efficiently.

He found the skeleton key and invaded the cramped confines of young Stanton's office. It proved but a few moments' work to locate the material on the Bimini Glyphs, then the previous drafts and the relevant note cards. He almost forgot: there were some computer files that would need to be deleted. No great difficulty.

Then he returned to the hall and rounded a couple of corners to the Special Collections room of the Institute.

The room was empty, as he knew it would be this time of day. With the door locked behind him, the professor searched a moment for the requisite key to open the cabinet in which the priceless and irreplaceable palm papyrus leaves of the *R'lyeh Text* were kept.

When these, too, were a mound of unrecognizable ash, he returned to his office, where he sat again at his desk, found yet another key and unlocked a drawer from which he drew an antique revolver and set it against his temple.

At first it seemed to Larry that no one was in the New Age store, though it was an odd time of day for it to be closed. Repeated knocking, at some cost to his knuckles, finally brought an answer. The proprietor had been meditating, his peculiar timing dictated by some harmonic cycle derived from Gurdjieff, and he did not much relish being brought back so rudely to Samsara.

But he admitted that, yes, Dr. Waite did have an office in the building. The trouble was that he steadfastly refused to see anyone except when he was on stage in his channeled persona. Otherwise, he was just a normal mortal like you or me, with no special secrets to share.

"Speaking of secrets," Larry insisted, striking at what he hoped would be a tender spot, "I'd like to trade a couple with the good doctor, secrets about the *R'lyeh Text*."

That did it. The door ceased in its closing motion and the crack widened again. "Well . . . Dr. Waite might in fact be interested in *that*. You just stay here and I'll see if I can get him to come down."

There wasn't long to wait. The rotund, perfectly bald and fulsomely bearded man hurried to the door and ushered him in and up a narrow flight of stairs with no delay. No pretense of aloofness such as his doorman had shown. "Come up, come up, Mr. Stanton. I can see you and I have much to talk about. No, I'm afraid I don't recall you from the other week. You see, I'm not myself on such occasions."

Dr. Waite's office was bland, laid with a shag rug, lined with pine paneling. The walls supported bracket shelves laden with the expected collection of Theosophical and Rosicrucian titles. Larry's eyes scanned them and paused only to note a couple of crudely bound, apparently privately printed volumes, called *Unter Zee Kulten* and the *Cthäat Aquadingen*. He wondered, not for the first time, what Waite's doctorate was in. Or what school had bestowed it, if any. No visible diploma provided the answer.

He briefly explained what his concerns were, aware that he was telling all he knew with no assurance of anything in return. But he couldn't figure how to open the game without tipping his hand, so he did and hoped for the best.

"As I stated earlier, Mr. Stanton, I'm afraid I can't answer your questions. But I know someone who can . . . if you'll give me a moment." With that, the huge man swiveled in his chair, turning his back to his visitor. He slumped over—so convincingly that Larry made to rise from his chair in alarm that maybe the fat man was having a heart attack. But no, here he came, swiveling around again. And Larry could swear the quality of the light in the room had subtly changed.

But that was not all. Waite himself had suddenly changed in some way hard to pinpoint. It seemed that he had been replaced by an identical twin who was nonetheless plainly a different man. There was a certain imperiousness, coupled with an odd clumsiness, suggesting the insane notion that the entity before him found the human body a singularly ill-fitting garment. The eyes rolled in a distracted manner, yet they were quite piercing when focused on the young visitor.

"Dr. Waite . . . or whoever, I, uh, came to see you a couple of weeks back with my girlfriend. You . . . did one of your past-life regressions with her, and she, she fell off the stage. That's not the problem; I caught her. But before she blacked out, she *said* some things . . . Some strange stuff that sounded a hell of a lot like the language of a very old artifact I had been translating. Something called the *R'lyeh Text*. Just snippets, syllables, but .. ."

The other spoke: "The . . . ? Oh yes, I know what you mean. Quaint, the way you pronounce it. Continue, please."

"Well, sir, that's just it. It's obvious you know something about this text. And I was under the impression it had never been translated, not really, anyway. There were a couple of hoaxes a number of years ago, but . . . Anyway, how did you get access to it? Is there another copy or something? And how did . . . ?"

"No, young man, I have never read it. I cannot read. Your speech is alien to me. Most of what you hear even now is the fool Waite. He is a docile instrument. Such as I cannot speak to you, no more than you might make your wishes known to a slug. But this slave of mine does his best. He is the Gate through which dreams may pass and clothe themselves in the words of mortals."

No more. Waite's form, suddenly vacant of whatever had momentarily occupied it, slumped forward, forehead smacking the desk top a good crack. Larry rushed to the man's side, lifting the unconscious form by the shoulders, holding him erect till he emerged from his stupor, like a wrestler in reverse playback, trying to unpin his man from the mat.

"Are you okay now, Dr. Waite? That was quite a performance, but I .. . "

"It was no performance, you young fool! Listen, I'll be straight with you. The past-life regressions are no trick, either. I represent those who are able to transcend the limits of the body and to search both past and future by mind-voyaging. The hypnotic regressions, as they are called, are research expeditions. Surely as an archaeologist of sorts, you can understand that."

Larry was puzzled, incredulous yet intrigued despite himself.

"Wh-what are you looking for?"

"What you have found: the lost words of the chants necessary to end the imprisoning of the Dead King of the Great Ones. Somewhere along the line the text was lost, destroyed, and with it the knowledge of the past."

A smile forcing itself to his lips, Larry tried to keep a straight face: "You mean, you were trying to get Barb and these others to *remember* those ancient formulae? What the hell makes you think they ever lived down there in Atlantis with you and your buddies? Of all the . . ."

210

"Your surmise is correct, Mr. Stanton. But they could not remember *enough*. The past they visited was too distant. We knew we had to try someone whose knowledge of the lost scripture was *fresher*, more *recent*."

Larry made for the door. "Oh no. You're not hypnotizing *me*, if that's what you think . . ."

Dr. Waite's stare transfixed him like a frog on a gig. He laughed a throaty laugh. "You're too late. Your regression is over, as of *now*." He snapped what looked like a webbed finger.

Larry's eyes opened on a harsh Pacific glare. His bare flesh felt unprotected from the red, vicious rays of the sun, which seemed to come from everywhere, reflected as they were off the choppy waves. He heard himself vacantly chanting the last of the sacred syllables, which, of all mortals remaining on the charred crust of the aged earth, stripped of its ozone mantle, only he knew.

As he caught sight of his arms, which seemed to have been gesticulating without his conscious direction, he knew they couldn't be the arms he had known since childhood: he didn't recognize the leathery reticulation. Where *was* he? *Who* was he? Some memory lingered of a time long ago when he was a creature known as Stanton.

And then the slippery masonry beneath, or perhaps beside, or perhaps above him, gave way, and he choked on the noisome miasma emitted from a suddenly gaping crater. As water flooded into the crevasse, he began to lose consciousness again.

His last thought was of a stray fact from a lecture he had once given maybe a million years ago, something about the digestive system of the mollusk and how it assimilates the tiny creatures it ingests. He was about to learn that lesson first hand.

–1995–

The Transition of Zadok Allen

Some time in the autumn of 1930 an Ipswich fisherman was hauling in his nets and noticed amid his flopping prisoners a metal cylinder which gleamed in the harsh sea sunlight. Leaving the fish to his sons who worked with him, he busied himself with the peculiar object. At first he thought it a stray length of pipe, but as he turned it over in his hands he found it was a sealed tube of exquisite workmanship, pale gold in color and carefully etched with the designs of fabulous fishy beasts and mermen. It was only a little corroded by the sea.

That night by lamplight, when he had a few moments to examine the strange artifact more intently, he found he could unscrew one end of the tube. Inside was an inscribed roll of an unusual parchment. My father (for I was one of his sons with him in the boat) soon decided to donate the metal case to the Newburyport Historical Society once he learned they already possessed a related piece, a golden crown of some type. I asked him why he did not attempt to sell the thing, but he seemed to feel it had wrongly come into his hands, and that he should be better off the sooner he divested himself of it. The written text, however, he kept for some reason. This I learned only years later when on his deathbed he bequeathed the scroll to me. I am fairly sure he had never even read it himself. But he could have. For it was in the familiar characters of our English alphabet.

Though written in English, the text was no less a mystery. I am transcribing it herewith in the hopes that someone with more information than I may yet read the brief account with more understanding.

Testimony of Robert Olmstead

I imagined I had seen my last of the town drunk Zadok Allen following the abrupt conclusion of my interview with him on the rotting wharfs of decadent Innsmouth in connection with certain events which have earned me a certain fame in some quarters and equal notoriety

212

in others. I had found the old toper a ready source of information especially once his tongue had been loosened by the ministrations of Bacchus. In such a state of inebriated eloquence he was quite the raconteur. At the time it did not even occur to me to take seriously his fabulous tales of Innsmouth's remarkable past, and yet now I am in a position to know that his yarns were scarcely half the truth, as distant from the wonders they shadowed as the child's picture of his parents' world is from the reality.

And such were the limits of my own self-blinded earth-gazing when I believed I had seen, or all but seen, the death of Zadok Allen, snatched away by his enemies for saying too much once too often. Following the trajectory of his panic-bulged eyes, I looked away for an instant, turning back but a moment later to find him having disappeared with a lightning speed impossible for however spry a nonagenarian.

It was only several months later, following certain monumental discoveries relative to my own life and lineage, that I found myself able to inquire further into the matter of my boozy companion's disappearance. I will now relate the true issue of those events, though in the nature of the case I cannot make the reader to understand certain references, and these may be more crucial to the meaning of the tale than I realize, myself taking many things for granted that once seemed utterly alien. So let our watchword in what follows be that phrase from the scripture, "He that hath ears to hear, let him hear."

As old Zadok asked me once with a shaking voice, "Ever hear tell of a shoggoth?" That fateful day I believe he found himself borne away in an instant in the embrace of one of these creatures, great amoebic clouds of living stuff, like unto the cloud-chariots of Jehovah and Hadad in the myths of old. Yet it was not his fate to perish either in the salty water or in the devouring acids of the thing's innards. Rather, like Jonah, he rode safe in the belly of a living vehicle, softly ferried within a bubble of wholesome air.

213

Even now I cannot guess at his feelings during this unearthly voyage.

And when he found himself confronted by one of those entities he had for so long feared and loathed, the Deep Ones? One feels certain that the direct presence of this being must have both horrified Zadok and calmed him. At once he felt the inevitability of the doom whose descent he had feared for decades, and yet also the relaxing sense of anticlimax that the reality can never be as dreadful as the expectation of the unknown. He must have questioned, as I had questioned earlier, whether his own experience were real or the product of radical delirium tremens. But then the fish-frog spoke to him.

"Friend Zadok, rememberest thou not thy old comrade? Does there yet remain no trace of thy childhood mate Hiram Gilman? Thou, too, art much changed with the passage of years. My pappy and thine were sailors together in the merchant fleet. Nay, 'tis not vengeance we would have with thee, but other business entire. I am sent to welcome thee."

First sure that it was some trap, Zadok at length was persuaded to understand the benign intentions of his captors. Surrounded by the deep, comforting hues of the deep, Zadok sat and listened, and many matters were made plain to him. Had he never questioned how he lived to so ripe an age, nigh unto the span of the biblical patriarchs? And why had he not long ago thought to flee a place he so feared as he did Innsmouth? Did he not recall what had been promised him as a lad when he had submitted to the Second Oath of Dagon? That rite had bound him to his town and his people. He had that day learned to shout the cry of the bacchantes of Dagon: *Iä! Cthulhu fhtagn!* which no infidel may chant. And his sacramental joining with Father Dagon and Mother Hydra had been enough to secure for him a taste of eternal life. Only so had he been able to last out the decades on the streets of Innsmouth, albeit in an increasingly frail human form. The Third Oath would have caused the eventual change, and Zadok might have joined his fellows in blessed immortality beneath the seas.

And even now it was not too late. He might still find beneath the waves the peace that had eluded him for many decades. He would require no more the false surcease of the surface dweller's alcoholic poisons.

Finally he and his companion (whose outlines no longer seemed so repellant and frightening to him) reached the crystalline portals of Y'ha-nthlei, whose roofless palaces and coral palisades seemed to him little less than the Celestial City in some allegorical tale he had read almost a century before. He was the Pilgrim, and he had at last reached the culmination of a long and meandering progress. The salt of his tears mixed with the briny water about him as the great Being which bore him alighted before the mansion that should henceforth be his own. He realized with a start that the supply of air had long since run out, but that he breathed, like a frog, with no difficulty at all.

From that glad day Zadok dwelt amid the splendor of a thousand dreaming sea-bottom peaks, each taller than any Everest upon the forgotten surface. He wandered, when the mood struck him, through the garlanded streets of submerged Atlantises whose ghostly bells swayed with the drifting currents. He called the fishes by name and patted their narrow heads, danced with the squids and rejoiced to plumb the depths of unguessed chasms where deeper worlds of Elder aeons still lay spread. Girded and crowned like Neptune or Nodens, he bore his trident and shepherded the peaceful flocks of dolphin and nereid. The ears of the Trilobite Kings were attentive to his counsel, and the phosphorescent eels eschewed not his company. Only the rotting hulls of sunken ships reminded him of the world he had departed and which he increasingly suspected of being a childhood dream.

Zadok Allen reigns there still, as he will world without end, notwithstanding that below the cliffs of Innsmouth the tides of the channel pitch and toss the broken-spindled body of an old man who had often used to stumble along the lanes of the half-deserted fishing village.

–1995–

UNDER THE MOUND

He looked at the ancient cylinder and was not surprised. Not even at the unusual caste of the metal, which was an indefinable hue of blue-gray. There was nothing like verdigris or tarnish on it, though, for all he knew, those who had unearthed it might have scraped away such encrustation before delivering it to him. Without having to spend time puzzling over how the tube was meant to be opened, as he had many times with other artifacts, he found the catch piece at once and unscrewed the top. Sure enough, there was a rolled set of sheets inside. These he reclined to peruse. This is what he read.

I was saddened, not particularly surprised, at the news of the death of the ancient Indian shaman Gray Eagle. I had expected it, dreaded it, for some time, for the medicine man was both ancient and dear to me. My connection with him is perhaps not unknown to you, my reader, whoever you may be, since my books sold well a dozen or so years ago. In *Gray Eagle Speaks*, I had simply interviewed the old man, as I wished to preserve the intriguing bits of myth and tall tales of the frontier days Gray Eagle had to share. Here was a genuine treasure trove of Native American lore with few parallels to anything previous ethnologists had been able to gather. In *Soaring with the Eagle*, I had recounted, with initial reluctance, some of the remarkable initiatory visions I had undertaken under the tutelage of the wizened sage. Though popular response was gratifying enough to justify a series of four more volumes on the same theme, the book destroyed any academic standing I had enjoyed among my colleagues. Most dismissed it as fiction. I cannot blame them. I knew the risk I was taking, but I believed that knowledge is gained to be shared. Not to publish my findings would have seemed almost a betrayal of some Hippocratic Oath that all researchers implicitly take. And I suppose that is why I am taking the trouble to write this account, and not exactly under optimum conditions.

On receipt of the news of my old mentor's death, I arranged at once to fly out to Oklahoma, even though I knew there would be no funeral, at least none that a white man would be allowed to attend. Nonetheless, I had duties to perform. Gray Eagle had told me that one day he would disappear into the wilderness to die among the spirits of his people. I assumed this had at last happened, though my informants had not known, or at least not said, whether his body had been recovered. In any case, the old shaman had instructed me in no uncertain terms what I should do. I was to undertake one last vision quest amid the silent and ageless buttes and mesas in the merciless sunlight and the impassive searchlight of the moon. And this I prepared to do. Few provisions were necessary, even by way of maps, for I knew the Oklahoma wastes well from my previous meditative sojourns there.

Once I had arrived in Oklahoma, I hired a car to make my way to the small settlement of Binger, a hamlet which seemed never to have experienced the expansion common to the towns of the region during the great days of the oil boom. Maybe it was better that way; its fate was to have started as a hamlet and, from the looks of it, to finish as one, somehow declining despite never having reached a higher point. No one there, though open and friendly, seemed to have any information to share with me. The Indians kept to themselves, even more than in the old days. At least I knew no corpse had been discovered. So I struck out into the desert, fully expecting to lay the old man to his final rest, though I did not relish discovering him in the state of decomposition he must by now have assumed. Unless, as I hoped, my informant had seen to the task.

I had thought I knew the full extent of the local terrain very well, having covered a great deal of it on foot and in the flight-visions into which Gray Eagle had initiated me. But now, looming above me, was the mute silhouette of an ancient Indian burial mound. I knew at once that it must be the place about which several local legends and rumors circulated, the haunted mound where a headless giant was sometimes observed standing guard, where Father Yig, the Rattler King, held court. With a shudder I got out of the car and approached it. What I felt was by no means fear, but a strange intuition of uncertainty. One never knows what to expect in a vision quest, else there would be no point to undertaking it. But I began to sense that what awaited me was something fundamentally more important, more powerful, if that makes any sense, than the already singular mission on which I had thought to embark. Would there be something atop the mound to justify my forebodings? Perhaps the wasted body of my friend? There was but one way to find out.

The ascent was easy enough, despite the unusual height of the mound, since such climbs are common in the work of the field anthropologist. Hunches, too, are the stock in trade of my profession, and I soon found that I had been half right, anyway. There was indeed a supine body at the

218

top. I cannot say that it rested in death, for its contorted posture announced that death had come at the end of a fierce struggle. What manner of wilderness predator had attacked the man I could not readily guess. The wounds had been horrific. There was no longer any head attached to the tattooed torso. After a few moments' careful scrutiny I concluded that the man had not been of Indian stock, nor had he been so hideously dismembered in the final struggle. Incredibly, the tissue at the end of the neck-stump looked for all the world like old scar tissue. This was a forensic puzzle like none I had ever encountered. How could the manifest death wounds on limbs and chest have looked so much more recent?

I looked over the edge of the mound to where my car was parked below and considered how best to load the carcass onto the vehicle. In order to avoid damaging the remarkable specimen further, I should have to arrange a makeshift harness and hauling line, though with the materials in hand, I could not see how this might be accomplished. So I left the problem for later and calculated what to do next. My directions to the place had been given me by Gray Eagle some years before, so it could not have been this strange corpse to which he had meant to direct me. There must be something else. And to that I must now turn. Archaeology would have to wait.

It was finally the shifting of the evening shadows, as the sun relented and began to sink, that revealed the open shaft leading downward. By a trick of optical illusion, the opening had been hidden in plain sight up till now. I unclipped my flashlight from my belt and did not hesitate to rush in where angels might fear to tread.

Given the aridity of the area, it was no surprise that the uneven walls of the descending shaft were free of nitre. At first I imagined that I was making my way gingerly through a natural crevasse in age-old rock—until I came to my senses and realized the obvious: that burial mounds are artificial structures. I had noticed details that might imply human craftsmanship, but these I had subconsciously dismissed. Now I realized they must indeed denote the hand of a designer, unless they denoted something quite fantastic. Could this possibly be a natural structure which happened to look like the work of the ancient Mound Builder cultures? Or, the crazy inspiration occurred to me, might this stony heap have served as the prototype for all the other mounds? Was it, like Moses' Mount Horeb, a natural edifice revered as sacred space because of its singular structural regularity, or because of some great event that had

219

taken place here so long ago that even ancient Indian lore retained no trace of it? I could be sure of nothing except that at this point, in this odd place, no possible explanation, no matter how far-fetched, could yet be ruled out.

Down and down I went, never finding the going particularly rough (again, possibly implying human artifice), until I began to perceive that my flashlight no longer cut so stark a swath through the surrounding darkness. Could my high-power batteries be failing already? No, for I immediately realized, switching off the light, that the darkness about me had itself lightened considerably. From whence could this misty vapor of radiance be emanating? Were there unseen fissures to the surface that functioned as ventilators? This could not be, however, as I noticed the light had a queer bluish tinge to it. It was not natural sunlight, then. As my eyes adjusted to the vague half-light, I found I could see the ceiling above me in closer detail. It seemed to be carpeted with a coat of luminescent fungus or moss. That added up to one mystery solved, but only by another. I knew of no such species. Not a professional botanist, I was nonetheless fairly certain that no such organism was known. This was a day of strange and unsettling discoveries, and this was by no means to be the last of them.

The colors of the illumination seemed to shift toward the purplish end of the spectrum and to brighten, the further down I went. My watch had stopped somewhere along the line, and I had unaccustomed difficulty in estimating how many hours had passed in my descent. My feet and back had commenced to ache, and this surprised me, implying I had spent a great deal more time here than I consciously marked. I began seeing great tree trunk-like pillars, which, to my relief, did not actually block my progress. At first I thought I had found definitive evidence of human artifice—until I noticed that the structures seemed to have been formed by the slow growing together of stalagmite and stalactite over many centuries.

The pillars, as I could not help regarding them, did manage to limit my field of vision until, suddenly emerging from between two of them, I stopped in my tracks, gazing slack-jawed at an astonishing panorama before me. Only a few feet away, the shaft widened drastically into the rim of a vast inner cavern. Traveling any faster along the rocky tunnel, I should certainly have plunged out unwittingly to fall to my death below, like water reaching the end of a drainage pipe and rushing with futile momentum in an arc to the surface below. As it was, it looked like I would have to use the greatest care to negotiate a sliding path down the precipitous, nearly vertical, wall of rock slanting down and away from the tunnel-hole.

I was a moment gaining my bearings. First I made sure of my footing and, before descending, I scanned the scene before me. It was good that I had troubled to secure firm footing, since what I next beheld would have been sufficient to bowl me over. I now saw not merely a cavern outstretched below and beyond me, but a virtual world. The actual extent of it could not even be guessed, but it seemed to extend for ever and ever. The tunnel mouth from which I had only just emerged was but one of many, as I could discern at least two others at irregular distances and varying heights along the gently curving cavern wall before it faded into the misty distance. The sky above seemed filled with an atmospheric nebula of the same bluish light-vapor that had illumined my way in the tunnel. It masked the cave ceiling far above, but the latter was probably too high to be seen anyway.

Turning to the level plain below me, I was relieved to see a winding road which eventually led to the tunnel mouth where I stood. In the other direction, I was shocked to see the outcropping clusters of villages and towns. Most of these lined the banks of a serpentine river, crossed and recrossed far more often than seemed necessary by a thousand basalt bridges of elaborate design. These I must examine more closely.

As I made my way carefully down the rubble-choked path, my eyes found it easier to focus. It immediately became evident that the place was populated—or had been. I did not at first see the bodies (numerous though they were) because, upon examination, they seemed to be somehow translucent, suggesting the ghostly likeness of certain deep-sea creatures. Some seemed oddly unstable, as if their tissues had begun to sublimate directly into the air. Needless to say, I had never seen anything like it. Who had?

I examined the clothing of several. The garments were marvelously well-preserved—but then I had no firm reason to believe them ancient, or even old. Most wore tunics or robes which seemed strikingly reminiscent of both Aztec and Greek designs. I shook my head, knowing that here I had found such evidence as every scholar half-dreads: that which threatens to reshuffle the whole deck of cards, to destroy the conventional picture of cultural evolution.

But a more immediately puzzling question presented itself. What had happened to these people? I saw nothing living in all the miles I walked, tireless with wonder and dread. I made for a large city in the distance. I

221

guessed it must be this place to which Gray Eagle had sought to direct me, since the specified way of ingress had probably brought me closer to the city than any of the other tunnels would have. Perhaps my answers, about the fallen race as well as the deceased Gray Eagle, lay there.

I passed a great number of the supine, translucent forms, so many that I soon lost count. All of them seemed to be fleeing from some menace, though the positions of some suggested desperate confusion, as if the poor wretches sensed the futility of their flight. As if there was no safety to be had in the whole of their underground world.

As the walls of the city, the name of which I would soon learn to be "Tsath," loomed up before me, my eyes were drawn by the huge sculpted bas-reliefs flanking the great city gates, one of which had fallen forward onto the ground, as if from some terrible impact from within.

The two great images faced one another, whether in menace or in friendly embrace, I could not tell, since the aspect of both was so alien as to be unreadable. On the left was an octopus-headed titan which seemed to lumber slowly forward to meet its neighbor. The image on the right was that of a vast serpent, coiled in an elaborate, almost Celtic-looking basket interweave. Mighty fangs, more like tusks, curved like sabers from the wide mouth, and scales shaded into feathers in a ridge or fringe along the creature's spine. I hesitated before passing through the portals into the city, half-fancying that the two carven behemoths might be alive, poised to rush together and crush me to pulp as I passed.

But enter I did, finding none but the dead and disintegrating to keep me company. Building after building had been carved or painted with murals mutely charading an ancient and horrific mythology. I could find evidence of no gods anywhere. All the figures depicted, when not plainly representing the perished underground race, were devils and leviathans, each more hideous than the last. Were any of these terrible figures supposed to be the gods of the subterranean race? Or had they worshipped nothing but devils? It was not a pleasant thing to contemplate—but then neither was the prospect of what it must have taken to send these monster-worshippers bolting in panic!

At length I began to associate most of the recurring images with aspects of the remarkable lore once taught me by Gray Eagle. He had spoken of certain matters only in evocative hints, but the clues were clear enough in view of what I now saw. I concluded that the octopus titan must be none other than the fantastic Tulu, who had first shepherded primordial humanity to the earth where they reigned in the kingdom called Kuen-Yian. The other being, the snake-creature, must be Yig, the Rattler King, prototype of Quetzalcoatl and the Hydra. Others were probably to be identified with the deities Nug, Yeb, and Nigguratl. Often these figures were shown mounted upon the rampant forms of lean and rangy beasts I knew must represent the dreaded Yith-Hounds. The names and their frightful tales were familiar from the arcane teachings of Gray Eagle, but even their forms were known to me, first-hand, from the visionary journeys upon which I had embarked into the intermediary realms between this world and the next. There I had beheld the frightful forms of the Wrathful Deities. I had never thought to see their effigies in this world.

And then, as I traversed a shadowy avenue of the great mausoleum-city, my eyes fell upon something else whose image I had never expected to behold again on earth: the wizened form of Gray Eagle. There he sat in the shadows, whispering so softly that I must have been only subliminally aware of the sound when I turned at no apparent provocation to spy the form of my teacher. He sat, cross-legged, in the drifting shadow, as if the darkness were only a greater thickness of the ubiquitous blue vapor. I hastened to bow to the pavement before the figure, scarcely able to believe what I was seeing. Like the dumbfounded disciples in the gospel accounts, I was speechless before my restored Master. I knew no words from me were required. I waited for him to speak.

When it came, the voice shook with the weight of unnumbered decades. It wavered more than I was accustomed to. There was also a strange tone as of buzzing or hissing in the otherwise familiar voice. But who could calculate the effects of such acoustics as prevailed here? At any rate, I gave little thought to the matter as I strained to catch every revelatory syllable. I will not reproduce verbatim what he said to me, though I believe I could, because some secrets are not good for mankind to know. What I will vouchsafe, though it will sound outlandish enough, was, believe me, merely the outermost fringes of the terrible secrets I heard that day.

The old shaman had a tale to tell surpassing the most extravagant legends he had ever regaled me with in years past. And it concerned the devastation of this, the underground world of Kuen-Yian, where scented gardens no longer bloomed, where the echo of silver bells on the wind was no longer to be heard.

The cavern-world's history receded back into remote antiquity and unto far-flung worlds of madness. The myths of Tulu bringing the race's progenitors to the new-formed earth were true enough, though the intergalactic journey was not made in physical form. The adepts of Kuen-

223

Yian had long ago mastered the art of mind-projection. It was in this incorporeal form that a group of them had joined Great Tulu on his slow, winging pilgrimage to this world. Upon their advent they displaced the minds of a primitive hominid race which, from what I gathered from Gray Eagle's sketchy description, must have been rather below the level of Neanderthal. The humanoid form took a bit of getting used to, but no doubt it was easier than the adjustment required of the poor primitive earthmen who now found themselves possessed of the original bodies of their usurpers: great, segmented millipedes. Ironically, the poor devils were doubtless as confused by the advanced technology of which they could make no use as by the primitive-seeming bodies they wore.

Once ensconced in their new domain, the dwellers in Kuen-Yian eventually grew uneasy with the confines of the underground world. They feared the surface world, always expecting a new wave of extraterrestrial colonizers like themselves, some variety of intelligent crustaceans (I realize my narrative only grows more implausible, and that I may well have lost any reader before now!). At an earlier stage, barely mentioned by Gray Eagle in his urgency, the men of Kuen-Yian must have suffered terrible losses in conflict with these "space devils." So when the lust for conquest struck them, they turned their attentions downward, to other, deeper cavern worlds of which they had become aware. Below the blue-lit world, it seemed, there lay another, filled with red radiance, this one called "Yoth." And below this there yawned a lightless abyss called N'kai, the ancient lair of the polar deity Tsathoggua. My mind was by now spinning with the knowledge of worlds within worlds and unknown universes beyond.

To conquer the reptilian denizens of the Yoth-world was a simple matter for beings with the psychic talents of Kuen-Yian. After the use of clairvoyant powers for reconnaissance, they would first assign the appropriate number of their own men to enter a fortified retention zone, then have them concentrate on those below, exchanging minds with the Yothians for long enough to place the latter's minds in their own incarcerated bodies. Then, wearing the scaly bodies of their captives, they would make their way to their own level and perform the soul-projection in reverse. It was a bloodless, yet entirely effective, maneuver. And yet perhaps the victory was not as definitive as it first seemed. One of the elder sages of Yoth had silently vowed revenge.

I had it in mind to interrupt to ask how on earth Gray Eagle could possibly have known such details as the inner thoughts of a member of a vanished alien species. Despite my years of confidence in the old man, my own faith in him was beginning to slip. I had accepted a great many outrageous assertions up to now, but I found myself listening as to a fictional tale (just as you, reader, must feel perusing my own).

The shaman, as he always had, knew my thoughts before I could voice them. And his answer to my implicit query was even more fantastic. Nonetheless, certain things began to fall into place, his astounding longevity, for instance. I had attributed his remarkable span in some vague manner to his occult disciplines, his knowledge of obscure herbs and medicaments. But this hypothesis I had never dared examine too closely. I suppose I had feared to hear something like this. Gray Eagle was no Indian. Instead he was none other than the captive Yothian elder himself. And his moment of vengeance finally came.

Signs of the religious preoccupation of the men of Kuen-Yian were everywhere, especially of the cults of Tulu and Yig, as I have said. Over the centuries, Gray Eagle recounted, the people had progressed from a literal belief in these deities (which Gray Eagle himself seemed to share) to a more philosophical creed in which Great Tulu and Father Yig had become allegories for various natural forces and ideal principles, much in the manner of the Stoic abstraction of lusty Zeus into the pantheistic Logos. This was followed in turn by a period of decadent ennui in which the more venturesome of Kuen-Yian experimented in a playful way with the old rites of Tulu and Tsathoggua. Gray Eagle saw all these developments, since he had been one of the elite among the Yoth-prisoners eventually to be received freely into the Kuen-Yian society, as occasional venturers from above or below had been for several centuries. And he knew well what the people of Kuen-Yian had forgotten.

These were no games they were playing. Consulting the ancient Yoth manuscripts plundered from below only served to confirm his fears, for he knew that the time was nearing when the constellations would assume once again their ancient configurations heralding the glorious return of sleeping Tulu. He more than half-suspected that it was the subtle influence of the stirring god that had awakened in the frivolous worshippers the peculiar desire to adopt the mummery of the old faith. And if Tulu should arise, the world would fall, both the world above and that below.

Though Gray Eagle had no love for those whom he still regarded as his captors, he resolved to turn them from this disastrous course. He was willing to share the world with even those of Kuen-Yian as long as there remained a world to share. He wasted no time in trying to convince any of the rulers; he knew he could expect naught but rude incredulity. So he returned to the study of the old Yothian scrolls, at last concluding that his only hope to stop the blasphemous consummation lay in an equally perilous move. He would summon the entity, N'Yog-tha, the dweller in the deep fissures of the earth. He was the last and the mightiest of the vanished race of N'kai who had in ancient days retreated below to unguessed chasms. He might be summoned to wreak havoc among one's enemies, as the dubious myths of Yoth related. Gray Eagle would invoke him secretly while feigning participation in the Tulu rites. The ensuing chaos should end the dangerous liturgies. And if somehow Tulu made his appearance anyway, if things had already gone too far to be stopped, why then, it might be that the two titans would meet in battle and annihilate one another.

Gray Eagle went ahead with his plans, and the results were still manifest. It was in flight from the rampaging N'Yog-tha that the doomed dwellers of Kuen-Yian met their terrible deaths, as I myself had seen. All this had happened generations ago. At that time, Gray Eagle had taken the opportunity to escape the ruins of Kuen-Yian and gain his first look at the surface world. There he had experienced little difficulty in taking a place among one of the Oklahoma Indian tribes. Changing his appearance, whether in reality or by hypnotic illusion, he took the name Gray Eagle and became a shaman and hierophant of the cult of Yig. He achieved great fame among his adopted people in the nineteenth century during the last stages of the U.S. government's take-over of Indian territories. Determined not to see the White man treat his adopted countrymen as the men of Kuen-Yian had dealt with his own people of Yoth, Gray Eagle became the leader of one of the smaller Ghost Dance movements who sought to turn back the invaders by magical means. Of course these efforts failed, at least the ones chronicled in the history books. But there was one unaccounted clash in which an entire detachment of U.S. Cavalry had simply vanished as far as anyone knew.

He lived thus in self-imposed exile for many years, an object of curiosity among frontier villagers and of tremendous veneration among Indians. All was well, if uneventful, as he rested content in the assumption that he had prevented the impending advent of monstrous Tulu.

But only months ago the old man's tranquility had been shattered by some arcane intimation that the appearance of Great Tulu had only been delayed, not stymied. The glacial progress of the turning stars allowed plenty of time, and now the time was near. Gray Eagle had returned to Kuen-Yian to wait and see what would transpire. His occult powers had grown much since his escape from Kuen-Yian, but he doubted they would be of any real use in preventing Tulu's return. What he planned, if anything, he would not tell me. I wondered if he planned again to summon N'Yog-tha, but he would say nothing either to confirm or deny the suggestion. Why then had he called me here?

The old man was silent, as if not sure how much to explain to me. Finally he spoke. His intention was that, in the event that Great Tulu were to be freed to ravage the earth, someone should escape the general dissolution to carry the knowledge of past ages into whatever future might someday evolve. I should be that messenger. But how?

Gray Eagle had managed to learn something of the astral time-voyaging practiced to such great effect by the men of Kuen-Yian. It was by these techniques, combined with his own Yothian clairvoyant and hypnotic abilities, that he had eventually discovered that the Kuen-Yian inhabitants had not really perished but managed to project their minds forward into the bodies of a far-future race. But they had found their new physical forms and environment (much more like those of their own ancient home across the galaxy) so amenable that they quickly settled into the familiar existence and actually came to forget their unearthly origins, claiming the heritage of the future race as their own history. And Gray Eagle, who had both seen and made so much history, could not bear that a whole planet should sink into lazy amnesia. He knew me for a scholar and a teacher who could not deny such an opportunity as he now offered me. He knew me well. My old mentor began to emerge from the murk of the shadow-mists, revealing a heavily beaded and mottled reptilian hide where before his powers of mesmerism had caused the image of a lined Indian face to appear. I had ceased to doubt his story, even though it had only become more extravagant as it lengthened. But now there was proof positive of his wild tales. I gazed upon the sole surviving visage of a reptile-man of hidden Yoth.

His hand reached for me with serpentine ease and rested with an icy touch upon my forehead. He continued to speak, but not in audible sounds. His thoughts appeared directly in my mind, in my memory, as if he were reawakening dormant recollections, something like déjà-vu. At any rate, I shortly knew what I had to do to make the jump. Like Lot, I took no time to consider what I was leaving behind, of what might be destroyed by an impending cataclysm. Gray Eagle allowed me no more time than was necessary to pen the narrative you are now reading. It was, I supposed, another attempt at preserving knowledge of the past in case my mission should fail, or perhaps to corroborate it should that be needful.

227

From here on in I can only look toward the future—and try to enter into it.

Here the inscribed sheets ended their peculiar story. It was not easy for him to roll them up and insert them back into the cylinder. So he left that for the archivists. Zkafka was one of the scholar gentry of the great insectoid civilization thriving on a strange earth with all her continents rejoined. Now he turned his eight facet-eyes away to survey his own chitinous form, as if suddenly seeing it in a new light. He had somehow known that one day the manuscript would surface. It had, and he had read it. Now he was certain, terribly certain, that the peculiar dreams of a past existence in the form of a hairy biped called "man" were no mere dreams, but memories. It was all true; that he could no longer doubt, since one of the most disturbing dreams had been that of writing this very manuscript.

–1995–

YOUNG GOODWIFE DOTEN

A crowd stood gathered just outside the iron fence of the Duxbury churchyard. They watched closely as John Doten shoveled the last spadeful of graveyard dirt back into the small plot and made to tamp it down. Then the young man, bowed with the effort of the task but more with the need for it, stooped and brushed away bits of flying dirt which had clung to the new marker, a somber stone tablet engraven with the familiar winged skull design. His young wife stood only a few feet distant and wept quietly, as did some in the uninvited multitude beyond. Others in that band, however, seemed to be shuddering more from fright.

All alike swiftly dispersed at the approach of the bereaved couple. The man had recovered his threadbare black coat and had his shovel slung over his shoulder like a musket. His other powerful arm rested tenderly about the still-heaving shoulders of his wife Prudence. One or two from the crowd extended a word of sympathy, knowing such to be a seed that never reached its mark to sprout. For what words can comfort the parents whose infant the Grim Reaper has claimed?

But others in the crowd sought comfort for themselves as they secretly traced the sign of the cross over gray and black-clad breasts. And it was their eyes which followed the slow progress of the couple down the street to their small, wood-frame house just off the town commons. So slowly and gravely did they move that almost they seemed a funeral procession in their own right.

The afternoon had grown late, and storm clouds encroached, as they did so often in the season. Before long not a soul lingered in the streets of Duxbury of the region of New Dunnich. All alike soon drew close around blazing hearths, some offering up prayers for the grief of their neighbors, others thanking the Good Lord that misfortune had passed them by this time. And others still clinging close to the light as if they feared the shadows.

For all of New Dunnich was in the grip of the witch-fright which had now spread all over the Massachusetts Bay colony, the contagion having spread outward from Salem and Arkham. Few misfortunes did not cause the fear either that the witchcraft had caused them or else that the

Almighty had levied punishment for deviltry. And thus were the townsfolk divided in their regard for young Goodwife Doten and her husband. Had some witch dame foully hexed her? Or was she herself another secret trafficker with Satan? For this was not the first instance of her losing a baby, whether before or during birth. Surely these misfortunes could be no accidents, and many pious village tongues had decided that her womb must be poisoned with the devil's gall.

Goodwife Doten had herself heard such whispers and paid them no mind, save that she bemoaned lost friends who durst not be seen with her. Indeed, few remained to comfort her in her latest hour of sorrow, only her fine husband. And John Doten contemned those whom he called old hens and vultures, the gossips of the town. His attendance at the meetinghouse was not frequent because his faith was not great, and he liked not to play the hypocrite, no matter the ill-will this might earn him from some quarters. He sat now before the raging fire alone, Prudence having retired to the bed. The day had been long and a heavy burden to bear. And besides, she was still weak from the ordeal of childbirth. John gazed into the leaping tongues of fire and let his mind drift into thoughts and dreams of the future which looked so far away.

Scant moments later, he was roused from his reverie by a firm knock at the door. Rising, he hastened to open the door and offer hospitality to whomever might wait upon his step. It had begun to rain, and he would be as good a host as Abraham had been.

The open door revealed the imposing form of the parson, the Reverend Abijah Hoadley. His impassive features did not relax as he entered, removing both tall broad-brim hat and heavy woolen cloak. These John took as the clergyman began to offer his sympathies for their loss, his stern visage belying the tenderness implied in his words.

"How I regret not being able to stand at your side in the hour past, but I fear the great number of ill congregants required my attention till late in the day." Thus he spake as he took a proffered seat before the fireplace.

Of a sudden Goodwife Doten appeared from the bedroom, pale of cheek, and both men rose to acknowledge her. All sat as the somber Mr. Hoadley addressed her. "My child, you have my heartfelt condolences. And my prayers as well, for I would not that the lack of God's blessing should cause men to doubt your sincere love for the Almighty."

"Then, good Parson, you do naught but echo both mine own hopes and prayers," replied Prudence Doten. "For 'tis true that I love God, and it taxes me to think why he may see fit to try me in this manner."

230

The parson rose, saying, "It is good to hear such pious sentiments from a pure heart. And sure am I that our Lord shall in due course reward such faith as he did the faith of Job. Now I must beg your pardon, as I have many rounds to make, even in such weather as this."

As he closed the door behind the belling cape of the Reverend Hoadley, John Doten could not hide his indignation. "His deceit is rank and fools me not. I doubt not that it is the Reverend Hoadley himself who is the chief rumor-monger! Note how his artful words ill-conceal his own belief that you bear the barrenness of Sodom's ground, cursed of God!"

Prudence rose to return to bed and made no reply. She hoped her husband erred but feared he did not. "True, he preaches of a Sabbath little else than the judgment of heaven against the wizard and the witch. Nor does he suffer a witch to live, and in his zeal, I am persuaded, the innocent suffer. They fall not before the wrath of the Reverend Hoadley's God, but of the Reverend Hoadley himself. And I like not the thought of incurring his wrath in my own case. But what is to be done?"

John Doten sat down upon the side of her thin mattress and took her pale hand in his own. "Beloved Prudence, we dare not wait any longer upon the grace of God. Nay, but let me speak," quoth he, motioning her to silence. "Mayhap there is a path open to us, and seeing the danger that looms, I say we must take it. And it is in no wise perilous, I feel sure."

She shaded her eyes with her hand. "You speak of old Goody Watkins, out by Briggs' Hill. Think not I have not oft times considered her. It seems to smack of heathenism and is more than a little redolent of Sarah's unbelief when she made Abraham go in and beget by Hagar. But it may profit us to consider her ministrations. It is said she is one of the Wise Women of old, and that she has knowledge of herb and root for healing. When my strength is restored, I will betake myself to her cottage. It may be that the Lord helps those who help themselves. But we must take care that none knows of it."

"Aye," agreed John, refreshed by new hope, "for it is naught but her keeping her distance from Duxbury that has spared her the zeal of the mob ere now."

Weeks passed before Goodwife Doten felt sufficient vigor return to make the trek out beyond the village limits. But she felt hale and hopeful as John made her comfortable in their small wagon and prodded the horses forward onto the Briggs' Hill road. They had taken care that all knew their feigned plan that Prudence should visit her cousin Elspeth in Zoar for a fortnight. John should return once he had seen to her safe arrival. As innocent as this might sound, suspicion, having once been kindled, feeds on any available fuel. So their wagon, as it drove out of sight, was followed by doubtful eyes. The road out this way was not well kept up, as few traveled it. Their progress over the rocky and weed-grown lane was bumpy but as swift as one might ask under the circumstances.

At length the time came to tether the horses, leave them munching a reward of carrots, and scale the steep incline leading to an almost hidden cottage resting against the face of Briggs' Hill.

John sought to gain a glimpse through the grimy window set into the oaken-boarded door before knocking. This effort proved futile, but even as he raised a fist to rap upon the wood, the great door came open with surprising ease. Before the startled pair stood a wizened, stooped form, chirping in a brittle but loud voice, "What business have ye w' Goody Watkins, she who but seeks to serve the Lord in silent retreat?"

"Old Mother," John began, unable to suppress a quaver in his voice, "we come to you for aid, for medicaments of a type. We . . ."

For the first time in their married life, Prudence Doten dared to interrupt her husband. Taking his arm, she stepped between John and the remarkable tiny figure and said, "Mother, my womb bears no fruit but thorns and thistles, children who do not live outside me. It is said you are able to help women such as I."

Old Goody Watkins appraised her with a calculating eye. "Surely you know what the Governor has done, how he has cut off the witches and the wizards from the land . . . not that I am one of them, mind you! Why would you lay a snare to bring about my death?"

"Aye," cried John Doten as he stepped again to the fore. "We know well what the Governor has wrought, a plague that rages and that threatens to take my good wife if she bear not a child! The fools charge her with diabolical trafficking, believing her misfortune the result of divine misfavor! Lady, we humbly crave your help, else there be no help for us at all. We await your mercy."

The old lady remained silent for a moment, during which time Prudence thought she heard the noise of scampering within the cottage. In these woods, that should afford no surprise.

"Very well. You shall have my help. Missy, you will share my modest accommodations for a few days. I see by your baggage you are prepared for that. Good. But no man may cross my poor threshold." Withal she placed her fragile arm about the younger woman's shoulder and led her into the cottage. John Doten could see his wife's furrowed brow as she gave him one last look before the closing door took her out of his sight.

232

He returned to the wagon, not without a sense of foreboding, yet not at all regretting their decision. He took the reins and turned the obedient horses about where they would head for a shaded creek. He would do some fishing to fill the time before heading back, so that none should mark a premature return for one making the trip to Zoar and back.

Goody Watkins proved an amenable host to her young charge. She bade her take her own rough bed, which was yet softer than that Prudence slept in at home in Duxbury. Old Goody would daily retrieve and mix certain dried roots and other substances hard to identify into foul-smelling broths and teas. These Prudence dutifully drank up, trying to conceal her distaste. Once or twice she remained alone while her caretaker journeyed into the woods or the fields to procure some ingredient of which she had run short, or which could not be kept in powdered form.

A week passed speedily before Goody announced, "Now ye be prepared right well. It is a toilsome affair. But one step remains. Dearie, I vow ye know those tales in the Scriptures where the barren conceive?"

"Oh yes, Mother Watkins, I have read them often and treasure them in my heart. They are the stories of Sarah, of Hannah, of Manoah's wife, of Elizabeth and Mary the mother of our Lord."

Goody Watkins tittered, "Well do ye know them of a certainty! A pious lass. Tell me, then, if you can, how the Good Lord did answer their prayers to open their closed wombs."

Prudence felt as if she were back in catechism class, but she was sure she had the answer ready to hand. "It was a miracle of the Lord whereby his Spirit did overshadow the holy women."

The arthritic finger wagged in mock rebuke. "I think ye hasten through the inspired text like a lass too eager to run from the schoolhouse and play! Think again, missy. Did not Jehovah send his angel to do the deed?"

Prudence paused in puzzlement. True, an angel had appeared from heaven to announce the birth in every case. But she had never taken the meaning old Goody now suggested. It seemed to her faintly blasphemous . . . But she had resolved to put herself into the kind old woman's hands, and so far she had seen no reason to regret her decision.

"You will understand better when midnight strikes. I will betake myself elsewhere. And you may expect a visitor who will complete what we have begun. Now, dearie, it were best you try to sleep." So saying, her strange benefactor gently closed Prudence Doten's eyes. At once she began to feel drowsy. Perhaps it was the effect of one of the herbs Goody had administered that afternoon . . .

She awoke abruptly in deepest darkness. The interior of the cottage seemed filled with rushing, airy presences. Had the window come open? No, in the dim moonlight she could see it was still securely fastened. And now she believed the cloud-dimmed rays of the moon faintly silhouetted a figure standing before her, at the foot of the bed. As clouds swept past the moon outside, the room grew a modicum brighter, and she could see it was not after all Goody Watkins, as she had momentarily assumed, but rather the tall figure of a man. And she could swear it was the form of a Caribbean slave which stood silently before her, his jet black skin of a piece with the enfolding midnight. But, no, as the room grew lighter still, she rejoiced to behold the familiar smiling face of her husband John!

He came to her and she welcomed his embrace. John Doten was a passionate man, and never more so than tonight, and yet she marked a certain coldness of member. But this she quickly dismissed as she felt herself yield to a thrill she had never before, as a Christian woman, dared to feel.

Goodwife Doten awoke the next morning under the watchful gaze of Goody Watkins, who sat and knitted. "Ah, my lass, I believe that now you understand Goody's exegesis of the Scripture, do you not? Was it not the rapture of heaven that visited you last night?"

Prudence Doten blushed crimson at the tittering of the old woman whose discretion should have withheld such a remark. At this, old Goody only laughed with greater vigor and shook her head.

"Where is John?" the younger woman asked, sweeping the small space of the cottage with wide eyes. "He must still be here, surely?"

"He will be here soon enough, my girl. My friends in the woods have told me so. Even now he approaches. But look."

Here came her husband up the hill, almost losing his footing as he squinted to see if he might catch some sight of her. Dizzily she arose, gathered her sleeping clothes and opened the door to greet him.

The big man crushed his wife to him with an enthusiasm she found surprising given their reunion of only scant hours before, but she was ill-inclined to complain. The two of them thanked their smiling benefactor and without a word John placed a jingling pouch in her claw-like hand. They departed, and Prudence did not like to admit the relief she felt at being away from the old crone.

Weeks passed, and husband and wife felt both joy and fear when it was discovered that Prudence was again with child. Would all turn out well this time? The village gossips speculated freely, but Prudence tried not to listen. She had other matters to consider and there was much planning to be done. The conviction grew in her, even as the baby did, that she would indeed bear a living, healthy child. Oft she would pray, "My soul magnifies the Lord, and my spirit rejoices in God my savior, for he has done great things for me, having taken away my reproach among women."

John came to feel more confident as well, though he could not keep calm on the day when it came time to summon the midwife. The distant baying of Squire Weston's hunting dogs hardly helped the state of his wrought nerves, and he paced nervously to and fro as the moment neared. How he wished he might somehow ease the pains of his dear wife whose moaning was loud enough for the neighbors to hear. He doubted not that most of the village waited without, fully as anxious as he. And then the loud moaning seemed to grow yet louder. Something must be amiss.

In the bedroom his wife emitted a throat-skinning shriek. He rushed in. Blood was everywhere. The screaming continued, and the midwife came close to knocking him off his feet as she bolted from the room. In shocked confusion he surveyed the close quarters of the room and his eye registered the tiny form of the new baby squirming on the bed, stained by a tangle of umbilical cord and thick blood.

He stooped to grasp the little bundle, his eye still half on his distraught wife. When he focused on the little one now cradled in his arms, he recoiled, slipped on the bloody floor and involuntarily threw the small form back onto the bed where its flapping, membraned wings and coiling tail spattered blood droplets in every direction.

For the first time in many a year Goody Watkins dared a stealthy entry into the village of Duxbury. She had heard of the unfortunate sentence passed against John and Prudence Doten, and now she had to see for herself their abandonment to the flames. All eyes in the commons were focused on the two smoking forms, though through the curtain of flames one could no longer determine which was which. With the crowd thus preoccupied she feared no danger for herself, albeit she kept an eye open for the Reverend Hoadley whose vigilance one might never safely discount. He himself had lit the fire which had consumed the Doten baby with the full blessing of the High Sheriff only an hour before.

It was all too bad, she had confided to her own son later that night, as she rocked him before the blazing hearth. "In his own way, I thought he was rather cute." As if to agree, her boy turned over on her lap and motioned with one rodentine paw for her to scratch his belly.

–1995–

THE SOUL OF THE DEVIL-BOUGHT
I

The telephone rang with a sound one does not typically expect telephones to make. This one sounded like a gong, and was in fact attached, in an arcane manner recalling the hammer and tympanum arrangement of the human ear, to a medium-sized brass gong somewhere in the surprisingly vast interior of the apartment. Muffled as it was by the many Oriental rugs and elaborate tapestries that insulated nearly the whole lay-out of the place, the mellow depth of the sound still managed to penetrate every inch of the strange domain. There would be but a single ring in any case, but this time, a dusky hand reached out to the dumbbell-like receiver in a second flat, as the giant possessor of the hand, a turbaned and taciturn Sikh, had been standing like a posted guard next to the intricately carved teakwood pillar-table on which the telephone sat like a museum antiquity. Akbar Singh spoke the monosyllable with something suggesting imperious urgency: "Yes?" Then, "What is your business with my Master?"

The statuesque Sikh stood apparently alone in the book-lined study, as if he were a cigar-store Indian included among the exotic collection of antiques, curiosities, and finely bound books crowding the place. It was not his own sanctum sanctorum, and yet he seemed alone in it—till all at once the highbacked leather swivel chair behind the great mahogany desk spun around to face him. And the face he saw was an accustomed one for all its peculiarity in the eyes of most of the few who saw it. His subtle Eurasian visage remained as passive as the Buddha's, yet his obliquely slanted eyes beneath a high, unfurrowed brow, seemed to smolder with adventurous expectancy. It was almost as if he was following the telephone conversation telepathically, as perhaps he was.

Dr. Anton Zarnak rose and reached across the cluttered desk top to receive the telephone from his servant. His eyes closed as he listened, as if meditating, as seeking to pick up signals from his caller that the other was not intentionally sending. The silver-white lightning zigzag that mounted up from his widow's peak to disperse through his otherwise jet-black mane of hair might have suggested, had Zarnak's imposing mien permitted the thought of levity, the drawing of psychic forces to his magnet-like brain.

"Yes, Mr. Maitland . . . soon to be *Doctor* Maitland, is it not? Yes, I thought so. I was expecting your call. Never mind how, but it was the next natural development. No, that's all right. I assume you are calling with reference to the Winfield inheritance? I am not without my sources, my resources as you might say."

Through all this, the giant Sikh let a small grin draw up the corners of his mouth. He was amused at the obvious confusion his master's prescience produced in such inquirers. He was no stranger to the feeling himself. And if he felt a hint of amused superiority now, it was not because he understood Zarnak's secret any better than the nonplussed caller; he had simply become accustomed to the inexplicable. And now Dr. Zarnak was handing him back the receiver.

"We will depart at once, my friend. I felt it best not to require our scholarly caller to leave his ivory tower to venture the shadowed courts of our Oriental Quarter. The Sanbourne Institute is no appreciable distance by car, and I suspect it will do us both good to get some fresh air." Akbar Singh nodded as he stepped away to fetch his master's coat. Fresh air indeed; he had breathed little but the drifting incense for some months now, half-suspecting that the fumes were meant to instill in him some psychic sensitivity or else protection. He did not really care to know more.

II

As the black sedan purred its way beyond the cobbled labyrinths of the Oriental Quarter of Santiago, its driver felt relieved to open up the throttle, at least for a while, till the famed Southern California freeway system, then in its infancy and innocent of the nightmare traffic jams of the next decades, brought them further inland to the Sanbourne Institute of Pacific Antiquities. To this institution the renowned Dr. Zarnak was no stranger. Indeed, it was from this place that he had earned the latest of his several doctoral degrees. His association with his alma mater was congenial, though he was scarcely the average alumnus.

Zarnak was, however, not infrequently called upon to date or authenticate certain relics obtained by the Institute from various questionable vendors on River Street, where the wharfs disgorged all manner of strange cargo brought in from obscure ports of call throughout the Pacific and Indian Oceans. There was no use in scrupling over how such items were obtained, since legality meant little in most of the places these traders frequented. The antique objects might as well have been

238

freshly exhumed from Davey Jones's Locker as far as any Westerner could tell. And if one or one's institution did not take advantage of such opportunities, it was not to be doubted that others would.

It was on a related matter that Zarnak was calling on Jacob Maitland, zealous young graduate assistant at Sanbourne, just nearing the end of his doctoral work and about to get his thesis in final shape to defend before his committee. He had done his work on a curious old document called *The Ponape Scripture*, a palm papyrus manuscript brought to the Sanbourne Institute not long before by the ill-fated scholar-explorer Harold Hadley Copeland. Maitland had occasion before now to contact Dr. Zarnak, whose acquaintance he had made during the last months of Zarnak's own work at the

Sanbourne. He had read Zarnak's dissertation, *A New Scrutiny of the Polynesian Genesis according to the Cthäat Aquadingen*. Young Maitland had at once perceived the crucial utility of some of his elder colleague's methods as applied to his own project, for he suspected that the obscure pages of the *Ponape Scripture* might be written in some lost variant of the Naacal language of fabled Mu.

Maitland's story, and his dire suspicions, began to unfurl as he welcomed Dr. Zarnak and his manservant into his tiny office. His name was stenciled onto a cardboard plaque taped to the pebble-glass of the door. As a graduate assistant he had little status and few prerogatives, and those few did not include spacious accommodations. Glancing at the massive frame of the Sikh, Jacob Maitland suggested perhaps the faculty club or even the library might be more conducive, but Zarnak insisted privacy was the more important consideration, and Akbar Singh modestly retired from the scene, announcing his intention to stay with their automobile outside.

It seemed that Maitland had been highly annoyed at a duty assigned him by his supervisor (manifestly because no one else with the right to delegate the noisome matter had any hesitation in exercising that right): he was to seek out a Mr. Winfield Phillips, heir to the property of one Hiram Stokely, an eccentric recluse for whom no living contemporary had any use—save for the famous Harold Hadley Copeland, himself the great benefactor of the Sanbourne Institute. Copeland had at some point managed the unthinkable, to purchase from the cantankerous Stokely two priceless old volumes, *Die Unaussprechlichen Kulten* of F. W. von Junzt and the *R'lyeh Text*, with which Maitland knew Zarnak to be more than familiar, together with some manuscript pages from an oddity called *The*

Yuggya Chants. How he had been able to persuade old Hiram to yield up these volumes no one at the Institute could even guess, unless, as some suggested, Hiram Stokely had found the books were of no further use to him, as if such relics could have any use other than bibliographic delving.

Copeland had eventually bequeathed his own vast collection of idols, manuscripts, modern volumes, maps, diaries, and what not, to the Sanbourne Institute for Pacific Antiquities. Once it had been discovered among his diaries that his copies of von Junzt and of the *R'lyeh Text* had come to him from Stokely's collection, the trustees of the Institute naturally wondered what else of similar scholarly importance might lie moldering in that late eccentric's library. Could not some arrangement perhaps be made with the heirs, a pair of the old man's nephews, Brian Winfield and Winfield Phillips? According to the local scandal mill the two had moved into the decaying hacienda-style estate of the hated Hiram Stokely some weeks before to set up an openly homosexual household to the outraged consternation of the poor white trash of the nearby town of Durnham Beach whose Puritanical scruples apparently did little to hinder their own squalid decadence and inbreeding.

Soon a new scandal had replaced the old. Perhaps rumor had merely substituted a new lie for one that had become old hat, but it was noised about that, whereas formerly the two young men had been inseparable on the few occasions they had ventured forth into town, now one caught sight only of Winfield Phillips, whose air seemed distracted in an ominous way, though no one, not even the gossips, could point to any specific evidence of foul play. Perhaps some lovers' spat between the two dandies had driven the offended cousin away under cover of night, or perhaps he had taken his own life in a moment of maudlin despair, as homosexuals were wont (or thought) to do.

Jacob Maitland found these reports half-plausible, having read somewhere of Phillips' keen interest in the Decadents. He judged no man for his private affairs, but the Durnham Beach gossip was more than casually interesting to him simply because it had fallen to him to make the first cordial contact with Winfield Phillips, and he feared on the basis of these reports that the man might be arbitrary and unreasonable in his dealings. When Maitland soon discovered, in addition, that Phillips had for a number of years been associated with the Miskatonic University in an analogous capacity to his own at the Sanbourne Institute, he began to dread that his counterpart might have designs on whatever precious volumes might remain, intending to donate the books to the Hoag Library of Miskatonic, and thus to strengthen his own position to gain a choice

240

faculty position. This possibility sounded all the more likely to Maitland, because he had hoped, by securing any such rare books for the Sanbourne's collection, to advance his own scholarly career. Well, there was nothing to do but drive up to the Hiram Stokely property and discuss matters as amicably as he could with Winfield Phillips himself.

Phillips had not bothered to restore telephone service to his uncle's house, apparently sharing some of the old man's eremitic inclinations. So Jacob Maitland had little choice but to make the long drive through the dreary mudflats and acres of stunted scrub pines to the old hacienda—and just hope Phillips would be home. Given the desolation of Durnham Beach and the surrounding acres, Maitland considered it unlikely Phillips would be busy at anything away from home. The peculiar look of the midget forest of scrub pine made him think of the legends of the New Jersey Pine Barrens which, according to local superstition, housed the fantastic Jersey Devil. Looking at the local equivalent of the Barrens, he could well understand how the desolation of a place like this would incarnate itself in legendary form.

He grimaced as he realized he was driving past the blasted acres of the infamous Hubble's Field, the routine excavation of which some years previously had yielded shocking revelations of many ages' worth of human sacrifice and mass murder. These ghastly revelations had effectively doomed the adjacent town to eventual desertion, as no one would move there. Even the surly denizens of Durnham Beach seemed to despise their ancestral habitat, though no appreciable number had ever sought to leave, not even a few years back when there had been a rash of strange disappearances, mostly of children. It seemed to Maitland that something kept the Durnham people rooted to their poisoned land, so that the thought of fleeing never even seemed to cross the minds of most. What could keep an outsider like Phillips here? It was no wonder that his boyfriend had left, no doubt deciding that he had had quite enough of these surroundings.

III

Zarnak listened with inscrutable silence as Maitland continued to fill the narrow confines of his office cubicle with details of his story. The younger man more than once paused to reprove himself for boring his guest with over-ample detail, but the latter assured him that no fact ought to be neglected. "Sometimes, my young friend, the memory is but a camera which records details which mean nothing to us but which may speak volumes to another who examines the picture it has taken. Go on."

Maitland had no idea what to expect when his knock was finally about to be answered. What would Phillips look like? Maitland had seen a poor photo of the man, standing literally in the shadow of his erstwhile employer, Dr. Seneca Lapham, a professor at Miskatonic, the subject of the photograph. But that was some years ago, in the aftermath of some queer business in Billington's Wood somewhere in the Massachusetts countryside. And who knew what effect some weeks of dwelling in this moldering old pile might have had on the man? Especially given the decadent habits local gossip tarred him with.

But the sight he saw was even more unexpected. It was not Winfield Phillips, nor even his reputedly vanished cousin. The figure before him, despite his undistinguished manner of dress, was plainly an American Indian (of the once-local Hippaway people, as Maitland would later learn). This taciturn man, whose prominent cheekbones shaded curious scar patterns, must have been taken on by Winfield Phillips, with some of his new-found wealth, as a factotum. That the man was an Indian might imply that none of the nearby townspeople would willingly work for him, though, God knew, there were few enough employment opportunities in the ghost-town community.

Each man momentarily contemplated the other in silence, Maitland at a loss for words, the Indian awaiting some remark to which he might reply. Finally, as Maitland began to sputter false starts of embarrassed cliché, the Indian, a much older man, simply pointed to himself, saying "E-Choc-taqus."

Maitland managed to get out his own name, albeit stumblingly as if he were not quite sure of it, and then a third figure joined them. This man introduced himself as Winfield Phillips. He did at least match the general impression of the man in the photograph, though he had somehow the appearance of being substantially older than his thirty years should have made him. Perhaps the unaccustomed duties of settling his late uncle's affairs had worn on him. The burdens of everyday life often took a greater toll on those whose minds were characteristically at home with scholarly abstractions, as Jacob Maitland knew only too well.

Maitland extended a hand and received a shake with a hint of reluctance. "Pleased to meet you, Mr. Phillips. I wonder if I might come in to discuss something with you. About your inheritance, you see."

The other's eyes narrowed in a combination of suspicion and interest. "The assessor's office? But I thought . . ."

242

"Oh, no, nothing like that, Mr. Phillips. I'm from the Sanbourne Institute."

"All right. Do come in. I'm afraid I've had quite enough of federal, state and local jackals appearing out of the woodwork, each expecting a share of the carrion. Forgive the imagery."

"Uh, surely," said Maitland, removing his hat and handing it to the Indian servant, who at first seemed not quite sure what to do with it.

The place was sumptuously furnished, mostly in Victorian style, something Maitland noted with a subliminal note of relief, for he hated to see homes where the inner decor belied the outer shell, or, worse yet, where the oblivious new homeowner had no sense of propriety and would mix styles haphazardly. But then he realized that Mr. Phillips must simply have had the interior of the old place cleaned out and repaired as necessary, not bothering to second guess his ancestor's tastes in furnishings. Still, that very effort implied Phillips' intent to stay and make the home his own.

Phillips had led his guest into the library and indicated a seat on one of the couches facing the fireplace, while his servant stoked the fire in the grate. Taking a seat in a wing-back leather chair opposite Maitland's perch, Phillips sat comfortably like the lord of manner, settling into the familiar contours of a favorite chair.

"At first, as you may know, Mr. Maitland, I came here from back east, thinking merely to attend my uncle Hiram's funeral and to take care of a few items of business over at the Sanbourne. I'm afraid I haven't got around to that yet. Affairs here have kept me unexpectedly . . . busy." He gazed emptily up at the high ceiling, as if looking through it to deeper gulfs beyond. "I had planned to sell the old place, but the longer I stayed here, the more I began to feel at home, I can't say just why. In fact, I almost had the feeling, silly isn't it, that I had *returned* home here after being away. No, I had never been here to visit Uncle Hiram, though I confess to feeling that I know him better, living among his things this way."

Maitland could not help noticing that in all this garrulous speech, Phillips made no mention of his cousin and companion Bryan Winfield. It sounded as if his cousin had formed no part of the events. Maitland wondered what else he might be strategically omitting. But then Maitland's role was simply to negotiate for some old books, not to play the role of detective.

"Well, to come to the point, Mr. Phillips, speaking of your late uncle's possessions, I am here to tell you that the trustees of the Sanbourne

Institute are curious to know whether his, that is, your library might contain any more old volumes like those Harold Hadley Copeland once purchased from Hiram Stokely . . .'"

"Yes," Phillips interrupted, "I know the ones you mean. And frankly, I can't imagine what it was that possessed Uncle Hiram to part with them in the first place. In fact, I've been considering asking for their return, so that the Stokely Collection, as I've begun to think of it, might be complete again. Of course you must have had photographic facsimiles made of them by now, you've had them long enough."

This was a blow! Maitland had come to add to the rare book holdings of the Sanbourne, and here he was, about to lose some of the crown jewels of the Institute. He should, he silently rebuked himself, never have come!

"This comes as something of a surprise, Mr. Phillips, but I can surely understand your viewpoint. I'm sure the trustees will be willing to consider the matter. I'm sure it can be settled amicably. Before I go, is there something I might help you with over at the Institute? You mentioned some errand you had there . . ."

"To be sure, Mr. Maitland, I did. But I really don't think I'll bother seeing it through. You see, it had to do with a fellow named Arthur Wilcox Hodgkins, a rather distraught man who appeared one day at Miskatonic, having come all the way across country from your own Sanbourne Institute. It seems he had a peculiar dread of one of the old Melanesian idols from the Copeland Bequest. He sounded more than a little paranoid, if you want my impression. Nonetheless, some of our faculty heard him out and thought it the most compassionate thing to let him take home with him one of our own lesser museum pieces, a star-shaped stone of curious workmanship, which he was convinced would function as some sort of apotropaic device to protect him from the occult doom he feared.

"Newspapers not long afterward reported that his terrors had gotten the best of him at last, that he had gone wild in the Sanbourne Museum Gallery, murdering a night-watchman and trying to set the place ablaze. All this transpired some eight years ago.

"My employer at Miskatonic, a Dr. Lapham, asked me, while I was out here for Uncle Hiram's funeral, to check into the matter, wondering if there were somehow more to the tragedy than the papers thought best to let on. But since coming into my inheritance, I have decided not to return east after all, and as for the Hodgkins case, I rather imagine it best to let sleeping dogs lie, don't you? The Sanbourne is hardly likely to relish the

244

prospect of the whole messy business being stirred up again for prurient public consumption, are they?"

Maitland had indeed heard of the bizarre tragedy of the unstable Hodgkins, whose time at the Institute had not overlapped his own. And he knew there was indeed more to the case, though what it might be, he neither knew nor cared to find out. And Phillips was right: it would be a blessing for the Sanbourne Institute not to have to deal with the publicity nightmare all over again.

"Your point is well taken, Mr. Phillips. Little is to be gained that way. We appreciate Professor Lapham's concern, but to be honest, we would appreciate your own more!" Both men laughed, thawing the stiff politeness of the conversation, though only in time for it to draw to its close. Phillips rose, as the old Indian entered the room.

"Echoctaqus, would you please show our guest out?" The Indian's features remained impassive, but something in his bearing said that the role of underling did not come easily to him. "I'll be looking forward to hearing from Sanbourne about those books, and please reassure your trustees that I'll be more than happy to reimburse the Institute for at least the amount Copeland paid my uncle for them. You won't forget? Good."

A bemused Jacob Maitland followed the Indian servant down the winding staircase to the entry hall and was halfway out the door when behind him he heard the raised voice of Winfield Phillips calling him back.

"Oh, and, uh, one other thing, Maitland, if you please! If you should happen to hear from Dr. Lapham or anyone else at Miskatonic, please be sure to give them my regards and to convey my apologies for what I now realize was a joke in rather bad taste. Thanks so much, old man."

Maitland felt surprisingly relieved to be behind the wheel again and retracing his path through the dismal acres of Durnham Beach and Hubble's Field, silently eating up the miles of the way back to the palm-girded campus of the Sanbourne Institute for Pacific Antiquities. And there his tale ended as well, as his voice trailed off into a question mark. He had asked Dr. Zarnak nothing specific, but both men knew that the whole story was in fact a question, a puzzle, the beginning of a story and not the end of one.

"First, my young colleague, tell me, have you brought Phillips' request before the trustees yet?"

"No, all this happened little more than a week ago, and the trustees won't be meeting for another month and a half."

245

"Good, good," nodded the other. "You must never relay that request, for Phillips must never regain those volumes. And I am sure that his uncle never yielded them to Harold Hadley Copeland willingly in the first place."

"Then how . . . ?" The rounding eyes and rising brows of the younger man finished his question for him.

"I am not at full liberty to say, Mr. Maitland. Suffice it to say that Professor Copeland possessed something well beyond a theoretical knowledge of certain matters that had occasioned his acquaintance with Hiram Stokely in the first place. Shall we say that there were at his service certain resources that enabled him to drive a hard bargain and to get what he wanted? Though you can see the good it did poor Copeland in the end."

"All right, sir, but what about the business of the 'joke' Phillips had made? That struck me as odd, hardly characteristic of the man's general mien."

"You are to be congratulated. You have the keen eye of the researcher. As for the so-called joke, I think I can provide a comprehensive answer there." So saying, Zarnak reached down for a leather valise he had carried with him, opened it, and deposited before Jacob Maitland a neatly typed manuscript of some forty pages. Alone on the top sheet, like a voice crying in the wilderness, stood the single terse line "Statement of Winfield Phillips."

"Go ahead, read it now. It will not take long, and it contains a number of things you will need to know for our conversation to continue. I shall meditate in the meantime."

So Maitland read, unperturbed at first, then with a growing sense of subtle alarm. The typescript began on a somber note, anticipating the writer's own imminent death. Phillips had composed the narrative in the very same house, no doubt in the same room, in which Maitland had interviewed him scarcely more than a week ago. He told of his mission to Santiago, his meeting with his cousin (and here Maitland could read between the lines some possible justification for the rumors of the pair's homosexuality), and their initial exploration of their uncle's mansion. Phillips' breathless description of his chance discovery of a shelf full of little-known classics of the Decadent movement left Maitland cold, as his own interests ran decidedly toward the scientific, not the literary, much less the polluted tributary of the Decadents. But when he got to the subsequent disclosure of centuried copies of John Dee's *Necronomicon* and Gaspard du Nord's edition of the *Livre d'Eibon*, his pulses quickened; here were the books whose hypothesized presence had motivated his trip out to the Stokely, now Phillips, estate. He was aghast at the implied death of Bryan Winfield and half-suspected that the narrator protested too much his innocence in the affair. All in all, much that had been unclear was explained in these mad pages, and yet somehow everything seemed even more mysterious than before.

Zarnak's eyes met his as Maitland at length looked up from the last page. "You are perhaps wondering whether Phillips gave in to the voices that beckoned to him in the end. But deep down, from what you have told me, I think we both know the answer to that."

"Then this is no joke? I was afraid it wasn't. What *was* the 'joke in poor taste', then? And how did you manage to get hold of this manuscript, Dr. Zarnak?"

"I came by it through unexceptional means. It seems that Winfield Phillips mailed the manuscript to his old employer, Seneca Lapham, no doubt immediately after typing it. It was his last act while in reasonable possession of his faculties. It was not long before he regretted having sent it off and wanted very much to allay the fears and questions his macabre account might have occasioned at Miskatonic. He wrote again, assuring Dr. Lapham that the earlier parcel had simply been an endeavor to fictionalize his visit to Durnham Beach for the funeral. It was the discovery of the various chapbooks and manuscripts of Henquist Gordon, Ariel Prescott, and the others that had inspired him to seize upon the macabre qualities of his visit, the funeral, the old, mildewed mansion, and so forth, and utilize them in a pastiche of his own. He claimed he realized only after having mailed it off that he had omitted a cover letter explaining the fictional nature of the whole thing and wanted to supply that lack now."

"To tell you the truth, Dr. Zarnak, I'm not sure I wouldn't have been satisfied with that explanation. But I take it Professor Lapham was not?"

"Correct. He had ample reason to know that truth is often very much stranger than fiction. And then there was the complete surprise of young Winfield abandoning his position at Miskatonic. And besides, even if the manuscript had been a piece of fiction, why on earth would Phillips ever have thought the staid and businesslike Seneca Lapham would have wanted to read its disgusting contents? He is not a man for such trifles, and Phillips knew that better than most.

"Dr. Lapham did not reply to either mailing from his former assistant but instead passed the manuscript on to me for my opinion. When I heard from you, I knew you must see it as well. It is certain that the narrative contains elements that the secretive Phillips now wishes had never been revealed, facts that somehow presumably may be used against him. For instance, did you notice Phillips's initial puzzlement over the unaccountable fact that his uncle, whom he did not know and had not met, should make him, and his cousin, his sole beneficiaries? Hiram Stokely had become estranged from both branches of the family to which the two young men belonged. What could have been his motivation? And something else: what was the reason for the hasty, closed casket funeral?"

Maitland lowered his eyes, covering his features with his hand. "Frankly, I'd rather not guess. But why bother with Phillips? If he turns out to be every bit as mad as that fellow Hodgkins, it's his own business, surely? Why appoint ourselves his inquisitors?"

Zarnak knew that the younger man was having second thoughts. His earlier forebodings were now giving way to fear, and this he sought to rationalize as much as to disguise. "Mr. Maitland, Jacob, why then did you call me into the matter, if not to get to the bottom of it?"

"My only interest in Winfield Phillips was in the rare books his uncle left him. I've told you, even in that errand I was only carrying out the wishes of my superiors here at the Institute."

"Come, Jacob, you don't even believe that yourself. I am a good judge of first impressions, and I realized when we met that you were a true delver into secrets. And we both know that most secret things are concealed for their danger. The righteous hide them away lest their disclosure prove dangerous, while the wicked hide them only till an opportune time, when the secret things would be most dangerous. You knew that from the start, and I believe you know what is at stake here, specifically."

"Hubble's Field. That's the problem, isn't it? The locals think the disappearances will start again, and they'll be next. And it will be Phillips who starts it all up. He'll keep his new allies, the Yuggya, well sated with their blood in return for who knows what rewards?"

"Very astute, Jacob Maitland. I see I was right about you. But what you have outlined is but the beginning of sorrows that will ensue if our friend Phillips is not stopped straightaway. For I am convinced that he was lured out to his uncle's property in order to continue the old sorcerer's terrible work somehow. My guess is that his vampiric allies had no concerns beyond ensuring a fresh supply of human sacrifices. Hiram Stokely had rather bigger things in mind, things hard for a sane mind to conceive of, though I have a few guesses.

"But it was a complex plan entailing much effort. And his devil's bargain caught up with him before he could finish his tasks. More than likely,

Professor Copeland had thrown Stokely's plans awry by forcing him to part with certain crucial volumes he required. You saw how eager his nephew Phillips was to regain them. Somehow, perhaps through the lingering psychic influence in the house itself, young Phillips has been enlisted to carry old Hiram's blasphemous schemes to their completion. At least that is my fear."

"What of the Indian?" asked Maitland, suddenly recalling how strange his presence had seemed. "Is it no more than Phillips having to go outside the radius of the town for help?"

"Would that it were so, friend Jacob. But in that case, one would still have to wonder why Phillips would trouble himself to locate an Indian, of the Hippaway tribe, I believe. There are none of them to be found in a radius of many miles nowadays. I cannot imagine there would be one on the list of any nearby employment agency. And especially not for such work. But his name is the real signal. Does it strike a familiar note with you?"

Maitland rose, put one fist to his hip, touching the folded index digit of the other hand to his chin, unconsciously striking the contemplative pose. "Yes . . . yes, it does, now that you mention it, though I was sure at the time I'd not heard the outlandish jumble before."

No, it would be something you have heard, or rather read, since your visit."

About to give up on the game, Maitland suddenly turned a quarter circle to face him and, with light dawning in his eyes, he almost spoke, then grabbed up the typescript and began shuffling through the pages. "Here it is! The old devil is named for the Field of the Conqueror Worm, *E-Choc-tah* in the tongue of the Hippaway. Hubble's Field. Good Christ! Why would anyone . . . ?"

Zarnak had stood to his feet now and was shaking the pile of pages together to even up their edges once more. "It is a very old tradition, Jacob. Our local burying ground, Hubble's Field, is only one of many such honeycombed horrors. The children of Ubb, Lord of Maggots and Corruption, are active the world over, as many traditions attest. The holy city Jerusalem, now part of the British Mandate of Palestine, had once been a centre of the veneration of Yog-Sothoth, and it was erected in olden times next to an unclean place of Ubb. The Bible curses that place as Tophet, Gehenna, and Akeldama, the Field of Blood. Of it Isaiah writes, 'the worm dieth not and the fire is never quenched.' The demon Ubb eventually seduced to his fealty Solomon, whose great treasures and

249

sorcerous powers are well known, though their true source remains unsuspected by most. In return, Solomon caused Ubb's cult to be established in the Jerusalem temple itself, where it remained till the reforming zeal of King Josiah swept the whole gallery of abominations away."

Zarnak fell silent as the shadow of his man Akbar Singh loomed against the pebble glass office window. The occultist lifted his valise and motioned for Jacob Maitland to precede him. Maitland had not planned on any outings today, but he felt he had little choice but to accompany the strange and almost spectral figure to his waiting sedan. All were silent as the tall Sikh, whose turbaned head brushed the ceiling of the automobile, made the night-black vehicle glide through the urban jungle like a panther on the prowl.

IV

Maitland next found himself standing in the entrance hall of number 13 China Alley, the dwelling of Anton Zarnak. The master of the house himself had quietly disappeared for the moment, and the wide-eyed guest handed his coat to Akbar Singh, who seemed to him as improbable a manservant as the old Indian Echoctaqas. Some mystery lay behind this arrangement.

But just now mysteries abounded. Poor Maitland scarcely knew whether he now found himself in an embassy of some Far Eastern empire or in a compact and overflowing museum whose collection of exotica far surpassed anything the Museum of the Sanbourne Institute had to show. Beneath his feet lay the huge skin of a white Siberian tiger. Suits of gilded armor stood to either side of a doorframe, and their make suggested no armorial style, no particular country or era he knew. He strained to read the small placard mounted on the base of one and thought he made out the odd word "Nemedian." Everywhere his eyes met wonders. From the walls of the corridor mounted animal heads gazed glassily at one another. One was avian, though far too large to be any ordinary species of bird; the other was apparently some kind of boar, but it had altogether too many tusks. He caught sight of what he first took to be a stuffed bat, but it was rather a flying reptile of some unknown type. In a daze, Maitland stepped closer and extended a finger. Yes, the stitching was that of the taxidermist, not of the toy maker.

The gentle touch of the mighty hand of Akbar Singh brought him to his senses once again. He shook his head and followed the direction the giant

250

indicated and soon found himself sinking into a plush chair facing that of Anton Zarnak, who sat with his hands together, like a tripod, his goateed chin resting on their point. On the desk before him was an old book. "I have here a rather remarkable volume called *Original Notes upon the Necronomicon* by an Englishman known to a small circle of readers as Joachim Feery. The text is actually less a commentary than an expanded edition of the terrible *Al Azif*. Where Lord Feery obtained his supplementary information, no man knoweth. But that it has the ring of truth about it, no one has successfully denied. And it has something of interest to say, I think, as to the matter before us. Let me read you something.

The nethermost caverns are not
for fathoming of eyes that see;
it is written in the Scroll of Thoth
how terrible is the price of a single glimpse,
for that the marvels thereof
are strange and awful.
Nor may those who pass ever
return, for in the transcendent
Vastness lurk Shapes of darkness
that seize and bind.
Cursed the ground where dead thoughts live
new and oddly
bodied,   and evil
the mind that is held
by no head.
Wisely did Ibn Mushachab bless the
tomb where no wizard hath lain.
But woe to that town whose folk omit
to burn the wizard and the enchanter at
the stake. I tell you, it will go easier for
Sodom and Gomorrah than for that
town. For it is rumored of old
that the soul of the devil-bought
hastes not from his charnel clay,
but fats and instructs the very worm that gnaws;

251

till out of corruption horrid life
springs, and the dull scavengers of
earth wax crafty to vex it and swell
monstrous to plague it. Great holes
secretly are digged, where earth's
pores once sufficed
and things have learnt to walk
that ought to crawl:
The Affair that shambleth about in the night,
the Evil that defieth the Elder Sign,
the Herd that stand watch at the secret
portal of every tomb,
and feast unwholesomely therein.
All these Blacknesses slither but
seldom from the moist and fetid
burrows of their loathsome lair.
And yet are they less than He That
guardeth the Gateway; that guideth
the rash beyond all worlds into the
Abyss of Unnamable Devourers. For
he is Ubb, the worm that dieth not.
These are the words of al-Hazrudin,
Imam of al-Illah.
The wise shall heed them.

"Well, what do you make of that, my friend?" Zarnak let the massive book fall closed.

The other's eyes had closed during the reading but now sprang open. "But wasn't the author of the *Necronomicon* himself something of a wizard? So Ibn Khallikan attests. And the *Al-Azif* has the reputation of a kind of occult Bible, forgive the comparison. I'm afraid I don't understand, Doctor Zarnak."

"I have thought long and hard on the very matter you mention. Here is what I have discovered, or at any rate surmised. To put it perhaps over-simply for the moment, I have concluded that the *Al-Azif* and the *Necronomicon* are not in fact one and the same. The former was the work of an eighth-century Yemenite demonologist, Abdullah al-Hazrudin. The more notorious *Necronomicon*, while it incorporates various bits and pieces of lore filched from the older *Al-Azif*, is substantially a new work, a series of mediumistic revelations made to Dr. John Dee while he gazed into his scrying crystal.

"Once he had transcribed the visionary material, he stood aghast at the character of it. Suspecting demonic inspiration for the larger part of it, he tried to disguise its true origin by fathering the work as a whole onto the obscure Arab al-Hazrudin. It was a day when the Christians of Europe commonly believed their Saracen rivals to worship idols and monsters such as Termagant and Iblis, so the attribution seemed natural. Dr. Dee dared not simply destroy the blasphemous text outright for fear of what vengeance might be wrought upon him by whatever alien influences had imparted the revelations to him.

"But afterward he petitioned his God for the gift of the tongue of angels, which he called the speech of the antediluvian revealer Enoch, that henceforth he might receive the oracles of God without admixture."

Maitland had been following all this attentively. "And, if I understand you aright, this Feery has rewritten the text in a similar manner, producing some markedly new result?"

"Basically, yes; though in some passages the result is a purified text, something much closer to the tenor of the original, a warning against the forces of darkness instead of a gleeful celebration of them. And I am fairly certain that in this passage we have some clues to our mystery. I will keep my own counsel about some of it till events corroborate my guesses, but I will tell you this. It would be a waste of time to approach Mr. Phillips again. He would surely grow suspicious, no matter what pretext we used to cloak the reason for our interest in his affairs. We must retain the element of surprise, and here is how we will do it . . ."

V

Midnight found a lonely trio trudging through an even lonelier landscape, as Anton Zarnak, accompanied by his servant Akbar Singh and the somewhat reluctant young scholar Jacob Maitland, made their way through the greater part of Hubble's Field, trying to get as near as they dared to the old Hiram Stokely mansion, yet not wanting to risk being seen in the wan moonlight. The farthest quarter of the vast and desolate expanse harbored a very old cemetery, with headstones dating in some cases to pioneer days. Excavations some years before had disclosed the shocking fact that pretty much the whole acreage of Hubble's Field had long been honeycombed with clandestine burials dating back further still, but of course none of these makeshift graves was marked. Work at the site had been suspended while the appropriate county boards met to decide what to do next. Finally, two considerations persuaded them to discontinue the operation and to reroute the planned utility lines elsewhere.

First, the presence there of ancient Indian remains made the place sacred in the eyes of the surviving Hippaways, who appeared as if from nowhere to make their case quite vociferously. Second, since there was no possibility of identifying any of the skeletal carcasses, some of them seemingly mummified, it was thought best not to re-inter them elsewhere. Best let the place alone, dreaming of its enigmatic past. No one came there any more, not even to lay flowers at the graves in the tiny cemetery that lay close to the mansion. Most of these graves were so old that none survived to memorialize dead relatives resting there. It was here that Zarnak chose to start digging. To Maitland's nervous questioning the unflappable occultist replied, "It is always easier when paying a visit to begin by locating the door. These even have their residents' names listed. Rather like your apartment house." It was a grim jest, but neither man laughed.

Akbar Singh's huge muscles swelled as he attacked the moldy mound of graveyard soil, unearthing the rotting lid of a coffin in surprisingly few minutes, as long as they may have seemed to Maitland, who was in constant terror, not of the supernatural, but simply of being apprehended by the local police—as if any were likely to be patrolling the God-forsaken area. He winced at every blow of the Sikh's shovel against the yielding wood of the old casket. Wood splintered as he pulled what was left of the lid free.

"Just as you surmised, my Master—nothing!" Maitland and Zarnak both advanced to the lip of the emptied grave. Maitland spoke first.

"You mean we've taken all this insane risk for nothing? I *told* you!"

"No, young Mister Maitland; please take a closer look. Don't be afraid. Indeed, the coffin is untenanted. That is as I suspected. But I believe we will find something else instead. Now, let's let Akbar Singh finish his work." The Sikh set to again, this time roughly tapping this and that section of the exposed coffin bottom, shredding what was left of the once-fine silken lining. Then a sudden splintering sound.

"The false bottom, sahib." Zarnak joined him, drawing forth an electric torch.

"And the steps? Yes, there they are. Not much, barely more than an uneven incline, I fear, but we ought to be able to make it. Come, gentlemen."

254

Jacob Maitland's reaction to this development may readily be imagined. With a quick prayer, the first he had uttered in many a year, the young scholar followed Akbar Singh, Zarnak bringing up the rear, down the stairs in the crypt. When they finally reached the end of the slippery ramp, which seemed to be a huge mud hill lent what little stable structure it possessed by an underlying heap of yellowed bones, the three venturers were glad to attain level ground again—until, that is, their descending feet splashed through fully a foot of scummy standing water. As they made their slow way forward, feet emerging from the mire with a sucking *pop!* each time, they tried hard to gain a sense of their bearings in case a speedy retreat should prove necessary. But that was of no use: the place was a labyrinth. And echoes defined the height of the ceiling variously the further they went. Once or twice, their heads bumped the rock above them, but then they would shortly hear the distinct sounds of leathery wings fluttering stickily far above them. Once they had to retrace their steps, losing an hour or two, when the ceiling began to close over their heads again and finally lowered to such a degree that passage was impossible. But eventually, they judged, they must be in more or less close proximity to the mansion. If so, soon there ought to be visible piles of gemstones, ancient coins and treasures: the gathered loot of the centuries mined and excavated by the wriggling scavengers who served the repellent Ubb, blasphemous totem of the eaters of the dead.

And, though none cared to point out the fact, it must be soon that they would encounter one of the nonhuman subjects of Father Ubb, unless of course the statement of Winfield Phillips had been a fiction or a macabre joke after all. But too much of it had proven out already for that welcome alternative to hold out much hope.

The moment delayed no longer, as fearful anticipation incarnated itself in the form of an obscenely glistening wave of corpulent viscosity, suddenly rising up before them from the underlying ooze, like a huge erect penis, as Maitland could not help thinking. The thing, which held its ungainly position for several seconds unmoving, had no visible countenance. In general shape it might have borne comparison to a single severed tentacle endowed with a life of its own. Great circular sucker-mouths quivered along its exposed underside, no doubt in eager throes of appetite.

All three men had crouched, bracing themselves for flight or fight, though each seemed equally futile. And it was then, in the midst of the cool detachment deadly danger brings, that Jacob Maitland realized what it must mean that the disgusting creature towered motionlessly, with its presumably more vulnerable underside exposed. It was trying in the only way it might to indicate peaceful intentions. He thought of the passage from the *Al-Azif* which ascribed some manner of craftiness, hence intelligence, to the servitors of Ubb. Without thinking, he blurted out his hunch to the others. Even with the echoes Maitland thus let loose, the posture of the hideous denizen did not change.

"Well done, Maitland!" cried the mud-smeared Zarnak, a ridiculous caricature of his usually impeccable appearance. "And I believe our host is satisfied that you have understood him. Look, there he goes, and I'd swear he means us to follow. Come on!" The bloated maggot-thing slid slowly through the muck and slime that covered the cavern floor, apparently troubling to keep the upper portion of its segmented jelly above the surface, so that it might be tracked and followed. Fully aware that they might well be following along like sheep to the slaughter, the three men saw little in the way of alternatives. And if the Yuggya, for such they must be, sought their destruction, a sudden and fatal ambush would have been a simple matter.

Before long, they began to recognize familiar-looking landmarks. They must, they now realized, have strayed far from their goal, and the beast before them had perhaps been sent to guide them to their destination. Soon the feeble glow of the waning flashlight began to magnify itself a thousandfold as its pale rays fell upon sudden heaps of ancient wealth. Here it was! The forbidden source of the wealth of Winfield Phillips, of Hiram Stokely before him, and of who knew how many corrupted souls in the ages before them? These thoughts barred any momentary flash of excited greed from any of their minds. What they saw was poison, not wealth.

And, as Zarnak had warned them, the real treasures of temptation were the promised secrets of elder blasphemy that lay beyond the veils of human ignorance. They were already getting more of those secrets than Maitland, for one, would have wished. He only hoped he might survive this adventure with a fair measure of blissful ignorance intact.

More than once nearly losing their footing, as their clumsy waterlogged steps landed on piles of underwater coins or fell on the open hinges of old chests that closed like toothless bear traps on their numbing feet, the weary party finally arrived at the chosen destination to which their nightmare sheepdog had guided them. All alike strained and squinted to grasp the outlines of a shadowed image that straddled the rocky cave wall in front of them. Was it some sort of statue? It seemed motionless enough, but then a low moan crept eerily from where its lips would be.

256

Emboldened, the men came nearer, semicircling the pathetic creature fastened to the rocks with a combination of rusty manacles and too-tight cords. It hardly stirred, and anyone could see it had severe anemia. Half-healed scars showed that the man had been often and deeply bled. It was a marvel that any spark of life lingered. But perhaps whoever, or whatever, had done this to him knew ways of prolonging life. Or, more to the point, prolonging death. Zarnak knew that in any case, life could not keep its toe hold here for long. He bent close, gesturing for the others to do the same. The flesh-scarecrow noticed and somehow rallied. A whisper struggled forth.

"Bryan . . . Winfield . . . still alive . . . wish I weren't, damn them . . ."

Suddenly the great worm-thing rose up again, splashing the noisome ooze in all directions . . . Again, it remained upright, directly across from the crucified man, with Zarnak, Akbar Singh, and Maitland between them. As they three involuntarily turned their heads to see the thing standing behind them, the dying man spoke again, this time with a greater steadiness he called forth from some unknown reserve.

"My cousin . . . Winfield . . . yes, *that!*"

Zarnak's whisper punctuated his own: ". . . fats and instructs the very worm that gnaws . . ."

Maitland was turning greener. "But . . . who was it I saw? Surely . . ." He trailed off into dumbfoundment, passive and resigned before one paradox too many. He began to totter, and the tireless Sikh reached out to steady him. Zarnak turned to him.

"Jacob, sahib Singh, unless I miss my guess, the man living in the house somewhere above is not Winfield Phillips, though he bears his face and form right enough. It is in fact none other than *Hiram Stokely!*" The wasted form manacled to the nitrous wall nodded with as much emphasis as it could manage.

"He had read the *Necronomicon* and must have reasoned that he would be able to cheat death by willing himself to linger in his decaying physical form till the maggots got to him. He must have arranged to let his 'impending' death be known, left instructions not to embalm him, and mandated an immediate burial. The sooner he reached the moist and tainted earth of Hubble's Field the better. He had already begun to change in a hideous way, hence the closed coffin ceremony. He exerted his fading will on the loathsome carrion-eaters, till they should have consumed him. Somehow . . ." and here he indicated the swaying bulk of the Yugg-creature, ". . . somehow *this* was the result. But who could abide

257

the thought of living on in such a form? This is where the ill-fated Winfield Phillips and his cousin Bryan came in.

"As young relatives and strangers to him, they could be assumed not to harbor the old family grudges, nor to know the reasons behind them. Old Hiram had chosen them as his heirs for no other reason, hoping to lure them to the old hacienda. His logic was flawless, I must admit. He trusted that they would not be long in discovering the secret of the cavern below the house, probably reasoning that sheer greed, if not curiosity, would impel them on a thorough search of the place for hidden caches of the old man's fortune. The thing that had been Hiram Stokely simply resolved to wait at the foot of the stairway the boys would sooner or later discover off the secret closet in the library, and he would seize the first that came in reach.

"This was the 'Red Offering', the blood his new body needed to maintain it. The first doomed interloper turned out to be poor Bryan here. The Stokely thing expected to be able to establish a telepathic link with whichever cousin remained, counting on a certain psychic predisposition that ran in their witchcraft-blighted line. It worked, and under the guise of promising him Faustian knowledge and wealth untold, he seduced the immature Phillips to damnation. In the end, he worked the wonder of supplanting the naive Phillips's very consciousness, trapping it forever in its own slime-coated body. His plan worked perfectly—until now. We must see to it that the old wizard does not live on to bring his terrible schemes to ultimate fruition, or the whole earth will become one vast Hubble's Field."

"And that, as you know, would be only the start." This was a new voice, and it came from above, no doubt from further up the same staircase the two cousins had perilously descended many months before. It was Winfield's voice, though not Winfield's speech. None of them knew what Hiram Stokely's voice had sounded like, but if they had, there would be no mistaking it now.

A flood light, or so it seemed to the sensitive eyes of the three below, enveloped them, making them a target for an unseen gunman. At once, Maitland went down, though there was no way to judge how severe the wound might be. The impact would have knocked him over, weakened as he was, in any case. Zarnak and Akbar Singh both made for the outer circumference of the beam as fast as they could stumble, while another shot shattered the lolling head of Bryan Winfield. If he had not already succumbed in the previous moments, his message delivered to someone at last, the bullet, meant for Zarnak, freed him. Other shots echoed and ricocheted, competing in volume with Stokely's outraged cries; he had apparently hoped to drain Bryan of a bit more blood.

As Zarnak and the Sikh each found shallow niches to provide a moment's shelter, neither could readily think of what to do next. They had few options as long as the Indian Echoctaqas, for it must be he, held his rifle. But there was one variable in the equation everyone was overlooking—until, that is, it broke the surface of the slime-lake and glided with amazing swiftness to the landing where the newly bodied Hiram and his confederate stood, the latter desperately firing futile rounds at the oncoming behemoth.

"Don't waste your shots, you old fool!" Hiram screamed, the voice of the younger Phillips cracking with the unaccustomed emphasis. As the wriggling missile bore in on them, it became clear that its object was Hiram, and the Indian, casting aside his empty rifle, sailed from the rocky precipice, half thrown, half jumping into the darkness. To his misfortune, he managed to land atop the waiting form of Akbar Singh, who proceeded to provide an appropriate welcome—with his fists.

Meanwhile, Hiram, wearing the form of his nephew, was struggling against a second layer of fleshy, pulpy clothing, as the greasy slime of the Yuggya body engulfed him. The great invertebrate gained new strength as its kissing suckers popped open dozens of veins and arteries all over the now-limp form of his enemy. The screams died down, the eyes glazed, the usurped body of Winfield Phillips shrank like a dried fruit rind. The vengeance of Winfield Phillips was complete.

All this Zarnak saw as he crept from concealment and ascended the stairs unnoticed. Below him, the Sikh and the Indian fought with surprising fury, Akbar Singh's titan strength dampened somewhat by many hours of dull exertion, the Indian's adrenalin pumping away to even up the odds. Still, Zarnak entertained no doubt of the eventual outcome. But as he ventured to approach the quivering mass of translucent, stinking jelly, lapping and bubbling over the desiccated form it had vanquished, Zarnak sensed a sudden and subtle change—for the worse. Something terrible was happening. The Yugg-maggot was regaining its form, its strength, its stature. And it seemed somehow different. Zarnak's sensitive instincts told him what had surely happened: in the moment of death, the demon-soul of Hiram Stokely had again displaced the psyche of Winfield Phillips and regained control of its previous host. Now it meant to pass into the body of Anton Zarnak himself! And the occultist seemed unable to thwart the other's design. He began to feel the separation, the drifting, the . . .

And then he went down, struck by something hard and wet, smacking into the back of his nodding head. As he struggled to hold onto consciousness, he saw from the corner of his eye what had hit him and broken the mesmeric hold the Hiram-thing had exerted upon him: it was the severed head of the Indian shaman Echoctaqas! Akbar Singh had wrenched it free of its moorings in one great effort and used it as the only thing available to disrupt the horror he could see transpiring above.

The desperate maneuver had worked, and now Akbar Singh came charging up the steps, dangerously slippery with splattered blood and ooze. He had seized a torch out of its wall bracket as he passed, and now he thrust it over the head of Zarnak, just rising slowly to his knees, and into the midst of the viscous larva before him. The thing made no sound except for the echoes of stones knocked loose by its flailing, ropy tentacles, the pseudopods randomly erupting from all over its violently quivering bulk. Then came the sound of bubbling and nauseous popping as molten pustules formed and vomited forth their unwholesomeness. Cleansing, obliterating flame swept in seconds over the glistening form of the thing, reducing it swiftly to a crumbling heap of caked ash, which kept collapsing as hidden pockets of mephitic gas imploded one by one.

Glad to turn away from the sickening spectacle, Zarnak and his rescuer made their way gingerly down the precarious steps to see to their third companion. Before they reached bottom, however, they ran into the staggering figure of Maitland, clutching the ripped flesh of a surface wound on one arm, but otherwise almost cheerful, given the circumstances. "What say we vacate the premises before any of Ubb's colleagues get wind of what's happened and come looking to settle the score? And this time, let's go through the house!"

So they did, taking one further precaution. After a quick search, Akbar Singh located a quantity of flammable liquids left over from the cleaning and renovation of the old hacienda. These he dispensed in liberal amounts over most of the extent of the interior. He had saved one of the torches from below the house. Once he was a safe distance from the front door, he warned the others, ignited the torch, and pitched it onto the veranda. Then he turned and ran as if the demons of hell were on his tail. Truth to tell, he wasn't entirely sure they *weren't*. Rejoining the others, he turned and watched the growing inferno. Beside him, Zarnak whispered, as if speaking to himself, "Blessed the town whose wizards are all ashes."

–1996–

DOPE WAR OF THE BLACK TONG

Eerie mists drifted through the place, as though someone had opened the windows and let in the hazy fog that always wandered up from the rotting wharves and sought entry at every River Street keyhole. But it was a different sort of mist tonight, one that bore the bitter tang of opium, and yet even this was not quite right. The low-ceilinged room was almost as dark as the street outside, lit only by the sputtering flames from tapers bracketed to the damp walls. The faint illumination revealed only the supine forms of the usual gang of River Street dope addicts. They shuffled from one hop joint to another, though in recent days several had entered this particular dive never to be seen again.

The narcotic Nirvana served up a counterfeit peace, one with a heavy price, but even heavier than usual tonight. The tableau held for a moment; then the heavy oak door burst inward as if suffering the impact of a medieval siege engine. Of course not even this disturbance could retrieve the attention of the far-gone dope victims in the place, but the sudden noise, like an explosion, galvanized several of the men who must have been feigning their drugged stupor. Throwing off concealing blankets and shawls, a handful of powerful, armed Orientals, their nationalities obscure in this rich gloom, sprang like Siberian tigers to meet the challenge of whatever army it was who had invaded their secret privacy. And it *was* an army: an army named Steve Harrison.

The one-man posse of River Street set his feet squarely, while the blue steel of twin automatics leaped into his fists and began to discharge a hail of white man's justice into the knot of Oriental thugs. When his guns were empty he cast them aside and reached for the Gurkha knife he had concealed in his belt Eastern style. It descended with the force of a guillotine, cleaving the skull of the first of the assassins to elude the rain of bullets and reach him. Himalayan blood spattered Harrison as he pulled the blade free of the sundered wreck of a head and managed to dodge a sword thrust aimed at him. Catching the still-plunging arm between his own elbow and side, Harrison trapped the man long enough to bring his own blade into play again. He hacked the man nearly in two, pulling his momentum only enough to avoid completely severing him and catching

261

the edge of the emerging knife himself.

Chance alone saved the detective from the next of his assailants, as he momentarily lost his footing on the freely flowing gore now puddling underfoot. Tripping awkwardly on a severed limb beneath him, he dropped out of the path of the blackjack aimed at his skull. His black locks whipped like lashes with the sweat of exertion, and below them his blue eyes glowed with hatred and determination. Letting go his blade, he launched a good old-fashioned punch at his single standing foe—who did not remain erect for long. The ham-like fist connected with the bearded jaw, making a loud snapping sound like that of a rotten tree branch.

Harrison stood alone, soaked now with his own profuse sweat and others' blood. His keen eyes swept the dim expanse of the den to check for the possible approach of more attackers—defenders, actually. None came. The place seemed to be littered with corpses, until Harrison realized most were the dreamily tossing carcasses of the clientele. With one exception. Sudden screaming sent chills down the spine of the big detective. Scanning the room again, now sure that the weird shriek must announce the presence of some devil from the Eleven Scarlet Hells of Oriental legend, he crouched in anticipation. A few moments more and he found the unexpected source of the unhallowed noise. It was one of the reclining heaps of doped-up flesh.

Narcotic lassitude had abruptly given way to maniacal lurching and writhing as if the man were bubbling on the griddles of Hell. Harrison had seen his share of bad dope fits but nothing like this. He approached the shaking cot and its terrible burden with a sense of superstitious fear which the earlier fight had not been able to awaken in him. Was the poor wretch demon-possessed? Fighting down the age-old dread of his Celtic barbarian ancestors, Steve reached forward and took the shaking form in his iron grip. Even Harrison had trouble holding him steady for long enough to see the face, and even then all he felt was a sense of dim recognition, as if it were a face he had not seen for many years. Something told him to take the poor devil to safety.

Harrison realized he had only moments to act. More of the Asiatics would surely be swarming in on him any moment. So he gave the struggling skeleton in his arms a quick shot to the jaw. This seemed to sedate him, all right, and the burly lawman hoisted the man over his broad shoulders like a sack of potatoes with no trouble. Quickly he sought egress by the same path he had entered. He knew the slant-eyed devils would never dare follow him out into the open in any real numbers. Even on River Street that would be too bold a move for anyone with a lot to hide.

Harrison's flesh, already mottled with the goose bumps of the uncanny atmosphere of the dope den, thrilled to the wholesome evening cool of the street. Even the clammy embrace of the river mists was a welcome relief.

Dumping his burden into the back seat of a waiting car, Harrison barked an order to the driver and assumed the shotgun position beside him, careful to keep an eye on the still-inert form behind him. As the roadster sped to St. Agnes Hospital on the edge of the Oriental Quarter, Harrison reached over and cupped the unconscious face in his huge hand.

"By Judas!" he exploded, startling the driver, an off-duty cop willing to cooperate with Harrison's unorthodox brand of justice. Almost unseated by the other man's outburst, the driver sent the car veering.

"I thought they'd discovered and killed him before I got there," Harrison puzzled loudly. "But it's him!"

"Who, Steve, who *is* it?" spat the nonplussed driver over his shoulder as he gripped the great steering wheel and tried to right the direction of the hurtling automobile.

"Jong-tso, the little rat of an informer who got me into this damn mess. I got a phone call from him in my office one night. Just happened to be there late. I pick up and it's Jong-tso. I ask if he's got a tip for me on that smuggling racket, but no, he says, it's somethin' else, somethin' big. Somethin' about a secret Oriental gang called the Black Tong. He says they're peddlin' some dangerous dope."

Pulling into a vacant spot near the emergency entrance, Bill Waterman, the driver, turned around with a look of incredulity in his eyes. "Him? Jongtso's about as likely to be upset by a run of bad dope as a Holy Roller is about a poisonous snake, Steve, and you and I both know it."

The two men pulled the sleeping figure of Jong-tso from the car, one taking his sandaled feet, the other his armpits. Steve replied, "Yeah, but to tell you the truth, that's why I was so interested. I figured it must be somethin' out of the ordinary. So I agreed to meet with him. Found him in one of the waterfront saloons and heard the whole story—or at least more of it. It's still mostly a mystery. Even more so now. Jong-tso said he was worried because he had relatives, friends, disappear after visits to certain joints, like the one we just patronized. Others came back but soon died. They knew something was wrong, but they didn't dare go for medical help because, scum like them, they couldn't be seen in public. Jong-tso and I agreed he'd take a turn, try to switch the dope at the last minute, see if he could sneak some idea of what's goin' on in there." The

263

conversation continued after the little Chinaman was admitted. The detective and the policeman waited in the room outside.

"But Steve, there's doctors in River Street who make their living off wharf rats like him when they need somebody to lick their wounds. Why didn't the chinks go to *them?*"

"Some did. Mostly the doctors wouldn't help them. Oh, they did at first, but then they clammed up, as if they recognized what was wrong but were somehow afraid to get involved. That's why I brought Jong-tso here, to a white doctor. He might not be able to decide what's wrong, but if he can, I'm betting he'll at least tell us."

At this both men lapsed into silence. Bill gave in to sleep. He had joined his friend after an already long day on the job. Harrison scarcely noticed the snoring as he unfolded a pocketed copy of a girly mag he'd picked up at the newsstand outside. But the charms of the wenches in its pages were not enough to distract Steve's racing mind. He could think of nothing now save the looming peril which hovered over River Street, a menace all the more ominous since its outlines were not yet visible. How can you prepare to fight what you don't know? Steve had never shirked a good fight, but he had to know what he was up against.

Where lust couldn't overcome Steve, weariness finally did. He joined his partner in Morpheus' grasp until he felt himself rudely shaken awake by the hands of a doctor who was saying something in urgent tones.

"Where did you get this man? And, more important, where did he get this . . . this . . . poison that's in him?"

Straightening his stained slouch hat and his crumpled necktie, Harrison blinked and stammered, "Why, Doc, I'm not sure I can tell you that until you tell me just what's ailing the little . . . er, what's ailing my friend. Sort of police business, you see." So Steve spoke, as he took out his Private Investigator's license, soon paired by the addition of Bill's hastily produced police badge. Now, if anything, the physician looked even more scared.

"I might have known! Officers, come with me, please." At this, the three men entered the swinging door and found themselves in a hospital corridor. The reek of disinfectant assailed their nostrils almost as foully as the opium had only a couple of hours before. They lingered here only a moment as the doctor whispered some instructions to a nurse, then rejoined them. "Let me introduce myself. I'm Doctor Randall Bennet. This way, gentlemen."

Another door opened into an oak-paneled office, the walls of which were thickly covered with certificates and diplomas from various institutes of medical learning. More than a few of these were apparently not American, if the languages were any indicator. Steve, a man with minimal education, glanced at them with admiration. He figured he had learned what he needed to know in the professional school of the streets, but he respected any man who took his trade this seriously. As his eyes turned to the fine mahogany desk where the doctor was now easing his spry frame into a well stuffed leather chair, Steve noticed the older man had withdrawn a huge and odd looking volume from a shelf and had it marked in a particular place.

"At first, I thought I must be mistaken in my diagnosis, but even a second test produced nothing that fit the usual possibilities. It was only on a whim that I took a look at this old thing. We doctors don't like to admit we're beat, you know, and sometimes we'll go to pretty nearly any lengths to avoid having to. So I saw this as my last resort."

"What is it, Doc?" Harrison grunted. "Some kind of a Bible?"

"In a manner of speaking, yes, Mr. Harrison." The doctor paused to wipe his glasses, as if seeking a moment to decide how much of a secret matter he could risk divulging to two strangers.

"I'm not sure I should even be telling you this. But you say your friend isn't the only one? If this is spreading, I guess we've got to try to put a stop to it."

Harrison leaned forward in his chair, impatient with the doctor's soliloquy. "A stop to what, Doc? I've got to know!"

"Very well. First I'd better tell you about the book. Otherwise the rest isn't going to make much sense." He indicated the worn spine of the massive book. "Do you read German?"

"Nope, just English. It's good enough for me. Suppose you tell me what it says."

"*Unaussprechlichen Kulten.* That's the title. It means something like 'Unspeakable' or 'Nameless Cults.' It's a kind of encyclopedia of madness and nightmare, compiled many years ago by an old German savant named Von Junzt. The man was possessed of a thirst for strange knowledge. His contemporaries compared him to the legendary Doctor Faustus."

"Are you saying this Von Junzt sold his soul for what's in that book?" quoth Harrison, skeptical and yet trying to fight down a returning sense of uncanny fear.

"Sold his soul? Why, yes, I suppose he must have. The book contains accounts of his travels to strange, forgotten places, some of which reputable scholars still swear are pure myth. In one chapter he claims that

Hell is a literal place somewhere on this earth, and that he was there. I won't tell you what he claimed to have learned there. I don't think you'd sleep any better than I do." Harrison's brow knitted in interest and in fear.

"How'd you come by this thing, Doc? I can't imagine it could be printed legally."

"You're right. It isn't. And I agree: It shouldn't be. What I've got is the Bridewall edition. Rare enough, though there are supposed to be even rarer versions with more text. I can only guess what horrors lurk in their pages. I came by this one not too far from here, in a hovel in your own River Street. I was called there on a medical emergency. Street violence, too late when I got there. A man shot down in front of a book store, actually a front for darker dealings in the back room. Apparently somebody had dumped a load of old books robbed from a mansion outside of town. Putting two and two together, I later decided they must have belonged to old John Grimlan. You've heard the name?"

Harrison was paying rapt attention. He had indeed heard the name— plus plenty of stories that still made his nape hairs prickle. He just nodded.

"The way I figure it, thieves broke into the house after his death and took the books for valuable antiques. They thought they'd be able to fence them easily but found no one wanted anything to do with them. On River Street people seem to know of things like this. They must have finally sold them off for pennies just to get rid of them. I happened to spy the title that day and bought the book for a ridiculously small sum. Certainly small compared to the price I've since paid for reading it.

"You see, the book had been the subject of rumor in medical circles for some years because of certain herbs and drugs Von Junzt was said to have catalogued, poisons mostly, worthy of a Borgia, but often the same substances can be used for medicines, too, in different doses. Even for anesthesia. I had never paid much attention. It seemed moot, since the very existence of the book was dubious. But once I saw it, I had to know. The rumors turned out to be true enough. I found the information in a chapter on assassin cults. You wouldn't believe some of the ways human beings have devised to kill each other. Many deaths today are dismissed as freak accidents because doctors don't know what Von Junzt somehow found out."

"Doc, are you saying Jong-tso in there has been given one of those drugs? Will he survive it?"

He shook his head. "No, I am afraid the Chinaman is already dead. And
266

it's good for him that he is. Believe me, he would be much worse off if he lived. But of course you are right. It was one of the drugs Von Junzt listed, something called the Black Lotus. And if somebody is spreading it around, there's a lot more at stake here than some local drug ring. And it's not even the drug, as terrible as it is, that's the real danger. It's the Powers who cultivate the drug and what they use it for. It wasn't designed for anything as mundane as opium dens, Mr. Harrison."

Steve rose to his feet, sensing the interview was at its end. "Well, what *was* it designed for, then?" The doctor was looking down at his desk blotter.

"The details aren't clear, I'm afraid. I told you my copy is one of an abridged edition. I've my suspicions, but they're much too vague to be of any real use to you. I don't have an answer. I'm just giving you a look at the puzzle you brought me when you brought in your dead friend."

"Thanks, Doc," Harrison grunted. As he turned to leave, Bill following him, more puzzled than ever, Steve said, "I think I know somebody who may have the answer or at least know how to get it."

Steve Harrison knew he was out of his depth on this one, far out. He didn't explain much to Bill, dropped him off home to a relieved wife, and continued back into the Oriental Quarter. It was late now, but Harrison couldn't afford to wait until a more civil hour. He guided the borrowed roadster down the more brightly lit streets of the Quarter, his headlights banishing slinking furtive shapes who feared to be transfixed in the beams. Parking by a local Buddhist temple, the safest place he could think of, he covered the rest of his route on foot. Here the layout of the Quarter bore the look of an ancient Eastern city, becoming a maze of aimless alleys and convoluted back streets and cul-de-sacs. No map would be of any help, and the cobbled pathways would never accommodate a car.

He had never had occasion to seek the address he now approached. He knew the man by reputation only, and he had always hoped it would stay that way. Still, when dealing with the mysteries of the East one had to resort to the ways of the East. Ofttimes those ways were inscrutable. Some secrets a white man could never learn, and then one had to seek allies. But the prospect was not a welcome one when the only possible ally was as fearsome as the enemy one sought to fight.

Harrison came to the corner of Levant Street where the dark mouth of an alley gaped like the maw of Jonah's whale. There was no sign, probably never had been, but he knew it for China Alley. His goal was number 13 along that shaft of darkness. Taking a deep breath, he plunged in. As it

267

happened, the dark was not absolute. A dim naked bulb cast its wan radiance over a small bronze name plate affixed to the grimy brick at eye level only a couple of yards down the alley. The plaque was corroded almost past recognition, but the outlines of the numbers just above it told him he had arrived at his destination. Just to be sure, he tried rubbing the name plate with the edge of his threadbare coat. Some of the grime reluctantly came away, and he could see enough of the name to fill in the rest like a crossword: ZARNAK. With a sense of resignation, Harrison pressed the buzzer.

Almost at once, as if his arrival had been expected, the door swung open. The well-lit interior blinded him momentarily, but in a second he could make out the silhouette of a figure fully as massive as himself. A moment more and Steve could see that the man before him was a Sikh, a member of one of the mightiest warrior races of Asia. He had had occasion to fight both against and alongside such men in his lifetime, both in River Street and in the exploits of earlier years when he had traveled East.

The tall man's proud head was surmounted by a twisting turban, his set jaw embellished by a full, jet-black beard. Between these perched a hawklike nose and the fierce sharp eyes of a mountain eagle. The statue spoke: "Mr. Steve Harrison, no? By Nam, we had expected you ere now." He motioned the baffled detective on into the foyer. Harrison obliged, taking his hat in his hand as he did so.

"So you know me. That I can figure. I'm well enough known in these parts. But you say you knew I'd be here, Dr. Zarnak?"

At this the swarthy giant's deep chest reverberated with the sound of distant thunder. Harrison supposed it was meant as laughter. "Ah, *sahib* Harrison, I am not that estimable person. It is my honor to serve him. He awaits you within. Will you accompany me?"

As he followed the factotum, Harrison could not help gawking at the exotic furnishings about him. The exterior of the building, a small two-story structure abutted on either side by taller, rotting tenements, gave no hint at all of the interior which looked more like a museum, or maybe the palace of an Oriental monarch, than anything else. The floors were thickly laid with Persian and Chinese carpets. The walls were similarly hidden by silken brocade tapestries depicting scenes from some mad opium dream. Chandeliers and candelabra bore intricate scrollwork and etchings that seemed reminiscent of unknown varieties of marine monsters and mermen. Bookcases everywhere overflowed with volumes bound in unusual materials with titles in who knew what heathen tongue.

268

The great Sikh seemed to move more slowly than one might expect, and Harrison wondered if he did so in order to allow him to take in as much of the place as he could. As Harrison found himself calculating just how far the narrow building must extend backward to accommodate such an interior, his guide was indicating a heavy teakwood door bordered in bronze. Zarnak, he said with a note of reverence, could be found within. And with that he vanished down another hallway. When Steve looked back at the door, he was surprised to see it standing open, where a moment ago it had been firmly closed.

His eyes swept the interior before he stepped in. Again his eyes had to adjust, as the room was but vaguely lit by two low-burning braziers flanking a great cluttered desk. Behind this desk sat a lone figure, head and shoulders slightly hunched. No feature of this occupant was yet distinguishable. As Harrison took the first step into the room, his feet silent not only from his instinctive cat-like tread but also from the thick lushness of the Bokhara rug, the figure at once rose to his feet.

"Mr. Steve Harrison, is it not so?" said a clear, firm voice of unusual timbre. "Let us have a better look at one another, shall we?" At this, the flames in the two braziers rose higher, as if controlled by an unseen agency. *Some trick,* thought Harrison. He had seen better.

In the brighter light he could see Dr. Anton Zarnak extending a hand to him. Harrison hesitated but a moment, and yet in that moment every detail of the other man's exotic appearance was imprinted upon his memory. He was of no more than average height, trim of build, serenely proud in posture. His form was draped in the folds of a deep violet silk jacket, lapels and broad cuffs encircled with rich quiltwork. A black ascot covered the distance to his neck, which was crowned with an unreadable face of Eurasian features. Above the slightly slanting eyes, which had the illusion of being mostly pupil, delicate brows arched. A high, intellectual forehead topped these like some mighty mountain fortress. His hair was fine and black, with the oddity of a single jagged tuft of gray and white blazing up from the widow's peak. His extended hand, like its mate, bore several rings, each engraved with a peculiar sigil. The one Harrison could make out best bore the device of a rooster-headed figure with curling snakes for legs.

Harrison took the outstretched hand, hoping to learn something from the man's handshake. It was surprisingly firm, as firm as his own. Steve was confused at his inability to judge the man's age, even approximately. Zarnak motioned him to take a seat across the desk from him. As he did so, Steve noticed the chair was comfortably close to the suddenly blazing fireplace. The workmanship of the mantel was fabulous, but what drew his attention was the collection of remarkable objects atop it. There were statuettes of various Asian deities, most of which Harrison had often seen throughout the Oriental Quarter, but many of them seemed slightly different in some queer way. There was the cross-legged, bloated figure of Ganesha, but his flap-ears looked to have tentacles trailing from them. Others were less readily identified. Here and there were inscribed clay tablets whose languages Harrison could not guess.

Above all this, like a great sun shining down on the smaller objects, was hung a large wooden face painted in garish red. There were three bulging eyes below a brow surmounted by a crown of tines bedecked with human skulls. Golden fumes or flames scrolled from its wide nostrils or drooled from the corners of the tusked mouth. Puffed cheeks might have denoted the monster's satiation with human flesh.

"I've seen that before," Harrison ventured. "Yama, the Tibetan King of the Dead, right?"

"Very good, Mr. Harrison," Zarnak replied with a subtle hint of a smile. "But in truth it is an older avatar of that entity, known in elder Lemuria as Yamath, Lord of Flame. The center of his cult was the metropolis of Patanga. Perhaps you have read of it in Dostmann's classic *Remnants of Lost Empires*. Here." The strange savant hefted a large Victorian-era book.

"No sir, I'm afraid that's a new one on me. I'm not so well read as you. No time for it. Justice is my business, and River Street keeps me pretty busy at it."

Zarnak dropped the book on a pile of similar tomes at one corner of his desk, raising a small mist of dust. "But then I see we are in the same business, Mr. Harrison. I do not read for leisure, you see. I am in the same line of work as you, and these are the tools of my trade."

Involuntarily Steve looked at the spines of the nearest stack of books. Like those he had spied in the hall, their enigmatic words meant nothing to him: *The Secret Book of Dzyan*, *The Ponape Scripture*, *Dhol Chants*.

"Please, Mr. Harrison, do not imagine I mean to belittle you. You employ your chosen weapons well, as I do mine. And I believe that it will require both our skills to deal with the menace we both face."

Harrison quickened. Talk was not his expertise, action was, and now they were coming to the point. "You mean the bad dope? I don't know how you know about my involvement, but I guess you probably have your informants." Another cryptic smile from Zarnak.

Steve continued, "I had a hunch you'd know the score if anybody did. Fill me in on what you know, and then we'll work out a plan. I think I can bring in police reinforcements if we need them."

"I fear their participation would be ill-advised," quoth Zarnak. He seemed to be taking his time as if explaining a complex matter as best he could to a well-meaning child. "First allow me to tell you what is at stake here. It will sound fantastic to you, but you have already seen much, perhaps enough to lend credence to my tale. We shall begin by sharing what each knows." Harrison, on the edge of the comfortable chair, settled back to listen.

"What can you tell me of your Chinese friend? What did he tell you, and what has become of him?"

"Dead, dead of the dope, the Black Lotus. That's what the doctor at the hospital diagnosed. Do you know of it?"

"I am surprised a Western medical man knows of it. But in River Street the mists whisper many things from far away to attentive ears. It may be that we are dealing with the Black Lotus, or we may not be."

"Doctor Zarnak, all I know from what I saw in that dope dive is that the poor wretches who are fed the stuff all of a sudden pass from a stupor to a state of wild agitation. Jong-tso was raving, saying all kinds of stuff in a language I couldn't understand, though I don't think it was Chinese."

"Presumably you know of the recent killing sprees in the Quarter?"

"There's always stabbings, garrotings, poisonings, mostly Tong wars and personal vendettas. That's standard stuff, though."

"These, then, are killings kept secret from white ears. Terrible butcherings, mutilations, the work of fiends possessed of berserk fury. These, too, are the result of the Black Lotus. Some who take it do not die, but kill. Thus far I have been unable to examine any of the bodies of those whom the drug itself slays. If I could, I would know what I need to know. Can you take me to have a look at the late Jong-tso?"

"'Fraid not, Doc. He had no known relatives. I think he's been incinerated by now. I won't tell you what they do with the ashes."

"I see. I am not surprised. Were you alone when you retrieved the Chinaman from the opium den?"

"No, my pal Bill Waterman was waiting outside in the car. What's he got to do with it?"

"I should like to question him, that's all. May we go and see him? I realize it is late. My man Akbar Singh will drive us." Both men rose.

Harrison countered the other man's offer: ""No, if you don't mind a few minutes' walk, I've got Bill's car parked not far from here. Might as well drive it back to him." So they departed. The car was unmolested, to Steve's relief. They got in, Steve driving. Along the way, he sat in silence, partly in the grip of a queer sense of foreboding, partly ill at ease in awe of the strange man beside him. The trip did not take long. As the roadster approached its familiar curb, Harrison's eyes widened to see police officers cordoning off the house and turning away curious, agitated neighbors. The car door flew open and Steve launched himself up the sidewalk. Zarnak followed with a more dignified gait.

By the time the erudite occultist had reached his gruff partner, Harrison was embroiled in a profane dispute with the police lieutenant, whom he seemed to know if not to like. "Damn it, Phil, you've got to let me see him! I know enough not to disturb the crime scene, for Pete's sake! At least tell me how Bill died! Was it a burglar? A revenge job?"

The policeman's eyes widened. "Look, Steve, you've got it wrong! Bill's *alive!* He's not the one who was murdered. It was Flora, his wife. We're trying to get Bill under control now."

Harrison grunted, eyes downcast, about the tenderest expression of emotion he was capable of. "Judas, but that's tough! Let me talk to him, Phil."

"You still don't get me," the cop protested. *"He killed her!* Poor devil must have snapped, killed her in her sleep. He's hopelessly insane. It took five of our burliest men to hold him down once they got the call from a neighbor. When they got there, he was . . . *eating* her." Here the lieutenant went pale, not for the first time that night.

Zarnak moved to the fore. He transfixed the eyes of the policeman as Steve watched, intrigued despite his shock over the news he'd just received. The savant spoke soothingly: "Lieutenant, I assure you that it is a matter of the highest urgency that we be allowed to see and, if possible, to question the poor madman. I can guarantee it will aid you in solving the case." Blank-eyed, the compliant cop said nothing but waved the two men through the police cordon.

Harrison dreaded the sight within. He was no stranger to spilt blood. He hadn't a weak stomach, but this was different, a stroke too close to home. Forensic specialists were already at work at the gruesome task of gathering up the savagely sundered pieces of meat that had until recently been Flora Waterman. Others struggled to get the flailing arms of a maniac with a slight resemblance to Steve's old comrade into a straightjacket. He was chewing at the gag. Zarnak at once insisted they remove it. He ignored their wide-eyed protests and began to reach for it himself. Harrison waved away their blue-coated arms.

"Do what he says, boys! If anybody can make sense out of what's happened here, it's Doctor Zarnak!" With an appreciative nod, the occultist stood silently, awaiting whatever shrieked syllables might issue forth from the tongue of the madman. He had not long to wait, as the ranter began to explode into sobbing cries of, "Iä! Iä! Lloigor fhtagn! Zhar! The swimmer in the Lake of Hali! Please, oh please! Ahhhhhh–!" The strange words gave out as Zarnak made eye contact with the poor wretch, seeming to fix him in a hypnotic lock. The suddenly limp form slumped over, giving the baffled blue-coats some relief but even more puzzlement.

Turning to the impassive Harrison, Zarnak whispered, "I have heard quite enough. It is even as I feared. Let us now return to my dwelling. I will explain everything." Eager to learn exactly what he had stumbled into, Harrison followed the older man out the front door with only an inexpressive grunt to the lieutenant who was now as reluctant to see the detective leave as he had been a few minutes earlier to let him in. Profanity followed him to the waiting car. "Doesn't look like poor Bill will be needing it," Steve muttered as they pulled away from the curb.

"I guess somebody must've tailed the car to Bill's house, somehow snuck in and administered the Black Lotus. In his sleep or not, I don't know. We both dozed in the hospital, but it couldn't have been then, or I'd have been fed the stuff, too."

"That would be my guess as well, Mr. Harrison. It is not unlikely that the same men traced the car to my neighborhood, too, but knowing of my near presence they felt ill-inclined to pursue you."

"Judas!" the great detective swore, suddenly swerving to pull the car over to a curb. "For all we know the yellow devils booby-trapped the damn thing!"

The bejeweled hand of his enigmatic companion rested like an alighting bird on his massive shoulder. "A wise precaution, my impulsive friend, but fear not. I would have detected such a crude stratagem when we first approached the vehicle. I assure you, there is no danger—not of that sort, anyway."

Underway again, the unlikely partners filled the short ride back to China Alley with what information they knew. Harrison had little to contribute. Zarnak, on the other hand, continued to explain as they re-entered his study.

"You have now seen for yourself a specimen of the Black Lotus's true power."

"More than I wanted to see, Doc. But tell me this: Why the hell would anyone, even a dope ring, want to smuggle this stuff to its customers? Where's the pay-off? I can see assassins using it, but who'd want to kill off the River Street scum?"

"I venture to say that those poor unfortunates could not evade their karma. But, as you surmise, no mortal agency willed them dead. It is evident that the local smugglers have intercepted a stock meant for someone else. The Black Lotus has a very specific use, and should it be employed otherwise, the results will be as we have seen tonight."

Harrison shifted in his leather chair uncomfortably. He was accustomed neither to such exquisite surroundings nor to such a thick pall of deadly evil as that which now seemed to surround him. "But what legitimate purpose could this infernal stuff possibly have?"

"That will take some explaining, Mr. Harrison, and even then I question whether you will be inclined to understand." Rising from his teakwood desk, the gaunt form drifted to one of the book-lined walls and extracted a peculiar-looking volume. It was quite large, reminiscent of that which Dr. Bennet had earlier shown Steve and his lamented friend at the hospital. But this one seemed not even to be printed in the familiar characters of the Roman alphabet.

"The text is rendered in Egyptian hieroglyphs. It is called *The Black Rituals of Koth-Serapis.* I doubt you have heard of it. It is little known in the West. Even the learned Professor Wallis-Budge makes no mention of it. It contains knowledge of many secret matters, including that of the Black Lotus. It seems the plant was first cultivated long ages ago during the black eons of prehistory, or shall I rather say, of history which has understandably been suppressed. Those who bred and used it were the sorcerer-priests of ancient Stygia, who discovered how it might enhance the worship offered to their secret gods, such as Set-Typhon and Golgoroth."

Steve's eyes narrowed with puzzled skepticism, but he continued to listen silently. He'd heard strange stories before that turned out to be all too real. This might be one of them. And the truth would have to be pretty strange to account for what he had seen this night already.

"The ages passed, and the blasphemies of Stygia were at length swept away by the flood-tide of younger peoples with scant patience for the decadent cults of primal magic. And yet the secret of the Black Lotus by no means died with Stygia. By unguessed routes and circuitous stealth the drug was carried East where the hierophants of Leng and Sung in the heart of Asia rediscovered its ritual value. At length it proved too terrible in its danger, too potent in its allure to those who dared pilfer small quantities of the substance for their own use. You have seen the results, and yet so great is the ecstasy that many counted even such a price as worth paying for a few scant moments of bliss.

"The khans of forgotten empires ordered the Black Lotus to be extirpated, but it lingered in use among the little-known Tcho-Tcho people of Burma. There it was successfully restricted to the orders of adepts who alone knew its proper use, those who still understood the prescriptions of *The Black Rituals of Koth-Serapis*. And as it had been meant to do, the Black Lotus opened the minds of the Tcho-Tcho epopts to behold their gods, Lloigor and Zhar. Some of them it sends into an insane killing rage. Such a priest, possessed of the deity, will turn on the bound sacrificial victim, whether beast or man, and rend it to pieces as you have seen this very night. The others present join the visionary in the cannibalistic orgy.

Harrison interrupted. "You're right, Doc. It doesn't make much sense to me—or at least not much of it did till now. I remember poor Bill screaming out those two names, if you can call them that! And the Tcho-Tchos! Every cop in the area knows them only too well: the latest wave of Oriental immigrants to clutter the docks. Damn near every single one of them connected with the criminal underground in one way or another. There are only a few, but even at that, there's too damn many of them if you ask me!"

"Yes, they have earned quite a dark reputation for themselves, both here and in their homeland. Few know of them; all who do both hate and fear them. They were certainly those for whom the stock of the Black Lotus was intended. By now I am sure they have exacted a terrible vengeance upon those who deprived them of the drug."

"Guess I gave them a head start back at the dope den. Then those Asians must have been the middlemen, really dupes who stumbled into a death trap. Must have been the Tcho-Tchos who caught up with Bill. But tell me, Doc, is all you've told me contained in that book? Most of your story takes place in the Far East, not Egypt."

"Very observant, detective. I see you do not miss many clues. No, my information comes by a rather different channel. You see, I *myself* once served in the remote Plateau of Sung as the high priest of the cult of Zhar and Lloigor. In fact, that is the meaning of the characters that make up my name: Zhar-Nak, the mouthpiece of Zhar."

Harrison's mouth fell open. "Naw, that can't be! You're not one of those squat little devils!" At least Steve hoped the man was lying. The chill of superstition returned and leaped down his vertebrae like a blue arc across electrical poles.

"I have not said that I was, Mr. Harrison. You should be aware that these dwarf-like figures belong to a warrior caste specially bred. Not all the TchoTchos are like them, nor have I expressly claimed to be of their nation. My origins shall remain my secret. They are not relevant to our purpose. "But I did hold sway over the sect until a crafty priestling called E-poh, a devil of a man addicted to the Lotus in small enough doses to stave off dissolution, stole the priestly tiara away from me by promising access to the drug to all who would join him. I have told you of the potent temptation of the drug to those who know of its powers. Thus degraded, the sect turned from me, and the Tcho-Tchos became the malevolent creatures you see today.

"It were a vain hope to regain my pontificate. What use to preside over such degenerates? And yet I must do what I can to prevent the sublime worship of the divine Lloigor and Zhar from being further profaned. You and I, between us, possess the means, I believe, to stop the blight of the Black Tong of the Tcho-Tchos from spreading its stain into the New World.

"Well, Detective Harrison, I have told you what I know. It is for you to decide whether you will fight by my side."

Steve remained silent for a few moments. He wanted very much to dismiss what the bizarre figure before him had recounted. It sounded like a drug-induced fantasy itself! And yet he could not deny it was the sort of shadow that tended to fall on River Street where the deepest darkness of the Elder World always seemed to collect. And if even half of what Zarnak had said were true it provided the only clue he had to ending an awful plague of crime and doom. And there were Bill and Flora Waterman to think about. He couldn't afford to turn down even the slimmest reed of a chance to avenge them. He rose and extended his hand.

"Doctor Zarnak, I'm with you. Lead the way. Somehow I think my usual methods aren't going to count for much in this case."

"Excellent, my young friend! But you are quite wrong about one thing: your abilities will prove useful indeed. While it is true we are ranged against more than human Powers, they are served by flesh and blood since it is the world of flesh and blood they would conquer. There are forces of dark sorcery at work here, yes, but I believe there is every chance at evening up the odds, as I believe you would say. Come with me."

He led the puzzled detective through the door and down the carpeted hall to a finely inlaid curio cabinet. It was a tall, glass-fronted display case, offering scrutiny of a set of rare Mediterranean antiquities. But Zarnak reached around the back, seeking for some hidden catch. A panel sprang open, revealing a peculiar staff bolted to a quilted recess. The thing was about three feet in length, some sort of stave. One end was sharpened, issuing in a deadly-looking spike. The other was delicately carved with the head of one of the great jungle cats. Zarnak quickly released the fastenings and passed the object to Steve. The latter was surprised at the weight and apparent hardness of the thing.

"It is a powerful talisman, once owned by an ancestor of yours. I believe you will find it as useful as he did."

Steve *did* feel a strange sense of familiarity, as if he had trained with the staff, as if it were somehow as natural to him as one of his own limbs. He looked forward to using it with terrible effect in the battle to come.

The day arrived for what had unofficially come to be known as the Mardi Gras of River Street, that day when several major and minor religious festivals of the many different sects represented in the Oriental Quarter spilled into the crowded avenues celebrating their favorite totems. It seemed as if time had rolled back and Steve Harrison, Anton Zarnak, and the latter's manservant Akbar Singh strode the convoluted alleys of ancient Tyre. Here four strong sets of swarthy arms bore up the tabernacle of an obscure Moslem *weli*, or saint, surrounded by a crazed throng of Muhammadans frothing at the mouth and lashing themselves as they recited Arabic verses from the Koran. There a band of equally god-intoxicated Siva devotees shambled in a trance state as they ran spikes and pins through their own seemingly bloodless flesh. Two Chinese paper dragons flowed gracefully through the crowds, borne up by hidden puppeteers. Steve knew that the festival was largely a cover for an open hunting season on tourists and the innocent. Oh yes, the cutpurses were out in full numbers, worshiping the only god they knew: Mammon.

Harrison, Zarnak, and Akbar Singh strolled through the crowds as inconspicuously as they might, swathed in concealing costumes. To any casual passerby, they must have appeared as a wealthy Easterner flanked by two burly bodyguards, not an uncommon sight. Akbar Singh wore only facial disguise to supplement his usual apparel, but his master had affected the fine silks of a merchant of the Old World. A veil masked his features, too, though few even in River Street would have been able to put a face to the well known but mysterious name of Anton Zarnak. Steve Harrison in his own way was fully as notorious, only his white face and dress were unmistakable in such surroundings. Thus on this day he appeared almost as the double of Akbar Singh, most of his mighty frame concealed in detail if not in outline. And it was Steve who first noted something curious in the scene.

"Hey Doc," he whispered, "will ya get a load of *that*! You ever seen a Chinese dragon like that before?" His gloved finger indicated a puzzling conglomeration of paper maché and brightly hued limbs twisting into view out of one of the side alleys. It looked more like it was supposed to be an octopus or a squid than anything else.

"Strange indeed. It represents the totem of no familiar sect or cult. Yet it would be quite out of character for the servants of the Old Gods so to show their hand. I wonder if it is not perhaps intended as a—"

"*Diversion!*" finished Steve, throwing the bulkier portions of his disguise aside. For out of the mouth of an opposite alleyway, dark as midnight even in the light of noonday, there now poured a stream of miniature juggernauts, the stunted but powerful forms of the dreaded Tcho-Tcho thugs. Harrison and Akbar Singh lost no time in unsheathing their weapons to meet the drawn daggers and guns of their squat opponents. A tidal wave of alarm swept through the crowd which promptly melted away, receding like a morning mist in all directions. Some sought the cover of storefronts, others manholes. And though neither Steve nor his Sikh companion had the leisure to note the fact just then, Zarnak had disappeared, too. Whether he had succumbed to the surprise attack in its first moments or decided that a diversion might be turned back upon its authors was impossible to judge.

The Tcho-Tchos were all over the two giants like hunting dogs on a lion. Terrible odds, but at least, Steve thought, the tactic made it impossible for any more to join the fray for the moment. The initial cluster of attackers functioned as a kind of barrier against others. Steve laid about him viciously with both Gurkha knife and staff. In the last few days of waiting, he had fine-tuned his performance with the strange weapon, and now it circled and thrust with merciless precision. Though he did manage a deep gash or gouge here and there, it seemed as if the lightest touch with the cat-headed stave was enough to disable many of the Tcho-Tchos. Zarnak had anticipated that the gang members, whenever they revealed themselves, would have sought to fortify themselves by means of black

278

sorcery, the same as that used to no avail a generation earlier in the Boxer Rebellion. Then British victory had been narrowly achieved with the secret employment of the same juju staff Steve used so devastatingly now. It seemed that the magical reinforcement of the Tcho-Tchos, like the Boxers before them, had actually made them more vulnerable to the counter-magic of the wand of Solomon.

Not daring to draw his pistols at such close quarters, Steve nonetheless rapidly evened the odds, cutting the forms of the malevolent dwarfs from him as if knocking the fruit from a tree trunk. His knife and his stave sought and found sheathing in non-Aryan flesh again and again. Their furious efforts stymied by the very denseness of their assault, the Tcho-Tchos wounded more of their own number than their intended victims. Though streaked with blood from a dozen minor cuts and grazes, neither of the giant combatants had yet taken a serious blow, though each had by now inflicted many. As he split one domed, bald Tcho-Tcho skull to the greenish teeth, Akbar Singh cried, "Such is the fight when cowardly assassins face warriors in the open air!"

But Steve had a different theory. It suddenly occurred to him that with this many well-trained killers arrayed against them, the two, no matter how valiantly they fought, must surely have met their doom ere now—unless their attackers had been ordered not to kill them at all! Suppose their orders were instead to *capture* . . .

He reached the conclusion of his thought with a blackjack punctuating his sentence for him. He didn't even know it when he went down beneath the swarm of gloating Tcho-Tchos. Nor could Steve see Akbar Singh following him only moments after.

A blank eternity later Steve Harrison felt the scene of his nightmare shift. Now he seemed to be lying prone and bound in a dungeon with only a dim hint of illumination. He tried to turn his body over and found he couldn't. He seemed to be tied to something that prevented him. He quickly realized that he was awake, that his feverish dreams had come to an end. Had they drugged him to keep him under after the effect of the blackjack wore off? His eyes began to adjust. Shapes were creeping inch by inch into focus. And so were smells. At once he realized he had been roped face to face with a corpse, and not a fresh one. Was it the sadistic joke of the Tcho-Tcho devils to let him die this way, the unwilling companion of one who had already been sent on ahead into Death's grim kingdom?

279

Harrison knew with the pragmatism of his barbarian ancestors that he dared not let himself be overcome with the horror of his situation. The only thing to do was to treat it as one more trap and begin looking for a way out of it. Then he could afford to think up a little sadism of his own. So he began to assess his position. Abortive attempts to flex his muscles quickly revealed that he was tied not at the wrists, as he had half-expected, but rather just behind the elbow. His forearms, and those that dangled listlessly from the stiff in front of him, were free. The same with his legs: They were lashed to the putrefying members of the other just above the knee. It might be possible, if he dragged the dead form to one of the walls, to hoist himself and his burden up to a standing position. Then, if he could keep his balance with this sack of rotten potatoes hanging from his front, possibly he could get to the cell door and see how secure it was. Maybe less than his captors thought.

Grunting, sweat pouring from him even in the musty cool of the cell, Steve had about half accomplished his objective when a new blow took the wind out of his sails. For when he was able to rise up into a fugitive gray beam of light coming through a vent in the oak door, he was aghast to see that he knew the face, or the twisted caricature of a face, of the man opposite him~it was Bill, poor Bill Waterman!

So the Tcho-Tcho Tong *had* gotten to him, gotten around the police surveillance (no problem, Steve himself was used to doing the same) and finished their business with their victim. This Steve realized as he slid to the ground once more, dragged by the bulk of his dead comrade. But as he braced himself for another attempt, he was startled again, and this was the worst of all. He could feel the corpse beneath him begin to *stir* with blasphemous animation. His nape hairs prickled with unnatural dread and chills swept over him. Here was the power of the lowest hell, the zombie conjure. Suddenly he felt that he himself was the burden, that his form must seem but an annoying impediment to the superhuman strength of the fiend who had come to possess the inert husk of his friend. The thing beneath him began to shiver, to shudder, then to buck with an almost serpentine litheness, to be rid of the mortal atop him. Steve could not drive from his mind the grotesque image of a rodeo ride astride the devil's charger! Could he somehow win the contest and save his soul?

Instinctively the detective knew that he must not let his opponent gain freedom of movement. The iron-limbed revenant had already broken one of the leg-bands and was working on one of the arm ropes. Steve knew he must try to keep him down and off balance. If he let the demon win free, he should never be able to survive its ripping talons. So he summoned his

280

knowledge of the wrestling ring, learned many years before in the amateur contests on board ship as he rode a merchantman from one South Seas backwater to another. He used the massive bulk of his body as a blunt instrument, shifting his weight to throw his macabre opponent off balance and onto the hard floor. He dared not reach with his unfettered hands for the throat of the thing that had been Bill, lest it seize the same chance and bring a more powerful demoniac grip to bear on Steve's own windpipe.

It was on his adventures in the South Seas and East Asia that he first learned of the antique evils he later felt obliged to fight in River Street. Among them was the dread rite of the *rolang*, the corpse who dances. In it, or so whispered secret rumor, the mystic adept voluntarily undertook the same contest in which he now found himself engaged. If he could hold onto his sanity long enough, he stood to gain great occult power through the ordeal. But what was the secret of finally disabling the necromantic ogre before it was too late? It had been long ago, and Steve, then young and in the grip of the naive rationalism of youth, had not paid much attention. If only he could *remember!*

Now the dead eyes of the *rolang* had come open, their lost pupils swimming back into view. They gazed at Steve with an utterly unhuman intelligence, straight from the Pit. The crumbling mouth began to open, and Steve knew not which was worse, the charnel stench or the cacodaemoniacal chortling. He felt madness and death were not far away from him now, and he was not far from welcoming their embrace. If only he could recall! And then came a voice, from some distance, and Steve took it for the voice of his antagonist, calling from the far reaches of Tartarus.

"The *tongue, sahib* Steve! Sever the tongue!"

But no, Steve realized through his superstitious panic, that was the voice of a living man! It had to be Akbar Singh! Somehow he had managed to free himself, and now he was trying to rescue Steve as well. What had he said? The tongue? That hardly made any sense. Maybe madness had come for him. But something bade him try the repellent suggestion. Gagging, Harrison opened his own clenched teeth and brought his involuntarily sneering mouth into an unspeakable kiss with his hellish counterpart. The depth of wretchedness came when he fished about in the cesspool cavity with his own tongue, seeking the shriveled stump of the dead man's. But he found it and seized it between protesting jaws, gnawing hard till at last it gave. He had it, spat it to the invisible floor beneath him, and felt the ghoulish form go limp, its sudden weight dragging him down with it.

281

But now the door sprang open, and the giant silhouette of Akbar Singh filled the doorframe. Stooping, he produced Steve's own knife to cut the remaining bonds. Bracing up Steve's unsteady form, he helped him from the tiny room and out into the hall. In the stronger light of the corridor Steve could see its length was littered with the savaged carcasses of Tcho-Tcho guards. The great Sikh's booted foot found an unattached Tcho-Tcho head and sent it smacking like a rotten fruit against the stone of the wall.

"There are greater numbers of the fiends than any of us had surmised, *sahib* Steve. But most of them are gathered elsewhere, where we are headed now." In answer to his companion's query, Akbar Singh explained, "They put too few of their comrades in charge of me. I led them to think I remained unconscious until I was able to take them by surprise. They had ingenious tortures prepared for me indeed, but Nam be praised, I was able to forestall them. Now the devils will taste of their own terrors many times over in the hells to which I have sent them."

Harrison was now fully able to trot alongside the Sikh down twisting halls surprisingly empty of any prowler but themselves. "I'm sure lucky you showed up when you did, pal! But what about Zarnak? Did they take him, too? Do you know where they're keeping him?"

"I have done a bit of searching, but the whereabouts of my master I do not know, unworthy slave that I am. And yet I did find *something.*" Withal, he produced from the folds of his tattered silk greatcoat a familiar-looking carved staff, handing it to Steve. He took it with gratitude.

"One thing I don't get, though, Akbar Singh. With this you could have made short work of that zombie yourself, no?"

"I think not. Not even Zarnak himself would dare employ the power of the stave. It may be awakened and controlled only by its destined wielder. And should I have interposed physically, I fear for my immortal soul, just as you feared for yours. The power of the *rolang is* great, and the means of stopping it are few."

The two figures had slowed their momentum, and Harrison followed the other's example in crouching to continue their progress on their knees. As they made their way through what seemed like an inactive drainage tunnel, Harrison whispered, "So where are we? I can usually get my bearings pretty much anywhere in the Quarter, but I can't place this joint."

"I will not swear to it, my friend, but I imagine we find ourselves in a set of tunnels leading from a warehouse to the waterfront. It seems likely that
282

the Tcho-Tcho devils stumbled upon it and found new uses for the remnants of an old smuggling operation. If I am correct, we have now returned from an area of holding cells, probably designed for the white slave trade, and are very near the warehouse itself. No doubt we have retraced the path by which they led us to our intended doom. Do you hear the chanting just beyond? Let us venture closer."

In a moment the two welcomed the chance to rise to their full height, though they did not decrease their stealth. As they eased open a wall panel in what appeared to be an old accounts office, they could hear more distinctly the sounds the acute ears of the Sikh had detected a moment before. Harrison envied the other man his wilderness-honed senses. It did sound like chanting, repetitive, antiphonal. Someone was leading, many other voices following. So there was a leader. Who might be masterminding the operation? Steve wondered, because whoever it was, he was a dead man as far as Steve was concerned.

The swelling chorus of guttural voices gave Steve a hint of his earlier dread. Deep down he knew that his Celtic forbears had driven the reptilian kindred of these dusky trolls away from the open spaces of human habitation. His knife thirsted for their stinking blood. He seemed to know that his statuesque companion shared his own primal hate for the Little People. Akbar Singh's ancestral mythology would know them as the Asuras, eternal enemies of the Aryan gods.

As both men inched toward a better vantage point, still well concealed, they hoped, they gained a better view of the single figure who stood behind an onyx altar stone placed atop a draped dais at one end of the two-story-high chamber. His arms were extended, occasionally upraised as in supplication. At first Harrison thought they were still too far away to make out the words he was saying, but soon he realized that the chant was in no language he knew, probably the same barbarous patois he had heard from Bill Waterman's raving mouth a few days before. Yes, there were the same words: "Iä! Iä! Lloigor! Zhar fhtagn! Cfyak vulgtlm vultlagn!" He felt vaguely nauseated at hearing the arcane vocables. They had a queer resonance, as if they struck a chord on some deeper, forgotten level than mere hearing.

Akbar Singh abruptly shook the giant shoulders next to him, startling Harrison out of the hypnotic torpor beginning to seduce him. "It is even as I feared, sahib Steve! He has opened the Gate, and Something has deigned to answer the summons!"

The sound of the chanting had subtly changed, taking on a subdued

283

quality, as of waiting and expectancy. The quality of the light had changed, too. It had something of the look of the pall announcing an impending tornado. And from this disturbed atmosphere there began to congeal a Form, hard for the mind of the observer to comprehend, but recalling in some vague way that paper squid shape during the River Street festival. There seemed to be a tangle of criss-crossing arms or feelers or tentacles obscuring whatever central body they stemmed from. There was a great splashing sound, though no water was visible. And the Shape was expanding, as when a cloud of smoke begins to dissipate. Only it did not dissipate; as it expanded it only grew more distinct. Its feelers now waved over the cowering dwarfs whose worship had summoned it. Of these, some trembled, overcome with religious awe, while others seemed ready to flee in terror, hesitating perhaps only for fear that flight might be the more dangerous course, not the less.

The scene held thus for a moment more before fully two thirds of the Tcho-Tchos bolted for the doors. The two eavesdroppers rose from concealment, their visibility now irrelevant, and made for the platform. For the shadowed hood of the mysterious celebrant on the dais had fallen away, revealing the sweat-streaked visage of *Anton Zarnak!* He had now lapsed into Mandarin, a tongue Steve had a working knowledge of. "O Most Holy Zhar, destroy these profaners of thy Mysteries, as once thou didst smite the men of Leng! Iäo Thamungazoth, for thy name's sake!"

That was all Steve could make out, as the litany of Zarnak was drowned by the screams of the fleeing Tcho-Tchos. For all their seeming clumsiness, the gigantic appendages of the glowing apparition struck swiftly and with deadly effect. The panicked goblins disappeared, one by one, enveloped in the smoky embrace of their indefatigable pursuer. The mouthpiece of Zhar had spoken, and his word had not been in vain.

Steve and Akbar Singh had arrested their reckless advance and now returned to their concealment, little knowing whether it would protect them from the questing tentacles of this Thing. When they dared look up again, after the shrieks had died away, the billowing death-cloud still hovered.

"I believe it is what my master called the *Tulku* of Zhar, the projected image of the god who sleeps in fitful repose in a grotto deep beneath the Plateau of Sung. But behold the master himself! I fear he is lost to us!" Zarnak stood erect, hands aloft, and with eyes wide. He no longer spoke. And the cloudy Entity continued to expand. Its quarry now accounted for, it began to extend itself in the direction in which the doomed Tcho-Tchos had made to flee. Was it going to round up a few of them that it had missed? But Steve would have sworn none of them could have made it that far. And that meant . . . He looked at the paling face of Akbar Singh.

"He can't send it back! Its hunger has been awakened, and it's going to head for River Street!"

"I fear you are correct, *sahib*. But what can we do? It were death to charge the thing, by Nam!" But Harrison did not hear him. He was again listening to the echo of what his ancestors once knew. The cat-headed stave in his whitening fist grew strangely warm. He knew that there was one thing he could try.

Standing erect, he whispered, "I'm sorry, Akbar Singh. Forgive me, Doc!" And with that he sent the sharpened staff sailing through the weirdly charged gloom like a javelin—*straight for the unprotected breast of Anton Zarnak!*

The great Sikh groaned in lament as the missile went home and Zarnak crumpled in a heap. But all at once, the spectral visitant from the shunned heart of Asia was gone, as if the sun had risen, cutting through the heavy morning sea mist. Confident they were now safe, the two men hastened to the dais. There was a body all right, but it was that of a bound Tcho-Tcho, no doubt the priest who had intended to preside over a very different ceremony. Zarnak must somehow have dispatched him before the crowd assembled. Harrison ripped asunder several yards of the fallen canopy which now draped the wreckage of the altar, on the chance that Zarnak's falling body might have become entwined in the stuff, but this, too, proved a disappointment. Nor was there any sign of the stave. Akbar Singh was content to let Harrison pursue his frenzied search by himself. He seemed resigned to the strange circumstance.

"May it not be that Zarnak returned with the avatar of his god to his adytum in Asia? I should suppose so. We will not find him, though I would not prevent you from searching further, my friend."

"What do you mean?" asked the nonplused detective, feeling that, after what he had seen, even the wildest theory of the Sikh might well be true. "Dead or alive?"

"I know as little as you. Indeed, it is not my business to know whether Doctor Zarnak himself was ever physically present among us. He himself may have been a *tulku*. I know not. I will simply return to his dwelling and wait. One day he may have use for my services again, and perhaps, who can say, he may require your own as well. Go in peace, my brother."

Without a word, Steve Harrison turned about and found the door. The Sikh had been right about one thing: The place was a warehouse, one of the oldest and outwardly most dilapidated on the waterfront. In a few minutes, silhouetted against the wholesome light of the breaking dawn, Harrison trudged the length of River Street, hardly noticing the strange looks from the few early risers whose honest affairs compelled them to be up at such an hour. As he walked on through the Oriental Quarter, his huge frame stooped by exhaustion, he felt for the first time, despite the exotic otherworldliness of the place, that on its ancient streets he had re-entered the real world.

–1996–

THE TREE-HOUSE
With W. H. Pugmire

John Whateley knelt in the semi-dark attic room that had been his father's study. A thrill of illicit excitement tingled his nerves as he shone his flashlight over the large cardboard box that sat before him. The box contained the journals of his father, Ebenezer Whateley, from the 1920's, the written accounts of a young man's life. His father had planned to destroy them, but found it impossible to do so. Although he did not want these records of his life to exist after his death, their destruction seemed almost an invitation to death; as though saying, "I have destroyed the records of my days on earth, now come smother my existence with your unyielding embrace."

Death caught the old man suddenly. He was now nothing but a memory and a putrescent corpse that festered underneath graveyard dirt. John Whateley shivered; the power to his father's house had been turned off, depriving him of warmth or electric light. No matter: what he sought was now before him. He searched through the box and found the journal dated 1928. That year had intrigued John Whateley all his young life. As a child, he'd had the odd habit of climbing to the top of Sentinel Hill on certain nights, of sleeping on the great altar stone and dreaming curious dreams. Dreams in which he saw oddly-formed shadows. Dreams wherein he heard the muted chants of alien words, words he could not quite remember. And when he was found, and when he spoke of these visions to his kith and kin, he saw faces twisted with horrible expressions; and, always, he heard whispered the date nineteen-twenty-eight.

On the occasions when he tried to learn something of what occurred in Dunwich on that date, he would become exasperated because of his failure. His relatives would pale and order him to be silent. Once he tried to discuss these matters with an ancient crone who belonged to the so-called decayed branch of the Whateleys; but she would merely smile and shake her head. It was from her that he learned of certain books, old books which spoke of fabulous legends. He read her books as best he might, learning bits and pieces of foreign tongues where he could. Once he had taken the trip into Arkham, the university town, and asked to see the most abhorred of the old books. He was allowed, somewhat to his

287

surprise, though a librarian looked on the whole time. As he reverently turned random pages, some of the words seemed familiar, but he was not sure where he had encountered them. And the Latin was to him a blank wall. Soon after, he had journeyed outside the region, to seek the assistance of a Catholic priest to teach him Latin. But John had been naive; barely into the lessons, he had let slip the reason for his interest, and the priest promptly ejected him.

He felt like a man standing in a field in which a treasure had been buried, but possessing no map. He was close to it, very close, but access was barred. So despite his studies, he never learned very much about his ancestral past and the incidents of 1928.

Now he would learn everything.

Old Ebenezer's handwriting was easy to read, and thus he scanned through the journal quickly. Many of the entries for January and February concerned the seaport town of Innsmouth, for which his father had a strong dislike. Mentions were made of the nefarious rumors concerning certain inhabitants of the town, and in February an entry recorded how officials from the Federal government made an astounding number of arrests, how whole families were taken away and never heard from again.

The other topic of especial interest was his father's cousin, Wilbur Whateley. It struck John oddly, the way his father wrote of this mysterious cousin. The writing seemed guarded, the words few and carefully chosen; as though to say or hint too much would be a dangerous thing. One entry was of more than usual length:

"I've just learned that Nathan Vreeland had been seeing Wilbur! And again since the disappearance of Lavinia. Damn the fool! I've confronted him about this, and he seemed amazed that people knew of his meetings. He won't tell me much, because—he says— he doesn't know very much. He says that Wilbur sought him out because of Nathan's reputation as a teacher. I guess that Nathan had been reading portions of dangerous books with Wilbur. God, the fool! His mania for occult study blinds him to other things, things that even a dullard like myself can sense. There's nothing I can do; when Nathan speaks of books he has seen in Wilbur's library, especially the English version of the damned N_____, his eyes glow with lust. He won't see reason. He scoffs at the rumors concerning Wilbur and Sentinel Hill.

"I'm confused and don't rightly know what to do. People are

becoming ugly in regards to Wilbur. I think that more than a few would be glad enough to see him dead. I don't know how much of that I can believe. I've seen, of course, the fires on Sentinel Hill, and I've felt the tremors and heard the rumblings. Nathan won't listen to reason, and we had quite a heated, bitter argument last time I saw him. I feel helpless."

Here it is at last, thought John. Here are names to be researched, and leads to be investigated. Oh, the stirrings of his soul as he read how another Whateley had felt the same attraction to Sentinel Hill. And he knew what the letter N must stand for. As if praying, as perhaps he was, he whispered the name softly: "Necronomicon." The very sound of it had a strange allure. He felt sure that he was on the correct path this time. Somewhere this English version of the book must still exist! With these thoughts whirling in his mind, he read on. The story that unfolded thrilled him with uncanny wonder, almost like what an amnesiac must feel upon the return of lost memory, lost identity.

The enigmatic Vreeland gradually became more than a name. It developed that he had moved to Dunwich years before to keep the hamlet's slovenly one-room school. As the number of students steadily dwindled, Vreeland had begun to supplement his income through private tutoring, willing to travel almost any distance over the rough roads of the region to meet with the woefully backward students. He had been engaged to tutor the much-rumored Wilbur, a strange lad who was at the same time both advanced beyond his years and shockingly ignorant of the most basic knowledge. From various oblique references, John began to surmise that Vreeland's calls upon the Whateley household did not decrease even when Wilbur and his grandfather were occupied elsewhere most of the time. Had Vreeland been tutoring the lonely Lavinia, Wilbur's mother? Or had something else been going on between them? But then Lavinia had disappeared one day. Rumor laid this to Wilbur's charge, but John's father had his own suspicions that the older Whateley had discovered Lavinia's true relation with Vreeland and secretly sent her away.

Even this did not put an end to Vreeland's association with the Whateley menfolk, for young Wilbur seemed to have passed some sort of threshold and was ready to expand his home education. Vreeland knew well that most of the youngster's training came from his grandfather's peculiar erudition, but the old man could teach no more than he himself knew. So Vreeland's remedial efforts were again required. Finally

Vreeland had himself been initiated into grandfather Whateley's queer curriculum. He had to be at least cursorily acquainted with Wilbur's studies in order to know how to assist him in the basic skills required. This marked the beginning of Vreeland's own obsession with occult lore, into which he began to venture like an explorer in a strange, new country.

When the journal recorded the news of Wilbur Whateley's violent death, John felt a stab of pain inside his soul. He had formed a subconscious link with Wilbur. Damn his father's prudential reticence! How had Wilbur died? And why? Had he at last been arraigned by the authorities for his mother's death?

Suddenly he found, folded between two of the journal's pages, a letter addressed to his father. The flashlight's glow was beginning to dim, and he held the letter near to his eyes, reading it carefully.

"Dear Eb," the epistle began. "I know you will not forgive me for the part I played in the horrible events that have taken place. I will not try and excuse my mad behavior. I am ashamed of it, and yet I cannot doubt that in the same circumstances I would do the same again. I will defend nothing and try only to explain certain things.

"You told me, during our final, most bitter argument, that when it came to my obsession with arcane books, I lost sight of all else, and this is quite true. I have discovered things, Eb, and this wisdom engenders a thirst for further knowledge. I do more than study these old books. But I do not want to write of this, particularly not now, while the town is in such a state.

"If I had realized more clearly who, or rather, *what* your cousin was, I would never have assisted him, but how was I to have known? Who in his right mind could have suspected? Despite our conceits, even you and I still know very little, and the authorities, knowing absolutely nothing of these matters, and eager to keep it that way, are prone to frown on anyone who is at all interested in Wilbur Whateley. And I have better reason than most not to want to attract attention. You spoke of certain visitors from Miskatonic who questioned you concerning certain rare books that belonged to your cousin. You were under the impression that the books in question had been misplaced and not yet found. (What I am telling you now I write hoping that you will destroy this letter after having read it.) When the shocking news of Wilbur's death came to me by 'phone from various men I know in Arkham, I acted quickly. There were three books of vital interest to me sitting on the crude, unvarnished shelves in the old shed where I met with Wilbur to tutor him in basic reading. Wilbur's grandfather had told me enough that I recognized their unique value, but he had never trusted me to read any of them for myself. Now I saw my chance.

"My desire that those books should not be destroyed or (which is the same) placed under lock and key at Miskatonic was like some intense fever. And so, in the dead of night, I stole to the farmhouse and broke into the shed, confiscating the precious tomes. One of them was Dee's imperfect translation. I acted blindly, with little sense. You may judge me slightly insane, but who would not have been after debating arcane blasphemies with Wilbur Whateley? Over many months of tutoring, absorbed in the work, I had learned to ignore the stench that oozed from above, the slitherings and fumblings and moanings from an unseen room. On that terrible night, as I invaded the tenantless shed in quest of the books, the sourceless sounds and the mephitic reek seemed magnified a hundredfold, as if whatever had kept them in check before had now been taken away (Second Thessalonians chapter 2, verses 6 through 9). Whatever was hidden there must have been the thing that soon ravaged the countryside. How little I then understood the magnitude of the risk I had taken that night! Needless to say, I lingered no longer than absolutely necessary.

"Nor will I linger further in this town. I am leaving Dunwich. Some of your relations may have told you of the Sesqua Valley, out West, to which they are preparing to journey. I am going with them. Come with us, Ebenezer. Dunwich is a dead town. Your name marks you, you must realize that. I need not remind you of what occurred earlier this year at Innsmouth, of certain families who vanished because their name was Marsh, because of a look with which they had been tainted. I believe that something of that sort may happen here, with Whateleys. I have myself had visitors from the government, as have many others; their furtive questions concerning your family are what moves me to fear for you and yours. We are young, you and I. Our lives lie ahead, and they can be good, long lives. Please consider what I have said, and I beg you to destroy this letter immediately.

"Ever your faithful friend, Nathan."

John Whateley folded the letter thoughtfully. He had indeed found that which he sought. No longer would he suffer familial suspicion or scorn; he would leave Dunwich for the far-off Sesqua Valley. Surely he would find the answers to all his questions with the help of his father's "faithful friend."

II

Nathan Vreeland frowned at the man who stood before him. He could see in John Whateley's thin nose and dark eyes a semblance of a long lost friend. But he saw something more in those dark, moody eyes. He saw a longing and a restlessness he had seen too often, years ago, in his mirror. Those eyes gazed at him now, intently, with keen anticipation.

"I was sorry to hear of your father's death, John. He was a good friend in my younger years. We lost contact after I left Dunwich. I confess that I am dismayed to learn that he did not destroy certain letters that I had written; although, from what you say, he may have intended to before his death. He seemed a troubled man after I left."

"Why are you putting me off?" Whateley's irritated voice sounded loudly in the small room. "You know from my letter why I am here."

Vreeland's eyes narrowed with annoyance. "I know well enough," he replied in a voice choked with conflicting emotions. He resented the youth's insolence, and yet he felt keenly how much like his own younger self John Whateley was. Vreeland felt almost tangibly the irony that he should wind up playing the role of Ebenezer Whateley, who had once tried futilely to warn Vreeland himself away from the same spiritual dangers. "Your letter quite . . . distressed me. You speak of feelings that are familiar to me. *Too* familiar! And yet, in spite of your studies, you seem to have learned precious little. I think your interests are too self-centered to do either of us any good."

"I've been trying to understand these things on my own, in the face of hostility from my family. Things have been kept from me. I feel this hunger, inside, and it drives me . . ."

"That's precisely why they're keeping things from you! The Whateley family has endured one tragedy after another because of that thirst for

292

forbidden secrets. It runs like a congenital disease through the whole family line. Oh, it remains dormant in some—like your father, though I sometimes think he must have been fighting down his own instincts when he opposed my researches so vehemently. But he was right, after all. You are dealing with forces you do not understand. You are being manipulated by things you will never comprehend. Now, in the last years of life, I am only beginning to realize their significance. We fool ourselves into thinking we seek wisdom, when in fact we are puppets in the claws of emotionless creatures who care nothing for us. 1928 was a long time ago, and yet the events haunt me still. And even that wasn't enough to convince me. I've made mistakes since then, terrible mistakes. My greed for knowledge blinds me still. And I am not the only victim. Your visits to Sentinel Hill, that mountain's lure for you—by God, the forces merely sleep, and even in slumber they rule over us, ever-waiting, ever-powerful. We seek their wisdom, but they never satisfy our need. Your own descriptions of the dreams you experienced are so vague . . ."

"Because I don't remember them clearly. Damn it, that's why I'm here! With your help, with the help of that copy of Dee you stole from my family, I will have the wisdom I crave. You offered your help to a Whateley in the past. Why do you hesitate now?"

"Do you really have to ask? Because of past mistakes! What is it you think happened in 1928? It was bad enough, but nothing compared to what *might* have happened! What in heaven's name are you asking me to do? Go with you to Sentinel Hill and call the frightful Name?" The old man's eyes were wild with unaccustomed emotion. His face was reddening, his breath coming in short gasps. His hands began to shake. He took hold of himself, knowing this was no good for his heart. In a moment he spoke calmly. "Do you really know *anything* of these matters, young man? Or are you merely an impatient child? I think you are like the foolish child who plays with his father's gun, thinking it a shiny toy."

"That's *enough!*" John Whateley yelled, his voice full of wounded anger.

"You're just like the others, old fool. You know things I have every right to know! It's my birthright! You stole this knowledge, and now you hold back! You make excuses . . ."

Vreeland pointed a gnarled finger at his unwelcome visitor. "I take precautions!"

"Then at least tell me where she is! If she's still alive, that is. You can't deny me that!"

A new wave of pain crossed the lined face, causing it to assume familiar, if tortured, contours. A tear escaped his eye, but he laughed, too, in a crooked way. "Yes, she lives. But she is quite mad, mad as a hatter. She didn't use to be. People said she was, simply because she knew things the others had only heard about. But now her mind is gone. And . . . yes, I believe I'll tell you why. You say the Dee volume ought to be back in the hands of the Whateleys? It *is*, young John, it is. I'm only trying to prevent what happened to her happening to you, too!"

John Whateley's colorless eyes widened. "You mean *she* has it? Why the hell didn't you *tell* me?"

"I just *did*, you idiot! Go to her if you must! What happens won't be *my* fault! You'll have brought it on your own head. To hell with you!"

Vreeland breathed a sigh of relief, though a shallow one, as his intruder, a living piece of his own past which had come back to haunt him, left in haste, repeating to himself the directions the older man had given him. Vreeland reached for his amber-colored bottle of pills. Life for him had long since become a labor, almost more of an ailment than the heart malady that threatened to put an end to it.

As he sank back helplessly into his threadbare easy chair, he was not aware of the face that watched him from the grimed window, a face which had witnessed the heated exchange, a face set in a grimace of determination and cunning.

III

It was late afternoon. The sun sat low, filling the valley with softened light. Looking around him, John Whateley admired the dreaming beauty of Sesqua Valley. It seemed an enchanted place. The refreshing wind smelled of forest scents, and the quiet gave him peace of mind, a sensation he hadn't felt in many years. He closed his eyes momentarily and took a deep breath. Looking about him again, he caught sight of a nearby mountain over which a pale mist was forming. The mountain's double peak almost resembled jagged wings folded on the back of a crouching daemon. Its white stone shone in the soft light. John Whateley looked at the mountain for a long while and began to feel a familiar stirring in his soul, the same sort of thing he always experienced when approaching Sentinel Hill in Dunwich. It was almost as if Sentinel Hill had followed him out here to the Pacific Coast. That was of course nonsense, John knew, but he could not help feeling as if the mountain were calling to him, flaunting the prospect of supernal wonders to be gained.

Walking casually, he took in the sights of the small town. It was in most ways little different from the many he had seen in his long trip hitchhiking across the country. But one house caught his keen attention. It stood upon a grassy knoll, a huge and ancient mansion such as one might find in New England. The boarded windows bespoke abandonment, although it had evidently been the home of a wealthy family in better days. Why had it been allowed to fall into such disrepair? At one side stood a grove of crooked trees. One of them, he couldn't quite be sure it was an oak, had been allowed to grow up so close that its trunk had actually damaged a portion of the antique residence.

He approached the knoll, suddenly realizing he had found his destination. This must be the house Vreeland had directed him to. Was it a trick? Obviously no one had lived here in a very long time. But somehow it felt right nonetheless. The air felt different, somehow, like the rarefied atmosphere atop a tall elevation. Whateley felt a momentary dizziness, and for a second his mind seemed to go blank. It was quite peculiar. But didn't this, too, remind him of feelings he occasionally experienced when he sat on the great altar stone on Sentinel Hill? He tried to remember, but his mind seemed disjointed.

As he came nearer the knoll, he saw that a tree-house had been built on the sturdy branches of the nearest tree. A ladder lay on the grass next to the tree. On an impulse, John Whateley lifted the ladder and propped it against the tree trunk's diseased, pebble-textured bark. The structure looked firm enough. He rapidly ascended the uneven rungs, then put a cautious foot onto the floor of its one large room. His other foot found the floor and he stood within.

The place was mostly veiled in shadows, though they seemed darker than the encroaching dusk should have made them. As his eyes adjusted he could make out more and more detail. Looking about him, he smiled at the humble signs of habitation. There was a low table and a milk crate which served as a chair. In one corner were glass jars filled with different kinds of powder. From the ceiling, hanging on a length of strong twine, swung the skeleton of what looked to be a frog; but as he scrutinized the object he thought the skull was weirdly misshapen.

A battered, wooden bookcase was stuffed with disparate volumes. He thought he recognized a series of dog-eared popular novels, including several of the breezy romances of Robert W. Chambers. Many others had no titles on their spines, seeming to be privately printed and crudely bound. But others had titles he recognized in an instant, though he had never even seen them, much less read them, as they were written in languages he did not know. These included the Latin *Malleus Maleficarum* and Remegius' *Daemonolatry*. But many others, the *Mnemabic Fragments*, *The Song of Yste*, Yergler's *Chronicle of Nath*, the Marquis LeMode's *Dark Visions*, the *Black Sutra* of U Pao—all these were completely new to him. One volume was much larger, and older-looking, than the rest. Its binding had been reinforced with tape many times, and it appeared to lack a back cover. It had been slipped length-wise on top of a row of other books, being too tall to stand upright alongside them.

He stopped suddenly, his mind whirling: what were these books doing in a tree-house that was apparently the play area of some child? The answer came in the slight, lean form of a boy who had silently climbed the ladder and who now gazed at John Whateley with questioning, yet somehow knowing, eyes.

"Who are you?" the boy asked.

"I'm a stranger," John Whateley replied, then wondered at the oddness of his answer. The boy climbed all the way into the tree-house, and Whateley saw that he was tall as well as lean. The boy was dressed in black, his clothes hanging on him as they would on the thin stick-form of a scarecrow. His shock of wild black hair looked as though it had never once been brushed.

"We don't get many strangers here," said the boy, seeming to phrase his words with hidden intent. "We don't like being *bothered* by outsiders."

John Whateley said nothing, not wanting to betray the defensiveness he felt.

"Looking at the books?"

"Yes. Yes, I was. I must say you've got odd tastes for someone your age."

"I'm . . ." The boy hesitated, then continued in a strange tone redolent of both offense and amusement. "I'm old enough to study these, and I understand them pretty well, I think. Old Mr. Vreeland has been helping me study them for quite some time."

The mention of Vreeland's name rattled John Whateley. So the traitorous old bastard was still in the business of teaching his secrets, just not to *him*! He must return to Vreeland and confront him. This time he would not be denied. All else momentarily forgotten, he turned to leave.

"Don't go." The tall, black-clad youth spoke in a quiet voice. John Whateley did not like that voice, or the eyes that stared at him. "Don't go. I'm sorry; I'm not being fair with you. I know why you're here. Maybe I can answer some of your questions. And, yes, you're in the right place." A sly grin played on the boy's lips. Feeling very wary now, still John could not very well turn down a promise of information. Every other channel seemed to have been closed off.

"What's your name?" he asked suspiciously.

"You may possibly know the name: Whateley. I'm called Didymus Whateley."

At this news, John began to grow numb. He leaned against the rough wall of the clapboard structure for support. Amid his total disorientation, one seemingly irrelevant observation quietly obtruded. There was something about the shape of the boy's head, he suddenly noticed, the wide forehead and small ears, that puzzled him. He looked at the misshapen skull of the skeletal frog, then again at the mysterious Didymus, and he fancied there was a similarity in form.

"You see, I live here, with . . . *her*." With this he pointed further into the shadows of the interior of the surprisingly capacious tree-house. Reluctantly, John turned his eyes in the direction indicated.

There sat, or lay, the shapeless white bulk of her who once fancied herself Queen Mother. No clothes encompassed the obese folds of her translucent flesh. Perhaps she had once worn the tatters of rotten gauze on which she now lay, strewn with her own filth. Every few seconds her corpulent mass quivered in rhythm with some interior tick or cramp. Only wisps of her frazzled hair, almost like old corn silk, remained clinging tenuously to her scabbed and mottled scalp. Yet for the apparent decrepitude, the pink eyes of Lavinia Whateley glowed with a feverish alertness. With these she looked unwaveringly at her newly-arrived kinsman.

"Ye've come to answer th' Call, hev ye, young Johnny?" The voice seemed to echo strangely, as if coming from a farther distance.

"Why, why . . . *yes*, Mother Whateley! I *have*! The old man Vreeland wants to stand in my way, though I guess he knows it's too late now." John's voice, despite his intimidation, grew stronger and clearer as he began to realize that here, for the first time, another had recognized his true destiny, his destined greatness. Then he began to venture much.

"Mother Whateley, everyone else believed you dead. Murdered by Cousin Wilbur. But I knew better. I read Vreeland's letter to my father, and it wasn't hard to read between the lines, to see that you and he . . . , well, that he stood by you when the others thought your usefulness ended. Is he . . ." (pointing now to the young man in black) "Is Didymus here

297

your son, I mean, yours and Vreeland's? I suspected something like that must have happened to explain your sudden disappearance, and Vreeland's following you later."

The voice of Didymus broke in. "He is clever, but cleverly wrong." Turning to his cousin John, he went on. "You know much, but as you yourself surmise, there is ever so much more that you do *not* know. That is why you have come seeking the *Necronomicon*. But tell us, what is it you hope to gain by such knowledge?"

"I think you know," John said defiantly. "Or at least Mother Lavinia seems to know. I am the next in line, the rightful heir to succeed Cousin Wilbur in his task!"

Unimpressed, Didymus Whateley taunted him: "See? I told you you are missing crucial knowledge, poor John."

"So *tell* me, damn you! Don't play games with me!"

"All right, but can't you guess? It is *I* to whom that rank, that destiny, belongs. Mine is the mantle of Umr-at-Tawil. I am he, the Mahdi of Yog-Sothoth, the Opener of the Gate!"

John suddenly felt childish, silly, as if arguing with a playmate over who would take what role in a schoolyard pretend-game. He didn't know what to say next. The first thing that came to mind was an unconnected bit of curiosity: "Uh . . . why a tree-house? Why hide *here*, of all places? She deserves better than this . . ."

"The house is built at the exact point of one of the Gates, a small one that occurs just above ground level. Living in the zone is what keeps Mother Lavinia alive, physically, I mean. So we had to be up off the ground, you see."

"But," and here John Whateley stepped toward the threshold, looking below. "Then why not a simple two-story structure? Why the hell build a defenseless tree-house, for God's sake?"

"*You* called it tree-house, not me, Cousin Johnny. I wouldn"t exactly call it a tree-house because it's not exactly a *tree* . . ."

"I don't care what you call it. It's a far cry from what she deserves, what *you'd* deserve if you were really entitled to be what you claim. Why not build onto the mansion? No use letting it lie empty!"

"Oh, I can assure you it is far from empty. Tell me, wise one, did you know there are goats that bear a thousand young?"

"Look! I've had enough of your riddles! Why are you joking with me? Show the proper respect!"

Didymus only laughed again. And this time, so did the white mass in the shadows. John Whateley was shaken. "But, look! Then what about 'the Call'? Why did you summon me, if not to take what's rightfully mine?" His voice wavered with the futile half-heartedness of one who seeks to argue with bad news.

"Because we knew you'd be trouble. Vreeland knew your father, and he knew what to expect of his son," said Didymus matter-of-factly.

"And," came the queerly resonant whisper, choked off every few syllables by a phlegmy chuckle that erupted into a cough, "I know what to expect of my son! Y'see, Didymus here is a might older 'n he looks. I guess yew didn't know. Hell, even Papa didn't know. On that night long ago, I birthed a fine set o' *triplets*, an' now Didymus is all I got left. Ain't that so, boy?"

With this revelation, John Whateley, suddenly having crashed down again to mere mortality, began to inch his way toward the door. Meanwhile, the beloved son fell to his knees and went forward into the shadows, arms extended for a loathsome embrace with that which lay festering in a pool of darkness.

But as John gingerly felt for the first plank step in the evening darkness, something found him instead. With breathtaking speed he felt his feet, his legs, then the rest of him, tightly wrapped with intertwining tendrils, sucker-tipped, boneless limbs that were not tree-limbs as he had first thought. The house perched upon the Atlas-like trunk only shivered slightly, the ground slightly more, as John's collapsing body whipped like a rag-doll into the open maw of the gnarled, living trunk of the shoggoth. At least that is what John Whateley thought it was called, though his knowledge of these matters was, after all, a bit sketchy.

–1996–

AQUADINGEN

Hrothbard of Thüringen kept his balance and did not fall from the battlement of the ruined Rhine castle. The place was reputedly haunted, but that did not affront him. In truth, that was why he had come. It was the wrath of flesh and blood he feared, not that of Principalities and Powers, for these were his allies, or so he supposed. This night would tell.

The moon was full, and its silver radiance made even the substantial slabs of the castle seem little more than congealed spectral mist. He knew, from his studies, that the moonlight was quite another thing from the radiance of the sun, emanating from a different source altogether, no matter what foolish philosophers might prate. The moon was Hekate's sun, the dark light in which certain subtle shapes and forms might be spied if only one knew how and where to look. And this he was sure he knew.

For Hrothbard possessed the Book. The Book that whispered these and other secrets no other book had ever told. Old Magda the Crone had shown it to him and had taught him what wonders it was capable of. She called it *Cthäat Aquadingen* and said no man knew its origin. Though its words were German, albeit of an odd dialect unfamiliar to him, the Book had been written by Other hands than the hands of man. The potent syllable "Cthäat" itself survived from the original tongue to attest its arcane source. More striking still was the binding of the book—in human skin, from the feel of it. This bespoke a race of Beings who viewed man as no more than leather-bearing livestock. He shuddered to think much further in that direction. Nor did he care much to contemplate what measures might have pried such a volume from such hands, but now it rested safe in his own.

Hrothbard knew well enough what measures had been required to wrest the Book from the old and withered claws of she who had owned it before him. It took all the magical skill and guile he had mustered during many long years of apprenticeship to Old Magda, but eventually she, committing the mortal sin of trust, had relaxed her guard, and he had acted. A well-placed word of insinuation to the burgomeister was all it took, and even the powerful old Witch had been, like Samson, found vulnerable and at
300

bay. Hrothbard had been careful not to be present, like Iscariot, at the moment of arrest, but he could not very well shun the spectacle of her drowning. As a witch, she had floated readily enough, but the burgomeister's men soon took care of that.

And it was their wrath Hrothbard himself feared from the corner of his dark eye as he dared stand erect on this clear and luminous night, atop the abandoned pile bequeathed to decay and cobwebs by the vanquished pagans of a bygone century. He made ready to intone the baleful liturgy called the *Nyhargo Dirge*, which, lapsed monk that he was, he had recognized at once as the Latin text of the Funeral Dirge of Isaiah the Prophet for the fallen Belshazzar, only in reverse order, and with certain peculiar rhythmic pauses giving rise to cadences of sound and potent silence in which ancient invisible letters might be spoken with the mind.

The *Dirge*, it was said, and as he knew well, had power to raise up those who perished in the sea, and whose carrion the waves had never yielded up. Clasped thus to the sea's jealous bosom, such souls would have been vouchsafed secrets, secrets that might make a man rich with the wealth of a thousand sunken galleons. And there were other chants in this *Cthäat Aquadingen* whereby one might enlist the underwater spirits to recover such treasures, even as Solomon had.

Hrothbard had once been dumbfounded to behold the dripping mass of seaweed mercifully cloaking he dared not guess what, which heeded the summons of his mentoress when the two of them had journeyed long to the coast of ancient brooding Tyre. She had told him that, in life, the Being had been the captain of a trading vessel that plied the old sea-lanes of the Purple Kingdom in the days before it had earned Ezekiel's curse and been destroyed whole in one night. Who he had once been, the Thing could not remember, but the treasure, and where it lay, amid coral reefs and rotting timbers, it would recall. Its mortal spirit occupied the centuries doing naught else but to count the coins it could never spend, but which others might yet spend. And Hrothbard and Magda had spent them. Among other fine treats, they had spent a goodly share of it on perfumed wine, and it was as the old woman lay vulnerable in her cups that the authorities had taken her.

The words of the *Dirge* were hard to say. They blistered the tongue, seemed an urgent foulness that the mouth instinctively sought to spew out. Their resonances echoed in the chambers of the head until it seemed to toll like a cathedral bell. He had once seen Magda stagger and nearly

301

fall from the weight of saying them. And now he, too, faltered. But he stood his ground.

Below him, a splash sounded, as if his speaking had fallen like a rock into the waters of the Rhine. He had seen no one else from his quick survey of the radius of the castle, but that meant little. There would be many places to hide. Could the sound mean he had been seen? That pursuers were closing in upon him even now? He could not resist taking a look, extending his head even farther into the clear air, where he might be seen and discovered.

And he did see something. Not a pursuer, but the glint of gold below. There was something glowing softly on a heap of rocks just a few yards' wading away from the river bank. It took a moment to register. His words had been heard! The old barons whose castle this had been and who, legend said, had hidden their wealth in clever adyta somewhere along the banks, must now have yielded up their hoard. The water nymphs of the Rhine had already answered his blasphemous supplication!

As Hrothbard, rejoicing in the riches that were to be his, hastened down the way he had ascended, his thoughts were filled with the legends he had heard as a boy of the Rhine's gold, protected by dwarves and dragons, so tempting and yet so elusive to those without the proper resources at their disposal. The moonlight guided his steps, and he curbed his enthusiastic zeal lest it cost him his footing on the crumbling masonry of the old fortress.

He reached the ground, picked up his pace as he made his way to the edge of the dry land, slowed again as he had to pick his way through the impeding thicket of tall-grown reeds. They seemed denser than he had imagined, almost a marsh. Mephitic vapors rising from who knew what decaying nether mulch began to steal his breath. But in a few more moments Hrothbard was through the noisome barrier and splashing into the shallows. The rocks, still glowing gold in Hekate's silvery fire, were rather farther from the bank than his loftier perspective had suggested, but still it was no great distance. Perhaps it seemed farther than it was because of the dream-like slowness that retarded all his movements. But did not time always seem to slow the more urgent one became?

At last, water coming up to his neck, Hrothbard made the rocks and began to clamber up onto them, guided like a moth to the gleam of his reward. He surmounted the crest of the rock-heap, made sure of his footing, and looked about. Yes, there was gold.

But it moved.

For a moment recognition refused to come, because his eyes had expected a different sight. But then they accepted what lay before them, long, shining sheets of golden hair. Draping the face of the rock like fish nets drying in the sun, the amazing tresses of a woman caught and gave back Hekate's silver luminance. He followed the golden tresses like sun rays, from their circumference to their center, fearing to look upon what he would find, such beauty as might dazzle the eye that gazes into the noon.

He saw her face and did not look away. She was *Lorelei*. She was the very vision of beauty. She was Aphrodite risen from the waves. Perhaps she had come to guide him to the treasure, for he could now see the rest of her. Her lower body was, in very truth, just as old tales had said, the graceful fin of a sleek fish! But no less beautiful for its exotic strangeness. Was she not a water nymph come to show him the lost gold of the Rhine? Or, the thought whispered itself, might *she* not be the treasure he sought? Such loveliness was treasure enough for Croesus, by all the djinn!

She said nothing in words, but her limpid eyes spoke well, as did her arms, lithely beckoning. Her delightful breasts seemed to move of themselves slightly, as if caressed underwater by soft, drifting currents, just as Hrothbard wished very much just now to caress them.

He dropped to his knees, never minding the hardness of the jagged rock, and made to embrace the comely form of the sea sprite whom his wishes had called forth. Her arms enfolded him perfectly with a strange boneless suppleness in a passionate embrace. She, too, must be eager for the touch of flesh on flesh, flesh entering flesh.

But who laughed? What unsteady cackle wafted like a scent over the surface of the night-calmed water? Hrothbard, kindling with rage that some upstart might dare spy upon his triumphant ecstasy, tore his gaze away from his prize to scan the bank. He saw well, as the shore seemed now to be as near to the rock as it had before. And on its slope stood a shapeless figure whose features were shadowed by the covers of a massive book it held open to the listening sky.

The Book!

Of course, he had left it on the river bank, fearing to lose the precious volume in the mud and the reeds. But who had taken it up? The small figure of some impudent child from the village? If so, he should have a lesson in manners he would not soon forget!

But the cackle had turned into a series of articulate, though still unrecognized, words. *Mein Gott!* They were words from the *Cthäat*

303

Aquadingen. One of them sounded like *Cthylla.* No idler would know how to say them. Hrothbard, now filling up with a cloud of confusion that barely veiled terrible realization, sought to free himself from the embrace which held him with a passion, the nature of which he was just beginning to suspect.

His back and shoulders commenced to scream with a thousand tiny stabbings, as their surface yielded to the terrific force of tiny suckers lining the steely coils he had thought were arms. His widening eyes caught a second sight of the expanse beneath the torso and saw that the streaming locks had veiled no mermaid tail but a mass of clumped and layered cilia, which now began to unfurl and to seek. As the squid-like thing flipped itself over to slide off the rock and glide back under the surface, the golden tresses seemed like nothing so much as a great tuft of corn silk protruding from an ear of irregularly bubbled corn.

Great draughts of red beclouded the water, then spread like a slick toward the shore. The stunted form set the book down on the grass, descended the bank, pale toe-stubs heedlessly squishing in the gray mud. Her knees followed them with a splash, and Magda cupped her palms to catch up the blood and drink.

–1997–

304

Annotations for the Book of Night

Here is the true account of the rediscovery and restoration of the long lost *Noctuary of Vizooranos*, an ancient parchment of great sorcerous potency by the testimony of the wizards of olden times. And though I, Eibon of Mhu Thulan, may justly claim credit for the exhumation of the scroll, the restoration was even the labor of another, the which I mean now to relate as a wholesome caution to whatsoever scribes may in future take in hand the transcription of these, mine own testaments.

Long had I searched among the libraries of what palaces and monasteries I might gain access to, and moreover inquired among my necromantic colleagues, in quest of a half-fabulous volume of occult lore, even the aforesaid scroll of the mighty Vizooranos, mage of elder days. Little was known of the exact contents of the writing, but legend held that the scroll bore revelations of a kind so black that Vizooranos must needs write them by night shrouded in the utter dark of the New Moon, with not a candle burning in the house. These oracles did he receive from certain devils of the Outer Darkness, the which did send his pen curling and swerving in all manner of eldritch hieratic scripts, yet supplying withal the arcane sentience wherewith to unriddle the same when he should peruse the screed in the dawn of wholesome daylight.

It was whispered that the revelations contained in this *Noctuary of Vizooranos* had been wrung from the fraying lips of damned souls dipped screaming into the magma pits of the Eleven Scarlet Hells of ancient myth. Such dread oracles were said to concern the secrets of infernal torture and how they might be wrought upon still-living flesh, as well as a catechism of the inconceivable lecheries and blasphemies for which these damned had been consigned to the boiling lakes.

For a time I set my search aside, for that no success appeared forthcoming, and other, more urgent tasks did press upon me. And so it was quite by chance some years later that, in the process of collating divers manuscripts treating of the deposition of wizardly relics, I found a clue. It is not exceptional that two or three sites may claim to be the final resting place of a sorcerer or sage of renown; nor is it rare for all these asseverations to have some merit, as the bones and possessions of such

305

men are often divided and distributed among their followers, who build shrines in divers places. But when it chanceth that two shrines should each aver to guard the whole of a great one's mortal bequests, the scholar must suspect either pious fraud or simple error. Haply may it eventuate that two ancient ones of similar names or epithets become confused as the memories of men, even of attendant priests, do fade. And thus had I identified twain mausolea professing to house the complete remains of the mage Lithondriel of Uzuldaroum. Some inner voice whispered unto me that more might lie at the root of the conundrum than mere error and misclassifying. And so I set out on pilgrimage to one site, then the other.

At the first shrine I besought the priests of the crypt to permit me to apply certain tests to the entombed remains of the supposed Lithondriel, and at this they seemed somewhat affronted, as if they themselves feared it might not be the venerable Lithondriel in truth who lay within. And should such prove out, they liked not the prospect of the fact being noised abroad and their livelihood withering even as the body within the tomb, whomsoever's it might be. But with appropriate pledges of silence I persuaded them, and much were they relieved when the trial did corroborate the tradition of their shrine. This left me the task of determining who might repose in the second tomb, as it were, of Lithondriel, and to this I now hastened, seeking out the second crypt in a village not far from the former.

Myself now being well apprised that the occupant of this second mausoleum was anyone but the dead Lithondriel, I was not such a fool as to vouchsafe these tidings to the custodians of that fane, but rather repeated those things I had formerly told the priests of, as it chanced, the true Lithondriel. These, too, gave assent with no great difficulty, and, with their help did I contrive to open the great sarcophagus.

The supine form of the one within was even one with the dust of the ages, the merest shards of brittle bone remaining unto him. But there in the sacred casket lay a metal tube, which I knew for the repository of a tight-rolled scroll! The corroded cartouche thereof gave me to think that my olden quest had borne fruit at last, for if my widening eyes deceived their master not, the faded glyphs gave forth the name Vizooranos. Claiming this treasure as the price of my service, I hesitated not in solemnly assuring the anxious priests that it was indeed the earthly detritus of the master sage Lithondriel who drowsed away the ages under their gentle care, and I was on my way again.

Having returned again to mine own tower of solitude, I made to open the cylinder, having first dismissed the guardian demons who, long since bored with their duties, were glad enough to depart and put up no resistance. Removing the cap, I tapped the antipodal end and gingerly took hold of the parchment roll within. Sanding away the waxen seal, I set about unfurling the scroll, mindful of its brittleness that it not shatter like the fallen egg of an archaeopteryx.

But to my dismay I saw how the parchment book lay already in tatters, veritably riddled with lacunae. Manifestly, someone had sought not so much to preserve the *Noctuary* of the wizard Vizooranos as to inter its forlorn remains along with those of its owner! It had suffered ruinous damage before being deposited with the corpse of the mage. I was no stranger to ancient and fragmentary texts, and I knew that with ingenuity and intuition, the clever scribe might make ample progress toward restoring what had been lost.

And yet what held true for ancient records and annals might not avail for such a text as this terrible *Book of Night*, for that the matters treated of in the parchment required adamantine certainty. One dared not trust to approximation and conjecture when in their zone of indeterminacy lay the difference between commanding a fiend and being devoured horribly by the same. One likes not to wager one's immortal essence upon a vowel point.

The hour was late, and mine eyes grew red and sore from much scrutiny by the green flame of my tallow, so I snuffed it out and retired. Mayhap, methought me, I should approach the task upon the morrow with clearer mind and quicker wits.

And even so it seemed to eventuate, for, having completed my mundane chores, from which even a wizard be not exempt altogether, such as feeding mine basilisk, reinforcing anew the warding charms containing the seven headache demons which would miserably afflict me if I kept them not at bay thus wise, and suchlike, I returned to the tattered scroll of Vizooranos, and I rubbed mine eyes in astonishment. Had senility in truth crept up so stealthily? For before me lay a scroll noticeably less decrepit than it had seemed the preceding night! But, faugh!, I chided myself and my errant imagination: it could be naught else than a mischievous memory which had overmagnified the plight. In the light of mid-morn the difficulty simply appeared less daunting to a refreshed spirit, and that was doubtless the whole truth of it.

Though the text was after all fearfully torn and decomposed, it did seem plainer to my gaze that these rare hieroglyphs concealed blasphemies which ancient rumor had not greatly exaggerated. A weight deposited itself upon the shoulders of my soul, and I commenced to musing that mayhap it were not so grave a tragedy as I had deemed it for such secrets as the mad Vizooranos had set down here to have perished. Almost I hoped that the remainder of the text might refuse to yield up its enigmas, though not once did I make to leave off my task. For knowledge must be preserved, its nature notwithstanding, and any who doth not what he may to prevent its perishing is surely a murderer and rightly so judged.

On the next day of my studies in the *Book of Night* of Vizooranos, I marked again the unmistakable reaugmentation of lost portions of the text, almost as if some scribe had secretly penetrated mine own inner sanctum, bearing with him a more perfect copy, and filled in what was lacking here and there, so that, while much remained in fragments, substantially more might now be read. It was evident to me, reading the newly recovered passages, that by far the blackest and most foul pericopae had been anciently effaced, and that not by chance. And, moreover, though the script be mostly alien to me, I fancied that the scribal hand was somehow familiar. Verily, the mystery of the repristination of the *Noctuary* had become even one with the secrets the text did purport to vouchsafe, though I confess I was no closer to solving the one than the other.

On the fourth day I found more of the missing text had been filled in, and even rents in the very parchment repaired in some wise not apparent. And I went back through those portions I had conjecturally restored. Where once I had thought to find gaps and erasures at crucial junctures, and speculated accordingly, I now found lines of script clearly and boldly legible. Moreover, on comparing mine own notes with the veritable reading of the text, I saw most dreadful errors which would shortly have spelled my doom had I proceeded to conjure on the basis of them.

As I pored over the scroll, what had formerly teased me became plain at last: the writing in which the corrections had been made was precisely like unto mine own! With this I did set quill and ink pot aside, resolving to wait till the next dawn when mayhap the scroll should have been altogether restored to its first state, whether by mine own hand or another's.

And forsooth, by the bulging belly of Zhothaqquah, it was! I sat, slowly and full of awe, before my reading stand, the fully intact *Noctuary of Vizooranos* spread out before me. Here was the fruit of long searching, won through despite the naysaying of rivals and brethren alike, who averred the *Book of Night* no longer lay anywhere upon this terrestrial disk. Now it was mine to delve into the disquieting secrets of mummified devils and aeon-perished Nephilim. But was it in truth a cup of poisoned wine I sought to

308

quaff, however sweet its vinous taste? For a time I dared not let mine eyes sink to the Gorgonic sight that might forever damn them to look upon steaming infernos of bubbling gore.

And softly did a whisper intrude upon my fear. Without articulate sound it bade me trace with pointing finger, as if another guided it (and I bethought me of the manner in which the scroll had first been transcribed by devilish afflatus), till I came upon a necromantic litany, even the frightful Disgorging of the Pit. As I read with silent trepidation its loathsome vocables, I began to sense the gathering of ectoplastic atoms and knew that so potent was the invocation that it had no need of being enunciated aloud! By doing naught but reproducing the words in my mind I had caused them to work their wizardry!

I staggered back, upsetting my heavy chair, as a Being materialized before me. Having never seen his likeness, I nonetheless knew the visage for that of old Vizooranos himself, smiling evilly.

A Voice issued forth, investing all things nearby with an ultrapolar chill. "Thou hast freed me, O Eibon, with the commendable zeal of thine erudition. Such was mine own in my day that I plumbed depths undreamt of before or since in gaining the ultimate knowledge, for all that it did forever blast my soul. Yet have I abided, all these ages, trapped in my mortal dust with the gaoler's key almost in reach. For the spell thou hast read ought to have called me forth, save that the dead cannot raise himself, and my disciples to whom I had entrusted the *Book* proved unworthy, letting it fall prey both to natural desuetude and to the violations of the faint-hearted and the inquisitor, till at last the potency of the thing was lost. But thou hast found the *Noctuary* and, bearing it away, thou hast borne me with thee also, and now I have caused thee to rise each night unknowing and restore what was lost, so that in the end, the spell might be there to be read again, as thou hast read just now, unto the freeing of my essence from this mortal sphere."

His translucent form began to drift away as mist in the face of the rising sun, but before it was entirely dispersed, of a sudden, I had scooped up the scroll and held it out to the vanishing spectre. And thus was the *Noctuary of Vizooranos* restored unto its owner and unto the Elder Night from whence it had first come. And I count myself in no wise poorer for the loss.

–1997–

The Burrower Beneath

It is said that immortality is for the gods alone, and with this precept I, even Eibon of Mhu Thulan, am devoutly inclined to agree. But it was not always thus with me. For in earlier days, ere I learned it were possible to grow weary of life, I dared to know if perchance mortal man might attain unto the immortal durance of the gods. Nor was I daunted in this quest, save only by the fulfillment thereof. But I speak in paradoxes and had best retrace my steps that my meaning may become manifest, for 'tis a lesson I would deposit here for the pondering of others.

It was in the first flower of my mastery of the esoteric arts that I did injudiciously reckon myself capable of any marvel I might conceive if only the proper technique be found, nor lacked I the boldness to fancy I might find or fashion the means to accomplish any task I set upon. Moreover, well knew I that much was discovered by the elder magi which has since been suffered to lapse into forgetful oblivion by those of too timid a disposition to pay the price of a glimpse Beyond. But I was possessed of no such qualms; hence I dared barter with certain unclean fiends, paying a fee I like not to name, for the recovery of long-interdicted screeds penned by devils in inks of molten blood.

Of these mayhap the foulest blasphemies lurked in that papyrus called *The Black Rituals of Koth-Serapis*, an enchanter dire who vexed the earth in the lost days of Acheron. For it was whispered in the banned and shunned circles of nether adepts that the unholy Koth-Serapis had contrived forever to cheat death. And, foolish novice that I was, despite my scholarly and thaumaturgical achievements, I determined to uncover the sand-blown path trod in elder days by dark Koth-Serapis. My reasoning was thuswise: if in truth that mage had attained unto the very secret of unending life, it must still, even with the passage of uncounted centuries, be feasible for one such as myself to make contact with him. That the attempt should not prove easy deterred me not a whit, and thus did I embark, defying the sage cautions of brother wizards my elder in years and much my superior in wisdom.

None of my sorcerous brethren had any clue to aid me had they wished to do so. Thus I knew I should have to seek what help I might through other, less dependable channels. I reasoned that, of all beings, the ones likeliest apprised of the whereabouts of a man made immortal would be those whom mortality had already claimed. Whether from envy or not, the dead might be supposed to know somewhat of one who had cheated the fate that had overtaken them, in like manner to earthly prisoners who lionize their cleverer brethren who have escaped the dungeon that still holds the rest of them. But I must needs seek the spirit of one who shared the earth with the ancient Koth-Serapis, and one who himself knew sufficient of the necromantic arts to guide me unto my hoped-for mentor.

At length I fastened upon the far-distant isle of Serendip for my most profitable goal, for that it did constitute one of the last-remaining fragments of sundered Lemuria, that primal continent from the dawn age of the earth, from whence the primordial Dragon Kings did reign before the fabled Mahathongoya did drive them forth, as is written in the hoary pages of the *Upa-Puranas*, after which they did take refuge, some in Valusia, some in mine own land of Hyperborea. There I hoped to find the ruins of the much-legended Tomb of Sharajsha, greatest of the magi of the pre-Cataclysmic age.

So I did book passage on a slaver's vessel embarking from the southern harbors of Atlantis and headed East. The adventures I encountered on the voyage may be told in their own place, but I must needs be on with my tale. Suffice it that I contrived, once or twice, to lure up from the deep in the lightless hours of the New Moon some few of the finny children of Dagon, who assured me that the Temple of Sharajsha still stood and told me of the most auspicious route there.

After many days our ship reached the shores of the island I sought, and I bade my companions farewell. Most sorry were they to lose me, too, for that my command of certain elemental spirits had more than once proved valuable in providing fair weather for sailing, and they should henceforth have to rely upon Nature's caprices as hitherto.

In the wave-beaten kingdom of Serendip I was cordially received by the ruler of the island who kindly put at my disposal all manner of provisions I should require for this last earthly stage of my quest. By way of gratitude I enlivened the evening's feasting with a number of simple conjurer's tricks which all present received with unbridled childish delight.

Early on the morrow, accompanied by a small party of dusky-skinned bearers, who did not cease to remark to one another upon my sun-paled Northern coloration, I set forth into the jungled recesses of the island. The unaccustomed heat I kept at bay by use of a cantrip learned from the dwarves of Hyperborea who spend much time amid subterranean magmic fires forging rune-inscribed arthame-swords like the one that even now slapped my hip as I walked.

After we had covered some distance amid the gorgeous jungle luxuriance, the like of which is not to be found in my own land, I directed my companions to depart from the well-trod pathways known to them, keeping to that course vouchsafed me by the scaly Dagonites. But at this suggestion, they were sore afraid, as the proposed detours must take us through certain zones anciently forbidden them under pain of dire taboo. I assured them they need not fear so long as they remained close in my presence, but some begged leave to camp where they were and await my return, seeing that I professed not to fear aught that might eventuate. For a primitive people their logic was quite sound, even though they might exercise it in the interest of base superstition, and in the end I insisted that they all linger there together and await me.

In truth, the ruined fane of the Lemurian mage lay not much farther away, and I gained the goal before the sun had set. In the slanting rays of the tropical sun I came upon what remained of the elder temple, which old scrolls made both mausoleum to the great wizard and altar of sacrifice unto his spirit. The weight of history bore heavily upon me as I stood in the presence of a mighty shadow from the epic past. Almost I felt that no ceremony should be needful, so powerfully did I feel his eldritch presence. Nonetheless I hastened to observe the ancient protocol prescribed for such solemn occasions, drawing forth from my baggage the brazen tripod for the offering of incense. Slowly I incanted the Great Necromantic Invocation and breathed deep the oracular fumes. The sense of time slipped from me and at some point I was made aware of a Personage standing before me, radiant with a strange penumbral fire.

"Why hast thou disturbed my rest, O man of the latter days?"

I fell to my knees before the mighty apparition and averted my gaze from his brow which seemed a darksome thundercloud. "Great Lord Sharajsha! I bid thee hear me out! I have come a great distance . . ."

"I have come a greater!"

"Yea, Lord, forgive my effrontery. I pray thee, tell me how I may find the undying Koth-Serapis!" In all this I dared not look into the face of That One I had dared summon.

"Thou wouldst call up a dead mage to find a living devil? His is a path no sane mind shall follow. I give thee this warning, O Eibon. Moreover, I shall grant thy boon, for that I see thou hast not in thee to take that which thou seekest once thou find it. And if the blasphemy of Koth-Serapis hath again become a lure unto mankind, it may be profitable for the truth of it to be revealed."

I returned to my faithful bearers, offering my regrets for having delayed them overlong, though in truth I had no sense for how much time had transpired. They gazed at me as at one mad, saying how I had left them but moments before, and that scarce had they sat to wait for me. We turned and made our way back to the palace of the Prince of the island in uneasy silence. I kept my counsel all the long months of my journeying back to the Hyperborean shores, assured now that my path lay clear before me, yet with a foreboding sense that the fulfillment of my desire would nevertheless not satisfy me. Little had I yet learned from the enigmatic oracle of the shade of Sharajsha. But all would soon become clear.

Back among the familiar surroundings of mine own sorcerous sanctum where fuelless flames and bubbling potions surrounded me with comforting warmth, I made ready again, with a weariness of soul, to take flight to a distant shore, though this time it be one supramundane, for that Sharajsha's revelation indicated no less a destination than the dread Vale of Pnath, the which I had not yet visited so early in my magickal career.

I made ready the needful preparations and in no time floated freely above my fleshly vessel. Freed thus from the blinders of the flesh, I now saw all manner of hidden things which circulate invisibly about us every hour, and which it is a mercy to have hidden from us. Likewise, a glance over to the stairwell leading from my chamber revealed what daylight obscured, even the onyx staircase of seven thousand steps to the Underworld of Deep Dendo.

Down these I rapidly made my way until I saw stretching before me the baleful expanse of the Vale of Pnath, a wasteland like unto the silvered sands of the Moon, where evil Mnomquah holdeth foul sway. I liked not what I saw and knew that even in mine astral form I might meet with untold dangers in such a place. Like a drifting specter I passed over the desolate and much-cratered face of Pnath, seeking a certain Pit, named in suppressed legends as the Abyss of Noth, whereunto the cryptical whispers of dead Sharajsha had directed me. I lingered a moment upon the Precipice of Noth to gaze at the fearful spectacle outstretched in the shifting infra-red vapors below me. For there lay none other than the blighted Necropolis of Nug-Hathoth of which the ancient lore-masters record naught that is wholesome.

313

I must needs take care to arrive no sooner than the fateful Hour of the Opening of the Under Burrows, the which I should know by the noxious Rising of the Black Wind which would bear up unto my ears the terrible gruntings of the Dholes as they issued forth in blind fumblings to commence their charnel feastings. I deemed it best to settle down upon the crest of the upthrust Tower of Narghan, and there to await the emergence of the eyeless slugs from their curiously asymmetrical burrows.

It was the sudden tortured wailing of unseen hounds that heralded the arrival of those unclean Ones whom I awaited. I made ready to descend to the nitrous tunnel mouths below when, of a sudden, there arose before me a jetting column of viscid loathsomeness, the titan form of the greatest of charnel behemoths, fully as tall as that high tower on whose pinnacle I stood! Its face, if such it may be called, betrayed no sign of sentience, its only true feature a sticky and unclean maw which yawned hideously and worked unceasingly, drooling with unspeakable poisons.

Great was my affrighted shock when the thing spoke in human accents! "Name thyself, mortal man, that I may know whom I am about to digest."

"Nay, King of the Dholes, thou mayest not feast upon my ectoplasm, as I am not the soul of one dead, but only on a journey, seeking for nighted wisdom and the mysteries of the worm. In truth, I seek for the undying wizard Koth-Serapis; knowest thou aught concerning him, O Burrower Beneath?"

At this, something perhaps intended as mirth escaped the fanged hole. "And wherefore wouldst thou find that one, O morsel?"

I liked his converse less and less and hoped he might unveil the knowledge I sought before I must endure more of his soul-upheaving stench, which even the senses of the astral body may detect.

"For that legends say he alone of all mortals hath attained unto immortality, and this secret I would know. Now I bid thee in the Bond of Pnath to tell me of the whereabouts of that Koth-Serapis, if indeed thou knowest."

That living pillar of cosmic foulness did commence fairly to quake with uncontrolled hilarity till methought its hideous bulk would shudder asunder.

"Know then that Koth-Serapis the mage learned that in no wise may the flesh of mortals retain a hold upon life forever. But it may yet cheat death by embracing the same the more fully. By force of adamant will may the wizard, if he but maintain the mindfulness thereunto at the moment of death, endure through the defilement of his carcass by the maggot's

314

tongue, till he passeth with the last shred of fleshly sustenance into the conqueror worm, whereupon may he bend the brainless vermin to his will, instructing the very worm that gnaws till he find himself reborn, new and oddly embodied."

Having gained the awful knowledge for which I had dared so much, I turned and fled in the most disgraceful fashion, leaving the mocking laughter of my informant echoing telepathically in my stricken brain. The shocking truth thus revealed to me cut short my journey, and I did start awake back in my chamber in the black tower of Mhu Thulan. Then well did I perceive the wisdom of Sharajsha, that only in learning the secret of immortal durance should I resolve never to pursue it more, and, though I have since not scrupled to prolong my earthly sojourn by certain esoteric means, when death at last does come to claim me, I shall look upon his visage as that of a friend and join him gladsomely. For in the last moment I knew the inconceivable price paid by ancient Koth-Serapis, in that it was his own towering, maggoty bulk which spoke to me!

–1997–

Feery's Original Notes

I

I sat, again, lost to the ticking hours, in the Reading Room of the British Museum, an institution which, though in general quite accommodating, just would not remain open long enough to suit me. The task in which I was engaged would have been simply impossible during a normal semester's activity at Brichester, but I was fortunate to have gained the boon of a grant substantial enough to allow me to holiday among the fragile pages of medieval sheepskin bearing the pen marks of one Dr. Dee. The material, though obscure and apparently alien to the area of my professional interests, was actually quite fascinating. I am by vocation a professional mathematician, though my need to understand mathematics from within a larger cultural frame of reference had led me to take on the history and philosophy of science as a second subject area of virtually equal interest. The astrological and kabbalistic intricacies of John Dee, court magus to Queen Elizabeth, might not seem to fall within either of my purviews, as I say, and I found myself rehearsing an elaborate explanation to every acquaintance who knew enough of my activities to find my occult delvings a surprise. At the point my story commences I had paused to rub my tired eyes, only to open them and behold yet another puzzled face. This time it was the curator of rare manuscripts.

"Pardon my curiosity, Professor Wentworth, but I cannot contain my curiosity any longer. Is not your specialty the history of higher mathematics and such matters? Of what interest can the vagaries of a medieval magician be to you? If your field were cryptography, even linguistics, I could see it, but . . ."

I knew it was time for my accustomed performance. I had again been called to account. And as I owe my reader the same explanation, I will undertake it here once again.

"Your curiosity is natural, Dr. Richardson. An incongruity like mine alerts a mind such as yours that, academically, the game is afoot. You know how one always finds a lost article the last place one can think of to search? Well, I have decided to jump ahead of the game by veering off to the last drawer first! If you were a colleague, why, I suppose I might

316

hesitate to tell you, but I know your position requires a clergyman's ethic of confidentiality."

"Indeed it does!" he laughed, "though I've never heard it put that way!" I was happy enough to take a break, so I pushed my chair back from the library table upon which my papers and books fanned out like the wake of a ship, though I wasn't sure this particular boat was going anywhere. Settling in more casually, I beckoned Dr. Richardson, a convivial enough fellow, to take the chair next to mine. I knew he would feel guilty about talking in a library, so I kept my voice low.

"My primary interest is indeed mathematical. I am sure you know of the important role played by Arabic savants in the development of mathematics, the old joke that the Arabs gave nothing to the world."

"Invented the zero, I believe."

"Exactly right. Which was like inventing the wheel if mathematics was ever really to get moving. The contributions of the Muslim scholars, especially the court scribes of the Abbasid golden age are inestimable, and not only in math. They kept philosophy alive, too, when the best minds in Europe were tying themselves into stubborn knots over the Trinity and the miracle of the mass. Where would we be if Avicenna, Averroes, and the rest hadn't rediscovered Aristotle and held him in trust for the rest of us?"

"Undoubtedly, Professor, but this ground has been covered before, no?"

"Indeed it has. But where some paths have been rather heavily trodden, there may be neglected paths, weed-grown and waiting to be traced out by the adventurous and the curious."

"In other words, by those who have a nose to sniff out tangents and byways."

"That's what I'm hoping. I first went astray, onto my present course that is, while paging through a copy of Mathers's *Greater Key of Solomon*. I forget now how I happened to be looking at it. What caught my eye was the series of elaborate magic circles and pentacles, all crossing double lines, labeled with strange-looking words in various alphabets. It reminded me of nothing more than textbook charts of geometrical proofs and theorems. At first I made nothing of it, assumed there was nothing to be made of it. But it wouldn't let me go. Finally I realized what my subconscious was telling me. I realized it might be a hunch worth pursuing to see if the resemblance I had remarked were more than superficial. Was it possible that these strange diagrams were intended as mathematical formulae of

317

some sort, if only one possessed the key? I decided to start with the old Arabic magic books by al-Kindi, So-&-so, etc."

"And were you right?"

"Still too early to tell, I'm afraid. As I say, there's the matter of the key. But I'm optimistic. I can't believe all that effort went into these things to no purpose."

"But there was a purpose, surely, method in the madness: they thought to summon up demons and things that go bump in the night."

"So they say. But I find it difficult to believe that magic was more than a cipher language. After all, how attractive could it have been after a few tries made it clear the stuff wouldn't work? Something must have kept the old boys at it."

"You're pretty sure it didn't work."

"Well, yes, as a man of science, I have to be."

"Excuse me, Professor, but aren't you indulging a bit of what Lewis called 'chronological snobbery'?"

"I think not. You see, I'm giving those old boys quite a bit of credit. I'm working on the assumption that they were speaking the language of science even as we are, but that their contemporaries couldn't understand it."

"Yes, but why the cipher? Why not make it understandable to their contemporaries?"

"My suspicion is that their speculations were well ahead of their time, maybe even ahead of our time, which may be one reason I haven't yet cracked their code. Even today there are heresies within the academy. Step too far out of the conventional parameters and you win the label 'crank.' Only in their day, scientific eccentricities were not so easily forgiven. Think of Galileo. What if the official scholars, with the patronage of the Caliphs, came to think of the current scientific orthodoxy as one with their religious orthodoxy. To step outside the one would be to step outside the other, and then you start to be pretty circumspect about who you share your theories with. You learn to speak your own language. Why the language of magic? Probably because that's what their enemies branded it."

"All very fascinating, Professor Wentworth, and I don't believe it will violate my pledge of librarian's confidentiality to tell you it's a new one as far as I know. No one else I know has perused our pages with this in mind. But you still haven't told me what the estimable Dr. Dee has to do with it."

318

"To tell the truth, it really isn't Dee I'm interested in. All his work in the Enochian language, crystal-scrying, that I leave to someone else. I'm primarily interested in Dee as a translator of the *Al Azif*."

A shadow crossed the archivist's face. It seemed we were no longer trading polite diversions.

"The *Necronomicon*."

"I'm afraid so, Dr. Richardson. What's the matter? Something seems to be."

"It's just that we . . . have trouble with people who request that book. But I'm sorry for my reaction. I'm afraid it's just reflex. You're obviously not in the same category."

"I hope not! Remember, what I'm after is, as you put it, the method in the madness. The math behind the madness. I've already been through the Olaus Wormius Latin and I've an interlibrary request in for Theodorus Philetas' Greek, though I'm pessimistic. Don't think I'll be able to avoid a trip to see that one. You'd be surprised to know what we don't have at Brichester, or what it is policy to say we don't have."

"Why so many translations?"

"In lieu of manuscripts. I'm trying to do a critical text of certain portions of the book. Ideally, I'd like to be able to compare surviving copies of the original Arabic or, failing that, the Greek, the earliest foreign language version. Only there just isn't enough manuscript evidence for that. As far as the authorities in the field know, the Arabic text has not survived, and there are precious few copies of any later version, many of them incomplete and freely interpolated—or bowdlerized. Really, it's chaos. But I need to get back as far as I can to see the pentacles and magic circles in their original state if I can. If there had been any mathematical precision in the originals, it would have been rapidly effaced the first time any serious miscopying or rewriting took place. I can trace some serious corruptions, enough to make me fear the task may be hopeless. But on the other hand, it stands to reason that it would work the other way, too. That is, if the diagrams were more than random decorations, anything close to a mathematically intelligible arrangement should allow me to restore the hypothetical original by adjusting the extant text to something that makes sense. Of course the danger there is creating supposedly ancient evidence in my own image. But it seems worth a try."

The venerable librarian shook his head in feigned exasperation, as if what I said were beyond him. A smile told me his good humor was restored, and I felt almost as if he were an uncle proud of the unexpected

319

ingenuity of a favorite nephew. He paused a moment.

"Well, now that you've told me what you're really after, there is another item I believe you might be interested in seeing. Something not listed under Dee."

I finished a couple of notes on my laptop computer as I waited in mild curiosity to see what new complication Dr. Richardson might throw onto the heap of my researches. He was a half an hour or so in returning. When he did he was carrying a shabbily bound volume bearing the embossed title *Original Notes on the Necronomicon*. Opening the loose-hinged cover board I sought the author's name. There it was, somewhat smudgily printed on the title page: Joachim Feery. It was not a familiar name. Lower down on the same page was the date of publication, 1943. I paged through, turning the coarse paper leaves, glancing here and there.

Dr. Richardson told me I might take the book with me, as copies were by no means rare nor sought after. I thanked him and decided to call it a day.

II

On the train back to the Severn Valley I dozed, as I usually cannot help doing on a train ride of any length, trusting to some inner alarm to rouse me before I miss my stop. But my research was much on my mind and invaded my catnap. I dreamed that I held the Feery volume open before me, deeply engrossed by the secrets it offered, secrets I seemed to be reading as a character in my dream, but to which I, as the observer, was not privy. And then, of a sudden, I found myself falling through the open book, as if its rectangle were that of an open window. I awoke with a shudder and a gasp, as if from one of the dreams of falling so common to our childhood years. My sudden coming to was noted with irritable looks by those around me, whose own dozing, I guessed, I had disturbed.

Taking the hint my subconscious had given me, I reached under my seat to recover my satchel and felt about for the book. It's cheap binding and general appearance almost seemed disappointing after the importance the book had possessed in my dream. But you know the proverb about judging a book by its cover.

It looked to be a strange sort of commentary on bits of the *Necronomicon*, nothing systematic, in accord with the title: notes, remarks, not a comprehensive treatment. It looked like Feery had worked from a copy of Dee, perhaps the same one I was perusing. But I could see at a glance that he had silently emended the text at certain points, adding whole sentences. Other times he had drawn attention to textual corruptions and supplied his own corrections, though he cited no manuscript authority. Sometimes he would simply overrule the text, as if the original author had it wrong and Feery knew better.

The whole appeared to partake of a kind of self-schooled erudition, genuinely learned, but apodictic. The author had simply expected to be believed on his own say-so. An analogy might be the eccentric Bible commentaries issued by self-appointed scripture scholars and television preachers to whom it does not occur to doubt that their whims and inspirations were any less than the illuminations of the Holy Ghost. I envied such writers their naiveté: direct inspiration certainly would be a short-cut! But there is no way to cheat in genuine scholarship.

Little of this would have interested me beyond serving as confirmation of Dr. Richardson's words that the *Necronomicon* had a habit of attracting the attentions of unstable minds. But then I stumbled on the section of ritual diagrams. I could see at once that the game I was playing had become at a single stroke both more complicated and more promising. Here were what appeared to be alternative versions, perhaps more faithful versions, of the mandalas of the *Al Azif*. And, to a greater degree than ever before, I had the maddening sense of half-recognition, as if these complex concentricities and spirals of enigmatic tables of Arabic and Hebrew characters held some encrypted truth, perhaps the secret of some unsuspected physical law or cosmic calculus. The diagrams had a powerful, almost hypnotic effect belying the crudeness with which they had been hand-etched.

The book engrossed me until I looked up again in embarrassed alarm, cursing myself, for I had indeed missed my stop! I exited the train at the next platform and studied the posted timetable. Ironically, despite their superficial resemblance to arithmetic tables, these things had long frustrated me. At length, with the help of station personnel, I determined that no train would appear to bear me back in the other direction for at least a couple of hours. A taxicab was a possibility, but what a waste of money. I already felt fool enough. Well, I reasoned, I had interesting reading; why not settle down with it to wait for a meal until the next train for Brichester should arrive? It would be a welcome reprieve from the cold and dark rooms that otherwise awaited me back at the university.

I had my choice of cuisines as I made my way down the main commercial street. Britain's liberal immigration policies had filled every

321

corner of the kingdom with a bewildering variety of nationalities. I had often reflected how we had not so much lost our empire as internalized it. Perhaps once we had conquered the ends of the earth, but now they had returned the favor. Some, it is well known, were not happy with this situation. But for myself, I rejoiced in the cosmopolitanism of the situation. If Sikhs, Nigerians, and Chinamen could be loyal British subjects on their own soil, why not on ours?

Such were my thoughts as I passed a storefront from which there emanated something quite other than the pleasant chaos of multi-linguistic dinner conversations and clinking dinnerware. The place was an Arabic restaurant-cum-nightclub, and apparently this evening the facilities had been let out for some kind of religious or political meeting. I can manage a decent smattering of Arabic from my studies, already mentioned, in the history of Arabic science and math. What I heard made me uneasy, as the speaker, who apparently saw no difference in function between a microphone and a bullhorn, railed on about Western decadence and the need for resurgent faith. Not all was intelligible to me, but I could make out enough, as I stood just outside the open doors as inconspicuously as I might, to conclude that the man represented one of the many militant Shi'ite sects who had been generating so much unpleasant news of late, both here and abroad.

One hopes such an audience's zealous reception reflects an expected lipservice from a casual crowd rooting for the home team rather than genuine political conviction. Otherwise, the scene was disturbing and made one think involuntarily of the rhetoric of National Front bigots who so fear foreign 'incursion' undermining the United Kingdom. There was much inflammatory invocation of terms like Dejjat ("Antichrist") and Iblis ("the Great Satan"). It hurt to hear my own beloved country, in which, after all, these people were welcomed as guests, vilified in such terms—if indeed, that was the drift of the incoherent rant I heard. A few minutes of this were enough. More would have spoiled my appetite, so I moved on, choosing, finally, a humble meal of good English steak and chips.

It was no mean feat to turn the pages of the curious Feery volume without ruining them with the grease of my dinner, so after a couple of attempts I set the book aside and gave my full attention to the dinner before me. As I made my way back to the train platform I again surveyed the various immigrant enclaves, wondering idly how different our 'common' world seemed to the residents of each. Perhaps, as the philosopher Leibniz had theorized, we all inhabit bubble universes adjacent to one another and never really interpenetrating. But here came the train, seemingly as weary as I felt.

The Feery volume proved to be more tantalizing than substantially helpful, though even tantalization is a kind of encouragement, and my poor hypothesis welcomed any encouragement it could get. I looked for the mysterious Mr. Feery in various registries and learned no more from books than that he had been something of a tarnished aristocrat of these latter days, of the kind who one reads are selling their ancestral castles as tourist attractions for want of funds to maintain them. Lord Feery, as I suppose he must be called, had attracted little in the way of public attention, having no record either of military service or of parliamentary involvement. He had managed, apparently, to keep the curtain of anonymity closely drawn about him. However, once it occurred to me to post an inquiry on the Internet, I came to learn that Lord Feery did have his share of notoriety, only not in the circles whose dull affairs were chronicled in those obituaries of the living I had consulted.

Joachim Feery, it developed, had once enjoyed quite some vogue among genteel occultist circles in Britain between the two wars. One might have heard Feery cited in the same breath with Edgar Cayce and Madame Blavatsky. These days, he, like the rest, had been eclipsed by other New Age luminaries. But his legacy had not been completely forgotten, as his currency on the Internet attested.

I planned another rail excursion to London and the Museum to wrap up a few final details on John Dee and his probable textual sources underlying his translation, but first I thought a stop into my Brichester department office incumbent upon me, to gather mail if nothing else. On the way over, I picked up a copy of the *Times*. It announced another terrorist incident. These had of late become so common as to be almost ignored unless one happened to be caught in the crossfire oneself. Thus my interest, since this one took place not far from the very street I had visited a week ago after missing my train stop. Though no one had yet claimed responsibility, something the numerous factions usually competed for, authorities put the blast down to one of the newly arrived Shi'ite sects, possibly a virulent import from Yemen. This sort of thing certainly put our many peace-loving Arabs in a difficult spot since the average Briton, his prejudices fanned by understandable fears, tends to view all Muslims as potential killers and spies. I felt for my Arab colleagues at the University.

Going through my mail, I quickly sifted out and threw away the administrative and interdepartmental junk mail. There were a couple of catalogues of interest, and finally one post card. It was a note from none other than Dr. Richardson, whom I had planned to visit later that afternoon. It seems he had a lead for me. If I wanted to know more about Joachim Feery and the *Necronomicon*, I might make the acquaintance of a certain recondite book dealer who sometimes supplied odd items for the special collections of the Museum, documents the Library authorities did not so much want to secure for their holdings as to keep out of the hands of anyone else. This last was an intriguing bit, and it made me feel we had not departed so far from medieval times as our conversation of the previous week implied.

As I passed through the faculty club for a cup of tea, I overheard a group of colleagues chatting over the latest terror incident. One of them, a literary man, called me over and asked if I hadn't been near the site of the incident. I confirmed that I had. It was no secret, as of course it was my own passing remark to a third party which had rumored its way to this man's ears. It seemed that BBC reports of the morning superseded what I had scanned in the *Times*, that the blame was now squarely pinned on a particular faction, the Yemeni sect already suspected. As one colleague, a political scientist, remarked, this news made the whole thing all the more baffling, since no one could think of any grudge the Yemenis might conceivably have against the West in general or against Britain in particular.

Our literary friend responded that in any case such groups hardly needed provocation, much less ideology, that Colin Wilson had rightly pegged such movements as "terror religions," and that nothing could surprise anyone after last year's abortive attempts at mass poisoning by the Japanese Om Shin Rikyo sect. Here was a sect that wanted literally to kill everyone on earth in preparation for some sort of Buddhist apocalypse! After that, nothing might be ruled out. I nodded my grudging agreement and as quickly resolved to put such grim considerations as far out of mind as I might, preferring to immerse myself in the niceties of my research, which seemed blissfully irrelevant to the increasingly beastly world of the waning twentieth century.

The train from Brichester to London tried its best to lull me to sleep, but contrary to my usual habits, I resisted its monotonous lullaby and stayed awake through the whole trip. I did not want to risk repeating the embarrassing episode of last week. Besides, I was busy examining the local map to be able to trace my way from the Museum when I'd done there, to the dealer Dr. Richardson had told me of. Once assured of my route, I settled back and sought diversion by looking at the passing scenery, none of it particularly new to me. Inevitably unwelcome thoughts began to

324

intrude, thoughts of the disturbing recent wave of terrorist violence. However, I must admit that it was neither worry for my own safety nor grief for the tragedy of those already stricken, but rather an element of nagging puzzlement that filled my thoughts. What was it about these events that kept, so to speak, tapping me on the shoulder? Why did it seem to me that I was dismissing it all too quickly?

I tried again to thrust the whole sad business from my thoughts and to concentrate instead on my researches. I began to review what I had researched concerning the background of the mad author of the *Necronomicon* and what in it might be conducive to my hypothesis of his mathematical interests. I recalled how, according to Ibn Kallikhan, a twelfth-century biographer, in whose encyclopedic collection of lives Alhazred had managed to secure a brief paragraph, the soothsayer had been discovered to be an apostate from the then-young faith of al-Islam, a secret diabolist worshipping some of the gods of pre-Islamic Mecca, Yaquth, Kthulhut, Nug and others. According to information provided a century or so later by al-Tabari and abd-al-Jabbar, Alhazred had served as the Imam of a forbidden Shi'ite cult, the Shi'a al-Dejjat. He had claimed the status of Bab, or Gate, visible representative of Hidden Old Ones.

Like the better-known Imams of Ismail'i and Twelver Shi'ism, his authority rested upon his esoteric interpretation of the Qur'an. The inference to be drawn from this tradition was that the *Al-Azif* itself had originated as a compendium of remembered hadith, or traditions, of Alhazred's inspired exegeses which came to him, he said, from the buzzing voices of the desert jinn, servants of Pazuzu, another of his Old Ones. His sect, understandably, did not find favor among the ranks of Islam which at this time were growing increasingly embroiled in sectarian strife. Alhazred's sect, located in Yemen, met with violent persecution at the hands of the Zaid'i sect, the so-called Fiver Shi'ites, who also had their greatest strength in Yemen. As a result of these unwelcome attentions, Alhazred had at length disappeared into seclusion for safety sake, the usual course of action adopted by the persecuted Imams of whatever branch of Shi'a Islam, all of whom, at one time or another, were branded heretics by the much more numerous Sunnis.

Sooner or later, when the last known Imam in hiding had not produced a son to succeed him but failed to reappear after a reasonable period, the faithful would proclaim him "occulted," hidden away by the power of Allah, perhaps somewhere upon earth, like the Seven Sleepers of Ephesus, or perhaps in heaven, either way pending his triumphant return at the end

325

of the age, when as the "Mahdi," the Rightly Guided of Allah, he would usher in a golden age of true Islamic theocracy. According to the pattern, Alhazred, presumably having died of old age in a seclusion unpenetrated by friend or foe, was declared the exalted Mahdi of Yog-Sothoth, and his second advent awaited. In this respect the histories of al-Tabari and abd-al-Jabbar superseded Ibn Kallikhan's report of Alhazred's fate, since Ibn Kallikhan, while admitting the currency of many stories of the mad Arab's passing, appeared to accept the account put about by the Sunni authorities to the effect that Abdul Alhazred had been rent limb from limb by an unseen demon in plain sight of a crowd of witnesses. Such a cautionary tale was an obvious attempt by the orthodox to warn the disciples of Alhazred to return to the fold of Muhammad lest they earn themselves a like fate to that of their wretched master.

Though the reports of al-Tabari and abd-al-Jabbar were later than that of Ibn Kallikhan, they had just recently been lent striking confirmation by certain still-unpublished documents discovered in the *genizah* of a newly excavated Mosque in Yemen, which also yielded many hundreds of pages of discarded copies of the Qur'an dating centuries earlier than any previously known. These manuscripts evidenced a radically different vowel pointation from the received text of the later Sunnite jurists, tending dramatically to corroborate the hypotheses of Lüling about a pre-Islamic "Ur-Koran." The same find had yielded fragments of a much earlier textual tradition possibly underlying the *Al-Azif*, namely certain portions of the legendary *Kitab al-Shirq* of Ibn Mushachab. It was these texts which interested me greatly, germane as they obviously were to my own researches, for I needed to see the earliest, most accurate transcripts of the relevant "magical" diagrams and charts.

The situation was maddening, since the Islamic government of Yemen were by no means eager to feed such information either to the scholarly world or to the press, since they represented "Satanic verses" of the sort that got poor Salman Rushdie in such trouble.

And then I realized what it was that had been trying to get my attention. Yemen, Dejjat, the Antichrist. The speaker I had heard ranting in the restaurant. The recent Yemeni terrorist episode. These might all be dots waiting to be connected the right way to yield their hidden design. But I could not readily imagine what that picture might resemble. And in a moment, I had dismissed the whole silly business, reasoning, after all, that Yemen was filled with Muslims, particularly Shi'ites, and that all of them would naturally believe in Dejjat as a minor article of their faith. And, yes,

Alhazred had been associated with Yemen, but then so had Sabbatai Sevi, since the major apocalyptic text of his failed sixteenth-century messianic movement had been penned there. I was beginning to see patterns where, surely, none existed. But then it was my stop, and I was glad to leave such extravagant speculations on the train.

III

The book and curio shop proved quite simple to find, even for one of my abysmal sense of direction. The street was lined with run-down looking shops, as if from a long want of business, and yet the sidewalks were far from empty. Perhaps this was because many of the storefronts had been occupied, a second glance revealed, by establishments of a rather seedy variety offering certain goods and services for which the demand seems sadly never to decline. I decided to remain outside as inconspicuously as I might for a few moments, observing the flow of clientele. Traffic was reasonably brisk, and I could only guess at what might be concealed in the plain paper wrappers most customers emerged carrying. Several, I noticed, made stops in other shops along the street either before or after their visits to The Middle Pillar, as the establishment was called. Finally I entered, deciding I was not likely to learn anything of value through amateur detective work.

I suppose I had seen shops like this one somewhere before; perhaps I just knew them by reputation. One side of the place was lined with glass jars and bins like those in a candy shop or an old time apothecary, which in large measure, I suppose it was, as the various containers seemed filled with herbs, powders, even divers types of rocks and salts. At first I imagined this merchandise to be culinary in character but immediately recognized it as a rogue's gallery of homeopathic medicines, the refuge of the desperate. On a moment's closer scrutiny, I saw that some promised aphrodisiac enhancement, financial blessings, protection from ill omens, or just plain good luck. Drifting across the shop I took in the sights of a small museum of curios, statues, some of them quite nice, representing the tastes of the more outré artists of the Victorian underground. And books. There were plenty of books, most of them in rather sad shape.

I glanced at the faded but finely tooled bindings of a few of them. In the main they appeared to be early editions of Cornelius Aggrippa, Trithemius, Fludd, Eliphas Levy, and of course the inevitable Aleister Crowley. Other cases held more recent printings of a few of these, but to my surprise, after a moment's reflection, I noticed the entire absence of the popular authors of New Age occult drivel. About this time I became aware of the presence of someone watching me, a tall and portly man, black-bearded with encroaching gray at his chin and on his thinning top. A lined face seemed to bear the marks of much laughter, though somehow I got the feeling he had done little laughing in the recent past. Wire-rimmed glasses completed the picture, and the man, the proprietor, spoke to me.

"I believe you're new to the Middle Pillar, my friend. Welcome. My name is Andrew Stiles. The store is mine."

"Thank you," I replied, extending a hand, which he took with a hearty grip. "I wonder you are able to compete with other esoteric shops. You seem to be short on the sort of stuff I expected to see, channeling, Atlantis, pyramids."

This remark elicited a chuckle. "We do all right. After a while one's clientele discovers one. And we cater, as you've noticed, to the serious occultist, people who know the difference between imagination and esotericism. Too many seem to be misled by the equivalent of stage magic. Now what may I help you with today?"

I liked the fellow, though I was fairly sure he would still fall into my own category of outlandish eccentrics. But he did seem like someone likely to be able to tell me something about Joachim Feery, so I decided to get right to the point.

"Mr. Stiles, I am told that you are something of an authority on a book called *Feery's Original Notes on the Necronomicon*. I had been reading it lately, and I wonder if you would be so kind as to tell me something about it." At this he seemed partly disturbed, partly amused. He nodded, unconsciously pursing his lips and motioned me to follow him back of the counter and through a draped doorway into a somewhat dingy sitting room.

The walls were mainly bare save for a few framed portraits and posters, one of them depicting the kabbalistic sephiroth, another the kundalini. An incense burner of unusual size stood in one corner, and to the side stood an ornate antique table, a church communion table, I believe, though with the usual DO THIS IN REMEMBRANCE OF ME replaced by another saying. But the most striking feature of the room was the presence of a spider monkey. This attentive creature sat atop a stack of identical volumes, missals of some sort, by the look of them.

Stepping over to a bookcase, he unlocked it, drew forth a familiar looking volume in worn dark, almost colorless, binding. Leafing through
328

the pages he recrossed the room, saw I was still standing, and indicated a seat, while he lowered himself onto another.

"An authority I am definitely not, Mr . . . ?"

"I'm sorry, my name is Wentworth. I'm on the faculty at Brichester, mathematics and history of science."

"Very well, Professor Wentworth. I am no authority when it comes to this particular book, but I am well-acquainted with it. What would you like to know about it?" His voice sounded suddenly weighted with a profound tiredness. I knew it must denote a story waiting to be told. But first I told him the tale I have already told you, of the nature of my researches, abridging it as much as intelligibility allowed. He followed it patiently and recapped when I was done.

"So what you want to learn is whether our Feery had any basis for his emendations, such as an earlier manuscript source for Alhazred's text. Is that pretty much it?"

"Yes, though anything you can tell me about Feery himself might be helpful. I appreciate this, Mr. Stiles. I know you must be busy." My informant arose to make sure the front of the store was adequately covered, then returned, poured two cups of tea, and sat back to try and answer my questions.

"You may know that Joachim Feery, an aristocrat of a fading line, had something of a following . . . I suppose back in the late 40s and 50s. He might have been comparable, I imagine, to Edgar Cayce or to Swedenborg. He was a modern visionary, and by that I mean that he claimed to be a man of science, as I might add all true occultists do. I don't expect you will credit that claim, Professor. Men in your position usually don't, I have found, but it is important at any rate that you understand how *we* understand it."

I felt I had to interrupt. "Don't discount my sympathies just yet! Remember, my hypothesis is that what masqueraded as superstition was science, higher math."

"Yes, that's true. That's good. But still, Professor Wentworth, I don't want to take too much for granted. I'll continue. Feery's interest in the *Necronomicon* was great, obviously. I take it his interest in it was not without resemblance to your own. But as far as I know, he had no other, shall we say, objective sources of information as to the text of Alhazred than you or I. My understanding is that his emendations were based on his own visions and revelations. He had, so to speak, gone to the horse's mouth."

I felt immediately disappointed hearing this, but only momentarily, since it implied that, like me, he must have suspected some genuine geometric/ mathematical basis to the original pentacles and mandalas and "corrected" them based on the same sort of inferences I was now drawing. That was still something worth exploring.

"May I ask, Mr. Stiles, what you make of Lord Feery's version of the *Al-Azif?* Do you dismiss it as a parasite on the body of a great work? Or do you find it . . . useful?"

"I may as well tell you, Professor Wentworth, that I place the greatest confidence in the insights of Joachim Feery, and that because of experimental confirmation. I will tell you the story if you care to hear it. I warn you up front that you will feel you must dismiss it." I nodded for him to continue. My interest was genuine, knowing as I did that even false or misinterpreted evidence may yet be important and relevant.

"The room in which we are sitting serves as a classroom and sometimes even as a ritual space. Until a year and a half ago, I ran the store here with the help of my partner and friend Malcolm Black. His picture is over there." I glanced at the frame he indicated. It was plain from the scene depicted there that he and Mr. Stiles had been quite a bit more than mere business partners.

"We offer classes and occasional religious services based on some of the esoteric traditions cherished by ourselves and our clientele. Many of our group are homosexuals, and in most cases not so much from natural inclination as by, how should I put it . . . by spiritual vocation. There is a kind of Tantric discipline that requires ritual coupling by way of macrocosmic-microcosmic emulation, mirroring certain planetary and astral conjunctions in the heavens, and this coupling must be devoid of the least particle of natural desire . . . I fear I risk offending you. But suffice it to say that our various ritual preparations did not in the end serve to fortify us against certain risks of a mundane nature. In short, Mr. Black at length confirmed that he had contracted the HIV virus, and then full-fledged AIDS. Thus far, I myself have tested negative.

"You have seen the many unusual chemical products we stock here, Professor Wentworth. I may say that none of them did the least good in forestalling the rapid advance of my friend's degeneration. Both of us knew there were other alternatives open to Malcolm, but neither of us spoke of them. They were not morally acceptable. But in the extremity of the situation, I am afraid that Malcolm grew desperate. So did I. And desperation casts a new light on things. We decided to bring in an

330

innocent third party, because the directions of the *Al-Azif* required it."

Here the large-framed man seemed almost to shrink into himself in obvious self-reproach as he continued with trembling voice. "There was a ritual, a technique, something akin to mesmerism, which promised to effect the trading of minds and bodies. I will spare you the details, especially since you have no doubt read the passage in Dee yourself. I only agreed to try the procedure because I believed the Dee text to be a garbled rendering. I thought nothing would happen, though I credited the efficacy of Alhazred's original, had we but known it.

"We chose an acquaintance, an irregular visitor to the shop whom we knew had few connections and no family to speak of. We knew he would readily agree to join us in an occult experiment, since he had in fact done so in the past, though this time we concealed from him the true nature of the endeavor. I felt guilty at the subterfuge involved, though I had no great fear of anything happening. It had not yet occurred to me, I can't say why, that the defective text from which we worked might prove dangerous rather than simply ineffective. Oh, I should tell you that by this time Malcolm had very largely collapsed. He was in a very bad way. He took no active role in the proceedings, and our guinea pig assumed the bed-ridden man was merely witnessing the operation. In fact, Malcolm's frail body bore a number of marks and charmed metal and cloth bits that should have prepared it to receive a new mind, while he silently repeated a prescribed mantra to send his own astral ego from its crumbling, disease-wracked façade into a healthier abode. In truth, it was the other man whose role was passive.

"The opportune hour struck, all was performed in exacting detail, but where I expected failure, worse occurred. Poor Malcolm, it is true, gained no egress from his tormented shell, but our guest did all at once lose consciousness, never to regain it. We made short work of his remains."

At this, Stiles' eyes dropped, and he shaded his face with his hand. His voice dropped to silence. He was, according to his own belief, confessing a murder, or a man slaughter. And I knew not what to say, since to comfort him I must needs belittle his beliefs, cold comfort indeed. So I merely waited for him to continue.

"I have said that Malcolm's symptoms, and his sufferings, were now very grave. The disappointment, and the guilt we both felt, seemed somehow only to accelerate his decline. We both awaited the end. It was not long in coming. For a time my friend awaited his fate with silent stoicism, but as his breathing grew noticeably more labored, more desperate, his eyes took on a strange fire and he seemed to beseech me silently to do something. To try the experiment again. At least that is what I thought he meant, though perhaps I merely attributed to him my own reckless thoughts. But he was slipping away too rapidly for me to make even such simple arrangements as were necessary. That is, if I were to secure the unwitting cooperation of another outsider.

"One alternative remained. What conscience required of me was that I should have laid down my own life for my friend, offered him my own body, such as it is, to continue his own life. But I confess I lacked the necessary courage for that. At the final moment, when I was committed, when forces had been set in motion, I faltered, and yet I did not dare stop altogether. So, God help me, I redirected the exchange. I excluded myself from the circuit and caused that another should after all become the new host for Malcolm's soul and receive his festering husk of a body in exchange. In another moment, the bloodshot eyes that had been my friend's opened wide with panicked incomprehension. The diseased limbs made to flail but lacked the strength. It was but moments before the mad fire raging in those eyes faded forever. The changeover had been accomplished just in time. The transfer had been successful. The difference was, this time I had used the formulae and diagrams as Feery had corrected them."

Here he fell silent again, save for repressed sobbing. The silence was hard to bear. There was something that had escaped me in his tearful story. "But, if I may, who was it? And what happened to your friend? I thought you said there was no chance of finding another subject in time? I'm afraid I don't . . ."

Wordlessly, Andrew Stiles pointed across the room to where the monkey had continued to sit, with patience remarkable for one of his scampering breed, during the whole recital. At first I still did not comprehend, thinking perhaps he meant to point out another photograph, but there was none to be seen. The monkey stood to its feet with a certain terrible intentionality and gazed at me.

IV

I sat now at my cluttered desk at Brichester. The interview with Andrew Stiles had concluded with nothing further said between us. Stiles seemed hardly in the mood to continue, while I could imagine nothing more to say. I simply rose in silence and found my way out of the shop. I made a stop at the Museum to round up a few remaining notes and to return the borrowed copy of Feery's *Notes*. I resisted the temptation to speak to Dr. Richardson of the strange visit with Stiles. I was sure he had not known what lay in store for me there, and I would have felt half as mad as I would have made Stiles sound simply by repeating his tale. More than this, however, I held the thing in something approaching awe, though not without keen distaste. It seemed something best not spoken of.

And thus I resolved not to speak of it either when I should ring up Mr. Stiles. For that I had now determined to do. I would just refrain from any comment one way or the other, while I pursued other matters with him. For one important question remained. All else had been swept from my mind as I sat listening to him a week before, but now I knew I had to finish my business with him.

He picked up and did not seem reluctant to talk with me. I don't know what I had expected, but I gather he must have taken the very fact of my call as something close enough to an acknowledgement of his uncanny tale. I now inquired whether he might know who had charge of Joachim Feery's papers, if such survived.

"I should imagine they remain in the possession of Lord Feery himself." This struck me as a bolt from the blue. It had not even occurred to me that Feery, of whom everyone thus far had spoken as a figure of the settled past, might still be alive. I asked Stiles where and how I might contact the presumably reclusive Feery.

"I would assume he still resides in the Oakdeene Sanatorium. I believe he still receives visitors on occasion, though these days few seek him out. If you want to interview him, perhaps I may join you. I think he will remember me."

"The Oakdeene Sanatorium, you say. Is . . . he . . . coherent?"

"Well, that's a good question. If you mean, is he lucid, I should say so. As to whether what he says will seem to make sense, that I cannot predict. In fact, you might think not, and I might think so. Are you game?"

I said I was. With Kafkaesque resignation, I was determined to see the increasingly tangential path through to the end now. Had Feery been confined because of aberrant behavior? Because of his beliefs? It would not have been the first time the visionary had been confused with the schizophrenic.

Stiles read my puzzled silence. "I did not know Joachim Feery before his confinement. All I can tell you is that there is a man in Oakdeene Sanatorium who claims to be Joachim Feery. I have no reason to doubt that claim, for all that it may be as much a delusion on my part as on his. One thing more. Occasionally he has also claimed to be Abdul Alhazred."

I agreed to the trip, my curiosity holding the reins, though I knew I might well be traveling with one madman to visit another. Andrew offered to make the necessary arrangements, and we agreed upon a mutually convenient time a couple of days hence.

Meeting him at the Middle Pillar, I waited for him outside. Rain notwithstanding, I did not care to lay eyes again on that monkey concerning whom poor Stiles harbored such shocking delusions. In a few moments, the large man emerged, turned, and locked the shop door behind him. "I doubt we'd have many customers today, given the weather."

Underway, we motored past a couple of news kiosks, whose headline boards announced yet another bombing. It had been sad decades since such news could really surprise, but most of that time the terror had been the work of the IRA. These days, newly open to negotiating, the Irish seemed to have passed the baton to Arab groups whose motives were less obvious. But we were soon out of London, and London's headlines were soon out of my mind. By this time I had toyed with the reported claims of the man we were set on visiting. What was the nature of his pretensions? Would he think himself the mad Arab reincarnated? Was his a shifting delusion begotten of Multiple Personality Disorder? Had his long study of the *Necronomicon*, hardly a volume conducive to mental health, finally unhinged his probably already tenuous reason?

"I don't really know. There's been nothing straightforward forthcoming under that heading. I do remember once his saying that 'Feery' was a derivation from the Arabic 'kaffir', infidel."

We fell silent, and I looked out over the green and pleasant countryside, over which the sun was beginning to smile as we left the rain clouds behind us. Before long, the regular hum of the motor and the gentle vibration of Stiles' smooth-running automobile lulled me like a baby into another of my traveling naps. On awakening I apologized, assuring my companion my dozing was no reflection on the company. He laughed and told me we had arrived.

Oakdeene was an old facility and had undergone various stages of expansion and remodeling in its time, the result a not unpleasant mixture of architectural styles. Fortunately, the older buildings had not been greatly modified to match the newer, and the strange Victorian combination of fortress-like institutionalism with cathedral-like grace rendered a reassurance of a firm yet healing hand. The imposing old structure bespoke at once the role of keeping its inmates safely confined away from society and yet of protecting its dwellers from an untoward world outside. The newer buildings had about them something of the euphemistic artificiality of rehabilitation facilities, as if to ward off Oakdeene's vague but longstanding reputation as a kind of Sheol for the most outré and perverse cases.

All this went through my mind as we parked in the designated visitors lot, a space both surprisingly small and significantly untenanted, and made our way to the administrative centre. After a few words passed between Stiles and a couple of white-coated men, we were given a pair of yellow cards, passes, and shown our way on a map of the grounds. An orderly accompanied us. Feery, it turned out, was to be found in the old part of the facility. Perhaps, I reflected, that denoted the length of his stay.

I was rather surprised to discover that our route took us not to a wing of cells or of hospital rooms, but to what had, in the days before the expansion, served as the office of the director! I soon learned that Joachim Feery, whose identity the staff took for granted as authentic, had been committed by his own request, and that he had arranged the outfitting of a well-appointed study and apartment in the old administrative section. His needs were met by the Sanatorium staff as he pursued his studies in the utter isolation he craved from a world he could not bear.

How had he managed such a unique arrangement? He had endowed the institution to a surprisingly generous extent, providing for most of that expansion which had left so much of the older space for his personal use. There were even hints of laboratory space being put at his disposal for experimental purposes, but of these matters the orderly who guided us either could not or would not say anything more specific. I could not help thinking of the old cliché about the inmates running the asylum! Was the committal of the old eccentric a mere charade? Or was not the very fact of it sufficient proof of its justification, since presumably he might have secured equal seclusion in a number of other ways and in a number of other places.

When we reached the great oaken door of Feery's domain, I was at once struck by the incongruity of what was manifestly the office door of someone of importance being elaborately unbolted from the outside! None of it made any sense, except that we were after all in the midst of an insane asylum! Given that, I decided that the usual rules might not apply. But how much stranger would things get before we were through?

The orderly, now seeming almost more of a butler, bade us be seated while he went to summon the "patient." I exchanged glances with Stiles, who did not seem as nonplussed as I. After all, he must have been through the routine before, though I suppose he had thought it better not to prepare me in advance lest the surprising information have the opposite effect and I back out of the visit.

Directly the young man returned, mumbled something about expecting Feery momentarily, and hastened away, locking the door after him, to my slight unease. After a few moments more, Feery himself appeared. I had formed no definite mental picture of the man, and was not surprised to behold a tall, slightly stooped and very lean man with an adequate tuft of thinning silver hair atop a lined and pallid face. His eyes sparkled with intelligence and with perhaps a hint of something else hard to name. His movements were slow but sure and unfaltering. The man reminded me of Bertrand Russell with a silver-white goatee. He wore nondescript clothing with a lounging robe over an open-collared shirt. I wondered at once whether he would offer a friendly greeting, but Stiles spoke first, saying something which struck me at the time as almost too respectful, as if some prior relation had obtained between them, as that of disciple to master. Feery nodded and glanced my way, then turned and left us to follow him down a paneled hall into his study.

This sanctum sanctorum was lined with volumes and punctuated by curios, in short, reminiscent of Stiles' own shop, albeit on a grander scale. But the lighting was so subdued, I could see nothing in detail and did not want to appear rude by looking away from my host. I was for the moment content to allow Stiles to fill the role he had assumed of go-between. I listened as he related the details of my research and my interests with remarkable accuracy. Feery listened silently, occasionally glancing in my direction and yet curiously never meeting my eyes, almost as if I were a photograph of a man instead of the man himself. It was a peculiar sensation, and slightly unsettling.

When Stiles was finished, Joachim Feery did not immediately reply but turned a quarter circle in his high-backed swivel chair to gaze out the French window to the Oakdeene grounds beyond, now bathed in the volcanic reds of sunset, at that particular moment when the red rays seem to be emitted from some hidden dimension usually unglimpsed by mortal eyes. When he began to speak, his gaze was still fixed outward, and his words were those of a soliloquy, addressing my questions, in some measure at least, but not addressing me in particular. His rasping, ancient tone did not falter or grow tired as he spoke on into the descending

336

darkness. His mantel clock occasionally sounded, but of this I was but absently aware. I will not try to reproduce his words, as I have ventured to do in the cases of words exchanged with Richardson and Stiles. I cannot quite recall them nor hope to convey the elusive effect they had.

But I may say that I never had or even sought the opportunity to ask specific questions that night. I half remember Stiles asking some, but I can no longer be sure even of that. I was hearing enough, or too much, as it was. My hypotheses, it turned out, were quite in accord with Feery's own understandings, and yet they formed but the edges of his ways. As I listened I found myself swept away into a giddy vista of universal forms, symphonic rhapsodies and fugues of number and dimension. Natural laws, as I had learned with the sophistication of the Neanderthal to regard them, now seemed so plainly to be no mechanistic structure, but rather spontaneous melodies cast upon the swirling æthers at the whim of some cosmic pipe of Pan. I gasped, beholding the secret of Riemannian triangulation whereby the way might be opened to undreamed of dimensions adjacent to our own, not in the spaces we know but between them.

Not a religious man, I nonetheless felt close to worship when told of the fantastic realities hinted at in the cyclopean muteness of Stonehenge. Legends of reincarnation and ancestral memory assumed crystal clarity as the Moebius loop of Time unfolded itself before me. The mysteries underlying the Stoic Logos doctrine and Nietzsche's revelation of the Eternal Return were enigmatic no longer. The character of the Buddhist paradox of the Void became clear, and I recognized that I had always known it but had failed to recognize the knowing. Einstein now seemed at one with the prancing shaman, and I, I loathed myself as a detestable snail crawling across the open page of the book of nature's sublimity, leaving only a trail of foulness to mark my passing.

When the voice stopped and I sat staring out the French windows into the dawning sun, I was a changed man. Feery had quietly departed without my staring gaze detecting the fact. I gradually shook myself back to a functional state, albeit with the queer feeling that I was awakening not from sleep, but from a state of infinitely higher waking from which I now sought surcease in the muddled perception of mundane awareness. Stiles had revived some minutes prior to me, and as we retraced our steps to the car and drove off the Oakdeene grounds, we began stammeringly to compare notes. I began to feel that neither one of us was in a proper state of mind to drive, so I suggested we look for some suitable place to break our fast. This done, we sat down to a couple of plates of something I cannot recall even sampling, and began to try to make sense of what we had experienced.

I was made to understand that Stiles had neglected to warn me of the likelihood of what might happen, not because he had not expected it, but because he had no words with which to convey it, something I could now understand well enough. I understood another thing as well; I reassured Stiles that I was now prepared to admit the validity of a great deal of that which I, as a man of conventional science, had hitherto been reluctant to credit. Now I simply saw how certain occult tenets only formed the hitherto unglimpsed undergirding for what I had understood as the truths of science.

At one point I marveled that Feery had never sought recognition from the scholarly world for the truths he had somehow attained unto, but as soon as I framed the question I knew the answer, for I knew that I should never be able to make understandable to my own colleagues the hundredth part of what I had been vouchsafed the previous night. Upon subsequent reflection I realized that this was due to the fact that somehow Feery's pedagogy consisted not at all in the gradual unfolding of evidences or the demonstration of theorems by derivation from first premises, but of the awakening of sheer intuitive beholding. There was, and remains, no other way to describe it. It was on the order of a mystical vision, and yet, once seen, no doubt could remain that what I had glimpsed, like the refugee from Plato's allegorical cavern, was the bright sun that I and my colleagues had formerly been groping toward with the tentative probings of a blind man.

V

Days passed as I sought to come to terms with my experience. I had begun with the hypothesis that what was called magic might really be science, and now I had come to feel that what I had called science was really mysticism. I recalled how Thomas Aquinas, possessed of the beatific vision on his deathbed, ordered that the reams of Aristotelian philosophy he had written over the years be consigned to the flames as the ploddings of ignorance. Was I, too, to dismiss the whole of the scientific method because of the remarkable experience I had lately shared with Stiles? In the end, it was a fortuitous happening that gave me perspective on the matter.

On a day trip into London I was awakened from my reverie by the sudden urgent bleating of an ambulance siren. As I would soon learn, it denoted yet another terrorist incident in the recent wave of violence that was now raising anxiety in the metropolis to an unaccustomed fever pitch. Oddly, the first thing to pop into my mind upon hearing the intrusive sound was a literary allusion. The image of Odysseus and the Sirens from the *Odyssey* came to me unbidden. I thought of how Odysseus, consumed with curiosity, rejected his own precautions, electing not to stop up his ears as he had ordered his crew to do so that he might hear the notorious song of the Sirens that reputedly summoned men ineluctably to their doom. Instructing his men instead to tie him to the mast and to pay no heed to whatever orders he might cry out while in the radius of the Sirens, he exposed himself to their witchery. As anticipated, he found their summonings so hypnotic that he begged, demanded and cajoled his crew to free him that he might heed the call. Luckily for him they obeyed his first order to ignore his second, and he survived. Once clear of their influence, his madness left him, and his relief was great that he had not been left to succumb to it.

I now saw the old legend as a parable. Had not the urge to abandon the ship seemed to Odysseus self-evidently right? Did that course not present itself to him as irresistibly and absolutely clear? Any reasoning to the contrary must seem the cheapest sophistries. And yet, once delivered from the Sirens' influence, he regarded his former certitude as madness pure and simple. In the same way the dreamer who manages to preserve what seemed the profoundest of nocturnal insights is often disappointed to find that daylight reveals it to be gibberish.

If one has experienced two states of apprehension that are incommensurable with one another, is one really entitled to prefer one to the other? If my visionary certainty under the influence of the mysterious Feery was not amenable to scientific verification, how could it overthrow scientific verification? Then I should be, in effect, preferring faith to reason, no matter how compelling the experience had been. And yet, might I not be rationalizing my way back from truth into self-imposed blindness? It was a serious business either way.

I have said that my preoccupation with intellectual puzzles was so great that I sought to seal myself off from the unpleasantness of the world around me, feeling that any attention I might devote to social crises could effect nothing but greater anxiety on my part. This insulation, however, was rendered impossible for me by the next developments. I thought to ring up my erstwhile companion Andrew Stiles to compare notes, to ask how a couple of weeks' distance from the events of our Oakdeene pilgrimage had affected his judgment. I was taken aback to hear the recorded announcement that the number was no longer functional. Had business been so poor that his service had been shut off? Another couple of calls revealed the answer: the Middle Pillar, together with several adjacent shops, had been fire-bombed out of existence.

I had not known Stiles well enough to mourn his passing, but I certainly felt a keenness of regret, and of rage. He had been a man of peculiar and eccentric beliefs, and of practices even more peculiar, but he was equally a sensitive, compassionate, and intellectually curious fellow, and he had taken time to assist me, a comparative stranger, in my quest. And now he was no more, thanks to the random violence of some fanatical sect with no grudge for which poor Stiles, or any of the other victims, could have been remotely responsible.

It had not yet occurred to me that the bombing might have been other than random, that the death of Stiles might actually have been the specific goal of the attack. How could it? I had not yet seen enough of the puzzle.

As the weeks passed I thought it best to let things settle, and I put the whole business of Feery, Stiles, and my once-cherished hypothesis out of mind as best I could, seeking immersion in routine chores. I could think of no other way to gain perspective. At length I had about resolved to put the whole project behind me as a failed effort and to take up my professional endeavors where I had left them off. But it was not to be. A letter in my box bearing the engraved return address of Oakdeene Sanatorium undid at a single stroke all my efforts at a return to normalcy.

My momentary thought to throw the thing away unread was vain. With fingers compelled with a leaden sense of fate I opened the envelope as if it were the sheath of a weapon. The antique penmanship of Joachim Feery greeted me in words curt with enigma.

> Stiles has finished his course, but yours has just commenced. Blessed are your eyes, for I tell you, many righteous men have longed to see what you see and have not seen it, to hear what you hear and have not heard it. O man of little faith, wherefore did you doubt?
>
> Yet I will suffer you even in this. Having beheld the substance, do you still seek the shadow? So be it. Here is what you sought. Remember, from him to whom much has been given, much shall be required. Stonehenge.

> –J. Feery

He had enclosed a folded sheet which bore the most complex of the

340

magical diagrams I had yet encountered. It was drawn freehand and by a man whose advanced age I could not venture to guess even after having seen him. And yet there was an almost mechanical regularity and precision to the drawing. The thing bristled with Latin, Hebrew, and Arabic characters set at strategic points within acute angles of overlapping seven-pointed stars contained within double and triple intersecting circles, and so forth. Rather than being daunting in its complexity, the fulsomeness of the figure depicted made the whole seem teasingly close to intelligibility. Here were, albeit among stubborn enigmas, several readily identifiable mathematical and geometrical tables if one but knew how to read them, as by now I thought I did. I did not so much resolve as acquiesce in the fact that I would accept Ferry's challenge to prove him out. In my hands was the final proof of my theory.

I set to work deciphering as much as I could, from which I soon understood two things. First, there was a date given in astrological code, the date, presumably, on which I ought to repair to Stonehenge for the experiment to which this diagram was somehow the key. Second, there were obscure words on the outer margins that were to be spoken during the procedure. I began to recognize the obvious: what Feery was prescribing for my edification was the performance of a medieval ritual of sorcery. Naturally, by now I understood that these much-maligned ceremonies had themselves been in the nature of what we should call scientific experiments, but still the notion presented me with a new hurdle.

In my mind, a geometrical depiction such as I was studying was a coded message descriptive of natural relations obtaining in the ideal world of mathematical laws, though reflected in physical reality. But their role was as signs to articulate to the eye and the mind an understanding of those realities. They were a written script conveying information. Beyond applying the principles thus set forth, one did not do anything to them or with them. What could I be expected to do at Stonehenge or anyplace else? What besides understanding some new depth of theory? And yet Feery seemed to regard what he had sent me as an instrument or device. I had now to decide whether this sort of approach even made sense to me. If it could not, then I should have difficulty making anything of Feery's challenge, to say the least.

I tried to reduce the problem to general theoretical propositions: what I was contemplating, put simply, was the notion that the knower could affect, even effect, that which was to be known, whereas we usually think

341

of the reverse being the case. But, come to think of it, why could it not work both ways? And, really, was this really any different from the now commonly accepted rule that the presence of the observer affects the outcome of the experiment he observes? I still had a bit of trouble with the notion that the utterance of certain syllables might somehow complete an unseen circuit and cause something to happen. But then, I reasoned, surely the very purpose of an experiment is to uncover that which was not evident before. Before long, I had seen my way to trying the ritual in what I judged to be a proper frame of mind. This seemed all the more important the more the experimenter was himself to constitute one of the variables!

The day stipulated by Feery was not far off. I cleared my calendar and gathered what few materials I should need for the project, contacting the proper authorities to make sure I should be able to get past the fences which had been erected about the monument only in the last decade. As a University scholar I had no trouble gaining access for research purposes. Luckily no one had questioned what sort of research I was about, for I should have been even more hard put than usual to give an answer.

I rented an automobile and ventured forth for a pleasant morning's drive north. Music occupied me most of the way, but eventually I switched channels, looking for some news. In the present troubled times things had been going from bad to worse. So it was with a sense of trepidation I listened to the international report. Another crisis in the Middle East, Saudi Arabia again. From what I could piece together, having tuned in after the report was underway, it appeared that some extremist group had occupied the Kaaba in the holy city of Mecca, the chiefest shrine of all Islam. Something of the sort, I vaguely recalled, had happened some time in one of the oil wars against Saddam Hussein, though I could no longer recall the details. One would have thought that event would have led to tighter security measures at the shrine, but then perhaps such would have interfered with the operation of the place as a site of pilgrimage, thus accessible to all and sundry.

As the news reader began questioning the hastily assembled panel of experts one comes to expect at such moments, I started to get a better idea of what was taking place so many thousands of miles away. The group had issued no demands, and had thus far slain no one but the guards who had tried to prevent them. No political manifestoes were being fed to an eager press. The goal of the occupation was yet far from clear, a thing all the stranger since such an act could not be anything but a suicide mission.

342

No more details seemed to be forthcoming, so the program passed on to other news stories. I stayed tuned, hoping for more information before I should arrive at my destination. For some reason, the situation seemed more unsettling to me than tumults in far corners of the world usually did, since one soon becomes numbed by the sheer number of them. Perhaps, I vacantly reasoned, it was because of my recent interest in things Islamic, a tangent of my research.

I saw by the road signs that I had come quite near my goal. For the first time it occurred to me that I might not be able to conduct my exercise in the desired privacy. Though I had secured admittance through the barrier that kept tourists at their distance, there was no reason to suppose that these should have been banned from the site. No doubt any who were present would watch my strange-seeming antics with great amusement. I would just have to deal with that, I supposed.

I found parking and made ready to turn off the engine when my radio announced an update of the situation in Mecca. Nothing more had happened as far as observers could tell, but someone had tentatively identified the occupying group as the Shi'a-al-Dejjat. This name meant nothing to the news reader or his informants, but I was fairly certain I knew the name in some other connection. But, as when one spies a familiar face in an unaccustomed location, I could not place it. Well, better to begin my errand. I could always catch up on further developments later, when more had accumulated.

The wind was rather strong, the air predictably chilly, as I showed my identification and was shown through the fences to the ancient circle of menhirs. Years of familiarity did nothing to dull the brooding wonder of the scene. Here in truth was the legacy of a past age, a message left by remote forbears, but one difficult to understand. That the careful arrangement of the vast megaliths was a great mute sentence spelled in massive runes, I could not doubt. It had kept its secrets through all the centuries curious eyes had studied it, no researcher ever being able to disclose more of the mystery than that the great cromlech's arrangement had some coordination with the sidereal calendar. Who knew? Perhaps I would persuade the structure to speak another whisper.

A small group of tourists, most of them bedraggled youngsters, followed my movements with interest as I unbuckled my case and extracted a curious collection of rulers, compasses, note papers and chalks of different colors. I set to work, aping the movements of medieval sorcerers, and more than a little self-conscious about it. If I was embarrassed to be seen

343

doing this by idle strangers who did not know me, at least I could take comfort than none of my colleagues would share the sight!

The requisite preparations were time-consuming not simply due to the intricacy of the designs I must trace in the hard ground, but also because of the great degree of precision necessary. After all, the diagram I was trying to reproduce was a thing of finite degrees and measures. If there were to be any efficacy in the thing it would have to be a function of exact mathematical relationships which could not be merely approximated. Before I was near finished, the shadows had begun to fall. I had not expected things to take this long, but I had come prepared just in case. So I returned to the automobile and broke out the flood lamps.

The work absorbed my interest, but the trip to the car told me that by now quite a considerable crowd had gathered to follow my slow progress. I supposed that it was the usual quotient of tourists, but that most of them had stayed longer than they would have otherwise because of the added attraction provided by the old fool and his antics at the center of the menhir. Now the thought struck me with a note of panic: what if one of these gawkers thought of alerting some local television broadcaster to what was transpiring out here? Such garish exposure was the last thing I needed! I forced myself to abandon these probably groundless worries and to get on with it. I had the figure done. Stepping back to take a look and, now that I thought of it, to get a picture of it, I was impressed with the beauty of the thing. With the various colors of chalk, the design was more than a little reminiscent of Tibetan sand paintings I had seen on television documentaries.

I was almost ready to begin. Taking a drink from my thermos, I unfolded my transcription of the formulae from Feery's sheet, which I had rendered in phonetic spelling, being no master of the languages involved. Out of the corner of my eye I could see that if anything, my unwanted audience had grown. I hoped I was providing them a show worth their money, because it should be over soon. What I expected to happen, I could not say. I suppose in retrospect I imagined I might somehow induce another affective experience such as I had shared with the late Stiles in Feery's study. The analogy with Tibetan mandalas suggested something of the kind, since their similar designs were intended as tools of yogic meditation. But I had no active expectation of anything, since any degree of meditative focus had been ruled out by the unforeseen presence of snooping busybodies outside the fence. I thought momentarily of packing up and returning some other time, but then Feery had seemed to think this particular place and time were vital to the success of the endeavor.

344

Well, there was nothing to be done about it but to proceed.

Turning and squinting into the suddenly magnified light flooding the scene, I saw that my worst fears of embarrassment were realized. Here were the television reporters, carnival barkers and sensationalists eager to use me as grist for their mill. Boom microphones were being arranged on either side of the fenced-off circle. Some of the coated figures holding microphones began to call out questions, which with increasing irritation mounting rapidly to fury I thought best to ignore. I fixed on the paper, took my prescribed position at the center of the elaborate grid, and began to intone the barbarous syllables. This simple task was rendered difficult now because the loutish newsmen would not leave off with their shouted questions. I hesitated momentarily, though, when I thought I heard one of them call out the word "Mecca." Then I began to realize that these were not the representatives of one of the burgeoning local cable hook-ups, but BBC reporters. Of course they were; the equipment they were using should have told me that. Did they somehow mean to connect my present experiments with the tense events taking place on the other side of the globe? There was seemingly no limit to the far-fetched connections the media jackals would draw in order to titillate their bored viewers. I continued.

As I chanted, feeling like nothing so much as a schoolboy parroting the noble cadences of classical poetry he could not understand, I began to sense a change in the air about me. My eyes burned slightly, I think. I felt a bit light-headed for a moment. The sounds of the television circus beyond the fence faded, and a muffling silence seemed to descend upon all things. I looked up at the crowns of the great stone slabs encircling me, half fancying that they glowed with a strange fire if only I could focus on it just right. And then the pit of my stomach began to churn as familiar perspectives vanished, angles shifted and expanded, as if a plain view were to blossom into a cubist representation. I began to see the accustomed three-dimensional shapes of the great standing stones as vestiges and extensions of vaster objects projecting out and back and up in hitherto-unguessed directions into unimagined dimensions. What had before seemed gigantic objects now revealed themselves as the merest edges and iceberg-tips of unseen continents of ineffable form and mass.

My wide-eyed gaze swept about in a circle which cost me my balance. As I tripped over my own dangling feet, I struggled to right myself and was grateful for the steadying hand of one who stood at my side. Before it occurred to me that there should have been no one with me, I sought the

345

face of my benefactor and saw the familiar yet terribly wrong features of Andrew Stiles. He wore a motionless frown, as if mourning his own death. But he was gone, and I seemed to be leaning against the stone gray wall of the Oakdeene Sanatorium. But it was instead one of the impassive pillars of Stonehenge. Bracing myself against it, I thought next that I heard an echo of laughter up high in the air, and a voice reciting in Arabic. I gazed upward into the starry sky and believed I beheld what looked like eight men bearing on their shoulders a great sedan chair of outlandish proportions and angular arrangements. Upon it sat One whose fantastic form and visage my baffled mind refused to register. There were blasting trumpets and wailing flutes producing a pulsating bank of almost tangible sound behind them.

Absently I became aware of a great deal of screaming and shouting at no great distance, presumably from the crowd. Could they see what I was seeing? I glanced about me but could make out little in the confusion of the great arc lights bathing the scene. Looking again skyward, I saw a new portent in the heavens. Now other forms seemed to be descending directly above me, breaking through the former apparitions and causing them to dissipate like smoky phantoms. The new arrivals came down fast and looked as if they would make no attempt to avoid me as they landed. Great harpoons of even brighter light shot outward and transfixed me. The noise was suddenly deafening. I reeled and tried to gather enough presence of mind to choose a direction to run, when I was stunned anew by the sounds of gunfire. Expecting to be struck down at any moment, I braced for the impact, for all the good it would do. When it appeared another few seconds were allotted me, I decided I'd best try to determine the origin and direction of the fire.

I now saw that the great juggernauts descending from above me were police helicopter gun ships. But as yet they were not firing. No, it was they who were the targets. The gunfire was coming from various points around the perimeter of the fenced-in circle. Thus far I had not been hit because the unseen gunmen were firing above my head, at the descending ships. At any moment, the latter were sure to begin returning fire. Yet if I made to exit the circle, I would only be running into the line of fire.

As the helicopters began shooting, I chose the shortest distance between two points and just dropped where I stood, regretting there was no lower I could sink. My life did not pass before me, though I fully expected to be chopped to mincemeat by the relentless crossfire. I had too recently been pitched between one unexpected reality and another. By now my own death would hardly be a more wrenching change than I had already undergone. I felt like an inert stone, willing patiently to endure whatever turbulence might next erupt above me.

The fire fight between unknown foes did not last long, and obviously I survived. I know not whether to lay my survival to both sides' lines of fire, or to the efficacy of the magic circle in which my body sprawled. But in a matter of moments, I found myself helped to my feet by a uniformed officer. The helicopters had landed off to the side of the Stonehenge menhir, and the police assault team were rapidly dispersing the crowd and, I gather, threatening the reporters and confiscating their videotapes.

VII.

I would soon learn that while I was naively conducting my experiment at Stonehenge, events had been unfolding at the Kaaba with an eerie symmetry. The Saudi troops streaming in to replace the fallen guards had quickly herded the crowds of pilgrims out to safety. With no more gunfire forthcoming from the ranks of the occupiers, the government troops had been content for the moment to hold their own fire, unwilling for needless damage to be wrought in that holiest of places. But it had been evident that something untoward must be taking place behind the vast black drapes covering the sacred stone fallen from heaven. In a moment, so swore the legions of panicked witnesses, the reverberations of thunder had sounded from the blue desert sky. Then the black curtains had fallen, consumed in an instant by engulfing sheets of strangely colored flame. There, for the first time in uncounted centuries, the blessed meteorite stood revealed to the light of day. Jaws agape at the blasphemy, the Saudi guards were galvanized into action, sure now that the terrorists were not some sort of misguided coreligionists. As they closed in on the collapsing ranks of the occupiers, who had apparently counted vainly on some sort of reinforcements, they could see that profane hands had dared touch even the sacred stone itself, tracing upon its ancient, pockmarked face a chalk mandala exactly like the one I had inscribed at Stonehenge.

As to what happened next, accounts differ radically, some witnesses insisting that the terrorists' blasphemies were expunged by a washing wave of their own splattering blood. Others swear with equal fervency that the angels of Allah took the rogues in hand, and still others say nothing of angels but avow that the intruders were borne away screaming into the ravening maw of an unseen demon. More dubious still is a rumor, denied with unusual vehemence by the Saudi government and the college of *ulemma* at Cairo, that when the Black Stone was cleansed of its profanation, close scrutiny detected the vestiges of paleologean carved lines forming the vague shape of a five-pointed star with the likeness of a great eye in the center.

The chance exposure of my own activity by curiosity-seekers alerting the media came quickly to the attention of British intelligence, already on the lookout for any clues to the unprecedented outbreak of recent MiddleEastern terrorism in the British Isles. The authorities, once set on the trail, lost no time in detecting the clandestine movement of a great number of armed men, nearly all of them Yemeni expatriates, into the vicinity of Stonehenge. The encroachment of these men had obviously not been prompted simply by media reports of eccentric antics at Stonehenge. No, clearly they, like their brethren at Mecca, had been prepared for something and must have known more what to expect than I, pitiful stooge of higher powers. My guess is that their leader had needed someone more capable than they of performing certain requisite preparations for what was to come, someone whose mind had been initiated and expanded so as to grasp something of the obscure forces to be manipulated.

Luckily it took little of my stammering to convince the police of my naive role in the matter. They were grateful for the information I was able to provide as to the background of the Shi'a-al-Dejjat, a sect long thought to be extinct. I could see they knew much more than I concerning the international machinations of the latter-day Shi'a. It soon eventuated that it was they who had assassinated poor Stiles, who must at some earlier time have been associated with their cause but afterward distanced himself from it. Any such connection seemed hard to credit at first, until I realized that the link must have been an indirect one, probably unsuspected by Stiles himself, who in his turn must have been quite as naive as I.

There were hints of other, similar incidents concurrent with those at Stonehenge and at the Kaaba, but these were somehow kept away from the public. I asked no questions; I already knew more than I wanted of the whole wretched business.

Of course one stone was yet unturned, and unturned it remained, for when the authorities arrived for a call upon Lord Joachim Feery at his private residence in the seclusion of Oakdeene, he had already vacated the premises and left no forwarding address. At this time he remains, shall we say, in occultation. I hope that he may remain so for a long time to come.

–1997–

348

The Green Decay

The History of Nabulus the Wonder-Worker

In the elder days of fair Hyperborea, when all things were possible for that men deemed them so, did one Nabulus win wide acclaim by a feat of thaumaturgy undreamt of and unmatched, even the infusing of warm life into a carving of bronze. And it happened on this wise.

Nabulus, a solitary figure of indeterminate age and arrayed, like any magus, with floor-length braided beard and flowing robes, lacked neither arcane power nor considerable renown. Unlike many wizards before and after him, he neglected not the simple mortals who abode in the settlements nearby, instructing them in such simple marvels of science as he deemed them capable of mastering, among which were the arts of medicine and irrigation, together with some rudimentary mechanical implements. Weapons he refused to grant, knowing that in this one sphere, increased knowledge made men more like unto the beasts, not less.

For these and many like boons was Nabulus worshipped by the humble of the land, nor did he lack apprentices drawn from among those astute enough to grasp that it is superior knowledge, and not divine fiat, which masters nature's secrets. By patient instruction and issuance of judicious challenges did Nabulus test his pupils' resources, for he knew that even wizards must one day perish, and he was desirous that his knowledge not expire with him.

Yet for all his benefactions and the gratitude of his people, Great Nabulus suffered a loneliness rendered the more grievous by reason of the very veneration in which he was held. For no man seeketh lightly to befriend a living god, and as such was he regarded. True, he did hold converse with extradimensional entities who regarded him somewhat more as a peer, but such fellowship held little of common human warmth. And most of all did Nabulus pine for the sweetness of the female.

Now the path of the mage is a solitary one, requiring the seeker to keep the strictest oath of chaste celibacy, lest his life-force flow into the wide and undistinguished river of mundane mortality. The sorcerer must needs apply his begetting desire unto ethereal and ectoplastic works, and to
349

expend one's energies in the pleasures of the flesh is to bind oneself to the way of all the earth. Even so had mighty Nabulus thought long ago to have cast out every sentimental pang for the gentler sex. But of late did his mind more and more repair to a forbidden notion: would not his triumphs be much the sweeter if he possessed a heart's companion with whom to share them? Was this too great a boon, in return for his many sacrifices? And might there not be some apt way to sate his longing, meet unto a wizard?

Upon the matter did Nabulus ponder much, turning a silent answer to those among his pupils with sufficient wits to detect his consternation. At length he arrived at a solution and charged his servants and apprentices to leave him undisturbed in his laboratory till his latest work was fulfilled. Of his disciples he would require the assistance only of the eldest, Aimoth the Acolyte, who should attend his supine form as his spirit vaulted high into the ultratelluric Zone of the Colossi, that akashic realm of eternal primotypes of which, Atlantean savants teach, all earthly things are material mirrorings.

Venturing thus into the dimension of pure essence, he resolved to capture a direct vision of the Eternal Female, the Divine Wisdom, for his own companion, then return with her to solid earth. His devotion to such a mate would be a love more celestial than the empyrean heavens, and no mere coupling of human breeding stock.

Nabulus lay upon a straw mat spread within a chalk pentagram of many strange hues, having placed at his head a full-sized brazen statue of a naked woman, flawless in every point. The mage had straightly instructed the youth Aimoth what he must do to aid in the ritual ascent. Many times he circumnavigated the mandala, uttering words of ancient Senzar and forming elaborate patterns with hand-held banners and veils in a prescribed order. All these were aids to his master's meditations. The apprentice showed his skill in a flawless performing of the rite.

Of the astral journey Nabulus would thereafter vouchsafe little, but it was soon known that he had not returned alone from his expedition into arcane realms. The Acolyte Aimoth had finished his share in the task and at length fell into a sound slumber, a natural concomitant of one's presence at an epiphany of the Other. But, he averred afterward, when he awoke it was to behold his master cradling the naked, statuesque form, for whom he requested his young assistant to fetch a robe, for the metallic homuncula forsooth had taken on living vitality. Great Nabulus had succeeded in causing the ultramundane Female Archetype to enter into a prepared vessel. Seeing her thus living and vivacious, the youth Aimoth at

350

once found his code of chaste impassivity a great vexation.

The feat of Nabulus the Wonder-Worker spread swiftly, both among his sorcerous brethren and among the common people. The latter rejoiced in their simple, good-hearted way, while the former took in the news with astonishment and some perturbation. For, though none sought to belittle the phenomenal magnitude of their colleague's feat, they liked not the notion of his casting aside so basic a tenet of the wizardly code as celibacy.

For his part, Nabulus deemed himself in no wise to have infringed on the ancient ways of the magi, as he sought naught but the spiritual love of a noble and chaste goddess. Besides, he liked not the hypocrisy of some of his detractors who were widely known to cavort with succulent succubae, keeping within the letter of the ancient law only by reason that their affections were lavished upon beings with no true flesh.

Alas, there were others of Nabulus' great household whose intentions were not so pure as his. For one evening, Nabulus having taken to his bed in exhaustion after a greatly taxing feat of exorcism in the village below, Aimoth the Acolyte, he who had of late found it more and more burdensome to pursue his studies with a single mind, chanced to espy the heart-shaking beauty of Nabulus' mate, the fair Akhamot, as she stood at the railing of the balcony gazing down upon the countryside of a world of matter to which she was still mostly a stranger. Aimoth waxed bold to approach his mistress and to speak.

"Of a truth did my master capture the very essence of beauty and bring it back to our poor earth, the which is scarce worthy of thy charms, my lady."

The Lady Akhamot craned her sleek neck a few inches to face the impertinent youth. But she did not rebuke the unaccustomed forwardness, that an underling and a youth should speak uninvited to a goddess. For in truth she did regard him with silent mouth and wide, awaiting eyes. Little was she accustomed to the ways of mortals, so far from ordinary mortality was her mate Nabulus.

Emboldened that she had not at once rebuffed him, Aimoth advanced to further outrages, mayhap misapprehending her silence. Nor did she resist when the lustful youth abruptly grasped her beauteous form and ravished her perfect mouth and breast with hot kisses. Even so she did not thrust him from her, though her bronze-born strength was sufficient to the need, for she yet observed events in pure puzzlement. All was new to her as noble Nabulus had not laid warm hand upon her form. Akhamot's rounded body had been fashioned from molten bronze, forsooth, but now it was flesh, and flesh, too, hath a molten fire. The profaner Aimoth knew little of the alchemical art, but he did know how to awaken the flame within his mistress, and ere long she was returning his passion measure for measure. And no great distance away the cuckolded Nabulus slept his sleep.

Weeks and months passed on, and from his love did Nabulus detect no sign of evasion nor of deception, for truly all she did was done in naïve innocence. Naught would she have kept back from Nabulus, had not Aimoth the betrayer warned her, with some cheap deceit, not to speak of it. But, being a vain and foolish fellow, Aimoth himself showed no similar discretion, boasting in secret, as he believed, of his conquest to some among his fellow apprentices, and even to a few of the household servants.

Not the lightest of Aimoth's sins was that his boastings fired the latent lusts of the other youth, yet new to the discipline of chastity, and many became corrupted in mind. And so the betrayer became the betrayed, for in no great space of days, several of his fellow-pupils had applied unto their mistress and enjoyed the same forbidden intercourse with her. For once ignited, her carnal fire, being archetypically perfect, could not be quenched.

How these degeneracies at length reached the ears of the cuckold Nabulus is not known, though there is no mystery to it. He required no scrying crystal to learn what all else knew, down to the lowliest milk-maid. Deeply did he grieve for the betrayal of his love and trust, but more for the defilement of the heavenly purity of Akhamot. She was too noble for the world nor could any act of hers be done with wickedness, but with Nabulus' tricky former apprentices, now traducers, it was another story. And, most unfortunate for them, Nabulus was by no means above the human lust for vengeance.

Naïve he might have been, indeed, very nearly so naïve as his Akhamot, but an utter fool he was not. So he planned a plan and continued in seeming obliviousness, making no one the wiser. What he did at last was to weaken, day by day, the binding spell that held the sky-born spirit of beauteous Akhamot captive to the material vessel into which he had contained it, so that little by little the cord linking soul to body was played out longer and longer. To her lovers was the process but dimly perceived as a slow lessening of her fleshly suppleness and a gradual ebbing of the tide of her ardor. But at first the decline was scarcely to be noticed. Nabulus would by this means at length unfetter her spirit and send it aloft again to that realm of pure possibility from whence he had unlawfully seized it. But that alone was not his plan. If he had sinned in overpassing the bounds between the worlds, his iniquity was light when weighed against that of his betrayers. For their doom's sake did he prolong the process. They must not suspect their awful plight till much too late, and to this end did the bitter Nabulus apply a second conjure, a mighty apotrope to turn away, for a time, the desultory effects of Akhamot's decline and to send them instead upon those who dallied with her, quite in the manner of the savage Voormi shamans and their hexes.

Thus, while fair Akhamot appeared to grow no worse, her suitors all alike commenced to mark a queer stiffness of the joints, a worrisome heaviness of limb, and a dismaying sluggishness of digestion. Akhamot seemed to have recovered all her vigor, but most of the apprentices of Nabulus sank deeper into deadening paralysis. And yet would they have traded much to retain even this sorry state, for as the weeks progressed, their very flesh did crumble away most loathsomely into patches of seeming verdigris, until at length naught remained of them but greasy piles of noxious green detritus.

The servants in the house of Nabulus the Wonder-Worker stolidly set about disposing of the heaps of filth the color of jealousy, but never were they apprised of the true cause of these astonishments, as, about the same time, the chief steward discovered the loss of both his master and his mistress. The mortal body of the wizard was found on his laboratory floor, by the looks of it, in the midst of an experiment that had gone wrong. But of the lady Akhamot there survived not a trace, nothing in fact but a curious life-like bronze statue of her.

–1997–

353

The Incubus of Atlantis

The History of Klarkash-Ton the Hierophant

It is said that the great arch-wizard Eibon, heretical proponent of the interdicted ancient faith of Zhothaqquah, had so faithfully served his slothlike master that the deity feared he should never find another so zealous for his divine dignity. Hence did the Lord Zhothaqquah take steps to ensure he should never lack the services of his favorite, though death gobble his mortal flesh. As all men know, Eibon was at the last assumed bodily into the heavenly sphere of Cykranosh whence his Lord himself had descended in ages past, so that Eibon should not succumb to death upon this earth. But at length death found him, restricting not his travels to any one world. And yet Zhothaqquah's plans for his son Eibon had but commenced, for the portly divinity had arranged that Eibon's soul should continue in his service by dint of metempsychosis, so that he should find himself again and again bearing a new mortal sheath when the old one had become threadbare.

In this manner, owing to the beneficence of his Master, did the one who had borne the name of Eibon pass the ages, sometimes recalling more of his previous existences, sometimes rather less. For if a man's memory begin to fade within the span of a single lifetime, how much the more over a succession of them? Much must be learned again and again as life passeth in succession after life, if it be relearned at all.

Now the seventh incarnation of Eibon the mage was as one Klarkash-Ton, he who served as high priest and sole devotee of Zhothaqquah in Atlantis during the ultimate generation ere her foundering. Shrewdly had the god foreseen his need for the services of the transmigratory spirit of Eibon, for had it not been for the admittedly somewhat lax devotion of the priest Klarkash-Ton, Zhothaqquah should have lacked any worship at all, and lacking worship, even the very gods may perish from neglect.

It is the lot of priests to take their living from the offerings rendered the deities they serve, and Zhothaqquah's cult having fallen into universal neglect, Klarkash-Ton found himself obliged to take other work unto himself to maintain a viable living. And in this endeavor his not inconsiderable scholarly gifts served him well. It was his sacerdotal duty to maintain the sacred lore of the myth-cycle of ancient Commoriom, which most had long since come to disbelieve save as merest myth, and to its literal truth not even Klarkash-Ton might any longer attest. Few would pay a silver coin even at festival season to hear him spin the tales of ancient Hyperborea. Thus it was that Klarkash-Ton expanded his repertoire to encompass droll and ribald anecdotes of sunken Mu far across the globe, great Mu which legend made the mother civilization of High Atlantis herself. Of Mu, to be sure, little positive evidence survived, but then the more rousing tales might therefore be told of her with no one being the wiser. From here did Klarkash-Ton yet further expand his canon of recitals as far as the prodigies of the distant star Antares and its circumambient worlds.

At length did the spellbinding talents of Klarkash-Ton bring him to the attention of the Tyrant of Atlantis, grim Pharnabazus, who summoned him to an official audience. Now this news was not pleasing to Klarkash-Ton, for the severity of the Philosopher King was well-known, to wit, that he frowned upon many even of the traditional sacred myths for that they portrayed the gods and heroes in a questionable light as the veriest rogues and voluptuaries. He had even been known to imprison or exile certain of the greatest of the Muse-inspired poets. So Klarkash-Ton much feared that, by reason of his extravagant tale-telling, King Pharnabazus might have devised unpleasant plans for him.

But the truth was quite different, and exceedingly palatable. During the royal audience did the Tyrant show his guest every deference and did invite him, on account of his great learning, to become official archivist of the capital. Knowing that his penurious worries should abruptly vanish should he accept his sovereign's offer, Klarkash-Ton wasted nary a moment in, as he said, acceding to the King's most generous command. With a deep and obsequious bow did the once-impoverished priest begin his career in the King's service.

In truth, everything about his new station delighted him, from the spacious apartments provided him to the scribal labors awaiting him in the Great Library of the King. Klarkash-Ton gloried in both the rich fare of the King's board and the rare manuscripts which it was his happy chore to study and catalogue. Here were true records of the ancient days and of lost kingdoms, even a priceless collection of Naacal Tablets from the court of ancient Ra Mu himself! The *Pnakotic Manuscripts* were not unrepresented, and there was a curious set of inscribed plates from ancient Uzuldaroum called *The Book of Eibon*, a strange name that

355

Klarkash-Ton somehow felt ought to mean more to him than it did. In these rare parchments and codices the priest delved tirelessly, his sateless curiosity growing jointly with his erudition.

As his command of the antique alphabets and cyphers grew, he discovered much concerning the methods of Elder Magick, and of the great boons a man might gain by their use. Of these the technique that intrigued him by far the most was the preternatural exercise of soul-projection whereby the mage might set his soul-substance soaring to other worlds of cosmic revelation, or simply undertake secret errands here on earth. And Klarkash-Ton thought how he might have use for such a skill and set out in all seriousness to master it.

Under kingly patronage, Klarkash-Ton lacked for no necessity and, in truth, for nary a luxury. But this left what little fruit that remained forbidden unto him seeming all the sweeter. And one night, having recently completed his studies of soul-projection (and emboldened somewhat, perhaps, by the great quantities of wine he had come to consume of late, it being freely available to him), he resolved upon an experiment. For he had decided he could no longer resist the alluring charms of the fairest in all Atlantis, for all that these were no common courtesans, nor even peasant girls, but the noble wives of the King himself and of his nobles.

It was instant death, all knew, for any man so much as to speak unto them without being first spoken to. And besides, Klarkash-Ton knew well enough that none of these fair ones would likely look fondly upon his spindle-shanked, scholarly mien. But another thing he knew was the art of astral travel. So upon that night he betook himself out of his fleshly body and glided upon the spring breezes into the most forbidden of inner adyta, even the royal bedchamber, where his majesty lay all naked with his fair queen, similarly arrayed. It looked to their invisible observer that their loveplay had barely commenced, and seeing them thus, he could restrain himself no longer.

The old scrolls had spoken truly! Klarkash-Ton now found himself behind the eyes of his lord the King and lost no time placing himself inside his lady the Queen as well. And all courtesy of the cooperative body of the King, the which he had borrowed. While after a few attempts KlarkashTon found he could not after all guide the movements of the body in which he sojourned, he could and did feel every sensation of that body, and this was more than satisfactory for now. Perhaps later he could perfect the method and come to control any form he might usurp.

After a night of fervid lovemaking, the priestly archivist returned to his apartments to find his accustomed form ready and waiting for him. Rising a bit light-headedly, Klarkash-Ton stepped up to his polished looking-glass and surveyed himself. He was in truth rather pleased with himself, for had he not managed to commit adultery with the Queen herself and all without displacing her royal husband or infringing upon his own vows of priestly celibacy? For his true bodily form had been resting quietly at home all the night.

Things continued in much the same manner for some months to come, as Klarkash-Ton showered his affections vicariously but no less passionately upon all the loveliest women of the realm. And it is to be feared that, complacent in his scheme, he overstepped himself in the end. For he ought to have taken note one evening, at the King's table, of a jaundiced eye cast steadily in his direction by one of the most powerful of the royal counselors, even the chief mage Mozillan, a man on whom little was lost and who had close familiarity with every magickal manuscript housed in the Great Library. And, too, he had a concubine of great comeliness.

Nor had she escaped Klarkash-Ton's epicurean scrutiny. Indeed, he had oftimes sampled her charms in his sorcerous manner, and soon he would come round to her again when he tired of the charms of certain others in his secret harem. One day as Klarkash-Ton went about his curatorial duties, he was accosted by none other than the Lord Mozillan, who required his assistance in locating a familiar manuscript. He had not yet grown used to the new storage system instituted by the archivist, who was glad to show him to the text he desired. Thanking the librarian, the mage caught him with a peculiar twinkle in his eye. "I'll wager you have familiarized yourself with much of the lore these scrolls contain."

"Verily, my Lord, the better to serve you!" So he bowed and spoke, but secretly Klarkash-Ton despised the proud sorcerer whom he, a mere stripling in the esoteric arts, had so easily outwitted. Yes, this very night he would betake himself to the bedchamber of Mozillan, and if he were not in an amorous mood already, Klarkash-Ton had honed his skills sufficiently to suggest and, if need be, impel, the first move loveward.

The golden moon was high over the breezy streets of Atlantis that night when Klarkash-Ton sent his wandering spirit forth on its latest erotic errand. He hovered a moment outside the window of the high tower of Mozillan's palace. Things were already well underway, the wizard's concubine moaning pleasurably, with the great broad back of her master, draped with the bedsheet, visible between her arched legs. Delighted at the sensuous spectacle, the floating soul of Klarkash-Ton dropped at once into the form before him.

And found his essence afloat in wine! Through the heavy crockery he could barely hear the triumphant shout of the cuckolded Mozillan, who had of course been wise to his devices. The wizard swiftly lifted the weight of the tall amphora from where his mystified but obedient concubine had been balancing it with some difficulty on her thighs. Rapping on the glazed exterior of the man-sized jar, the mage Mozillan mocked the errant spirit he had confined within it.

"I shall see to it, O Klarkash-Ton, that your vacant body is suitably disposed of, for, the gods know, you shall be having no further need of it! You shall bide the ages in the confines of this ensorcelled wine pot, a besotted genie in a bottle, till some poor fool of future days may chance to dredge your prison up from the wine-dark depths where I shall shortly drop you!"

And not long thereafter, as he felt himself falling over the rim of a boat and into the sea, Klarkash-Ton had cause to reflect that there surely were worse ways to spend the centuries than pickled in fine Atlantean wine.

–1997–

The Shunpike

Business brought me to North Central Massachusetts, as it had many times before. I make my living in the admittedly inglorious profession of grocery supply and field supervision for a medium-size chain of food stores sprinkled throughout the Commonwealth with another few franchises in Rhode Island and New Hampshire. It is my task at appointed intervals to visit and inspect these establishments, to check on their managers, their supplies, and to diagnose the problems of failing stores. Our chain was once considerably more widespread, having since lost business to burgeoning competitors, so it behooves us to keep a finger on the pulse. Like the circuit-riding preachers of old, I knew my rounds well and could almost have driven them, in my capacious Packard, blindfolded. Aylesbury, Arkham, Ipswich, Fenham, Wilbraham, and others: they were almost like the furnishings of a great room to me, so familiar and, generally, comfortable were they to me. Despite harsh driving conditions during certain parts of the year, I rejoiced to circle the New England countryside and viewed my unspectacular employment primarily as an excuse to tour my beloved homeland.

Thus it was that surprise, no, shock overcame me as I approached a toll station along an oft-traveled stretch of road leading to the Berkshire region; I spied for the first time a crude and weathered signpost, peeping out from behind a shock of recently pruned foliage. Its haggard letters spelled a single word: SHUNPIKE. It was one of those old rutted paths, invisible on any printed map, creations of the ingenuity of the poor who lacked even the small sum to pay the modest toll and yet could not drive their burdens overland through open country. As my automobile approached more closely, I slowed my pace for a better glimpse. The dense roadside growth had been cut back much more drastically than usual, and I found that a significant stretch of the makeshift road was visible before it began to make its inevitable bend to rejoin the main road somewhere on the other side.

On a whim I pulled the Packard over to the side of the road. I was still yet some yards from the toll station and could not tell whether my pause had excited the notice of the toll collector, or whether he might be asnooze, not unusual for this section of road where the press of traffic was

359

not great. I quickly reviewed my schedule of appointments and decided that I could indeed spare some time. I had no fixed deadline in such a leisurely part of the countryside where grocery proprietors habitually passed the days with friends around the cracker barrel. And besides, how much time could it take? The only danger might be to my tires, for who knew what degree of desuetude might afflict the neglected road beyond my field of vision? So, as my patient reader must have at once surmised, I made for the unofficial turn-off, feeling my way carefully and possessed of a sense of adventurous expectancy.

What I anticipated finding I could not then have explained, and probably I felt more of idle curiosity than aught else, but as I have said, the wonders of the New England countryside, as well as its small towns, are the refreshment of my spirit, and I am always willing to try for a look at some new corner, cove, or glen I have not heretofore seen.

The road surface was surprisingly smooth, as if heavier traffic of an earlier day had succeeded in packing the ground and smoothing it. Subsequent muddying rainstorms had apparently done little to erode it. And thus I found I had actually to slow down in order to take in the adjacent scenery. Driving presented no real difficultly. I had struggled along paved roads with more trouble from time to time.

Another thing I had not counted on was the sheer extent of the thoroughfare. While it would be natural for the tributary to linger before rejoining the mainstream, so as not to make the illegitimate circuit too obvious, the duration of the drive along the shunpike seemed a good deal longer than necessary, almost like a real back road. In a few moments I began to worry about getting lost. I considered simply turning around and retracing my path, paying my toll, and being on my way to my next stop. But something bade me continue on, just a little and ever a little more.

I carried on for what must have been twenty minutes in this trajectory when I again felt the electric jolt of total surprise, for before me appeared another signpost, this one unobtrusively pointing the way to the town of Foxfield some undisclosed distance from the road I was driving. A turn-off from a turn-off? This struck me as very singular. I had to assume that what I had discovered, including the shunpike itself, represented the vestiges of an earlier and largely effaced road system swept away by the construction of the highway on which I habitually traveled. And yet it was hard to imagine the people of a town permitting themselves to be so completely cut off from common traffic. True, there might be some connection between the settlement and other open roads on the other side, but I felt sure that in all my travels and on all my maps I had never seen a town of

360

Foxfield.

Almost fearing to look at my fuel gauge, I was relieved to see that I had a fair safety cushion providing the town were not far away, for of course I had determined to seek it out. I made the turn and motored down the road. This one suffered as little from encumbrances as the last, surely an oddity in both cases, given their little use over so many years, but the gravel with which it was covered made for a bumpier ride. Nor did I relish the sounds of impact as tiny gravel missiles ricocheted off the recently repainted side surfaces of my automobile. And yet I kept on.

Though I knew the place must be a ghost town by now, I rationalized this waste of company time with the vain scheme of searching out the viability of recommending a new franchise in Foxfield should the hamlet still somehow manage to thrive. Why should the natives, if there proved to be any, not welcome the prospect of reestablishing closer contact with the outside world? I could think of no reason.

My heart sank as I saw a gasoline station coming up on my left and, nearing it, found it a weed-grown relic. Only then, at the pang of disappointment I felt, did I realize how strongly I had harbored the folly that the town might still flourish. Now it seemed plain that it could not. And yet I continued. I can give no real account why. I suppose I simply felt stubbornly inclined to see the thing through to the end, unspectacular as that must now surely be.

It turned out to be a day of surprises, since not five minutes later I slowed down to a stop along a cobbled street of a small but living and active town!

My arrival made me the magnet of ill-concealed stares from adults and open gaping by the gathered children who had been playing amid the leisurely progress of their elders down the street of the place.

They gazed at my automobile as if they had never laid eyes on one. While trying to appear friendly and inoffensive, I did not at once try to speak with anyone as my eyes were involuntarily drawn to the architecture of this, apparently the main street. I began a leisurely stroll down this thoroughfare, bare of cars though liberally sprinkled with fresh-faced villagers. I crossed one bridge over the rushing river below, the Miskatonic, I imagined, and noticed the crumbling remains of another, older structure which had once spanned the waters further down their course.

Foxfield looked like a living fossil from a previous generation. There was evidence of modern amenities here and there, but on the whole the place had the air of the turn of the century. The same was true of the costume of the natives, as I was soon to notice. Yet nothing suggested any conscious attempt to preserve or to affect the past out of a sense of nostalgia such I myself felt. It seemed rather that here one might visit another time just as we are accustomed to visit other places and to observe there a fully-formed world of fashion and custom consistent in detail and yet without conscious artifice.

To my request for direction to a good restaurant, a young man, whose dress suggested unmistakably a member of the cloth, perhaps returning from lunch himself, replied with a stammered recommendation punctuated with a pointing hand. I thanked him and proceeded down the block, smiling at those few who made eye-contact and otherwise taking in as much as I might of my surroundings. I became aware that the clothing of most around me attested the same anachronistic design. Most of the clothing, however, partook of the banal functionalism of the dress of most working people and was little distinguished as to style or period.

I will not dwell on the unexceptional decor of the eating establishment I had chosen. I need only note the puzzling character of the menu and of some of the items on it. For one thing, no prices accompanied the entries. This detail usually denotes the exorbitant prices left diplomatically tacit in the most expensive New York restaurants, but this place, really little more than a pleasant cafeteria, could scarcely be charging so much. Or so I hoped as I made to choose between a number of enigmatic dishes. There was a surprising percentage of orders involving venison, even bear meat, very little in the way of beef. And some of the vegetable items bore names utterly unfamiliar to me. Feeling in an adventurous mood, I finally settled upon one of these and waited to discover what familiar greenery the local names "starflower" and "angelroot" might conceal. As I waited, I could not help but notice the inquisitive looks aimed in my direction by most of the other patrons. None seemed hostile, only curious, no, perhaps apprehensive might be a better word.

My lunch was not long in arriving, and I greeted it ravenously. I was intrigued to see that on the salad plate rested at least two vegetable species with which I was wholly unfamiliar, though they looked edible enough. So I set to. Starflower and angelroot were tasty enough, quite distinctive in fact. And here my head for business began to return. Could not my own grocery chain regain some of its dulled edge in the competitive field if we could arrange to become the unique distributor of some canned variety of these delicious and unique treats? Our own label, and the profits to be split with local farmers? More than another local franchise might be at

362

stake here. I made up my mind to seek out some greengrocer in the town and make some inquiries.

I had gotten no further with mercantile speculations such as these when my gustatory reverie was interrupted, pleasantly enough, by a visitor. It was the very man who had only half an hour earlier directed me to this very lunch counter. His face was unreadable, but his manner was polite as he asked if he might join me. I rose and extended a hand of welcome. Then we both sat down. I am, I suppose, naturally friendly, but many years in my profession have reinforced my belief that friendliness is the best policy, smoothing many a feather and soothing many a brow.

"Pleased to know you, Reverend . . . Or is it Father . . . ?"

Shaking his closely trimmed, brown-haired head, the young cleric corrected me. "Actually, I am called Elder, Elder Renfrew. And may I know your name, stranger?"

"Of course. I should have introduced myself. My name is Howard, Howard Willet. I am a traveling field supervisor for the N_____ chain of grocery stores, and I am delighted to have discovered your fine municipality."

This seemed to set my interlocutor at ease, just a bit, but he retained the air of unease. "I should say that 'discover' is quite the word, Mr. Willet. Few outsiders find their way here. Few even know of Foxfield any more. May I ask how you made your way here, and why?"

It took only a moment to supply him with the details of my story, and I saw no reason to hide my business interests. All this he took in without remark. I took advantage of the lull in conversation while he thought over what I had said. "Elder Renfrew, I suppose you could say I am something of an antiquarian, and I must say the aspect of your town charms me immensely. I should much enjoy a tour of your church if you can spare the time this afternoon."

His eyes brightened, and he almost smiled, as if by some word I had unwittingly made things easier for him. "That would be a splendid idea. In fact, Mr. Willet, I might as well tell you, it's not my church. I am only the assistant there. The Presiding Elder is Elder Thorndike. I told him of your arrival. As I said, it's quite an event when an outsider visits us in Foxfield. And Elder Thorndike asked me to invite you to his study. I was afraid you might think it a bit queer, your only having arrived in town."

"Not at all, my good man. By the way, precisely which Christian denomination do you and the Elder Thorndike serve?" At so simple a question the young clergyman hesitated.

363

"I think you would not have heard of us. And besides, we don't really have a name. There are no other churches to distinguish ourselves from in Foxfield. But Elder Thorndike can explain all that better than I can. As I say, I am just his assistant. Pretty green on fine points of theology, I'm afraid."

Knowing the name of one's sponsoring religious body did not strike me as a particularly fine point of theology, but I elected not to press the point.

"I was just finishing up anyway, so we might as well leave," I said, rising and reaching into my vest for my billfold. But my companion forestalled me with a gesture of his own.

"No, you're our guest. Let me pay it."

I thanked him and couldn't help but notice that the young man seemed to place himself between me and the woman at the cash register in such a manner that I would not be able to see the actual exchange. Had the meal indeed been prohibitive in its cost?

I feared he did not want me to know how much his courtesy, to which he may have felt obliged, had burdened him. Knowing that most rural clergy live like church mice, I could not allow this. So I stepped forward and retrieved my billfold.

"Really, Elder Renfrew, it's most kind of you, but I can't let you . . ." My eyes fell upon the notes in his hands which I at first took for some antique issue of the Treasury Department, but were not. He rapidly passed to the woman two or three pieces of odd-looking scrip which almost looked to have been hand-drawn. Did the isolated village have its own system of currency?

I had no choice, then, but to let him pay, thanking him again for his generosity, and politely pretending I had seen nothing out of the ordinary. Whatever the reason for it, alternate local currency would certainly complicate my embryonic plans for a profitable relationship with the town of Foxfield. I realized I had a lot to learn about the strange settlement. As we exited the building and made our way down the block I realized I would very soon have an opportunity to satisfy many of the questions that assailed me.

The outward aspect of the church, a white, wood-frame structure typical all over New England, was unusual in one respect only. Indeed it bore no name board, though two signboards stood at either front corner of the lot, one announcing the title of the week's sermon, the other bearing a scripture quotation, though I could not at a glance identify the source of the text: "Secret things shall be made manifest, and hidden things shall

364

come to light." A good Congregationalist layman myself, though my travels forbid me regular attendance in a single local church, I have committed many portions of scripture to memory and tried my best to memorize this one as we passed it.

The front doors of the church were open, and we proceeded quietly down the nave, trying not to disturb the two or three elderly parishioners who had stopped in for midday prayer. We turned left before the pulpit and, after another turn or two, arrived at the door of the pastor's study. Elder Renfrew's knock brought a swift response. The oaken door opened on a small cubbyhole of an office. The diminutive Elder Thorndike welcomed me in with a broad sweep of his hand. His battered desk bore opened and marked books, of which the wall shelves were full as well. Most seemed crudely bound, and the open volume was, I would swear, hand-written. But my eye was drawn to a strange contrivance of square gold or brass plates, each thin rectangle inscribed in strange glyphs, the whole stack being connected by two thin arches of iron wire threaded through two holes along the edge of each plate.

"I see you fancy books, Mr . . . Willet?"

I assured the parson that I did indeed, treasuring the library bequeathed me by my maternal grandfather, a collection of musty volumes dating from the last century, dear old books from which I had learned much in my precocious youth. Some of these tomes looked to date from about the same period, I suggested, indicating one of his full cabinets.

"And so they do, Mr. Willet. Sit, and let us talk, shall we? Good. Now I would very much like to know how you chanced to come among us." My story was repeated at no great length. And again, I saw no reason to conceal my hopes for reopening commerce between isolated Foxfield and its Novanglian neighbors.

"That, I fear, would be a problem," commented the parson, as if the idea were a foregone impossibility. "You see, Mr. Willet, it's not as if we are so completely shut off as you might think . . . It isn't easy to explain to someone who's not one of us. Well, Foxfield people decided a long time ago to try and protect ourselves from the worldly influences beyond our borders." His jowled chin rested, cupped in one hand, elbow propped on the table. I could tell the man was choosing his words judiciously, as if trying to satisfy me without really telling me anything.

Perhaps I might get somewhere by changing the direction of the conversation

. "Elder Thorndike, would it be possible for you to introduce me to the mayor of Foxfield? I mean no disrespect, but it might be that he would have a different perspective on the matter."

"I'm afraid that would be impossible, or rather, I should say, unnecessary. You see, sir, I am the leader of the community—the civic leader, I mean, as well as the spiritual leader."

I replied that this arrangement was certainly unusual, though not entirely unprecedented, and that I had not intended any discourtesy by my request. The Elder only laughed pleasantly.

"Our ways must seem queer to you, I know. And that's part of the problem here. Too much time has gone by. We're too out of touch with the fast-paced world out there. Oh, we tried it. The machine age reached us here in Foxfield, and we played with its toys for a time. But in the end we decided we liked things better the way they used to be."

I thought of the Amish and Hutterites of Pennsylvania, not to mention the derelict gasoline station I had passed earlier. But he had not finished speaking. Rapidly I sought to regain his train of thought.

"Besides, it's not as if we're ingrown or anything, no inbreeding, God help us." Even so, I had noticed no marks of that taint among the fine-looking people of the little town. There was something slightly exotic in a feature here or there, perhaps a trace of immigrant blood, but nothing more.

"I surmised that you must grow and hunt a great deal of your own food, but you don't even seem to use Federal currency . . ." Here the older man shot a glance of dismay at the younger, the latter subtly flinching. "And I am quite sure the name of Foxfield appears on no current maps of the area. How do you manage?"

"Actually quite well, thank you, Mr. Willet. Much better than we would manage if we were once again to risk contamination by the world. We cherish our ways, our faith, and there are some things the common run of mankind just does not understand. Alma says it well enough, 'O ye workers of iniquity; ye that are puffed up in the vain things of the world, ye that have professed to have known the ways of righteousness nevertheless have gone astray.' Of course, not you personally, Mr. Willet! I simply mean to . . ."

I reassured him that I took his point, and that it was hard to deny it a large measure of validity. I thought to ask how much the younger generations of Foxfield even knew of the outside world, as well as how many of them might make their way there, but some prudent instinct bade me forbear. Instead, I thought it better to salve my itch of curiosity on another point: "I fancy myself a student of scripture, Elder Thorndike, and yet the text you quote is unfamiliar to me. Oh, the sentiments are common enough throughout Holy Writ, but I cannot quite place the words. Would you be so kind as to enlighten me?"

Here young Renfrew caught his eye with a look of grave concern which made the older man hesitate as he reached up to the nearest shelf. But: "I'm sure it will be all right. Aren't we commanded in scripture itself to make the truth of scripture known like the pealing of a bell?"

His stubby finger tapped several spines in near-sighted scrutiny till he found the one he sought, and handed it to me. "It's an extra copy. Take a look at it, though I'm afraid I can't let you keep it. You'll find the passage in there; here, I'll mark the page. But let me tell you a bit of history."

Something seemed to have changed the old parson's mind about telling me what I wanted to know. Now he seemed fully as eager to enlighten me as he had been only a few moments ago to keep me in the dark. This fact made me a bit uneasy, but at the moment my curiosity was uppermost and I did not think his sudden garrulousness as odd, indeed as ominous, as I might have.

"Mr. Willet, the New York State border is no great distance from here, as I'm sure you know, being a great traveler and all. Unlike us shut-ins, I mean. You asked about our religion here in Foxfield, and I'm going to tell you. In fact, it's something you'll be needing to know. Now where was I? Oh, yes. Along about the mid-eighties the whole region was ablaze with the fire of revival. The evangelists and preachers were through here one after the other, crisscrossing the map like traveling salesmen—no implication to be taken, you understand. Folks were getting saved, sanctified, filled with the Holy Ghost.

"Only they didn't all cleave to the same church. Families were split as to who got converted by the Methodists, who got dunked by the Baptists or the Holiness. When the preachers left to go elsewhere, the region was fairly busting with religion. There wasn't a town in Eastern New York or Western Massachusetts that hadn't got religion—and lost it again—two or three times over. In fact they took to calling the whole area 'the burnt-over district.' Ah, I see that rings a bell with you. Good. Well, there was a lot of strife, I'm sorry to say. You know how it is with religious folk: sometimes they're so busy being Christians they lose sight of how unchristian they're being to one another. Well, about that time, there must have been several of the younger men in the towns of the burnt-over district that just couldn't see strife as the handiwork of the Lord, so they betook themselves

367

to quiet places in the hills and took to praying for hours at a time that the Lord would show them the way. Which church to join."

I had indeed heard of the notorious 'burned-over district', and things began to fall into place. What the clergyman had just recounted was the beginning of the tale of Joseph Smith, the controversial seer of the Mormon Church. Having had a cousin convert to that faith, I had had ample occasion to learn more than I wanted to know about his religion.

"I see it in your eyes. What I'm telling you isn't unfamiliar. But let me go on. One man, named Phineas Hoag, a Foxfield boy much taken with the use of seer stones and water-divining, used to go out to the megaliths on the other edge of the town—you'll be wanting to take a look at them, I'll warrant. And he fasted for forty days, beseeching God all the while. And at the end of the forty days, a great shining Being revealed himself to Phineas. He announced himself as Moroni, from the men of Lomar. He entrusted to Phineas a set of plates, like these; they're a copy, of course. What you're holding is a translation. It's called the *Pnakotic Manuscript*.

"And it told the history of the Land of Lomar and its fair-skinned people, how they built a mighty citadel in the lands far to the north, and how they were finally driven south by the squat, hairy Gnoph-kehs. Also calls 'em Voormis, which is a little easier to say. These critters, ape-men, I guess you'd call them, kind of like what those evolutionists talk about, they caught up with Moroni's people hereabouts. There was great bloodshed, but the men of Lomar called upon the Lord, Avaloth, they call him in the *Manuscript*, and he delivered them. He showed them the Place Between the Rocks, the very place Moroni appeared to Phineas Hoag. And there the people of Lomar found safety in a hidden world, preserved from their enemies."

I couldn't help interrupting him with a question, "But Elder Thorndike, isn't this the story of Joseph Smith you're telling me? *The Book of Mormon*, the war between the Lamanites and the Nephites? Are you telling me you and your people belong to the Mormon Church?"

"No, my friend, I am not. You see, Moroni appeared to several who took refuge in the hills. Some were not worthy, others failed to understand. Some confused the revelation they heard. But, yes, there is a connection. It was only Phineas Hoag who proved a fit vessel for Moroni and his people. Only Phineas was vouchsafed the secret of the Place Between the Rocks, where the men of this earth we know may commune with those of Lomar. I told you we're not exactly shut off. It's just that we seek higher company. We hold truck with the Old Ones, we eat the bread of angels, if you will."

I had never heard of this sect, but I knew enough about that period of fervent revivalism he mentioned not to be surprised at most of what he said. It was plain that I had stumbled upon the source from which young Joseph Smith had derived most of his mythology. Skeptics had long pointed to something called the Solomon Spaulding Manuscript, an old religious novel in handwritten draft, as the basis for Smith's artificial scriptures, but here was surely the actual fountainhead of his creed. So he had pilfered it from a local rival sect! I had here discovered something of real historical value, and I resolved to feign only casual interest. Later I would try to contact a scholar at the Miskatonic University with whom I might share what I had learned.

But the Elder was talking again. "I know I've given you a lot to think about, Mr. Willet." He looked out his window and continued, "The sun's about to set. I hope you'll accept our hospitality for the night."

To do so would put me behind, though not seriously; but in fact I was by now fairly certain that I should not be allowed to leave the village of Foxfield in any case. My stay should be an extended one, most likely a life sentence. The town, as I have said, held distinct attractions for me. It was a place a man of my tastes might even consider as a retirement home. But to be detained there against my will was another matter entirely. And yet I knew discretion for the better part of valor. So I thanked the good parson for his offer and promised to take especial care of the borrowed volume, which, of course, he had supplied as part of my orientation to my new life in the pious community of Foxfield. He dispatched his young assistant to accompany me to the Manor House, the largest and perhaps the only hotel in the town.

During our walk to the hotel, I was quick to observe what I could of the reactions of the townspeople we passed. This time, seeing me freely accompanying the well known Elder Renfrew, most faces seemed less uneasy. One or two even smiled or nodded. Despite my position, I could feel nothing against these people, who, as far as I was concerned, shared my plight whether or not they knew it. Even young Renfrew was hardly to be blamed. His mentor, the Reverend Thorndike, no doubt acted from sincere motivation as well, but then so had Torquemada, I did not doubt.

I thanked Elder Renfrew for his company and bade him good night. He seemed to hesitate a moment, as if on the point of saying something, a warning perhaps, but then he must have thought better of it and departed.

As I unpacked my valise and lay half-clothed upon the comfortable bed, it occurred to me to wonder at such a state of careful preservation of a hotel for which there could be no conceivable use in a town in which visitors were feared and shunned.

Shrugging off this curiosity, I deemed it best to pass the time absorbed in the book Elder Thorndike had given me, the *Pnakotic Manuscript*. Mark Twain had once characterized the *Book of Mormon* as "chloroform in print," and I hoped its apparent prototype might not be the source of its soporific quality. I opened the book and began to read. There did seem to be a fair amount of dreary dogmatizing, which I quickly decided to skim superficially. Various pithy sayings were quite striking, though, especially those attributed to a prophet named Kish of the Land of Mnar. As in the canonical Bible, there was no dearth of ceremonial instructions, and even though these had been translated into familiar English, some terms had simply been transliterated, there apparently being no appropriate English word for this ritual instrument or that sacrificial beast. The implication, of course, was that the text did in fact stem from an alien time and setting. Or at least some forger had been clever enough to include such artifice.

What interested me the most, once I finally located it, was the historical account to which the Elder had referred, not that of Phineas Hoag, a modern figure, of course, but the saga of the men of Lomar and their epic struggle with the degenerate Voormis. The habits of these latter were hinted at with euphemistic reserve which did not manage to conceal terrible depravity and bestiality. Who either of these peoples were and how they might have been harmonized with orthodox ethnology I could not guess. But then it was all quite likely fantasy and fiction, though the more I read, the more often I had to remind myself of this fact.

The loathsome Voormis, it seemed, had worshipped a particularly repellant demon called Tsathoggua, whose ultimate origins were not of this world. It was this foul Being, described in the *Manuscript* sometimes with the features of a great bat, other times as more nearly a massive, tentacled toad, who had raised the loping Voormis from their original animal state into a shambling parody on the clean lines of true men. The Lomarites, on the other hand, were presented in terms suggesting the Greek demigods of the *Iliad* and the *Odyssey*. The stilted prose did nothing to silence the ringing echoes of tales in which strapping swordsmen of Lomar sank their blades and axes deep into stinking Voormi flesh defending their homeland in a doomed attempt to whelm the invading tide of the pelted half-men. Of any eventual fate of the detestable Voormis there was no hint, something only natural, I supposed, the rest of the chronicle being written from the standpoint of the men of Lomar, whose miraculous deliverance severed any contact with their subhuman opponents. It was fascinating. And despite the superficial Christianization of the whole business implied in Elder Thorndike's monologue, I could find in the text no attempt to connect this mythology with the biblical tradition. It was quite a puzzle.

By this point it is clear I had indeed become enthralled with the remarkable book. Some portions did indeed merit a Twainian reproach, while others, no doubt the work of unknown bards and poets, gave me to believe I had discovered a genuine, though hitherto unknown, epic tradition having barely survived the fall of some prehistoric Northern civilization. Had the book done its intended work upon me? For, though still disinclined to believe in any present-day Lomarians locked in an unseen dimension adjacent to rural Foxfield, I had about come to the conclusion that the *Pnakotic Manuscript* must represent an ancient tradition, albeit mythical.

So absorbed had I become in the book that it took me a few moments before I realized someone was knocking insistently upon the door. Reaching for my shirt, I wrapped it about me, stuffed its tail into my trousers and approached the door. Without stood my assigned companion, Elder Renfrew. I welcomed the agitated man in, indicating the single chair in the room, while I seated myself upon the edge of the bed. At first I thought he had returned only a few minutes after his departure, perhaps to add some final, momentarily-forgotten detail of his mentor's instruction. But then I noticed his dripping overcoat, which he hung on the closet door hook. There had been no rain earlier, and suddenly I realized that nearly three hours must have passed while I had paged through the Foxfield scripture.

"I see you've been reading it," Elder Renfrew said, with a nod toward the volume. "What is your impression?"

"I must confess I am quite impressed with your *Pnakotic Manuscript*. It appears to be a genuine discovery of some importance. I wonder that your Phineas Hoag did not try to make it more widely known. Was he perhaps overshadowed in his effort by his more successful rival Joseph Smith?"

"I'm not sure I would call the heretic Smith successful. He was, after all, lynched in the end."

I laughed. "Yes, *there's* a point!"

Only a hint of a smile relaxed the man's face, which then returned to an expression clenched with foreboding.

"I expect you have surmised that you are never to depart Foxfield, Mr. Willet." This he stated quite matter-of-factly. In the same tone I replied. "Yes, that was my inference. I see I was not mistaken. Will you tell me why I am to be detained? And how? Will they make room for me in the Foxfield jail? Or is my life sentence to be a short one?"

"Neither. They hope in all good conscience to win you over so that no coercion will be necessary. But none is needful in any case. Foxfield is quite small enough that any attempt by you to escape would be noticed and stopped. Elder Thorndike has already alerted our roaming hunters to keep close surveillance. There are a number of armed men in the surrounding fields most of the time anyway, you see, so guarding you presents no problem, not even any special effort."

"I see. Then at least my confinement would be more in the nature of house arrest. But I must warn you I cannot abide being kept against my will. And I am beginning to suspect that you are tired of it, too. Am I anywhere near the truth, Elder Renfrew?"

His eyes widened and he hunched forward in the creaking chair. He said nothing but waited for me to continue. I did. "I thought you employed the word 'they' a bit too often, Mr. Renfrew. And now please tell me why you are here."

He seemed confused, vacillating between hints of despair and of renewed hope. "I hope I am not a book so easily read by Elder Thorndike! But I think he cannot suspect. It is moot, though. I will tell you that I had planned on returning to see you with a plan of escape. You see, it was I who contrived to have the underbrush trimmed back so that it would no longer obscure the entrance to the shunpike. I hoped someone would come, not knowing exactly what to do if anyone did. It would have been better if a large group came. Frankly, that's what I had hoped, that it would be your police. It is possible that a large armed force might make the difference.

"You see, Mr. Willet, as a clergyman here I am privileged to know certain things about the outside world that others never learn. Ironically we must know about the outside in order to remain ignorant of it, isolated from it at any rate. Still . . . it must be futile. I have stooped to grasping at straws."

"Don't be so quick to despair," I sought to reassure him. "It is not impossible even now that, my presence being missed, a party will be sent to find me. My itinerary is known, and witnesses will remember having seen me at my last stop. So surely there will be a search party in the area. Once they discover the shunpike entrance as I did they are sure to explore it."

"It's no good. Your presence here will lead our leaders to make sure the entrance is somehow hidden again, and the highway authorities will probably not even notice. And suppose a party of outsiders did make it this far. There are the men of Lomar. You're not taking them into account."

My sense of bafflement returned. "What can they have to do with it, my friend? Surely you're talking about mere characters in a book. Forgive me if I seem to offend your faith, but the Lomarians, if they ever existed, are long dead." At this he seemed to look over his shoulder nervously, but he went on, in lowered tones. "Mr. Willet, I only wish that were true. I can assure you, the men of Lomar are quite real. I mean physically real. I have seen them."

"What do you mean? In a vision?"

"No, they are as physically solid as you or I."

"But all this about their passing into some adjacent dimension of space. Surely that denotes heaven and angels."

He shook his head. "They are not angels, Mr. Willet, though there are devils worse than them." The young man pulled his chair closer, drew himself up, and interposed a seemingly unrelated question. "Does it not seem strange to you that a town as xenophobic as our Foxfield should maintain so capacious a hotel as the Manor House?"

"To tell you the truth, I had wondered that, yes."

"The rooms in this establishment are maintained for the occasional visits of those from Lomar." He could, I am sure, read the incredulity written broadly across my face, but I said nothing for the moment and let him continue. After a pause, he said, "They do not often venture outside their secret zone, nor for long. Where they dwell is a timeless realm, more akin to dream than to waking life. And outside of it they will age just as we mortals do. So they are loathe to leave it. Favored members of our community are allowed to enter their dimension at the Place Between the Rocks, but, again, not for long. They are permitted to take sparingly of the game and the crops of that strange world, but the possession of timeless immortality those of Lomar preserve strictly unto themselves. Only one in the town of Foxfield have they taken to themselves and allowed to remain among them, even Phineas Hoag, to whom they revealed themselves."

I shook my head in amazed disbelief. "Are you telling me that the descendants of the ancient nation of Lomar are alive somewhere outside of this town?"

"No, sir. I mean to say that the very men of Lomar themselves, those of whom the *Manuscript* tells, are alive on our borders."

"You know," I said impatiently, "you're only making it more difficult, not less, for me to believe any of this. For one thing, what could either party gain from the strange alliance you describe? A few vegetables? Immortality, I could see that; but that's not part of the package. Except for your prophet. And why not suppose even that to be anything more than a legend that grew up after he disappeared? For all you know, maybe he met the same end as Joseph Smith!"

"You have asked me two questions; I will give you two answers. It is true, the return for our fealty to the Old Ones of Lomar is not great. They manage to supply us with what we lack from the outside world, and to some they supply certain articles we would consider very valuable, though little esteemed by them. Gold, for instance, though our circumstances set certain limits to what can be purchased with it. There is an irony in that, but I can tell you, Elder Thorndike's private residence is quite something to see. Like the dwelling of a medieval king, for whatever good it does him.

"The town of Foxfield first kept to their bargain largely out of fear. The power of those from Lomar is very great. It is a power easily able to repel and destroy any armed force from the outside world, though they would hardly welcome the attention that would bring.

"The last few generations of Foxfielders, however, have never known anything different, and only rarely does a renegade like myself grow dissatisfied. The tales of those few, once they are discovered, are terrible to hear. Whether they met their whispered fates at the hands of the town's rulers or those of Lomar, we do not know. It does not matter. But by now the bond with Lomar is simply a fact of life, like the air and the water.

"As for what our unseen masters reap from our service, it is rather simple. Just as there is a Gate to their hidden dimension, there are other Gates to other dimensions. Foxfield's misfortune is to have been founded near one of the places where these Gates meet. It is our task to see that they are not opened contrary to the will of Lomar. There are certain secret keys, words of binding and loosing, known only to myself, Elder Thorndike, and a few others.

374

"And, as for the immortal continuing of Phineas Hoag, the revealer, the covenant-maker, I have as little choice to disbelieve it as I do the existence of the Lomarians themselves."

"Yes?" I challenged, still hardly satisfied. "And what is the source of your certainty, if I may ask?"

Elder Renfrew abruptly stood to his feet, startling me; he strode briskly to the door and pulled it open. Extending an open hand toward the hallway without, he said in exasperated tones, "Both Phineas Hoag and three of his ancient masters are elsewhere in this building at this moment. Come, I will take you to see them if you wish it."

I was galvanized with an unexpected current of fear. Reason told me that Renfrew must either be trying to hoax me with the aid of a handful of rustic impostors, whose pretense would be immediately exploded, or himself have been deceived by such cheap chicanery. And yet, who could seriously hope to bring off such a trick? And why resort to it if my confinement were assured in any case? For the first time I began to feel creeping coldly upon me a terrible sensation that the absurd, the preposterous, might actually be substantial and terribly real. The bare thought of the proximity under the same roof of fabulous immortals and, even more, the blasphemous survival through more than a century of a contemporary of Joseph Smith, chilled my spine. I stood but remained silent, dumbfounded. Renfrew slowly and quietly closed the door again. We resumed our respective seats.

"I . . . your word is enough . . . for the present," I said, struggling to regain my composure. "But what are we to do?"

"Friend Willet, I said I had hoped to discuss escape with you, but now that seems past all chance of succeeding. Tomorrow, like it or not, you will be taken by myself and Elder Thorndike to the Place Between the Rocks. No, do not fear, you will not be harmed. Not physically. But you will be shown the inner realm of the Old Ones of Lomar. I cannot predict how the sight will affect you, but it is likely you will think no more of escaping the hospitality of Foxfield. Beyond that, I cannot tell you what to expect."

"But surely you have seen this sight yourself," I reasoned aloud. "You must be able to give me some idea of what is in store?"

"Mercifully, I have not seen. I have never dared. But I fear, should my insubordination after all be detected, that I may share whatever fate awaits you. I thought you should know. Try to prepare yourself. Perhaps there is little to fear. I only know that some have not returned sane from the encounter. And now I must go, lest the length of my absence itself invite suspicion. Good night to you."

There was nothing more to say, and in an instant, no one there to whom I might say it. Here I was, a shaking wreck, who had only ten minutes before relegated the whole fantastic business to the follies of religious delusion. And now, God spare me, I had come to share it. I strove all night, in lieu of sleep, to have reason regain the upper hand, to reassure myself of the reign of sanity and the security of the mundane. When these efforts failed, I merely sought to tell myself that the night fears which make us all children would vanish with the dawn. Even the usually calming monotony of the rain at the windowpane did nothing to soothe me. At last sheer fatigue overruled and mercifully threw me the crumb of an hour's slumber.

Waking again with the light, I dragged my aching body from the bed and washed myself cursorily. With an anvil of dread hanging over me, I dressed and sat down to wait. Vacantly I flipped the pages of the *Pnakotic Manuscript* for some unmarked duration, probably not long, till I heard a knock upon my door. I rose wearily, my limbs numb from insomnia and resignation, and reached for the knob. I hesitated a moment, suddenly imagining who or what might await me on the other side.

To my considerable relief the hallway held only the two black-frocked Elders Renfrew and Thorndike, as well as a burly town policeman, whose uniform shared the quaint signs of anachronism characteristic of Foxfield as a whole. I gathered from an overheard remark some minutes later that the personages whose presence I had dreaded had returned to their accustomed dwelling sometime during the night.

"From the look of you, Mr. Willet, I fear you did not sleep well," began Thorndike, with the unctuousness of the practiced clergyman. "For that I am sorry. I believe my young colleague has told you of our destination." Here he took my shoulder in what seemed to me a mockery of fatherly reassurance. "I can assure you this will be a morning to remember, for us all." With this remark he looked a moment in Renfrew's direction. I said nothing, having none of the energy needed to frame an adroit rejoinder. I simply accompanied the small party down the stairs, through the lobby, and up the streets till we reached the open fields on the edge of the town.

Not far away I could see the silhouettes of one of the massive rocks about which so ominous a cycle of legends, or even more ominous truths, had developed. When we had come nearer to it, I could see others nearby. One could not tell whether they were purely natural phenomena or rather some sort of artificial structures. But in either case, still closer proximity revealed the presence of somewhat faded but deeply carved glyphs. Those on the pair of megaliths we approached were evidently of the same type as I had glimpsed on the metal plates lying open on Thorndike's desk the day before. I reflected that it must be such relics as these which had given rise to the many eccentric theories about Norsemen or ancient Phoenicians visiting New England's shores. As if the truth were any less fantastic!

"This is," began the theocratic ruler of Foxfield, "the very spot on which Phineas Hoag first beheld Moroni and received the *Manuscript*. It is sacred to us, so I must ask you to remove your shoes before we enter the Place Between the Rocks." The whole party, myself included, then performed the incongruously quaint-seeming ritual of unlacing our footwear. Well, Moses had not scrupled; why should I?

As we took a few solemn steps forward, I confess I did feel an odd sort of atmospheric disturbance, as well as something more. I began to fancy that I could almost make out certain rushing shapes in the air about me, from the corner of my eye, so to speak, nothing to see straight on. Noting my confusion, Thorndike explained. It seemed he had the natural tendency of the preacher, to interpose commentary at every opportunity, requested or not.

"They are all around us even now. The Old Ones walk serene and primal, not in the spaces we know, but between them. But you shall shortly gain the gift of second sight, Mr. Willet, and you will be one of us. Come, there is nothing to fear."

I traded apprehensive glances with Elder Renfrew at these words. I still had no clear idea of what to expect, what might happen to me. But I was not eager to find out.

"Elder Renfrew, I believe it will be your task to open the Gate. I will, ah, stand back here so as to be out of your way. I believe you know the liturgy for the occasion."

The younger man stepped forward gravely. He bowed, then knelt on the ground without regard to the moisture and mud. He rose and made a slow progress back and forth between the two great stones which rested about fifteen feet apart. Under his breath he was chanting the words of some memorized formula. I could not tell whether the words were in English or in the unknown tongue of the *Pnakotic Manuscript*, though I supposed the latter.

The feeling of disturbance increased, and I felt a ringing in my ears, also some reverberation which I can only compare to thunder sounding afar off, though I cannot swear it was truly sonic in nature. And then, between

377

the rocks, the light of morning began to take on a strange reddish tint, like one sometimes sees in the night sky above a great fire in the distance. I wanted to look away but could not. I fancied that between the rocks I could catch a hinted silhouette of several tall figures, mostly male, and with a suggestion of a great many more behind them. I began to feel the powerful tugging of an instinct to weep, perhaps from awe. There was something undeniably majestic to the vague but potent scene taking form before me.

I had lost the sound of Elder Renfrew's monotone chanting. I had even lost any sense of myself and my position, so overcome was I with the epiphany. But in another moment, there was an outburst of cries and shouts. And then gunshots! That must be the police officer who had accompanied us. Involuntarily I wheeled about, losing my balance and stumbling to the wet ground. I saw the form of Elder Renfrew collapsing to the earth as well. It was he who had been shot. Instantly I supposed his disloyalty had been discovered and punished, though in more mundane fashion than I had expected. But I was soon to realize there was much more at stake here.

Now the thunderous crackings had magnified in intensity tenfold, sending disabling echoes through my tortured skull. I saw that Elder Thorndike had given into the same sudden pain and writhed upon the damp earth, while the confused policeman wasted his remaining shots firing into the air, aimlessly, as I momentarily thought. But then the senses of some in Foxfield were keener than mine where certain matters were concerned, and I realized he might be seeing something I could not. I looked back to the Place Between the Rocks, where the glowing portal between dimensions had seemingly vanished again.

But the same aura of eldritch half-light now spread as if with the strokes of a great brush across the whole horizon. And in it the eye strained to fill in the implicit lines of a great mass of struggling forms. I knew not what to make of this mute pantomime of heavenly battle. Coming to myself, I regained sufficient presence of mind to make for the moaning form of Elder Renfrew. Knowing the dangers of moving an injured man, I nonetheless decided I must attempt to hoist him up and drag him as best I could back toward town, away from the wildly firing gunman, who had now brought a second weapon into play. The wild-eyed policeman must have known no mundane weapons could reach the target he sought but continued to obey the dictates of panic nonetheless.

Our pace was maddeningly frustrating as I sought to regain the town. Shoeless on the bare ground, my speed was even less than it would have been. Anxiety bore heavily upon me, as I knew not but that any moment might send down upon us whatever Entities strove in the heavens above us. I now moved as in a nightmare fantasy, especially as I experienced in reality the same molasses-slowness that retards the would-be runner in a dream.

But at length we did make it to town. The bleeding Renfrew was able to make me understand how to reach the local physician, who, it turned out, had already been roused, like the rest of the townspeople, by the celestial cannonade. There was not much to be done, alas. The policeman had had little danger of missing his shot at such close range, and Renfrew was fading fast. I begged him to tell me what had happened and, more important, what might yet occur. His blood-drooling lips parted in a whisper.

"I told you there were other Gates, other worlds . . . Last night I decided something had to be done quickly. Knew how to get access to secret portions of *Pnakotic* . . . Knew there was a way to open other . . . Voormis, too . . . Waiting all this . . . In the end, decided . . . let them finish the job . . . Chant . . . opened both . . . into each other . . . Thorndike heard . . . too late, though. Over soon . . . for me, too . . ." And this was the last of it. My ear had been close to his stammering lips, but now I rose to look into the baffled face of the fearful doctor. I closed the lids of my poor friend's vacant eyes. I tendered no word of explanation to the nonplussed country practitioner, but turned and ran for the main street of the town. My automobile was not where I had left it the previous day, but it did not take me long to locate it. It reposed before a particularly opulent private home a street or two away, which I surmised must be the palatial residence of the Reverend Thorndike. I only prayed no one had thought to disable the motor. Climbing into the driver's seat, I saw no key but retrieved the extra set I always keep about my person. The machine shuddered into life, and with none of my usual automotive caution, I barreled through the cobble-paved streets like Barney Oldfield, sending the pathetic Foxfielders scattering in every direction. I made for the shunpike, resolving that no recently interposed barricade should long detain me.

As it happened, I met no opposition. My guess was that all the roving hunters and patrolmen, alarmed by what was taking place in the skies above them, had rushed home to see to their families' safety. Once I regained the hard earth of the shunpike, I ventured to look back toward the town I had so precipitously abandoned. Most of the phantom Armageddon had apparently run its course, the long-delayed conclusion of an ancient saga of hatred between two races who had far outlived their appointed time.

Ahead of me, at long last, was the reentry point to the main highway. I rejoiced to see it, and as I turned the wheel to regain familiar paths, I craned my neck momentarily for one last glimpse in the direction of Foxfield. The horizon over that way seemed almost normal now, save for a rapidly dispersing shadow that might have been a vestigial storm cloud from the previous night's rain, or might have been something else, but which suggested the rough outlines of a vast, squatting toad.

The Strange Doom of Enos Harker
With Lin Carter

STATEMENT OF PAXTON BLAINE

I

In 1931 I graduated, with modest honors, from Miskatonic University in Arkham, Massachusetts, and for some months thereafter, sought gainful employment without success. It was my intention to continue my studies and seek a degree upon the completion of my thesis, which was concerning obscure cult-survivals in certain parts of the East. Very much research remained undone, however, and employment in those Depression years was scarce and seldom remunerative; since I required part-time employment, my search was futile.

At length, however, I noticed an item in the personal columns of the *Arkham Advertiser*, placed therein by Dr. Enos Harker. He offered a comfortable subsistence and free room and board in his home for a private secretary able to organize his notes and prepare a manuscript for publication. The opportunity seemed nothing less than a godsend, and I applied forthwith.

Dr. Harker had rented a seaside house, barely more than a cottage, on Cairn's Point. Once a fashionable oceanfront resort for the wealthy merchants and older families of the seaport town, the neighborhood was largely deserted by now, and even rather desolate. But the streetcar connected the suburb with the downtown area, and it was not difficult to find my way.

My potential employer was an unusual figure of a man in his late sixties, I assume. Inclined to corpulence, he affected a severe clerical suit of drab black, and even a clerical collar. I soon discovered that he was, or had been (I never quite learned which) a preacher in one of the more obscure of the Pentecostal sects; a missionary, in fact, who had spent many years in India and parts of Burma and Tibet. Portions of his face and hands were curiously swathed in surgical bandages, and he informed me at our first meeting that he suffered from a skin condition similar to scrofula or

381

eczema, for which a local physician was treating him. It was this disability that necessitated the hiring of someone to handle the paper-work, for I gathered that it was his hands which were most seriously affected by the disease.

"Blaine, Blaine," he murmured, with a slight, thoughtful frown. "I wonder if you are by any chance a relative of Dr. H. Stephenson Blaine of the Sanbourne Institute of Pacific Antiquities, in Santiago, California?"

"I have that honor," I acknowledged, "for he is my uncle."

"Excellent, excellent!" Dr. Harker made reply, in that oddly hushed, almost whispering voice of his, which made me wonder, a bit squeamishly, if his peculiar affliction had not somehow affected his vocal cords as well as his face and hands. "I have read a monograph or two of his. A scholar of some reputation, I believe."

Our conversation soon terminated. Dr. Harker seemed to be satisfied with my credentials and I was, as I have already stated, happy with the terms of his employment. I was to begin my work the following Monday. We parted and I returned to my small flat on Parker Street in a mood of considerable elation.

Over the following weekend, it occurred to me that perhaps it would be wise to look up my employer in the various reference works available at the library at Miskatonic, which I did. He had been a graduate of the Byram Theological Seminary in Kingsport with a Doctorate in Theology, had traveled and lectured widely, and, as I have already remarked, spent many years as a missionary in the East. An amateur anthropologist of some note, he had published a number of papers on certain aspects of Asian archaeology and upon certain of the cults of the Far East, which interested me greatly, as my own interests, of course, lay much in that area of study.

Apparently an explorer of some repute, he had penetrated into portions of Inner Asia seen by few white men, and was one of the first to explore the ruined stone city of Alaozar in the Sung region of Burma, and had traveled extensively, it would seem, in the more northern parts of Tibet.

All these things made me certain that we should enjoy a mutually profitable and interesting relationship.

Why, then, did I feel an uneasy qualm that warned me to shun this unusual personage? A qualm almost to be named with the name of . . . *fear*.

II

My tasks were simple enough, and did not require extensive labor. Until his progressive disability had robbed my employer of the fullest use of his hands, he had been compiling notes towards a scholarly work of great length and complexity. It became my primary duty to take down by dictation further data as he gave it in his soft, weak voice, and also to journey to the library of Miskatonic University and the Kester Library in nearby Salem for further research.

Many of the books I delved into for this purpose were tomes I had already consulted in the course of preparing my own thesis. I refer to certain volumes such as the *Unaussprechlichen Kulten* by the German occultist, Von Junzt, the Comte d'Erlette's *Cultes des Goules*, Von Heller's *Black Cults*, the original German text of the *Unter-Zee Kulten*, and the heavily expurgated treatise, *Le Culte des Morts*. I had also to look into the abhorrent pages of the old *Necronomicon* of Alhazred for certain references to a singular corpse-eating cult in a place called Leng.

This particular volume is as notorious as it is rare, and its rarity is nigh fabulous, generally kept under lock and key. My connections among the faculty of the University gave me free access to the damnable volume, although some of the ravings I glimpsed within its thickly-written pages were to haunt my dreams thereafter.

In general, my employer was seeking references to a cult or tribe called the "Tcho-Tcho people," rumored to linger on in certain of the more inaccessible parts of jungled Burma and in Leng—wherever Leng was supposed to be, for I could not find it in any atlas. They were believed to worship gods or devils with names like "Zhar" and "Lloigor," but so little about them was known for certain, that many authorities seemed to consider them to be merely legendary.

I was also to search for any and every reference to Leng itself; to a certain Tcho-Tcho lama who veiled his visage behind a mask of yellow silk and dwelt in a "prehistoric" stone monastery; to Inquanok, which seemed to be both a people and a place, the place being adjacent to the plateau of Leng; and to certain sea-divinities or maritime demons with uncouth names like "Cthulhu," "Idh-yaa," "Zoth-Ommog," "Yeb," "Ghatanothoa," "Ubb, Father of Worms," "Ythogtha," and so on. None of this research was particularly demanding of my time, but it was oddly disturbing. This was not only because my own researches had led me to many of these

383

same sources, but because of certain events in the recent past which were still whispered about by the townspeople, but which had been hurriedly hushed up in the newspapers—the effect being that no one quite knew whether they were wild fable or contained a germ of horrible truth.

What really happened in the old Tuttle house on Aylesbury Road near the Innsmouth Turnpike, and why was the account published in the local papers so oddly cursory? For what reason did Federal agents dynamite and burn several blocks of decaying waterfront tenements in nearby Innsmouth back in the winter of 1927-28, and why did a U. S. submarine discharge torpedoes into the underwater chasm off Devil's Reef? And what really happened to Bryant Hoskins in that cabin in the woods to the north of Arkham, that led to his death as a raving madman in the County Sanatorium in March 1929?

Nobody really knew; or, if they knew, they didn't speak of it.

And why was Enos Harker so interested in this obscure, damnably ancient mythology?

III

Some of the information I extracted from the old, crumbling books excited my employer to a pitch of feverish intensity. For example, I returned from one such trip to the library at Miskatonic, with two quotations which seemed to me to be little more than innocuous, but which kept him up all night, pawing through his sheaves of notations with those bandaged hands of his, muttering under his breath, the visible portions of his features flushed with unhealthy and febrile exultation. For the sake of me, I could not guess why!

The first passage from the *Necronomicon* read thusly:

It was from fabled Sarkomand the Tcho-Tcho people first came into the Waking World, that time-forgotten city whose ruins bleached for a million years before the first true human saw the light of day; and its twin titan lions guard eternally the steps that led down from the Dreamland into the Great Abyss, whereover Nodens reigns as Lord, and the Night-Gaunts that serve Him, under dread Yegg-ha, their master.

The second was a fragmentary ritual, apparently quoted from another source, which went thusly:

Aye, was it not written of old in R'lyeh that the Deep Ones await their followers, and we must not fail to be present at the Great Awakening? It is written that all shall arise and join with them, we who carry the Emblem and those who have merely looked upon it. From the ends of the earth cometh the Summons and the Call, and we dare not delay. For in watery R'lyeh Great Cthulhu is stirring. *Shub-Niggurath! Yog-Sothoth! Iä! The Goat with a Thousand Young!* Are we not all Her children?

When I delivered these notes to Enos Harker he virtually snatched them from my hand, holding the pages close to his face (for his eyesight had recently grown weakened, perhaps due to the progressive degeneration caused by his disease), and scanned them with fierce intensity.

"Of course!" he mumbled in that weak voice of his. "From Sarkomand they came . . . all the way to the Sung plateau, to build their ghastly stone city in the jungles! I should have guessed it from—" but here his voice broke off and he glared at me with wary suspicion, almost as if he thought me spying upon some private thing. Then he went into a screened front room, which faced on the beach, to scan the notes in private.

When I retired, a little past midnight, his light was still burning.

IV

It had by now become quite obvious to me that my employer's health was failing very rapidly, although I still did not understand the nature of his complaint. I knew that a local physician, a Dr. Sprague, had been treating his scrofula—or whatever it was—with zinc ointment and with a substance called cortisone, then generally unavailable, as it was still in the experimental stage of being tested and had not yet been released to the general market.

None of the medications seemed to halt the spread of the skin condition. In addition, his features became bloated and puffy, and his person, which had been normally corpulent when I had first begun working with him, soon became grossly obese. He had difficulty in walking at times, and gradually the white bandages spread over his swollen, pasty visage until he was virtually masked with bandages, like an Egyptian mummy. There was also a peculiar *smell* about him that was singularly repulsive . . . a nauseating stench, as of seawater gone foul and rancid, or like the bloated, rotting corpse of some marine creature exposed to the harsh air and the cruel sun.

385

But perhaps I exaggerate. The cottage stood so close to the empty deserted beach that the salt wind penetrated every part of it, and the reek of the stagnant seawater in the tidal pools and among the gaunt rocks filled my nostrils night and day. Besides, Dr. Harker's weeping wounds and odorous ointments accounted for his unusual smell.

Harker became increasingly dependent upon me for many of the small necessities of everyday life. It was no trouble for me to ride my bicycle into the edge of town and buy groceries, nor to wash the dishes and remove the garbage and handle his bills as already I was handling his correspondence.

This correspondence ranged all over the world, for Enos Harker was continually in touch with certain scholars in places like France, Peru, India, and even China, who had made a special study of the weird old mythology that had become his life's work. This mythology, by the way, had as its central belief the notion that the earth had been visited by strange and demonic intelligences from other worlds and galaxies, and even from beyond the Universe itself, from the very remotest of ages, long before the evolution of humankind. Not being made of matter as we know it, these "Ancient Ones" or "Old Ones," as they are known, were deathless and unaging.

Æons before man, they were pursued to this part of space and time by their former masters, a race known as "the Elder Gods." A titanic conflict ensued, and at its terminus, the Elder Gods were victorious over the rebels who had been their former servants. Unable to destroy the Old Ones, they imprisoned them with powerful spells—and, in particular, with a potent talisman called "the Elder Sign"—and in their charmed imprisonment they, presumably, rage and roar to this latter day, for all the world like the Fenris Wolf and the Midgard Serpent in Norse legends.

They are served, even in their imprisonment, however, by their minions or subject races, few of which are to be considered even remotely human. The devils which mostly concerned Enos Harker were the sea-entities Cthulhu and Ythogtha and the rest; their minions are called the Deep Ones and the ancient books of this system of superstition describe them shudderingly as huge and bloated things, half froglike, half snakelike, partly squamous and partly rugose, with ghastly protuberant eyes, and gills.

The Tcho-Tcho people, also among his prime interests, are followers of another group of divinities, not sea-elementals at all. They are associated with the "shunned and evil" plateau of Leng, which some texts discuss as though located in "the black heart of Secret Asia", and elsewhere mentioned as near the South Pole. This doubtless makes as little sense to

386

the reader as it did to me at the time.

But there was an uncanny *coherence* to all of this: on the surface it seemed a mad, chaotic jumble of nightmarish legend, but underneath it all was a basis of something sinister, age-old and time-forgotten . . . but hideously *suggestive*.

For who would expect myths centuries, even millennia, old to concern themselves with intelligent creatures from other planets, distant stars, remote galaxies, or weird dimensions beyond the three we know?

V

Most of the correspondence concerned a particularly rare book called the *R'lyeh Text*, for which my employer was searching with a furious need that went far beyond mere scholarly or scientific curiosity, and approached the proportions of a fixation.

Copies of this curious old book, while rare, were not unknown; indeed, several redactions (for the book had never been printed and existed only in manuscript copies, furtively circulated between the members of obscure cults) were to be found right here at the Miskatonic. The problem was that, while the *R'lyeh Text* was written in the letters of the common alphabet, the language itself was no longer known or understood. It apparently consisted of rituals or invocations to the devil-gods of this mythology, which were read or chanted aloud by their worshippers, hence they needed only to pronounce the uncouth verses, but did not really need to understand what they meant.

Few scholars, if any, could read the "R'lyehian" language, and it was for some of those that Enos Harker was so desperately searching . . .

I have previously alluded to the strange mystery surrounding the death of Bryant Hoskins, who died in 1929. While the case attracted considerable attention in the public press, the authorities seemed to have hushed the whole affair up, but it had taken place so very recently, that there were still people about who possessed information concerning what really happened in that secluded cabin in the woods north of Arkham.

By purest chance, one day about six months after I began my employment as the secretary of Enos Harker, a clue to the mystery came to light. A muckraking journalist on one of the less reputable Boston papers began digging into the case, and turned up a sensational story which most people, I suspect, dismissed out of hand as wild speculation.

But one item emerged from the newspaper story which sent my employer into a frenzy of excitement. Young Hoskins had been employed at Miskatonic in the capacity of private secretary to the Director of the Library, Dr. Cyrus Llanfer. In July of 1928, the Library had received, as part of the Tuttle Bequest, not only a priceless copy of the *R'lyeh Text*, but a document in what was believed to be Amos Tuttle's own hand called the *R'lyehian Key*, the very existence of which went unnoticed for some time, until Bryant Hoskins chanced upon it by accident. It had been found at the end of another manuscript volume, something called the *Celaeno Fragments*.

It would seem that the late Amos Tuttle had been one of those few scholars on earth who was still able to decipher the mysterious, ancient language in which the *R'lyeh Text* was written, for his *R'lyehian Key* was none other than a glossary of the ancient language, together with some speculations on verb-forms and grammatical structure.

Hoskins, who had become fascinated by the mysterious *Text*, spent the last months of his life translating it into English. The labor had broken his health, both in mind and body, but when he was taken away to die raving in the asylum, the manuscript of his version of the *Text* was salvaged from the cabin.

According to the reporter's account, the "Hoskins Translation" now reposed in the secret shelves of the Miskatonic University Library. And thither I went, bright and early the next morning.

VI

I was ushered into Dr. Llanfer's office, and he greeted me amicably enough, for we had had dealings over the past few months, during which my employer had sought access to the *Necronomicon* and other books. While these abhorrent old volumes are strictly forbidden to the general public, they are accessible to qualified scholars. Moreover, I was by this time well acquainted with Dr. Llanfer, so I imagined I should encounter no difficulty in gaining access to the Hoskins translation. I was in for a surprise.

"Mr. Blaine," the white-haired archivist said to me with a troubled note in his weary voice, "come with me if you will." He motioned me to follow him into the Special Collections room, then through a double-locked door. Proceeding across the carpeted floor to a metal set of shelves, he unlocked this, too, and displaced two or three metal strongboxes of various shapes and sizes (some of which could hardly contain books, I mentally remarked). He turned toward me with one of these metal cases, unlocked it, and opened it as gingerly as if he were a lion tamer parting the jaws of a ferocious beast.

"Here it is. Not much to look at, is it? Just a set of scribbled notes on pad paper not a year old. No ancient artifact, though God knows we house enough of those. This is the translation you're looking for. I have no plausible pretext under which to bar you from reading it, though I half-wish I did! This text has meant madness and death to at least three men of my own acquaintance. And so far as I know, all they did was to read it. As for myself, I have not perused its contents, not even after young Mr. Hoskins made reading it so much easier. Do not misunderstand me. I have the love of learning, of recovering lost knowledge even as these men did. But unlike Amos and Paul Tuttle and Bryant Hoskins, I do not have a suicide urge. I hope that you do not have it, either."

Taken aback by this monologue, I scarcely knew how to reply. "And what of the Reverend Harker? It is he who has sent me. I am only his emissary. If the book is not available to him, it will be my duty to tell him so. This I will do without qualm. But you must realize that he will not rest until he has had a chance to consult that book. Especially since, as you say, you can hardly deny a qualified scholar access to the official holdings of the library."

"Yes, all that you say is quite true, Mr. Blaine. Quite true. Only promise me that you will play your role as disinterested stenographer well. Read and transcribe what you must. But hold it within you only as long as it may take you to get back to Harker's home and tell him. I fear he has already progressed too far down his path to be helped. And it would be cruel to prolong his agony. May the forbidden knowledge of the text of R'lyeh deliver the inevitable blow swiftly and mercifully. Here. Take what you need."

I proceeded to avail myself of Dr. Llanfer's oddly grudging generosity, intimidated by now at the prospect of whatever shocking revelations I should meet with. What could a mere text, however ancient and recondite, contain? I opened my notebook and commenced jotting down the greater part of the translation, feeling more and more a sense of anticlimax the further I went. At long last, after a couple of hours, I finished my task with something akin to a sense of disappointment, almost as if I had failed to find something I had sought within the text.

But then of course I had no idea what it was my employer might be looking for. I knew not whether he should recognize whatever he sought in these strange litanies, nor whether disappointment might not be better than satisfaction, given Dr. Llanfer's manifest opinion of the ancient screed.

When I returned to the Reverend Harker's manse that evening, it was plain he had been waiting with intense agitation, for he fairly grabbed the notebook from me and, without a word, turned and closed the door of his study. I was half-minded to linger just outside and listen for any demonstrative reaction within, but I rebuked myself for such juvenile scheming and retired for the night.

My curiosity had by now reached a zenith, its fires only banked by the silence in which the old clergyman shrouded the whole business. He only grew less and less communicative as his baffling condition worsened, seeking to make himself understood chiefly by monotone mutterings and waves of his bandage-mittened hands. Yet even such charades as these made it evident to me that somehow we were running a race against time. But was it a race to attain some goal, still unknown to me? Or was the race to escape some frightful doom worse even than the physical debilitation that seemed rapidly and steadily to be consuming him? Strictly speaking, it was no business of mine. Certainly the Reverend Harker never sought to share his burden with me.

I had more than an inkling that the reticent Dr. Sprague knew more than he dared say. He approached his ministrations with what appeared to me a hint of fear, though mixed with a greater dose of resignation, though this made no sense to me at the time.

On one occasion I had exchanged pleasantries with the elderly physician as I made to leave the house and make another bicycle trip into Arkham to consult again the volumes in the University library. Upon learning my destination, Dr. Sprague offered to drive me into town on his way back. I felt some revelation to be at hand, but as it happened I was disappointed. As he seemed to expect, I asked him about the precise nature of my employer's mysterious malady. But, contrary to my own expectation, he had little to tell me.

"Beyond the physical symptoms which are as evident to you as they are to me, I can only say that what plagues Dr. Harker is something more in the nature of a *spiritual* affliction." He plainly wished not to discuss the matter at greater length, but I had the very definite feeling that he had meant by his cryptic words to warn me of some danger. Could the old missionary's pestilence be somehow contagious?

VII

As the days passed, I began to mark new symptoms plaguing Dr. Harker, chiefly an inability to sleep through the night. Though he denied it, it was clear that nightmares were displacing his nocturnal respite. Once I believed I heard him chanting one of the Psalms, as if to ward off his nightly nemesis, "He giveth to his beloved sleep . . ."

Once his agitation passed over the line into actual screaming, and of such urgency as to awaken me, asleep as I was at the opposite end of the house. He himself remained asleep, and seemed to calm somewhat as I crept softly to his bedside, knowing that, despite my good intentions, such an invasion of his privacy might lead to my immediate dismissal. But I had to be sure the old man was all right. His breathing had slowed somewhat, but I noted that his nightmare flailings of a few moments previously had disarranged the gauzy wrappings of his face. The disturbance was but slight, and yet what I saw disturbed me profoundly. I have said that the Reverend Harker had been quite plump on my first sight of him and had, with the progress of his disease, continued to bloat in a most unwholesome fashion. This I vaguely attributed to the side effects of some medicine he must be taking, since otherwise one would expect advancing degeneration to shrink and wither the body. But nothing I had seen prepared me for what I saw now.

His face, which he had lately taken to veiling almost completely, was partially visible, and it had suffered shocking disfigurement. His eyes were almost totally obscured by grotesquely swollen puffs of blue-veined pasty flesh. His nose, which admittedly I had never seen unswathed, seemed to have expanded to an astonishing degree. But here the change was not due to swelling, for the very structure seemed to have been altered, the bridge oddly broadened, the nose itself, still covered at the tip, absurdly elongated. His hair, always thin and wispy, was mostly gone, some of it visibly scattered around the pillow.

Though I felt utter repulsion, my curiosity was stronger still, and I actually found myself reaching hesitantly to pull away yet more of the loose bandaging. As I stood frozen with indecision, startlement shook me: the muffled voice spoke. "It appears I am found out. But I think you have

391

discovered enough for one night." As he spoke, he made to rearrange his futile disguise, and he sat up.

"I am most sorry to have disturbed your sleep, my young friend. Return to your bed. I doubt that sleep will return with you, but try to get some rest. We will talk, and talk plainly, on the morrow. I would have taken you into my confidence ere now, save that I feared you might become drawn into the web that holds me fast."And with that, he turned his obese form over on its side, shaking the bed frame as he did.

There was nothing more to be said for the moment, so I turned and found my bed again. I resigned myself to some sleepless hours before the dawn and gazed out of the window at the cold white orb of the moon, which, I fancied, looked down upon secrets it knew but, like the intimidated Dr. Sprague, would not, or perhaps dared not, reveal.

And yet, despite my shock, I fell asleep almost at once. As if the moon had been the swaying watch of a hypnotist, I seemed to have passed without noticing into a dreaming state. And the wan, bluish radiance of the lunar disc seemed to narrow and to gather in intensity. It seemed even to go on and off periodically, though at very long intervals, as I watched and watched, seemingly for endless hours. The contrast with the surrounding darkness was great, so that the strange light illumined nothing but itself. I seemed to know that the unseen landscape was not that which I would recognize in the light of day. As with a false memory, I felt I knew the lay of the shrouded land, and that it must be a vast, bleak mountainous plateau. And with equal tacit certainty I felt that the light I watched was set to guide the path of someone or something on its way home.

With this . . . glimpse, I awoke to find the sun streaming on my face. Ordinarily I should have awakened with the light much sooner, and I found I shook off Morpheus with unaccustomed difficulty. I arose, showered, and dressed with a lingering sense of oppression. At the same time I eagerly anticipated whatever the Reverend Harker might have to tell me. It was with some distraction that I made my way through the assigned tasks of the morning. My researches had come increasingly to seem like a charade. Of what import could fine points of exegesis of obscure old texts possibly be in the face of my employer's obviously impending collapse? Mustn't there be more significant things I could do to make his remaining weeks or days more pleasant? I resolved to make the suggestion whenever Dr. Harker should summon me. The day waned, and I suspected the old clergyman's lack of sleep had taken its toll, and that I should have to wait till the next day for our promised conversation.

To my surprise, the buzzer sounded in the library to summon me to his bedside at 9:45 in the evening. I rose with haste and paced rapidly to his door, knocking before I should venture to enter. Some moan from within I took as my invitation and turned the handle, opening the door into almost total darkness. After what I had seen the previous night, I did not wonder at the reason.

A tired but surprisingly steady voice began to recount the strangest tale I had ever had occasion to marvel at. It is possible the disorientation I felt was due in some measure to the altogether unaccustomed tone and timbre of what should have been a familiar voice. I could not imagine what tumorous occlusions could have grown so quickly as to affect his formerly clear and rather comforting voice. I will report as accurately as I can what the doomed man confided in me, as there no longer seems to be any point in keeping it to myself. The essentials are right, I am sure of that, though I will hardly blame you if you wish to accuse me of exaggerating.

VIII

Enos Harker had entered into the study of divinity at Byram Theological Seminary rather later in life than most of his classmates, having felt a dramatic "call" to the ministry in early middle age. Previously he had earned a modest reputation as a regional historian of the New England and Middle Atlantic states. One evening while crossing town, he had felt strangely drawn to one of the storefront congregations of a small Pentecostal denomination. What attracted his attention was the sound of the sobbing hymns and shouted "prophecies" emerging from behind the painted glass of the large windows that had once displayed merchandise in the days before the neighborhood had run down. Wandering through the door and down the central aisle, he knelt with the circle of moaning seekers in what revivalists call a tarrying meeting.

Suddenly the Holy Ghost struck one of those present like lightning. She seemed to explode into almost orgasmic ecstasy, her arms flung skyward, her head thrown back, and unleashing a torrent of nonsense syllables, what Enos Harker would learn was called "speaking in tongues," ostensibly divinely inspired oracles in genuine foreign languages unknown to the speaker in a normal waking state. Harker watched in growing alarm and yet unable to turn away. One by one, all those in the circle succumbed to the spittle-spewing frenzy, as if electrically wired in series, until it finally and ineluctably reached him. When, in the wee hours, he found himself back outside on the street, he was a changed man. He began to pore over the scriptures, the copy provided him by the elders of his new religious fellowship. Not the King James Version, this Bible had been newly translated by the founder of the sect, himself under prophetic inspiration.

He returned to the shabby sanctuary every night for the next month or so, his conviction of new purpose and new destiny reinforced and focused, till one midnight, the sweating, straining knot of believers, their hands clasping him about the head and shoulders, began to shudder and sway, and one of them blurted out a prophetic declamation. Brother Enos, it announced, had been set apart by the Lord to take the Full Gospel message to foreign climes as a missionary.

This duty the earnest new convert did not shirk. But the sect was tiny and militant, eschewing, as is the manner of such conventicles, any cooperation with other churches varying from their own doctrine by the slightest degree. By themselves, the sect, its name a jumble something like "the Fire-Baptized Temple of the Apostle of God," had neither the numbers nor the resources to maintain a theological college or a missions board. Thus his attendance at the staid Byram Seminary, theological training being a prerequisite for any reputable missionary agency. The years of dreary dogmatics, homiletics, and biblical languages did little to dampen the fires of Enos Harker's zeal, and upon graduation and ordination, he lost no time in choosing his mission field. Though, in truth, it was not really his choice, the location being divulged to him, as he assumed, by the Holy Ghost during a dream. His destination would be a little-known recess of darkest Asia, a place of which he had never heard, a high and airless plateau called Leng.

Dr. Harker did not pause to explain how he managed to gain the cooperation of his missionary agency to journey to such a remote outpost without demonstrating any competence in the local languages. I gather, however, that with the mountain-moving (some would say "fanatical") faith of the Pentecostalist, he simply dared to believe that the "gift of tongues" would suffice him, that when the moment came to speak the words of the gospel message, the Holy Ghost would quite literally supply the words. He knew it would be no easy thing even to gain access to his goal. He knew how the first Christian missionaries to China and Tibet were cruelly tortured and martyred, but should this be his eventual fate, he would not shrink from it, welcoming the martyr's crown for the glory of his Lord. He had then imagined, you see, that such might be the ultimate sacrifice in the service of God. He was later to discover horrors far worse.

394

As the night grew deeper at the old man's bedside and I found myself, ironically, taking the role of father confessor, I was no longer so certain I cared to plumb the mystery further, but I knew it was too late to withdraw. I had the curious feeling that something more ominous awaited me than even the severest shock a mere story, even a true one, might deliver.

Enos Harker's reading while in theological school had been wider than the narrowly prescribed list of standard works drawn up by his professors. And before his conversion it had been wider still. He knew that other Westerners had managed to penetrate into the secret heart of Asia without molestation. Showing the proper respect for a culture in which they were visitors, and which they plainly admired, pilgrims like Madame Alexandra David-Neel and the artist Nicholas Roerich had actually been welcomed and given generous freedom in the usually off-limits regions north of the Himalayas. But they had come to learn the esoteric wisdom of the East, and he had come for quite a different purpose: to teach and to preach the glad tidings of the Holy Ghost. Still, if he came as a holy man seeking out holy men, he was sure he could make himself understood, and that he might even find a ready hearing. Such was his faith.

Dr. Harker, whose wasted constitution forbade him to enlarge upon any point not absolutely needful to relate, passed over the no doubt colorful details of the long sea voyages and difficult treks over land by the most primitive conveyances. He never expected divine inspiration to make it any easier to arrange for transportation or knowledgeable guides without him knowing the tongue-twisting languages of the many tribes and clans along his path. But somehow he made his way to the shunned Plateau of Leng.

Then a man of hardy physique and robust health, he had found the climb up to the frigid table land a bracing challenge. He had picked up a smattering of Tibetan and Nepalese phrases necessary to make certain rudiments understood, but his grasp of these languages utterly failed him in understanding the sudden reluctance of his guides and bearers to complete the journey up and across the plateau itself. Apparently the man who had hired them for the missionary had withheld the fact of their ultimate destination in order to get them to agree to go even this far. So all fled him. But this, too, thinking of the missionary travails of Saint Paul, he took in stride. And on he pressed, finding that the way to his object was after all clearly marked, at least at night, when, from a distant structure, vague against the mist-shrouded horizon, there emerged periodically a beam of light like a beacon, he assumed, to welcome distant pilgrims to a place of holy retreat. As soon as he saw it he thought of

395

Moses and how God had guided the children of Israel through the wilderness as a pillar of fire by night. The redoubtable Dr. Harker took it as a good omen.

It took several days to cross the plateau, the total flatness of the place robbing him of any sense of distance. Despite hours walking, the squat complex of buildings never seemed to get any closer, until all at once, it loomed on the horizon. Structures began to dot the blasted landscape as he approached. Most were the broken teeth of once-proud pillars and obelisks which bore wind-eroded carvings. Upon examining one of these in the light of his lamp, Dr. Harker found long vertical columns of letters remotely resembling Tibetan, of which he had seen quite a bit during his recent journeyings. But this was not precisely Tibetan. Subsequent research would disclose that what he had seen was a linguistic ancestor of the Naacal language of fabled Mu. Alternating with these mute stelae were queer carvings of unrecognizable marine creatures, some of which suggested nothing so much as the submarine behemoths of the Permian Age. But surely these carvings had represented no actual models, and only recounted heathen myths native to the region. Still, it was singularly improbable for marine motifs to occur in the religion of a plateau in the mountainous heart of Asia.

A stiff wind suddenly blew up from out of nowhere and pummeled the intrepid missionary as if Aeolus himself would prevent him from nearing the grim pile of brooding buildings. But Harker had an inner drive of his own and would not be kept from his destiny. He pressed on indefatigably. He had nearly reached the closest of the buildings, a low, unadorned structure made of huge stone blocks that had so settled together and been smoothed by the howling winds of countless generations that they seemed almost the natural mass of a megalith.

And then, without warning, a pair of stocky humanoid shapes loomed up through the ubiquitous gloom that seemed to hold daylight ever at bay. The men, for such they must have been, were completely swathed in great fur cloaks and cowls against the ripping talons of the plateau wind. They accosted the weary traveler, whether in hostility or rescue, he could not yet surmise, and half-guided, half-carried him the rest of the way into their compound. And though the windy torrent whipped away their words like autumn leaves in a hurricane, Harker believed he caught the word "Leng."

He remembered little else until he awoke inside a dimly lit cell whose only illumination came from a small butter lamp on the floor in a corner. Of comfort there was none, save for a threadbare Yak hide beneath him, which hardly softened the naked stone floor. For a moment he feared he

396

had already been consigned to some already-forgotten dungeon reserved for any so foolish as to violate the chaste isolation of the place. But then he realized the dwellers in this awful place must be a monastic fellowship of ascetics, and that they had no doubt assigned him quarters no more Spartan than their own. He resolved to be sure to try and communicate his gratitude for their rough-hewn hospitality—provided he ever saw another of his hosts.

IX

Several days might have passed. The absolute silence, together with the lack of any hint of sunlight, made it impossible for him to gauge the passing of time. Sometimes when he would awaken from a longer or shorter period of sleep there would be a meager portion of food awaiting him, which he gratefully consumed.

And then one day, he guessed some two or three months later, he awoke to find himself, not in his accustomed cell, but in the center of a circle of silent, seated forms amid a large meeting hall. Butter lamps provided the only light here, too. And none of the shapes could he see distinctly. It was disorienting to behold a robed figure seem to be sitting or reclining, then begin to move laterally without rising. Movements were few, and bodily outlines were mostly obscured by generous folds of draping cloth, but something in the perspective suggested that occasional arm or hand motions presupposed the wrong anatomical angles.

Once in a while, there were low exchanges of unfamiliar words, though sometimes he could not be sure whether they were sounds of intelligent conversation he heard, or rather the hypnotic drone of distant insects. The ring of the men of Leng held thus for some hours, apparently in the performance of some spiritual exercise. Looking about him at what little the soft and hazy light revealed, Harker was taken aback to notice what looked like a shadowy dais off to one end of the low but vast chamber. Atop this structure, which seemed imperceptibly to merge with an outcropping of stalagmites rising from the natural stone floor, there sprawled a shifting heap of living matter. Upon this figure Harker tried now to focus, hoping that as his eyes adjusted to the gloom he might be able to scrutinize the form more clearly.

All at once he became aware of a low susurration that had only just broached his threshold of hearing while very gradually increasing in volume. The monks were chanting. And the illumination began to grow the least bit brighter, though nowhere could Harker spy anyone adding fuel to the many small lamps or otherwise adjusting the light.

No matter; at least a better glimpse of the figure on the throne had become possible. And still his head mildly ached with the frustrated effort to put some familiar construal upon what his eyes reported. For the shape shrouded in luxuriant layers of yellow silk seemed amorphous. He had once or twice seen individuals with thyroid conditions that made them dangerously obese, women from whose limbs sagging pouches of redundant flesh depended. In these cases the conventional lineaments of the human body had become obscured like an ancient fossil encased in mud. But this comparison only began to hint at the appearance of the Hooded Thing before him. Three great bell-like funnels of lemon-yellow silk seemed to veil thick and stumpy protrusions, presumably a head and two arms, though no recognizable flesh was visible. And there were strange . . . *shiftings* among the folds of the massive cassock that Harker found himself wishing the shadows still hid.

The chanting died away as quickly as it had begun. And now Harker felt that the still-unseen visages awaited some word from him. Sooner or later he would have to speak, else why had he come among these strange heathen people at all? So he up and spoke, knowing that in no case could his audience possibly know his language, but trusting in the promise of scripture that the Holy Ghost should fill the mouth of the one who preached the gospel. "My friends, you whose lives, like mine, are given unto spiritual things; I have journeyed far to bring you glad tidings of great joy. For unto you has come this day a Savior, who is Chr . . ."

"*Ta tvam asi!*" came back a voice as if to punctuate his words. He knew from his seminary studies in Comparative Religion the meaning of this phrase. It was a famous quote from the Hindu *Maha-Upanishads*. It meant "That thou art" and referred to the identity of the individual self with the divine Brahman. Did one of those present mean to counter his preaching with a counter-gospel? Or had the Spirit made them understand his English syllables, even as God had translated for the multitude at Pentecost so that each heard the gospel in his own native language? Did they indeed understand him? But if so, what was the sense of the Hindu formula?

He had barely a moment to ask himself these questions, and then he felt a spiritual onrush such as he had not felt since that first night in the storefront temple. His tongue and vocal cords were no longer his own as

398

he yielded to the impulse of the Spirit. He blanked his conscious volition and uttered forth the glossolalic syllables: *Pnglui ngah Cthulhu fhtagn!*

And in a moment all the figures seated about him were bowing and prostrating themselves before him, or at least that was what he thought. Given the confusing body shapes and motions that met his eye, he could not be sure what they were doing. But it seemed like obeisance more than anything else. He had been merely the mouthpiece for his God, no more than a messenger handing over the sealed message. It was not for him to know what words the message contained. But he thought and hoped he had somehow prophesied the glad tidings of salvation, and that his audience had found themselves cut to the quick even as Simon Peter's hearers at Pentecost were. He would soon find it was not so simple as that, but whatever he had said, it had certainly met with their approval, and their attitude toward him was henceforth of the most positive and even reverential.

The Reverend Harker had made his apostolic journey to distant Leng to plant the banner of the gospel where it had never flown before. He came to teach, and yet henceforth he found himself playing the role of learner. His mysterious hosts made that much clear, providing him with scrolls and block-print codices in great numbers. He had, as I have said, already picked up a smattering of the Central Asian languages required to make his way into the remote hinterlands, but this proved a meager basis on which to build competency sufficient to plod through lengthy and turgid volumes of metaphysics and yogic disciplines.

Once or twice the monks of Leng managed to secure the temporary services of Nepalese or Chinese outsiders who might facilitate the missionary's progress in learning, but nothing was systematic. Nonetheless, after many days (which turned out to have been years!) Harker found he could understand something of the spoken language of the men of Leng, less than one might expect given the time spent among them, for it was a strange whistling, buzzing, even grinding sound hard for a Westerner to understand or reproduce. The written languages, particularly the proto-Nacaal, were easier to grasp.

And these studies supplied the key to a vast repository of ancient and esoteric learning. Dr. Harker was soon amazed at the wealth of ancient lore that slept in the vast subterranean libraries of the monastery. Heathen lore it might be, but he was not such a boor as to scoff at the gathered wisdom of a civilization that was ancient when his own ancestors were still huddling in caves. Some of what he read seemed so bizarre that he could not really construe it well enough to know whether to agree or to disagree

399

with it. Other texts betrayed fairly close kinship with certain Hindu-Buddhist doctrines just then becoming more widely known in the West through Max Müller's *Sacred Books of the East* translation library. Still others held surprising parallels to the familiar doctrines and commandments of his own faith.

X

The turning point came, the light dawned, when at length he was presented with a very ancient parchment which, as his widening eyes deciphered line upon line, purported to be a contemporary account of the apprenticeship of Jesus of Nazareth among the adepts of Leng! Here appeared to be the answer to the long-standing riddle of the "lost" years of Jesus between his youth and his baptism in the Jordan. Everything the bemused Harker had learned up to now, no matter how *outré*, had not really touched him personally. But *this* . . . this struck at the heart of his faith. And yet was it a threat to his belief? Or a *supplement*?

Was it possible that he might be on the verge of discovering a new, or long-forgotten, dimension of the gospel? Was this why he had been so strangely drawn to the virtually unknown frontier of Leng? Was he preaching the gospel to these people? Or were *they* preaching it to *him*? It did not take him long to resolve that Providence had vouchsafed him a unique opportunity to learn, and that he had best take full advantage of it.

They brought him more scrolls, more scriptures, which he now devoured with a newly-stoked spiritual hunger. He mastered the *Upa-Puranas* almost effortlessly now, and the *Black Sutra* of the legendary avatar U Pao opened its secrets to him. *The Book of the Sayings of Tsiang Samdup* remained stubbornly mute to him no longer.

All throughout the years he was allowed but brief and rare glimpses of the shrouded figure he surmised to be the abbot of this arcane fraternity. Never a word did he hear from that almost amorphous personage. It appeared that he spent most of his time in mystic contemplation. Then one day Brother Enos (as he had come to think of himself) was startled to hear the shimmering crash of a great gong reverberating throughout the nitrous, low walls of the monastery. He knew something momentous must have occurred, and he half-expected one of the brethren would come to his cell to inform him what had happened. Yet it was with a mounting sense of alarm verging on panic that he roused to the bitter whine of the bone-trumpet summoning him at the midnight hour to join the brethren for a procession down unfamiliar halls and ramps leading to an obscure quarter of the vast hive-like complex, the full extent of which he had never been given to suspect.

Butter lamps rested in niches along the halls, giving scarcely any illumination at all, though perhaps it was enough for eyes long accustomed to the byways of the night. The mourners carried on a low chanting in some language that seemed alien to Harker even after all his studies. After a great deal of this transpired, the group, numbering a dozen or so, filed into a chamber that rose a good deal higher than almost any other he had seen in all his time there. In the midst was a broad wooden table ringed with candles. At the center of this was a veiled heap of irregular outline. He wondered that the old abbot did not preside over what looked more and more to be a sacramental feast. And then he realized what the silken veil must cover. The masked hierophant had finished his business in this incarnation.

What would happen next? What was the nature of this ceremony? Was it a simple memorial, designed to speed the soul of the late lama to his next incarnation? Or would it somehow decide the succession to the holy throne? He would have to wait and watch.

One of the hunched, cowled shapes now held a book whose opened pages shadowed his spread hands. A new chant rose, this time in the more familiar tongue of Tibet.

Fly, fly, O Nobly Born, from this house of clay, and thou shalt behold the Obsidian Night! The Maw of Chaos! From it thou camest; tend thou unto it. Know it for the Void of thine inmost Self! Skirt thou the perilous slopes of Sumeru and seek instead the gates of Sarkomand. Shun the ravishing sights of the Elder Deities, and know thyself as one of the Wrathful Deities.

On and on it went, and Harker began to recognize it as a hellish parody of the notorious *Bardo Thödöl*, the Tibetan *Book of the Dead*.

At last silence returned. And now the celebrant, having put down the book, held aloft the inscribed and rusty blade of a ceremonial knife a foot long. Others lifted up a section of the silken cloth, and the priest began to cut, to slice. Enos Harker grew increasingly terrified, sensing what was coming, yet unable even to consider the possibility with his conscious mind.

401

The gloved hand held out the quivering, putrescent flesh to him, with a few muttered syllables. Involuntarily, Harker's mind supplied the gospel words, "This is my body; take, eat."

And he did.

It seemed inevitable, and he even felt ashamed of his qualms, thinking of Father Abraham obeying God's command to slay his firstborn son.

(As my employer related these shocking events, I could not help but recall vividly how he had earlier required me to fetch for him the disgusting passage from the *Necronomicon* concerning the "corpse-eating cult of Leng." Apparently he was quite well informed on the subject already.)

XI

In the months that followed, the destiny of Enos Harker was made clear to him. Since his return to the States, Dr. Harker's researches had been devoted in the main to corroborating the secrets of his initiation from Western occult sources, and to finding some way of understanding them in light of Western thought which again formed the inescapable atmosphere of his thinking.

First of all, he had managed plausibly to locate the mystical philosophy of the men of Leng as an apparent hybridizing of Manichean Gnosticism, which, as is well known, penetrated both China and Central Asia well before the tenth century, and the shamanistic Bönpa faith of Tibet and Mongolia. This accounted for the strange, inverted parallels to Vajrayana Buddhism, which had largely supplanted the Bönpa in neighboring Tibet, as well as the striking dualism that opposed a set of Elder Deities with another set of Wrathful Deities. It seemed that, on a penultimate level of being, higher than that of waking perception but lower than the Ultimate Oneness of the Void, there existed a whole geography of dream-continents and oceans, with exotic names like Sarkomand, Ikranos, and Mount Sumeru. It was from this strange realm, the home of the Ancient Old Ones, the Undying Masters of the Leng sect, that dreams and revelations came.

The highest point of the bizarre pseudo-Buddhistic cosmology was the Universal Void in which all supposed truths were revealed to be half-truths and fell away. Here chaos without form or name, beyond "Namarupa," held sway. All beings were considered illusory, momentary refractions of this Bliss-void, which certain scriptures named Azathoth, others Achamoth, or Vach-Viraj. But there was a series of divine demiurges, half-real personifications of the Chaos to provide a face to whom mere humans might relate as worshippers to a god. Of these there might be many or few, depending upon the tasks and the needs of the time.

The most important of these were a pair of entities called Lloigor and Zhar, though their secret names were Nug and Yeb, and they were also known, when the stars were in certain configurations, *which they now approached*, by the names Klulu and Nyarlathotep. These were the avatars they wore to ring down the curtain on the present world-cycle. They might walk among men in human form, sowing madness and chaos, for these were deemed by them spiritual enlightenment. Nyarlathotep had appeared once in human form as the Egyptian Pharaoh Nephren-Ka, while Klulu strode the doomed shores of Atlantis with the gaunt visage of the priest-king Kathulos. This was long ago, but at the end they would emerge again, Klulu rising from the subconscious depths of hapless human minds in a torrent of fatally maddening night terrors, while Nyarlathotep would come forth in human form again. But in the meantime he would by no means leave his sons, the men of Leng, as orphans. In every generation he would live among them, psychically projecting his essence (or *tulku*) into a chosen vessel. This, of course, was the hierophant of Leng.

The indwelling of the deity caused a gradual transformation of the natural flesh into an exalted substance which took on more and more the original likeness of the entity within, which was not to be seen by men. Upon the death of each vessel, the successor would be chosen by manifest signs. And the sacred essence would be passed to the new avatar by means of physical ingestion. Then the acolytes would present to him the Yellow Sign, the Pallid Mask, and the Silken Mantle. He would pursue a life of telepathic linkage with the Klulu avatar on the Dream-Bardo, so as to know when the end of the age was imminent. The time had to be soon, for the faith of the cult of Leng, which had once (as they believed) spanned the globe, had now retreated to this single monastery, a predestined ebb such as occurs towards the end of every cosmic cycle.

There were other Byzantine complexities, such as the multi-tiered organization of the men of Leng, many of whom were not privy to the deepest secrets and doctrines of the sect but acted chiefly as passive mediums for the voices of the Ancient Old Ones who made their directives known from time to time. But the great revelation, which the reader will by now have surmised, is that Enos Harker had been chosen as the latest, and apparently the final, avatar bearing the *tulku* of Nyarlathotep.

XII

He had returned to the West only a few short years ago now, feeling the desperate need to think upon all he had heard, upon the responsibilities that now rested upon his shoulders. Those devoted to him as their priest-king, indeed as their living god, dared not question his departure, though they cannot have been very enthusiastic about it. For all they knew, he might have sensed the call to go forth into the world again, even as former avatars had done in times past, to prepare things for the final advent of Chaos when mad auroras should roll forth and blast all things with merciless, wasting light.

As I should imagine it, the very sophistication of the vessel, an educated man of the West, which made this incarnation of the *tulku* so very potent, also made it less predictable, less manageable than previous pontiffs, who had all been ignorant Asians born and raised in the back of beyond, dwellers in a virtual stone age bereft of culture or human contact. We are all of us, to an unsettlingly large extent, creatures of peer opinion. The world we live in is like an atmosphere we breathe, and it is notoriously difficult not to do as the Romans do when in Rome. Thus Dr. Harker's confusions and nagging doubts, once he returned Westward, quickly blossomed into a crisis of indecision in which his loyalties to rival pictures of reality nearly tore him asunder. He tried to control his thoughts through the preparation of the scholarly monograph which I had been hired to put into final shape. His urgent wish to consult texts like the *Necronomicon* and the translated *R'lyeh Text* was really a last-ditch effort to disconfirm his own beliefs and experiences as illusions and delusions. Perhaps he had been brainwashed by the cult. He now hoped so! Better that than that the insane things he had come to believe should prove true!

But prove true they did. He had hoped that the utterances he had once thought bits of the uncouth tongue of R'lyeh would turn out to have nothing in common with what appeared to be a tangible relic of that language, translated by an objective third party. The terrible truth was that some of the same phrases he remembered hearing (and saying!) were there, and were defined exactly as he had come to understand them. There was no chance now that it was *not* true.

As for me, I must admit I found myself one step behind the elderly clergyman. I felt very afraid that the noose of the truth was closing about my neck as well. But I desperately hoped that of which at any other time I should have felt unquestionably certain: that the man before me, plainly suffering from delirium, was raving insane. But I also realized it was too late for that, too late for sanity.

XIII

I now knew well enough the nature of the affliction that was fast ravaging the physical form of Dr. Harker. He was not after all degenerating. He was *transforming, transfiguring* into the likeness of the Apostle of the Last Hour, Nyarlathotep. And when that transformation was complete, that hour would have struck. The Kaliyuga was at an end. And whether the Apostle emerged on this side of the world or that made little difference. Once he had sloughed off the last clinging vestige of his host Enos Harker, a human being with a human conscience, the last hopes of preventing his apocalyptic mission would vanish, too.

Silent until this point, I stammered a question to my employer, though to think of him in such terms now seemed frivolous. How could he be so strangely calm? Had he simply resigned himself to his fate? And to the grim fate to be meted out to all mankind? Or was there some last shred of hope that he had thus far kept from me?

"It may be. It may be. Earlier this evening I had a visitor. It was his coming that made me delay so long to call you here to my side. He is a man who is knowledgeable in these matters, in some ways more knowledgeable than myself despite all I have seen. He is the Swami Sunand Chandraputra, or at least that is what he requests to be called. He understands the situation quite well. He left me this."

The bandaged, paw-like protuberance held forth an abnormally large key of tarnished and elaborately carven silver. "With this, I may venture to escape. I cannot save my life. My fate was sealed the moment I partook of the blasphemous sacrament. But it may be possible to go where the emergence of the Thing inside me will do no harm. I shall take hold of the Key, and I shall enter a state of dream more real than the illusion we now share. And there I shall pass through a door, the mountain portal of Sarkomand. The Tcho-Tcho devils will be waiting for me and will try to bar the way. But if I may hold firmly to this, that they are but the groundless phantoms of my own mind, then I may win through. What will happen then, I do not know. But the way back for the avatar will be long, too long for him, having assumed the cumbersome mantle of gross flesh. *Listen!* The time is at hand! *His* dreams begin to impinge on the waking world!"

I had been vacantly aware of some increasing reverberation for some minutes, but it had not yet obtruded upon my conscious mind. Now the sound, if hard to put into words, was plainly to be heard. There seemed to be a slow and steady tread as of great steps, the steps of Leviathan shaking the earth, though I felt no physical tremor. They resounded from deep below the ground, as if from some unsuspected caverns under the earth. But as the minutes passed, the echoing steps seemed to rise gradually along the bending curve of the firmament till it was close to reaching the zenith. I sat thus, my eyes fixed upon nothing in particular, waiting, listening. I jumped as the mantel clock sounded midnight. I turned to look to Dr. Harker, I suppose for some signal of guidance, *only to find an empty bed.*

But not entirely empty. A key, of blackened silver, and of outlandish proportions, pressed its bulk into the disheveled bed sheets. Instinctively I grasped it, turned, and made for the door. I paused not, nor entered my room again to retrieve any of my few belongings, but headed inland with all the desperate speed I could muster. I had little thought of what might happen next, only that I must flee like Lot from Sodom.

I must have found my way to the University campus where my rappings gained me entry to the dormitory where a friend lived. I can remember little of what passed that night or the next day, nor was I a witness of what happened at Cairn's Point, of whatever could have happened there. As I have said, the district is largely deserted, and that is merciful, in light of what finally transpired. But a derelict who chanced to be staggering down the streetcar tracks toward the beach related how he had first seen a strange flash of bluish light erupting from the top of what I am sure was Dr. Harker's rented cabin, as if it were a lighthouse on the shore. Then there was a widening flash of light in which there appeared to be a knot of several figures struggling in shadowed silhouette, one larger than the rest. The authorities put that part of it down to alcoholic delusions. But not even they can deny that *something* turned the whole of the beach into a great sheet of glass.

And whatever agency, whatever force, was responsible, something the chemists at Miskatonic are still debating, it also reduced the beach house of Enos Harker to a thin layer of wind-scattered soot. No search has been conducted for the missing Dr. Harker, since his infirmity was well known, and Dr. Sprague has assured the police that he could have been nowhere but in bed when disaster struck. The drifting ashes must therefore include his own. However, I know better, and I am not alone. Dr. Sprague, not for the first time, seems to know more than he is willing to say, and Dr. Llanfer seems not to be alarmed, but rather almost relieved, as if a drama had reached its denouement. All the others are naturally upset at not being able to file away a mystery they cannot solve. But the greater mystery is that of which they have no inkling, that of the strange doom of Enos Harker.

-1997-

The Transition of Abdul Alhazred

Transcribed from the Dee Edition

Hear then, O my disciples, mine own testimony to the true events, much rumored and also much falsified, touching my departure from this mortal sphere into the Depths of Chaos and Truth.

It came to pass that in the ninety-eighth year of the Hegira that I betook myself upon the lonely path of the Black Hajj unto thrice-damned Chorazin, that place distinguished by prophecy as the natal site of Dejjat, the Son of Perdition that shall come in the Latter Days before the Trump of Jibreel shall sound to waken those who sleep, when even death shall perish. There I journeyed alone to venerate the last standing shrines and chapels of the interdicted Gods of the Arabs, even Yaghuth, Wad, Sowa, Ya'uq, Gog and Magog, all of them cheated of their due reverence by the Prophet of ill-fame.

Others whom I shall not name did greet me there, some of them pilgrims like myself, others sojourners who passed their days in the holiness of desolation, offering sacrifices of prayer and meditation when they could find naught else to render up. But the Gods who teeter upon the very brink of oblivion do not sneer at whatever shadow of sacrifice they be offered by the few cherishing their once-mighty names. I had in former years made the Pilgrimage more than once, and each time did I mark how the number of the Congregation of the Shadows had waned.

I spent no appreciable time choosing my humble lodgings, as, even with the sparsity of unfallen shelters, those who dwelt thereunder were fewer still. I entered upon the obeisances required for the occasion, chanting the forbidden liturgies of al-Manat and of Eblis, whose sacred words have ceased echoing in Mecca, that great city. I proceeded to the graves of the holy martyrs, slain as they confessed the faith of Yazid and of Melek Tous. Finding a small gathering of the shrouded faithful attendant upon the ruins of the Black Mosque of Our Lord Shaitan, I sensed that they awaited my word, and I did oblige, leading them in the unhallowed litany of execration of Allah and his Prophet.

In those days, though I must needs assume the outward cloak of Moslem piety so as to conceal the truth from the prying eyes of those unworthy to

408

know it, I had gained a fair modicum of esteem in certain select circles by reason of my far questing and mine insatiable thirst for ancient secrets by the which I thought, by some means as yet undisclosed, to restore the Old Faith of the days before the Prophet of the jealous usurper Allah, indeed before the days of men.

And it was as mendicant and pilgrim that my co-religionists received me and deferred to me. I had, as can be seen from the preceding tales, learned more of the dangers than of the glories of the strange paths I sought to tread. I had considerable yet to learn, and as yet naught to teach. And it was this path of surceaseless inquiry that had led at length to the Black Hajj of Chorazin in the days of which I now tell.

No sooner had I concluded the anathemas sacred to our rite than I began to pace my way in silence back to the hovel I had chosen as my own. Many followed me, perhaps thinking me to be in progress to some other holy place. We had entered through the tumble-down stones of an ancient gateway into what had once been a thriving bazaar and still served as the central place of paltry bartering of bare necessaries between the destitute wretches who dwelt here. And straightway was I stricken by an unseen blow. As a circle of wide-eyed faces did commence to form around me, I dropped to the ground and did flail in much blazing agony. As some now say, methought I contended in vain against the superior might of an unseen Jinni who shook me like an empty wineskin. I was taken up for dead, and some took pity, securing my return, supine and oblivious, to the city of Damascus. Straightway the word was noised abroad that some Devil had devoured my soul, that I had recapitulated the hideous screaming doom of my aged master Yakthoob. Indeed, in the years to follow, the tales of master and disciple were not infrequently confounded together.

And in truth I did find myself to have quit the confines of this mortal tent. My shade did voyage upon a subterrene ocean of blackness, sure of one thing only: that I was bound for the lowest of the Eleven Scarlet Hells, where the forfeited souls of the damned do serve as morsels for the dread Yamath-Cthugha, Lord of Fire.

But that homecoming was not yet to be mine, as in the fullness of time I came to myself again, new and oddly bodied, for that presently I was much amazed to find myself resident in far stranger housing and on a far stranger pilgrimage than that upon which I had embarked unto fabled Chorazin. The feeble limbs of a man had fallen away, and mine immortal essence indwelt the ungainly form of some great cone from which sprouted twisting, serpentine appendages, like unto those of the cuttlefish.

Such images and worse had I beheld ofttimes in dreams and visions under my master's guidance, and in unbidden nightmares even more. What I heard in that unknown realm I may not repeat, and much I confess I remember not, for that some secrets are not good for the fleshy minds of men to know. From some truths the soul recoils, and like oil introduced into water, the twain forever balk at mixing.

But I may say that, during my visionary journey, I found myself, even as I had in mundane Chorazin, amid a group of fellow pilgrims, minds like mine own, who had been seized up from their own times and climes and borne away hither, both to teach and to learn. For it was made plain to us that we were the guests of the men of Yith who, like us, had made their temporary abode in the snail-like bodies of the cone-things, supplanting whatever intelligences might at first have inhabited them. These they sent back to their own dying world, beyond the rim of the outermost sphere. They fain would not abide here amid the crude forms of the cone-beings forever, this mode of existence being most vexing to them, but meantime their task was to amass a great library of knowledge of all the eras of their adopted planet, for that they were able to voyage through Time as well as through Space, and would one day choose some future aeon in which to live. To this end did they barter minds and bodies with chosen men from many ages.

While we lingered in their underground city somewhere in the unknown antipodes, transcribing the extent of our wisdoms, the Yithites in our own accustomed forms would learn of our age and leave behind selected bits of their own advanced knowledge in exchange, all the more to their own considerable advantage, since in this manner they might influence the course of future ages in directions more amenable to themselves, preparing the way for their own advent in the future world.

I hesitated not at all to share mine own deposit of esoteric learning with these fellow-seekers in the path of knowledge, though at length I came to suspect that what I inscribed in curious inks upon thin metal-leaved codices told the Yithites little if anything they did not already know or surmise from their own delvings done aforetime, albeit my knowledge, given Yakthoob's death, was perhaps the greatest among mortal men. Doubtless the volume of my record yet remains buried in that unknown city of the cone-race.

Though they likely had naught to learn from me, much did I learn, not from them, but from my fellow sojourners. Though most was forgotten during the harrowing journey back to this body of familiar flesh, as one's dreams, though vivid, flee before the morning, well do I recall certain soul-

410

blasting secrets reaped from the captive minds of sages, savants, and shamans of divers ages and lands. Of these I did esteem most highly the acquaintances of the minds of one Vonjuns from among the German kafirs of whom Tacitus telleth, and one Prinn, disciple and slave of mine own Saracenic brethren in time to come, yea, and of the fabled mage Eibon from polar Hyperborea, whom I confess I had half-believed to be mere legend.

One day, amid a great tumult of unaccountable whistling and crashing, neither a sound easily made by the ungainly forms of the cone-shaped entities, my sojourn came to an abrupt end, my blasted consciousness finding itself hurled dizzyingly, sickeningly back into its accustomed habitation. What the looking glass showed did most fully corroborate the tidings of the Damascenes, among whom my body had abided these eight long years! Only, as I soon was made to understand, my form had not been supine, nor my absence noticed. All alike swore that I had been feverishly engaged at a scriptorium, which they hastened to shew to me, at work on what they took up in shaking hands, a great codex, written within and without in a great number of iridescent inks. This tome I took from the hands that held it out to me, as they believed I had received it from the hands of the Old Gods Themselves while in a mantic trance. I retired to my hut, and by the light of a lamp I began to read.

The scribal hand was doubtless mine own, albeit with some unaccountable touch of unfamiliarity. And what I there did read has filled my head with clashing shrieks which do never cease to ring among the empty caverns of my soul even to this hour. Here were the unbearable truths of elder, outer entity, of the Black Aeons before the dream of sanity was first made the retreat of cringing mortals. There were many hundreds of tightly-written pages, and no correction or error that I could find anywhere among them. It was a revelation indeed, and by no means least unto myself. Here I learned of the Doom that must come at last upon all men, and here I learned equally to rejoice in it.

It must be that some of the men of Chorazin, who had not abandoned me, had heard and read these Oracles from the Pit as that entity dwelling behind my visage promulgated them. For when after many days I again arrived in that ruined city of abominations, the multitude, which I now did see had grown appreciably during the time of my visionary journey, awaited my word and hailed me with one mighty voice as Dejjat himself, the Mahdi of Yog-Sothoth.

Here is even the truth of the matter, and what follows is that portion of the revelations I have deemed fit to share. I make to reveal my mysteries to

411

those who are worthy of my mysteries. Count the cost, I admonish thee, before that thou delvest, and mark well these lessons I have sought earnestly to teach unto thy profit in the ensuing narratives.

–1997–

Wrath of the Wind-Walker

With James Ambuehl

I The Survivor

Revenge is a dish best served cold, or so the Spanish say, and nowhere is the truth of this maxim better born out than in the unreported story of the Professor Jonah Winslow, late of Royceton University. It is altogether fitting, even an understatement, to call it a chilling tale.

My name is James Joseph, "J. J.", Hanley, reporter for the *Braving Bulletin*. I had received from my editor what first seemed a routine assignment for a human interest column. I was to interview Professor Winslow at his residence just outside the nearby farming community of Laren. Like the shunned hamlet itself, which most think has more than enough to hide, the man was reclusive. Or at least he had been. But now he had a story to tell. It seemed that it was his idea, not my editor's, to do the interview. I discovered this only once I arrived at the old Winslow farmhouse, a rambling, ill-kept structure on the edge of Laren. His forebears had been farmers in the town, local barons, really, who valued the privilege of education which a hard-striving life had denied them and made sure their young scion Jonah would not be similarly deprived. His education had taken him to some of the finest seats of learning in Europe and instilled in him a love for archaeology as well as a wanderlust to pursue it. Some of this background my own spadework had revealed, the rest disclosed by the man himself.

As the gaunt and wizened figure of Professor Winslow greeted me in his foyer, I noted how his appearance as well as that of the interior of the old house matched that of the exterior perfectly, a matched set of shabby genteel relics. I also noticed, and it took no particular investigative acumen, the large number of exotic souvenirs from many a research trek, his own or others, but probably his. The place was festooned with them, as if the man were operating an antique shop or a museum. This feature impressed me but did not surprise me, given my host's profession.

A third thing I noticed, though it may sound ludicrous for it to be remarkable in what some characterize as the Minnesota tundra, was how

413

cold the place was. Colder in a subtler, more penetrating way, than in the open air, and this inside a house whose radiators were audibly whistling with the effort of keeping the frosty air at bay. But there were other ways of doing that, and the old savant poured me a liberal glass of brandy after indicating a well-stuffed if threadbare easy chair in front of his raging fire.

"You may know, Mr. Hanley, that it is my custom to shun the light of publicity. My expeditions have been carried out more to satisfy my own curiosity than to make my reputation among scholarly colleagues. And yet that is not the principle reason for the obscurity of one particular venture of which I have now decided to speak. Yes, Mr. Hanley, I will answer both questions presently: why it was kept secret, and why I am silent no longer. As for the latter, the story must be told now if it is ever to be told, since I am the last who can tell it, and I fear I shall not be available for the task much longer. As for the former, you will shortly deduce the reason."

Anyone whom I may allow to read this notebook will have thought it odd that I have bothered to polish the style of this account beyond the brief notes I took at the time. I have decided to write it out in connected form here despite the fact that I realized almost immediately that I should never be able to report what the professor told me. It was a tale most would decry as fabulous fodder fit for tabloid scandal sheets and hoax-mongering rags. I would make my apologies to my editor but write up the story anyway and "publish" it only here. After hearing it, I felt I owed it to Professor Winslow at least to set his story down in writing and thus make it possible for it not to die with him. Whether it will ever reach a wider audience I doubt. But at least I have allowed its echo to resound one more time.

II THE TEMPLE OF THE WINDS

"I will tell you," began my host, "the tale of an expedition which yielded the most spectacular discoveries of any in which I ever participated, and which I have nonetheless kept as quiet as I could. It was early in my career, the ink on my doctoral diploma scarcely dry, and I lacked both the institutional backing and the patience to go through the proper channels to obtain it. Besides, I knew that with official backing came control by those whose money came with strings attached. So I used a disproportionate amount of my family trust to hire a rather dubious group of men to accompany me on an expedition deep into the jungles of Cambodia. They were neither the typical crew of interested scholars nor of

414

obedient, long-suffering native bearers. I was unwilling to wait out the shifting squalls of political unrest which plagued war-torn Cambodia, or as it was called at the time, Democratic Kampuchea, so, in order to afford protection from the rapacious Khmer Rouge butchers, I had been forced to hire a gang of mercenaries at least as skilled with guns as with tools and gear. And for all the precautions, we made it most of the way to our goal without incident. And the goal?

"While pursuing my graduate studies on the Continent, I had, contrary to the owlish advice of my research directors, 'wasted' quite a bit of time studying some of the earlier and long-discredited writers on the subject of Asian and Pacific ruins. Dostmann's *Remnants of Lost Empires*, Colonel Churchward on Mu, LePlongeon, that sort of thing. There were persistent hints, drawn seemingly from independent sources but nowhere corroborated by modern field research, suggesting the survival in inner Asia of the most outlandish cult. Have you heard the old joke about the missionary who went and preached to the Eskimos of the dangers of Hell's fires—and they asked him how they could get there? Just so, the legends told of an anomalous jungle cult worshipping a god of snow and ice, concepts which one would have thought lacking from their very language and world view!

"What made me take the whole business seriously, however, was the occurrence of the same themes in an indisputably ancient record, something called *The Eltdown Shards*. Ah, to tell you the truth, I'm surprised you've heard of them. They are, as I suppose you know, ancient metallic fragments of various sizes that form a fragmentary record inscribed in some proto-Semitic tongue. The scholarly mainstream dismisses them as an imposture, like the similarly named Piltdown Man hoax, despite the fact that Carbon 14 dating makes them blasphemously old. Far older than there should have been Homo Sapiens loping along on the planet. And that is why they are ignored. They give the lie to the rules of the conventional game, and those who are presently winning the game do not relish changing the rules. But, as I say, I was young in the field and had no reputation to worry about preserving, though I suppose I should have been more concerned about building one.

"Thus it was that I decided to look for the cult, or for its remains, for the *Shards* hinted of a temple where the god of snows and winds, whom some called Avaloth, and others called by another terrible name, had deposited his treasures. He held the keys of the treasuries of heaven, the legend said, and while comparative mythology would suggest this must

415

denote the heavenly storehouses of the snow and even of the stars, often such myths were protective euphemisms for the fantastic treasuries of very real gold and gems the priests had extorted from their bullied flocks through many generations. It was this part of my theory which enabled me to interest my crew of paid adventurers, some of them local natives, others known to certain museum officials of my acquaintance as suppliers of exotic items legal and illegal. I intimated to them the possible existence of a store of treasures should we locate the ruins. Leaving the precise arrangements somewhat vague, I simply hoped I could bring back enough relics to prove the truth of my reports, whatever plunder my associates might feel entitled to appropriate. Oh yes, I know how disreputable it all sounds. And, believe me, I am not defending it.

"Let me spare you the travelogue. You have guessed that we must have found the vine-clad set of ruins I sought, for Cambodia is rich in such sites. Only these were not precisely ruins. At first I was not sure we had even found a man-made structure. What seized our attention was what first appeared to be a strange outcropping of naked rock amid the jungle, strange I call it, because it was white. What sun rays penetrated the green canopy glinted off the mass with surprising brilliance. Closer examination suggested the impossible, the absurd: it was *ice*. An ice-encrusted building of compact rounded stones, as a matter of fact. The whole structure was veiled with streamers of vaporous fog which unfurled eerily as the surrounding heat made some of the frost sublimate directly into restless steam. I think most of us imagined ourselves the victims of some lesser-known type of mirage. Were we so sick of the heat and enervating humidity that our tired minds supplied the refreshing cold we coveted?

"Daring to touch the frigid surface with cold-blighted fingertips convinced us that what we were seeing, and feeling, was no dream or hallucination, unless simple hallucination had already given way to complete delusion. As we spread out and surrounded the edifice, things only got less explicable. Voices could be heard from within the deep-freeze. As might be imagined, the voices had the distressing sound of deep shuddering from the cold. But that shivering, teeth-chattering sound had a sort of fantastic and doleful cadence to it, and it repeated. We all looked at each other, as if seeking assurance that at least we were all sharing the same madness. And then one man of our party, more foolhardy than the rest, ventured into the opening, for the ice-shroud was not complete. There was a door, and one could see from it how a foot-thick layer of ice overlay the black stonework below it, as if it were an intentional and permanent structural design. What sort of beings might congregate

416

within? I was ostensibly the leader of the expedition, however unorthodox a venture it was, so I shortly regathered my wits and hastened to catch up to the man who was making his way cautiously inside.

"There was actually a ceremony in progress. Here was all the evidence I required to know whether old legends spoke truly or not! Here before me were no ruins, no relics, no vestiges or fossils—but the rumored cult itself! In some small measure I felt as Schliemann must have felt when his spade lay bare sleeping Troy. Indeed, we were all so dumbfounded, surrounded by impossible realities, that we were momentarily oblivious of the strange and fearful impression our advent must make on those assembled for the rites. The last thing I was thinking of before I beheld all eyes turning in the inner dusk in our direction, was how the scene resembled the biblical scene of the Day of Pentecost, when the house in which the apostles sat was suddenly filled with the sound, though none of the felt force, of a mighty wind. The interior of the rock igloo was echoing almost painfully with the raw, wild sounds of the screaming wind, though not a candle flame flickered unduly.

"The chanting stopped abruptly, changing to urgent exchanges in a language none of us, in all our studies or travels, had ever heard. The worshippers began a few tentative steps in our direction. I thought I glimpsed one seated figure, on a dais raised above the general level, somewhat removed from the congregation. He remained enthroned.

But then my attention was seized by the sudden fusillade of gunfire without! My initial assumption was that my latent fears had been justified; that some trigger-happy thugs in our party had flown off the handle. Wheeling about, I rushed the few feet back to the portal and stuck my neck out. Retracting it like a frightened turtle, I realized what had happened. Despite our vigilance, we had been clandestinely followed by a Khmer Rouge patrol. Their savagery, I am sure you know, was unmatched even by the semi-legendary Tcho-Tchos of neighboring Burma. Needless to say, a bloodbath ensued in which most of my men were lost as well as, I am happy to say, just about all the Khmer Rouge. The wounded among them we summarily executed. Later, when I had the leisure to think of such things, on the long march back, I congratulated myself for having recruited seasoned veterans, not merely strong backs.

"You will think me hard-hearted, but among all the deaths the only ones that struck me as particularly tragic were those of the tribal cultists, for none of them survived. They were canny enough to remain within the recesses of their strange fane, huddling about the throne of their leader as soon as they heard the gunfire. None of them fell victim to the Khmer

417

Rouge assault, and probably none would have in any case, as they had after all remained unmolested by their countrymen thus far. No, I am sorry to say it was our own gunmen who, their bloodlust excited by the Khmer Rouge ambush and not yet abated, turned on the natives, reacting to the natural apprehension they had of us, in view of the circumstances. Nor can I deny that the treasures of the little temple, which had indeed proved quite literal and material, exerted their own attraction. My mercenaries proved more rapacious even than I had feared.

"As the handful of survivors quickly made the circuit of the profaned sanctuary, gathering their blasphemous loot, of which I resolved instantly that I wanted none, I examined the fallen forms of those whom my protests had proven impotent to save. I wanted to see if any spark of life or breath remained, and in the process I was startled to observe the physiognomy of the dead, for they seemed more Caucasian than Mongolian in racial type, their long noses betraying but the merest, recent admixture of local, native blood. Later I was able to remind myself that the phenomenon was not entirely unprecedented, as witness the problematical Ainu people of northern Japan and the extensive collection of mummified, red-haired Caucasian figures discovered in Western Xinkiang in 1993.

"My search for lingering life was rewarded in the single case of the hierophant of the cult. He lay before his bullet-splintered throne, his eyes fixed in a state of shock rapidly slipping into final extinction. I kneeled beside him in the widening pool of his own gore, my chest weighted by a burden of sorrow and guilt that could hardly have been greater had I myself pulled the trigger on the old man. He recoiled at my touch, mumbling some strange words that trailed off into a death rattle. It was as if he held a weapon he had previously lacked the opportunity to discharge—until now. And, having done so, he could let life go.

"I sat gazing at his recumbent form, my scientific curiosity taking over again momentarily, and traced in my mind the lines of his remarkable physiognomy. Then I remembered my camera! I retrieved it as fast as I could from my gear and returned to the old priest's side. My lens revealed a hideous transformation. In no more than a minute and a half the wizened form had utterly degenerated in the most loathsome manner. He had not, strictly speaking, yielded to the depredations of rapid decomposition, which itself would have been singular enough, God knows; rather, he seemed to be succumbing to the blackening leprosy of frostbite. And in the last moments before mere skeletal stumps remained,
418

I could have sworn his feet, which I had not thought to examine before, had something of the shape of broad hooves.

"You see why this expedition was never reported to the press. We had trouble enough, given the results, shielding our endeavor from the watchful eyes of the U.S. State Department, to say nothing of the Khmer Rouge government. And then there was the profit motive. As I have said, I refused to claim any share of the tainted spoils, even for purposes of research. Displaying any of the artifacts, in view of their origin, was out of the question. My mercenary partners would see to the melting down of the gold, lest dangerous questions be raised about it. But, over their initial reluctance, I was able to photograph pretty much all the plundered objects on the way back to our jumping-off point in Turkey. Here, Mr. Hanley, are a representative set of the photos. You have my permission to publish them if you see fit.

Obviously, I am breaking my silence at long last, though even the pictures will ultimately prove little of my story. I suppose I kept the whole miserable business secret as long as I did in hopes I might evade some measure of responsibility for the terrible crime my poor judgment occasioned. At least, I suppose, I hoped some unnamable providence might thus understand that I sought not to gain either fortune or fame from my deeds. As part of my penance I purposely sought professional obscurity in the anthropology department of an unsung school like Royceton.

"And so, I prayed, perhaps I might be spared. But I have abandoned that hope. This sheaf of clippings may hint at why. You are a journalist, a kind of detective. I believe I shall leave it to your investigative instincts to draw the proper conclusions from the evidence. Then, if you feel you have a story, you may feel free to print it, sparing no one, least of all myself."

III THE DEATH-WALKER

Professor Winslow was courteous enough as he bade me rise and escorted me to the door, but his insistence was firm that the interview was over. He judged he had revealed his secret, though I found myself aswim in unanswered, and I feared, unanswerable questions. They transfixed me as I drove along the unlit rural roads back to Braving. I did not even consider sleep but made a pot of strong coffee and sat up reading the file of news clippings.

419

It was a mixed lot, and without benefit of the professor's narrative I would have lacked any clue to seeing what most of them had to do with one another. On the whole, I came soon to feel that I was reading through Charles Fort's notes for a new collection of anomalies like his famous *Book of the Damned* and *Lo!* Here were brief notices and extensive studies of bizarre weather phenomena most of which had altogether escaped me, though I pride myself on staying as current on world news as my time and resources allow. Most of them recounted, without much in the way of examination, stories about local temperature plunges, aberrant harvest failures due to unseasonable frosts in the most improbable places. Some treated of air disasters. Others had to do with obscure cult survivals in farflung places. Some of these were quite detailed and had been torn from professional academic journals in the fields of anthropology and comparative religion. And still others, *à la* Fort again, concerned mysterious disappearances and freak deaths.

I made notes on several items I wanted to research further, but four clippings in particular struck me as more suggestively sinister than the rest. They belonged to the category of unaccountable deaths, and I quickly began to believe I knew what Professor Winslow meant to tell me in his circuitous way. For certain factors made me infer that the remarkable deaths were those of the surviving members of his expedition.

One of the adventurers, now financially independent, perished in 1975 while leading some associates on a mountain-climbing venture. In view of the man's skills his tragedy would have been a bit surprising, but by no means mysterious. As often in such cases, the culprit was unanticipated foul weather. The unusual thing, though, was the precipitousness with which the squall of wind blew up from nowhere, as well as the restricted scope of it. For the rest of the climbers watched in horror as their leader was abruptly dislodged from his perch by a single, immensely powerful puff of chill arctic wind. His struggling form had actually been lifted clear of the mountain, plunging in a steep arc through the frosty air without striking the rocky mountainside along the way. There was otherwise no storm.

Stranger still was the sworn testimony of witnesses and medical examiners that, upon hitting bottom, the body shattered as if it had been instantaneously frozen through. Something eerily similar had occurred two years later when another of the men had fallen over the side of his yacht (all the men had become quite wealthy as a result of their ill-gotten gains). Again, that he should have drowned was unexpected, given the

420

considerable athletic prowess and experience of the man, a professional adventurer like his fellows. But, once more, the startling aspect was not the death itself. The incident took place, of course, in sunny summer weather, but the body, once recovered, was enveloped in a thick casing, really a block, of solid ice. You can see the trend.

1986 saw the death of a third man. Inclement (which, remember, means "unmerciful") weather was again at the root of the thing. The fellow had invested heavily in an oil operation in Alaska and was on site overseeing some rigging problem when he was all at once swept up, like Dorothy in the gale in *The Wizard of Oz*. The radio had warned of the approach of tornado-force winds all the previous day, but they were still supposedly many hours away across the desolate northern plains. And again, the icy cyclone which claimed the man was preternaturally circumscribed, localized, snatching nary a shingle from a roof (though, true to the weathermen's predictions, the next morning witnessed hellish fury from the skies across the whole region). Again, there were witnesses to the event. And though all knew how capricious hurricane winds can be, sweeping away a fortified building here but leaving a flimsy shanty unmolested there, driving a pine needle through a steel wall, etc., none of them had ever seen the like of this. The boss was pulled apart by the ripping force of the spiraling cocoon which held him. Spinning loops of intestines and internal organs and gore were all that remained of the once-robust man as the cyclone spun itself out and deposited the raw mass almost at their very feet, like, some said, a cat laying a caught mouse at the doorstep. They thought of the phrase "wind-devil" and wondered.

The fourth, and last (a few more men had survived the original battle in the Cambodian jungle but perished in intervening years under unknown circumstances) met his fate five years later while flying alone across British Columbia. The man, a reckless adventurer at all times, was not scrupulous about maintaining appropriate radio contact with the ground, so it was a while before anyone knew something was amiss. The black box, recovered from the crash-site, showed the pilot had frantically sought to communicate in his last moments. His wings had suddenly taken on a shroud of heavy ice and begun to plummet. At least his fragmentary cries seemed to imply such.

And there was something else. Right at the end he had stammered something about a pair of stars he had never seen before, a pair of purplish stars that seemed to loom up out of nowhere. Some more eccentric commentators on the event suggested a connection with decades-old reports by airline pilots of strange lights following their aircraft. But no one was really in a position to rule out eccentric hypotheses, since the search through the wreckage revealed no corpse. Like the prophet Elijah who had been taken up in a flaming chariot, no trace of him was found, though a radius double the usual width had been meticulously combed. Some who listened to the cockpit recording swore they could detect the echoes of flutes, but more level-headed investigators dismissed this as the simple result of the frantic whistling of the winds through the fuselage of the plane which must already have been breaking up.

For some reason, perhaps a hunch that these reports would make more sense after reading the clippings, I turned only now to the file of photos. The artifacts, hardly photographed under optimum conditions, and with the equipment of thirty years ago, were allusive and ambiguous in detail but damnably clear in broad outline. There were stylized depictions, I would swear, of igloos, bas-reliefs of the Northern Lights, snowflake designs, and other northern motifs. Carved and chiseled faces suggested nothing of the Asian. Eyes were round, noses straight, brows high. More than a few evidenced distinct expressions of fear and panic. The possible source of those expressions appeared in a few photographed statues somewhat reminiscent, in a prescient way, of the sculptures of Alberto Giacometti, foreboding in their sense of utter alienation and looming menace. This, I knew, must be the icedemon Avaloth, he that was invoked also by some other name which Professor Winslow seemed curiously reticent to speak. For a god, the figure was depicted with a singular lack of beneficence and majesty, only stark fearsomeness. I resolved to look more deeply into the anthropological aspects of the question, reasoning that, for all his avowed secrecy, old Winslow might possibly have let a few hints drop to his colleagues at Royceton University.

That would wait till the morrow. I turned out the light and rolled over to sleep. Late as it was, though, sleep came reluctantly, barely able at the last to silence my speculations. Winslow had decided he was marked as the next and final victim of whatever inexorable doom had overtaken his fellows.

The whole thing sounded too superstitious to credit, and it did not take me long to realize it would never bear publication. But I could hardly dismiss the evidence of the manner of all the deaths. Any one of them would have been freakish enough, but the pattern of them taken as a whole left little room for blithe dismissal. Though Winslow had said nothing of surviving members of the cult or of the peculiar racial enclave among whom it flourished, I wondered if somehow they had managed to catch up with their despoilers. It seemed fanciful, though hardly more so

422

than the alternative. About this time I finally fell asleep. I refrain from describing my dreams.

IV GONE WITH THE WIND

Inquiries among the faculty at Royceton University revealed little I did not already know. As it happened, Professor Winslow had not shared his secrets with anyone I was able to find, though a number of senior faculty, hearing my questions, nonetheless shook their heads knowingly as if certain long-standing puzzles now made new sense. I did manage, with their help, to locate certain resources in the University Library that provided a few (ultimately useless) clues. An old copy of Dostmann's *Remnants of Lost Empires*, one of the books that had first set the then-young Winslow on his tragic quest, at least supplied the secret name of the ice-god as Ithaqua, and a cross reference suggested a possible identification with another polar demon, one Aphoom-zhah, the Cold Flame. Of these the standard dictionaries of mythology knew nothing, but then I guess that is what so intrigued Professor Winslow about the whole business.

A specialist in Oriental religions was able, almost by accident, to shed an additional ray of light on another aspect of the mystery. What was a cult of worshippers of a god of Arctic winds doing situated in the middle of the Cambodian jungle? It turned out that one early theory of the Rig Vedic scriptures placed their origins within the Arctic Circle, largely on the basis of the astronomy implied in the Vedic hymns to the sun-god Savitar. Certain references implied the sun to be visible to the original poets for months at a time. Most scholars believed that the Vedic religion belonged to a group of migratory conquerors from the north who swept into India bringing their faith with them. Could they have originated so far north? No one could say for certain, but the theory was still held to be viable, if not unchallenged. And of course, one would have to conclude the same sort of thing had happened in the case of the sect of Avaloth/Ithaqua. Only it was impossible not to suspect that, given the nature of their frightful totem, the group might well have been the object of repeated persecution, scapegoated as the magical cause of natural weather disasters. Such persecutions would have kept them moving south over many generations.

It was all beginning to make a certain kind of sense, at least on one level. And yet what could one make of the assurances of Professor Winslow, a man who, despite his morbid preoccupations with a guilty conscience, certainly seemed still to be sound of mind and balanced in reason, that he had found in the steaming jungle of south Asia a stone temple sheathed in a thick coat of ice? And, similarly, there were the bizarre deaths of all the parties to the desecration of that temple. No band of jungle natives, no matter how fiendishly bent on revenge, could possibly orchestrate such phenomena. Had it not after all been somehow the result of the potent malediction of a dying shaman?

Though perhaps a bit more enlightened, I had essentially reached a dead end. I saw no way to be of help to Professor Winslow, not that he had requested any assistance from me. I still believed that any danger he might face would be the self-infliction of a superstitious belief in his inescapable doom, like that of the recipient of a Voodoo curse, driven to heart failure by his own fear. But I could hardly even attempt to dissuade him of phantom anxieties, since his own evidence, plus my subsequent corroborations, left little room for any alternative of which I might try to convince him. At length I admitted to myself that I could do nothing but let the matter drop. I made excuses to my editor, explaining that the story was too technical to maintain the interest of the average reader. I returned to my work, covering the run of the mill events of the Braving-Laren environs, not that these are without their own sometimes dark and ominous dimension.

Thus things stood until one summer day when a note crossed my desk asking that I write up the obituary for none other than Professor Jonah Winslow of Laren, Minnesota, aged 70, trapped in the collapse of his burning farmhouse in the middle of the night. I felt an odd sense of relief at the sad news, a sense I suppose of a release of tension, as if the other shoe had at last fallen and I need not strain my ear waiting for it any longer. Still, I felt a pang of genuine remorse, for the old and lonely man had confided his life's great secret to me, passing it on to me, that it not join him in the oblivion of death. Insofar as I recorded his last testament and even kept it alive by my own reluctant belief in his story, I guess I did in fact render him the only aid he had sought.

I speak even now of reluctant but real belief. By now one might have expected mere distance in time to have clouded over the details and made belief seem less compelling, given the tendency of the human mind to gravitate to the familiar and the comforting. But there was one more fact that sealed the matter for me. You see, I was not satisfied knowing

Professor Winslow had died by fire. Indeed, his old wooden house was most likely a tinderbox, and many such structures perish the same way every year. And he might have, as I suspected, finally have subconsciously done his imagined Fate's work himself by carelessly allowing a fire to burn out of control. This seemed odd. The other survivors of the Cambodian expedition had all died by the touch of deadly cold. And had Winslow burned to death?

I decided to drive out to the charred ruins of the house. And when that proved fruitless, I looked up the coroner, half ready to hear that, like the crashed pilot, no body had been found. But instead what the man furtively whispered, after I assured him I would never mention his name in connection with the information, was that old Professor Winslow's corpse had been found prone in the cinders of the old house but rigid and covered with a shell of frost.

–1998–

The Thing from the Trenches

An Untold Tale of Herbert West

It is from the depths of self-loathing that I write, and for no eyes but my own, all in a vain attempt to assuage my ever-present guilt. They say that confession is good for the soul, that is, if one still has a soul, and I fear I have long since bartered mine away in the slow process of acceding to the dominant will of my partner, my master, Dr. Herbert West. West and I had been fellow students in the medical college of the Miskatonic University in Arkham, Massachusetts. From the beginning we were drawn together by our openness to theories beyond the normal range of convention. We never truly became friends but knitted a perhaps even more solid bond by becoming colleagues each indispensable to the other. There were precious few in the field of medicine, theoretical or practical, who showed any positive interest in the paths down which we could not wait to race.

For we looked into the future of medicine, and the beckoning future of mankind, a path which only daring medical risks might help us to blaze— for the eventual good of humanity. Who knew what advancements might be possible, both in the repair of fleshly injury and in the accelerated evolutionary perfection of the species? As medical theorists, West and I circled the enemy territory of the Unknown, looking for some beachhead to begin our conquest. West's chosen point of entry was that of restoring the life of the dead. West was by no means a religious man, being by disposition and conviction a mechanical materialist. For him, it was no matter of necromancy, but rather of extremely complex machine repair. He felt sure he could eventually determine a fit method for jolting the stalled mechanism back into humming motion.

So promising did West's early successes seem to me that I shortly dropped my own amateurish half-ventures into the frontiers of medicine to become his assistant, or rather, his accomplice. For the lines and methods of research we were obliged to pursue made the needful extremities of the oldtime "body-snatchers" look innocent indeed. We required an abundant supply of corpses, and the more recently slain the better. For a time the medical school provided for most of our needs, but

426

those circumstances also mired us in administrative red-tape, to say nothing of prying suspicious eyes. We made our greatest advances in times of community crisis, when the freshly dead were ready to hand and the attentions of the authorities were elsewhere. Upon graduation we had set up practice in a small town near the graveyard and within easy reach of local gin mills and prize-rings, all manner of haunts of the lower classes, whose injuries and even disappearances were more or less expected and never too much marked by the law.

Our greatest stroke of luck came, however, when West and I joined the Medical Corps in the Great War. Stationed in bloody Belgium, we found ourselves virtually hip-deep in experimental subjects. I rejoiced when our ministrations were able to alleviate the wracking agony of the butchered soldiers we treated, though our efforts seemed wholly futile given the scope and extent of the wartime carnage. West, it must be admitted, never gave any poor sufferer less than the full measure of attention and effort his case required. And yet I often found myself regarding him as a ghoul masquerading in a lab coat, eager to escape mundane medical tasks and to get on to what really interested him. But I reminded myself in such moments that even here, as distasteful as West's goals and methods had alike become, his ultimate motivation was to push back the bounds of medical ignorance to the eventual blessing of a suffering mankind. At least I could hope West still worshipped such gods. It became apparent soon enough, though, that he held other idols in reserve and served them on errands unfathomable to the run of mankind. It is of such an adventure I now undertake to tell.

Herbert West had in truth made certain strides in surgical method which, due to his own subsequent vicissitudes as well as the ethical squeamishness of a quailing majority, he had not yet shared with the wider public. There were two in particular. First was West's theory, soon to be amply vindicated, that consciousness was merely most greatly concentrated in the brain, being in fact distributed, albeit in a state of general dormancy, throughout the nervous tissue. Thus the body itself provided its own redundancy systems if one only knew how to flip the toggle to awaken them. And, God help us, West thought he did.

Second, there was a kind of living, organic tissue paste West had derived from reptile flesh. It could be used with singular effect to patch wounds where adjacent tissue had been blown away or gone necrotic. This stuff he steeped in kettles and pots with a foul reek. Surprisingly, the maintenance of the substance required no very peculiar conditions or close oversight.

Many, perhaps even most, of the wretches sent to us in our field hospital near the front lines were hopeless and left our custody merely patched, not healed. But West's twin discoveries, as well as perhaps others to which I had not been made privy, did work veritable miracles on more than a few grateful Allied soldiers. Just what he did with their German and Austro-Hungarian counterparts was less clear, and no one in authority cared to pursue the matter. Remember, these were the awful days of mustard gas and trench warfare, and lists of casualties, wounded, missing, and killed in action were largely conjectural everywhere.

At the end of a particularly trying day when the weather made it unlikely that further combat or bombardment should preoccupy us, West and I had the opportunity to make a brief visit to a tavern in the nearby town. Most of the buildings were deserted or ruined, and it seemed that the pub was maintained largely for reasons of community morale, like the one remaining church in the town. We sat there in the dim light customary to stalls in such dens, and West surprised me by extracting a crumpled handkerchief to wipe down the beer-circles on the table-top before laying flat a pair of similar-looking leather books, diaries so nearly alike that they might have come from the same set.

"Look at them, Dan. In fact, take them and read them . . . at your *leisure*." We both chuckled at this bitter jest, but I did take up first one, then the other, and glanced through a few of the hand-scrawled entries. One was written in neat, precise German. So fastidious was the scribe that he had even gone back and erased false starts rather than crossing them out, at least toward the front of the volume. The look of it became more haphazard the further into the diary one paged. It was evident that the later entries took the writer into the war, closer to danger, and he could afford less attention to his creation. The entries were dated farther apart, too, till they ended altogether, the night before the most recent battle. I knew what that had to mean. As well, I knew where West had obtained the item, no doubt the both of them.

The second journal was written in French, whether by a Frenchman or a Belgian, I could not tell without closer scrutiny. He had not taken such care for appearances early on, so there was less difference between earlier and later entries, but this diary, too, stopped with a terribly suggestive abruptness. The two volumes would make for interesting and poignant reading, and I thanked West for their loan.

"But, West, what is your interest in these diaries? I know you for a close student of human nature, indeed the most penetrating of all, but this is hardly your typical avenue of investigation . . . ?"

428

"It is a most singular circumstance, my old friend, that in the same day fate should have supplied me with two so closely similar documents, stemming, as you shall see, from two so similar personalities. And this singularity has given me the idea for an experiment. Tomorrow, time permitting, I shall show you what is left of the two young men who have donated their last testaments to us in this fashion, and I will ask you to venture a guess as to what I have in mind." We went on with our drinking, welcoming the respite it provided, toasting the day when this wholesale human slaughter should cease, and the researches of science might be free again to pursue their courses unhindered.

Despite the liquor I consumed, I found it difficult to sleep that night and, hoping my full waking faculties should not be too early required upon the morrow, I turned up my lamp and began to squint at the pages of the German diary. Perhaps this would help me find my way down the onyx steps to slumber. Here, translated, is a passage I select at random, more or less equivalent in style and feeling to the original.

How dreadfully the once-beautiful countryside has changed since my childhood visits here with Uncle Heinrich and Auntie Trude! Where once banks of sweet-smelling flowers thronged the country footpaths uncultivated, now there are only ditches of mud and human blood. Graceful barns and inns, which even in their one-time desuetude used to testify to the kindliness of days gone by, are now cut down, their timbers drafted for ugly, utilitarian use. And is it any different for us human beings, the crown of God's creation?

Can we have been intended to serve as targets for infantry practice? Pawns in a chess-game played by silver-buttoned generals nursing at their Meerschaum pipes? I cannot believe it. Nor can I forgive it! If I survive this hellish slaughter, I vow I shall henceforth take more interest in the affairs of state which once I so devoutly ignored, thinking it all so far beneath the dignity of an artist such as myself! I have lived, I fear, as a fool. I now fear equally that I shall die as one.

I put the book aside, my head throbbing. Sleep did come quickly now, but only because depression tends to benumb the sufferer. I was stricken anew at the terrible waste of life, not merely of shed blood, but of souls snuffed out by pointless violence. That a dumb bombshell should prove the superior of a man! Well, enough for tonight. Morning would be coming for me too soon now.

The next day, for some reason, afforded more leisure than any for weeks past. There were still plenty of recovering patients to be seen to, but we did not have to treat their ills in spare moments snatched from attending to carcasses fresh from the battlefields. Had there been a brief truce? I knew not, but was grateful to Chance, the only deity I could any longer accept. So in the afternoon, following a nap, I took up, this time, the French diary book. The ink was superior, but the paper cheaper, so that the writing often threatened to penetrate the verso of the leaf. Because of this, the diarist had soon taken to writing only on every other page, which certainly made for easier reading.

As it happened, the poor man needed even fewer pages than he had available. I began to read, and it was not long before I found myself wondering if I had after all delved into this text the previous evening but forgotten, having become so drowsy at the end. But no. I realized the apparent redundancy resulted from the astonishing similarity in sentiment and expression between the two diarists, who might almost have been translating into their respective languages from a common original! Rare as it was to find such a sensitive spirit in such circumstances, it was truly extraordinary to discover two, and trebly tragic to remember them both rudely cut down in the muddy mayhem.

At first my eyes, red and staring into the distance of idle and accustomed despair, did not notice the presence of West, though he had not approached with any particular stealth. "Quite remarkable, are they not? Despite, I mean, a certain romantic naiveté from which both suffered. Twin Werthers, one might call them." Such jibes, intended as such, I knew, were nothing new to me.

"What you say is true, West, though I confess I have not yet mastered your admirable degree of scientific detachment. But what is your interest in these two unfortunates? You are not like that plump chap we knew at school—Derby? Will you perhaps seek side-by-side publication of both diaries in some literary journal? No, I thought not. What, then?"

West wordlessly motioned me to the rear of the large tent we used as an operating room and supply closet. Behind it he had caused to be erected a secondary tent, poorly lighted, which showed the silhouetted forms of various apparatus I had never seen him use on any of the soldiers. Indeed, my first thought was for how he had gotten it all transported and set up, given the strict assignment of personnel for necessary tasks. I recognized vats of the loathsome, bubbling reptile tissue, mainly by its unmistakable

430

smell, and then I saw West's shadowy form, long accustomed to this veil of darkness, motioning me to what might elsewhere have suggested a meat locker in a butcher shop. Within its heavy doors lurked divers body parts ice-packed in various stages of integrity and preservation. Labels, unreadable to me in the darkness, classified and identified the parts and, I supposed, their donors.

"Do you see these two sets of . . . pieces?" West said, his voice assuming the best clinical monotone. "They represent the earthly remains of our two autobiographers. There is not enough of either of them left to merit an attempt at bringing either back. It would be cruel even if there were any chance of success. You shudder—I can see why! They must have fought like tigers, despite the refined sentiments displayed in their journals. If you have read to any depth in their pages, you will know that they were no pacifists at heart. No, their disdain of modern warfare was fueled partly by a longing for the imagined chivalry of an earlier, more gallant age. And each seemed to blame the other's country for the ruination the conflict had wrought on their beloved Europe. Thus, when their time came, they waged war quite valiantly—if one believes in that sort of thing. As a result, there is not much left of them. And, you'll find this interesting, I'm sure. It looks as if the two young heroes may actually have killed *each other!*"

My head swam at the way West apparently savored the irony of two men of refinement nonetheless possessed by the most ancient demons of savage conflict. Oh the futility of man! Did West really see human life as worth preserving and extending? Or was it all a macabre joke, mere gallows humor, to him? I know I was long past laughing.

"Well, old friend, what is your plan for them? What good can these piles of human refuse do you now? I might as well know."

"For, yes, you are to be a part of it. Whatever should I do without you? For now, just study the remains. Catalogue them in your memory. Inventory the possibilities, for what I intend is to try to make from the two mighty warriors, neither without lively intelligence, *one new man*, greater than the sum of his parts! I have already administered a preliminary dose of the reagent directly into the brains, significant and complementary portions of which seem to have survived nicely. I am hoping thus to stave off the decay of the rational faculties as much as I can. In this manner I may have the wherewithal to cobble together a fighting man able to execute commands with efficiency and to question them not at all. That is a fine set of traits, don't you think?" He didn't need to say it was precisely this combination of useful weaknesses he found so useful in my own case.

431

I left the inner adytum of West's lair, squinting at the light outside it, which, though fairly feeble, was stronger by far than the gloom enfolding the area just vacated. And as my eyes adjusted, focusing on whatever they first chanced to strike, I noticed an odd bit of trivia. There was a rumpled pile of French and German uniforms in various stages of filth and bloody degradation, together with scissors and a sewing kit. Had West, besides his medical duties, taken on the role of camp seamstress, too?

Sleep kept me waiting that night, once again, as it pursued divers errands elsewhere, no doubt closing many pairs of eyelids permanently before arriving for the gentler work of nudging me to slumber. And as I sat waiting, I took out the Frenchman's diary.

> But when has it been different? Has not the German, the Teuton, ever been a plague of locusts, existing downwind from civilization, waiting for a scent of anything better or higher in order to ravage and destroy it, to feed off it? What is the Teuton but a vampire leaving all it battens on a desiccated husk? For the Teuton is the eternal Beast, jealous of Man, always seeking to devour him, lest man put him where he belongs: in the cell, the cage, the circus tent, so that all may see plainly what he is. And yet everyone does see it already, save of course, for the swaggering Beast himself!

Here was the childish combination of enlightenment and schoolyard pride West had spoken of. It was the fuel of duelists in the academies, young fools who have yet to learn the sad wisdom of the physician, that no scar is a badge of honor. In the case of this French soldier, one could detect the contempt he felt for the Prussian foes who had long before aped French culture for the lack of any genuine German arts of their own. All the while, the young Germans, once such admirers and imitators of Parisian fashions, were now encouraged to judge these very traits as marks of their rivals' decadence and effeminacy. Vanity of vanities! And yet, given more years to mature, surely such youths, by no means slow of wit, would have learned to think on higher planes. But such maturity they would now never reach. Whatever futures lay before their salvaged bodies now was presumably that of mere fighting drones, for whom remnants of national or cultural pride would be needless distractions. So for West, denier of the soul and spirit, this is what human flesh in the end came to: living weapons, engines of destruction designed not to enrich human life but to grind it underfoot.

At length, Morpheus came and relieved me. As he took up watch, I sought relief in dream but found only nightmare. How odd that the next morning when West awakened me, the nightmare only seemed to grow worse.

It was a difficult day, growing worse the later it got. The shelling had been particularly bad, and it seemed the stream of casualties passing through our hands would never mitigate its fury. In the midst of all the carnage, Herbert West performed, as always, with machine-like efficiency. Once or twice he disappeared into his inner sanctum to retrieve some of the reptilian mass needed for particularly bad cases of shrapnel damage. It was true: his methods could work miracles. One could only pray that after the European hostilities had ceased, he might have the opportunity to persuade the medical world of their value. We would see. But he was capable of other medical marvels which he dared never unveil.

Finally the surging stream of blood and battered flesh reduced itself to a trickle and then petered out. The both of us cast away our reeking surgical garb and sponged away what we could of the wasted lifesblood in which we had swum all day. But then, West quipped, it was time for the *real* work to begin! With a crushing sense of dread, I knew what he meant. Nothing more delayed our delving into whatever charnel blasphemies he had planned for the remains of the French and the German diarists, to whom we now turned.

In what followed, I struggled to keep the fatigue back from filming my eyes and from causing my hands to tremble. Equally, I tried to keep my gorge down. And manfully, I did so by managing to focus my attention on each intricate task West assigned me. It was blessedly easy to lose sight almost completely of the larger whole whilst necessarily preoccupied with the minute details of knitting and clamping alien flesh. In such procedures as West specialized in, one never quite transcended the initial queasiness besetting the novice surgeon.

Of course an experiment as extensive and as detailed as this could not be the work of a single night, and West and I gladly stopped when each corner was turned. There were, however, many, many such corners, and we whiled away countless sleepless nights in the ghastly business. Sometimes the burden of the next day's labor was merciful, sometimes not. I can only hope in retrospect that our daily patients did not pay the price for it that I did in frayed nerves and bodily exhaustion. After one long session, ending as the sun rose, I was startled by the realization that I did not even know how far along we were, so great seemed the ocean of minute procedures we must needs perform. I did my work as assigned and never had a comprehensive vision. In fact, most of the fleshly mass over which we labored was covered on each occasion with surgical sheeting, with only the active area exposed. I had no complaints about it, I can tell you. Indeed, I came to hope I should not have to behold the final product once we were done!

But I was not to be so fortunate. West woke me in the middle of the night. Through the pounding of my sleep-deprived head, I sought to fasten onto his words. ". . . done tonight! Let us ready our protégé for some practice shooting! It should be rare sport!"

I muttered, as I pulled my shirt on, "Shooting! Are you mad, West? They'll . . . !" "Of course I jest, old man. But I do have a rifle here, not loaded, and I want to see how our man can handle it, how much of the motion of the soldier the reanimated creature can remember." By this time we were halfway through our operation room and on the way into West's clandestine lab area. As he opened the draped screen door, I could make out the silhouette of a sitting figure, motionless like a statue. As West gradually turned up the kerosene, whether to spare my eyes or those of this creature I knew not, I first noticed that the seated soldier wore the most peculiar patchwork of a uniform. It seemed that West had sown together scraps from cast-off uniforms of both armies! Surely, I thought, pondering the least significant detail of the matter, a full uniform could not have been so difficult to scrounge. But then I saw what he had actually done: the man's uniform was German on the right side, French on the left! What use this jest, I wondered—till I stole a glimpse of the thing's face. I had not shared in the surgery on it, nor yet even seen it, but now it emerged fully from the shadows.

The creature as a whole was built, or rebuilt, on analogy with the uniform! He had most of the German soldier on the right, most of the Frenchman on the left! The split down the face was nearly exactly symmetrical. I knew the path of juncture must zigzag wildly the further one went down the body, and that one leg and most of the other were the donation of the German. I had known the creature was to combine both fragmentary sets of remains. Of course, that was the whole point of the experiment, determining the possibilities of wholesale patchwork reconstruction and reanimation. But I was unprepared for this ghastly spectacle!

"Stirring, is it not, my old friend? Have we not discovered here the very path to peace between long-warring foes? Let us commission our recruit henceforth to turn his, their, united resources against the common adversary—Death!" I saw that he had secured a crystal goblet and was raising it for a toast.

I stood in silence, trying to assimilate what I saw. I accepted a glass of wine from West, hoping it would help calm my nerves. West then took a third glass and looked at the steadily breathing specimen sitting between us. "Why not?" he said, as he poured a taste of the black liquid and handed the drink to the slowly extending hand. I noted with keen interest that its motion was regular and even. There was nothing jerky or hesitant about it. Motor control seemed excellent if this were any true measure. He took the glass to his mismatched lips and drained it.

"Let's have more light!" quoth West, and he turned up the lamp. The figure in its harlequin uniform arose slowly, evenly, and looked about the still dim room, taking in the array of clutter. Was he a sleeper awakening? Or an automaton awaiting his first command? How much of the brain tissue of the original men would function independently? That would tell the tale. What technique would West use to find out? Unless he already knew more of these matters than he had let on. That was usually the case.

West could have addressed the soldier in passable French or German had he wished, but he chose neutral English in case the creature might have residual knowledge of it. "For whom do you fight, my man? Who pays you so well? The Kaiser? Or the French? I cannot tell from your uniform, you see."

Withal, the man looked down at his clothing. Not color blind, at least, he started with reaction, raised his stitchwork face, opened his jagged mouth and spewed forth an indescribable gibberish such as I had never heard, whether in psychiatric training with schizophrenics or from the lips of our terrible experimental failures from the graveyards. It seemed somehow intelligent and yet utterly without sense, almost as if I tried to separate two clashing radio signals. If a shouting match could emerge from a single mouth, I heard it! And, as you may guess, there were from time to time heard *plain French and German* syllables amid the mélange.

I feared now that this strange hybrid being, whose tragic irony had been but exaggerated by Herbert West, must turn his rage upon us, whether he recognized us as his tormentors, or merely lusted for nearby prey. I looked about for a viable weapon, some knife or other. West stood his ground, as if expecting what was to happen next. I do not think he had it planned, but I must feel that he had by now an almost prescient instinct where

435

these awful matters were concerned. He stood passively while the reeling monster before us commenced to come to death grips *with itself!*

With insane and elemental fury, hands shot out to rip flesh, to gouge eyes, to deliver blows to the selfsame physical form, only each punishing stroke was delivered from one side of the body to the other! From the German to the French, from the French to the German! In an instant the composite uniform was again a collection of bloody rags, and after only a little more time, so was the still quivering body. In a terrible final gesture, both hands, a finger missing here, knuckles bare of skin there, somehow grasped onto the opposite sides of the face, hooking into cavities of mouth and eye, and pulled the head itself apart like a bloody piñata, showering brains and their foul reptilian mending paste like the pulpy slush of a crushed melon.

Herbert West poured himself another drink, downed it, and stooped to start the nauseating chore of gathering the now-lifeless body parts. As I bent to join him, he quipped, "Well, I suppose there are just some enmities too deep and too old to be mended, eh?"

−2000−

From the Pits of Elder Blasphemy
With Hugh B. Cave

There were drums tonight—or was it thunder, so far off he couldn't yet tell the difference? But then he could hardly hear them. Not only too far off, but suddenly drowned by something closer at hand, something admittedly less ominous, but with more raw irritation—the barking of dogs. It started, his bedside clock documented, at precisely 3:15 in the morning, putting an end to any hope of slumber. One dog would bark somewhere in that part of Port-au-Prince in which he had rented a room at the Pension Étoilé. Half a dozen others would follow, scattered throughout the city, at first with an almost tentative note, as if a great canine orchestra were tuning up for a concert. But when they started in earnest, it was more like a shouting match, each bark answered by challenging rejoinders until the whole city was set ahowl. Dismissing the momentary urge to add his own barked "Quiet!" to the melee, a weary Peter Macklin gave up in disgust and got out of bed. Shrugging himself into his clothes, he opened the verandah door to let in any breeze that might be passing by. It was July, and Haiti—this Caribbean land of *vodun* and poverty—was as savagely hot as its people were gentle in their unspoken surrender.

He had expected the city to be hot in July, of course. As a graduate student of anthropology, that fascinating study of man's veiled origins, struggling development, and kaleidoscopic cultures, he had twice before visited Haiti to write about *vodun* and its believers. By now he could speak enough French to carry on conversations with the country's elite, as well as sufficient Creole to communicate with the masses. And he had had ample occasion in his work to do both. His studies had evidenced enough early promise to merit a modest travel stipend included as part of his scholarship, but it was close to exhausted, and he had comparatively little to show for it. After all, *vodun*, "voodoo," had long attracted researchers, both serious and sensationalist, because of its inherent exoticism, and his academic advisors warned him of delving into a dried-up well. He was beginning to fear they had been right. What else was there to say about it?

This time he was here on little more than a hunch, based on a rumor he had heard in Miami's Little Haiti while visiting his parents in Florida. He had once heard of something similar in hushed whispers among the Rasta communities of Jamaica, too. The rumor involved certain of the magicians, or shamans, as anthropologists were careful to call them nowadays, *bocors* and *houngans*, belonging to a secret cult whose members were in touch with unknown deities, terrible gods from the sound of it, who might be called upon to do terrible things. The infamous zombie legends went back to such people. They existed as religious outlaws on the margins of *vodun* society and theology, operating much as contract killers who claimed magical means to do dirty jobs. But until now no one had ever heard of them banding together in a religious society of their own. Was it something new? Or perhaps something very, very old, only now becoming known for the first time? In either case, here was a new wrinkle, a new aspect of the matter. And his research took on a whole new relevance. Here was his chance not only to avoid reploughing a depleted field, but even to gain a precocious reputation among his peers by a major discovery. If, that is, he could make it more than a rumor. There would have to be interviews, participant observation, and before that—some actual, personal contact.

And here he was in luck, for it turned out that the brother of a young Haitian in Florida, who did odd jobs for Peter's family, claimed association with this mysterious cult, and Peter was awaiting the arrival of this man, one Metellus Dalby, who would bring him news of the group's latest meeting. He did not have long to wait. It almost seemed as though the barking of the sleepless dogs had been prophetic, an oracle wrung from them by some supernatural influence on their keen other-than-human senses. Within fifteen minutes there came a knock on the rickety door of his room.

Leaving the little verandah where he had gone for a breath of air, only to find more of the crowded city's suffocating heat, Peter advanced the short distance to the door and opened it. The man confronting him was a Haitian, tall, slender, and very black.

"You're back already?" asked Peter, startled, in Creole. It came out almost like a rebuke.

"With good news, *m'sieu*." Nodding briskly, Metellus Dalby stepped past him into the room, then spun about to face him. "There is to be a big meeting of the cult this very night. You must accompany me to it!" The bright gibbous moon illuminated the scene of two men, one white, one black, staring at each other. Then the Haitian spoke again, more slowly. "But there is something we must do first, *mon ami*." From a pocket of his baggy trousers he withdrew a pint bottle of some dark liquid.

Peter nodded. "How long will it take?"

438

"I will apply the first coat now, another about noon, and a third before we begin the journey." His smile broadened into a shining crescent moon. "You will look like one of my people when I finish, I promise you that. And while it will itch, a little, it will not inconvenience you."

"What about my sharp nose, my thin lips?" For the first time, Peter saw them as he feared a non-Caucasian might see them, not handsome, but marks of alien origin.

"Haitians come in all shapes, my friend. Some of our ladies on the Mardi Gras floats could win prizes anywhere in the world. You've seen them."

The Pension Étoilé was on the Champ de Mars, and, that being part of the Mardi Gras route, Peter involuntarily glanced out the window, as if half-expecting to see the marching bands and gaudy floats in full force. His companion smiled again, showing those whiter than white teeth.

"It may burn a little, this vegetable dye," Metellus warned. "But not for long. You'll be comfortable again soon, I promise." Peter wondered what sort of errands had made Metellus so familiar with the stuff and its use. Whatever they might have been, they only made Metellus exactly the sort of person who would know how to help him on a gambit such as he contemplated. Like the CIA, anthropologists sometimes had to deal with people who could get things done when there were only dubious ways to *get* them done.

Peter took the two or three steps to the bed, removed the top part of his pajamas, and lay down on his back. Pulling the cork from the bottle and leaning like a masseuse over his client, this man he looked on more and more as a friend, Metellus began the process of darkening those parts of the white man's body that would be revealed by short-sleeved attire. As he did so, he talked.

"What is to happen tonight, *m'sieu*, will interest you, I am certain. These people plan a special meeting in which they will call upon the Old Ones to present themselves. There is a line you will hear, and you must be ready to join in the first time you hear it. That is not dead which can eternal lie, and with strange eons, even death may die. I heard it from Tiburon, on the Southern Peninsula, who told me it was not for the ears of just anyone. You do not want to sound like it is new to you. That is not dead," he repeated, coachingly, "which can eternal lie, and with strange eons, even death may die."

"Meaning?" Peter asked with a frown.

The Haitian shrugged. "Who knows, exactly? But *they* know its meaning, never fear. And perhaps after tonight we, too, shall know." He fell silent,

439

giving the white man the chance to repeat the formula to himself silently till he knew it. When the bottle was empty, Metellus stepped back from the bed to look Peter over, then nodded. "We should plan on being there before dark, so we can show my work off to best advantage, eh? We can use my Jeep to take us as far as Furcy, then we'll have to walk a few miles. Those mountain trails are not easy, as I believe you know."

Paying as little mind as he could to his tingling skin, Peter looked at the mirror while speaking to his partner. "What time did you leave there tonight?"

"Just after midnight."

Peter glanced at an alarm clock on his chest of drawers, subtracting the minutes it was off by. Its lazy hands now stood at five minutes to five, and Metellus had been here how long? Forty-five minutes? A little more? "So we want to be there when?"

"I should plan on picking you up about three o'clock this afternoon, I think."

Nodding matter-of-factly, Peter opened the top of the chest of drawers, a storage place with absolutely no security, to take out his billfold. From it he handed the Haitian some gourde notes. "Fill up the gas tank, Metellus. Better put some food in the Jeep as well. There's no telling what we may be getting into, eh?"

"Thanks, boss," he answered with a note of irony, noticing that there was more there than needed for the tasks Peter had stipulated. He left, and Peter's sole companion was once again the humidity, which by now seemed to have gotten the better of the dogs, who had fallen silent. Maybe he'd be able to get some sleep now. When the dye on his skin seemed to be dry enough, Peter returned to his bed and dozed till mid-morning, knowing he would probably not sleep at all in the night ahead of him. Who or what, he wondered, were the "Old Ones" his Haitian friend had talked about? Old gods, older than the conventional Obeah pantheon, to be sure. But which gods? What kind? It later seemed vaguely to him that his dreams that morning tried to give him some hint, but he could not remember.

Come five minutes to three that afternoon, Metellus turned his Jeep into the Pension driveway, and Peter, standing ready, stepped right into it. Several of the little hotel's other guests had stared unabashedly at Peter as he had descended the staircase from his second-floor room and walked through the downstairs hall to the door. No doubt they were startled at a white man having becoming a black one, but none questioned him, perhaps feeling it safer not to. As he slid onto the seat beside the driver's, his Haitian friend nodded approval and said, "The dye worked well, I see. If I were you, I might be wondering how long it will take to wear off."

"I have thought about it, now that you mention it." Peter smiled as he made himself as comfortable as possible. The Jeep was an old one, open, with a fabric top to shield its two occupants from rain or sun.

"You may continue a Haitian for three or four days," said Metellus, with the air of a doctor, showing his white teeth again in a grin. "I can think of things I'd less rather be."

"Eh?"

Peter realized he probably hadn't phrased the remark properly in Creole. "Just so long as it works tonight," he amended.

"Yes," replied Metellus with surprising and sudden gravity, as he backed out of the Pension's drive. "Just so long as the Old Ones don't know who and what you really are." Peter thought about that remark from time to time as the two of them traveled up the winding road to Petionville, where so many of the country's wealthier citizens lived to escape the heat and squalor of Haiti's capital. It lingered in his mind on the even longer climb over a narrow blacktop road to the mountain village of Kenscoff. And it jabbed at his mind now and then as Metellus, a skilled and careful driver, took the little vehicle up the final twisting climb to the end of the driving road at Furcy. At various times during the journey Peter had turned in his seat to peer down through the heat-haze hanging over the roofs of the capital, as if trying to penetrate the opaque mists of antiquity. He wondered why he was doing what he was doing. Did all anthropologists live dangerously? It was only missionaries who wound up in cooking pots, wasn't it?

His companion brought the vehicle to a stop in front of a peasant cottage, and Peter snapped out of his reverie. "We leave the Jeep here," Metellus announced. "These people know me." He glanced at the watch on his wrist. Peter had earlier observed that he wore a Rolex or some such, which one would think out of the range of any legitimate income. But he had wisely traded it for a more modest Timex for the occasion. "Are you hungry, my friend?"

His eyes concluding a sweep of the cottage and what lay beyond it, Peter barely caught the words but replied, "I hadn't given it a thought. The heat takes away my appetite. But perhaps we ought to eat something, eh?"

Metellus slid from his seat and leaned into the back of the Jeep to lift out a bag of food. It turned out to be a strange mixture of fruit, vegetables, and the worst sort of greasy junk food. More of it than they could expect to eat. And there was alcohol. Metellus opened the bag and gave him his choice. Peter grabbed a couple of apples and a roll. Metellus took even less. Just then the cottage door opened, and it was an attractive, middle-aged black woman who greeted them both with a smile and a happy "Bonjour!" Metellus handed her the rest of the provisions. Trust him to think of everything, Peter thought.

From there they walked. And Peter soon discovered and appreciated why Metellus had judged it wise to arrive at their destination before dark. The trail was a footpath. It was a snake twisting through the forest. At times it would be blocked by fallen tree-limbs, mostly pine, and by boulders that must have come crashing down the mountain. Peter hoped there were no more like them at home. It seemed endless.

Peter was tired, his companion scarcely less so, when the pair finally arrived at a cluster of huts in a clearing that, mercifully, turned out to be their destination. But there was to be no rest for them. People came striding from the huts—men, mostly—and Peter had to be introduced to them by Metellus. Had to smile and remain standing while his companion explained that Peter was a Floridian, a friend of Metellus' brother, and that he was deeply interested in the Old Ones. Also that he was eager to participate in the night's proceedings, at least as an observer. Peter momentarily started at hearing the exact truth from the other's lips. He had expected more pretense than this, though he could think of no real reason it should be necessary.

By the time the newcomer had been introduced all around, it had grown dark enough for lanterns to be lit and hung in the surrounding trees, and *vodun* drums began to throb. No one seemed suspicious of him, and the only looks in his direction that he noticed appeared to be polite and friendly. He returned the smiles he saw and hoped for the best. He asked if he might do anything to help prepare, was told that he was a guest and should not busy himself with such tasks. This he took for permission to nod off for a brief nap.

Once he felt Metellus nudging him awake, he realized he had slept for at least three hours. The moon was high, and the clearing was now crowded with eager figures darting to and fro, creating almost a strobe effect as they passed rapidly before the blazing lamps and lanterns. He got rapidly to his aching feet and looked nervously to make sure his sleeping posture had not revealed any pink flesh. Metellus's grin anticipated him and let him know all was well. The two of them hurried into the circle and looked for good seats, close to the action, whatever action there should be, yet not too obtrusive, lest any surprise or reluctance on their part be noticed. Here at the scene itself, Peter wondered for the first time how many of the celebrations of this sect Metellus had actually seen? He spoke enigmatically about it, as if he knew little, and yet he appeared to be well enough known to those gathered. Perhaps he had received only a preliminary degree of initiation and could only guess, as Peter had heard him do, at the real secrets of the cult. But didn't that imply that Peter, an outsider, could not hope to see anything much out of the ordinary? Well, there was nothing to do but wait now.

He scanned the close-packed crowd. The scene was familiar, as were the expressions of adventurous expectancy on the black faces gleaming with sweat and firelight. Then with a start he hoped no one noticed, he saw faces of a more ominous cast, weathered and haughty visages whose peculiar lines betrayed habitual emotions and exaltations of a kind he could not guess. Some bore ritual scars, others faded tattoos and paint. There were earhoops of strange workmanship, too, some suggesting the forms of strange sea creatures. Here was something new. Might he perhaps interview these old men, who were certainly those curiously allied *bocors* and *houngans* rumor had described as improbably coming together for some frightful purpose? He sensed somehow his chances of that were slim.

His eagerness dulled to disappointment once the congregation hushed as if by some tacit signal and the service began. The celebrant, an aged fellow with a wrinkled face and a voice little more than a fatigued whisper, droned out the singsong of the usual introductory prayers. He drew the usual *veves* around the base of the central pole or *poteau mitan*. Still droning, as if wearily reciting a child's nursery rhyme, he called upon the usual string of *vodun* deities: Legba, Ogoun, Erzulie, Damballah, and the rest. Peter had seen and heard all this too many times before. And yet the gathered cultists appeared to be all the more eager, as if their favorite part were on its way.

At once the rote character of the display vanished. The preliminaries, perfunctory, were over. Gestures in the crowd became rapid, even violent, aimless jabs, striking heads and torsos oblivious of the impact. Eyes rolled up, people blindly rising, shrilly chanting, joining a frenzied follow-the-leader snake-dance. At Metellus's urgent signal, Peter joined in as best he could. He strained to make out the words being sung, and because of the number of voices, twenty-five or so, it was difficult. Especially difficult for one to whom Creole was not a primary language. Yet he understood some of it. And to his surprise, these black bacchantes were calling not on the traditional gods of *vodun*, whose names he had heard mere moments before, but on someone, something, far more ancient. The names were altogether new to him, and he realized this was why it was so difficult to understand. Some of the . . . names? were so bizarre, and were barked and screamed past comprehension. *Tulu* . . . *Nigguratl-Yig* . . . *Nug* and *Yeb* . . . And the cacophony was rapidly giving way to some alien language, perhaps speaking in tongues. Less and less Creole.

An intuitive flash told him what must be going on here. Old Ones. He knew, anyone knew, that the nominal Christianity of Haitians and other Caribbean peoples thinly masked the African religions of their pre-slavery ancestors. They might call the object of their ecstatic devotion Saint This or That, but they were really invoking Damballah, Baron Samedhi and the others, gods of ancient Africa. But what he was beholding here was something else—these Old Ones had to be the unthinkably archaic gods and devils to whom screaming sacrifices had been offered in the dawn ages before Zimbabwe and Benin and Opar, deities whose worship had at length been banned and driven underground to take refuge under the names of the more wholesome gods of Zulu, Ashanti, Shona, and other tribes. Behind their myths the Things of Elder Blasphemy still lurked and ravened, as the benign spirits of African faiths would later hide behind the haloes of Catholic saints. In a moment he knew.

The chanting and the drumming continued. So did the dancing, as the cultists formed a rough circle and continued to move their feet—some in flat-soled sandals, others quite bare—in a shuffling processional. The celebrant, whose torpor had long since vanished, hopped into the center of the circle and began to rotate, his glazed eyes following the crowd as it spun round him. He shouted something once, twice, stabbing a finger in the direction of two of the entranced mob. One of these, who could hardly have even been aware of the summons, a teen-aged girl, broke from the group and fell to the ground. She was instantly followed by a second, this one an old hag. Further uncouth vocables erupted from the voodoo priest's raw throat, and the two females obediently threw off all restraint, their faces still strangely vacant, and began a savage death-struggle. Gouts of blood and torn-off flesh flew everywhere, and Peter's stomach roiled. Fistfuls of human meat, an eye, another, scattered into the air. Blood somehow splashed over him from the direction of the two women as if thrown from a paint can. The young anthropologist found his consciousness tottering. Rousing a moment later, he realized he had fallen into the arms of Metellus. He prayed no one else had noticed this failure of nerve, but a quick glance told him no one was paying any attention to him, nor would they.

Parts of the two ragged forms surrounded the old priest, who now sank to his bony knees and began to scoop up the blood and apply it to himself,

444

a gory baptism, finally falling down and rolling in the crimson pool. The others grew silent, watching intently, Metellus and Peter no less than the rest. The old man regained his knees and remained in a posture of supplication, his blank eyes showing only their whites, intoning some throat-kinking chant.

Peter knew that in an ordinary *vodun* ritual, one would next expect the ecstatic possession trances to begin, nothing very sinister, not far removed from the goings-on in any Appalachian Pentecostal ceremony. But he was in for a surprise. From one of the nearby huts a strange figure appeared. The crowd wheeled as one to face it. The drummers poised motionless with hands upraised over their drumheads. Into the clearing there slowly advanced, on claw-like feet each some fifteen inches long, a body like that of a chicken but as big as a barrel, with the head of a human male. And it did not seem to be a costume. Behind it in single file came half a dozen other monstrosities. In absolute silence (Peter absently noted the distant cachinnations of forest insects) the cultists widened their circle to give the summoned newcomers enough room.

Then came another, all by itself. A creature anthropologist Peter Macklin recognized from his reading, or thought he did. What was its name? He could not remember. His mind was in too much of a turmoil to function properly. But the thing was like an octopus. A huge one. You couldn't see all of it because it seemed to sprout a number of weaving, waving tentacles. They moved with supreme ease despite the lack of any fluid medium. Everything about it seemed to be in motion, hypnotic motion. Some of the tentacles moved it forward; others writhed and trembled above its bulbous body, glistening greasily in the lantern light that illumined the whole clearing. Then as it came closer Peter saw that he had been wrong; in truth it was more like a huge sea-serpent, with ugly-looking big claws on some of its arms—or were the arms really feet? All he knew for sure was that a name for it came into his mind.

The monstrous Thing joined those that had preceded it. It was no longer certain what was or was not hallucination. To Peter it somehow appeared that he was looking at a line of gigantic creatures seen from a great distance. But then they seemed to be standing here, with their human worshippers, in this Haitian hilltop clearing. Metellus, beside Peter, now on his left, leaned toward his companion, who was plainly paling beneath the dye. He said in a low voice, "That last one is the dreaded *Tulu*, my friend."

The name which had come into Peter's mind was different. It was *Cthulhu*. But he only nodded. And then he felt two pairs of strong hands take his elbows and guide him quickly out of the circle and into one of the huts, not that from which the entities had emerged. Momentarily, amid his sudden panic, it occurred to Peter to wonder how any of the tiny huts could have contained the great creatures he saw. A familiar voice spoke in the intelligible accents of Creole. It was Metellus.

"Do not worry. The ceremony has reached a point which we may not see. Here, take your rest." Metellus indicated a soft straw mat on the ground. Peter felt himself sinking fast into sleep. Perhaps he had in truth been hypnotized, or perhaps the emotional shocks he had experienced were proving too much for him. He put up no resistance. He did not notice whether Metellus lay down beside him or returned to the festivities.

Peter slept dreamlessly, or at least he remembered no dreams, and this with a strange sense of relief. He was awakened by a hand shaking his shoulder. He was led wordlessly by a couple of big Haitians into another of the huts. There, cross-legged and completely cleansed of the previous night's defilements, sat the wizened priest, who silently motioned him to sit on the ground opposite him. His two retainers assumed waiting positions on either side of the structure, seeming to blend in with the barbaric figures depicted on hangings that draped the circular walls. Peter felt no fear, only a sense of nervous anticipation, much as he had felt defending his Master's thesis before his committee.

The old man's Creole was clear, his voice steady. "Young sir, I think you would like to join us. Have you not come among us for that purpose? A simple initiation will be required. Don't worry. No harm will come to you, despite what you perhaps think that you witnessed last night. Then, and only then, can our true secrets be revealed to you."

Peter did not hesitate. Indeed, this was more than he could have hoped for! He had seen something disturbing the previous night, at least he thought he had. But he could not remember what. Maybe he had dreamed after all. At any rate, this would be an unparalleled opportunity for participant observation. This was his chance to do original research into a virtually unknown Afro-Caribbean religion! His academic career would be off to a flying start!

"It would be an honor, Grandfather. I must tell you, though, I must eventually return to the States where I have obligations. I would not be able to be present as regularly as I would desire. May I still join you?"

"Your friend Metellus has told us you would divide your time between here and the United States. That poses no difficulty. You bring to us new blood. I believe your coming to be a boon both to yourself and to our

446

divine lords. Indeed, I have no doubt but that it is they who guided your path to us."

Peter smiled and answered, "I'm sure you are right, Grandfather." He secretly wondered how delighted the old man or any of the others would be when he published his research on their cult. He hated to betray a confidence in that way, but it was sometimes necessary if knowledge were to be shared with one's colleagues, and with the world.

"Go and rest now, young Peter, till tonight, when you shall swear the First Oath of Damballah. Remain in your hut until the sun sets. Then these brethren" (indicating the two giants who still stood silently like sculptures) "will pick you up for the ceremony, when you will become one with us." He smiled. Both men rose. Which man was concealing more from the other?

When he returned, Peter was glad to see Metellus waiting for him.

"Tonight I'm to be initiated, Met!"

"Me, too," the Haitian replied, making his friend's eyes widen.

"I half-suspected you were already a member, the way everybody knows you here."

"The truth is that I took the First Oath when a young boy. I took the Second when I reached manhood, at age thirteen. I learned more then than you know now. But the Deep Things, as they call them, are revealed only to those who take the Third Oath of Damballah. That is what I'm to take tonight. I hoped I would. But now I'm beginning to wonder, to worry. I think maybe I've already seen too much."

"You mean, last night?"

"Yes, that's exactly what I mean. Except that I don't know what I mean. I can't remember much, except for some nightmares afterwards. I don't know what was dream and what wasn't. Do you?" Peter shook his head, a frown settling across his stained face. "I'm not sure I want to go through with it, Peter. And I'm even less sure you ought to go through with it."

"But why not, Met? It seems like a once-in-a-lifetime opportunity!"

"Oh, it is—for them!"

"I don't follow you."

"About the only thing they don't know about you, mon ami, is that you are white. I doubt they would care about that any more. You see, I think they want to use you, your position in society back in the States. They know that you will have connections they could never get, influence they wish they had."

"For what?"

"Oh, the cult is very old. They once had power and influence on a scale

447

you can't imagine. They would love to get it back. At least that's what the Old Ones are telling them in dreams. I know, because since the Second Oath, I share in some of those dreams. And they think you can help them get their old power back again. And I'll tell you something else—I'm quite sure they'll never let you publish the facts of what's really going on here. Only a kind of toned-down version. I'm sorry to upset you, Peter. I'll leave now. I want to scout about the camp a bit. I'll see you tonight before the ceremony. Till then, you think about what I've said, okay?" Metellus left without giving Peter a chance to respond.

Peter did give the matter some thought, though nothing he could think of persuaded him to change his mind. He had too much invested in the thing now. And what harm could come of it? Metellus seemed to have survived it with no difficulty. And what was he worried about all of a sudden? It was dark in the hut, and, while not quite as hot as in the countryside below, the place was still pretty sweltering. So Peter did what he often did on such days. Without actually deciding to, he slept.

He dreamed. In his dream, Metellus returned earlier than he had said he would. He had a sense of great urgency about him, said he had managed to remember something. But the more he pleaded with Peter to get up and leave the compound with him, the deeper Peter seemed to sink into slumber. It was a strange dream, and Peter began to forget it as soon as he felt hands shake him awake. They were black hands, Metellus's he thought at first, but no. The priest had sent him the two unspeaking escorts as he had promised. Peter was happy to join them and surprised, once the door opened, to see that it was already dusk. And no sign of Metellus. Well, probably he was on his way to the ritual area where the crowd was beginning to reassemble. Metellus, too, he remembered, was due to undergo an initiation this night.

Smiling faces greeted the outsider, about to become an insider. The throng parted like a curtain to let him penetrate to the center, where the old priest, in ceremonial finery, stood holding a ceramic cup. He was already chanting. It did not sound like Creole. The postulant met the old man's glance, smiling and, he hoped, reverent. But he could not help stealing a glance here and there to check on Metellus's presence. Still he did not appear. Peter was made uneasy by the strange language, filled with gutturals and grunts, yet also with tongue-twisting, liquid-sounding accents, almost melodious, and yet somehow bestial.

It became clear, as the priest neared a crescendo, that he was reciting the conditions of an oath, the Oath to Damballah. Peter knew he should shortly have to assent to whatever it was they were requiring of him. If

448

only Metellus were here to help him make some sense of it all! But then, he thought ruefully, he was the anthropologist! He should be able to figure it out. Well, there was nothing for it now but to go on with the drama. When the priest stopped, looking expectantly at Peter, the latter nodded and bowed, hoping that would suffice. It must have, for the old man said something else unintelligible to his congregation, and they broke into wild applause and joyful shouting. Women and children came forth to place flower wreathes around his neck, a laurel wreath upon his sweating brow. Several dipped their fingers in the cup the old priest held, then made crosses on Peter's face and forehead with the red substance contained in the cup. After all had their chance, the old man offered the cup to Peter and bade him, this time in clear Creole, to take a drink. Peter knew by now that it must be sacrificial blood. But he was not one to be shocked or disgusted at alien mores, much less alien diet. As a field anthropologist, he could never afford such scruples. So he took the cup and drank of the salty beverage. More cheering followed. He guessed he had successfully taken the First Oath of Damballah. Now he need only wait to discover what secrets the initiation entitled him to. It was a cross-cultural constant: initiates into any cult received catechism about the inner truths, though still deeper secrets might well remain, pending further degrees of initiation, degrees he dearly hoped might not take him too long to attain. It was all a matter of research, and of making friends with these people. And that shouldn't be too hard. Like all Haitians he had met, they were plainly good-natured and friendly.

The drums began to throb, and his pulses involuntarily picked up the pace. The priest gestured toward one of the huts, and Peter realized the ritual was not over after all. He looked at his initiator, then in the direction he had pointed. Shrugging, he decided he was game, and started for the hut. Now he noticed the drummers were moving into a circle around the small structure. As the shaman walked beside him, Peter ventured to whisper to him, "Grandfather, you do me great honor. But where is my friend? Was not, he, too, to receive initiation tonight?"

The oldster smiled and bobbed his head enthusiastically. "So he was. And so he did, less than an hour ago. You will see him soon enough. And now, my son, you will learn the secrets of life and death. First life. The Second Oath of Damballah." So saying, he pushed open the flimsy door. Peter went through it and gazed around the close quarters. There was room for a pad on the ground, and it was not unoccupied. Her black flesh gleaming in the light of banks of candles, the very incarnation of Haitian female vitality stretched out invitingly. His pulses hammered, his hormones surging. The drums outside did his thinking for him, though thinking had little to do with a situation like this! She was naked, and in a moment, he was, too. As he mounted her, as impatient as she of preliminaries, he got a good look at her face and saw two things with a gasp. He recognized her as the woman at whose cottage they had left Metellus' car. And her eyes were completely vacant, whites showing, lost in a rapture that was at least as spiritual as sexual, probably more. Peter understood that she was in the midst of a possession trance, no doubt believing herself to be indwelt by the spirit of the love-*loa* Erzulie. He had never imagined making love to a woman in such a state. As he entered her, pumping madly, he found she was like a volcano, a bucking mustang. It was all he could do to hold on, to gain purchase and drive himself home again and again till explosive release came. It was glorious!

He was winded, rolled over, felt her lithe limbs shuddering, shivering, coming to a gradual relaxation. Still she said nothing. And in the post-coital silence Peter could detect the low tones of an antiphonal chant. On one side of the hut, he could make out male voices. They repeated an invocation, *Nigguratl!* Then the female voices responded, *Yig!* He wondered what it meant specifically. He knew what it meant generally: he had just participated in a holy rite older than Baal and Asherah, the *Hieros Gamos*, or sacred marriage between god and goddess, between heaven and earth. It was supposed to be a magical guarantee of fertility for the fields. As this went through his mind, he realized for the first time he had exposed his piebald, half-dyed flesh! But the woman had been past noticing.

He had barely managed to wipe himself down and replace his clothes when the old priest swept the door open, exposing him to the laughing, eager faces of as many of the cultists as could get a view inside. The old man beckoned him to come out, while a couple of older women rushed past him to see to the woman, who was beginning to rouse from her trance. He was still reeling with ecstasy and exhaustion, but there was evidently to be no break.

Eager hands ushered him into a smaller hut, this one with smoke ebbing from the door corners. He dimly observed that it was no doubt a sweat lodge, part of the universal pattern of the rites of passage. You could find them in preliterate cultures the world over: Amerindians, Siberians, Melanesians, Amazonian Rain Forest dwellers. All of them did it. In Peter's preconscious mind rested the knowledge that the smoke hut symbolized the womb of the second birth, birth unto a higher plane. It would be an ordeal, designed, through oxygen starvation and sensory deprivation, to produce visions, usually visions mirroring the traditional totem-masks of the tribe. What would he see, if anything?

Half-stumbling, partly due to the shoving of his escort, partly to his residual light-headedness, Peter fell to the ground inside the fire-lit hut. The ground was plain but not hard. The light flickered with its source. He felt a great urge to surrender to sleep. When had he slept so much? He could not remember. He drifted, drifted. He supposed he was asleep again, because now there appeared to be a row of figures stooping and sitting before him, too long a line for the small space to accommodate. He thought that he ought to know them. There was surely something familiar about them. And then he remembered he had marked their faces the previous night, at that ceremony he had largely forgotten. Maybe he would remember more of it now that they were here again, the *bocors*, the *houngans*, the tattooed and branded sorcerers of the cult. The firelight did strange things to their outlines, that was for sure, but it seemed to Peter that it was their shadows that were strangest of all. They did not seem remotely to correspond with the bodies casting them. The man in the middle, with the hoop ear rings and the worst scars along his neck: the shadow that loomed above him reminded Peter vaguely of the outlines of Great *Tulu*, the pincers attached to lolling necks and appendages. The others were all different but equally ill-fitting. Yes, the Old Ones . . . He was beginning to remember . . .

The spokesman for the group opened his eyes, and Peter saw no iris or pupil, only an empty expanse of glowing green, as when a ray of sunlight penetrates the sea water above a diver. The figure started to speak. It seemed as if he had been speaking for some time, as if someone had turned on a radio in the middle of a speech. But the content was definitely directed to him. "We know it is knowledge that you seek. The true seekers come to us sooner or later, as you have come. Here they learn the higher path, the path to the past. Which can come again. But you are special, Young Sir. The Old Ones have sent you to us for a purpose. You can help us to bring back the past of the Old Ones."

Peter felt he should be sitting in a posture of respect or veneration to these old saints, these elders of the community. But he was utterly empty, barely able to grasp what was being said. He lay there like a limp doll, hoping they would take no offense.

"We know you want to learn our secrets so you may gain fame by betraying them to the outside world. That you cannot do. But you will gain your fame. You will write your book. We will tell you what you may say. Others will even be able to verify what you say. And when you have

451

your fame, we will have it. And then we will send one to you with something else you may tell your world. It is a world that loves the drugs. Substances." A ripple of laughter followed this.

"In that day, maybe two, three years down the road, when you are the so-famous professor, you will tell them you have discovered something great among us. You will tell them the old island witch doctors are not so stupid. That they have chemical secrets from the rain forests. Powders that can lift the spirit, than can extend the manhood, that will shrink the fat from the white man's ass. And it will. And it will do other things their tests will not show. And in this way, you, my son, will open their hearts to love the past of the Old Ones. And in that day you white men will sing as we sing: That is not dead which can eternal lie. And with strange eons, even death may die!"

He didn't see them leave. Maybe he had blacked out, lost consciousness even within the dream. But at length he roused again, sure by this time that he had been secretly drugged, even before being brought here to the sweat lodge. Now the fumes were making him cough. That's it—he had coughed himself awake. There was something in the smoke that was playing hell with his sinuses, that kept him confused, too. But that, of course, was part of the regimen. It didn't worry him unduly. But it entered his head to wonder about Metellus. Was he elsewhere in the camp, undergoing something similar?

And then: there he was! Peter flinched with shock, as welcome as the sight of him was.

"Peter! I made a big mistake bringing you here!" The image of his friend hovered nearby. The man must be kneeling to look into Peter's sodden face. Peter smiled and reached out to touch the other's shoulder in reassurance, but he could not reach him somehow.

"No, no, Met. It's all going well! Better than I could have . . . Say, that's quite a scar you've got there . . . How'd you . . ." The black visage, curiously dim and gray in the smoky interior of the hut, waited for Peter to compose himself, to get his thoughts straight.

"Hear you passed your initiation rite, or test, or . . . Give me a minute . . ."

"Yes, *mon ami*, I took the Third Oath of Damballah, all right. With the Third Oath one renders oneself entirely to the Old Ones."

"Well, I can tell you, buddy, the Second Oath's not s' bad! I never had such a . . ."

"What about the First Oath, my friend? Did you taste the drink? The salty cup?"

452

"Yes, it was blood, I know. I knew it would be. Very common in these things. Probably one of their goats."

"I think it was a goat named Metellus," the black man said, closing the mouth in this face and opening the new lips of his throat into a horrible grin. "It is no mere scar. You now have my blood in you. That is why I may come to you in this manner, while your mind has been opened to the influences. I have little time left. *You* have little time left."

Peter was shaking himself awake, shruggingly gathering himself into a sitting position. His wide eyes looked on the face of his dead friend, and the greater his sobered clarity became, the dimmer the features of Metellus became. "No, Metellus, I . . ."

The words came as a sourceless whisper: "You dare not leave and disobey the Old Ones now. They will not permit it. Do not openly defy them. But do not serve them. I will . . ." And there was no more. But Peter was now very definitely awake. His head pounded without benefit of drums. The smoke was about dispersed, which, he figured, was probably what allowed his head to clear. He lay down for a second, found that this only made his head hurt worse. So he rolled over to kneel and stand, but as he rolled, he encountered a supine form and recoiled. At first, his memories mixed up, he imagined it was the woman from a few hours before. But it wasn't.

He sprang backwards away from the machete-butchered carcass of Metellus. It hadn't been just his throat. That must have been only the beginning. He hadn't looked like this in the dream Peter had just awakened from. But he could no longer begin to guess, in this place, what was a dream and what was waking reality, or even what the difference was supposed to be. Anything was equally real, it seemed.

He flung open the fragile door and staggered out. A semicircle of the cult elders, a couple of their musclemen, and a few little boys awaited him. His dramatic appearance caught some by surprise, awakened others. The little fellows scattered, their interest in the stranger at an end for the time being. The others, rising to meet him, seemed subtly to come too close, their chests hoisted as if to signal threat, forming a cordon around him. A strange way to treat a guest and a new brother in the faith! But they must have a pretty good idea what was going through his mind. Mustn't he be weighing his old loyalties against his new ones? He would in a short time seal off the past and identify fully with the cult. That would be easier, of course, the longer they could keep him here among themselves, isolated from his professional colleagues and family members back home.

He met their polite questions as to his welfare with equally empty

453

answers. He knew he was meant to see the corpse of Metellus. It must somehow be part of the ritual experience, "the secrets of life and death." It also no doubt stood for a warning that the same thing could happen to him should he have second thoughts. Peter thought better of expressing his sorrow and rage at the ritual murder of his friend. It could only increase their suspicion. Better for the moment to let them think, as they no doubt did, that as a white man (oh yes, they knew all right: "you white men"), he regarded Metellus merely as an expendable hireling.

"I . . . saw great things. Heard great words. Words of destiny . . ." The older men smiled and looked at one another. He knew they had been waiting to hear something like this.

During the long afternoon, Peter listened and took extensive shorthand notes as the oldest of the cult elders fulfilled the promise made to him, that initiation should carry the privilege of disclosure. He got an earful of the lore of the cult. There was very little about the history of the group. Life changed very little in their tiny world from year to year, even from century to century, with the exception of the disruption of slavery. But the faith could go on and did go on, with only the temporary lack of sacrifices, in the slave quarters.

By far most of their lore concerned the Old Ones, old gods, as he already knew, but now he sat entranced with morbid fascination at tall tales and weird theogonies unlike any he had encountered in his wide study of folklore and mythology. It was a treasure trove, and a genuine ancient tradition. There was far more here than he had dreamt of when he first dared hope there might exist in remote Haiti an untapped trove.

Most of what they told him, he was made to understand, he would be permitted to communicate to the outside world in the form of scholarly monographs. It was a sacrifice of traditional secrecy, to be sure, but even that was necessary to pave the way for the past of the Old Ones to come again. All men must know their Masters so that they might render them a fitting welcome when the great day came. Peter understood that there were yet greater arcana to which his two degrees of initiation did not yet entitle him, and of these he dared not ask, nor were the elders likely to permit them to be spread abroad.

Nor was Peter especially eager to advance farther along on the cult's path of discipleship, given what he knew had happened to poor Metellus at the climax of his initiation. He kept thinking of those last words his friend's shade had uttered in the dream vision. He had left him a dilemma, a riddle. He dared not give any sign of resisting or renouncing his role in their insane conspiracy, yet neither could he afford to become their

454

accomplice, really their puppet, in it. He waited, as if for a signal he knew could never come: a signal from a dead man.

The catechism went on for days and then weeks. He could hardly imagine there was so much to the religion! It must be ancient indeed for the legendry to have become so complex, so fulsome, so baroque! There was no way of knowing how old the belief was. Their own lore said that it went back, of course, to the Old Ones themselves, and that they had come to this planet from somewhere else entirely. But here history had shaded off into mythology. The true story would never be known. Peter found he was beginning to think like an anthropologist again. He found himself, as he looked over his notes by firelight each evening, musing over possible methodologies to make sense of the seemingly confused symbols and myths. He felt even Levi-Strauss would find himself outwitted by these old mythmongers! Well, one thing anyway: if he managed to get out of here alive and unharmed, he had more than enough for a monograph, no, a series of them that would make Victor Turner's famous studies of the Ndembu look like a kid's description of a birthday party!

If only he could leave it at that. But a dark pall hung over him. There was little chance, he now realized, that they would hinder his return to the outer world (he once would have called it "the real world," but who knew what that was anymore?). Indeed, his role in their plan depended on that. But how many more atrocities must he be implicated in before he left? Back home, he could put that part of it out of his mind. Cultural relativism and all: who was he, a Westerner, to judge their ancient customs? And so on. But there was a ritual tonight in which the Old Ones would be invoked, and believers would receive their expected foretaste of the ecstasy of the past of the Old Ones, a past which now looked closer than ever to returning, thanks to their new brother. He knew he could not stand seeing any more of the poor wretches picked out of the crowd to die in a bloody holocaust as part of the ritual. Yes, he now remembered all too well what had transpired on that first night.

He had a seat of honor alongside the ranks of shamans and *bocors* inside the circle. Behind him gathered a number of children, whom he hated to contemplate seeing what he feared they would see, though he knew they must be hardened to it by now. Peter was a favorite of the children, especially as his skin, free of the dye, had begun to lighten and lighten, until it approached very nearly its original hue. This fascinated the children, who followed him around like baby ducks. The time came, and soon, as he feared, one of the priests began to intone the familiar invocations. He was interested to note that, even though they no longer had to be judicious in the presence of outsiders, the crowd persisted in the ancient formula, calling on the names of the *vodun* deities that masked the terrible entities they actually served. He knew that traditions endure even absent their original rationale. So here came the names: Legba, Ogoun, Erzulie, Damballah, Samedhi . . .

As before, the crowd's enthusiasm was pent and building. But suddenly something surprised them. Something was going on at the rear of the circle. Peter craned his neck, trying to see over the shoulders of the old men. In a moment he could tell that the same thing, whatever it was, was going on all around the outer perimeter. Instinctively, he turned to his young entourage, gathered behind him, and sternly told them in his clearest Creole to get out, go to their homes, even out of the village, now.

The commotion was building. He could hear numerous physical impacts—bodies falling? Crowds clashing in battle? Was a riot beginning? Were some already intoxicated? Screaming began, and not just screams of alarm or of pain. There were shrieks of holy terror that ripped through the cotton humidity of the jungle night. Peter was on his feet, moving around aimlessly, uncertain what to do. If it was a fight, what side should he be on? How could a company of men approach the compound undetected? He began to slip on skids of blood on the packed ground, then to trip over bodies. A bloody harvest was progressing with amazing speed. He guessed that he, too, would momentarily fall under the scythe. Lanterns swung wildly and were extinguished. Torches bobbed and some went out. Some were swung as weapons, but ineffectively.

Suddenly, in the midst of the melee, Peter was sure that his sweat-stinging eyes glimpsed the impossible visage of Metellus, his livid gash gaping. But the gross wound did nothing to impede his prowess with the machete. He hacked and hacked without the fatigue of the living. Dead, he had himself become the Grim Reaper. But he did not fight alone. Like a gang of laborers chopping down jungle growth to clear a field or the path for a road, there was a whole crew of forms wielding knives, clubs, machetes. All silent. None of their faces was visible given the bad lighting. But the nearest one seemed incongruously to be sporting a top hat and sun glasses over a gaunt form one would not have thought sturdy enough to inflict the blows he was dealing.

The *bocors* and cult priests, taken by surprise, began to rally. They had no earthly weapons, but Peter could see their hands and arms flailing as if they bore deadly cudgel and sword. He knew they must be conjuring. It looked like superstitious pantomime, but Peter could tell something was happening because of what he heard, or thought he heard. He seemed to catch the echoes of explosions without the explosions themselves. Aftershocks of invisible eruptions. Something was occurring on a plane he could not see. But whatever it was, it had little effect on the invaders. One or two seemed to vanish, not to fall smitten, but just to disappear. But then perhaps they were leaving of their own accord now that the massacre was near its end. In the hacking fury of Metellus's vengeance, with the aid of his mysterious hosts, tattooed heads flew like coconuts in a windstorm. Blood rained down, and Peter found himself spitting it out as he could not prevent a good bit of it entering his nose and mouth. Indeed, there seemed a red fog which made him gag and cough till he thought his lungs would burst.

He made for the edge of the clearing, where he could see the terrified yet curious young faces following the whole ghastly business. Their eyes grew even wider, if possible, as he approached, a wild and terrifying sight, he knew. But once he was upon them, and they kept looking past him, he knew another was the object of their gaze, and he turned to face it. It was Metellus. He gave a look to his dripping machete and cast it away, into the trees. He extended an arm toward Peter, but when the latter made a move to join him, Metellus waved him off. He tried to say something, but there was no sound, and Peter could not read his lips. He knew it was a final parting gesture, though. And then there was no one.

Peter's ears felt the pressure of sudden and total silence. None of the adults could have survived. But neither were their conquerors anywhere to be seen. Yet he knew where they were: wherever Metellus was. The true *loa* had taken their revenge, and Metellus had shared in it. As for him, Peter knew what he must do next. He would round up the newly orphaned children of the village and, with them in tow, begin the long journey back down the mountainside to the cottage. A few could return with him to town in the Jeep; the rest could be picked up by the authorities. He hoped they could all find homes, and anything would have to be an improvement.

He paused for a moment, looking in the direction of his hut. His papers and notes were there, even a tape recording or two. His book, yet unwritten, was there. His career was there. But now who would believe any of it? The myths and rituals of a small community—now all dead in a massacre? A massacre he alone had survived? How would any of that look? He turned his back on the village, counted the children, and started for the foot path.

–2000–

The Ghoul's Tale

The Fifth Narrative

The nethermost caverns are not meant for the eyes that see the light of day; nay, but the revelations thereof are reserved unto those, for whom, like unto the eyeless fish aswim in the subterrene grottos, darkness has become as light. And such was I, Alhazred, spiritual son of the mage Yakthoob and Opener of the Gate whereby the Spheres meet. I had long since become even as one with the creatures of night and shadow, and it was the smiling of the sun that I cursed. Oft had I ventured into earth's cancerous bowels in search of the secrets of the grave, and thus it was that I came to delve beneath the ruins of elder Ægypt into the honeycombed netherworld of Amente itself, wherein sits enthroned for all æons to come the desiccated shell of the Acheronian sorcerer-king Nephren-Ka. Whispered legends had it that all the destiny of the ages had been vouchsafed unto the Black Pharaoh, and that the secrets of Trismegistus Nyarlathotep were traced upon the copious lengths of yellowed linen that now enclosed him. It was this artifact that I sought in my folly. For though many esteemed me master of the eldritch arts, the greater wisdom was that of my novices and acolytes, none of whom dared follow me.

Passage was easily enough wrought, providing one but knew the hidden paths, and such knowledge was mine, for had I not bargained with Those who chart the topography of Hell and of other realms more dreadful still for those unwilling to wait till death should take them there? Like unto the ancient mage-king Solomon ibn-Daud who adorned his courts with apes and peacocks and thought no cost too great for these fancies, neither did I estimate any reckoned price too dear for the secrets held out to tempt me, as I have related aforetime. I shudder even yet at the fearful tribute of one eye that fetid Nug exacted of my Master Yakthoob for the secret of the Elixir of the Angels, and no less at the demand of Tsathoggua, the Abomination beneath Memphis, whom naught less than mine own manhood would satisfy. For the knowledge of Irem the City of Pillars I ceded a full score of years from my life yet to come. The price of the map to the throne of buried Nephren-Ka I care not to repeat, save that the leather scroll I scrutinized by the flickering light of my torch was

458

tanned from mine own back. And this was but the beginning of sorrows. But so much and more I judged to be small in exchange for what powers might be mine if I were to gain for myself that winding sheet.

The hieratic glyphs lining the walls about me, preserved by the arid heat of Ægypt's blazing sands, mutely proclaimed the original purpose of the shaft I now half-trod, half-slid down at a steep angle. In ages past, the place had served as an initiation hall for those who sought to plumb the deepest mysteries of Set-Typhon and Gol-goroth, secret Gods of antediluvian Acheron. I scrupled not to defile these holy precincts with my passage, since was mine own errand not a pilgrimage for knowledge? I, too, would possess the secrets of the Ancients.

Hours and days became nigh indistinguishable to me as I made my continual descent. Sorely did I require sleep, but no opportunity was found, and at all events, I had years before bartered the power of restful slumber for some esoteric secret or other. Truly I did commence to fancy that I heard the noise around me as of some foul vermin scuttling somewhere beyond the scope of my vision. But this uneasy awareness I sought to dismiss, reasoning instead that the sounds must be merely those of mine own slow progress downward, distorted and partly magnified by the peculiar shape of the passage by which I sought ingress.

In the fullness of time did I gain my sought-for destination. Before me yawned vast doorposts and lintel wrought cunningly of black and polished stone. Glyphs in the tongue of Acheron announced the place for that terrible vault in which the withered mummy of Nephren-Ka, earthly avatar of the Crawling Chaos, did drowse away the ages. Again I scarce could dismiss the uneasy feeling that crafty eyes tracked my movements, but so great was my eagerness to despoil the tomb of what lay within it that I spared thoughts for naught else, waxing bold to enter.

The shadows in the adytum were doubly thick, and the torch I bore did little in truth to dispel them. Still, the object of my quest was plainly manifest. I stepped silently toward the figure seated on a dais at the far extreme of that charnel chamber. But, soft!, a sound that was verily no mere echo brought me up short. Doubtless, another was with me in the place. I stood still, then turned warily about, seeking to detect my living shadow. I had not long to search, for the silence of the ages was straightway vanquished by the echoing of a voice soft and sly like unto the voice of the Edenic serpent—and it did hiss mine own name! What guardian demon had apprehended me?

"It is I, old friend, thy fellow apprentice, Ibn-Ghazi. I dared not believe mine eyes, but of a truth, thou canst be none other than Alhazred!"

He stepped forward into the narrow circle of fading light cast forth by the torch I grasped. And in the feeble luminescence I saw that the past had forsooth yielded up a ghost I had thought never to behold again, even that false-hearted betrayer who had seen fit to sell the soul of our Master, the venerable Yakthoob, merely to satisfy his carnal appetites. Seeing him now brought no joy to my heart.

"Praise be to Iblis that thou hast come at last, O Alhazred! Oft have I prayed for deliverance from the curse that hath befallen me. For long have I paid dire penance for the deeds that disgraced me."

I would fain know how the infamous Ibn-Ghazi had happened upon this place, since scarce could I imagine he had either sought or gained occult erudition like unto mine during the many years since we had learned together at the feet of Yakthoob (upon whom be peace), for that he preferred the ways of Dionysus to those of Hecate.

"'Twas the merest luck, O Alhazred, that brought me hither, though ill luck, to be sure. Like you, my brother, I sought the Elder lore among the houses of silence, but I chanced to attract the unwelcome attentions of a pack of meeping feasters upon the dead, even the muzzled children of Anubis al-Ghul. Meseems their pickings to be slim insofar as they have of late waxed exceeding bold to pursue the living, there being insufficient carrion to satisfy them. And in my flight I took whatever winding paths and tunnels I might, at length successfully eluding the mangy devils. At yon shadowed portal they recoiled with much yelping and slunk away like the craven curs they are. And now, forsooth, I do confess I fear to depart, lest, in their great hunger, mayhap it transpire that they linger, waiting to pounce upon my person."

"Ibn-Ghazi," said I, "I marvel that these loping feasters reckon thee not among their own number, as thou hast most abundantly proven thyself the most craven of jackals. But then little do they know thee as I know thee. Nonetheless, thou canst readily see how I myself penetrated even unto thine hiding place without molestation, howbeit I did think to hear furtive sounds upon my way. But if what thou sayest be true, how was it they did not beset me?"

Ibn-Ghazi answered, saying: "That I wot not, O brother in Al-Monsin Metatron! Save that I suspect thine own aura of occult sanctity hath repelled them even as hath that of this holy fane."

Somewhat in this reply pleased me not, and I inquired whether it was in truth mere happenstance which had brought him to the resting place of the avatar of Nyarlathotep. Mayhap he had contrived to steal or cheat his way to this secret adytum, knowing full well the value of that which lay within. Yet his fear was most palpably real.

"If, old comrade, thou hast, by the providence of those Powers we serve, come so far on some errand of discovery, then permit thine humble acolyte to serve thee in this venture. All I shall beg in return is thy protection in passage from this dark place. What sayest thou?"

My torch had now grown exceeding dim. And as the darkness waxed thick, certain shadows commenced to shift and to circle about us twain. The sounds of nameless chittering and cachinnation were now unmistakable, and for all that did the fear which had plagued Ibn-Ghazi seem to depart the closer did the loathsome ghouls approach.

"Meseems thou hast underestimated the power of these surroundings to keep yon parasites at bay. Well do I now discern thine insidious craft, how, trapped by the ghouls, thou didst bargain with them to spare thine own worthless life in return for thy services in procuring for them human meat. Then would they at length suffer thee to depart with the Shroud of the Black Pharaoh."

"O Alhazred," the traitor mocked, "thy reputed wisdom never faileth! Albeit it may dawn a moment too late." With this did the coarse forms of the ghouls draw fast about me, as my flesh, friend to a thousand abominations, did nonetheless quail from the loathsome caress of their drooling muzzles. Next did they force me to my knees as Ibn-Ghazi, whose villainy exceeded their own for that it was freely embraced and no necessity of nature, made for the recumbent form of the husk of Nephren-Ka, drawing his dagger with the which he might more swiftly despoil the rotting cadaver of its wrappings and be on his way.

But it was not for naught that, whilst Ibn-Ghazi had wenched and drunk away his energies over the years, I had devoted myself with ascetical ardor to the scrutiny of the Elder Records filched from the very bog of Ubbo-Sathla. Unlike my torch, my resources were far from spent, and I did utter forth the binding spell of Anubis, the totem of those feasters upon the dead. Straightway there concatenated a nimbus of light of no familiar hue. Even as the mongrel hounds of this world do fall back and cringe before the sound that surpasses human hearing, so did the ghouls fall back in agony, and I was free of their noisome clinging.

I was astonished past all measure to behold Ibn-Ghazi halt in his course, as if seized by an unseen hand. Slowly he made to turn, sore racked with pain, but having taken up his evil cackling again. Only now that chilling laughter issued forth from canine jaws, from which poisonous spittle did drip. So IbnGhazi was himself one of the ravening pack! His trap had not been as I surmised, though of a certainty it was nonetheless treachery most

461

foul. That he was not thoroughly whelmed by the magic I had summoned I ascribed to whatever vestiges of his sorcerous apprenticeship he had retained from his early days of tutelage under the venerable Yakthoob. And now therefore I made ready to deal with him.

Only that as it eventuated, this task was made moot unto me. For all at once did the rangy form of Ibn-Ghazi fall limp in the grasp of a towering figure looming up from behind him, even, as the fading radiance of mine cantrip shewed, the shuffling lich of the Ebon Pharaoh, whose millennial rest our interloping presence had disturbed! Deep did his bony talons sink, cutting into the leathery flesh of the ghoul-changeling and choking off his blasphemous cackle. Stinking, sluggish blood overflowed the mummy's hands as his ineluctable grip inexorably severed Ibn-Ghazi's head from his neck. I beheld the dead visage changing once again into the semblance of human features even as the head dropped to the dusty ground like an overripe fruit.

I stood as nerveless as an embalmed mummy ought by rights to stand, transfixed as the hideous eyeless gaze of Nephren-Ka turned in my direction. He made no sound, but the tiny writing scribed upon his funereal bands was eloquent in its mockery. I knew I should have the lavish boon of the Gods should I escape with the treasure of my own life, if not my soul. And that is what I did, abandoning the tomb of the revenant forever, so do I swear by Al-Illah or whatsoever Gods may yet deign to hear me.

–2001–

The Elephant God of Leng

Dedicated to the shade of Frank Belknap Long.

It seems to me I once read in Plutarch that the only difference between the atheist and the superstitious man is that while the first believes there is no god, the second believes there is but wishes there wasn't. Then it struck me as something of a joke. But now that I recall the remark, it seems to me truer words were never spoken. I have read something else, *seen* something else, in the intervening years that brought the ancient quip home to me with genuine force. I used to be an atheist. Now I guess you could call me superstitious.

It was winter back home but felt like summer as I crossed the great steppes of Siberia, headed for an obscure destination in the secret heart of Central Asia. It's possible that Aeroflot once ran an occasional plane out this way, but I doubt it, and since the Union of Soviet Socialist Republics fell, there was no route out here except the ancient one: camelback. I felt like Haliburton himself with my hired retainers, a ragtag bunch of bearded mutterers, most of whom had drifted (or been pursued) for so long that they'd probably forgotten what dusky national origin they once had. There were, thankfully, a few other Westerners with me, mostly technicians along to operate the film equipment for the PBS documentary we were shooting.

The whole thing had seemed the wildest of goose chases from the start. I'd never have taken on the assignment if my job with the production company weren't already hanging by a thread. Well, if the rumors proved out, we'd get plenty of ratings on this one, by God, Public TV or no. It started when one of the directors, a typical limousine liberal given to the delusions of the affluent, described a conversation she'd had with a member of her Theosophist group. Somewhere in the jungle of Blavatsky's *The Secret Doctrine* there was a reference to ancient Cyclopean ruins in Asia, supposedly left over from a colony of ancient Mu or Lemuria, or maybe it was Oz. As the network exec described it, it didn't matter who built them, but if there really was a neglected set of ruins out there, maybe a city, the Theosophical thing would make a good hook for an otherwise dull archaeological documentary.

463

Trouble was, there was absolutely no solid evidence. Everybody that's studied it knows that Blavatsky was at least half-charlatan, and that half of what she wrote she made up. But how would we know for sure if we didn't go take a look? That's what we were doing under the blazing sun, in the exact middle of nowhere: taking a look.

We found nothing, except, that is, for some lost Afghan rebels who didn't seem to know their war was over and thought we were the enemy. Lucky for us, some of our bearers who turned out to be Afghans themselves, were able to calm them down. As the drift of their parlay became evident, chiefly by the lowering of gun barrels, a bright idea occurred to me. So I emerged from cover and sauntered out to where the men stood, still talking. Once there, I asked our man Achmet to ask the other man if he and his compatriots had spotted anything like what we were looking for. After all, I figured, they must be pretty well used to all manner of secret paths and shunned quarters after years of skulking and guerilla warfare.

The news was both good and bad. First, there was nothing else, nothing at all, the way we were headed. But there was indeed something, possibly an old hermitage, that sounded kind of like the name of Blavatsky's Brigadoon. But whatever it was, it involved a hike up to the top of a plateau some leagues in a completely different direction. The trouble was, I knew good and well that if I returned to the States with this job left hanging, I'd be finished in the business. No one would consider mitigating circumstances. That's the only reason we decided to keep going. I knew what Moses felt like wandering in the wilderness for all those forty years.

We traded the camels for donkeys at a bazaar along the way. Better for the climb. Weeks passed, and we came in sight of the place, the Plateau of Tsang. It wasn't on any map I could find. So I guessed that made it a good enough candidate for the site of a lost city. Or temple, or whatever.

Finally we had to leave the donkeys with one or two of the bearers on a lower ledge and get out the climbing gear. It was clear that if there'd been some sort of monastery up there, the monks weren't kidding about isolation from the world. At the top, we found ourselves so exhausted, even the hardy hill men in our number, that we all decided to take a siesta before striking across the surprisingly small surface of the plateau. It appeared to extend for not much more than an acre. At the far end there was a visible structure, or the remains of one, but unless it extended underground, it didn't look like much. It would wait.

I was awakened by the sounds of gunfire. It seemed a couple of our men just couldn't wait to get a look at whatever valuables the plateau might conceal. Thinking there'd be a treasure, or maybe a leftover cache of Soviet weapons, a pair of them had snuck off. And they'd found something. Something worth fighting over. I jumped to my aching feet and ran for where the shots had echoed. I didn't hear any more of them, so I hoped the coast was clear.

By this time everyone was awake, and the others, hardier specimens, beat us Americans to the spot. By the time we caught up with them, we were greeted by a cacophony of wailing gibberish. It seemed these men, many of them kneeling, were calling on Allah, perhaps in mourning, perhaps asking for protection. I elbowed my way through the suddenly pious crowd to get a good look at the two bodies.

There had been shooting, all right, but they hadn't been shooting at each other after all. A later scrutiny of the scene would show bullets having knocked some chips from the stone ruins that loomed over them. But what *had* the men been shooting at? I had to assume, at whatever killed them. But filling in that blank did not look to be an easy matter. The dust of the ground had been stirred and disturbed by the footprints of the panicked bearers as they had first surrounded the corpses of their fallen comrades, then sprung away in panic. But between the troop of foot prints, I thought I made out fragments of a broad sweeping motion, as if huge ropes or snakes had dragged the ground in a semi-circular motion.

But the corpses, carcasses really, of the two poor bastards were the most mystifying. The throats and wrist of one had been torn away, possibly scraped away, while the other's heart had been pulled out of his chest. His chest hung wide like an opened clam. I didn't call on Allah, but as soon as I could reach a place with a ham radio I did call the network office to tell them that we were headed home. Needless to say, the documentary was as dead as the two guides. And the network was fretting, last time I heard, about possible suit from the survivors of the two men.

I arrived home in New York free of two worries: I wasn't going to die parched in the desert, and I still had my job. At least for now. Nobody could say I had botched the project, so at least I had a reprieve—until another batty exec had a fool's errand to send me and my crew on. But maybe it wouldn't come to that. For, you see, the trip wasn't entirely a waste after all.

I said we were wrong in our first guess that the two bearers had killed each other. But we were right about them having discovered something before they died. It was lying there between them on the ground, only partly stained by their flying blood. They had dug up a stone box, even opened it. It was nothing that interested either of them, couldn't have been, not that they had the time to do much calculating before whatever it was took them by surprise.

It was a book, and after my first decent hot shower in many weeks, I settled down in a nice soft robe with a glass of scotch and opened its covers. Not that I could really read it, mind you. But I knew what it was, and it was something to look at. The thing was an elaborate wooden codex, varnished boards enclosing bound pages of some tough parchment. The characters seemed something between Sanskrit and Tibetan, maybe that Senzar language Blavatsky had written about. Maybe she wasn't lying. She hadn't been lying about the ruins, that's for sure.

The text was block-printed the way they do it in Tibet and Nepal. The volume might be valuable as an artifact, and if worse came to worse, I could try to sell it, though I suspected the network would claim possession of it as soon as they heard of its existence, which, thanks to me, they hadn't yet. But then it occurred to me that if I could get the thing translated, it might hold the clues to future archaeological digs that would ensure my reputation for years to come. I could see myself not only on PBS, but the Discovery Channel, too, hell, maybe even at a university post. It wasn't out of the question.

About this time I was jarred from my boozy musings by the sound of someone out in the hall. I put my slippers on and went to the door. No one was there anymore. But then from the corner of my eye I could have sworn I saw someone out on the fire escape. Again, no one. By now I was plenty spooked. Could someone be trying to break in? Or was I under surveillance? New York began to seem to me altogether as creepy as the shunned Plateau of Tsang. Hell, maybe I'd be safer there. I double locked the doors and windows, then searched the apartment, every square foot, all the while assuring myself it was just jet-lag and the jitters. I wanted to believe this, and I had just about got myself believing it till I took another look over in the foyer area and saw something sitting on the mail table.

It was an unmarked videocassette, no box either. I held the cool plastic of the thing, puzzled, my tired mind somehow failing to connect it with the suspicious noises and glimpses I'd just been investigating. Instead, I tried to remember if I'd rented the tape before going away and considered what a hell of an overdue fee I must owe by now. But I didn't think I'd rented anything. Could somebody have dropped a home video through my mail slot? Might I have absent-mindedly picked it up on the way in from the airport? Didn't recall that either. But by now, my relaxing was ruined anyway. I was tense and edgy, both from the long trip and from my

466

probably imaginary suspicions. So I popped the video into the machine and reached for another scotch. Maybe between the two of them, they'd put me to sleep.

No such luck. The tape had no trailer, no intro, and as it developed, no real plot either. I began to wonder if what I was watching had been taped starting halfway through a sci-fi movie on late night TV. But there was no dialogue, no voice over. The film was grainy, but the effects were, I had to admit, quite well done, maybe computer graphics? Anyway, first there was just the expanse of space. One star grew slowly (far too slowly for good cinematic pacing) larger until you could see it was a spacecraft. A queer combination, from what you could see of it, of egg-shaped pods and a central disk. They didn't make the stars move behind the ship, a common but scientifically inaccurate gimmick. Without any transition you could see into a view port. The scene was bouncy but it seemed like the helmets worn by the pilots were strangely oblong. But who said they were supposed to be from NASA?

Another long shot. Now you could see this ship wasn't landing, just floating, orbiting I guess, with the planetary disk well below them. But then you could see closer to the surface. There was a kind of ghostly light or lambency, just enough to show the texture of the world, again amazingly well simulated. The terrain was parched, crumbling into dust. There were interlocking webs of impact craters. But, off center on the screen, you could see a large body different in color from the rest, and, yes, more regular, a geometric shape: a broken cone or pyramid. Was it supposed to be the last building left standing, or some natural formation? A volcano of some type? I suddenly caught myself taking it for reality.

And from the drifting pall of desolation on this barren surface, there was suddenly motion, too fast for the eye to follow. The transition back to the orbiting craft was abrupt, painful to watch since the camera seemed to quickly follow whatever had moved, dizzying and confusing the viewer. Somebody needed some direction help here. Now what was happening on board the ship? You saw agitation inside the view port, and the whole craft began to bob and dip. It was as if it had been lassoed. And then a wider shot showed that it *had*. The silver bulk of the thing, confusing to the eye even when moving smoothly, was apparently trying to escape what looked like a fleshy web or rope that entangled it and tugged powerfully.

But this was the most ridiculous thing of all: how were you supposed to believe this lariat could extend from the planet's surface into outer space? Next the camera backed up, letting you see the space ship nearing the planet, falling out of the sky and bursting into flame. No transition this time, but now you could see the opening of that cone—yes, it was a cone. The debris of the ship was being swallowed, like dust bunnies going into a vacuum cleaner. And now you could see a little bit of the rope up close. It seemed almost to be flexing and shifting like a living appendage. And there might have been suckers on it.

All this abruptly stopped and something else began—also in the middle, by the look of it. I guessed that someone had taped what I just saw over this, some footage of a ritual some relative of the guy with the camera must have been involved in. It was Buddhist or Hindu. I couldn't see any faces through the thick, clinging smoke. People had red robes, tasseled hats. Some held banners or standards aloft. Some bowed down before an idol, which I thought I could recognize. The elephant head—let's see, who would that be? I'd seen it plenty of times in a local Indian restaurant. The Hindu god Ganesha, I was pretty sure. But somehow different in detail. And then, for the first time, there was sound. Coming up gradually, it seemed, not surprisingly, religious chanting. Reminded me momentarily of the terrified bearers up on the Tsang Plateau. What were they saying? A foreign language; I just tried to remember the sound of syllables: *Chaugnar fhtagn.*

The tape was over. I hit eject, and out it came. Like the old automat sandwiches, I thought. Had one when I was a kid. A glance at the clock showed nearly two hours had gone by. That didn't seem possible. I couldn't have been watching it that long. It was kind of engrossing, I had to admit, but I couldn't have lost track of time to that extent, could I?

Well, that could wait till tomorrow. The tape had worked; I was drowsy and headed for the bed. I wasn't sure I could stay awake long enough to get under the covers. I slept like the dead. If I dreamed at all, I don't remember it.

Next day I dropped by the studios, said hello to a few friends who'd heard of the strange deaths and were worried about me. I told them I couldn't do much by way of satisfying their curiosity about the two mangled men. There had been no question of keeping the bodies with us on the journey back, and so we had the Asians bury them on the plateau, which they did with amazing efficiency. Guess they didn't want to look at them any longer than they had to.

The execs were waiting to see me. But really there was nothing any of us could say, no questions I could answer. I was relieved that they did at least credit me with the effort to make it across that hostile terrain. Maybe we'd even be able to work some of the footage shot on the way into some other project. I told them I doubted it, since there had been no way to stabilize the cameras on camelback for very long. Most of it no doubt looked as clumsy as that video I'd viewed last night. And then it occurred to ask whether any of the execs had sent someone to drop that cassette off. Was it supposed to be part of someone's trial project? I didn't think we were in the business of sci-fi entertainment. But, no, no one professed to know anything about it.

I checked in at a couple of my favorite bars, to say hello to a few people, and a few martini glasses, that hadn't seen my face for a while. Time passed, and I returned to the apartment. Sending my hat across the couch like a Frisbee, I began loosening my tie and looked over to see if the message machine wanted to talk to me. For once, nothing. There was a movie I wanted to catch on cable, but that wouldn't be on for an hour or so. I went to get the book from where I'd secured it. Suddenly thinking of the strange things I half-imagined I'd seen and heard the previous night, I got worried it might not be there. After a moment's panic, like I get when I feel for my keys and think I've lost them, I reached around the interior of the lock-box and was relieved when I felt the smooth surface of the lacquered boards.

I thought a closer look at the thing wouldn't hurt. Clearing some space on the kitchen table (the book was pretty large), I opened the covers, intending to take a good look at the illuminations, which I remembered as showing fine workmanship. My eye followed the margins, the colored inks still quite brilliant, until I happened to pause on a square inch of text. I felt instantly confused, felt maybe I was seeing double. A headache exploded out of nowhere, and I found myself falling back against the cushion of my chair. What had happened? I was afraid to look at the page again. Was there something written on it that was somehow just too terrible for my brain to let me see? No, that was absurd—I couldn't even read the language!

I was wrong. When my eyes rested on the page again, with only a mild wave of disorientation this time, I *could* read it! Now let me tell you, I had forgotten the little Spanish I'd had to take in high school. On the trip to Asia I couldn't read a sign for an airport restroom unless somebody translated it. And now I could read and comprehend a language which only the night before I could not even recognize.

My nerves were calm in the face of it. The impossible sat before me like an impenetrable block. All I could do was to stare dumbly at it. My eyes slowly gravitated to the page again. What it would have said had it been in English was *"The Testament of Mu Sang."* I didn't read any more. I somehow felt as if I were reading someone else's mail. By rights I should never be able to read it, and so I was afraid to. I got up, got myself a drink, paced. Turned on TV and stared at it blankly. I guess my cable program came on, but I never knew it.

Finally it occurred to me to phone up Joey Aronson, a pal from the network who designed foreign language programs, concentrated language learning programs for adults. Luckily he was home. I interrupted him watching the same show I had planned to see. He didn't mind. It took me some minutes to figure out how to ask my question, a few more for him to realize just what I meant. It seemed so absurd. Yes, overnight I learned a language, and yes, without even trying.

Joey had never heard of anything like it, but on second thought, he suggested maybe some sort of sleep-learning program. But I dismissed that: wouldn't I remember having taken it? *Not remembering something . . . ?* Ironically, that rang a bell somewhere. Joey hung on, probably more convinced by the minute that I had gone crazy over there in Central Asia.

"Look, Joey, come to think of it, last night, something strange *did* happen. Somebody left me an unmarked video. I watched it, some confusing movie footage. But when it was over, I was missing at least an hour and a quarter by the clock. Is there any way the tape could have . . . hypnotized me? And while I was under fed me knowledge of this language?"

"To be honest, Ed, it sounds impossible, but I don't know. We have language immersion weekends for people to pick up a language before they go abroad. And then there's sleep learning, like you mention. I've never heard of the pace being accelerated like this, though. Listen, I just thought of something. Ed, can you *speak* this language? Get the book and try reading something to me."

I reached over for the book and opened it at random. Again, it made sense to me. I started reading as if it were the morning newspaper.

"Hold on, Ed, you're reading me English. I don't want you to translate. Just read it."

I gazed at the page.

"Sorry, I wouldn't have the faintest guess how you'd say any of this stuff. It's like it just comes right into my mind what it means."

"Try this: what's the word in this language for 'book'?"

"Can't tell you. Doesn't that beat the hell out of you!"

"Tell you what, Ed. Bring the book down to my office tomorrow, and . . ."

I interrupted him. "Sorry Joey, but for reasons of my own, I'm not sure I want anybody seeing it just yet. Would it work if, say, I just traced a page or so of it?"

"Okay, whatever. I'd like to take it to somebody I know at the Museum. If it's a known Asian language, he'll be able to read it or know someone who can."

"Fine, but, Joey, that's not the trouble. *I* can read the damn thing. I just don't know how come!"

"Yeah, I understand, but let's do it my way for now. Get copying." He hung up. I got out some onion skin paper and started tracing, trying not to read much of it as I went. I was still wary of it. This wasn't my mail; whose was it?

Bright and early the next morning, I stepped out of the taxi in front of the network building. Joey was waiting for me at the curb and suggested we bundle ourselves right back into the cab for the ride over to the Museum. It was a cold day, our breath steaming even within the confines of the car. We tried to talk about in-house gossip. Somebody was about to be fired for sexual harassment, but I couldn't remember who. I could sense Joey shared my eagerness. Traffic was fairly light given the New York snow mounds, and we made it there in no time.

A knock on the pebble glass window of Dr. Harding's office fetched a quick response. As the genial man extended his hand, I realized I'd met him before in connection with one or another documentary I'd assisted on. He was in his late fifties, heavyset, graying, ruddy face, few wrinkles. Surprisingly, he remembered me, too. I was happy to let Joey do what explaining he could, all the time thinking to myself that it was probably a psychiatrist's office, not a linguist's, I should be sitting in.

The professor interrupted my encouraging train of thought. "This all sounds most intriguing! And now may I see the text?" I unfolded the sheet and began to read. Even though it was in English, it still sounded like outlandish gibberish, even to me. Then I handed Professor Harding the paper. Donning a pair of reading glasses, he regarded the cryptic symbols in silence for some time. Finally, he looked up and spoke.

"Mr. Banning, I am afraid there is no Senzar language, any more than Joseph Smith's Reformed Egyptian was a genuine language, ancient or modern. But this," he shook the paper, "*is* a real language. It is a sort of primitive Pali, an earlier stage of what Gautama Buddha would have spoken. Linguists have hypothesized such a tongue, but until now, no actual examples have ever been found. Whatever manuscript you have discovered will be of great scientific interest."

"Wait a minute, Professor Harding. Are you saying that this book is pre-Buddhist?"

"That I cannot judge without seeing it; of course, it may be a more

471

recent copy, though still quite old, of a very ancient literary work. But yes, that work would have to antedate the birth of the Buddha, unless the primitive Pali continued alongside the more developed version, which I would have to judge unlikely."

"I assumed it was an artifact of some Central Asian Buddhist monastery."

"If not for the peculiar dialect, that would be a good guess. Many such manuscripts were buried by monks to keep them safe against the advance of the Mongol armies."

Joey interposed, "Is it something you can read, professor?"

"Yes, there is little problem there. It is close enough to standard Pali for me to make out most of it. But naturally there is far too little in this copied fragment for me to understand just what is going on in the passage. Perhaps if you would let me see the complete manuscript?"

"Tell me one thing. How good was my translation?"

The professor removed his reading glasses again and paused, looking at Joey who seemed to know what he was going to say next: "I am sorry to say that your reading bears absolutely no relation to this piece of text. Of that I feel sure."

If there is some square before square one, that's where I'd been left standing. Having crumpled up the onion skin sheet, I tossed it and rose, taking my hat and coat, leaving the others protesting as I slammed the door and sought the steps. Making for the subway, I knew there was one thing left for me to do. Read the whole manuscript. Or, since apparently I was not exactly reading it, I guessed I would simply be picking up the receiver and letting someone talk.

Once home, I retrieved the great wooden volume and placed it before me. I turned on every light in the place and disconnected the phone. Then I opened the covers and began to "read." This is what I thought I read.

THE TESTAMENT OF MU SANG

This is the oracle of the one born of Hanuman's womb. These are the words to confirm what has gone before and what is to follow. Blessed is the one who grasps their inner meaning, for only the inner eye may read.

In the fifth month of the year of the badger, my office was that of first attendant to the Feeble One, the century-old master of our sect, and his bloated vice-regent, the Mad Prophetess. For many generations we had occupied the forlorn lamasery of Tsang, whereupon no worldly man may enter. Our chief task was the keeping and copying of scrolls, which were housed in abundance. Many were written in scripts none could any longer read. Most were traced upon parchment dried from the skins of High Lamas, stripped from them on their deathbeds.

When on occasion one of the brethren might dare to read what was contained within certain carefully guarded scrolls, dangerous doctrines might arise within our ranks. But such heresies as reared their heads were quickly dispatched by means of the tortures which were our other inherited trade. By these two arts, the copying of scrolls, and the slow flaying of human hides, was the lamasery much enriched over many generations. Many of the mountain chiefdoms required copies of the scriptures as well as discipline for their prisoners.

We went along peacefully in this fashion year after year until the return of one brother, Zinxong, who had spent many years away from the community while serving as the court torturer for Qwon-ling, the most powerful of the mountain chieftains. At first he was received back with great rejoicing, as for a long lost relative. Little we knew that, even as the traitor sat at table with the aging Lama and us, his attendants, the warriors of the chieftain he had lately served and still did serve were swarming over the low walls of the lamasery, quietly slaying all who opposed them.

As the sounds of fighting were heard in the dining hall, we rose to our feet, all but the Feeble One who was past rising and indeed had to be carried from place to place. And our false brother went to greet his brethren in perfidy, the chieftain himself as well as his shaman. It was now all too clear that his tribe had made alliance with our traditional rivals, the Brotherhood of Leng. Their silken yellow caps glowed in the soft light of the butter lamps. Their very presence here was blasphemy. I clutched my robes of holy crimson, the true color of enlightenment, and sought egress as the sword of the traitors unerringly found the brittle breastbone of our revered master the Feeble One. A second stroke silenced forever the raving mouth of the Mad Prophetess who was ever at his side.

In truth, I confess I mourned not greatly at the passing of the Feeble One. His voice had not been heard in many a season, since the Mad One had grown to dominate him. And her dispatching I greeted with positive elation. She had abused us for the last time. But this meant I stood next in line for the pontificate of our sect, the Red Hats of Tsang.

Thus it was that I resolved that the heretical Yellow Hats of Leng should by no means usurp our holy monastery and its riches for their own. As the attendant of the High Lama, I knew well the secret paths of escape, that might even that day have availed the Feeble One had he not been so palsied and under the fell dominion of the Mad Raving One. But secure behind thick tapestries I made my way silently down hidden stairs to the Inner Adytum far below the surface.

There I knew that I must call on the aid of our gods to vindicate and protect those few remaining Red Hats from the bloody hands of the blasphemers.

None had dared approach the hall of shrines in many a year, as the curtains and ropes of cobwebs made manifest. I bent and peered close at the writing upon the bases of the statues. Legend had it that the divine images had been brought here from the stars and were themselves older far than the monastery, which had been later erected over this very cave. Genuflecting, I passed quickly by the squat representations of Nug and Yeb, of Lloigor and Zhar. I shuddered and lingered not at the chapel of Dark Han. The image I sought was that of elephant-headed Yag-Kosha, whom our forbears had worshipped in ancient Khitai. Alone among the brethren I had been given access to the antique scrolls of summoning and now sought to call out of the dimensions the terrible form of Yag-Kosha, that his righteous fury might take vengeance upon the usurping devils of the Yellow Hat.

At last I saw that I had reached a web-festooned image which seemed clearly to bear the outlines of the mighty elephant, the chosen avatar of the blessed Yag-Kosha. There were the flaring ears, the gracefully bending trunk. The engraved name plate at the base of the statue had been too much corroded with verdigris to be legible, but no matter. I knew I had found our savior. Setting down my butter lamp, I prostrated my form, casting aside my crimson habit so that my naked form might be seen to be covered with penitential scars and tattoos as offerings to the divine Yag-Kosha whose epiphany I sought.

So absorbed with mystic rapture was I in calling upon the deity that I scarce marked it when the sound of sandaled footfalls approached. It seemed that a few of my surviving brethren had surmised my destination and made to rejoin me. At once they prostrated themselves around me and sought as best they might to repeat the ancient vocables after me.

The musty air began to stir. The sole butter lamp flared like a torch, and from somewhere we all alike heard the slow grating of stonework being forced apart. Dared we hope that our supplications had found a receptive ear?

We regained our feet and stared about in the lightening gloom.

For a moment we yielded to faithless fear as we saw the villainous Yellow Hats and their retainers pouring into the far end of the chamber. They had discovered, no doubt with the aid of the traitor Zinxong, our place of refuge. They lost no time in locating us and sending armed men, their scimitars already upraised, to finish their slaughter. This they did, sparing only my own humble person so that I might guide them to the treasury of the Red Hats.

The devil Zinxong approached me and warned his master Qwon-ling that it would not be easy to torture the secret out of me, as I myself was as expert in the art as he and knew secrets of resistance that few could break. As for me, I rejoiced at the prospect of silent triumph over the white-hot sitting spike, the drill of the eye, the slow nibbling of the flesh.

But this contest was not to be mine. The flabby, debauched faces of Zinxong and Qwon-ling alike were drawn in terror by the terrible bellow that now sounded through the chamber like a thousand bone trumpets. The flaggings of the floor beneath us began to spew forth like froth from the cataract. As many of the godless Yellow Hats succumbed to the rain of stones, the two traitors released me and sought futile shelter. More Red Hats, having procured their own weapons, rounded the corner into the hall and stood transfixed at the sight that greeted them.

Where moments ago only cringing and fleeing human forms had stood now towered the form of a god. Its massive bulk rolled with surprising speed over the piles of bodies now collecting on the floor. With fleshy tendrils and ropy coils it grasped hapless monk and heretic alike, as a frog might retrieve a juicy fly. Even for the steeled eye of a master of torment it was not easy to look upon men's skulls as they crumbled from within, sucked empty of all contents. Once-firm limbs shrank and bonelessly rolled up like emptied sleeves and stockings.

Why, I wondered in pious horror, did the blessed Yag-Kosha not distinguish between the righteous and the wicked? I stood aghast, panting in terror against the base of one of the support columns. So far the swinging tentacles had not sought me out. For this I could not account, except it be that the great lord understood that I had summoned him and had mercy on me alone.

Then it was that I beheld the half-torn form of the perfidious Zinxong being slowly borne by a mighty arm toward the ravening maw of the feaster. "Fool!" he gasped. "It is not who you think! It is Chaugnar you have summoned, the doom of us all!" And with that his skull snapped like a cracked almond.

And now I perceived that the terrible form before me bore but faint resemblance to the noble lines of the mighty elephant. What had seemed the fan-like ears were in fact rudimentary membranous wings. What seemed an elegant trunk was a central proboscidian tentacle. All else was madness with no comprehensible form. Now at last I understood the ancient parable of the blind men and the elephant. The form of Chaugnar was such that no mortal eye could grasp it and retain sanity.

When it was over, I, Mu Sang, stood alone and vindicated as the keeper of the sacred monastery of Tsang. Mine was the honor to have opened the portal of worlds to Great Chaugnar, to have awakened him from his sated sleep of ages, and to have summoned him from that distant world where he alone remained alive, all its creatures having fed his eternal hunger.

And now I was chosen. My task it is to serve him as he sleeps content and full. But the ages must pass, and one day he shall awaken again, when the gnawing pangs grow too great.

This is my prophecy, and now I go to seal it up for the day that he shall find it whom Chagnar has chosen to succeed me.

Iä! Chaugnar fhtagn!

I read and re-read the thing. Dawn came up. Noon passed. Realization grew upon me. I not only understood what the strange manuscript meant, I also understood what it meant that I understood it. It was I who had brought the party of men to the Plateau of Tsang and disturbed its dust of ages. In fact, I guess it was I who provided bloody Chaugnar with his breakfast after his long sleep. Where was he now? From what I had read, I knew he could hardly be confined to space as we are. Maybe Madame Blavatsky would have known how to explain it. I didn't. But I knew it had to be waiting.

I took some pills and finally got some sleep. The next day I began wondering what might have happened to all the rest of the bearers. Did their wailings to Allah protect them in the end? There's no way to trace them. I didn't even know most of their names. But I did make some calls to my camera men. The tearful wife of one of them told me he had been inexplicably mauled in Central Park. When people rushed to the scene there had been no sign of the assailant. None of the others could be reached, but I had a hunch I'd be hearing similar stories soon. All these poor bastards had actually trespassed on Chaugnar's sacred ground, where the priest Mu Sang had brought him. I was the only one to get away. Maybe now it would be over. Maybe I was able to flee the destiny after all. But what if I hadn't?

I got a sick feeling when I thought of Joey. Haven't got up the nerve to call his wife yet. I'm hoping Professor Harding's okay, but I shouldn't kid myself, I guess. I had, I now realized, randomly chosen to copy and then read aloud the part of the manuscript which includes the prayer of summoning for Chaugnar. He must have made the trip. I guess it'll go on till he's satisfied again and sleeps like I do after Thanksgiving dinner. It took only a few dozen before. Maybe it won't be many more this time. But what about old Mu Sang? Did he finally escape? How do I know how long he lived after he finished his manuscript? I'm just about done with mine. For all I know, I may be next on the menu.

–2002–

The Horror in the Genizah

I am as yet undecided what to do, where to go from here. My researches can never be published: their drastic and explosive nature guarantees the impossibility of them even being taken seriously in the scholarly community. My colleagues would tell me this fact alone should give me pause, should make me rethink the whole thing, since I cannot possibly be correct. It is true, if someone else arrived at my conclusions and put them forth publicly, I should dismiss him at once as a crank and shake my head at the tragedy of a once-sound scholar going off the deep end. But the point is moot in any case, since I have attracted the attention of a terrorist cell whose zealous members I cannot ultimately evade. I am the object of a *fatwah*, and against it I know no government security agency can shield me. So I doubt I should survive long enough to see to the airing of my findings. All I will attempt is the present narrative, and whether it will turn out to be a good-bye letter on the eve of flight or a suicide note I do not yet know. Like the reader, I fear I will have to wait till the end to find out.

The whole business began two years ago with a proposal at the annual convention, in Boston, of the American Society for Oriental Research. Someone belonging to the Koranic textual criticism work group suggested a team of us locate a series of very old mosques throughout the Arab-speaking countries whose *genizahs* were still inviolate. A genizah, or "treasury," is a narrow space or small room enclosed at one end of a mosque, behind the pulpit and platform area. It would have a slit in the wall through which the presiding elder would push detached leaves of old, worn out copies of scripture when time for their replacement came. The Muslim veneration for each copy of the Koran is hard to exaggerate and can be compared only with the traditional Roman Catholic reverence for the sacramental host. For, just as the Catholic believes the consecrated wafer becomes in essence the very Body of Christ, so does the Muslim hold his well-thumbed copy of the Koran to be somehow one with the "Mother of the Book," the heavenly prototype of the text from which the angel Gabriel dictated the Koran in piecemeal form to the Prophet Muhammad. As such it may be said that, in some sense, even a dingily-printed copy of the holy book is itself eternal! Whatever one may think of such a belief, it explains this otherwise peculiar method of disposing of the texts. One cannot simply burn or destroy the sacred page. So it is instead "retired" by permanent storage in the "treasury," a kind of retirement home for superannuated copies of scripture. Mosques had borrowed the custom from Jewish synagogues that gave the same treatment to tired old copies of the Torah scrolls which similarly must not be burned because they contained the name of God.

Manuscript discoveries tend to occur mostly in hot, arid countries, where the climate is ideal for preventing decomposition of papyrus. Thus the longevity of the Dead Sea Scrolls found at Qumran in the Judean Desert in 1947, the Nag Hammadi library discovered in Chenoboskion, Egypt, in 1945, and the manuscripts found in the Cairo Genizah in 1896, some of which turned out to be copies of texts later found at Qumran. The proposal at the ASOR meeting was that permissions should be secured from the governments of Iraq and Saudi Arabia to search out any of their ancient mosques with their genizahs intact to examine their possible contents. Who knew what manuscript treasures might not lurk within? Piled ignominiously in dusty heaps there might await us unprecedented manuscript evidence as to the earliest state of the Koran.

For the reader uninitiated in these matters, let it be known that the text critic's task is a difficult one as it bears on scripture, and this is equally true no matter what religion's scriptures one studies. Because of the widespread use of the texts many of them will have survived, far more than of "secular" works of ancient literature. But most of these copies will be near-worthless, because most of the significant alterations to any holy texts will have been made in the earliest period when a scribe might "correct" or embellish the text with impunity. Such was possible because there were fewer copies to check, and the texts would not yet have come to be regarded with such absolute reverence as would soon render them untouchable. And, naturally, the very fact that the texts had been altered in the service of changing orthodoxies militated against the preservation of earlier forms of the text which had retrospectively become "heretical"! For example, Islamic tradition itself records that the Caliph Uthman caused all extant copies of the Koran to be gathered, collated, and standardized, and then for the collected copies to be destroyed and replaced by the new, official "textus receptus." Despite the existence of several fluid and poetic translations of the Koran, it is the dirty secret of Koranic scholars that the Arabic text is often nearly incoherent. Günter Lüling and others suggested that this was because the primitive text had been heavily altered, and often simply by virtue of repunctuating the consonantal text. That is, like

479

ancient Hebrew, ancient Arabic had no explicit, written vowels. Later scribes began to abet liturgical public reading by adding vowel points. And usually the choice of them was obvious. But in a surprising number of cases, a whole new sense, worthy of the imagination of a Kabbalist, might spring off the page if one substituted a hypothetical string of alternate vowel points. And, besides this, of course, whole words might have been changed, added, deleted, replaced. Only access to actual, tangible written copies from the earliest days could settle the question, and the genizah proposal seemed an ideal way, probably the only way, of approaching the problem. The whole issue was made more urgent by the eruption of controversies over scholars like Lüling, whose radical theories of a pre-Islamic "Ur-Koran" had made him an outcast from the scholarly community.

In 1972, during the restoration of the Grand Mosque in Sanaa, Yemen, workmen discovered great heaps of precious parchments which included, in whole or in part, literally thousands of copies of the Koran, some dating from the eighth and ninth centuries CE, the first two centuries of Islam. Study of these manuscripts commenced in earnest in 1978 under the direction of Dr. Gerd-Rudolf Puin, who reported interesting variations of wording and order of the materials, and most importantly, differences in punctuation. We still await the full results of this research. It is slow going, since, given the volatile sensitivities of the Muslim authorities, should anything very controversial become widely known, further access to the texts might be restricted.

In view of the political upheavals in the Arab world occasioned by Jihadist terrorism, our scholarly guild felt we must redouble our efforts and proceed as quickly as we could. Our greatest break came from the new, post-Baathist regime installed in Iraq by her American conquerors. Though the mullahs in charge of several of the most ancient Shi'ite mosques were understandably rather prickly about it, they did at length cooperate. It helped that we were able to tell them truthfully that whatever paleographical materials we found we intended to display in the country's own museums as national treasures of the Iraqi people and the Shi'ite community. Photographs of the texts would be quite sufficient for our scholarly task. Or so I supposed at the time. In any case, we were canny enough to watch our backs. If the mainstream clerics tolerated us with qualms, there had to be extremists who looked upon our work with seething disfavor and might do something drastic to stop it. I think it best not to supply the name of the village where I made my discovery. I do not want to bring them further trouble of any kind. Suffice it to say that several of us quickly struck paydirt. Remember, this was not quite what one usually pictures when one thinks of archaeological expeditions. We had no need to find and unearth buried buildings or to reconstruct rubble into likely outlines of vanished structures. No, we knew where the relevant buildings were; it was simply a question of getting into the manuscript graveyards built into them and trying to do as little damage to holy shrines, most still in at least sporadic use, in the process. Once "in," we would readily find what we were looking for, or not, and that would be that. It was pretty simple and straightforward. And, as I say, several of us working at different sites had some luck. There were occasional copies of this or that biblical writing in hitherto-unknown Arabic translations, but, as we expected, most of the material was Koranic. Though it was too early to tell how significant the particular manuscript leaves might prove, some peculiarities, much like those reported from the Sanaa mosque, were evident at once. At the very least one could say, and one had to say it gingerly, that the evidence had greatly increased for a very different primitive form of the text. And that is about as much as has ever trickled out to the non-scholarly public.

I shared the excitement of my colleagues at their finds, as we called back and forth on our cell phones with new bits of news. But when I made my own discovery I deliberated long as to whom I ought to call and in the end told no one. Some students and I found the initial pile of papyrus pages and organized them, cleaned them up, and treated some of them to save them from further disintegration. I took the photographs. And it was I who took the materials back to my shabby hotel room for safekeeping that night. I had fully expected to spend the night sleeplessly, energized by the excitement of discovery and unable to wait till the morning to begin deciphering what I had found. But the combination of nonstop excitement and fatigue vetoed this plan, and I fell asleep fully clothed, despite the oppressive heat.

And as I slept I had the strangest dream. The content of it was peculiar, as I will relate in a moment, but what struck me as so odd was that the dream seemed to be purely auditory, with no visual element whatsoever. Perhaps such dreams are common enough, but I know that I had never experienced one. As for what it was I heard, that is difficult to say. I recall it fairly clearly; that is not the problem. Nor was it phantasmagorical like many dreams which cannot even be repeated coherently on waking. It was rather that what I heard while asleep seemed pregnant with meaning, but I could not quite discern it. Perhaps this meant my subconscious mind was trying to tell me something, I don't know what. But in the dream I found myself feeling breathless in claustrophobically close quarters. It was physical confinement, though I was not especially aware of bodily discomfort. And what I heard was muffled voices. I might have been hearing them from a distance, or they may have been nearby, but on the other side of whatever wall confined me. It was impossible to make out specific words, but I think it was Arabic, and it was chanting. It reminded me of the *Muezzin's* Friday call to prayer, which I had certainly heard often enough in the past weeks from every local minaret: *Allaho-akbar!* "God is most great!" And though I do not recall making any sound at all in the dream, I had the odd feeling that these voices were in some way trying to drown me out, even to keep me at bay.

Freud somewhere says that one ought by no means complain of dreams that disturb the sleep, for they are the mind's way of dealing with worse phantoms of the subconscious. It is like the ruckus created by the arrival of the police: a ruckus, yes, but better than the menace that occasioned their intervention! Perhaps it was so in my case. But it was not conducive to regenerative rest, for I woke suddenly and, despite the fatigue, could not get back to sleep. It did not take much convincing of myself to get up and start examining those manuscript leaves.

The students were naturally eager the next morning, pressing to know what I had found. I told them some disappointing lie to make it sound like there was nothing very noteworthy in the discovery. For what I actually did find was, to say the least, disturbing. Elementary paleographic considerations proved the texts to be very early indeed. And I very shortly came to see that the papyri did much to confirm the theories of Lüling, at least insofar as they showed there was radically different punctuation at an earlier stage of Koranic evolution. Lüling's contention was that as much as one-third of the text was founded upon a palimpsest of Christian strophic hymnody, and that this was only subsequently altered by scribes to comport with later Islamic orthodoxy. But as to just how "unorthodox" the underlying Koranic Ur-text was, Lüling had not even begun to imagine.

The pattern became evident to me almost at once, but I dismissed it as the coincidence it had to be. I thought of the pseudo-messages that eccentrics occasionally claimed to discover by analyzing strings of letters in the Hebrew Bible, coded predictions of contemporary events such as the assassination of Israeli politicians. In the same way, I felt sure I must be reading into the text the stray contents of my memory. But as page after page proved to yield the same sort of sense, I could no longer deny it. And in the same moment, I knew I could never dare make my findings known to the scholarly community, much less the public. There would be some who would laugh me to scorn, then refuse even to look at the data, like the stubborn cleric who refused Galileo's invitation to gaze into his telescope. There would be others who would think me history's greatest blasphemer and would howl for my blood. It is easy to despise and denounce the bigotry of those who would censor and suppress knowledge that clashes with their cherished dogmas. But what if one finds oneself in the same position? Suppose, for instance, anthropologists were to stumble upon some sort of data that would effectively prove one race inferior to another? Such knowledge would be so loathsome to us that we would judge it best unknown. Of course, there is no such evidence for such a repugnant conclusion. But I had discovered something equally detestable.

For what I had found amid the familiar consonants of the Arabic text, coiled there like a serpent ready to strike, communicated by a shocking distribution of unmistakable vowel points, was the text of another Arabic work, far less familiar, but well-enough known to most Arabists: the *Kitab al-Azif* of Abd al-Hazred. It was a shock, but a shock of recognition. I had been through the consonantal texts of both and had never before recognized the identity between the two. I can only say that one perceives what one expects to perceive, and that, under the "guidance" of the traditional vowel punctuations I had simply experienced different texts. And now the scales had fallen away from my eyes.

The crisis I now felt I faced would be dismissed by most workaday people, naive and happy in their servitude to the needful mundane, as a tempest in a teapot, a disturbance in the tranquility of the ivory tower. I wish I could share that perspective. But it is impossible, since I had begun to imagine, however reluctantly, the large ramifications of the find. I feared they should reverberate far beyond the ivory tower, that is, after wholly demolishing it.

And yet even I was rudely torn from my fearful reveries and forced to cope with the "real" world. Early the next morning I found myself awakened in mid-flight, the strangest sensation, I can assure you, as a mighty explosion hurled me from my bed. The hotel, where it was known several of us stayed, was bombed. I still grieve to think of my students, killed there. Such fresh faces, lit with the zeal for learning! Such promising careers to be cut short so pointlessly! But not quite pointlessly, since they could truly be called martyrs to the cause of truth, and so I memorialized them to the microphones of the swarm of cable television reporters who at once descended upon the scene. It was mere chance that none of the veteran scholars, my colleagues, were seriously injured by the attack. But this fact did not go unnoticed, and the Jihadists soon attacked again. It was obvious enough that they would. What fools we were to insist, against the warnings of the local authorities, that we stay on the job for as long as it took!

Again, I was there to witness the act. With the small hotel reduced to rubble, we had resorted to tents nearer the site of the old mosque. Rising early, we set to work and hoped to be finished shortly. In fact, we were packing up the manuscripts when our assailants appeared. This time, fearing to destroy the holy site, they used no explosives, satisfying themselves with machine guns. As I saw colleagues and old friends fall before the fanatical assault, I thought for a fleeting moment of how my father must have felt in the Korean War, seeing the same terrible harvesting of the dead day after day. But there was no time for reflection as I instinctively sought shelter in the one safe place available: the mosque itself, which I prayed they would not violate.

I rushed past a couple of the clerics who worked as caretakers of the old place. Their eyes were wide with panic, as they only now began to realize what was taking place on the street outside. They found places to hide themselves while they kneeled and prayed. I do not know that they would not have cheered the gunmen had not they themselves fallen under danger from them. But I made my way into the genizah, I suppose because it was the area of the structure the most familiar to me: any port in a storm.

I can only say that, as I huddled down there, listening to the fire-cracker-like popping of the guns outside, wondering when the terrorists would run out of either victims or bullets, I felt an unaccustomed sense of familiarity with the place, more than I would have thought should have come from my labors there of the last few days. And as the gunfire became more sporadic, enabling me to hear more of the fearful chanting of the custodians of the place, I experienced an unaccountable sense of irritation, really of fury, at hearing it. This, I guessed at the time, must be a delayed and thus misdirected reaction to the attack of the zealots outside, the only reasonable object for my feelings.

But then the gunfire began again. I reasoned that it must mean the police had arrived and were shooting it out with the attackers. This should have made me feel relieved, but it did not. I felt no less fearful and alarmed than before. I remember thinking that it seemed most likely that the terrorists should seek refuge as I had done in the mosque itself, betting that the authorities would not fire on it. And when they found me, I should be killed at once or held as a hostage. The urgency of a cornered

484

animal was rising within me now. Without conscious volition, I heard myself beginning to chant Arabic phrases and, with a peculiar passive detachment, I observed that they were phrases from the texts I had been studying, that is, the terrible words, now reconstructed, of the *Azif!* In a moment, I was actually screaming them! Without thinking of it, I had moved closer to the opening we had made in the genizah wall and, as I peeked out now, I could see the clerics had arisen and were running for the outside, and this though the gunfire had by no means abated! I am quite confident of this, for I noticed that a moment or two later, the bullets did stop, almost as if the appearance of the custodians outside the mosque was a signal for the gunmen to cease fire. That made no sense, and I recall thinking it was like a movie out of sync, with the soundtrack coming in too late, for surely the clerics must have waited for the guns to stop blazing before they left. Who would not? Surely nothing inside the mosque could have so scared them?

I waited a few moments before likewise exiting the old structure. I saw then that the battle was indeed over, and it appeared the police had quite expertly taken down the terrorists, whose inert forms now lay scattered about the radius of the mosque. I usually decline to look upon the gory remnants of auto accidents and the like, but this time I was irresistibly drawn to take a look at the slain bodies of those who had been so intent upon slaying me. As I approached one of them, dazedly ignoring the solicitous interrogation of the police, was I all right, and so forth, I noticed first that the dead men did not lie in the proverbial pool of blood. Looking at their swarthy, bearded faces beneath one's burnoose and another's knit skull-cap, I saw at once that these men had been overcome not from without but from within. It was bacilli, not bullets, that had finished them: they bore the unmistakable marks of the terrible Bubonic Plague! I tried to convey this to the intrepid, bull-like policemen, but they seemed willfully impenetrable. At first they seemed not even to grasp what I was trying to tell them, though my command of modern Arabic is pretty good. Then one of them asked if I were a medical doctor, to which I replied in the negative. That was good enough for him; he needn't trouble himself further.

Miraculously, none of my colleagues, and no more students, were killed in this second ambush. But we had learned our lesson. We all left Iraq the next day, for Germany, where we would rest up for a few more days, then head home to America. I deeply surprised myself by lying to my colleagues about my discoveries. My slain students were the only ones who had known I had made any discoveries. But my more serious deceit was to smuggle the manuscripts out of the country. This was accomplished with surprising ease, though not without a fairly hefty expense, which I rationalized as falling under the necessary costs of the expedition. It would not have been the first time momentous manuscripts had been secured in dubious ways. But then I did not intend to share my discoveries. I even toyed with destroying the papyri but could not bring myself to do it. I was divided, in that I dreaded lest any other eyes should see these strange pages, and yet I felt they must be preserved, and I could not be confident of their safety if I left them in the hands of the authorities in Iraq. Perhaps I was thinking of those museum robberies during the first days of the overthrow of the Baathist regime.

I have never had the slightest difficulty falling asleep on plane rides. I find I do not even need to recline the seat. I simply close my eyes, and the next thing I know, I have arrived at my destination. It reminds me of the science fiction conceit of being placed into suspended animation for the duration of a long space flight. And so it was on the flight to Germany. Only this time I dreamed very vividly. I want to call it a recurring dream, a repeat of the one I had dreamt a few nights ago in the hotel room. Only this time it was not simply repetition. For one thing, this time I could see what transpired, not merely hear it. But I seemed to view it all from the standpoint of a spectator, not as an actor in the scene, even though I was in the scene. I'm sure you have experienced the same sensation. What I dreamed was that I was being imprisoned somewhere, some very narrow cell. There were pushing hands, hastening to be rid of me, free of the touch of me. But "I" was not myself, the person writing the present narrative. It was as if I were playing some other character in a drama. I can recall no use of my limbs to resist, though I did seem to make some efforts to strike back, futile ones, turned back in some equally subtle and indescribable way. All the while there was that familiar chanting. And I think it was the chanting of verses from the Koran, that is, in something approaching its now-conventional form. I remember something about Noah, *Nuh*, and the angel Gabriel, *Jibreel*. But there were many voices, chanting various verses.

I awakened as we touched down, instantly certain that I knew the secret of the alteration of the primordial *al-Azif* into the more familiar, and far more wholesome, *al-Qur'an*. Quite simply, the ancient savants had sought, quite effectively, to subvert and stultify the reading of the *Azif* by the process of repointing the consonants with different vowels, creating a whole new sense, and many times, nonsense. As Lüling, Ibn Warraq, and others had argued, much of so-called classical Arabic was the invention of

Koranic exegetes who had basically created arbitrary rules for making the oft-incoherent text seem to say something. Something *else*. Crone and Cook, Schacht, too, had come close to the astonishing truth, that the earliest version of so-called Islam was a very different cult than the final product which, as we know it, is an elaborate attempt by third- or fourth-generation Muslims to create something like Judaism and Christianity so as to coexist with these two and to coopt their theological pedigree, all in an effort to replace something earlier and quite disturbing.

What, then, had been the role of the Mad Arab, as an earlier generation of Eurocentric scholars knew him, or better: the inspired poet al-Hazred? He has been credited with the authorship of the *Azif*, but it seemed more likely to me now that the man must have been something very much like one of the Shi'ite Imams, an inspired heir of the Prophet, entrusted with the esoteric meaning of the Koran. And the true import of this claim would have to be that he had preserved or restored the original punctuation of the text. I saw at once how this reconstruction comported with the wild claims of a dangerous Syrian sect that the French colonial authorities had wiped out in the nineteenth century: they believed that al-Hazred would one day return to the earth, revealing himself as the "Mahdi of Yog-Sothoth." All this was considered the vilest blasphemy by both Sunnite and Shi'ite communities, who had lifted not a finger to protect the heretics in their midst.

My head was swimming as I passed the days until our return to the States. I declined colleagues' invitations to join them for a drink, a meal, a show, any token effort to regain a sense of normalcy. They must have decided I was still a victim of emotional shock at the loss of students and colleagues, not to mention my own close brush with death. But I confess, these concerns had been crowded from the stage of my mind, at least for the present, by the enormous puzzle I was trying to solve. And the puzzle was less my outrageous historical hypothesis about the Koran and its sinister alter ego than my absolute confusion as to what I ought to do next. Reveal my conclusions and be dismissed in disgrace from my position and from any esteem from my peers? Or try to ignore what I now knew and continue on as if I had never made the discovery, though that would make my professional activities henceforth a total sham? Scylla and Charybdis.

As it turned out, events forestalled any of this, taking the decision out of my hands. As our airliner, a luxurious 787, took wing to cross the Atlantic, the fuselage of the plane shook to a powerful impact. At first I thought it was the wake of some explosion outside the plane, perhaps the crash of a landing plane. But then I saw the flames and smoke inside the cabin, billowing with astonishing speed! Later examination and the interrogation of witnesses on the ground revealed that it was no bomb; security had been vigilant enough to prevent that. No, it was a surface-to-air missile, shoulder-launched by a new airline employee of Middle Eastern descent, hired only days before. He was shot trying to escape, and his background-check information yielded no hint of any such deadly potential. Nor did any terror organization ever claim credit for the disaster. Obviously, I survived the crash, and with minimal injuries. It was almost as if Providence had spared me in particular. No one else survived their injuries more than a week, and many of course died on the plane.

The box full of manuscripts did not survive. Indeed, I am quite certain they were the real target of the terrorist strike. I have come to believe that the import of my discovery had somehow leaked out. Or perhaps the custodians of that mosque had inherited knowledge of its secret. And it was devout Muslims, not members of some unknown esoteric cult, who sought to eradicate the terrible truth. It was not the use of the *Azif* they feared, or so I surmise. The existence of the book was well-known to scholars, though few were very interested in it. Most dismissed it as one more of the many medieval Arabic books of magic and superstitious lore. No, what these zealots sought to keep secret was the proof that the book of al-Hazred was the original text underlying the Holy Koran!

These desperate men must surely know I survived the attack. It was a matter of worldwide news. So for a while now I have been waiting for another attempt to finish me. None has yet been forthcoming. But perhaps they will leave me alone after all. They must realize I could never hope to convince anyone of my theories if I tried, and that even to mention them would invite accusations of crack-pot insanity. If so, they are quite right.

But it is not as if the story is yet a closed book. There have been developments. Further dreams, for one thing. And in these new dreams I have come slowly to realize who, or what, it is that is being shut away in the genizah. It is, of course, the manuscript pages of the Koran, or the *Azif*, for they are one. And they are—*it is*—a living entity in some sense I cannot fathom. I say it is a living thing. It thrives like a parasite. And I am its host. For some days now, I have found it difficult to read any book, any magazine I open, as if at this late date I am developing dyslexia. The letters swim and fade. Until I see before me pages of Arabic letters, and punctuation. For my eyes, every page of every book is a page of *al-Azif*. And when I sleep, though that is no longer frequent, I behold in three or more dimensions the realities which the text sets forth.

I fear there is something to the myths of a return of al-Hazred. Not literally, of course. But it may yet be that the insidious text ever seeks its bearer. Its apostle? It is not a fate I can embrace. It is too much for me. Let some other drink this cup. For now I have decided. Writing this account, which I of course cannot proof read, since it appears to my red eyes as just more Arabic text, has made clear to me that it is after all going to be a suicide note. And, again, I know there is a greater force behind what I thought were my own actions. I feel certain in these last moments that I have been moved to write this as a means of securing my successor. It is he or she—it is you—who read this account. It is no doubt too late even now, and soon you will find that no matter what *nor is it to be thought that man is either the first or the last of earth's masters, or that the common bulk of life and substance walks alone. The Old Ones were, the Old Ones are, and the Old Ones shall be. Not in the spaces we know, but between them . . .*

–2002–

THE MARK OF YIG

Colin Gilman sat at the desk in his crowded study. The room was neither especially large nor small, but it seemed almost like a phone box because of the choking jam. Books and journals were crammed everywhere. A surprising number of these were his own published works, for Gilman was an avid and prolific writer in many fields. His titles spanned, it seemed, the whole register, dealing as they did with subjects as diverse as literary criticism, the history of violent crime, systems of esoteric thought and theology, parapsychology, and deviant sex. He worked, and sold, in both fiction and non-fiction genres. Yet despite their great diversity, the close reader of his *oeuvre* would not be long in discovering the common thread that tied all his many works together. Colin Gilman was a pioneer on the frontiers of consciousness.

He found the tether binding humanity to the conventional five senses altogether too restrictive. Concerned friends often joked that reality was just not good enough for Colin; rather, he would retort, he was convinced reality is bigger than most people think, and he wanted to see more of it. Thus his intensive and extensive researches. His books he regarded as so many research reports which he shared with the reading public. Reviewers called him a popularizer, damning him with faint praise, but he understood himself better: as a synthesizer. Today's scientific establishment, he reasoned, was too much blinded by its micro-specializations, and it took a look through the other end of the magnifier to see how their many insights fit together. This he tried to do.

Just now he was concerned with split-brain research and what it meant for the nature of consciousness. He had penned a couple of tomes about it already, hazarding the theory that efficient thinking and increased creativity might be enhanced if we would learn to play the two brain hemispheres off against each other, rather like both feet pedaling a bicycle. But now he was beginning to glimpse another possible step that no scientist had yet taken. What if the supposedly vestigial reptile part of the brain had more activity going on in it than the textbooks said? He had in fact come to suspect that it ought to be regarded as no less than a "third hemisphere" of the brain. The challenge, then, was to figure out just what role it played along with the two others.

The trouble was that Colin was no medical man. In matters such as this he was dependent on the researches of others. But why must he wait for crumbs to fall from their table? Why not try to prod research along a bit for once? It might work. Colin sat back, spun the swivel chair half-way round, and gazed up to the ceiling, which had a number of posters tacked to it, but he saw none of them. He was searching through the vault of possibilities, the steamer trunk of schemes. Why humans look upward when they do this, he did not know, but it might make for a good book sometime, if Desmond Morris didn't beat him to it, that is.

Possibilities began to take shape and branch out to touch one another, like the ganglia in the brain. Hmmm. A call to his old friend Allen Enslin over at Oakdeene Sanatorium might yield some fruit. He had first come to know Allen while researching an early book called A *History of Perversion and Violent Crime*. He had arranged to interview some of the criminally insane patients at Oakdeene, and that with great profit. Allen seemed to understand and appreciate Colin's work. He might be willing to join him in an experiment now. Perhaps he could be brought round to see how it could assist in his own work, since Colin's provisional theory was that the old reptile brain harbored the most primal and atavistic impulses. If one could isolate these, even extinguish them, what might the future of the human enterprise be like? Perhaps no more leaden progress with two steps backward into savagery for every one into the light.

Colin was firm in his opinion that a certain vanguard of the populace, maybe 5% of them, possessed an extra something, call it the X Factor, that lent genius to some but seemed to make others into maniacs and madmen. There was a genius to evil, too, sometimes. Hitler had had it; so did Charles Manson, Jim Jones. But what made the difference between the superman and the monster? He now suspected it might be the degree to which this X Factor was filtered, channeled, through the reptile brain. It was certainly worth an experiment, and there was no point in putting off the call. Now where was Allen's extension number?

Colin did his best sell job, something he had a lot of experience doing, every time he took a new manuscript idea to one of his publishers. It was not long before he had Allen sold on the project. Basically what Dr. Enslin saw as their best option was to take one of the "lifers," a serial rapist perhaps, and administer a serum to suppress the activity of the relevant portion of the brain. Since there should be no immediate reaction, the best procedure would be simply to have the man under observation for a few weeks. In view of this, Allen assured him, Colin hardly need appear in person to witness the injection. There would be nothing to see. But Colin

Gilman hated to be restricted to the sidelines, so he insisted on being there, and to this Allen had no significant objection.

Half a week later Colin stood outside the two-way mirror opening into the padded cell of one of the brutish inmates of Oakdeene, a man well known as the Camside Ripper. He had not hoped for so ideal a test subject. He knew well the sanguine career of the Ripper, as he had devoted fully half a chapter to him in his book *The Children of Whitechapel.* Dr. Enslin had just administered the drug and was joining Colin in the observation booth while a couple of orderlies tried to soothe the big, hulking man who retained the childhood fear of inoculation. They seemed to have succeeded, and, though the men lingered in the cell just to make sure, Allen and Colin had begun chatting in the booth, expecting no immediate reaction.

Colin was just telling his friend which of two directions his next book might take, depending on the eventual outcome of this test and others like it, when suddenly it appeared that they might not be in for so long a wait after all. The human beast at bay in the glass cage before them was getting agitated, very agitated indeed. Something seemed to be wrong with the microphone, so the ensuing scene was played out in eerie silence, at least from where Colin and Allen stood in helpless paralysis. Other orderlies had appeared from nowhere and were frantically trying to get the cell door open, but for some reason it refused to cooperate. One of the men inside must have somehow jammed the thing in a desperate attempt to exit.

With incredible speed the Ripper had exploded into a supernova of violence. Springing upon the orderlies, he proceeded to vivisect them, tearing their muscular forms to great, ragged hunks of gore. Very little wall space remained the original shade of hospital beige, most of the surface now running red. Before the impotent and incredulous eyes of the men safely outside the cell, the man-monster began to greedily devour the nearest charnel fragments. By the time, moments later, that the security officers managed to burst the door in and shoot him dead, the thing had seized what remained of the buttocks section of one body and was enthusiastically raping it.

Colin had seen enough, enough both to sicken him and to destroy his first hypothesis. Allen stared at him in shock, almost as if he blamed his friend for the tragedy, though there was no way either man might have predicted it. The doctor darted through the door and around the partition to gaze firsthand on the shambles of flesh, as if his skills could be of any use. As for the dumbfounded Colin, as soon as he could collect his wits he judged it best to leave without further words. He would call within the week to apologize. He only hoped he hadn't made things unbearably difficult for Dr. Enslin at the Sanatorium.

Back in his flat, he tried to slough off the shock of what he had witnessed with the aid of a good, stiff drink. The drink didn't hurt, but, as usual, the most effective healing balm proved to be speculation. He could give his emotions the night off by taking refuge in the intellect.

He now found himself firmly ensconced at square one. Ought he to abandon this line of research completely? But no, whatever had happened at Oakdeene, it surely meant there was something to his idea of the power of the reptile brain. He soon felt a new hypothesis beginning to gestate. The Camside Ripper had erupted into savagery precisely when the emissions of the reptile brain had been *blocked*. Was it possible, then, that the relation was the opposite of what he had first suspected? Could it possibly be that the source of the animalistic passions in the human breast was some part of the "advanced" *mammalian* brain? If that were so, it would imply that the role of the archaic reptile brain was instead to *hinder* these impulses, to dilute them, to cool them down with the slow, calm logic of the cold-blooded reptile.

The thought staggered him. What if the task *were* to inhibit the passions of the mammal brain? Here we might be talking about a significant twist in the evolutionary path. Before, he had considered it a matter of eradicating the baser instincts by cutting them off at their source. But if the negative passions were simply one of the vivid colors on the palette of the dual mammalian brain, who knew what drastic effects might come from tampering with them? What would happen to the other emotions?

One thing seemed sure: he would get no further help from Oakdeene. One choice faced him. Would he dare to use *himself* as an experimental subject? The Faustian lure was something he'd lived with all his life. He didn't imagine that in the final analysis he'd be able to resist it now. But it would be a moot point unless he could find out what sort of chemicals would do the job. He'd have to give that some thought for the next few days. He must have *some* contacts *somewhere* who'd know what to do. And there were other things to be busy with in the meantime. One of them was a good night's rest.

He awoke mid-morning and clicked on the television, looking for regional or local news. And there it was: the atrocity of the day before. He'd been afraid they wouldn't be able to keep this one hushed up, despite the fact that Oakdeene's administrators had learned over the years to do some surprising feats of public relations and media disinformation. He listened for a few minutes, then sampled a few other television and radio broadcasts, and finally turned both machines off, satisfied that his good name was not being connected with the Oakdeene business, at least not yet.

After a shower, Colin fired up the computer and typed away for a while on a new, revised edition of one of his earlier books, *Heroes of Heresy*. It was a rogue's gallery of spiritual dissidents who had dared reject the conventional understanding of the world, and tried to make the world over in the image of their own sometimes peculiar visions. There were Swedenborg, Jan of Leiden, Enoch Bowen, Joanna Southcott, James Jezreel, and the Ghost Dance Prophet Smohalla: a motley crew, to be sure. He let himself get lost in the not unpleasant job of dialoguing with the earlier version of himself who had written this book so many years ago. If his other projects allowed the time, he'd love to rewrite the book completely; some of his subsequent researches shed interesting new light on the subject of outlaw religion. And then the phone rang.

Surprisingly it was Allen Enslin. Even more amazing, he wasn't furious. "Listen, old man, I'm sorry for my attitude yesterday. I know you weren't to blame. It just rather blew my circuits, I'm afraid. I see a lot in my line of work, but nothing even in the Ripper's previous repertoire came close to what we saw. In fact, the outcome of the experiment has made me more convinced that you're onto something important. No, don't worry, I'm in no trouble. I grieve for those poor bastards he took with him, but nobody's going to be very surprised a chap like our Ripper goes wild and kills people."

Colin's eyes widened. This seemed impossibly good luck. Here's hoping it held.

"That's a relief to know, Allen. Still and all, I'm quite sorry the way it turned out. I must say you handled yourself superbly with those reporters. And thanks for keeping my name out of it. But tell me this: if you're still willing to help me in this research, can you give me a bit of insight . . . ?"

In the end Allen's surmise was that the more hopeful approach was not to suppress the mammalian instincts but to increase the output of the reptilian brain, just the opposite of what they'd done before. Such advice as this Allen was happy to give, but he simply could not subject any more of the poor devils in the asylum to such guinea pig treatment. Damned souls they might be, but it was not his privilege to play games with them. "I realize that, Allen, and that's not what I'm asking. If you can administer the necessary drug, I think I'd be willing to undergo the process myself . . . Yes, I rather doubted your professional ethics would accommodate that, either. Let's put it this way: can you tell me, purely theoretically now, what

494

one would do, just speculatively, if one wanted to set up an experiment like this? Let's say it's for one of my books. Maybe I won't try it myself. Maybe some animal experiments first."

"All right, Colin. I'll assume you mean that. You'd have to be crazy to try it on yourself after what happened to the Ripper. And if it's animal experiments you want, I could help you with that. Let's try to get together in a couple of weeks, shall we?"

In a day or two, true to his word, Allen had written up a rough prospectus of what chemicals might be required for a series of experiments and posted it to his friend. But of course Colin Gilman was not in the least interested in animal experiments. What he wanted to test was the effect on the human disposition if the reptile brain was stimulated, and no amount of tests on lower animals could ever tell him that.

So, list in hand, he was off to some alternative medicine people he knew in this or that far quarter of the city. London harbored a great many things in its nooks and crannies invisible to those not expressly looking for them. Over the years Colin had had reason to search out a good number of them. Just now he betook himself to a man, sort of a modern shaman, who dealt in all manner of unorthodox substances used by the AIDS underground. These wretches would try anything in hopes they might chance upon the Philosopher's Stone of a cure.

As luck would have it, most of the substances he needed were ready to hand. Feeling optimistic, Colin even hinted at his intention for the drug, only to find a keen interest on the part of his benefactor, a "doctor" Albert Phineas. The man had once been a practitioner of orthodox medicine but had lost his license over certain experiments with drugs and obscure surgical procedures. The good doctor continued his practice unofficially, circumspectly presenting himself as a dealer in exotic health food and dietary supplements. Colin had come to know him a couple of years earlier when working on an article on homeopathic medicine and faith healing. Phineas denied none of the risks that so concerned Allen Enslin, but he shared with Colin the pioneer spirit and was quite willing to assist him.

The day arrived, and Colin, sleepless all the previous night, greeted it with a mixture of anticipation and fear. He was fairly sure that, whatever happened, he would soon mourn the loss of his old self as he knew it. Even should he find himself advancing to a new evolutionary plateau, the cost might be great in terms of those gentle emotions that made life livable. But in one way or another, he reasoned, it was a sacrifice all pioneers of science had to be willing to make. There can be no advance,

495

no adventure, without risk.

When Dr. Phineas arrived, he announced that there would be little actually to do. The administration of the drugs would not even require sedation. Colin insisted on the application of firm wrist restraints he had secured from a nearby S-&-M shop. He didn't want to chance any repeat of the horrors of the Oakdeene experiment, no matter how unlikely they seemed. These precautions Dr. Phineas dismissed with a laugh, though in the end he humored him. He did warn, however, that there would be a danger of temporary blindness. Given the meandering circuitry of the brain, a temporary obstruction of the optic nerves was not unlikely, though this should clear up in a week or two. Even then Colin would find himself abnormally light-sensitive and should not venture outside without appropriate cover.

"Here goes, then," was all Colin could think of as he prepared to enter the stream of scientific destiny. The injection was no more daunting than donating blood. He did feel drowsy and soon fell asleep. When he woke up some hours later, his familiar time sense apparently gone, he was indeed quite blind. A small price to pay, he hoped, assuming the results would compensate him. Hearing him stir, Phineas came to his side and gently assured him that all was well. He stayed there for a few days, as it happened, feeling it his obligation to supervise his charge and see to his needs, until finally Colin announced he cared not to detain him further. Anticipating the blindness, he had for several days made a project of learning to navigate the interior of his flat, as well as the immediate neighborhood, blindfolded. He now felt sure he was able to be largely self-sufficient.

The days passed slowly. Yes, he could navigate the blocks around his flat, but reading and writing were beyond him. Colin played his entire collection of recordings two or three times until he grew sick of them. He grew mad with anticipation. At first there was relief that nothing overtly drastic had occurred. After that, he began to feel disappointment that nothing of any kind seemed to be happening except, of course, for his blindness. But then his impatience began imperceptibly to dwindle. A mood of increasing equanimity crept over him, finally something approaching impassivity.

As he grew reconciled to the waiting game, he decided to keep alert by a form of mental gymnastics. Why not attack a couple of the old windmills? The Ontological Argument of Saint Anselm, for instance. There was a brain-twister that continued to exasperate professional philosophers fully a millennium after the old Archbishop of Canterbury had tossed it, like the

Apple of Discord, into the philosophical tea party. That ought to keep him busy for a while!

But it didn't. Colin was at first sure that he had forgotten some turn of the argument, for it seemed so childishly simple that he was certain he must be doing the saint a disservice. But, no, that was it all right: "that than which nothing greater can be conceived." Special Relativity? Nothing to it!

It struck him suddenly that something had happened after all. He was able to inventory the contents of his mind and to analyze them with a clarity he had never before dreamt of. It seemed, in fact, that any direction in which he now turned the searchlight of his thought disclosed jigsaw puzzles with the hitherto-missing pieces ready to hand, Gordian knots which were as easy to unravel as a recalcitrant shoelace.

And yet he accepted all this with not the slightest hint of exultation or even excitement. This was his first signal that he had indeed paid an emotional price for his intellectual gain. Even this realization might have been expected to occasion alarm, but it was with a cool and detached curiosity that he began to contrive ways of testing his emotions. First he sought to exhume some tender scars of the past, the frustration from the old days before his recognition as a writer and thinker, when he had lived in the most makeshift of dwellings and spent his days, like the young Karl Marx, reading through as much of the British Museum Library as he could before closing time. But there was nothing there, just frozen memory, like accessing a data bank. Neither the echo of bitterness (they had called him one of the "Angry Young Men" back then) nor even nostalgia for a simpler time.

Not even lust answered his summons, as he tried to think of the women he'd bedded once he'd realized that even academics have their groupies. No remembered vision of breast or bottom titillated him in the least. No question: he had changed. He had, among other things, lost the ability to regret the loss. But then no harm done. He began to view the passions of the mammalian brain as an addiction well broken.

As the weeks passed, Colin Gilman came to relish the cool darkness as a most conducive atmosphere for quiet contemplation. But his sight did begin to return, recapitulating, he mused, the gradual dawn of light-sensitivity among his remote pre-reptilian ancestors. With the return of vision, however, came sharp pains, so he was in no hurry to open his eyes again. Finally Colin contrived a type of heavy veil through which he could just about see his way before him, though reading was still impossible. He judged that he would not need to wait much longer before making his discovery public.

And for this he thought he already had the suitable forum. He was scheduled to speak at a city auditorium to a group of business, academic, and civic leaders interested in questions of futurology: charting out the rapid impacts of new technologies and social trends. He had always found such audiences receptive to his lectures, as he was one of the few who kept his finger upon so many pulses at once. His promised topic was that of the utility of the computer in enhancing the learning ability of students, soldiers, and employees. He had been engaged to develop certain suggestions, first broached in his book *The Computer in your Skull*, to the effect that mastery of the computer would function like bio-feedback enabling the user to employ the learning systems of his own brain with increased efficiency.

Now he had, to say the least, found something of a short-cut to the same end. And there was much bigger news where that came from. Later he would be prepared to submit to whatever testing the echelons of science might require of him, but for now he would reveal himself to the same audience he always addressed: the interested layman.

His sight had improved still more when the date arranged for the lecture arrived. He did his best to get dressed up for the event, nonetheless sure that he looked a mess and must be as pale as an albino from his long seclusion. Summoning a taxicab, Colin made his way to the auditorium. The day was cold and, for him, acutely uncomfortable. He had foreseen this and located an old pair of gloves, which clothing he usually eschewed on account of their clumsiness. He did not need a set of lecture notes and could hardly have read them in any case. He intended simply to describe the series of events (skipping the unfortunate mishap at Oakdeene) and the results to which they had led.

Once arrived at the auditorium, he asked to be led to the gentleman who was to introduce him, a prominent educator at one of the city's technical institutes. Colin apologized for his peculiar appearance and requested that, given his still-painful sensitivity to light, there be no spotlight on the lectern. He would take off the heavy veil so that he might be heard, but then his tender eyes must have protection. His host readily agreed and explained to the assembled crowd as he introduced the renowned Mr. Colin Gilman.

Colin stepped hesitantly up to the podium with rather less ease than he had expected. But he got there. He grasped the edges of the podium and began to speak, thanking the audience for their kind reception, commending them on their forward-looking interest, assuring them that their evening would be an investment of time well-spent. A silent note of tension from the audience greeted his announcement that he would be taking certain liberties with his assigned topic. But he had them on his side again when he promised them, as it were, front page news. He had started to outline his original thinking about the suppression of the reptilian brain when the trouble began. Later he guessed that the word had not gotten to one of the men in charge of power and lights in the facility. Thinking the lack of a spotlight an embarrassing error, someone must have sought to rectify it. Colin found himself in mid-sentence when the spotlight fell full force upon him. The half-blind speaker reeled from the ocular pain as if struck by a fist. The audience groaned with empathy, but this turned at once into a sea of gasps and screams as they panicked.

Colin's own lancing agony gave way to fear, as the sound of shrieking told him something had gone dreadfully wrong. Had the flash come from some electrical failure? Whatever was going on, he was absolutely vulnerable. He tried to sort out his confusion by calling out questions which no one seemed to hear or to answer: was the hall on fire? Was there a sniper? Anything might have happened. Only his new cold-blooded equanimity, rapidly returning now, saved him from bolting in panic like the rest. For him flight would have been as deadly as whatever threat might have descended, since he could scarcely see where he was going.

But then it occurred to him that he *could* see, better than he had expected, at any rate. Though still sensitive, his eyes must have recovered a great deal of their former strength after all. Colin had timidly lingered among the shadows for too long. Now he found he could easily behold the fast-emptying auditorium—*and the puzzling absence of any apparent threat!*

A gunman might crouch concealed in the balcony, he theorized, so he made at once for stage left, from whence he had first emerged. No one left here either! Lurching about, bumping painfully into a half-dozen shadowy obstacles, he finally tripped and fell head-on into a full-length mirror. It came free of its hanger and fell to the floor with a bang, but miraculously it did not shatter.

Colin stood puffing and gave the mirror a look. It would be the first time he had seen his familiar features in many a week. He expected to see a scabby outbreak of itchy psoriasis which had irritated him for days. But he saw something else.

In fact, he saw some*one* else, or thought he did. Staring back at him was something on the order of an iguana's head perched atop a rumpled suit of clothes. He had not the emotions to share the revulsion experienced by the crowd (he now knew its occasion). But he was numb nonetheless. His

499

first thought, when one came, was simply to realize his eyelids had days ago stopped blinking. Up to now he had not marked it.

He looked for his discarded veil but could not locate it. It was getting dark out, the short winter days doing him a favor. He had remained selfconsciously gloved, since the temperature of the place seemed too low for him, and now he pulled up his coat collar and hoped he could get back to his flat unnoticed. Calling a cab was obviously out of the question, so he decided to walk it, keeping to the back streets, no easy task with the limits on his sight. But neither did he relish encountering either unsuspecting wayfarers or the police who must soon come investigating. He took the plunge, hastening out the door and down the sidewalk.

Colin passed glowing tavern doors and red-lit brothel windows, reflecting with inhuman calm that he should have no more welcome in the havens of the once-kindred human race. He felt no sorrow at the fact, only observed it. But there was a sense of emptiness. He was now truly a loner among the common run of humanity. And he did not expect they would easily tolerate his strange company. But where to turn?

One street looked almost familiar as he neared a sidewalk church. There must be scores of these, Salvation Army storefronts and obscure Holiness sects, all over London. But he doubted there would be any welcome for such as he under any of their roofs. For here he was, the serpent of Eden in person! But someone was coming out the door, a drunk, oblivious. Colin turned away as if to avoid a blow and almost lost his footing with the surprising momentum of his own motion. Righting himself, he paused to risk a glance up at the half-familiar sign on the door.

Yes, he had visited this one some years ago while researching *The Far Reaches of Religion* for the BBC. There would be a cheaply appointed chapel within, manned by a caretaker who doubled as pastor of this tiny flock, The Church of the Ophite Gnosis. Some impulse made him enter as he effortlessly retrieved the filed-away memories of that interview long ago.

The portly, unimpressive-looking rector had assured him that his church represented a revival of the real Christianity as taught by the ancient Ophite Gnostics whose belief was that Christ was like Prometheus. He had visited Adam and Eve to bring them enlightenment against the peevish threats of Jehovah who wanted to keep all knowledge as his private preserve. "Yea, hath God said ye shall not eat of the tree which is in the midst of the garden, lest ye die? Nay, but your eyes will be opened, and you shall be as gods, knowing good and evil." The little, pot-bellied man in his preposterous ceremonial robes had proudly shown Colin the various books of lore which supposedly proved all this, from *The Hypostasis of the Archons* to some treatise of the church father Epiphanius, to the infamous *Book of Dead Names* by the medieval heretic Martin the Gardener. At the time this sect had not impressed him more than a dozen other fringe-religions whose eccentric members believed themselves in touch with flying saucers or the ascended masters or Essenes from Lemuria. But now some inkling made him change his course and step inside.

The sounds of traffic and of loud revelry from nearby pubs and bawdy houses seemed somehow far away in here. At first he was alone. But then, perhaps drawn by the signal of some unseen electric eye, a custodian appeared from behind a beaded curtain. It was the same man, a little grayer, a little plumper, Colin thought. Also a little blinder, since the man made no move to recoil from him as the others had. Instead, embarrassingly, the little man went to his knees, gingerly doubtless on account of his arthritis, and began to mumble a prayer. Colin then realized the man was praying to *him*.

The old fellow hoisted himself back to his feet by supporting himself with the edge of one of the chairs they used for pews.

"I *knew* you would come, my Lord," said the man, not venturing to meet his guest's eyes. And yet it did not seem his reluctance could be laid to fear. If anything, it was reverence.

"You remember me, do you? I'm surprised, as it's been some years. I thought I did fair by you in my book." The scene was absurd. Colin felt like Scrooge speaking to the materialized ghost of his own past, a phantom of reverie. "But how *can* you recognize me after what's happened? You needn't worry, I'm not going to harm you. You must help me, though."

"I rejoice to serve the Lord Yig, the revealer, even that Old Serpent whom men blaspheme as Satan. Let my Lord command."

"Look, my friend, I don't know what you're on about, but . . ."

"Your arrival was foretold to us by your brethren. You will soon understand if you do not now. It is mine to direct your steps."

"Direct me? Where?" He knew not how, but Colin had begun to sense a rightness in what the man said, as if an after-effect of the experiment had been to reawaken deep and dormant memories. "I suppose direction is one thing I could use. Everything's gone topsy-turvy for me, that's for sure."

The man motioned him to silence, then drew back the curtain and opened a hidden door. He indicated Colin should go on in, and then followed immediately. "I will show you the Holy of Holies. None but our eyes may see it save on the High Day of Initiation." Now he had produced a small metallic box, baroquely inscribed, that came open with some rusty resistance. He pressed a button, and a dim blue ray shone down from a hidden place amid the hanging drapes. The light fell directly upon an asymmetrical block of basalt no more than 10 inches round at its widest diameter. It was like a distorted dice cube, and every black surface bore peculiar carved runes. After a moment's scrutiny, Colin rather half-fancied he knew the thing. He turned to the man and uttered one word:

Ixaxar.

His companion nodded.

Colin shifted his gaze again, staring off into the unillumined recesses of the sanctum. He felt the first hint of emotion he had felt for a long time. There came a mental image of happier days among the brilliant green hills, of sunning oneself and feeling the caress of rocky bank, crystalline fountain, and grassy blanket. And then there was the longing of regret and loss after the coming of those who had shown no mercy to any not of their kind. His people had been driven underground only to emerge stealthily and take sporadic revenge against their usurpers. They had been vilified as the Little People of the hills, their once great glory reduced to a story to scare infants off to bed.

For some time Colin stood transfixed, gazing again at, or into, the strange angles of the Black Stone. When his reverie was done, he knew what he had to do, where he had to go. Without further words, words which he sensed his vocal apparatus was less and less capable of forming, he strode over to the cellar staircase and found his way into a hidden opening in the basement wall. From there a newly recovered instinct led him to thread his way through a series of forgotten tunnels connecting many of the tenements and alleyways in the district.

Exiting a drainage tunnel hours later, he made for box car transit into the Welsh hills, where he headed unerringly for certain coal shafts long ago abandoned on account of unexplained disappearances there. Beneath blind lanterns and the shells of naked bulbs strung from the ceilings, he picked his way through rotten boards and ore heaps, penetrating at last into the unknown windings that led to the deep glories of red-litten Yoth.

The London news made much of the strange disappearance of famous author Colin Gilman. Fanciful theories circulated wildly. Even the relatively sober *Times* suggested the disappearance was part of a hoax designed to heighten public interest in a new book the author must have written about flying saucers. No doubt he himself would turn up hale and hardy, claiming to have ridden in one. The tabloids framed with lurid color shots of naked women a supposedly "inside" report that poor Gilman had met a bad end while researching another of his sex crime novels.

Allen Enslin and Dr. Phineas each wondered which report to credit, though both had inklings that something far stranger might have happened. But all such newsprint rumors only caused the old caretaker of the Church of the Ophite Gnosis to smile. It was a poor world whose wildest fancies paled next to the truth. Clutching the latest of the news editions in one hand, with the other he retrieved a crumpled note brought to him by secret means. In it he was pleased to read that one who had been known as Colin Gilman now sported in the pale currents of unguessed grottos in the serene company of souls untroubled by the degradations of hot mammal blood. Always a loner, he now rejoiced to be an outsider among those who still claimed the name and heritage of man.

–2002–

ACUTE SPIRITUAL FEAR

The great Gothic edifice of the Chapel of Miskatonic University's School of Divinity rose like some primal granite cliff through the frozen fireworks of the brilliant autumn leaves. Philip Brown reflected, on his way to the Great Hall, that sights like these were almost reason enough to have chosen the venerable old New England Seminary. Miskatonic's divinity program attracted few students these days, since most who aspired to the ministry in the Congregational Church, its sponsoring body, were impatient with the conservative traditionalism of the place. Here the debates between Calvinism and Arminianism were still in fashion, and the echoes of the old Puritan divines had not yet completely died away. This was the theological cosmos in which Philip delighted to live.

It was New Student Orientation Week, and as he inspected the various displays of campus clubs, he naturally gravitated to some and equally avoided others without a second thought. The Solidarity with Central America Caucus was not for him, nor the Liberation Army, an updating of the old Salvation Army in light of Latin American Liberation Theology. The Feminist Sisterhood left him cold, too. He was cut from traditional clerical cloth and viewed the role of the minister much as it had existed in the previous century: something of a hybrid between personal counselor and pulpit theologian. Social activism was all right for some, but Philip did not see his call to the ministry in these terms. Nor was this the only respect in which he felt himself an outsider in his generation. Perhaps the old ways lingered longest in New England, but he had to admit that they were passing even here.

Philip had all but decided, by the time he reached the end of the in-door bazaar, that none of the student organizations suited him. But then he noticed one intriguing hand-lettered sign. It said THE MISKATONIC SOCRATIC CLUB. This name he recognized, for one of his favorite authors, C. S. Lewis, a champion of traditional orthodoxy if ever there was one, had founded the Socratic Club at Oxford. His goal had been to provide a forum for discussing the great philosophical issues of the day. If that's what the name denoted here, he would definitely be interested. He picked up a leaflet which looked hopeful, as he waited for someone to return to the booth. In a moment, a middler or senior appeared with a

504

steaming cup of coffee and offered a friendly hand.

"Name's Glenn Bridley. I discovered the Club when I was a freshman, too. It certainly livened up my years here in sleepy old Miskatonic. They started the Club ten years ago because some students felt they needed to hear more perspectives than they got in class. Just the old-time religion there, if you know what I mean."

"I happen to like the old-time religion," Philip replied, a tad defensively. "But I see your point. There's a big world out there, religiously like every other way. We need to know about it, I guess."

The other's smile returned. "That's the true Socratic spirit, Phil! We're having a debate next week. Why don't you stop by? The schedule's in that leaflet you're holding."

Philip gave the pamphlet a glance, then looked up. "Eschatology, huh? The doctrine of the end of the world. I just might come! I cut my teeth on that stuff. Hal Lindsey, all that kind of thing."

Glenn smiled knowingly. "Don't tell me; you're one of us 'Afghanistan War babies'?"

A blank stare. "What do you mean?"

A lot of us were 'born again' back in 1980 around the time when the Soviets invaded Afghanistan. Lindsey and a lot of the other paperback prophets had everybody on the edge of their seats thinking Armageddon was right around the corner. Had *me* convinced. I 'got religion' and started praying hard to escape the Great Tribulation. The whole thing blew over, but, hey, at least it's coming into the faith with a bang, huh?"

Philip laughed, too. "I know just what you mean! I've never heard the phrase, but I guess I'm one of them, too! War babies, that's a good one. You know, Glenn, when I look back at those days, sometimes I feel like a real jerk for getting so excited over a silly scare like that. But I can't deny that when I thought Jesus was coming back any moment, I had a zeal for the Lord I've never been able to recapture since."

"Yeah, right, Phil . . . ," the other mused. "I know what you mean. You 'put away childish things,' but you're sort of sorry to see some of them go. And the Lord said that it's the ones with the faith of a child that make it into the kingdom of heaven. Where do you strike the balance?"

Philip thought a moment. "Sometimes I think that it's striking a balance that's the problem. Jesus wasn't balanced. People called him crazy. Mother Theresa's not balanced. Neither was Gandhi. Maybe 'balance' is another word for compromise."

Glenn's eyes were fixed on the newcomer with a certain gleam. "I think you'd make a great Socratic Clubber! And not a bad friend, either!" They shook hands again. Phil went on to the library with a new sense of at-home-ness. The Miskatonic campus no longer felt such an alien place. He thought he'd heard there was a student position open at the Hoag Library, and he wanted to verify this. Maybe he'd apply for it.

The next two weeks were a whirl of activity. There were last minute registration mix-ups to iron out, permissions to get for admission to closed classes. Philip felt he just had to get into that seminar on the lesser-known Puritan theologians. He had long been intrigued by the life and writings of the Reverend Abijah Hoadley, a Congregationalist parson who had served one of the oldest standing Congregational churches in this region. Hoadley had written a lesser-known counterpart to Cotton Mather's notorious *Magnalia Christi*. It was called *Of Evill Sorceries donne in New-England of Daemons in no Humane Shape* and it promoted much the same sort of fabulous rumor and superstition as Mather's volume. In the places where the two compendia of marvels overlapped, there were curious differences of a striking nature. Philip thought he might try a research paper running down local sources of some of the legends. Had there been any remotely factual basis to any of them?

His classes started out unspectacularly, with the calm dogmatism he had expected and indeed appreciated. Over lunch at the Arkham House of Pizza, a local franchise of a small statewide chain that served up the best Greek-style pizza he had ever tasted, Philip got into a friendly debate with Sue Millman, a fellow first-year student. He had taken exception to Sue's characterization of the faculty as "a bunch of old mossbacks."

"I don't see how you can speak that way, Sue. After all, aren't they just 'defending the faith once for all delivered unto the saints', as Jude says?"

"That's how they dignify the fact that none of them has read a new book in the past thirty years. Get real, Phil! History passed this place by long ago. They say Dr. Nicole actually falls asleep in his own lectures! Once he was half-way through his notes before he realized he was in the wrong classroom! And old Dr. Kline! You know why he's so sure Adam and Eve were literal people? 'Cause he knew them personally!" He couldn't help chuckling at this, and that broke the building tension.

Claude LaValle entered the fray. He was one of the few students in the ministerial program who signed up for courses in the seminary's vestigial Biblical Studies program. He would pursue a career in teaching, not a parish, when he was done. "Sue's right. I'm thinking of transferring over to Harvard Div. The Bible profs here hardly know what historical criticism is. I asked about D. F. Strauss once last semester and Dr. Stuart thought I meant the composer! I even hear there are important biblical manuscripts

506

here that the faculty never even consult, probably don't even know about."
Philip had to admit this might be true. He knew they still used the old
King James Bible in classes. Even he had switched to the New American
Standard Version some years ago.

"I'm beginning to see the need for something like the Socratic Club."
Philip suggested. "Are either of you planning to go to their debate this
evening?"

"What's the topic?" asked Sue.

"Eschatology. You know, the end of the world."

"Yeah, right. Like I'm going to worry about that. Count me out,
Phil."

"Sorry, old man," added Claude, "but I've got prior plans, too."

The trio split up, Philip and Sue heading off to their respective field
work assignments. Sue was working with a battered women's center.
Philip's task was more traditional. He was filling in for the semester as a
youth minister for a small congregation over in Saugus. And if he didn't
get moving he would be embarrassingly late for his first session. So he
checked for his road map and headed for the parking lot.

As he drove the narrow, winding New England lanes, punctuated as
they were with green and white road signs for towns with quaint names
like "Pride's Crossing" and "Folly Hill," he almost felt he had left the
quiet expanse of Essex County for the living pages of Bunyan's *Pilgrim's
Progress*.

He turned on the scraping wipers of his feeble Volkswagen Beetle to
scatter the tears falling from the lowering Puritan skies. As he did so, he
began to reflect on whether he, too, was something of a "mossback."
(Actually that had been only one of the least colorful epithets Sue, an
excitingly modern woman in every sense, had used for religious
traditionalists.) Maybe the way to recapture some of the excitement that
had marked the early years of his spiritual pilgrimage was to experiment
with new ideas.

But could anything new thrive here in these old precincts of Cotton
Mather and Abijah Hoadley?

As was so often true in dying parishes like this one, the youth of the
church were few and scarcely interested in their parents' religion. For
most, MTV was their church, various decadent Rock and Roll stars their
idols. Philip could see he had his work cut out for him. It was hard to
relate to them; when he was their age, he had been busy studying scripture
and trying to decipher whether Henry Kissinger or Yuri Andropov was
more likely to be the Antichrist. He had precious little in common with

the few teenagers who showed up for the meeting. This first session had made that abundantly clear.

So it was not with much enthusiasm that, some hours later, Philip parked outside his dorm and rushed, skipping dinner, over to another dorm lounge where the Socratic Club must already be underway.

He found the door and tried to edge his way in as inconspicuously as he might. He was surprised at the number of seminarians, plus a few of the other University students, crowding the lounge. Who would have thought the end of the world would be so popular a topic? But perhaps the recent turmoil in every corner of the globe, wars and rumors of wars on every newscast, had made it a live question again. Two speakers stood at borrowed classroom lecterns. The first, white-haired Professor Jenkins, was just finishing up. Philip heard enough to know it was the predictable party line: Christ would return at the close of the Millennium when the gospel would have permeated the whole earth, defeating the powers of evil once and for all. He had to admit it did sound a little stale.

As the venerable old academic seated himself uneasily on a flimsy piece of lounge furniture, the other rose to speak. He was a youthful-looking man named Winthrop who pastored a Congregational parish in the nearby town of Foxfield. Philip didn't recognize him, but he thought he remembered the leaflet saying the man was a Miskatonic alumnus. And it was beginning to get interesting.

"Let me suggest a rather different perspective than the one so ably set forth by our previous speaker. I wonder how many of you are familiar with the Gospel of Thomas." Here he raised a thin brown hardcover book and opened it to the middle. "This is a collection of sayings attributed to our Lord, fully as old as our New Testament Gospels, but excluded from the biblical canon in the fourth century. It was rediscovered in 1945 in the sands of Chenoboskion, Egypt. Here's a passage germane to our subject, in saying number . . . um, 51. 'His disciples said unto him: When will the repose of the dead come about, and when will the new world come? He said to them: What you expect has come, but you know it not.'

"Suppose that's true. Suppose in the providence of God this scripture has come to light in our day to warn us we ought not to be looking *forward* for the kingdom of God, but *backward*. Can it be that the Second Coming of Christ has indeed already occurred? And that, just like two thousand years ago, we, the religious know-it-alls, failed to recognize him?"

The earlier speaker could not contain himself. Rising as if by reflex, he sputtered, "Now, listen here, young man! Our Lord has made it quite clear in Matthew chapter 24 that his glorious Second Advent would be
508

unmistakable, that his coming would be as when the lightning flashes forth from one end of the firmament to the other, that every eye shall see him!" His face had purpled, and he seemed altogether too outraged to speak further.

The Reverend Mr. Winthrop was not flustered. "Dr. Jenkins, with all due respect, I'd say you have your quote from Jesus and I have mine. Him who has ears to hear, let him hear." With that, the tempestuous exchange came to an abrupt end.

The student crowd began to disperse, some apparently deep in thought, others no doubt eager to get back to their reading assignments. Those immersed in biblical Hebrew and Greek courses, poor devils, could think of little else. But Philip, who certainly had work of his own to attend to, nonetheless made it a point to seek out the heretical Reverend Winthrop.

"Excuse me, sir."

The man turned with an expression of affable interest. "Yes, young man?"

"To tell you the truth, I almost feel guilty talking to you. You see, I suppose I agree with Dr. Jenkins. At least that's the way I've always been taught. But what you say is intriguing, fascinating, really, and I'd like to hear more. Do you have a few minutes?"

The Reverend Winthrop looked at his watch. "Well . . . I do have to be back for a deacons meeting at six, and I've got to check in with a parishioner in Mercy Hospital . . . but, yes, I think I can spare twenty minutes or so. How about a cup of coffee over at the snack bar?"

Once the two of them were seated, ritually consuming a pair of coffee and Danishes, Philip spoke all in a rush, as if to a confessor. "It's just that I miss that zeal I once knew when I believed Christ would come again at any moment. I eventually admitted that was naive, that Christians have been predicting the Second Coming for 2,000 years, and they were always wrong. But what you said, well, it does sound heretical, like Dr. Jenkins said, but maybe Sue is right, and he *is* a mossback like some of the faculty."

Winthrop burst into laughter. "You said it, I didn't! He was the same when I was a student here. He's a good man, but you're not liable to hear anything new from him, that's for sure."

Philip smiled and continued. "If what you say is true, it would be just electrifying! Amazing! It would like being back with the original disciples following the Lord Jesus himself!" The wistfulness, the growing will to believe, was evident with every word, and none of it was lost on the older man.

"Congratulations, young Mr. Brown. Unlike some, you can see quite clearly what's at stake here. It becomes far more than a matter of theology, of whose doctrine is truer. We would be talking about the rebirth of the Christian faith. And what does St. Paul say about faith turning into sight?

"Look at the time! I really must be going. But, here, let me give you my number. Let's talk again. Meantime, why don't you look up this verse of scripture and think about it?" He scribbled a brief citation on a napkin, folded it and passed it to Philip.

Back in his dorm room, Philip hastened to his desk and grabbed up his Bible. During the walk back he had tried to place the chapter and verse number, but with no luck. Here it was. Matthew 17:10-12. "And his disciples asked him, saying, 'Why then do the scribes say that Elijah must come first?' And he answered and said, 'Elijah is coming and will restore all things; but I say to you, that Elijah already came, and they did not recognize him, but did to him whatever they wished. So also the son of man is going to suffer at their hands.'"

Philip looked up from the text, perhaps staring into space, perhaps praying. But in a moment his reverie was interrupted by a knock at his open door. "Phil! I saw you at the meeting. How'd you like it?"

"Glenn, I have to admit, it's really set me to thinking. I'm entertaining new ideas I would have rejected out of hand only days ago. And I don't mind telling you it's not very comfortable!"

Glenn sat down on the bed next to him. "I know what you mean, old buddy. I've been there myself. I remember my first semester. I came in here thinking I had it all sowed up. God had called me, and I just needed some practical know-how, or so I thought. It wasn't long before I was doubting everything I ever believed and then some! Theological education does that to you, and it's good that it does, I think. No other way to maturity."

"I suppose you're right, Glenn. But this idea that the Second Coming of Christ has already happened . . . ! That he came again and went unnoticed, and, if I'm reading this passage right, that he might even have suffered again . . . I don't know. That's tough to absorb!"

"Again, Phil, I've been there. I know what you're going through."

At this Philip turned and stared at his new friend with wide eyes. "What? You mean you believe this? That Christ has already returned?"

Glenn laughed and said, "Don't look so startled, for Pete's sake! I was the one who arranged for Reverend Winthrop to come speak, though I did think he'd have a bit more of a chance to air his views!"

"Does the whole Socratic Club believe this way?"

510

Glenn paused to consider what seemed to Philip a simple question. "I'd rather not speak for anyone but myself. But I'm sure I'm not alone."

"Okay, Glenn, then I've got to ask you this question. I wanted to ask Winthrop, but he had to rush out. You must have some specific idea of who it was, don't you? I mean, if Christ returned already, was it somebody you have a name for? Or are you trying to identify him? Waiting for him to reveal himself?"

"Yes to all of the above," Glenn replied. It's complicated. But let me give you a couple of clues. Maybe you'll guess. We think that the pattern of his coming would be the same both times. So you have to look for a candidate, so to speak, who was born of a virgin, a humble country girl. There would be signs in the heavens to signal the birth, maybe not a star necessarily, but, let's say, thunder and lightning. And that's where Dr. Jenkins's Matthew quote fits in: that's the lightning flashing from one end of the skies to the other.

"And he'd be marked by physical ugliness, because Isaiah predicted, 'He had no form or comeliness that we should look at him, and no beauty that we should desire him. He was despised and rejected of men; a man of sorrows and acquainted with grief; and as one from whom men hide their faces he was despised, and we esteemed him not.' You'd even expect him finally to be set upon by the authorities and killed, then to rise from the dead and ascend into heaven to rejoin his Father."

"And you're saying this has happened to somebody else in recent history?" Philip's initial incredulity had returned with a vengeance.

"I'm saying more than that, Phil." Every trace of casual conversation had drained out of Glenn's voice now. "I'm saying it happened to somebody in this very state. Some of it even happened on our own campus."

What Glenn said began to strike echoes in the recesses of Philip's brain. He had heard something, something that sounded like this, but he never saw the significance in it that Glenn seemed to see.

"You're not talking about that Whateley guy, are you? That must have been, what . . . fifty years ago?"

"Sixty-seven, to be exact. What do you already know, Phil?"

"What I saw was some kind of 'In Search Of' show on TV. It was one of those Loch Ness Monster kind of things, where they 'investigated' some local sightings of a creature. As I remember, it boiled down to some horribly deformed lunatic, somebody that looked like the Elephant Man or something, right? And he was killed on campus by a Doberman. And this all happened to occur just before a hurricane up in Dunwich, right? The survivors they interviewed were full of wild tales of the guy being born

511

without a human father, having an invisible brother who rose into the sky . . . I'm surprised I remember that much of it, to tell you the truth. All rumor and exaggeration, like the Bermuda Triangle."

"You know what you sound like, Phil? Just like one of those modernists, the Bible critics who have an explanation for everything, 'cause they just can't believe in the supernatural. Do you think Jesus walked on the stepping stones in the Sea of Galilee, too? And the resurrection appearances, they were probably just hallucinations, weren't they?"

Philip was not used to having such accusations leveled at him. It was precisely to avoid that kind of teaching that he had sought out this, the most traditional of theological seminaries. "You know that's not how I believe!"

"Phil, be careful that you don't wind up like the old scribes who dismissed Jesus as a devil and a madman. Don't close your mind like they did. If it happened once, it could happen again. And what if it *has* happened again? Wouldn't you want to be a part of it? I know for a fact you would!"

For this, Philip had no answer. As outlandish as the thing sounded, he still found himself excited by the prospect—just like the old days! He suddenly realized he wasn't really arguing with Glenn; he was really trying to fight down his own rising desire to believe in what Glenn said, what Reverend Winthrop had said. It did make a seductive kind of sense.

"Look, Phil, as I said, I remember feeling just the way you do now. Take some time to think about it, pray on it some. And in the meantime let me lend you this."

He held out a dog-eared copy of a crudely printed paperback book with a stenciled title: *The Diary of Wilbur Whateley.* "There's a group of us that meets to study it. Really, it's become a kind of Third Testament for us. You'll see why."

It was time to hit the sack. Both men had early classes the next day.

Morning in the dorm kitchen witnessed a frazzled Philip Brown mumbling a hello to Sue Millman, who seemed enviably bright-eyed. She must be, Philip quipped to himself, living the righteous life, not flirting with heresy like himself. "How's your clinic work going these days, Sue?" he asked with a bit more animation.

Her large brown eyes narrowed, and she brushed her bangs aside. "I'd be lying if I said I enjoyed it. Every day I see women come in bruised and bleeding because they said something that set their husbands off. Most times they don't even know what it was that tripped the land mine. And their husbands, most of them, aren't boozers or criminals. They're

512

doctors, lawyers, professionals. It really makes you sick, and there's no way to distance yourself from it without losing your humanity. But I feel I'm doing important work. I'm even thinking of going into it full time. I mean, instead of the parish ministry. Maybe I'll quit the Div School and switch over to Aylesbury State for a Masters in Social Work."

"I'd hate to see you do that, Sue!" said Phil, his interest now patently genuine.

"What, you don't think there's a need for the kind of work I'm doing?" She began to bristle.

"No, that's not it at all, Sue. It's just that . . . I'd . . . miss you, that's all. But you're the one to find God's will for your life, not me, that's for sure." He was turning red, and she saw it. It seemed to amuse her, but for a moment, Sue looked at him with a funny expression, as if seeing him in a new way, assessing him in a new light.

"Well, I guess you're right about that, Phil. Hadn't you better get to class?"

"That's right!" he said, looking at his pocket watch, one of his many odd affectations. "I've got that Puritan seminar, and it's starting right now!"

"Sounds like fun. Don't let me keep you from it." she said with a chuckle. He grabbed his satchel and trotted up the steps and across the wide, leaf-littered lawn.

It was not Philip's best day of the semester. He found himself uncontrollably nodding off in class. One student paper on old Preserved Cromwell of Newport only augmented his drowsiness, but when the name of Abijah Hoadley came up, it woke him like an alarm clock. Cromwell had apparently exchanged a few letters with his colleague. The import of this Philip missed, but it suddenly struck him that Reverend Hoadley had served in Dunwich, the very place from which the mysterious Wilbur Whateley had hailed. It had been called New Dunnich at the time, but he was sure it had to be the same place.

The seminar presentation had more to do with some polemical theological tracts circulated by the combative old preachers, something to do with the Halfway Covenant debate that racked New England Puritanism for a generation. The paper steered clear, perhaps from embarrassment, of the controversy over Reverend Hoadley's pulpit battles against Beelzebub and Dagon. Philip's own research for the seminar had acquainted him with this darker side of Puritan theology.

He left the seminar room after an apology to the professor for his inattention. Philip reflected that he had some time on his hands today. He had planned to drive out to the Wilbraham area to do a bit of research for his project on Abijah Hoadley, but the skies had clouded up already. As he made for his dorm room, the target of the first practice shots of the rain volley that was to follow minutes later, he decided he'd spend the day, after a quick nap, with a different sort of research. He was itching to get into that odd-looking paperback Glenn had loaned him.

Unusual for his cat naps, Philip dreamed. It wasn't the first time he had dreamed himself in the role of one of the twelve disciples, but there was something different about this dream. He couldn't quite focus on the Lord, as if it were one of those too-reverential movies where they didn't show the face of the actor playing Jesus. But now he was going somewhere with Jesus, up a hillside, while most of the other disciples slept. There were a couple of others with him. Upon awaking a few moments later, he would realize he had been dreaming about the story of the Transfiguration on the mountaintop.

In silence the three disciples and their Lord continued till they reached the top. Then, wordlessly, Jesus stood apart by himself and looked up to heaven. Now his face could be seen. He looked as Philip had always imagined him: slender, of medium height, inappropriately European of feature, and with chestnut brown hair and forked beard. But suddenly he was surrounded by a nimbus of light and hard to look upon. Two other figures appeared as if hovering in the air on either side of him, but their shimmering shapes frustrated the eye. Perhaps there was a suggestion of a star-shape up top.

But then it seemed that the Lord Jesus himself changed. He grew to a height of some eight or nine feet. And it was hard to penetrate the light cloud that enveloped him, but he seemed to have too many limbs, like the statues of Hindu deities, but the arms rolled and flowed with boneless grace. The face, what could be seen of it, seemed vaguely elongated. And the eyes flamed as with a flame of fire.

A peal of thunder spat explosively: This is my Son; hear ye him!

And Philip awoke. He jumped from the bed and stood sweating, head aching, heart hammering. It was the most vivid dream of his life.

He thought at once to get down on his knees and pray, as he usually did whenever he came to a crisis point. Somehow this seemed to qualify. But it wouldn't calm him. He couldn't seem to get past empty words. So he did the next best thing, went down the hall to the dorm lounge, vacant at the moment, and clicked on the TV. Alpha waves were what he needed, and right about now Philip was willing to take them where he could get them.

514

After a couple of sitcoms of which he remembered nothing at all, he felt better. He felt he could thrust the disturbing dream from his mind if he could distract himself. So he decided he might as well go back and pick up that Whateley book. See what all the fuss was about.

As he had it in his hand, he realized he might be opening Pandora's Box. But he had come too far to turn back now. He did not try to start from the beginning, but instead felt he stood to get a better idea from a random sample. So he opened the book, which, he now saw, had the loosened spine of a volume much read. Ironically, it reminded him of those early years when, as a young believer, eager to divine the guidance of God, he would "cut scripture," just let it fall open anywhere, assuming the Holy Spirit would pick the page.

Back from the Zone of the Colossi, just as Grandfather said, in the twinkling of an eye. Folks hereabouts don't know of those worlds. Don't know even of that world they live on. Had no form in that Zone save as vortices of violet gas. Saw much of the past there, also much of the future. Grandfather says time does not flow there but is frozen like the Miskatonic in February. Now understand that chapter in Dee.

Mother took me out to the woods, said I'd been spending too much time with my nose in old books. She and Grandfather argued and shouted for a spell, but in the end Grandfather told me to go with her, said we wouldn't put up with sech womanly interference forever. She packed a basket and said she meant to have us a picnic in a clearing she used to visit when she was a young'un like me. Only she got confused and said maybe it weren't there no more. We kept going till she said this one would do. So we sat us down and spread out the cloth and the food. But then she saw what the trees looked like, how the branches wasn't like other trees, how they had little mouths, and didn't stay still. She left it all where it was and got up running. This was funny and I got to eat the chicken by myself.

Inside the Voorish Dome today. Took shape when Grandfather said them words in the Aklo and danced the Mao Game. I will learn that dance,

too. We was up at the hilltop between all the tall stones, and then all at once the stones reached up and closed like fingers when a body prays. Grandfather says it is I who will be the King of the Kingdom of Voor, whence the earth was first stolen. One day I will ride its winds alone.

Looks as if That above will play host to me fine. I asked Grandfather why he wouldn't use it hisself, but he said, No Willie, it's for ye 'cause it's like unto ye. He said that in that day I should see it is myself and nothing else. Then my Name from them in Yian-Ho shall be BuggShoggog, and his will be Kamog. And then Grandfather bowed down in front of me, and I laughed at him.

Philip's first impulse was to throw the crazy text aside, but he stopped himself. It wasn't his own book, after all. But there was something else. There was a sense of something more than strangeness. These words were not the product of anyone's conscious artifice. They didn't make enough sense for that. It was like half a telephone conversation. You felt you were eavesdropping on something utterly alien and frightful. And the fact that the diarist didn't seem to sense it himself, that he was so, well, accustomed to this terrible cosmos of nightmare hints and cryptic enigmas—that's what made it chilling. And that chill was almost, no, it was spiritual in nature. He couldn't rightly use any other word for it. Here in this crudely duplicated paperback lurked the Dark Mysteries, a sense of defiling, demonic holiness. So he handled the book with a reverence as great as the loathing he felt for it, and put it back on his desk.

It had stopped raining. More than ever he needed something to bring him back to terra firma. In another moment, he had it: he decided there was still time this afternoon to head over to the library and apply for that opening. As bookish as he was, it would be the ideal job for him. His field work didn't pay enough to cover his various fees and leave him any pocket money. His head seemed to clear like the skies above once he got out under them. As it happened, he was in luck. No one else wanted the job. It seemed most of them spent enough time among the musty stacks as it was and couldn't stand spending an extra minute there. Fine with Philip. He would have to start work next week. That would make his schedule even tighter, so he'd best get his research done while he could. Maybe tomorrow would afford a better chance to make it out to the west of the state.

The day was cool yet sunny. Philip grabbed a writing pad and a guidebook. He headed for the Massachusetts Turnpike and rapidly passed into the familiar mental state he called "driver's Zen." The miles sped by, and soon he was looking at a local map for the Wilbraham-Hampdon-Monson Historical Society. He hoped they might have a collection of the papers of the Reverend Abijah Hoadley, or at least maybe they'd know where to send him next. He didn't trust the telephone, because experience told him you couldn't trust a curator any more than teenage store help to know what they had on hand. He wanted to look for himself.

The inconspicuous white wood-frame building was disappointingly small, but it was occupied. Philip had to wake the curator, who resented it. He was willing for the young man to putter around. "Just don't steal anything." Mere moments revealed there was nothing here. Philip paused on the steps outside to consider how he might salvage the trip. He walked to the gas station across the narrow street and got a Coke out of the machine. It was still a quarter in this backwater.

Then it occurred to him that the Congregational church in Dunwich itself might well have some relics of its famous former pastor. It had been his last parish, since Hoadley had mysteriously disappeared, most thought killed by Indians whose ways he openly condemned from the pulpit. So he looked at his map again and made a couple of notes.

It proved no easy matter even to get into Dunwich. The roads to the place had only recently been reopened and cleared of encumbering growth. The town had been completely shut off from the outside world for decades. It was only a Commonwealth flood relief effort that had caused access to be opened again about fifteen years ago, and the roads were all but unpaved. The rutted paths veered crazily among the steep shoulders of bulbous, tall hills, and one rounded corners with heart in throat for fear of invisible oncoming traffic—until one realized there was no such thing. No cars came out of Dunwich, or into it—except for his own.

As he drove over a recently but crudely reinforced covered bridge, he noticed one steeple stabbing crookedly above the low and sagging skyline, and it turned out to crown an old church made over at some point into a Dry Goods Store: OSBORNE'S, as a faded sign proclaimed. It had been long ago abandoned. So he drove down the ghost town streets a bit further. No one was in evidence. Perhaps they were such xenophobes that they hastened out of sight upon the entrance of an outsider, like roaches fleeing when you turn on the kitchen light.

But turning down another block or two, he did manage to find the structure he sought. It was an old meeting house with nothing as pretentious as a steeple, in the unadorned style of the early Puritans. He pulled the Beetle over, noticed the antique absence of a parking meter and carefully climbed the front steps of the church. Modern church buildings had office entrances, but he knew such a relic as this would not. So he pulled at the bell and wondered why he bothered. There was no way anybody but a ghost could be home. If he were lucky it would be the ghost of Abijah Hoadley. He turned to go and call it wasted day.

He had turned the ignition key when the half-oval of the church doors split and then opened wide. Philip jumped out of the car and strode up the steps, hand extended. He faced a small, stooped man who looked little inclined to return his friendly gesture. He was vested as if a service were in progress, though no sound from within suggested activity. And these were certainly no Congregationalist trappings. The robe was faded and colorless, but the bug-eyed man's oblong pate was adorned with a curious golden tiara. Philip's eyes could not trace the delicate workmanship of the thing without impolitely looking away from the man's flap-lipped, expressionless face.

"Help?" grunted the cleric tonelessly.

"Uh, yes, Reverend. My name's Philip Brown. I'm a seminary student with Miskatonic Divinity School, and I'm doing some research on Dr. Abijah Hoadley, who I understand once preached here. I hate to trouble you, but I wonder if the old church might house any papers, you know, sermon notes, pamphlets, letters by him."

"Papers . . . hmmm, might at that. Come on in."

Philip felt a slight sense of foreboding at stepping into the shadowed narthex. It was really pitch dark, though the odd little man didn't seem to mind. In a moment an antique kerosene lamp sputtered into flame, and the peculiar cleric led him past the decrepit sanctuary, barely visible, into the church office.

"Been cleaning it out. About to dump this. This box, old records. Take a look if you want." Philip lost no time stooping to examine what he could see in the flickering dimness. He guessed it was this or nothing. Whatever papers were in the box were so brittle and yellowed that it seemed not unlikely he should find what he was looking for. And yet they could date from any time in over two hundred years since Hoadley's day. What were the chances? Still ... he remembered how Tischendorf had discovered the precious leaves of the *Codex Sinaiticus* in the garbage can of St. Catherine's Monastery.

518

"Since you're only going to throw them out anyway, why not let me take them off your hands?"

The other man signaled his assent (or so Philip interpreted) with a vague wave of the hand. Philip picked up the carton and carried it to his car. Just as the man was about to seal himself back in his empty church, one more silent relic among so many, Philip had an inspiration.

"Uh, one more thing, if you don't mind." The impassive face paused in its retreat into the dark.

Philip was back up on the steps. "Would you know anything about a man named Wilbur Whateley? I understand there was some big ruckus over him back in the Twenties. I was curious . . ."

"No, never heard of that gent. Young sir, I dun't know the taown much. Bishop jest sent me here from another town to get th' church goin' agin. Not much interest. Dun't know whut's amiss. A lot o' church-goin' in my town. This Whateley go t' church much?"

"I don't know. Good question. Thanks anyway. Good luck with the church!" Philip drove off with the blank face staring after him.

Hours later, Philip lugged the old box into his room and collapsed onto the narrow bed. He ached from the dullness of driving. Ordinarily he would be sound asleep in seconds. But here came something loud, dragging him reluctantly back into wakefulness.

"Phil! Good! I was afraid I'd missed you! Come on! It's starting!"

Glenn Brindley practically dragged his befuddled friend out of bed.

"What? What *is* it, Glenn? Another Socratic meeting already? For Pete's sake . . . !"

He was soon accompanying Glenn down the hall and out of the dorm. It seemed on balance the easiest thing to do. He was too tired to protest much.

"Hope you don't mind, old buddy; I took the liberty of picking up that copy of the *Diary* I loaned you. Have a chance to look through it yet?"

"Yeah, as a matter of fact, I did. But where is it we're going?" He had begun to get pretty steamed, friend or no friend.

"Think of it as a Bible study meeting, Phil. Remember I told you a group of us gather to study the *Diary*. Well, tonight's something special. We have a guest speaker, and he wants to meet you." Philip stopped in his tracks. "Meet *me*? You've got to be kidding. I'm going back and get a nap." He turned, but Glenn followed.

"Really! It's a professor, the only prof on campus who sees things like we do. We've told him about your interest, and he says he'd like to meet you,

519

maybe answer some of your questions. Now there's an opportunity for you!"

Philip stopped again. One of the mossbacks? It seemed impossible.

"Yeah? Who is it?"

"None of us knows. You see, he can't very well reveal his identity. You and I can accept a new idea and not much will happen. The Dean will shake his head if he hears of a student becoming a modernist or a Pentecostal or something, but the faculty have to sign a doctrinal statement or they get fired. You know that."

"You mean he's teaching here under false pretenses!"

"Come on, Phil! What's the problem? Don't you want to know more about the doctrine?"

A moment of silent musing, then the inevitable: "Sure. You're right, I don't know what's eating me. Just exhausted, I guess. I'll go with you, Glenn. Come on."

They entered one of the classroom buildings that had the hall lights on, but no rooms were illuminated. They entered one of them nonetheless. To Philip's surprise, once his eyes had adjusted to the gloom, the place was full. At the desk, shrouded by strategic darkness, was the heretical professor, the coreligionist, the mentor of the campus sect.

"Ah, I see our new friend has arrived!" The voice was artificially hoarse. Philip could make out little detail belonging to the seated figure. The outlines suggested none of the few professors he knew, but that meant nothing. This was his first semester.

"Glenn tells me he's lent you the book. What did you think, my young friend?"

Philip sensed every eye upon him. He wondered who the students might be. How many of them had been eyeing him for days as a potential recruit?

"To tell you the truth, I couldn't make much sense of it. But I didn't start at the beginning, just flipped the pages and read here and there. But I admit there's a real power to it even without understanding it." It was his answer that made little sense, but in the circumstances he couldn't think of much to say. The shadowed man spoke again. "And that's what you're looking for, isn't it? Spiritual power. I think that's what we're all looking for. A greater experience of Christ, a Christ at hand, here with us, not two thousand years ago, not just in the pages of the Bible."

"Yes, sir, that is exactly how I feel. Glenn's probably told you. But there's something I don't understand. Why this Whateley man? What reason is there . . . ?"

520

The dark whisperer cut him off. "Son, if you're looking for proof, you're not going to remain any kind of a Christian for long, are you? Do you think you can prove Jesus of Nazareth was the Christ? You know what they used to say, 'Can anything good come from Nazareth?' That's what folks hereabout say of Dunwich today! 'We did esteem him stricken, smitten of God . . .'" The voice trailed off.

One of the hitherto silent students chimed in here: "It's an act of faith, Phil. You can't escape that. But that's what Christ asks of us, isn't it?" The voice sounded familiar, but without seeing the face, he couldn't hazard a guess.

"Yeah, I guess it is." Phil found creeping over him the familiar feeling of conviction. He had felt it a hundred times over the years of his Christian life, seated in the aisles of a chapel or spiritual retreat: the speaker pressed home the message of repentance, surrender of the will and recommitment to Christ. The laying aside of every proud idol that stood in the way of total dedication to God. Many times he had been obedient to these calls to the deeper life. Now he felt it again, that magnetism of inevitability, that weight on the conscience.

"Tell me one thing, though. I know about the virgin birth, the stories about it, anyway. But was Wilbur Whateley raised from the dead? How could that escape notice?"

"It didn't, young Mr. Brown," the professor replied patiently. "He died, as you probably know, right here at Miskatonic. But certain once-sealed records written by eyewitnesses reveal that the body vanished within seconds. And then, look it up in the local papers if you don't believe it, an Entity burst out of confinement up in Dunwich. That was Wilbur, returned in his glorious resurrection body, in his true form. The theological term for it is a 'shoggoth', the form he had before he condescended to come down among men. He appeared in his greatness to make a final appeal, but again they persecuted him. 'He came unto his own and his own received him not'. Shortly afterward, he left his powerless persecutors behind. Calling on his Heavenly Father, he ascended into heaven, just as he did before, as we read in Luke chapter 24. Surely you know that text."

The pieces were beginning to fit together at last. It was still terribly hard to believe, to accept, but then Philip had felt exactly the same way when he was first challenged to accept the resurrection of Jesus and the miracles of the Bible back in 1980. He had taken the leap of faith then. Why should it be so hard now?

The professor, as if sensing his hesitation, spoke again: "You work at the library now, don't you Philip? We have someone there who has access to the rare book room. I want you to ask him to give you a look at the Bible manuscript kept there. He'll know the one you mean." He said the name, and Philip recognized it at once. It was the staff member who had hired him only the other day. He didn't doubt there was a connection. Philip was silent for the rest of the meeting, content to listen to the professor's detailed commentary on selected passages from the *Diary*. But he could make little of the arcane exegesis of the equally esoteric texts.

When it came time to go, he was relieved and ached for some sleep. Glenn walked him to his room, keeping up a steady flow of pep-talk chatter. Philip promised him he would seek out the manuscript as early as he could the next day. Finally his pesky friend left him alone and he dove for the pillow.

Philip appeared at the library yet fully three hours before he was due to work. As a staff member he used his privilege to get into the rare books collection. He found the man who had hired him. The latter now regarded him plainly with a look of silent recognition and led him to a locked cabinet. He opened the doors and from within carefully lifted a huge vellum codex of great antiquity.

"I don't need to tell you how careful you have to be with this. It's old and it's priceless. See, the label says 'Codex Miskatoniencis.' Have you heard of it, Philip?"

"No, but I'm not that familiar with textual criticism. I know of *Codex Sinaiticus* and, let's see, *Codex Vaticanus*, one or two others."

"Right. They're from the fourth century. The time of Constantine, the first Christian emperor of Rome. This one's from the same general period, at least they think. It's so rare because it's one of the Bibles that escaped burning, maybe the only one."

"Huh?"

"You see, Constantine was the one who convened the Council of Nicea, where they decided which books ought to go into . . . and out of the Bible! Once they made the final selection, he had an edition of fifty deluxe codices prepared for his bishops—and then burned the others, the older ones that had different books. This is the only one known to have survived."

Philip's eyes were round now. "How . . . how did we come to have it?"

"Some decades ago, one of our professors, old Dr. Bowen, found it on an expedition to Egypt. He was looking for an ancient gem of some type,

522

which some say he actually found and kept in a church he pastored up in Providence after his retirement. He had found the *Codex* almost as an accident and, incredibly, he wasn't really that interested in it! So he donated it to the library as a bequest when he left."

"And it lies here unknown?" Philip marveled aloud.

"That's not such a mystery. This Bible has some striking textual variants, some altogether different books! Local clergy were invited to examine it when it was first brought here. After flipping a few of the pages, they shuddered and urged that it be burned at once. Obviously, the school wasn't going to let that happen to a priceless manuscript, but in the end they did agree to hush the thing up. Remember, the Congregationalist Church endowed this place and still supports it heavily. They couldn't have the local ministers badmouthing the seminary. But you're here, as I understand it, to take a look for yourself. Be my guest. But for God's sake be careful, okay?" With that he left Philip alone and returned to his cataloguing.

Philip turned the pages with a sense of dumbfounded awe. He had been vouchsafed a privilege such as few students of the Bible ever had. Luckily he had taken New Testament Greek during his undergraduate years and could work his way through much of the text without great difficulty. The book had been opened to the Gospel of Mark. There were few surprises here, few departures from the canonical text thus far. Here was something: a resurrection story reminiscent of Lazarus, but it ended in a strange way. Jesus, it said, spent the night with the resuscitated man, the two of them clad only in linen sheets, Jesus initiating the man into the Mysteries of the Kingdom of God. That sounded vaguely odd, even offensive. But he could find little else out of the ordinary and was about to turn to one of the other gospels when his eye fell upon what seemed to be the Transfiguration story. Here were some difficult Greek constructions.

One unfamiliar word stumped him, so he got up and fetched a Greek lexicon. He was surprised to see that the word denoted some type of sea creature, a squid or . . .

Suddenly stunned, he forced himself to read on. It read almost as a transcript of the shocking dream he had dreamed the other afternoon! He tried to proceed further down the page, scanned a chapter in which Jesus encountered Simon Magus and revealed his saving mission to him . . .

Philip was becoming dizzy now. He shut the book with a thud, the noise not escaping the librarian, who flinched and came running. He began to admonish his new assistant. He really must take better care . . . But when he noticed Philip's ashen face, he calmed himself and quietly urged the

523

young man to take the day off, return to his room and pray about what he had read. Philip left without further comment. He had some thinking to do, once he could do any thinking again, that is.

Halloween came mid-semester. Philip was not in the habit of celebrating it. His piety had never allowed him to be comfortable making light of devils, witches, and the like. But this year was different. Still not an occasion of revelry, to be sure, but he did have special plans for the evening, at the campus chapel. All Hallow's Eve, All Saints' Eve, was after all a church holiday. It was dedicated to commemorating the holy heroes of the past and their victories over the Powers of Darkness. That's what he and his newfound compatriots would be doing tonight, but that was to understate it. He could hardly contain his excitement.

Sue Millman noticed his anticipation that afternoon and asked whose party he would be attending. None, he had replied sanctimoniously, he was going to church. Sue gave him a puzzled look and left the snack bar.

But now the time had arrived, and Philip picked up his copy of the *Diary* and headed over to the chapel. There would be a preliminary period of prayer and study, kind of a miniature retreat, as they sought to ready themselves for the Epiphany. This should occur at the stroke of Midnight. He did not know exactly what to expect. None of the others were willing to tell him. He wasn't totally sure any of the veterans, even Glenn, had seen one of these events. They had said something about needing Philip to complete the circle of twelve, symbolizing the original disciples. Maybe only the professor, whose identity Philip still did not know, had been here long enough to have seen the last Epiphany of the Returned Christ.

All any of the other students seemed to know for certain was that there would be something analogous to the resurrection appearances of the Gospels. And this was enough for Philip. Tonight he would find out once and for all whether he had been correct in the leap of faith he had at last decided to take. And he felt sure his decision would be vindicated. It would be the high point of his spiritual life. Thus he reflected as the chapel clock struck the quarter before the hour. It was time to make the circle and start the liturgy.

He stood next to Glenn Brindley. Across the nave he could make out the hooded faces of Reverend Winthrop and one other. Squinting, he saw with some surprise that it was Claude LaValle! Claude had never let on that he belonged to the campus sect. Perhaps he was another novice and did not know of Philip's recruitment either, until tonight.

All linked hands and began with the Lord's Prayer. The rest of the litany seemed actually pretty conventional, though he noticed the phrase
524

"Principalities and Powers" kept recurring in it. The circle bent like one of Salvador Dali's melting watches, extending up the chancel steps and into the sanctuary proper. There, still in shadows, the lights turned off up there, was the professor, their mentor and celebrant. After a chanted reference was made to the Nine Angles, or something like that, everyone went silent and waited with held breath.

Philip could hear the distant baying of dogs in the sudden silence. Then the professor began to step forward into the light. Philip was expecting something, something spectacular, but even so, this was a surprise. He couldn't believe a professor who had kept his identity a secret for so long would take a risk like this. Why would he dare being discovered? Suppose some outsiders were secretly watching? He had been afraid of someone recognizing him for the same reason. He was willing to suffer for Christ if need be, but neither was he particularly eager to be expelled from divinity school.

It must have been an effect of the confused lighting pattern in the cavernous place, but Philip thought he saw the form of the professor growing taller as he entered the lit space. But perhaps that was only because he had thus far misjudged the height of a man he usually saw sitting in the shadows. Then the face became visible. There was time only for a brief glimpse. It was definitely no one he had ever seen on campus.

The face changed. For a split second Philip had the absurd idea that the man's beard grew longer even as he watched. But no, the face was elongating, like something he had seen in a dream once . . .

The shape of the figure, who was now raising his voice and saying something in a language Philip didn't know, was vague and seemed to billow out. His liturgical robe, of course . . . unless . . . There was now plainly visible an extra pair of looping arms, each holding a communion chalice. And now the voice spoke in familiar English, with familiar words: "Peace be unto you. It is I myself. Do not fear."

Philip's spine now froze with the thrill of numinous fear. He dimly heard Glenn announce something about consecrating the body and blood. Philip lowered his eyes. Like Moses in Exodus, he was afraid to look upon God.

Glenn released his hand, which fell nervelessly to his side, and Philip bowed to the ground. Thus he posed in reverent awe, losing count of the minutes. He no more knew what to say or to think than poor Peter did on the Mount of Transfiguration when he had stammered empty words about building booths for Jesus, Elijah and Moses. Best to bask in the divine Presence.

And then from somewhere in the narthex he began to notice the trespassive sounds of yelling and cursing. Philip felt, almost like a physical blow, the sense of sacrilege that some profane person might dare to disturb the holy gravity of this occasion. The noise, instead of abating, was actually growing nearer and more strenuous. Despite himself, Philip could not resist the reflex to look back and see what was going on.

What he saw was Glenn and a couple of the others, with more hastening to assist them, holding a naked and fighting woman. As they came closer, he had the crazy idea that it looked like Sue Millman. They were trying to get her wrists into a pair of handcuffs, but she was going down fighting. It *was* Sue.

Wait a minute! What was going on here? What could she be doing here? Spying on him? Maybe—but naked? And what were the other brethren doing with her? He looked back to the One on the chancel steps. That One beckoned hideously with waving arms and empty cups that seemed to be parched for some liquid to fill them. And then he saw the gleam of the knife.

He snapped out of it, almost felt like the deaf man in the gospels who could suddenly hear again. It was as if some spirit of animation had decided to transfer itself from one host to another, for in the same moment Sue went limp, perhaps from some blow he could not see, and Philip was galvanized into motion. Acting on instinct, he jumped up, ran for the knot of robed figures who carried her now-compliant body through the silent nave.

Apparently this move took the rest of them as much by surprise as Sue's appearance had startled him. He barreled into them clumsily, like a ricocheting bowling ball, but the blow was effective enough. They dropped Sue among them—and she landed on her feet. Philip realized she must have been playing possum, hoping for a chance to surprise her captors. Philip had provided it for her, and now the two of them made the most of it. They implicitly agreed not to waste the time trying to fight the larger group, now augmented by the other stunned worshippers. Better just to make a break for it.

Bolting for the twin half-doors, they evaded one or two stumbling attempts to catch at their pistoning legs and cleared the nave, then the narthex, finally bursting through the doorway and into the chill night air. They ran a few more feet before Philip turned about for a glance at the chapel to make sure no one was following. As might be expected, the campus was alive with festive activities, some of them not entirely sober. Those in the chapel, he reasoned, would not pursue them in the open, revealing themselves as a ravening lynch mob.

He paused for a breath and in a moment had stripped off his ritual robe to cover his friend's shivering nakedness. Wordlessly, he took the hand of the traumatized woman and led her back to his room.

In another few moments, Sue, clutching her unaccustomed garment, was her old self again. "What the hell was that?"

"I might ask you the same thing," Philip replied, his seminarian prudishness reasserting itself. "I can smell the alcohol on your breath. You were at one of those fraternity mixers, weren't you?" As he said this, he was busy pulling out an old carton from beneath his bunk and hastily sorting through some old papers inside it.

"That's none of your fucking business, Phil! I'm about sick of your pious bullshit! You and the others—you're just a bunch of old . . ."

"'Mossbacks'? Is that the word you're looking for?" mumbled Phil as he scanned a piece of yellowed manuscript.

Both were abruptly brought back to their present dilemma with a sudden pounding on the door. A voice came, Glenn's, speaking in measured tones, as if trying to control itself: "Hey, Phil! Is Sue with you in there? You must have misunderstood! It was just part of the drama of the thing!"

Sue spat back, "What was I supposed to be doing—jumping out of a cake? Get out of here, you bastards!" Then, in a whisper to her friend, "What are we going to do? Go through the window?"

There was the muffled sound of a huddle of people deliberating on the other side of the door. Then one voice emerged. This time it was Reverend Winthrop. "Look, you two, let's open the door and talk before the campus police get mixed up in this and we all get into trouble over nothing." No answer.

Another knock came, this one with sufficient force to splinter the door. And judging from the height of the impact point, the blow must have been thrown by a freakishly tall figure. More blows came.

Philip was studying another old paper. Sue's eyes widened. "Jesus! What the hell are you doing? In a minute they're going to . . ."

"Sometimes it's the old mossbacks who have what it takes, Sue. Here goes. All I can say is, I hope my Hebrew's good enough!"

What followed was a snaky string of unrecognizable syllables. Among them Sue thought she recognized the divine Names Adonai, Jehovah and Tetragrammaton. Then others with a similar ring but no familiar meaning: Buzrael, Lucifuge, Demogorgon. The words made her wince, spun about her the queasy aura of a migraine's onset. She seemed to be missing part of it, as if some other wave than ordinary sound were intersecting the frequency of Philip's voice and canceling it. Then she began to see spots, then the shrinking into tunnel vision. She focused on Philip and saw the tiny lines of blood trickling from his nose and mouth.

Then there was the peculiar sensation of hearing the echo of a mighty scream without the scream itself. And perhaps something had popped disgustingly in the hall outside (though subsequent investigation revealed no residue). There were confused sounds as of stumbling and falling, dragging and footfalls. And the sound of a body falling somewhere behind her.

Sue turned to see the limp form of Philip spread ungracefully on the floor. She tried to get him onto the bed, decided just to prop him sitting against the bunk. She looked quickly about and grabbed up a baseball bat, then tentatively opened the dorm room door. No one. Then she called down the hall for someone to get campus security. No one answered, apparently all out celebrating or praying. Or just too scared to get involved. So she opened the window and called out.

The campus police were not long in arriving, having apprehended a couple of the slower, more dazed cultists as they made their way across campus. It seemed that Sue's disappearance had not gone altogether unnoticed when she had been seen leaving the party with a young man no one in the fraternity recognized. It seemed seminarians just could not help appearing incongruous at such events, so someone noticed a "creep" leading the half-inebriated Sue Millman away and fumbling with her clothes. Though too drunk to intervene himself, the student had possessed the wits to call security from the lounge pay phone. The ruckus at the chapel had already sparked another call, so the police had gone there from the dorm.

The scene there was inconclusive though suspicious, so the officers had begun to patrol the campus till they spotted several robed figures in an apparent state of semi-shock. Mere Halloween revelers? Few could speak coherently, yet none appeared to have been drinking. And then they had heard Sue's screamed summons.

It was a matter of just a few minutes till Philip was brought around. He and Sue tried as best they could to explain what had happened, though Sue was almost as much at a loss as the police. Philip spared them those details he knew that, as worldly men, they would never believe. Sufficient to say he'd blundered into what turned out to be a lot more than a Halloween prank. Sue was quick to confirm that her friend hadn't been a part of it and had helped her escape. In the next week there were more questions to be answered and, this surprised even Philip, there were bodies to be identified. He found himself nauseated at the sight of the strangely . . . distorted bodies of Glenn, of Claude, of the librarian he worked for—and of the Reverend Winthrop. No one could say precisely what could have killed them. Oh, it was some sort of severe impact, almost as if the bodies had been selectively crushed at close range, like the old Puritan witch pressings. But in a dormitory hallway? And why were not all of them affected the same way? For some were more mentally affected than physically. Only one or two had after some days begun to return to lucidity, and their memories were spotty, unless they were lying.

No one was expelled from the divinity school, to the initial surprise of the campus community, for the simple reason that none who survived were in any condition to continue there. The parishioners of the Reverend Winthrop took the news with surprising equanimity, almost as if some such denouement might have been expected. The people of Foxfield were always known to be queer in their beliefs and it seemed that nothing surprised them very much.

It took a few days, but at the end of the week Philip was satisfied that all the Miskatonic divinity professors were alive and well, harrumphing at all the campus mischief. He was by now persuaded that the rasping mystagogue he had met was not one of them.

The dean had a lot of explaining to do to the grief-stricken families of the slain students, though he had little in the way of explanation to offer them. Philip was just glad that job was not his, though he did try to come up with something to write on a sympathy card to Glenn's mother. Best she not know what devilish business he had been involved in. So he said one late November afternoon, just before Thanksgiving break, to Sue Millman as the two spent the afternoon in her room talking.

"One thing I haven't asked you, Phil; I know from my work at the Women's Center that people sometimes need time before they can talk about their traumas. But I'm dying to know. You were affected by that . . . blast, too. I saw you bleeding. You were knocked out. But how come you weren't killed or . . . driven insane like the others? And why wasn't I affected?" She took Philip's hand. "And, well, Phil, what the hell were you doing reading those old scraps of paper while they were trying to kill us?"

He laughed. "They weren't just scraps. Those particular scraps happened to be some of the letters of Abijah Hoadley, you remember, my research topic. I found them in that box of documents I scavenged from the Dunwich church. Most of it was old bills and ledger pages, nothing much. But it turned out my hunch had been on target. There were a couple of letters by old Hoadley, even draft pages of his famous book. What I was reading was a letter to him by a colleague, a Dr. Ward Phillips, over at a Baptist church here in Arkham. He knew of Hoadley's one-man crusade against witchcraft in New Dunnich and warned him he was getting in over his head. So he sent him copies of certain old cabalistic spells he said might protect him."

"Must not have worked, though," Sue interrupted. "The one thing I do remember you saying about Hoadley was that he disappeared under dubious circumstances, right?"

"Oh, they would have worked all right. You saw the evidence of that on Halloween night. That's what I was reciting. That's what got rid of our pursuers. Hoadley just didn't use them. The old mossback rebuffed Phillips' advice, said it was all too Popish, too superstitious, and he would rely 'onlie upon the strong Name of the Saviour.' That mistake cost him his life. His soul, too, I'd guess."

"What's the difference?" Sue muttered. "Well, I don't know what to make of it. Maybe you're right, but your 'explanation' sounds just as crazy as what you're explaining."

Philip shrugged. "You've got me there, Sue."

Sue got up to fetch another cup of coffee. She took advantage of the momentary discontinuity to change the subject. "I guess you could see this coming, Phil, but I've decided to leave the seminary. It all seemed less and less relevant the more deeply I got involved with people's problems, out there in the real world. I'm going to look into that Social Work degree I told you about over at Aylesbury State."

Phil rose and looked out the window. "You're right, Sue. That doesn't surprise me. But this may surprise *you*. I'm leaving, too."

"What? Why?" She rose and stood beside him. He turned to face her.

"This is going to sound even crazier than what I just said, but here goes. Right after Halloween, I had to rethink everything. You remember all the business about the second coming, about . . ."

"Yes, I remember," she said, putting a hand on his shoulder. There were deep wheels turning here, and she knew enough to be a sensitive listener.

"At first, given what I saw that night in the chapel, and then what happened in the dorm, I decided I had been lured into a cult. I'd seen the same thing happen to friends of mine who joined the Children of God cult, Guru Maharaj Ji, you know the type. I prayed and asked Christ to forgive me. Especially when I realized what almost happened to you . . .

"But then I remembered the dream, and what I read in that biblical manuscript. Even now it makes too much sense. It all fits together too well!"

"Phil!" she gasped, "You don't still believe it's *true*, do you?" He could sense her body stiffening, reflexively withdrawing from him as if he'd just confided he had a communicable plague.

Philip laughed bitterly. "I *do*, Sue! I *do* believe it's true! But I don't want anything to do with it! It's like having God appear to you and hearing him tell you his name is Satan. In fact, it's not *like* it—that *is* what happened! The 'real' Christianity: I wanted it and I got it. But I don't want it anymore. You see the irony of old Hoadley's position. Poor fool! To think the name of Christ would protect him. He needed to be protected from *it*!"

Sue's eyes were round. She had to regather some presence of mind to try and fill the bomb crater of ensuing silence. "So . . . so, what will you do now?"

"I'm open to suggestions. Got an extra copy of that brochure on the Social Work program?" Smiling a small smile, Sue said that she thought she did.

–2003–

The Devil's Steps

Alice Spenser waited patiently through the routine. She stood on the rich but faded carpet in the oak-paneled reception office while the Great Man's secretary verified her appointment. Of course Alice knew Miss Briarton knew that Dr. Ap-Rhys was expecting her. She was a regular visitor. As the President of the Graduate Students Association at the Brichester University Divinity College it was her task to make regular reports to him as to the academic progress of her student colleagues, to make suggestions for the improvement of the program from the student point of view, and generally to keep the lines of student-faculty communication open. This she did well, for it had not taken her long to learn that despite Professor ApRhys's frosty exterior, a vestige from the days of pre-War Old School decorum, he was actually quite warm and truly interested in the progress of the tiny band of apprentice scholars training at the prestigious school. The two had quickly developed a friendly working relationship.

"You may go on in now, Ms. Spenser," said the bespectacled matron, one of that tribe of devoted secretaries who seem to eschew marriage as infidelity to her beloved professor.

With an appreciative nod, Alice passed through the door, as many in her position had done over the years. She was no longer intimidated by the look of the place, for it had the appearance of an old library in which a process of spontaneous generation caused new books to appear atop old ones with preternatural rapidity. She did half fear being caught in an avalanche. Knowing that this office, too, must be oak-paneled, she could nonetheless no longer see much of it, seeing that most of the vertical space was book-covered or festooned with framed photographs of the likes of C. H. Dodd, F. F. Bruce, T. R. Glover, Sidney Lampton, and other greats of British New Testament scholarship, Dr. Ap-Rhys' own field of study.

And yet she could not stop her eyes from wandering to the shelves for a moment before settling on the owlish visage of the professor, looking up from a shapeless stack of books and papers.

"Good day, Ms. Spenser. I've been expecting you. I suppose you'd say we're in the mid-term doldrums now, so we may have little to discuss. Any news on the Colloquium speaker for next year?"

532

"Not yet, sir. We're still waiting on Dr. Marshall, but his duties at Edinburgh keep him pretty busy. I hope to know before the end of the month, though. I know that's cutting it close. Dr. Lincoln at Sheffield is another possibility."

"Very good. It's never easy. It will come out right in the end. Always does. Now what else is on your mind, Ms. Spenser?"

"As you say, sir, there's little else to report—except for one bit of news that I think will surprise you."

"Yes?"

"It concerns that fellow Tedrick."

"Oh yes, the poor chap who can't seem to arrive at a thesis topic. How long has he been at it?" Dr. Ap-Rhys sat back in his leather chair. He could not repress a note of amusement, though he did feel for the young man. Every few years there would be someone like him, with a substantial command of the scholarly lore, but with no discernible originality. British scholars were accustomed to the task of the archivist and the apologist, unlike their German rivals who made innovation their watchword, but some creative insight was necessary. One must after all prove oneself with a dissertation, and a dissertation had to have something new to say.

"I don't know, sir. He was here when I entered the program. But he's apparently come up with something at last, and he promises to unveil it at the seminar tomorrow." This last was a regularly scheduled but unofficial function where the graduate students would meet to share ideas and to present paper drafts for the scrutiny of their peers before handing in their final version to the professors.

Dr. Ap-Rhys gave it a moment's thought and asked, "I don't suppose it would intimidate the lad unduly if an old faculty member were to sit in?"

"I can't rightly say, Professor, but then I should imagine he'd be flattered at your interest. And it's certainly your prerogative." The interview did not last much longer.

The next afternoon the small circle of students were indeed surprised when Professor Ap-Rhys stepped into their lounge just after the start of the meeting. He nodded and quietly took a seat. Mr. Tedrick could be seen to swallow hard, but he betrayed no other sign of nervousness as he launched enthusiastically into his presentation, setting forth the basic concept of the book-length paper he hoped to begin writing as soon as the appropriate committee approved his thesis prospectus.

All were silent, keenly interested, and, Alice began to think, even vaguely alarmed. For Mr. Tedrick's researches had taken a peculiar direction indeed. Alice could not read Dr. Ap-Rhys' poker face, but then it rarely evidenced any real emotion anyway.

Tedrick had reached the final lap. "Here's the meat of the thing. In both Synoptic versions of the Beelzebub Controversy, the scribes charge Jesus with 'casting out demons by the prince of the demons', and he refutes the charge. But he does it in quite different ways. Mark's Gospel has him begin with a rhetorical question, 'How can Satan cast out Satan?' The 'Q' source underlying Matthew and Luke lacks this and instead substitutes two subsequent hypotheticals: 'If I cast out demons by Beelzebub, by whom do your sons cast them out?' and 'If I cast out demons by the finger of God, then the Kingdom of God has come upon you.' This complex is plainly a secondary midrash applying to Jesus' case the Exodus story of Moses' triumph over Pharaoh's magicians who finally had to acknowledge Moses' superiority, saying, 'This is the finger of God.'

"So, bear with me now, if you omit both Mark's rhetorical question and Q's midrash, you get close to the primitive tradition lying behind them both. And what's left is no refutation at all! Indeed, we must take Jesus' words as an admission and a defense of his practice of 'binding the strong man.' In other words, he *did* bind the power of Beelzebub to do his bidding. He was at first regarded not as the Son of God, but rather, as Celsus and the rabbis maintained, a magician who used the power of Satan against Satan, so that Satan's kingdom would come crashing down. I can adduce plenty of parallels from the magical papyri to show how well it would fit current practice, but I think you get the idea. Any questions?"

All eyes swung over to the impassive face of Professor Ap-Rhys. After a moment he spoke, as if sensing the others needed him to speak. "Well, Mr. Tedrick, it's original, I must say, however unorthodox. Let me give some thought to the matter."

Through all this, the young researcher seemed not one whit apprehensive, though he might have been expected to shiver at the prospect of being shot down in flames before his peers by a judge whose verdict was to be feared only less than that of God himself. But instead Tedrick seemed positively eager to finish and almost disappointed when the comments were so meager. When Dr. Ap-Rhys rose abruptly to return to his office, Tedrick took this as his clue to exit as well, as if he cared not a fig for his colleagues' suggestions. This left the rest of them more than a little dumbfounded and feeling abandoned.

"Well, Ian, what did you think of it?" asked one blank face.

"To tell the truth, the word 'blasphemy' comes to mind. I'd laugh it off if his reasoning weren't so bloody cogent."

Alice paid little attention to the interchange which was beginning to take on a more heated tone. She rose to leave, feeling a strange urgency, yet unaware of her goal. She found herself walking at a brisk pace across the campus, through the venerable stone archways and past the megalithic, ivied halls devoted to Science, Archaeology, Literature. She could not get the shrunken figure of Hugh Tedrick off her mind. She knew little about the man. He was thirtyish, ill-kempt with the obliviousness of one who lives in his mind rather than in the world. His straw hair was usually greasy and chopped for convenience rather than style. He kept to himself, and, as far as anyone knew, his only diversion from his studies was his habit of taking moonlight walks through the wooded hills just beyond the campus.

Dr. Ap-Rhys turned in early that evening, feeling strangely fatigued, even, he might even have said, spiritually fatigued. As he prepared himself for bed in his rooms at the University that night, he reflected gravely that today's students tended to seek novelty for its own sake, no matter that they stood to upset the faith of the humble in Christ's flock. But the church had, after all, weathered the teapot tempests of her own bishops, Colenso, Robinson, Jenkins, even that Pike fellow over in America.

Once abed, despite his exhaustion, he had unaccustomed difficulty falling asleep. He dreamed, but upon rising with the dawn, the Professor had no recollection of what he had dreamed. And at this he felt somehow relieved. He reflected that he might as well betake himself to his office and make an early start.

He had hoped to spend several hours at work on a new manuscript to deal with the theology of the Pastoral Epistles on the hypothesis that they had the Writer to the Hebrews for their author, as a few scholars held. Several verses might be viewed in a new light if one might make significant cross reference to a much larger corpus of material by the same author. But his plans were cut short with a burst of frantic pummeling on the door. It was too early for Miss Briarton to be at her post fending off annoying callers, so there was nothing for it but to answer the knock. He was readying his polite but firm dismissal when he saw who awaited him.

Alice Spenser stood without, disheveled and hysterical.

"Come in, my dear, and by all means tell me what has happened. Here, take a seat. Go ahead while I stoke the fire."

It was a moment before she could compose herself sufficiently to answer. By this time, Professor Ap-Rhys had pulled up a chair beside hers so as not to have the width of his great desk as a barrier between them. He took her hand and held it firmly, as he had done with his own daughter in earlier years.

"I still don't quite know what happened myself, Professor," she gasped between sobs. "It was yesterday afternoon, just after Tedrick's presentation . . . the bastard! He left shortly after you did. Then I left. I suddenly felt like I had to. I couldn't think of anything but his greasy face. Not his presentation, just him. Before long I found myself knocking on the door of his rooms. I hadn't even known where he lived, but there I was. He opened immediately, said he'd been expecting me. What kept me? I was already confused, but this made me feel panic. I can't explain it, but outwardly I was calm.

"He reached for his coat and said he supposed I'd be warm enough as I was. Then he said he knew I must be wondering where he'd gotten the idea for the thesis, and that he wanted to show me! We would be going for a little walk. When we got back outside it was beginning to get dark. He took my hand and held me close to him as we walked. I was disgusted and wanted to run away. Somehow I couldn't, though, and we walked on past the edge of the campus and into the woods. We climbed a ridge and stood there arm in arm. Inside I was protesting, but I swear I couldn't make my mouth say what I wanted it to say. Then we . . . Oh, Professor, I'm so dreadfully embarrassed to be telling you this . . . we started kissing! I couldn't help it; it was as if someone else were in control of me.

"As we stood there, the moon rose. It was getting colder, and a breeze was rising. I guess he thought it was romantic, almost as if he'd orchestrated it. Then he took me over to a clearing and pointed out what looked like a set of footprints set into the ground. The soil thinned out there, and it seemed like these four footprints were set in solid stone. The moonlight made it easy to see the contrast of shadows. He smiled and said, 'Alice, this is where I come to get my prayers answered. It always works here. I just discovered it. I suppose it's something like Eliade's theory of Sacred Space. Some places are just more powerful than others—if you know how to use them.' I remember everything he said, because I was beginning to be afraid of what he would say next. I knew something awful was about to happen.

536

"He continued: 'I wasted all that time, years, I guess, waiting for some idea to pop into my head so I could get to work and receive my degree. And then I learned about this place. Here's how it works. All you have to do is put one foot in one of the prints, then say your prayer, and it works. Why, it was no sooner than I prayed the first time that the idea came to me, the one you heard earlier today. You can only pray for three things, and I've got one more. And I'm not greedy. I guess it would happen anyway, but I'm going to pray that my thesis becomes accepted, not just by the committee, you know, but by everyone. I'm praying it will become 'critical orthodoxy', and that on the strength of it I'll be offered a post at the Divinity College, or maybe at Cambridge. What do you think?'

"For the first time I felt able to say something, so what I said was, 'But you said there were three prayers allowed. That's only two. What was the second?' He said I was. Then I couldn't say any more, couldn't scream like I wanted to, and . . . and . . ." She broke off into sobbing again.

"I think I can guess the rest, my dear," said the professor. He helped her over to the couch and put her feet up, then went to fetch a cold drink. "Now, you just settle down, Alice. I'm afraid I'm going to have to ask you a few questions when you feel able to answer them."

Alice Spenser grew calmer and then slid rapidly into slumber. This Dr. Ap-Rhys was pleased to see, and in the meantime he stepped into the outer office where he found Miss Briarton settling in. She was quite surprised to see him already at work, then more surprised when the Professor explained as much as he felt he might vouchsafe. He instructed her to secure fresh clothing, a few medicaments, and to have the number of the campus infirmary at the ready. Meantime he must not be disturbed. She must clear his appointments, make up any excuse she liked.

Then he busied himself at research among the volumes in his study. Something Alice had said gave him an idea. He took down several volumes of local folklore, more on historical demonology. These he had seldom had occasion to use, but he was glad now he had kept them. When some hours later Alice had awakened, he was ready to offer her a possible explanation.

"Ms. Spenser, I wonder if you have heard of 'the Devil's Steps', because whether you have heard of them or not, it is certain you have seen them."

Alice looked puzzled. "You mean those footprints in the rock?"

"Yes, quite," continued her benefactor. "Local legend has it that these were the footprints left by the devil as he fled the gospel preaching of John Wesley when that good man canvassed these parts some two centuries ago. But, to apply the words of St. Luke to the case, it would seem that Satan had departed only until a more opportune time presented itself. For darker cycles of local legend indicate that the site of the Steps themselves became a place to seek out the devil. If one arrived on the night of the New Moon, one had only to place one's feet into the steps one after another, making a wish, which the devil promised to grant. One dared not surpass the third step, for the fourth would cause the foolhardy to come to the devil in person, where there would be hell to pay. Most of the stories are, as you might imagine, cautionary tales, showing how this or that poor fool was led by his overweening greed to chance the last step for a fourth wish, only to be damned horribly."

"So, Professor, you think Tedrick had learned of this legend, and that his prayers were prayers to the devil?"

"That, of course, is exactly what I think. Ms. Spenser, I realize that you and I belong to different generations, and that your contemporaries, even when devout, are little inclined to the beliefs of my era. It is surprising that young Tedrick believed them, but perhaps desperation and ambition drove him to trying the legend for himself. And I am inclined to judge it more than legend, especially in view of what happened to you this evening past."

Alice looked into the fireplace, the embers of which still lent their comforting warmth to the chill morning. "The truth is that I had pretty much consigned belief in the devil to St. Paul's bin of 'childish things' to be put aside. But now I have to wonder. He didn't hypnotize me, I'm sure of that. Suppose there is a devil at work here, Professor, one besides Hugh Tedrick, I mean. What is there to do? I've been raped, at least that's what I'd have to call it, but I can hardly press charges! There won't be any marks of violence. I couldn't exactly resist him. And no one would believe my story. How can I make sure he doesn't do it again?"

"My dear, I doubt you have much to worry about on that score. He doubtless believes that his 'prayer' secured your slavish obedience in perpetuity, else he would never have divulged to you all that he did. That he was wrong is evident from the simple fact of your presence here. I cannot believe he would employ his last wish to bring about another encounter. And yet he may become upset and do something rash if he realizes that, knowing what you know, you are no longer under his control. So we will have to move quickly."

"Move quickly?" she parroted. "You don't mean you're going to help me get revenge on him?"

"That is not my intention, no. 'Vengeance is mine, saith the Lord, I will repay.' And yet the end result may not be altogether different. You see, my dear, there are far larger issues at stake here, forgive me for saying it. Don't you realize the implications of Mr. Tedrick's other wishes? He has as much as admitted that his blasphemous notion of our Lord leaguing himself with Satan was inspired by Satan himself! I mean, directly."

Here the old scholar rose and walked to the casement window overlooking the University Chapel. It was a tall and stately structure, built at the center of the campus, though subsequent expansion had thrown it off center. That was a sign of the times, he had more than once reflected. Christ and his Kingdom were no longer given the central place in the University and her affairs.

"And that is only the start of it. He has said that he will use diabolical means to secure universal acceptance of his heresy. I doubt that our vain Mr. Tedrick has in view any more than his own personal renown. But 'We are not ignorant of his devices,' as St. Paul said. I am sure there is something altogether more far-reaching in significance here. And we must seek to forestall it if we may."

Here Alice begged leave to return to her own rooms, assuring the Professor that she could see to herself and did not require the services of the infirmary. She promised to call him the next day. By this time the afternoon had far advanced, and Dr. Ap-Rhys felt the encroaching return of the previous day's lassitude. He locked his office, and his forgotten monograph, behind him.

This time, he was barely able to climb into bed before sleep overwhelmed him, and he began to dream at once. He found himself robed for a convocation, marching with his colleagues down the great nave of the Chapel. He usually did not dream in color, but this night he saw the vivid and garish hues of the stained glass windows. These were not the accustomed colors of those widows to the celestial world. Now they opened on infernal sights, as one beheld depicted in their frames the frightful images of Korah, of Absalom, of Judas the Iscariot, Simon Magus, Sodom and Gomorrah, even the molten chasms of Hell itself. The Great Harlot Babylon flaunted her lewdness, while demoniac satyrs and unclean nymphs sported in depraved revelry. Here the apostles engaged in unspeakable acts, while there the Blessed Mother of God stood rouged and beckoning. And all the while the unseen organist kept up a mad storm of dissonance that fairly mimicked the screaming damned in Hell.

Struggling to keep his feet as he continued in the line of march, the dream counterpart of Ap-Rhys steadied himself against the shoulder of the man ahead of him. To his surprise their robes were deep red velvet, not the traditional subdued blue-black. And the face of the man, as he looked back over his shoulder at him—why, it was the smiling countenance of Professor Hugh Tedrick!

They had seated themselves now, and the crashing cacophony of the insane organ subsided as the Chaplain of Brichester began to speak. Ap-Rhys could hear no words, but only the roaring as of a great furnace. And now the dream changed: the Chaplain seemed to be presiding at the Holy Eucharist, but it was a crying infant he held aloft to consecrate. Dr. Ap-Rhys could not watch and so shoved aside those around him, emerged unsteadily from the end of the pew and lurched stumblingly back down the nave to the outside doors. There stood Miss Briarton, grotesquely naked and obscenely tattooed, warning him with a finger to her lips, not to disturb the service. He lunged past her and collapsed onto the handrail, half walking, half falling down the long steps.

He staggered onto the green lawn before the Chapel, narrowly stepping aside when he noticed he was about to trip over the squirming bodies of two students locked in sexual congress out in the open air. As he looked around him, the whole of the yard was covered with such scenes, several of the fevered couplings between members of the same sex, some involving animals. He made his way to the broad sidewalk where he hoped to find a clear path. The massive slabs of pavement were defiled everywhere with spray-painted graffiti obscene in the extreme. It nauseated him to look upon the scrawled filth.

Finally he sank to his knees and raised his old eyes to the beckoning heavens. They, too, had changed. Above him he saw a low dome of roiling red, as if the heavens had turned to magma. He regained his feet, old knees aching with the effort, and made to run again, as far as he might. After only a few yards, as his heart began to pound dangerously, he dropped himself by the base of a statue whose shadow loomed over him. It should be a statue of the Savior, his arms beckoning. In relief he clasped the knees of the stony Jesus. He lifted his eyes to meet the haloed visage—only to flinch at a horned and grinning Antichrist.

Then it was that he woke up screaming, torn shreds of sweat-soaked sheets held tight in his white-knuckled fists.

He sat for a while at the edge of the bed, this time remembering every vivid detail of the nightmare. At length he turned on the radio to nothing specific, counting on the crackling noise of the mundane to make him feel part of the real world again. He went to the cabinet and opened some brandy. He did not seek more sleep for fear of what it might hold. As for what he had dreamt, he did not doubt it qualified as a true vision, much like those recorded and discussed in such detail in Lampton's classic *Apocalypses: the Apostolical and the Apocryphal*, though from what source they stemmed he was not yet sure. Neither could he discern whether the vision were purely symbolic or actually descriptive, but in either case it surely heralded what might be in store—if young Mr. Tedrick were allowed to proceed with his third wish.

Earlier in the morning than he would ordinarily have considered proper, Dr. Ap-Rhys rang up Alice Spenser. She was surprised to hear his voice since neither was it the professor's custom to make telephone calls himself, unmediated by Miss Briarton. The professor, whose voice sounded to her strangely hoarse, as if he had missed too much sleep, simply requested that she drop by his office at her convenience sometime that day.

Miss Briarton appeared worried as Alice entered the outer office, whether more concerned for the young woman in view of her recent ordeal or for the haggard-looking Professor Ap-Rhys, Alice did not know. She thanked the older woman for her silent hand-clasp of sympathy and progressed into the inner sanctum. There the professor had dozed off, and she gently prodded his arm to wake him.

"Ah, Ms. Spenser, I regret my inattentiveness. I have not been sleeping especially well, you see."

"Nor I. And I daren't tell you what I dreamed, Professor."

"I think you needn't. Then we are in this together." This terse pronouncement Dr. Ap-Rhys punctuated with a rare smile. "It is clear we must act against the too-deeply delving Mr. Tedrick. By all means we must prevent him from taking the next action he has planned. We must contrive to be present when next he treads the Devil's Steps. That must be one week from now, as he is limited to the night of the New Moon. Until then, you will have little choice but to meet him. I suggest, my dear, that, insofar as you can manage it, you feign a romantic devotion to him." Here Alice reflexively rose to her feet.

"Doctor Ap-Rhys, I don't care what's at stake, I'm not about to suffer the advances of that . . . that . . ."

541

His raised palm, quietly interrupting her. "Of course not, Ms. Spenser. God forbid! But if you can bring yourself to speak to him as if his spell had taken hold, I believe he will not doubt his continued hold on you even when you make excuses not to accept his advances. He is smitten with infatuation, and any young man in that position finds it difficult to understand the actions of his young woman. The sweetness of your words will be enough to sustain his illusion even if your behavior frustrates and surprises him. As I have said, he is unlikely to spend his last wish regaining your obedience."

Alice nodded her head soberly. "And in the meantime maybe I can find out more information."

"That would be most helpful, except that I think we probably already know enough."

"Why, Professor, what do you have in mind?"

"Let us wait till the night of the New Moon, shall we?"

The week passed more quickly than Alice expected. She actually saw little of the hated Tedrick, and when the two did meet, he paid her scant attention. She was relieved no little at this turn of events and speculated that he had simply been interested in the initial conquest, that now his beloved thesis again occupied him totally. She was only disappointed that she had no more opportunity to gather information helpful to the professor. And it was he that she now went to meet, this time at the Field House.

There he was, his stout form incongruously wrapped in black pants and turtleneck sweater. Alice, too, had remembered to wear the color of the night to pass unseen among the trees. She knew the way through the woods all too well from the adventure of the previous week and led the way once the dusk began to deepen.

The odd pair stopped some yards from the radius of the clearing and crouched down to wait. The professor, fatigued as he still was, was not long in falling asleep. Luckily he did not snore, so Alice smiled and decided to let him sleep till she heard or saw anything out of the ordinary.

It was about midnight, as they had half-guessed, when Tedrick appeared. He was alone and, like them, clad in black. He showed no sign of noticing their presence. He fumbled in the dark for a few minutes, while Alice gently awakened her mentor. Then both watched as Tedrick set up a small platform and made a peculiar arrangement of candles atop it. These
542

burned strange colors, some greenish, and they cast a baleful light over the scene. The two watchers were made uneasy at the increase in illumination, but they had hung back at a sufficient distance to remain unseen—or so they dearly hoped.

It was now evident that Tedrick's garb was a black robe, probably one cribbed from the Choir College, but this he soon shed, revealing a scrawny body painted over most of its surface with astrological and alchemical symbols. Alice suppressed a titter. At the same time she felt a shudder of disgust and rage, recalling the last time she had seen that naked body, albeit unpainted.

"Look," Dr. Ap-Rhys whispered, "he's taking out a book. That begins to explain how not every common fool who knows the legend has been able to gain his wishes from the Steps. There must be some ritual. I'd advise you not to listen."

But that did not stop the old academic from listening himself. The chant was in Latin, and though Tedrick had a workable knowledge of the Koine Greek of the New Testament, it was clear he had only a passing acquaintance with Medieval Latin. The longer the Professor listened, the more audible snatches he could pick out. Yes, it was a copy of the Gospel of Herodias, the scripture of the Witches' Sabbath. He had to credit Tedrick with one thing: he had certainly done his research well this time.

He felt a tug on his sleeve and turned to the wide-eyed face of the worried Ms. Spenser. "Why aren't we trying to stop him? When are you going to do something, Professor?"

"My dear," he replied as calmly as if fielding a classroom question, "I have already done it, as you shall shortly see."

Tedrick had seemingly come to the end of his chant. He now placed his foot gingerly in the first footprint, and the second, and then he paused, possibly getting the wording straight in his mind, so that his wish would come out right. Finally he took the fateful third step. More fateful than he realized, as it happened, for instantly he seemed seized by an impotent panic. In another second, as inertia carried him down to complete the step, his body seemed to be enveloped in light, then to half-disappear, as if he had passed halfway through a door. As his form stepped or fell completely through, a terrible cry was heard, and the two hidden observers were momentarily blinded by a flash of sulphurous cloud.

"It's all right to stand up now, my dear. There was light, but thank God, no fire, at least not on our side!"

"Where is he, Professor?"

"Where he would have ended up sooner or later in any case: in Hell."

"But, I mean, it was only the third step . . . !"

"In fact, it was not, Ms. Spenser, though like yourself, the late Mr. Tedrick thought that it was. You see, it took no elaborate sorcery to defeat the likes of him. Last week I simply engaged a local sculptor to come up here and camouflage the first step while carving into the ground a fifth footprint. Thus our unfortunate Mr. Tedrick thought to step into the third but actually stepped into the original fourth print. And in the bargain he stepped into Hell where he and his hypothesis belong."

–2003–

A MATE FOR THE MUTILATOR

Things seemed to be converging toward a Halloween to remember. At least that's how it seemed to the participants in the scenario that was now gathering like a bank of lowering storm clouds. It would turn out to be a lot more interesting than any October 31st any of them could remember since childhood. And that, of course, is just what they all wanted, though they were in for some surprises. Let's start with Miss Rose Gabriel, queen of campus whores at out-of-the-way Chesuncook State College, in remote Maine. There was little in the way of diversions to be enjoyed in this dreary locale, a place set so far out into the ancient New England wilderness that it had not even been reachable by paved roads until the late 1970s. Even today it lacked the most basic amenities of most college towns. There was, for instance, no multiplex cinema, nor even much of a town for a movie house to be in. Basic necessities were available if you didn't mind a trip down the highway. A single Italian restaurant supplied what pizza orders were phoned in, and more than one customer guessed the place merely reheated frozen pizzas fetched too long before from a supermarket. But there were no better alternatives, so one made do. All this students learned as soon as they arrived on campus. Promotions for the school didn't highlight any of these facts, since the advertising for the school centered mainly on the liberal admittance policy.

Chesuncook State was pretty much a last chance gas station along the educational highway. The best students here were decidedly mediocre, and that's why most of them were there, needing some sort of a diploma, and getting only some sort of diploma. These young men and women mostly majored in having a good time, which is what got most of them there in the first place. They were only in college at all because their parents thought they ought to be and insisted that a sheepskin in anything would at least elevate them a notch above manual labor. The only exception, which stood out like a sore thumb, was a small group of students majoring in environmental studies, a specialty that took natural root at Chesuncook precisely because of the remote and rural character of the place. The surrounding wilderness was a living laboratory. There was also a small but thriving computer science program, the pride and joy of the administration, since it promised, if successful, to improve the reputation of the college. If not precisely intellectual, the computer science majors were at east brainy, and these days, with the economy the way it was, that was plenty good enough. So this gives you some idea of the place and, generally speaking, of the people.

Ms. Gabriel could be found primping before the mirror in the apartment she shared near the campus, above an old drugstore, in town. Her boyfriend Jerry was not very particular in his standards of fidelity. Oh, Rose did not think he'd ever cheat on her. She had little to worry about there, she often reflected. It was just that he seemed to have no old-fashioned qualms about the approach she was taking to working her way through college. It paid the rent, that's for sure. Rose did not consider herself a prostitute, not exactly, since she viewed it only as a career stepping stone, not a vocational goal in itself. For that she would scarcely need a college education. But it sure came in handy *paying* for a college education. And there were other forms of payment that came in pretty handy, too, such as passing grades from professors. Rose was a pragmatist. You had to be in today's world. And Jerry seemed to view matters the same way. He was glad enough to get the money.

And though the couple was not exactly your typical nuclear family, Jerry's expression of concern as he admired her from behind sounded like that of a sitcom husband from the fifties. "Rosie, you sure you want to be going out tonight? I mean, Halloween brings out the crazies anyway, but that guy, the killer, is still at large. The 'Mutilator.'"

Rose was focusing on her mascara. She wanted to look tasteful, not like what she was. "You are so cute when you're worried! But I'll be fine. Personally, I don't even think there *is* this 'Mutilator.' I think it's a scare tactic pumped up by the cops to keep college kids out of mischief. A curfew to keep 'em behind closed doors studying."

Jerry wasn't convinced. "I don't know . . . You can't deny there have been bodies. Parts of bodies. How is that a hoax?"

"Oh, I know people have turned up dead, and they might even be murders, but I don't think there's one particular boogie-man lurking around. Remember where we are, after all. This place is uncivilized. It could be that wild animals are killing these people. Nobody's seen the bodies except the police. That's why I'm thinking conspiracy." Jerry laughed ironically, his voice still grave.

"And to you this sounds like there's nothing to worry about? It's a little too dangerous either way, isn't it? I can't stand the thought of anything happening to you . . ."

"Oh, you're sweet, but I can take care of myself. I mean, something could happen to you anywhere you *go*, right? It's a crap shoot. Even if there *is* a Mutilator, he can't be everywhere at once, can he? What, are you not going to fly on the remote chance the plane might crash? I used to feel that way till I realized there wouldn't be stewardesses and pilots holding those jobs if it was really all that risky, right?"

Jerry's tone lightened a bit, and his laugh held a note of real levity this time. "But how many times have you had the same stewardess on two different flights, huh? Maybe they *do* chicken out, and they have to replace 'em every time! But you have your cell phone, right? Call me if you need me, okay?" She kissed his bestubbled cheek and went out the door, headed for the house by the campus where the geeks would be awaiting her.

It was a sort of unofficial fraternity. Most students seldom bothered with official organizations, as if they needed to claim to be a service organization to have an excuse for drinking and partying. But these guys shared a dilapidated old home owned by the uncle of one of them. There were at various times eight to twelve guys crammed into the confines of the house, the dimensions of which would have seemed generous with fewer people in it. They were the brains of the student body, our aforementioned environmental engineers and computer geeks. The kinship they felt expressed itself in nothing more wholesome than occult role-playing games. You didn't have to look very hard in the common TV room to spot both a DVD and a cassette of *Animal House*, plus most of the *Revenge of the Nerds* movies. It would have been hard to tell whether these guys consciously drew on their cinematic counterparts for role model inspiration, or if they enjoyed jeering at those clowns because it let them imagine themselves superior to *someone*. It would have been equally difficult to say which attitude would count as more pathetic. Winners they might one day be, with lucrative careers that would leave their

Chesuncook campus mates in the dust, but for the present, they were losers. They called the place Delta House, but everyone else dubbed it Dildo House. It fit so well, you didn't even think of it as a joke anymore.

Well, the brothers of Dildo House were, in their industrious but haphazard way, preparing for the evening's entertainment. They didn't chip in for female pulchritude just every night. No, they were still kids enough at heart to want to have a good Halloween time. Just now, having farmed out chores among his easily bullied hangers on, Chet, whose uncle owned the place, relaxed in his room, larger than the rest of the bedrooms, and pored over a pile of gaming manuals. There were scenarios he might choose from involving medieval devil-worship, Greco-Roman pagan sacrifice, jungle fertility rites, all sorts of stuff that might be fun. He was pretty late in deciding what game to play tonight, but it had better be one they could use their usual assortment of props for, as well as something that the visiting Ms. Gabriel would agree to go along with. Chet knew from experience that Rose wouldn't mind being the nude altar for a mock Satanic mass, but that seemed a little tame for the evening. How would she feel about being tied up?

Tossing the modules aside, he went to dump out his book bag. He remembered a library book he had just received on interlibrary loan from the Maine Historical Society. He learned that many years before, there had been in this very vicinity a survival of old Salem-era witchcraft rites, or at least local rumors of them. Chet loved this sort of stuff. Yeah, there it was. There was a section of pages from an old police transcript from when they had busted in on what the papers said was an occult ceremony but which Chet imagined was just a local speakeasy or still. But wherever it came from, there was a transcript of a ritual, a litany, that local history buffs allowed did have some connections with attested Indian rites suppressed by the Commonwealth governors back in the days when Maine was part of the Massachusetts Bay colony. Hmm . . . there were voice parts for several different people. He still had time to run over to the library and make copies. And there was a role for Miss Gabriel too. She was probably game for it. If not, maybe a few more bucks would make her willing. Now, what else did he need to do? He just hoped that idiot Wassowitz would come back with enough pizzas this time.

The sun was descending as Rose decided on a parking space and as some of the Dildo House guys were polishing off some last minute homework. Slovenly rejects they might be, but good grades being the only thing they had going for them, they didn't often risk screwing them up. And the profs didn't generally delay exams just because the night before was Halloween. And less so since campus security had announced a curfew in view of the business about the Mutilator. They had credited him with the death of a couple of coeds on or near the campus. They really didn't have the authority to make a curfew stick, nor the needed manpower, and the town authorities weren't in the mood to help them. So Dildo House, not to mention Rose Gabriel, made plans as usual. And they weren't the only ones.

It was good and dark now. The kiddies in the crossroads town had long since retired from their feeble show of supervised trick or treating over the length of a single neighborhood and were safely inside getting stomach aches. Most houses by this time, as most dorm rooms, were illuminated within by the light of TV screens displaying monster movie reruns and jack-o-lantern documentaries. It seemed harder and harder to catch the spirit of the season these days, when Christmas decorations already festooned department stores before Halloween was in its grave. But there was an exception. As the wind began to rise, a lone figure of vague outline rose, too. Swathed in heavy, muffling clothes, he regained his feet as if he had been kneeling in prayer. Now his vague silhouette stood out in the icy moon glow against the tall dry grass like a weathered tombstone. Then he began to move. He was headed in the direction of the campus.

There were a number of curfew flouters this evening, Halloween proving to be too tempting. One could always count on seeing a gaggle or two of high school and college girls laughing to and at themselves as they rang doorbells, glad enough to receive candy bits and to evoke a leer from tired old dads who appreciated the sight of them and the scanty clothing they usually wore to spurn the night chill. After all, were you ever too old for some Halloween fun? No indeed. That's what the Mutilator thought, too, as he walked past the back fences of a residential row, looking for a house with no lights. Any dark house, even from the back, no kitchen or bathroom lights, was most likely empty, its occupants taking a powder at a steakhouse in the next town to weather the storm. Soon he chose a likely candidate and went over the fence and up to the back porch. The door was easily breached, and it was the sort of place he knew would never waste the money on an alarm system. His creaking footfalls aroused no one. The place seemed unoccupied. So he went to the front and flipped on the porch light, sat down and waited for the tricker treaters. He'd have a treat for them, all right. Or was it a trick? It all depended on your perspective. He polished the blade on his shirt tale till he could sort of see his face in it, then pulled down his ski mask. Had to be ready!

The porch light attracted tricker treaters like a flame draws in moths, equally doomed. Here came the giggling girls, trying to look their cutest, knocking tentatively on the door. He guessed, not having seen the front of the place, that there weren't any Halloween decorations in evidence. But the light was enough. They came. Well, if there weren't any scary skeletons on display now, there soon would be. As he opened the door, he could smell the booze on their breath. Some innocents. As for him, he never drank when out and about his rounds. Not safe. Didn't these girls know that? Didn't they teach them anything in school? It was time for a well-deserved spanking, that is, if you could still call it spanking if, instead of the flat of your hand, you used the point of your butcher knife.

Screams? Sure there were screams. What do you expect on Halloween?

Chet was showing Rose to what he called her dressing room, the downstairs bathroom, more or less scrubbed for the occasion. She had taken the costume and accepted his explanation almost wordlessly. He gave her a xerox of the ritual script, not that she had anything to say, more of a prop, really, though irreplaceable, that's for sure. As she passed, some of the guys looked up from their own photocopies, saw her, and clapped. There was nothing fake about their enthusiasm. She couldn't help feeling flattered, but she also couldn't help groaning. At least she wouldn't have to look at their faces.

Poor Wassowitz nearly dropped the pizza boxes as he tried to balance them exiting his car. He knew he would catch hell from the guys if he let the boxes tip, because then all the cheese would slide over to one side, and it would be a mess. That's one reason he liked 'em well done, more cooked, so that wouldn't happen. But then they'd yell at him for burning the damn pizzas, and he couldn't win. But this wasn't why he was nervous. You see, Wassowitz had never been laid before, and tonight was supposed

550

to the night for him. You see, it was only virgins who got stuck with the gopher chores, by the rules of Dildo House.

But now he had dropped his goddamned keys into the darkness, and he was precariously close to dropping the pizzas, too. Turning to place the increasingly damp, limp boxes flat on the roof of his car, he stooped down to grope for the goddamned keys. That's when he spotted the gleam of the street lamp on the reddened knife blade. Wassowitz was slow on the uptake, despite his considerable skill when it came to electronics, and what crossed his mind was some improbable nonsense about this being one of the guys ready to slice the pizza. But it wasn't. Wassowitz missed the party. His pals hardly missed the pizza, though, having other things to think about. Naked things. Guess which ones.

A lone Chesuncook student, I can't think of his name, one of the serious ones, so serious he didn't have time for the kind of shenanigans we have been observing so far, was spending Halloween, which he wasn't even aware that it was, out in the deep woods of Chesuncook. He was cataloging some remarkable local forms of wildlife and foliage. There were interesting standing stones, too. But it was too dark now. The moon was up, but it didn't afford enough light for the close work he had in mind. He'd have to come back tomorrow, which would be a royal pain, given the distance from the campus. Maybe he could find a motel closer. Hadn't he seen one on the way out here? He shouldered his rucksack and headed for the car, trying to remember what direction he had come through the trackless tall grass. The chorus of the frogs became noticeable in the distance. Of course, that didn't mean anything. Who would think it did?

Back in Dildo House, the geeks were getting ready for the main event. They formed their rough circle, all clad in cheap theatrical robes, inherited from the campus drama club which had disbanded a couple of years ago for lack of interest. The guy assigned to chalk the circle had forgotten to do it, so now he had to draw it, unevenly, around the guys as they stood there. The geeks were all naked beneath their robes, a fact one or two probably felt self-conscious about, guys who had always felt uneasy about having to take showers with everyone else back in high school. But this

551

was their big night for Rose Gabriel, and they wanted to be ready, so to hell with everything else. Papers shuffled as they all tried to find their proper places. Some of the crap looked to be unpronounceable, but what difference would that make as long as everybody tried to follow along on paper? They'd know what you were trying to say. And who else would be listening? All for fun. But not nearly as fun as what they were expecting.

They parted like the sea when the estimable Ms. Gabriel entered the room. This time she was suitably naked and rouged. Wow! Damn! These creeps knew that, sexually, their futures would most likely be downhill from here, after tonight. She knelt, ass toward Chet's face, as he knelt and placed his big book (probably an old Britannica volume with the xerox laid flat on the open pages) on her tasty-looking butt. He began to read, stammering with anticipation. It looked like he was trying to make a good show of it, trying not to leave any of the peculiar words out or say them too badly, but you could see he was already getting an erection. And he wasn't the only one. It was all the brethren could do to keep their minds on what they were supposed to be reading, and Chet had to bark a rebuke at one of them when the guy just couldn't seem to take his bulging eyes off Rose's bulging tits long enough to find his lines.

A voice from the circle complained, "For Chrissake, Chet! It's just a fuckin' *game*, for Pete's sake!"

"No!" Chet yelled back, "No it's *not*, Goddammit! We're not like those stupid *jocks*! There's more to it than *fucking*, I tell you! It's *performance art*, Goddammit!"

This got laughs as if it was supposed to. Rose couldn't keep her face straight, and few others could, either. But they piped down and tacitly decided to humor Chet. Besides, the screwing would have to begin pretty soon.

It did. Chet was the first. He struck it in as far as it would go, and he seemed to be in a trance all right. That was no acting. As he came, and it happened pretty fast, he shouted some gibberish, culminating with a word like *Kamog*, or like a frog bleat. Which wasn't on anybody else's copy of the sheet. But who cared? It was somebody else's turn now.

Rose's mind was happily engaged in counting cocks, figuring up how much she'd be due for each one. A good business woman, that one.

By this time, many miles away, our student, the one who didn't even know it was Halloween, had checked into a Holiday Inn he was surprised to find open. All the lobby vending machines were defunct, and there was no kitchen for Room Service, a phrase that seemed preposterously out of place there. He wished he'd brought a sandwich and decided to turn in early to make a fresh start in the morning. It would be a trek back to the site, but not nearly the trip it would have been had he gone all the way back to the dorm. He opened the window to freshen the air in the stale room before turning his lamp out. Funny, those frogs he had heard tuning up before were really rhapsodizing now! Maybe glad to be rid of him. Well, he was glad to be rid of them, or their racket, once he closed the window again.

He turned on the local news. That damn Mutilator again! Why couldn't they find this son of a bitch? Sleep would not be denied, and our boy was shortly out like a light, snoring as if he had been one of the frogs.

Rose was about done, or rather the geeks were about done with her. All flaccid and content, as content as the children in the town with their tummies full of candy, the Dildo House brothers were mostly passed out on various couches and chairs, some with the aid of post-coital substances in which the house was amply stocked.

"Well," she mused, aching and ready to change position, the carpet chafing her knees, "I guess that's your whole gang, huh?" But it wasn't. Another shaft was suddenly insider her, as rough as a square peg in a round hole, painful, yet somehow very familiar. "Hey, who? That's going to cost you extra, you know . . ." Clamp-like hands attached themselves to her shoulders, which now seemed very fragile, despite the pounding her buttocks had stolidly taken. The newcomer flipped her over as if she were a sheet on a bed he was changing.

She choked with panic, gasped spit down her throat and coughed as she saw that one gloved hand now held a large knife. And eyes glared at her from the holes in a ski mask. A ski mask she momentarily thought maybe she had seen before. But once the other hand ripped the mask away from the face of that figure whose knees now pinned her down, she knew why something seemed familiar.

It was Jerry.

Some Goddamned sense of humor. His little joke? But the slash across her left breast argued against that hypothesis. She looked around frantically to see that the geeks were asleep all right, but they would never wake up. She felt their blood pooling, reaching her like spreading rain puddles. But Jerry was talking now, demanding her undivided attention. "Damn it, Rosie, I *told* you to watch the fuck out for the Goddamned Mutilator! Now he's got you, you stupid slut! You and your dickless pals! I. . ."

He was gone, very quickly, like a TV effect where they make a guy disappear by pausing the camera while everybody else stays stock-still and the one character leaves the stage. You've seen that one a million times.

Rose, still properly alarmed at the blood flowing from her sweet flesh, heard the impact of Jerry's body smacking the wall of Dildo House and of plaster clattering off onto the floor. Who had saved her? Who could have? Not the bony little chicken Chet or any of his scrawny followers, that's for damn sure.

She made to rise, to go to the bathroom and try to do something about that cut. She'd have to get to the fuck-damned emergency room, for Christ's sake. But—there she was, flat on her back again! Oh Christ, who *now*? A weird pin-wheeling of shadows strobed the light above her. Her limbs were pinned to the rug again, but by what felt like soaking-wet pillows. Like maybe pillows freighted with lead, if that makes any sense. And let's not forget the intolerable, humid breath that came in great gales as if from an exhaust duct. Sweat and blood stung her eyes, and she couldn't focus them. Closer and closer to her open-mouthed face there leaned in a beak with a tongue, croaking a single word, if it *was* a word: *Kamog!*

–2004–

THE PRYING INVESTIGATIONS OF EDWIN M. LILLIBRIDGE

The recent recovery of the final remains of *Providence Evening Telegram* reporter Edwin M. Lillibridge, long resting uneasily as if coveting a friendlier refuge, has occasioned much speculation as to the means of the newsman's passing from this world, as the condition of the bones speaks volumes, albeit in an unknown tongue. His disappearance as long ago as 1883 caused some comment at the time, but in those days any mysterious doings connected with the shunned Free Will Baptist church on Federal Hill were deemed best left alone. Besides, Mr. Lillibridge had been a bachelor with no surviving family, and, with the eventual expiration of his sponsoring newspaper, there seemed no one left with a vested interest in discovering his fate. It was, as is well known, only the recent exploration of the old church ruin preparatory to its ordered demolition that led to the fortuitous discovery of Lillibridge's troubled bones. And when the coroner disclosed their singular condition, including the odd *charring* and in some cases acidic *dissolution* of some of them, it was quite naturally deemed a case better left closed, if only by time and ignorance.

An unexpected discovery of my own has now led to the disclosure of the odd facts leading to the vanishing of the lost reporter, and I feel it incumbent to share the information thus recovered with any whose curiosity about Lillibridge's life and work may still linger.

In his cramped office in the *Telegram* building, Edwin M. Lillibridge fanned himself to ward off the early autumn heat. He listened with growing interest to a set of local parents who had much more serious preoccupations than the temperature. The man and woman, as Lillibridge could easily tell, had been through their story many times already, and without the satisfaction they sought. There had been in recent years a subtle but disturbing increase in the rate of missing children incidents, and it was a matter of persistent ill-rumor in the old town that the disappearance had something to do with the theosophical sect nested in an old Baptist church building crouching atop Federal Hill. When the couple's young son failed to return home after school detention, they took the matter to the local constabulary but were surprised to meet with a combination of unease and indifference, as if the stance represented a studied but regretted policy of the department. Mr. and Mrs. Alsop, for that was their name, soon gathered from wider but informal inquiries that the police had their own reasons for taking such reports less than seriously. The bereaved parents took this to mean the police were being paid for their lack of curiosity, probably by the well-endowed Starry Wisdom Church. The congregation's wealth was rumored to be very great, stemming from the mysterious discoveries of their pastor, the Reverend Doctor Enoch Bowen.

This clergyman had himself been affiliated with the Free Will Baptist denomination until a sabbatical trip to the Near East, on which he aimed to pursue a hobby in amateur archaeology, had issued in the chance discovery of a horde of antique treasure somehow hitherto unmolested by the local Arabs. It had been shortly after his return to Providence, curiously reticent to discuss the nature of his find, or indeed even to verify the report of it, that Dr. Bowen had returned his ordination credentials to his denominational office and instituted a new regimen of theology and worship at the familiar building, with the full backing of the then-dwindling congregation. That his discovery had at least included some modicum of the legendary wealth of the Pharaohs seemed certain from the sudden campaign of building renovation that gave the old pile a new lease on life. It was at that time, for instance, that the older stained-glass windows with their conventional themes had been replaced by subtly different religious symbols and cameos, some of them mystifying and a few downright disturbing to pious neighbors not belonging to the new sect.

Dr. Bowen himself, a man of abstemious habits, did not change them in any outward respect, continuing his Spartan lifestyle to all appearances. No one accused him of enriching himself, and this, plus some strategic charitable giving to the neighborhood poor, served to deflect suspicions from the unorthodox Church of Starry Wisdom. After all, it was a time of religious fermentation all across New England and New York, and the appearance of one more new brand on the metaphysical shelf occasioned gossip for only a short time till more titillating topics soon replaced it.

There was certainly nothing sinister about the reputation of Pastor Bowen, a bookish man whose repute for counseling the distraught was well-deserved. If anything, his new theology only enhanced his reputation as a local Swedenborg or Quimby. Thus it had been no difficult decision for Mr. and Mrs. Alsop to pursue their inquiry with the man himself. They found it hard to credit any implication of involvement in their tragedy on the clergyman's part, and, besides, must not any accusations of Starry Wisdom's role in the child-snatching fire their minister with a zeal to get to the bottom of the whole wretched business? Or so the couple had hoped. In the event, they found the silver-haired Dr. Bowen quite forthcoming with his trained listening ear, ready to extend well-worded sympathies, but oddly reticent to lend any practical aid. Then again, he proposed, prayer was a mighty weapon, and he should be sure to wield it in their behalf. The couple left with a feeling like that which they now inspired in the reporter: that Dr. Bowen's words were well-rehearsed, a script familiar from repeated performances. There had, after all, been those numerous other disappearances.

Lillibridge listened patiently until it was his own turn to repeat himself, for he had more than once found himself listening to very much the identical story. He had already tried to dig into the mystery, but to no avail. The chief impediment to his investigations, investigations which the police, not he, should be pursuing, was the surprising development that not long after confiding in the reporter, most of the affected parents had quietly *joined the Starry Wisdom Church* and were henceforth reluctant either to maintain any inquiry or to cooperate in it. Of course, all said it had been the compassion of Enoch Bowen in their hour of need that had attracted them to Starry Wisdom. It sounded reasonable after a fashion, but Lillibridge could not help thinking it odd.

He saw them out, wishing them well and assuring them of further news should he find any, and then made his way down the block where he hoped an old friend, Officer Shaunessy, might be found. Lillibridge and the policeman had more than once traded tips that came in handy. Besides, the doughty Irishman was too upstanding a man to take part easily in any departmental corruption, and Lillibridge decided he must now ask his help, hitherto reluctant for fear of raising a dangerous subject: an honest policeman in a corrupt department walked a narrow line, and Lillibridge did not want to give him a shove into personal danger. But now he knew he must do something, and he decided Officer Shaunessy could surely take care of himself.

Sure that he saw the tall, broad form of the man he sought a pair of blocks ahead of him, Lillibridge quickened his step until he reached the great Irishman and tapped him on the shoulder. The larger man spun about with reflexes surprising for one possessing his stature and weight. As soon as he beheld the familiar features of the reporter, the constable relaxed, his red face lit by a widening smile. "Eddie, me b'y! 'Tis good t' see ya! It's off duty oi am, and oi'd be pleased if y' were t' join me f'r some refreshment."

Withal, the ill-matched pair continued together for scant further steps before turning in to a local tavern, through whose swinging doors they passed. Lillibridge scanned the dim, smoky interior, looking for a booth or table where men might converse with no one eavesdropping. Finding such a redoubt, he waved to the burly policeman, who made his way across the crowded floor balancing a couple of glasses of beer.

"Bill, I wish I were here for a social occasion pure and simple, but I'm afraid I'm seeking you out on business, a bad business. I'm hoping you might have some information to share."

Setting his mug down, the patrolman quickly shed the mood of relaxation he had begun to allow himself. "Aye, there's always bad business o' one sart or t'other to keep us busy in moi loin a' work! What's troublin' ya, Eddie?"

Lillibridge looked around before continuing. "It's a sensitive subject, Bill, in more ways than one. But I have to ask. Today I was talking with another couple who'd lost a son. Here on Federal Hill. The only lead I've got is the Starry Wisdom Church. I know the police have . . . thought it best to deal with Reverend Bowen with kid gloves. But if you know anything you could tell me, I should truly appreciate it. I hardly need to tell you I would keep your name out of it."

Bill Shaunessy had already sat back against the upholstered bench, leaving his beer to drink itself. His genial smile was gone. He did not appear to be angry. What pained his round, wide-boned face looked more like a sense of dread and pain. One could tell he was trying to decide how to say that he would not be saying anything.

"By the Saints, Eddie. You've brought up a sahr point. Not as I blames ye. But there's a lot mahr to the thing than ye know. Oi know ye think we're paid t' look t'other way. And some are. That oi know. But oi know, too, that things could get a lot worse. A *lot* worse. So bad that missin' a few of our dear ones now an' then wouldn't seem so great a sacrifice."

Lillibridge turned pale, so pale that the change was visible even in the shaded interior of the saloon. His friend's face remained frozen to stone. The reporter moved his mouth as if to reply, but it hung idly for a moment, then closed again. Shaunessy resumed his low-voiced, reluctant words. "But this oi'll tell ye. There's a man ye might talk with, though not t' quote in the paper. An' don't be after tellin' him oi sent ye."

If Officer Shaunessy had his beat to pound, so did Edwin M. Lillibridge. He was used to following a story down any dark alley it might take him. This time it took him to one of the oldest and most stately dwellings on College Hill. He had seen the place but had no associations with it. The inhabitant was largely unknown to him, despite the fact that Lillibridge had occasion at least to catalogue the name and face of most of the prominent members of the community. This one was *only* a name and face. He was a successful businessman, involved somehow with shipping, but neither he nor his trade had ever before proven newsworthy. As he rang the bell and was shown in, the reporter was surprised to observe the halls crowded with packing cases, with most of the rest of the sumptuous furnishings draped with blankets and tarpaulins. Plainly, the master of the house was busily engaged in leaving town, from the looks of it, for good. Lillibridge wondered, only half-seriously, if the sudden instinct to migrate might have anything to do with the matters into which he now found himself looking.

Harold R. Collins III made his appearance with hand extended, though apparently in no welcoming mood. He was quite evidently preoccupied. He bade his visitor state his business and come to his point. Not wanting to be rude, he nonetheless had much on his mind.

"As I do, Mr. Collins. So I appreciate all the more your seeing me on such short notice—and apparently just in time!" The other man looked a bit nonplussed, as if something in Lillibridge's words had obliquely suggested danger to him.

"I mean, I wouldn't have wanted to miss you. Mr. Collins, I am told you have lately resigned your membership in the Starry Wisdom Church in Federal Hill."

"*You're* not a member, are you?"

"Oh, no! No, sir, I'm not. Nor a detractor. I am merely curious to get to the bottom of certain rumours that have raised their heads again of late. I'm not really looking for a story. I think public interest in Starry Wisdom peaked some years back. I'm more interested in the welfare of some friends, and they told me that Starry Wisdom . . . might be . . . of help."

"Then I should say you have come to the wrong man, sir. As you say, I
559

have strayed from that particular flock. Whatever concerns *it* no longer concerns *me*."

"But, there you are! That is just the perspective I'm looking for, Mr. Collins. I am hoping that perhaps you will know certain things that you will no longer feel honor-bound to keep secret, if you know what I mean."

"You are clever, my good man, but surely one is all the more bound by honor to keep vows made to those in whose debt one no longer stands. How does scripture put it? 'He sweareth to his own hurt and changeth not.'"

"Indeed, sir, one of the Psalms, as I recall. My mother used to quote it. But it is a matter of danger . . ."

"I should say that it is! And I don't mind telling you, it is not merely honour which compels my silence."

"Just as it is not mere wanderlust that motivates your impending departure, no?"

"As I say, Mr. Lillibridge, you are clever. But I am afraid I can be no help to you." And yet, with these words, Collins reached out to take the reporter's hand and silently placed something cold into his palm, closing the other man's fingers around it. "Now I fear I must return to my preparations. You can show yourself out?"

That is what Edwin Lillibridge did, and he waited, in case eyes should be following him, till he got back to his office before opening his hand. For a second he thought he might have held a coin, but then he realized it had to be a key. Lillibridge now sat there, gazing at the thing. He hoped it might prove indeed to be the solution to the puzzle facing him. And he thought he knew where the key would fit. But it was nonetheless puzzling, since the same place was open to the prying eyes of the public.

And so Lillibridge decided he must next do something he had not done for a good many years, before journalism became his religion. He would attire himself in his Sunday best and attend the services at the Starry Wisdom Church of Providence. He felt no particular foreboding at the decision. He was undaunted at the prospect of attending the meeting of an eccentric sect. Any city that took pride in housing the Mother Church of the Christian Science denomination of Mary Baker Eddy could hardly flinch at the presence of the Starry Wisdom sect.

Lillibridge sat himself down in a sturdy pew about halfway down the nave and scrutinized the place during the service preliminaries. The sanctuary, nearly eighty years old, was in excellent repair. Then he remembered the refurbishing campaign financed by the Reverend Bowen's Egyptian delvings. Of the once-controversial stained-glass designs he could make little, especially since the morning was cloudy and no artificial light source illuminated the windows from behind. All that struck him as being out of the ordinary was one tall window framing what looked like a procession of monks. The artist must have had trouble with full-figure representation: the pacing, robed forms bore odd proportions, almost simian. He knew portrait painters often had difficulty with the rest of the human form when rarely called upon to depict it.

The congregation was surprisingly large, given that the sect had a few years earlier left town under a cloud of suspicion not unlike that which prompted Lillibridge's own investigation. There had never been provable charges; the congregation feared, and not groundlessly, vandalism and lynchings, should some agitator whip the local superstitious Catholic immigrants into a frenzy. Under assurances of police protection, which the department could hardly refuse, Dr. Bowen and a number of his disciples did finally return to the city a few years later to take possession once again of the old Free Will Baptist church into which they had poured so much energy and resources.

But Lillibridge was even more surprised at the strikingly diverse racial composition of the church. For next to stolid Yankees sat squat and swarthy Asians or East Europeans, Lillibridge could not quite tell which. Nor were Negroid and mulatto faces unrepresented. He reflected that this racial tolerance would of itself have been enough to cast a pall of scandal over the congregation in the eyes of society's proper mavens. Lillibridge himself, despite sympathies that had necessarily grown with experience, found himself momentarily taken aback with a mild feeling of distaste and disdain. But then he could not have sworn the origin of it was mere reflexive bias. Something in the general mood of the place disturbed him on a level so subtle it was practically instinctive. But then again, that might as easily be the product of his long alienation from organized religion. No wonder he felt out of place.

For the same reason, he guessed, he felt mildly uncomfortable with the hymns, though the congregation sang them rousingly enough. There were occasional odd references, names he thought sounded vaguely Egyptian, but then again, he had not heard, much less sung, any hymn in years. All of them would have struck him as equally bizarre, especially those of the famous Ira Sankey, which one sometimes read quoted in news reports of

Dwight L. Moody, choruses celebrating the blood atonement of the Saviour in almost primitive terms. It all brought back to him what had alienated him from churchgoing so many years ago. And now, here he was back again, albeit as something of a spy.

Now the Reverend Bowen was ascending the hourglass pulpit. Some parishioners moved along the crowded pews from where their position behind the gathered columns, like indoor oaks, had impeded their adoring view of their shepherd. Lillibridge could see the aging clergyman, still visibly hardy like Moses, with undimmed eye and unfailing strength on into advancing years. As the old man's smiling gaze swept the familiar faces of his flock, Lillibridge thought he saw the preacher pause a moment longer on his own upturned visage. This reaction must be entirely natural for a minister noticing the unaccustomed face of a visitor. The reporter reminded himself to betray no trace of suspicion, but to display only the genuine curiosity he felt.

Dr. Bowen was by this time reading the scriptural text upon which he would expound. Again, it was wholly unfamiliar to reporter Lillibridge, but he was not a religious man. He would likely fail to recognize a reading from the Bible if someone told him it was Shakespeare.

"A veil is stretched out between the world above and the realms that are below. And shadow came into being beneath that veil. And it came to pass that the shadow became matter; and that shadow was projected apart. And it took shape in the matter: like unto an abortus. And it did take on a plastic form molded out of shadow, and it became an arrogant beast resembling a lion. Opening his eyes, he beheld a vast quantity of matter without limit. And he did wax arrogant, saying, 'It is I who am God, nor is there any other apart from Me!' And a voice came forth from above the realm of absolute power, saying, 'You are mistaken, Samael,' which is interpreted, 'God of the Blind.'"

And there was something about the "Urim and Thummim," the divination stones through which God had made known his will in ancient Israel.

Lillibridge, who might have been tone deaf to scripture, at least had a sensitivity to writing and communication, and he could make nothing of these strange words. Even less could he discern the import of the tedious sermon that followed. What the text might have had to do with it was hard enough to determine, but the sermon was principally a tedious mass of specialized jargon of which no sense might be made by the outsider. Even a secretive sect need not close its doors to the public if it so concealed its revelation beneath a thick blanket of theological code. The chorus of *Amens* made it clear that the faithful had understood the disquisitions of their beloved leader well enough.

A smiling Lillibridge shook hands with a few congregants as the meeting dispersed, but no one was eager to exchange more than bland pleasantries and polite invitations to return for another visit. That was to be expected. It was neither the time nor the place for searching questions. The reporter hoped at least for a direct look in the eyes and a handshake from the pastor, but in this, too, he was disappointed. Unlike most clergy who position themselves at the church door to bid parishioners goodbye, Dr. Bowen had exited the platform through one of the doors flanking the chancel. Either he was not comfortable with crowds or he sought thus to increase his mystique. No one but Lillibridge seemed to mind.

Sitting at a lunch counter, in a row of suit-clad church refugees, Lillibridge fingered the key in his pocket as he looked over the menu. Absent-mindedly, he ordered some sort of sandwich and planned his next move. He now knew why the nervous Mr. Collins had thought the church key, for such it must be, was needful, since the limited access to the truth Starry Wisdom allowed a Sunday visitor was not likely to be worth much. Yet Lillibridge had picked up one choice piece of information. It seemed that services would be suspended for the next month while the greater portion of the congregation embarked upon a long-planned cruise to the Holy Land, with Dr. Bowen as their guide. Through his researches, Bowen must know the region well, and such trips were not uncommon in affluent congregations. Lillibridge knew, as Collins must have, that the temporary absence of the Starry Wisdom faithful would afford him a rare advantage to gain secret entry into the old stone pile atop Federal Hill. It was an opportunity of which he meant to take full advantage.

Edwin Lillibridge had plenty with which to occupy himself, attending to his ordinary reportorial duties, anticlimactic as they might now seem, as he waited for the Starry Wisdom congregation to follow their leader safely out of the country. He laid no special plans for his infiltration of the sanctuary.

By the expediency of sham inquiries made to the office, pretending to seek an appointment with church staff for the purpose of demonstrating new office equipment, Lillibridge had ascertained that the staff would be absent during the cruise, those not aboard the ship taking the time off locally. He felt sure there would be night watchmen on duty, but during the day he should be able to venture boldly into the sanctuary through the front door. To any casual passerby it must seem business as usual, as neighbors not attending a particular church seldom bother to keep apprised of its schedule. He expected to have uninhibited access to whatever might lie behind any doors through which his skeleton key might admit him.

The day came, and the reporter made his way to the courtyard which stretched before the elevated plot of ground on which the Gothic Revival bulk of the Starry Wisdom Church stood, as if perching on a platform to come closer to heaven. There was a normal day's foot traffic, as he had expected, and he tried to look his most inconspicuous as he crossed the cobblestone expanse and inserted the key, first, into the iron gate. It swung open cooperatively, and he ascended the stairs, aware of occasional eyes resting on him from the street and reassuring himself that it meant nothing. He did not take the rest of the stairs ahead of him all the way up to the huge sanctuary doors, reminiscent of those of a medieval castle. Instead, he took the sidewalk around to the side, where he thought he remembered the office door being located. The key fit this one, too. He guessed that Mr. Collins must have been some sort of deacon or vestryman to be entrusted with this key. He had managed to retain it upon his departure from the group. Lillibridge wondered how amicable a parting it had been, and he speculated whether representatives of Starry Wisdom might not yet seek to reclaim the key from the man, who after all had appeared to expect some visitation he earnestly hoped to avoid.

He was able to gain access to the church office, but not to the desk drawers or locked files. Nor did he dare to force them. He dreaded leaving any evidence of his visit, much less blatant proof of prowling. So he quit the office and walked softly down the hall. He passed the entrance to the sanctuary for the moment. He felt he had seen what it had to offer when he had visited before. So he continued to the next door, which should lead to the sacristy, the "backstage" area adjacent to the chancel, behind the pulpit and choir loft. It would contain access to the immersion tank traditionally used by Baptist churches, which this had once been. He doubted Starry Wisdom had much use for it these days. But who knew what he might find in the preparation area of the sacristy, which, as he seemed to recall, would have been the room through which the pastor would have made his post-sermonic exit.

The door cracked, then creaked, open, in obvious want of oil. Lillibridge flinched at the noise, hoping he was the only one in earshot. He could not know for certain that he was alone in the building. He was surprised at the size of the room, which seemed to double as the pastor's study. Nearby was a large desk, with a bookcase surmounting it against the wall. He paused here and could not resist scanning some of the exotic titles. He had never heard of any of them nor had he the faintest notion of their contents. The *Necronomicon* might be an actuarial compendium for all he knew, if not a collection, of death certificates. The language appeared to be Latin, which Lillibridge had never spent a minute studying. Likewise the tongue-twisting *De Vermis Mysteriis*. Two "i's" in a row? He thought perhaps he had once heard of *The Book of Dzyan* in connection with a magazine feature on Madame Blavatsky, but he couldn't be sure. Reluctantly, he replaced the books and looked for any paper scraps that might bear revealing or incriminating notes. Nothing seemed amiss, much less suspicious.

Another table, closer to the chancel door, bore a set of neatly stacked and polished vessels, apparently communion dishes, but also other odd-looking tools or liturgical devices whose use he could not guess. All bore exquisite, yet disturbing, workmanship, including delicately stylized representations of marine life forms out of some ancient poet's imagination: he thought of the Norse Kraken and Homer's Scylla—and shuddered. But what did he know of such things? Was not the fish a very ancient Christian symbol? So he turned and saw another, inner door that opened upon the baptismal pool. For some reason, he felt drawn to take a look.

Here was an odd thing. The tank had been made over into a large aquarium. Obviously the rites of Starry Wisdom no longer included baptism by immersion. Lillibridge himself maintained a small aquarium at home. He was fascinated by what he now saw and momentarily sought for the inevitable containers of fish food but decided against feeding the shy denizens of the tank, who hid in the reeds at the bottom of the large structure. He did not want to disturb anything the night watchman, who must be assigned to feed the fish, might notice. But he did allow himself a pleasurable look into the depths of the miniature habitat. The waters were oddly murky. It was difficult to make out more than vague motion inside. But at once, some of the waving sea weed parted, revealing a kind of crustacean, yet octopoid, chimera he had never seen before, even in books. It disappeared as quickly as it had revealed itself, and Lillibridge staggered back from the glass pen with revulsion.

Regaining his composure with a silent self-rebuke, the interloper made for the door, re-entered the uncarpeted hallway and began to ascend a flight of stairs which he calculated must lead to the bell tower. He knew he should likely find nothing there, but it should afford a nice vantage point for the enchanting panorama of Providence below.

Creaking stairs took him to the door of what he first took for a store room built into the capacious shaft of the upthrust tower. He knew he was not high enough in the structure for this to be the level where the church bell hung. It was even a bit low for the ringer to stand and grab hold of a bell rope. More than likely, a storage room in such an improbable place would house cast off objects and furniture from the old Baptist days, items for which the present congregation no longer had any use. At any rate, he should have to enter it if he were to find access to the higher levels of the increasingly claustrophobic tower.

The investigator's initial glance seemed to confirm his guesswork, as the first thing he beheld was a group of elegantly upholstered high-back chairs of the kind that line the rear wall of the chancel in old churches for the sanctimonious posteriors of church deacons or some such. Perhaps their style was no longer considered tasteful, or perhaps they were judged too ostentatious and had been retired here. But, no, that would not explain their arrangement, for a second look showed Lillibridge that the throne-like seats were arranged in a perfect circle, some seven of them, surrounding a squat table of unusual design. On closer examination, the reporter saw that the central object was an asymmetrical stone pillar, plainly an ancient artifact, no doubt one of the treasures retrieved from Egypt by the delving Dr. Bowen. Outside the circle of chairs, pushed against the walls, were seven large head sculptures of primitive design, such as could be found on Easter Island, though these looked to be plaster copies, like stage props. This was plainly a ritual space unto itself, the site for celebrations or meditations of a more private type than the public services such he had lately attended. He knew at once he had found the place where the real business of the Starry Wisdom Church was done. Now—what *was* that business?

The light was poorer up here, and dust augmented the denseness of the shadows, drifting as it seemed from the boards above, the ceiling of this level and the floor of the one above, the interior of the steeple. Once Lillibridge's eyes made the adjustment, he looked more closely at the central altar stone, if that was what it was, and at the object displayed upon it, which he had not noticed at first. There was a polished metal box, open in the manner of a jewelry shop display, and nestled in it~no, held within a peculiar metal band in such a way that none of its facets actually touched the velvety cushions of its container—was a strange, dull gem.

Not without a certain witch-fire glow, albeit of the subtlest kind, the polished surface of the stone was cut into the most irregular shape, none of its various faces possessing a right angle to share with is neighbor. It was somehow frustrating, baffling, to look at the thing. And yet one could not look away. Though opaque, the object yet seemed to possess a strange *depth* into which the eye was irresistibly drawn. Abandoning his studied caution, Lillibridge now sat down in one of the great chairs, not moving his gaze from the black, red-streaked gemstone. He brought a finger near the stone but withdrew the digit when he felt a kind of radiant electricity emanating from it.

For a moment his rapidly drifting mind recalled Joseph Smith, the Mormon prophet, as he wondered if it were not such a gem, a "seer stone," that Smith had used to discern his revelations. But at once that thought was lost, crowded out by what he could have only called false memories, vivid, timeless glimpses of a past that seemed to unfurl into an impossible distance, yet all redolent of memory's familiarity. His mind was now in some manner anchored to the stone. Perhaps he was sharing the memory of the stone . . .

Lillibridge's mouth gaped wide and his arms hung limp, crookedly propped on the heavy, carven arms of the great ecclesiastical chair. In such a state he did not, needless to say, hear the soft scuffling sounds emanating from the unseen steeple interior just above him.

In the unnamable world in which his spirit now drifted, Edwin M. Lillibridge confusedly acknowledged the strange feeling of having been *joined* by some unseen companion. Shortly he found his stupor dissipating, as he began to see with a sight that must have imagination as its vehicle. He appeared to be the center of attention for many pairs of eager eyes. But the eyes waved from chitinous stalks. They were very far from being human. But they did seem intelligent. He felt like an infant being held up in the delivery room of a hospital for the mother to behold. One of the odd beings surrounding him in this dream held what appeared to be a sharp-edged tool, though at first it had seemed no more than a further extension of its arachnid anatomy. A chorus of the most peculiar buzzing, as of a summer's wealth of crickets, albeit with some sort of electrical distortions admixed, filled the space they shared. Before long, he felt "joined" again, this time by another presence who seemed to represent the curious spirit of one of the entities.

It seemed to him, again, by a misplaced sense of memory rather than perception, that he was located, not on the fair earth, but on an unspeakable world of impenetrable blackness, a hell of onyx, obsidian, and pitch through whose crevasses slowly oozed rivers of black lava.

But then he knew a different sort of endless blackness, as he seemed to be transported, in company with a great horde of the crustacean things, through fathomless space. He sensed more of their insane buzzing, though the vacuum of space allowed for no true sound. At length the caravan of beings exchanged dead blackness for blinding white. The vestigial Lillibridge-consciousness understood, with a knowledge to which his sense perception would have been inadequate, that they had arrived at earth's south pole. The time was many thousands of years in the remote past, though recent enough for the all-encompassing ice fields to have smothered all life.

At some unknown time later, there was a great conflict, warfare between the lobster-like invaders and another, already-resident species, one, if possible, even more mind-blastingly alien. For these beings looked like great scaly barrels surmounted by quivering star-fish heads, and with membraned wings sprouting from all sides of their trunks like the leaves of huge vegetables. The two races fought by means of energy beams directed at one another and at their respective citadels. The human part of him assumed the bizarre space-explorers were fighting, as earthmen did, over territory, though he could not imagine what value anyone would see in the sterile ice desert. But then he realized that he himself, that is, the entity contained within the oddly faceted gem, was the true object of the contest. They were warring over the gem from the steeple tower!

It must be a talisman of terrible potency or of some equally great value. At length one side prevailed: the starfish things exterminated all but a relative few of the things from the black planet who, it seemed, had originally fashioned the jewel of all knowledge. The straggling remnant of the lobster-race abandoned their Antarctican outpost to seek refuge further north where they should in future restrict themselves to curious mining operations, looking for substances unavailable on their own lightless world.

Meantime, the living gem found itself the object of great and elaborate rituals of veneration among the Antarctican creatures, who offered ichor-streaming sacrifices upon oddly-angled altars, seeking to plumb the artifact's depths in search of knowledge that might help them secure victory in yet another conflict, this time against certain amorphous entities of their own creation, viscous masses of protoplasm teeming with eyes that moved questingly in every direction, like some real-world counterpart to the Argus of mythology. But from this, all they gained was the knowledge of their inevitable defeat beneath the onslaught of the monsters, and Lillibridge shared the vision of the attack of the things, including their eventual overwhelming of the temple of the gem. But the Antarctican vegetable-race had contrived a metal box of curious design to house the thing, for they surmised that darkness such as the inner entity had known on its parent world would unlock its guardian spirit with incalculable power. And in their last extremity, the high priest of those doomed aliens managed to shut the box! From its lightless interior came the Avatar of Darkness, which Lillibridge's spellbound, purely passive awareness now recognized intuitively as the external form of that consciousness with whom he shared location in the striated gem.

An awful mountain of smoky tenebrousness sailing forth on a pair of vaguely defined bat-wings, the god or devil swept its gaze over the ranks of triumphant rebels with its surmounting cycloptic eye, a deadly orb with three overlapping pupils. From it a withering death ray projected, crisping the flabby masses of the creatures that had overwhelmed their creators and masters. As it returned, like Aladdin's genie, into the narrow confines of its container, the juggernaut left behind it outspread acres of ruined masonry which soon began to be reclaimed by the drifting snow and ice, to await possible discovery by the children of men.

Aeons passed as the Lillibridge-consciousness sank back into dreamless sleep-within-sleep. But then he heard the strange, sibilant chanting of a new race, scarcely less outré than any other he had seen, for these had the form of reptiles that had somehow evolved into near-humanity. Their explorers had unearthed the case containing the mystic gem from its grave amid the dead snow fields and transported it back to their home on an antique continent lost even to the most archaic mythologies of mankind: elder Valusia whence one day King Kull should arise. These crafty beings soon surmised the nature of the treasure they had found and made the sacrifices in cold blood that the Thing inside required as barter for the knowledge that it offered. From it the serpent-race snatched the secret of assuming any shape desired, or rather, of projecting it onto the receptive minds of those among whom they wished silently to pass. And yet in the end they lost their advantage, as envious factions gained access to the gem and begged of it ever superior skills in besting their rivals, until the ensuing intrigues spelled the obliteration of the greater part of their people, only a few managing to linger on in impotence alongside the new race of men in future centuries.

And one of them, having learned no wisdom from the dangers of too much knowledge, carried the box and the gem with it across jungle-garlanded Africa to adjacent Lemuria, where it was lost sight of till the first Cro-Magnons stared dumbly at its pale aurora and erected about it flimsy curtains of mammoth-hide hung from a crude lattice of tusks and antlers. From its hypnotic glow the cave-men received unbidden promises of great boons in hunting and warfare. And they were glad to pay the price in squalling infants and shrieking maidens. And thus was the enhancement of the brain of man accomplished, sparked by an infusion of death-dealing and death-bought wisdom from the Avatar of Darkness. And thus was man's bloody path established forever: the incessant seeking of knowledge and the application of it to ever greater death and destruction.

Sensations were crowding upon him too fast for the human consciousness, who had by now lost track of its own name and identity, to register them all. But at some point he grasped that the immortal gem had found its way from continent to continent, from one civilization to another, in the manner of a deathless *atman* traveling from life to life concealed within the shifting soul of mortal man. And next it seemed he dwelt in Plato's Atlantis, where the champion Kull had caused the stone to be set into the pommel of his broadsword. It gave him victory over all enemies, but when he seized the throne of Valusia and was nearly destroyed by the lingering serpent-race who contrived to regain the gem and with it their dominion from of old, the king had the gem removed and cast into the ocean.

But of course that was not the end of this small token which survived where whole continents foundered. Many centuries later the thing was cherished anew, by another mighty king, the tyrannical Pharaoh Nephren-Ka, whose native diabolism enabled him to put the stone to the greatest advantage yet. For from its depths he purchased the knowledge of all the future history of his realm. But the first bit of the future he saw was his own overthrow by his decimated subjects who could stomach no more of his butchery, as a whole generation had perished as the price for his revelations. Henceforth his name was never spoken and was chiseled from all monuments.

And it was in the concealing wreckage of the tomb of Nephren-Ka, a perverse structure with its apex pointed down, dug into the sleeping earth below, that the intrepid Enoch Bowen had lately recovered it, drawn by a seeming instinct he could not have disobeyed had he possessed any inclination to do so.

"Lillibridge. Edwin M. Lillibridge." Yes, *that* was the name of his fleeting human consciousness! He remembered! Someone was repeating that name, trying to rouse the shattered man from his stupor of too much knowing. Then the reporter had *not* been alone in the building. But who was it, standing before him now? Pulling himself as erect as he could, Lillibridge squinted, unaccustomed to real, ocular sight. The tall, silver-haired figure carried a lantern to dispel the gloom that enveloped them both—and others. It was night. Hours had passed. But no. The man before him was the Reverend Bowen. He was back from the congregation's cruise trip. This meant Lillibridge had been sitting there, overcome, for long *weeks*. His growing physical enervation had no doubt only made him the more receptive to the nightmare visions that had assaulted him during these terrible days.

The clergyman was replacing Lillibridge's press credentials in the reporter's coat pocket. The exhausted and disoriented man knew he would have a lot of explaining to do. He had violated the sect's Holy of Holies, that was true, but he had done no real harm, taking nothing, leaving virtually no mark to betray his passing—until the minister and six of his elders chanced to discover him as they entered the shrine to perform whatever rites were customary to the secret place. Well, Lillibridge now knew what it was he had come to discover, but he had no evidence that would stand up in any court, unless he could find where the childish bones were buried in the convenient churchyard.

But what proof did Bowen have that Lillibridge had done anything of a criminal nature? His presence was proof of his trespassing, true, but then to prosecute Lillibridge must lead to the public exposure of the suspicions against Bowen's sect, and in such a case the discretion of the police would be of no avail. All this passed swiftly through the mind of the reporter, forced to take stock of his indelicate position with the instinctive alertness of a cornered animal. But it shortly developed that Dr. Bowen had no such plans. Plans, though, he did have.

"My dear Mr. Lillibridge. I had expected to make your acquaintance sooner or later. Warned of your interest by the gem, I arranged to have you followed, as it turned out, to the house of the backsliding Mr. Collins.

He is not good company to keep, Mr. Lillibridge. Mr. Collins is a disciple who looked back while plowing for the kingdom of God. Thus he went off the straight path. And he has led you off the path, too, I regret to say. But rest assured, Collins has been made to see the error of his ways, for all the good it will do him. And I gather from what I see here that you, too, have come to a fuller apprehension of the truth. Indeed, I should say that, given what you have no doubt seen, you walk no longer by faith but by sight, isn't it so?"

"So what is it you plan to do with me? Sacrifice me as you did all those children? Am I worth a few more hallucinations to you and your sycophants?"

"I cannot say as I care for your tone, Mr. Lillibridge, but, yes, essentially that is it." He gave a curt signal to his assistants, two of whom bound the limp and unresisting interloper to the chair arms, following which two more dragged the huge seat back and across the floor until it rested squarely beneath the trapdoor leading to the recess of the steeple. The noises of shifting and knocking were now unmistakable. The Thing up there must have hungered to get at him for weeks now. But its impatience would soon be at an end.

Here it came, dropping through the suddenly gaping portal like a load of reeking tar dumped onto a raw street surface. It enveloped the screaming man, smothering his protests, mercifully cutting off his oxygen and his consciousness before it sent something resembling a hollow horn through the top of his skull to suck at his brain.

But Edwin Lillibridge did not in fact lose consciousness. Instead, he merely found himself displaced, and restored to a state of mind now familiar to him. He found himself again at one with the intelligence within the stone, though the stone no longer housed it. As he directed the billowing Avatar of Darkness to turn its ravenous attentions to the wide-eyed humans trapped in the narrow room with it, the Lillibridge-facet had but a single thought: *I am It, and It is I.*

—2004—

Original Appearances

"Twas the Night", *Blasphemies & Revelations*, 1ˢᵗ ed., 2008

"Beneath the Tombstone", *Footsteps* IV Summer, 1984

"Saucers from Yaddith", *Etchings & Odysseys* 84 #5 October 1983

"Black Eons", *Fantasy Book* Vol. 4, no. 2, # 16, June 1985

"The Antique Coffin", *Tales of Lovecraftian Horror* # 1 May, 1987

"Wilbur Whateley Waiting", *Revelations from Yuggoth* # 1, November 1987

"Ashes to Ashes", *Tales of the Episco-Pals* # 1 1988

"Midnight Mass", *Tales of the Episco-Pals* # 1 1988

"The Deprogrammer", *Cerebretron* # 3 March 1987

"A Thousand Young", *Eldritch Tales* # 18 Winter, 1989

"The Dweller in the Pot", *Dagon* # 27 June 1990

"Exham Priory", *Crypt of Cthulhu* # 72 Roodmas 1990

"The Round Tower", *Vollmond* # 3 Autumn 1990

"The Strange Fate of Alonzo Typer", *Nyctalops* # 19, April 1991.

"Behold, I Stand at the Door and Knock", *Cthulhu's Heirs: New Cthulhu Mythos Fiction*, 1994.

"The Beard of Byatis", *Made in Goatswood: New Tales of Horror in the Severn Valley*, 1995.

"Down in Limbo", *Deathrealm* # 24, Summer 1995

"The Transition of Zadok Allen" in *Cthulhu Cultus* # 1. (nd).

"Under the Mound", in *Lore* #3, Winter 1995.

"Young Goodwife Doten", *100 Wicked Little Witch Stories*, 1995.

"The Soul of the Devil-Bought" in *Cthulhu* Cultus 1996 #5

"Dope War of the Black Tong", *The Disciples of Cthulhu*. Second revised edition, 1996

"The Tree-House", in *The Dunwich Cycle* 1995

"Aquadingen" appeared in *Blasphemies & Revelations*, 1ˢᵗ ed., 2008

"Annotations for the Book of Night", *Mythos Online/Al-Azif* # 2

"The Burrower Beneath", in *Fungi* Vol. 2 # 16 Fall, 1997

"Feery's Original Notes", *Cthulhu Cultus* # 6 1997

"The Green Decay", in *Night Scapes* # 2, July 1997

"The Incubus of Atlantis", *The Sorcerer's Apprentices: New Tales in the Tradition of Clark Ashton Smith*, 1998

"The Shunpike", *Return to Lovecraft Country*, 1997"The Strange Doom of Enos Harker", *The Xothic Legend Cycle*. 1997.

"The Transition of Abdul Alhazred", *Mythos Online* # 1 June 1997

"Wrath of the Wind-Walker", *The Ithaqua Cycle* June 1998

"The Thing from the Trenches", *Blasphemies & Revelations*, 1ˢᵗ ed, 2008

"From the Pits of Elder Blasphemy", *Acolytes of Cthulhu*, 2001

"The Ghoul's Tale", *The Song of Cthulhu*, 2001

"The Elephant God of Leng", *The Tindalos Cycle*, 2010

"The Horror in the Genizah", *E'ch Pi El: Chilling Tales of the Cthulhu Mythos*, 2006

"The Mark of Yig", *The Black Book*, 2002

"Acute Spiritual Fear", *Disciples of Cthulhu II*, 2003

"The Devil's Steps", *Blasphemies & Revelations*, 1ˢᵗ ed, 2008

"A Mate for the Mutilator", *Eldritch Blue*, 2004

The Prying Investigations of Edwin M. Lillibridge", *Hardboiled Cthulhu: Two-Fisted Tales of Tentacled Terror*, 2006

www.ingramcontent.com/pod-product-compliance
Lightning Source LLC
Chambersburg PA
CBHW032253020726
47495CB00001B/90